MEN OF LONDON

Volume Two
Books 6 – 10

Susan Mac Nicol

www.BOROUGHSPUBLISHINGGROUP.com

FLYING SOLO
DAMAGED GOODS
HARD CLIMATE
SURVIVAL GAME
NOT SO SECRET SANTA

ISBN 978-1-951055-26-4

FLYING SOLO

To those people with nowhere to go, the homeless of the world who struggle to survive:

We do see you. It's simply that sometimes we can't acknowledge you're there. To do so would mean feeling uncomfortable and having a conscience. We should all try harder to help you and make sure you can always be seen.

Also, to those who care about them, the charities and people who help without judgment: You are the true heroes. Never forget that you do make a difference, and for that we are all forever grateful.

ACKNOWLEDGMENTS

The character of Maxwell is loosely based on a friend of mine called Warren Joseph Allen. We've had some conversations I can't repeat here, because I'm a lady, and he's taught me a few things I really didn't need to know, but enjoyed learning about all the same. He's sassy, a diva, but much like Maxwell in character—I believe, anyway. Thanks, Warren, for allowing me to use certain personal insights, quirks and habits in my story. I won't tell which ones are true, if you won't. :) Hint: He can be bribed to tell all for the price of a pair of Andrew Christians.

The game Gibson is designing is a bit of fun. *Camp Queen* sounded like a rollicking good game, though, and if anyone fancies developing it, let me know. It could be a lot of fun.

AUTHOR'S NOTE

Last winter, when I worked in London, I tried to give my coat to a homeless man who was barefoot in the snow and had only a thin jersey around his shoulders. He was in his sixties (or maybe younger, we all know living on the street ages people) and he shook his head.

"Madam," he said, "you're a woman. I can't take your coat. I'm a gentleman."

He took the coffee I bought him and walked down the street, still barefoot, before I could give him anything else. That sense of pride and dignity has stayed with me.

Those people on the street once had a family, a life. They have a story to tell, and there but for the grace of God go I.

FLYING SOLO

Prologue

Snowflakes drifted past Mooch, peppering his already freezing face with pinpricks of icy spite. Huddled under his tattered blanket, he pulled his threadbare jersey and jacket tighter around his shuddering body. The shop doorway he and Levi sheltered in was scarce protection from the heavy flakes blanketing the dismal London streets.

In the corner, curled into a foetal ball, Levi slept, face under a bright red cover sprinkled with stark white. Mooch had recently returned from a bit of dumpster diving to find his street partner sleeping. Despite his ire at that fact—Levi was supposed to be watching their stuff—Mooch hadn't the heart to wake him. Sleep came grudgingly to Levi. Instead Mooch had checked they still had their meagre belongings and had given a sigh of relief when he confirmed they were intact.

As for food, he'd found nothing other than half a sandwich already green and mouldy and not worth eating. Mooch had standards and he wasn't prepared to risk another bout of gastroenteritis for himself or Levi.

He reached over and tucked the grimy blanket over Levi, making sure the hand out in the open was pushed back under the thin covering—a hand already blue and cold, its fingernails ragged and bitten and spattered with cuts and nicks.

Mooch was tired; the cold had invaded his body like a sly enemy trying to wear him down, trying to make him acquiesce to the demand he simply lie down and never wake up.

"Not going to happen," he muttered through chapped, torn lips. "Bitch is not going to get the better of me." He glanced over at Levi. "Not while he needs me anyway."

No matter how he'd tried to cajole Levi off drugs with sex, love and threats of leaving him, nothing made a difference. If

Mooch thought it might help, he'd find Levi's dealers and punch their lights out, warn them to leave him alone. But Mooch knew, as soon as one went down, another low life sprung up in their place. At least Levi had one woman he trusted who was better than a stranger. It was safer for him that way.

A passer-by glanced at them, a faint look of disgust on his face. Mooch sneered, willing the stranger to pass so Mooch couldn't see his look of contempt, and at the same time imploring him to toss a few coins their way so he and Levi could get something warm to eat. It wasn't to be, and Mooch got his first wish watching the retreating back of the man clad in heavy, warm clothing and sturdy boots.

"Bastard," he mumbled. "It's nearly Christmas. Couldn't you spare a few pounds? You could certainly afford to lose some."

He cackled at his own joke, his amusement turning to a hacking cough threatening to rip his insides out through his throat. Once his coughing fit had subsided, he hunkered down further inside his blanket and watched the few commuters passing. He was close to sleep when a soft hand fell on his shoulder, and when he looked up, the kindly face of an older woman stared at him as she pressed a five-pound note into his hand, along with a steaming cup of coffee.

"You look as if you could use this," she whispered. "I wish I could do more. You're a kid."

She smiled sadly and went on her way as Mooch managed a stuttered, "Thank you."

He grasped the cup greedily, warming his hands, and then put it down reverently as he tucked the money into his secret jeans pocket. He resisted the impulse to gulp down the coffee. He'd wake Levi up; they could share the warm drink and perhaps the five pounds might go some way towards buying them something warm to eat. Mooch scowled. He'd make damn sure it wasn't being given to Levi's supplier.

Buoyed with a sense of making the night better for them both, he leaned over and shook Levi's shoulder. Perhaps the warm coffee might put back that sparkle in Levi's green eyes and bring a faint smile to his haggard face.

"Babe? Wake up. I have coffee, and I'll go get us something to eat. It's an early Christmas present."

Levi slumbered on.

Mooch extricated his leg from under his blanket and kicked him. "Hey, sleepyhead, wake up. I need you to watch the stuff again while I get us food."

There was still no response. Mooch swore and scrambled over to pull the blanket away. He shook Levi's shoulder. "For fuck's sake, wake up."

It was only then Mooch noticed the open, bulging eyes, the open mouth clotted with vomit and the look of nothingness on Levi's face. Mooch had seen that look before.

Gut churning, he pulled off his worn woollen glove and touched Levi's face. It was ice cold, and marbled, his body as still and lifeless as a damaged mannequin tossed out into the rubbish. Mooch gave an inarticulate cry and shook Levi harder, willing him to be okay, to still be alive even though Mooch knew it was hopeless. Stricken, he noticed the needle still stuck in Levi's arm.

Mooch cried out in grief as he buried himself into the corner while pulling Levi's skinny, stiff body onto his lap. He stroked Levi's stringy, black damp hair, ignoring the puddle of cold, stodgy vomit on the blankets, currently being smeared over Mooch's clothing and hands.

"Wake up, baby," he crooned to the dead man in his arms. "I need you. Please don't leave me here. You're all I've got."

He was still sitting there clutching his friend and lover to his chest when the police arrived two hours later to take him away. One of the policemen was kind and sympathetic and told Mooch they'd take good care of him and Levi, but they needed him to come with them.

From then on Mooch knew life would never be the same again.

Chapter 1

Vomit had never been something Maxwell Lewis could stomach. However, in his job as senior flight attendant with Target Air, it was something he had to deal with ad nauseam. Faced with a rabid bull intent on eating his testicles or a whiny, crying child with pseudo-vegetable soup spewing out of his mouth, Max would take the bull anytime—even though he loved his testicles *a lot* and preferably where they were, with a man's mouth wrapped around them.

"Max, do you think you could get your head out of the clouds long enough to help me here?" The exasperated voice of fellow cabin crew colleague Fiona Randall interrupted his randy dream and Maxwell scowled.

"Fi, you know I hate this part of the job," he whined, batting his eyelashes at her. It worked sometimes, but from the look of wrath on the face of the woman in front of him, not this time.

"We *all* know how you feel about it," Fiona said, her hands busy with the bag as she tried to capture the flow of copious, foul-smelling projectile matter gushing forth from the bug-eyed kid in seat 16C. "But I think I need another bag. Do you think you can grab one?" The sarcasm in her voice made Maxwell tut as he rummaged in a nearby empty seat for an empty sick bag.

"Not helping, gurl. Sarcasm is the lowest form of wit, remember? We've had this discussion before." He pulled the bag out with a flourish and handed it over. Fiona promptly shoved the full bag of sick in his hands and he wrinkled his nose in disgust. The other passengers around him looked a little grossed out too. Maxwell popped the bag into the waste bin underneath the cart he'd been pushing down the aisle when the kid had decided to go all Vesuvius on them. He couldn't move back to the galley until Fiona had finished her clean-up operation.

A few minutes later, the kid, who turned out to be a ten-year-old unaccompanied minor, had been shuffled off to the bathroom for a wash. The area around the kid had been sanitised with air freshener and antiseptic wipes and Maxwell was pushing his near-empty trolley into the galley so he could ready it for landing.

It was a short flight and they were only fifteen minutes from touch down at Frankfurt Airport. There, Maxwell would take a twelve-hour break as he waited for the plane to fill with the next contingent of passengers and luggage. Once all were on board, he'd be flying back to London City Airport where he was based.

He loved his job mostly—the travelling, the people he met, the anonymous blowjobs in the bathroom—but he was feeling a little jaded by it all. At twenty-seven years old, he was nearing the age when both the constant travelling and the hurried sexual hook-ups were starting to lose their glitter. His favourite fuck buddy and good friend Oliver Brown was out of the running, having pledged himself to Leslie Scott, the kind of man Maxwell could only aspire to have one day.

Maxwell heaved a deep sigh, wishing he had his cute occasional-travelling-partner-in-the-air, Finchley 'Finch' Morton-Harcourt the Third, on the flight. Finch was adept at sucking Maxwell's balls down into his pink, angelic mouth and performing the blowjob of the century in the bathroom. Sometimes they used the quiet recess of the first-class cabin when it was fairly empty. Both of them had learnt to hold in their moans and gasps when they were at work. Thoughts of that greedy little mouth around his cock made him harden in his trousers and he smiled dreamily. His number one flight attendant narrowed his eyes at him.

"Max, are you ill? You have a weird expression on your face, like you have gas. Please don't tell me you're going to puke like that little horror earlier," said Grant Tooley—and yes, his boss knew all the jokes there were about his unfortunate name. Grant took a voracious glee in levelling a fierce stare at a would-be joker before ripping them to shreds with his rapier-like tongue. He also wasn't fond of children, preferring his King James spaniel, Melissa, to any human. This included his wife of three years, Annie. Maxwell never quite knew how she could play second fiddle to a yappy dog, but acceptance of her place in Grant's life was something Annie dismissed with a wry grin.

Maxwell sniffed. "I was thinking. It happens occasionally, you know. I'm not just a pretty face."

Grant snorted. "The day you think about anything more serious than whose cock you're going to suck when we land, or which guy you're going to plough next, will be the day I give up my membership in the Spaniel Appreciation Club and buy a Rottweiler." He shuddered. "Never going to happen."

Maxwell squinted his eyes at Grant in sympathy. "Are you sure you're straight? I mean, the Spaniel Appreciation Club. You sounded so gay there I thought we might be having a moment."

He evaded Grant's angry thump to his arm and hightailed it out of the gallery, narrowly missing Fiona as she carried bin bags to the disposal area.

She opened her mouth to say something, but the intercom blared and the captain's announcement they were about to descend echoed in the air. Maxwell escaped to his seat and buckled in, sticking his tongue out at his friend as he did so.

When they landed, he'd get something to eat, change his shirt, and take the time to chill out. Maybe he could even find someone to hook up with.

***

Getting home to his studio flat around midnight was like being given a Nigella Lawson cheesecake. Maxwell loved Nigella. If he'd been straight, he might have married her, or at the very least had her as a sugar mommy. She was sexy, comforting, familiar and the very thing to make a rainy day brighter.

It was raining a May downpour as if God had smirked and flushed the celestial toilet not once but twice. Maxwell was weary and stank of sweat and puke because some old dear had heaved her insides all over his shoes soon after landing. It had obviously been National Puke on Cabin Crew Day.

He splodged into the hallway of his small, ground floor flat near the docks less than half a mile away from London City Airport, and switched on the table lamp in the narrow hallway. He left his suitcase propped against the wall. Locks of normally gelled and immaculate hair fell in wet streams down the side of his face, dribbling cold water onto his already chilled neck and back.

The area Maxwell lived in wasn't the best or safest place to live, but it wasn't too bad in his opinion. He'd been in far worse situations and could take care of himself. He'd had no trouble to date and most of his neighbours were friendly, if a little suspect.

Luckily the downpour appeared to have kept the various bad elements indoors, something for which Maxwell was thankful. Despite its uncertain location, it was still expensive, but affordable. The flat's most attractive feature was the fact he could walk to work without relying on public transport. A friendly taxi driver called Boris occasionally gave him a lift in return for a six-pack of Sol beer. Boris hadn't been out on the route tonight so Maxwell had walked home.

And now he was pissed off. It had been a boring stopover with no envisaged hook-up because he'd fallen asleep for hours when he laid down for a quick nap. It was raining and his flat was cold—the fucking heating hadn't come on again—and the only thing cluttering his fridge was a salad that looked as if it was being terraformed.

Maxwell was fed up with coming home to an empty place.

"Yes, ladies and gentlemen, I, Maxwell Christopher Allan Lewis, past confessed slut and major player, want a man to share my life with. No one is more surprised at this revelation than I," he grumbled as he watered his half-dead pot plant. Perhaps it might rejuvenate by some kind of miracle. If not, it would be delegated to the corner of the room where so many of his other plants ended up. He could have built a compost heap with the desiccated remains of his not-so-leafy friends.

He couldn't even have a pet, for fuck's sake, because he travelled too much. He'd love a goldfish, but his friend Leslie told him fish were 'sensitive souls' and needed a lot of upkeep. Leslie's aquatic friends passed on at an alarmingly rapid rate and the man had claimed airily that 'it was just the way fish were.' Maxwell grunted. He didn't think he could cope coming home to a floating corpse in the fishbowl time and time again.

"I guess I'd have it for a *little* while at least," he muttered as he set about cleaning out his fridge and battling with the heating to turn it on. Maxwell had a bad habit of talking to himself. Sometimes, far beyond in his past, he'd been his only company and he'd broken the loneliness by holding conversations with himself. It had gotten him some trouble when he didn't pay attention to his words.

He had a weekend break now, which was a blessing. Maxwell wanted to kick back, drink, dance, fuck someone, be fucked, and try get out of the ridiculous doldrums he was in. He blamed his ex-fuck buddy Oliver and Oliver's adored boyfriend, said fish-killer Leslie, for his current mood. Seeing them so happy together had awakened something in him. The knowledge you could come home to someone special, who'd listen and be there for you when you needed them instead of being just another bonk in a bed; Maxwell wanted that emotional connection to a man so badly. It was a desire he thought had been tucked away into the murky closet of his past and not brought out in a while.

His less-than-idyllic teenage years had meant he'd learned to be self-sufficient. Having a home with heat and running water, a way to put food on the table instead of rooting in rubbish bins or begging, and a warm bed to sleep in without the demand of 'added extras' were things he would be forever thankful for despite the lack of any significant love life. Sometimes small pleasures were enough to live by.

He changed into comfortable sweats and a ragged tee shirt picked up off the sideboard in his bedroom—he didn't believe in putting all his stuff *inside* the wardrobe. He made himself a cup of coffee, and out of habit, checked his sex worksheet. Maybe he could find someone worth asking for a booty call.

This sheet, appropriately named *Sexcella* was a work of art on which he recorded most of his sexual conquests. Casual one-off relief in the plane, airports and bars for blow- or hand jobs were excluded. There were physical descriptions and pertinent details about the man in question, like the length and girth of his cock, how good his blowjob skills were, his sexual performance in actual fucking and what their potential relationship factor was. The higher Maxwell rated them overall, the odds got better he could see himself with them in a longer term relationship. He was picky; nothing less than a five suited his needs. All the men so far ranged no more than a three and a half. Finch was a three and a half. Relationship-wise, he didn't cut it. He had an understanding partner at home who didn't mind his up–in-the-air escapades as long as Finch came home to him. Maxwell didn't think he could ever be in an open relationship like that.

His list was longer than a shopping list but shorter than a listing of the Top 25 Eligible Gay Bachelors. He'd started it years ago. He'd bigged it up to his friends and colleagues, telling them loftily it contained a lot more names than it did. It had become a self-fulfilling prophecy and he'd gone along with the game. His friends thought he was a man slut, but the reality was he'd been quite discerning in compiling it.

One day, he'd find a Five, and he'd no longer need it. Unfortunately, tonight was not the night and he couldn't even dredge up the enthusiasm to call a Four he knew.

There doesn't seem to be any point...I'm destined to be alone and horny.

Instead he switched on the television. He wasn't in the mood to play *Mass Effect* on the X-Box; he needed to alleviate some tension and watching porn was a good way to get relief. Watching Nicky Starr's porn films were even better. The man was a god. The fact Nicky was also his friend Oliver in his porn star persona didn't deter Maxwell at all. He and Oliver had had an arrangement until Leslie came along. Max didn't begrudge Oliver his new happy status; he bemoaned the lack of his own. Watching Nicky's tight, sexy body getting it on with a Leslie-like twink always made Maxwell horny. What was the fun in having a world-class adult actor as a friend and ex-fuck buddy if you couldn't watch them in action?

As Nicky pounded the twink's delectably tight and perky arse, Maxwell imagined himself sandwiched between them, seeing Oliver and Leslie in his head. He knew he was a bad boy fantasizing about his friend and his boyfriend, but he didn't care. A man had needs.

Later, sticky and sore, as he'd been rather enthusiastic in tugging his poor dick, Maxwell opened up the sleeper couch and went to bed. The jacking-off activity had done nothing to assuage the empty feeling inside him.

He drew the duvet over his head, hugged a spare pillow close to his chest and tried to forget he was sleeping alone.

Chapter 2

Gibson Henry hunkered down in his uncomfortable aeroplane seat on the aisle, scowled and made sure his earphones were tightly pressed against his ears. Even with the pounding rhythms of Black Sabbath blaring in his ears, the wails of the baby in the seat in front of him was akin to long-nailed fingers being scraped down a chalkboard. The infant's squalls sent chills down his spine, making him edgy. Depending on his mood, Gibson either listened to classical music inspired by video games, or heavy metal. Today was a heavy metal occasion.

He had to grin and bear the flight because if he ever wanted to see his family, the journey to where they lived in Cramond, outside Edinburgh, was a necessary evil. His mother, father and brother had moved up there about five years ago for his father's job. His only sibling, Richard, had insisted Gibson travel to their parents' thirtieth wedding anniversary this weekend. Their dad had been ill recently and Richard thought it would help his recovery to see his youngest son.

Gibson didn't travel well in a car, getting bored at endless hours behind the wheel without anything to keep his fingers busy. Not to mention the fact he didn't own a car anyway. Driving a hire car from Canning Town, where he lived, to the seaside village of Cramond had not been an option. Sitting on a plane he could at least work on his game design.

Gibson muttered in irritation. "I wish that kid would shut up. My damn ears are bleeding."

He ignored the look of outrage levelled by the old dowager sitting beside him and went back to his custom-designed supercharged laptop. He was working on the latest version of *Camp Queen*, a game he hoped would be another best-seller for him. Gibson was currently trying to mould the character of his sexy, wisecracking diva-assassin Phoenix Astor into something the fans would like.

There was a tap on his shoulder and he looked up in irritation. Alluring chestnut eyes framed with long lashes met his and for the first time since Gibson had boarded the plane, there was a stir of interest in his journey. The attendant looking back at him ticked all his boxes. Taller than Gibson's five-foot-four, Mr Yummy had broad shoulders and thick, coiffed rich chestnut hair swept back behind what Gibson thought were cute ears. The man sported a well-trimmed goatee framed around generous lips made for kissing or blowjobs. Gibson could *so* see them wrapped around his cock. His groin appreciated that thought too and he was glad he had his food tray down.

"Nice," he murmured.

The attendant blinked. His mouth moved and Gibson removed the earphones. "What? Sorry, didn't hear you. Mega music mix going down here."

He was flashed a wide grin. "Not a problem, sir. I asked if you wanted anything to eat." His voice was deep and well modulated. Gibson thought the guy would make a fortune on chat sex lines with the soft accent. He'd pay to listen to it.

Gibson nodded. "Are you on the menu?" Over the years, he'd been told he had no sense of decorum by friends who refused to go out with him to public places.

Luckily the guy can't clock me one here in the middle of the plane if the gaydar is off.

The attendant gave a wolfish smile. "Not today, sir. I have sandwiches or croissants though, whichever takes your fancy." One eyebrow rose in question and Gibson's jeans grew even tighter.

Fuck, this guy is cute. I'm pretty sure he's one of us too.

"Nah, I fancy something a little meatier. Something I can get my mouth around, you know?" He was pleased to see his words made the attendant swallow and close his eyes in what looked a short-lived rush of lust. The woman next to him gave a gasp of *whatever*.

Gibson grinned up at the attendant. He'd got this guy's measure. Gibson knew his slight frame, elfin face, spiky mid-length platinum hair currently streaked with red, and wire-rimmed glasses perched on his nose ticked boxes for men who liked his look. He cast his eyes down towards the man's groin and smiled. Yep, this guy was definitely one of them.

Gibson peered at the name badge on the man's lapel. "Maxwell, my man, I'm not hungry for food. I'll have an orange juice, though, if you've got one." He rummaged in his man bag and pulled out a few one-pound coins.

Maxwell nodded and selected a bottle of Tropicana from his cart. He handed it over to Gibson with a plastic cup. "Two pounds please, sir."

"That's what you guys charge for a tiny bottle like that? That's scandalous."

Maxwell shrugged his shoulders in apology and accepted Gibson's money. Their hands touched and a shock ran through Gibson.

Crap. This is such a short flight. I'm sure if was longer I'd convince him to meet me in the toilet. Maybe next time....

"Thank you. Enjoy your flight, sir. We hope to see you again soon."

"I'm sure you will," Gibson murmured. "I'll be travelling quite a bit on this airline over the next few months."

Well, he would be now he'd met Maxwell. Target had become his preferred airline of choice.

Maxwell smiled politely and moved away. Gibson made no bones about the fact he watched the attendant's arse as it made its way down the aisle. Maxwell had an exceptional derriere and Gibson could see himself between those cheeks—mouth, fingers, dick, he wasn't fussy.

Twenty minutes later the landing announcement came on, and Gibson was buckling himself up. Maxwell had walked past him a couple of times and they'd shared a few sly, knowing smiles. Gibson grinned to himself. He had a long flight coming up to attend a gaming conference in New York soon. He wondered idly if Maxwell would be on that one. He hoped so. A lot could happen on a transatlantic flight.

***

It had been ten days since Maxwell had seen the sexy figure of Gibson Henry—yeah, he'd checked the flight manifest—aboard one of his designated flights. That platinum head was hard to miss. The red had gone but when Maxwell spotted the familiar flash of pale blond seated in 12C, his pulse quickened. The man had a preference for the aisle seats it appeared. He'd been in the galley when the passengers boarded and had missed greeting the man.

Gibson had gotten him hot and bothered from the minute Maxwell had seen him the first time. The other man's small, tight, wiry frame and pink tongue stuck out at one corner of his mouth as he focused on his laptop screen, had been all kinds of hotness. Designer glasses perched on the end of a snub nose was a particular kink for Maxwell.

And when he'd looked into those cheeky bright green eyes, Maxwell was a goner.

The 'misappropriated' Edinburgh passenger manifest had some of Gibson's personal details, which Maxwell had stored on a piece of paper in his wallet. Gibson lived in Canning Town, not far from Royal Docks; his date of birth was July 7, 1990—so he was twenty-four years old—and for good measure Maxwell now had his mobile number. He knew it was highly illegal and unethical but he'd been securing cute guys' numbers for years and no one had found him out yet. When he'd seen the man's name on the manifest for the New York flight, Maxwell had believed, like Sherlock, that the game was afoot.

Once the plane had levelled out and the drinks carts were ready to go, Maxwell made sure he was the one serving 12C. When he arrived with Ginny, his colleague, Gibson was huddled over his laptop, his face scrunched up adorably, earphones on, concentrating on some Photoshop-type programme.

Once again Maxwell tried to catch his attention by lightly tapping his shoulder. Gibson scowled, his glance upwards barely registering who was in front of him. He flapped a hand in a go-away gesture and Ginny rolled her eyes at Maxwell. They both knew passengers weren't always that polite but to see this coming from Gibson made Maxwell peeved as hell. The man hadn't even acknowledged his presence.

Huffily Maxwell moved on, smiling and joking with passengers even as he steamed with righteous anger inside. An older man in seat 21F decided he might be having a heart attack, and all thoughts of Gibson vanished in the urgency of the incident. Luckily it turned out to be gas. An hour later Maxwell finally got to see Gibson again when he delivered a drink to his fellow passenger in 12A, a stalwart man of African origins who looked as if he played rugby forward for the Teletubbies, only with muscles. Maxwell sympathised with the woman squashed between Teletubby Man and Mr Gibson 'Rude Bitch' Henry. The woman was engrossed in her Kindle and looked up and smiled at him as he passed the drink to her seat passenger.

Gibson looked up too, and gave him an unexpected yet radiant smile. Maxwell's insides fluttered—as did something else.

The blond pulled the earphones away. "Maxwell, my man, how *are* you? I didn't know you were on this flight."

Maxwell's jaw dropped. "I was here earlier. You waved me away. Sir," he added hastily.

Gibson frowned. "I did? I was probably drawing. I tend to get grumpy when I'm doing that." He shrugged. "I don't take notice of anyone when I'm in the zone. You could literally die right before my eyes and I wouldn't give a fig."

Maxwell blinked.

Well at least Gibson Henry was honest.

"I'll try making sure I don't expire then," Maxwell said. "I'd hate to decompose while you're in the drawing *zone*."

They grinned at each other. Maxwell knew he'd better move on before he got a fierce glare from his boss for dereliction of duty.

"If I can't get anyone anything else, I'll leave you in peace." He moved away and stifled a chuckle at Gibson's *sotto voce* comment.

"What I want you can't give me right now."

Maxwell's groin heated up at the comment. He flounced his way happily down the aisle, answering passenger questions and taking drinks orders, and arrived at the galley where he began to fulfil the requests.

There was no time to make an excuse to go back to visit his cute passenger again, and finally he went on his break, having a well-deserved cup of coffee and a pastry from the cart.

When he went back to his post, it was approaching midnight. His boss for this flight, Larry Moreton, grinned at him. "Max, could you please check out Mr and Mrs Doherty in first class? Their bell went off a few minutes ago for service and I'm in the middle of sorting out another rather difficult passenger." The first-class section was surprisingly empty for a long haul flight, with a passenger quotient of eleven.

Maxwell rolled his eyes. "That old pervert and his wife? The guy goosed me earlier when I went to check on him, and his wife thought it was funny. I swear if he does it again, I'll deck him."

Larry chuckled. "You have such a cute arse. Irresistible." He pretended to inspect Maxwell's backside. "I'd fondle it." Larry was bisexual, but *so* not Maxwell's type with his smarmy pickup lines and breath smelling of pear drops. Maxwell wasn't a fan.

"Good to know. Fine, I'll see what he wants. As long as it's not me." Maxwell made his way to first class, passing Gibson on the way who winked at him.

"Hey, Max. Going somewhere?"

"To sort out a passenger in first class, sir. Can I get you anything on my way back?"

Gibson shook his head. "Nope, I have some self-service planned." He winked again. Maxwell didn't even want to begin to wonder what he meant.

He entered first class to find Mr and Mrs Doherty fast asleep. They were in their eighties, wrinkled and…old. Their service light still winked on and off and Maxwell switched it off. He crinkled his nose at the drool coming out of Mrs Doherty's thin-lipped mouth. He decided to check on the other passengers while he was there. None of them needed anything. The cabin was quiet, dimly lit and most of them were sleeping. He thought while he was there, he might as well check everything was good with the bathroom.

His hand was already on the door to open it when fingers grasped his right butt cheek and squeezed tightly.

He closed his eyes and took a deep breath as he turned around. "Mr Doherty, I'm going to have to ask—oh, it's you." A

pleasant thrumming began in his cock as Gibson's hand
continued to hold his arse tightly.

"I told you I was looking for self-service." Gibson's husky
voice sent a shiver down Maxwell's belly to his groin. The hair
on Maxwell's stomach rose with static.

Maxwell looked around. Everyone slept on and the couple
of passengers who were awake were either reading, had on
headphones or were watching the late-night film. No one seemed
to notice the two men eye-fucking each other outside the toilet.

Gibson nodded at the door. "Open it. I'm sure we can both
fit in there. I'm only a little guy—well, in height anyway." He
smirked as he took his hand off Maxwell's butt and gently pulled
down the lever. Raising one pale eyebrow, he motioned Maxwell
inside then followed him in. It was a tight squeeze—nothing
Maxwell wasn't used to, having been in this situation before—
and then they were both face to face, bodies squeezed against
each other. Maxwell's cock was raging to be set free and he soon
got his wish.

"I doubt we have much time so we'll have to do this
quickly." Gibson reached down, unzipped Maxwell's trousers
and reached inside, gripping him in small, yet strong fingers.
Maxwell squeaked, the feeling of a hand on his needy dick
sending a jolt of electricity to his toes. He still couldn't speak.

Gibson knelt down, pushing his own loose sweats and briefs
down his hips and unleashing what for his size was an
impressive cock. Maxwell's mouth watered at the sight of the
pink and purple cut goodness jutting up from a groin laced with
blond curls. He wanted to taste it, lick it and make Gibson
scream.

However, as Gibson's wet, warm mouth encircled his cock
and began a slow, steady suck and pull on the head, Maxwell
thought he might be the one doing the screaming. He watched
the head bobbing up and down on him, and Gibson's hand curled
around his own cock as he jerked himself. Maxwell tried
valiantly to suppress the rising moans and groans in his throat.

He panicked after a while when he realised the door hadn't
been locked and reached over to slide the lock to closed.

"Good move," Gibson said through a mouth full of cock, the
reverberations of his voice tickling Maxwell's dick to new,

heady heights. "And may I say, you taste as good as I knew you would. Tell me when it's time." His mouth shut up, but his eyes lifted to meet Maxwell's and the cheeky glint in those green eyes caused a head–to–toe shudder to course through Maxwell's body.

"Oh, God," he breathed, resisting the impulse to fuck Gibson's swollen, pink mouth. He didn't think it would be polite. "You're pretty good at this."

Gibson shrugged. "Practice." He leaned forward and took Maxwell deep, lips brushing his shaven pubes. Maxwell surrendered to the sensations and closed his eyes, chest heaving as he was thoroughly blown.

He'd no idea how much time had passed but the feeling of his swollen cock head brushing the back of Gibson's throat as he took him deeper was the last straw.

"Going to blow," he gasped. Gibson gave one list lick then removed his mouth. He stood up as his fingers squeezed Maxwell's dick, stroking it roughly. With a noise resembling a grunting moose in heat, Maxwell unloaded white ropes of come onto them both. Gibson gave a much manlier grunt and fisted his cock fiercely before pressing against Maxwell and unloading warm, musky fluid onto Maxwell's once pristine uniform.

They stood pressed together, gasping as bodies came down from the orgasm high. Maxwell nearly had another one on the spot as Gibson raised his fingers to his rosebud mouth and sucked off what was on them, eyes never leaving his.

"God, you are one dirty boy," Maxwell managed to get out. "You look sexy as fuck."

Gibson grinned, eyes dark and hooded. "Yes, I've been told." He pulled one finger out of his mouth with an obscene, popping sound. Maxwell couldn't even move to zip himself back up. He was boneless and on such a high, he didn't think he'd ever come down.

Gibson laughed. "Let me help you." His fingers deftly tucked Maxwell's half-hard dick back into his trousers and zipped him up. He then sorted himself out and patted Maxwell's cheek.

"Thanks. See ya."

He opened the door and was gone before Maxwell could say anything else. His jaw dropped and he stared at the empty cubicle.

What the fuck? How rude was that?

What they'd done was nothing too drastic but surely there should be some banter exchanged, perhaps even a lingering kiss—Maxwell liked kissing—before they disappeared? Maxwell had at least hoped to exchange a phone number and see if they could meet outside of being in the air. And seeing as how he was looking for something more permanent, he'd hoped...Maxwell sighed at the loss of said hope.

"I don't simply zip myself up and say 'see ya.' I have manners,'" Maxwell grumbled as he cleaned the spunk off his clothing and wiped his jacket clean with a handful of paper towel. He squinted in dissatisfaction at the papery speckled trail left behind on the fabric. His feelings were still hurt at the speed at which Gibson had left.

"I was right the first time. You *are* a rude bitch," he muttered as he left the bathroom. He took a quick glance around to see whether any of the passengers had noticed anything but they all looked much the same as when he'd gone into the bathroom—he checked his watch—ten minutes ago. It had been a record blowjob indeed. He normally took a little longer to get his rocks off.

He passed Gibson, back in his seat, earphones on, captivated once again by his laptop screen, and oblivious to Maxwell. He wondered spitefully whether he could get away with spilling a drink on the man's computer. *That* might make him sit up and take notice, especially if his balls had a chance of being fried.

Sadly, Maxwell didn't follow up on his pipedream because he valued his job. Instead, for the rest of the flight, he took to watching Gibson out of the corner of his eye, and trying not to show his in-flight sex partner he was pissed off.

Before the flight was due to land and Maxwell was on rubbish duty, he stared hard at Gibson as he packed up his laptop bag.

"Should I slip him my number or not?" he muttered. "After all, Canning Town isn't too far away from me. It's conceivable we could meet up again. Perhaps it might all work out."

Deciding on the affirmative, Maxwell wrote his number on a scrap of paper with the words 'Love to meet up again for a drink' and as he neared Gibson, he slid the folded scrap onto his lap as nonchalantly as he could. Gibson frowned, looked down at the paper, back up at Maxwell then casually pushed it back into the black bag Maxwell sported.

"Thanks but I don't do repeats," Gibson said with a shrug. "It's kind of a one-off thing, you know? Thanks anyway."

Maxwell's jaw dropped at such blatant rudeness as Gibson turned to look out of the window. Trying to hide the embarrassment of rejection, he carried on and kept the hurt off his face to show Gibson he didn't give a fuck.

Crap. He'd met his match in the flesh. *Obviously he's a tosser of note, a cocksucker, a player and in short, a douche. He is so going on Sexcella at a two rating. Great BJ. Post-coital— bleh.*

Hours later, as he tossed and turned in the bed in his hotel room on the overnight layover, the ignominy of the careless gesture still stung. He'd also decided not to participate in any more anonymous sexual escapades in the air. It was time to start thinking about his future and find someone steady he could come home to. It'd be better than a damn fish.

Chapter 3

"Fucking useless piece of shit!" Gibson threw the tablet he was using against the wall of his dining room and watched as it fell apart. It made him feel a little better.

His best friend Jack Cunningham rolled his eyes and took a sip of his beer. "You're a twat, Gib. What the fuck did you do that for?"

Gibson stormed over to the pieces on the floor and kicked them. "It's so bloody slow, and keeps freezing on me. I can't even get my mail up on it. What good is it to me?"

Jack pursed his lips and inclined his head thoughtfully. His long, brown hair swung down the sides of his face like swathes of faded velvet. "That's why I don't do tablets. Give me a laptop or a desktop any day. I mean, you can hardly even watch porn on those damn things the time they take to buffer. By the time the guy's giving it to the big tits dolly bird, it's like watching it in slow motion." He mimicked the action, making a circle of his fingers and driving another finger in and out in an exaggeratedly slow and filthy gesture. "Not worth it."

"My laptop's busy rendering some images and my desktop is downloading some new software." Gibson snapped as he paced around. "All I wanted to do was check my mail and see if Everett had got in touch." He picked up a slice of carrot from the veggie platter and bit it savagely.

"Everett the Egghead." Jack chortled. "The big, hairy, fuck buddy from Canada."

"Fuck. You." Gibson spat. "He's not that hairy. And does Beth know you make disgusting gestures like that whole finger thing you had going on?" Beth was Jack's long-time girlfriend.

Well, maybe Ev is a little hairy-like but he has a great dick and he knows what to do with it.

Everett Talbot was one of the few people Gibson fucked more than once, which was usually only once a year anyway when they attended the Gamez Geek Ultra event in Brighton. The GGU was the prestige event for game developers and designers and one Gibson never missed. Everett was also a master at coding and programming and both Gibson and Jack relied on him as one of the many freelancers they used for the development of their games.

Jack snorted. "Beth knows she's the only one for me. Doesn't mean I can't watch porn. And dude, Everett is like the epitome of a bear. Have you seen the two of you shimmying it up on the dance floor? It's like Chewbacca and Peter Pan going at it. Scary." He shivered theatrically.

Gibson narrowed his eyes. "He has a nice pelt on his chest, and a beard. What about the bird I saw you with once PB"—PB was code for Pre-Beth—"who had a damn moustache and looked as if she'd got a pair of udders on her front? No, fuck that. Double udders."

"Hey, her name was Annie, she was cool," Jack threw a disgruntled look at Gibson who stared back fiercely. "And she was a real sweetie. She had a few hormone problems at the time."

Now it was Gibson's turn to roll his eyes. "She nearly poked my eyes out when she tried to hug me. I could have died from suffocation."

The two friends glared at each other then as smiles curved their mouths, they fell into peals of laughter.

"Oh my God," Gibson managed, eyes streaming. "We had Chewy and the Pneumatic Bearded Lady as dates…"

Gibson's bad mood dissipated. Jack was always able to get him out of hissy fits by distracting him. They'd been friends forever, since secondary school. They now worked as a team in a game design company they'd formed called Anomaly Media. Jack was the writer and also a technical whizz kid at programming and code and picking out bugs. Gibson was the creative one, drawing, designing and developing the game characters and the worlds they lived in as well as coding. It was a partnership that worked well and they'd built two successful games so far, *Blockshock* and *Dust and Souls*. *Camp Queen* was Gibson's dream, his concept.

They shared the flat in Canning Town and used the spare room as their office. Jack had money behind him from a gaming business his father had owned, which saw them through the lean times—although those were not often, as their games sold well. Jack was built like a linebacker and he'd saved Gibson's arse more times than he cared to remember.

"What are you waiting on Ev for, anyway? Anything special?" Jack wiped his eyes and picked up a desiccated sandwich from the plate between them. Gibson winced as Jack munched away on dried ham and hard cheese between what looked two pieces of brown cardboard.

"Yeah. There was this bit I couldn't get right in the animation for Phoenix and he said he thought he knew what the problem was. I sent details over to him to take a look." Gibson checked his watch. "He said he'd get back to me by three pm and it's already half past."

Jack thrust the whole half sandwich in his mouth. "Well, now you're going to have to check your damn email on my computer. Seeing as how you threw yours against the wall. Like you did with your phone the other week." His voice was non-judgmental.

Gibson sighed. He did have a tendency to get pissy when his gadgets didn't work for him. "Sorry. I'm not sure I need a tablet anyway." They smirked at each other. "I suppose I could do without for a while and use my smart phone. It's the screen is a bit small sometimes to see anything, especially all the techy stuff and I don't want to strain my eyes any more than I have to." "Whatever." Jack took a swallow of his beer, finishing it off and gave a burp as he set the empty bottle down on the table. He grinned. "Of course you could stop fucking breaking stuff, you impatient arse."

Gibson stuck a tongue out at him and Jack lunged, trying to catch it. Gibson skipped away nimbly.

"One of these days," Jack growled. "I'm gonna catch that little pink thing, rip it out and pickle it."

"Ooh, bloodthirsty," Gibson teased as he picked up the shattered pieces of his tablet. "How am I supposed to rim guys if you rip out my tongue?"

Jack's face went green. "Shit, don't put those images in my head, you bastard. I don't want to know..." his voice tailed off and he scowled and put his earphones in. A few minutes later he was swaying to what Gibson imagined was the sound of Alex Clare and the concentration on his face meant he was probably checking code.

Gibson poked him on the shoulder. "Oi. I thought you said I could check my emails?"

Jack ignored him and Gibson gave a deep sigh. It looked like he'd be relegated to using his phone to see whether Ev had sorted his problem. He wanted the issue fixed before his next flight out to Dublin to meet with an investor who was interested in promoting *Camp Queen* in his gaming boutiques and online. The demonstration needed to go well.

Thoughts of the impending flight in a week's time made him recall the brown-eyed, sexy guy called Maxwell he'd blown in the toilet on his New York flight. Gibson had to change his flight back to another airline because of a delay in NY and hadn't seen the guy again. He'd been cute and decent; Gibson had some deep-rooted guilt at blowing the guy off—no pun intended— when he'd tried to give him his number. In hindsight, it had been a shitty thing to do. The hurt in the guy's eyes had rankled a bit. Gibson might be a slut but he wasn't a cruel tosser. He'd meant to find the guy and apologise, but then he'd got sucked back into his game and that had been that.

Shoving aside his regret, he was overjoyed to find the answers he sought from Ev on his mobile, with a laconic, 'Miss you buddy, I'll be in UK in a few months and maybe we can get together' message. Gibson grinned. He'd make sure there were more Chewy and Peter Pan antics at the club to piss Jack off. Maybe a little half-naked grinding and wet bear kissing. That was sure to give his friend the heebie-jeebies.

***

Gibson stared at his friend Cruz Castillo with growing trepidation. "Let me get this right. You want me to wear this outfit and drape myself all over your buddy Pete to make Craig prove I'm not interested in you. Is that my instruction for tonight? And how far do you want me to take it? Pete knows about this plan, yeah?" Cruz's boyfriend Craig had some crazy idea Gibson and Cruz were doing the horizontal mambo and Cruz had a plan to convince him otherwise. Pete was Cruz's friend from the gift shop where he worked as a sales assistant, and was joining them tonight at the opening of a new gay club in Soho called Innuendo.

Gibson stared at the outfit laid out on his bed and then back at his other best friend with jaundiced eyes. Cruz stared back at him, big doe eyes dark and serious, his full lips pursed.

"Sí, dipstick." It came out 'deepsteek' as Cruz's Spanish accent made itself known, normally more when he was stressed. "Pete will play along. If Craig sees you with Pete dressed like *that*"—he waved a slim, brown hand and bit his lip imploringly—"he will *have* to believe I am not interested in you or you in me 'that way.'"

Gibson huffed and glanced down at the outfit with a sense of unease. The silver hot pants complemented his hair, although they would cover virtually nothing of his arse or his hips. And as for his dick…he shivered. He was cut, and wearing those, the whole world would know about it. The black mesh tee shirt with straps and buckles was, well, tight, but wearable. As were the shoes. A pair of glittery, two-inch-high silver boots, with red laces, which he thought he was supposed to tie around his calves.

Cruz sighed. "It's a theme evening tonight, bebé. Gladiators and Glad Rags. You don't own anything like this so I had to borrow this outfit from someone for you. I couldn't loan you any of my clothes or Craig would think we are together."

"Tell me again how making Craig think I'm fucking someone else when I'm not is going to help you get him back?" Gibson and Cruz had never had that sort of relationship; Cruz was like his brother, but for some reason, Cruz' ex had never accepted it. The pair had had a heated argument over it a week ago.

Cruz rolled his eyes and blew a strand of ink-black hair off his forehead. "Because he will see you and Pete making out, and I will be like"—he draped a dramatic hand to his forehead—"I don't care, I want you, and Craig will realise what he is missing and that he adores me, and then we will make mad, passionate love at the club."

Gibson thought there might be a flaw in this plan somewhere. "And Pete isn't going to take this too far, is he? I mean, you said he's a nice guy but I don't want to have to get serious with him."

"Sexy dancing, bumping, your usual slutty stuff," Cruz said helpfully.

Gibson scowled. "Yeah, thanks for that." He heaved a sigh. "Fine, I'll do it. You are *so* going to owe me one."

Cruz's face sparkled with a smile showing off white teeth. "Thank you, sweetie. I love you." He leaned forward and planted a smacking kiss on Gibson's cheek. "Now I need to go home and get ready. I'll meet you outside Innuendo at nine. I have our VIP tickets so we don't need to queue, but I left them at home." He waved goodbye and flounced out of the bedroom.

Gibson heard him calling to Jack. "Bye, Het Man, please make sure Gibson gets dressed on time."

Gibson suppressed a grin at Jack's snarl at his hated nickname. Cruz loved to tease him. Jack loved superheroes and had often enquired plaintively why he couldn't be 'Muscle Man' or 'Sex God' rather than 'Het Man.'

Hours later, after showering, man-scaping, shaving and moisturising, making sure he could fit all his man bits into the clothes he was wearing, Gibson was ready. He looked in the mirror and took a deep breath.

The man looking back at him was willowy, yet toned, with broad shoulders and strong muscled arms from swimming.

Gibson might be short but he was all in proportion. His fair-skinned legs were devoid of hair—he only had faint blond wisps on them even when he didn't shave—and his mousse-styled platinum hair was artfully sculptured. He'd changed his glasses to his clubbing pair, a trendy pair of dark silver frames, which enhanced his green eyes. He couldn't wear contacts; his eyes were too sensitive to use them for long.

He twisted around and gave a grin when he observed his arse in the mirror. Tight and perky. Just the way he liked it—and others did too. There was quite a lot of his cheeks and crack on show but there was nothing he could do about it. He sat on the bed, and pulled on the boots, wrapping the long laces around the bottom of his legs.

For good measure, he slid in a barbell to his pierced belly button. The shirt and shorts didn't meet over his stomach, leaving a vast expanse of pale, toned skin and the start of a four pack, of which he was quite proud. He popped another earring into his ear and wrapped a few leather bracelets around his wrist. The final look was damn sexy, slutty and, even if he said it himself, mighty fine. He pursed his lips in the mirror and blew himself a kiss.

"Pete, my man, you are not going to know what hit you tonight. Make sure you know the boundaries or I'll have to kick you in the nuts."

He picked up his bum bag, stuffed in what he needed and hot-footed it into the hallway. He ran into a muscled man mountain on his way out and gave a startled cry.

"Jack, I didn't know you were still here. I thought you'd gone to Beth's." Beth was Gibson's favourite lady other than his mother. He liked the spritely red head.

Jack stepped back, his eyes wide, mouth open in what looked like gob-stopping alarm.

"Gib, what the hell? You can't go anywhere dressed like that. Someone will kick your arse." He pushed long hair behind his ear as he stared at his friend in trepidation.

"Who are you, my mother?" Gibson said in irritation. "What the hell?" He pushed his glasses up his nose with his middle finger, hoping Jack got the hint.

Jack's eyes roved down his body in disbelief. "You...you have hardly anything on. I mean, I can see your damn dick, like..." His Adam's apple bobbed as looked at Gibson in dismay.

Gibson threw him a fierce stare. "Yeah, what about it? It's a Gladiator party, and I, my man, am one sexy gladiator." He twirled around and took great glee seeing Jack looking ready to faint. "Come on, you've seen me in club wear before. What's the big deal?"

"Not like that." Jack's voice was faint. "I mean—half your arse is hanging out."

"All the better to feel me up, or stick it in," Gibson quipped.

Jack blanched and Gibson took pity on him.

"Oh for God's sake. I'm wearing my long coat over this outfit. You didn't think I'd get on the tube dressed like this, did you? Credit me with a little bit of sense."

He stomped into the entrance and grabbed his long trench coat off the peg.

Jack's eyes narrowed. "Well, 'scuse me for worrying my best friend is going to be fresh twink bait for the bears and haters out there. The coat makes you look like a damn flasher."

"Jack, I'll be fine, promise. I'll get a lift home anyway, if I come home. I might get lucky and it's Saturday tomorrow, so no work. I'll text you, though, if I don't come home." He shrugged into his coat and fastened it.

"You'll have them lining up to do you that the way you look tonight," Jack grumbled.

Gibson narrowed his eyes. "You know, I might think you were jealous if I didn't know you were a very straight man and my best buddy since forever. What gives?"

He was shocked to see Jack looked apprehensive. They usually teased each other about Gibson's lifestyle but not to this extent.

"Have you been watching the news lately?" Jack asked quietly, all traces of teasing gone from his tone. "Every time you switch it on lately there's something about some gay or lesbian being bullied or beaten."

Gibson sighed. "Sure, it happens. I can't live my life worrying about it though."

"I worry about you. I'm a big guy; people think twice about trying to take me down. But a little shit like you…"

Gibson's heart ached and he stepped forward and laid a hand on Jack's arm. "Hey, nothing is going to happen to me." He motioned to his bag. "I have a whistle, a can of Mace Cruz gave me, and I can run fast. I'm prepared."

Jack's eyes were still shadowed. "Please be careful, Gib. That mouth of yours can sometimes run away with you too and I'd hate for you to attract some wanker's attention." He grimaced.

"Especially given what you're not wearing. Promise me you'll watch out for yourself."

"I will," Gibson promised. A surge of affection at his friend's concern made him lean forward and kiss Jack's cheek. "I have no desire to become a victim. "He punched Jack on the arm. "'Sides, I'll sic you on him afterwards if anyone tried anything. And no one wants the Sex God coming down on his sorry arse."

Jack looked unconvinced. "Let me know if you stay out or I'll worry."

Gibson nodded and crossed his chest. "Scout's Honour."

"You were never a scout, half pint," Jack said with a slight smile.

Gibson pouted. "Neither were you, Het Man." He dodged Jack's punch and flung open the door. "I'll text you if I get lucky," he yelled as he made his way to the lifts.

He didn't have time to hear what Jack shouted after him as he stepped into the lift and the doors closed.

Chapter 4

Maxwell stood sipping his strawberry daiquiri as he watched the dancers writhing on the dance floor. The new club was heaving and he already regretted coming. He'd been given a ticket by a friend, and if he hadn't used it said friend would be as pissed as hell. The tickets were rare, like a Willy Wonka chocolate bar.

Maxwell was quite a fan of dress-up, but he thought the Gladiators and Glad Rags event sounded a little ambitious for a collection of ragtag patrons dressed in cut-off sheets and leather belts and straps across sweating bodies. He'd tried his best though. He looked down at his own outfit. He'd spent some of his hard-earned pennies online to get himself a passable tunic crested with gold thread and a pair of Roman sandals. A sword and dagger had been offered with it but he'd not had the money to waste for those. His hair was styled into some semblance of mussed-up magnificence and he'd trimmed his goatee to a light shadow. His hairy, muscled legs stuck out from his short tunic and had already gotten a lot of lip-licking attention. He'd had a few offers tonight. First, he'd been hit on by a huge guy he'd nicknamed Bearzilla; dressed in full Roman regalia, he'd been looking for a willing sub for the night. While Maxwell wasn't averse to the idea usually, Bearzilla wasn't his idea of someone he wanted holding him captive.

The guy who'd approached Maxwell afterwards hadn't been great either, as he'd been with his partner, looking for a third. He'd been spaced out and Maxwell knew the guy was on something. The one thing Maxwell had no tolerance for were drugs and people on drugs. He had a pathological hatred of them and anyone who dealt them. He didn't even like taking medicine.

Maxwell's recent dissatisfaction with the way his love life, or lack of it, was turning out made him wonder if anyone else here tonight was looking for the same thing: a little stability in a relationship and not a series of one-night stands.

He muttered to himself, "Hell, yeah right. Like that's going to happen. I shouldn't have even come here tonight. I should find a Scrabble club somewhere, maybe a ball-dancing group. That's more likely to deliver dividends for the start of a relationship than this place."

He stared idly out at the crowd, noticing a small, sexy, blond-haired guy in silver micro shorts grinding against a tall, well-built Asian man. The blond was familiar in some way, cock-stirringly tasty and very much Maxwell's type; he even wore glasses. The Asian guy was hands on and Maxwell grunted. It was what you'd expect in a club like this, but he wished it was his hands all over the blond's pert little arse. He mused whether to go over and cut in, thinking he might as well have fun while he was here and who knew? Perhaps the guy was looking for something a little longer term.

He was about to make a move when he saw the Asian guy's hand reach down and grip the blond man's crotch. Maxwell sniggered when the smaller man pulled away, stomped on the other man's foot with his silver boots, not once, but twice. He snapped something, pushed the grimacing man away then whirled to make his way towards the bar. As he drew nearer, Maxwell's heart stopped.

"Gibson?" God, the man was sex personified up close. Maxwell's cock swelled under the tunic, his mouth watering at the vision of a pale-skinned, pale-haired pixie with a scowl on his face and green eyes flashing anger at the world.

Gibson didn't appear to hear him and gestured to the bartender. "Dan, can I have a Vampira please?" He took off his glasses and started cleaning them with a bar napkin.

The bartender nodded. "Sure, honey. One Vampira coming up."

Gibson put back his glasses, tapped his fingers impatiently on the bar and the slow burn of something dark welled in Maxwell's chest.

Doesn't he even recognise me? Am I that unmemorable?

"You don't remember me, do you?" He stood a little closer.

Gibson frowned and peered through glasses already steaming up again. "You do look familiar—wait—oh, Maxwell, right? From the plane? Wow, small world. How are you?" He shrugged apologetically. "Sorry, my glasses were mucky earlier from dancing. I couldn't see properly."

Maxwell was gratified Gibson at least remembered his name. "Yeah, that's me." He gestured towards the floor. "Looked like you handled yourself okay out there with that guy."

Gibson rolled his eyes. "Yes, he's okay but he was getting a bit too hands on. I warned him not to take the bloody charade too far but did he listen? Nooo…"

He smiled at Dan, took the drink the bartender gave him and slid a ten-pound note across the counter.

"Charade?" Maxwell watched as Gibson slid the change into the white leather bag he had strapped around his hips. A belly bar twinkled in the light and Maxwell was mesmerised by the sexy shimmer. And the flat, toned stomach it belonged to. And the cheeky curve of Gibson's arse.

"Yeah. I'm here, dressed like this, which isn't my usual outfit by the way, dancing with Pete, to make *that* guy realise I'm not having it on with my gbf." Gibson gestured towards a couple on the dance floor, a short, dark-skinned guy in his early twenties who was busy excavating the contents of the mouth of a broad-shouldered black guy dressed in leather.

"Gbf?" Maxwell said in bemusement.

"Gay best friend." Gibson sucked at his drink through the straw and Maxwell was mesmerised by the sight of pink lips around a candy cane piece of plastic. "He's the little guy. Craig is his ex-boyfriend, but from the looks of it, whatever I was doing with Pete worked. They look as if they're enjoying themselves and hopefully Craig now realises I'm not into Cruz."

They watched in companionable silence as the two dancing men's groins undulated against each other, and as their kissing on the dance floor grew even hotter.

"Christ, I shouldn't be watching them," Gibson grumbled. "It's making me hard and in these shorts that's a bad idea. My dick might split the seams these things are so tight."

At those careless words, Maxwell's cock flagged to attention harder and more aching than before. A quick flick down towards

Gibson's groin confirmed he clearly didn't have much room to manoeuvre.

"You got some time off from flying then?" Gibson cocked his head with a knowing grin, probably having seen the direction of Maxwell's eyes.

"I have a whole three days off before my next shift. I heard about this place opening, decided to check it out. It's pretty cool."

"Yeah, lots of new talent." Gibson gave a noisy slurp of his drink then peered at Maxwell over his glasses. Maxwell's stomach clenched in appreciation.

"I don't normally do this, but do you fancy a repeat? There's a bathroom on the left we can slip into."

Maxwell drew in a deep breath. He was *so* going to regret this, he knew it. He had to take a stand somewhere though in his search for everlasting love.

"Thanks, but no. You're not the kind of guy to get involved, or so you said when you blew me off last time, so it wouldn't solve any purpose except for a quick bit of pleasure. I wasn't really in the mood for this tonight but I promised a friend." He drank up what was left of his cocktail and put the empty glass on the bar.

Gibson looked shame faced. "Yeah, about that. I'm sorry. I shouldn't have been such a git. I wanted to apologise to you on the plane afterwards but then things ran away with me and I got distracted."

Maxwell was heartened by the apology. That took balls. "No problem. I understand. I'm at a bit of different path in my life. I'm tired of the fuck 'em and suck 'em. I want someone to come home to. Maybe it's a stupid pipe dream but I have to start trying to find someone somewhere, right?"

He smiled at Gibson, who stared back at him with a strange expression.

I bet he isn't used to being turned down. Maybe I'm being an idiot.

Maxwell wondered if his newfound principles were worth it. He might have to reconsider.

Someone shoved against Gibson, causing his drink to go flying all over the back of another man standing at the bar— a very big man in a shiny dress suit, flashy jewellery and what looked like a permanent scowl etched on his wide face. He turned around and grabbed Gibson's wrist, causing him to cry out softly in pain.

"What the fuck? You've messed up my suit," Shiny Suit growled.

Gibson tried to wrench his wrist free. "Hey, you ape, let go of me. I'm sorry, it was an accident. Someone knocked me."

"Yeah? Fucking twinks. You think all you have to do is bat your girly eyelashes and a man will forgive you anything. I ought to—"

"Let him the fuck go," Maxwell said evenly. His blood was heating up like lava in Pompeii at seeing Gibson being manhandled. His temper was slow to burn but when it did, oh boy. Maxwell was quick to go from slow denotation to supernova I'm-going-to-fuck-you-up-so-badly status. He controlled it—mostly. When he'd been on the streets, it had taken all his self-control not to become an animal like some of his friends had. And sometimes an animal had been what you needed to be to get by.

"What did you say to me?" Shiny Suit's lips twisted. "Punk, you think you can take me on?" He let go of Gibson, who stood rubbing his wrist with a worried expression.

"Max, leave him. He's not worth it. He's a douche bag in a suit. Let's get out of here—" Gibson's voice was cut off as the other man reached out and slapped him on the cheek, the flat sound echoing in Maxwell's ears like the knell of doom. Behind the bar, Dan motioned to the bouncers across the room to come over.

The rushing blood in Maxwell's ears grew to rock-concert crescendo and he moved forward in front of Shiny Suit, standing between him and Gibson. At the sight of a red handprint on Gibson's fair skin, and the look of shock on his face, Maxwell now wanted to hit someone. He took a deep, centred breath to calm himself down. The last thing he wanted to do was scare Gibson away.

"I might look all soft and cuddly," Maxwell murmured, "but beneath this gorgeous and drool-worthy exterior lies the heart and soul of a primal beast."

Shiny Suit's eyes widened in confusion and Maxwell thanked the gods he seemed to have a dumb one here. Brawn and no brains were always so much easier to bring down. Years of fighting his own battles against bullies at school, hanging out with street gangs and learning to fight dirty had often proven his salvation at times like these.

And there was one way he'd found to distract a bully and calm himself down that was almost fool proof.

He adopted his *Karate Kid* stance—the Crane Kick. He stepped back, curling his arms and hands into position. Gibson's face was a picture in astonishment and Shiny Suit looked confused. Maxwell lifted his one leg and gave a blood-curdling screech. The bully stepped back with a look of panic.

Out of the corner of his eye, Dan the bartender was laughing like a loon. Maxwell had no idea where the bouncers were but hoped they'd get here soon before he had to kick arse. Immediately around him, the crowd had hushed and faces stared at him in anticipation.

"What the hell, are you fucking crazy?" Shiny Suit looked around the bar as if asking for someone else to agree with him.

Maxwell did. "Why yes indeed, kind of you to notice. I'm the baddest motherfucker you ever laid eyes on and if you don't apologise to my friend for hitting him, right now, I'm going to kick the ever-mighty shit out of you."

Gibson's eyes were like green dinner plates. "Maxwell, are you sure you're okay? Did you take something?"

"No I bloody didn't," Maxwell huffed, straining to keep his position. His upraised leg ached and he was sure his signed Andrew Christians were showing under the tunic. "I want this arsehole to say he's sorry for being such a dickhead. Quickly. Before my foot finds his knackers and pushes them into his throat."

Shiny Suit looked down at his groin and winced.

The man next to him, a slim, older man, clutched his arm. "Chris, apologise and forget it. The guy didn't do it on purpose and I can clean your suit, baby." He tugged at Chris's arm and Chris scowled.

"Running out of patience, people," Maxwell growled. In reality, his leg was aching. "Either say sorry to my buddy here or face the wrath who is Maxwell Unleashed."

Gibson's mouth framed the words, 'Maxwell Unleashed.'

The sight of his name on those beautiful lips and the adorable look of stupefaction on Gibson's face made Maxwell determined to follow through his threat. He gave another yowl and kicked out his foot, narrowly missing Chris's groin. "Next time I connect," he yelled.

Chris was yanked back by his seemingly irate partner. "For God's sake, let's go. I want a drink and a dance, say the fuck you're sorry already, you buffoon."

Chris stared at Maxwell then at Gibson then at the bouncers who now stood beside him, arms folded, waiting to see what happened next. Chris seemed to know when he was beaten.

"Fine," he spat, turning to Gibson. "I'm sorry I hit you. Take your crazy friend away from me, and let's call it a night, right?"

He turned and was pushed through the crowd by his partner who mouthed a 'Sorry, guys' as he left.

Maxwell put his leg down and watched them go with a smirk. Around him, people started clapping and cheering, and he grinned and took a bow. He stood up quickly as he realised doing that showed his arse to the world. "Thanks, my esteemed audience. Glad I could entertain you."

"Hey, crazy guy. These are on the house." Two huge cocktails stood on the bar. Dan was chuckling fit to bust a gut. "Your boyfriend is one lucky guy. That was some crazy shit you pulled there for him."

"He's not my boyfriend," Maxwell said, a little longingly. "He's a—" He didn't even have time to decide whether he was going to say friend or fuck buddy when he found his lips being claimed by a soft, searching pair. Gibson framed Maxwell's face in long fingers and kissed the crap out of him. Maxwell yielded—he was only human after all—and all sound ceased until there was only the scent and feel of the man pressed against him. His glasses dug into Maxwell's cheek but he didn't give a fig.

He tried not to get too handsy; Gibson did have boots on, after all, and wasn't scared to use them. But the feel of the smaller man in his arms, his lean torso and kissable lips and the hardness pressed against his groin led to a memorable moment indeed.

When he was released and Gibson stepped back, lips swollen and wet, Maxwell tried to gather his brains back into his head from his crotch so he could form a sentence. He was still trying to when Gibson spoke.

"What you did for me back there…no one's ever done something like that for me before. Well, apart from Jack. He's my sbf."

"Sbf?" Maxwell was proud he'd managed to speak three whole letters. And what was it with this guy and all the acronyms?

"My straight best friend. You are one insane dude. That guy could have hurt you."

Maxwell shrugged. "When you've lived on the streets, you learn how to take care of yourself."

Gibson drew a shocked breath. "You were on the streets?"

Crap. I didn't mean to let that out. Best gloss over it.

"Yeah. So, you kissed me."

Gibson smiled slowly. Maxwell's heart gave a ping and beat faster.

Gibson grinned. "Yes. Problem?"

"Hell no. Best kiss I've ever had."

Gibson looked shy. "Thanks. I like kissing."

"It's one of my favourite things to do too." Maxwell leaned over and gently kissed Gibson's cheek where the pale pink of the slap still showed.

Gibson drew in a soft breath and Maxwell was sure as they looked at each other in the clamour of the club, and only having eyes for each other, that they'd had 'a moment.' From the uncertain look on Gibson's face, Maxwell wondered if he was mistaken.

He'd be upgrading Gibson to a resounding four and three quarters on his spreadsheet, based on his kissing skills alone. The small deduction was because he needed to leave some room for improvement and maybe, with time, he might get there. If Gibson was into a repeat performance and wasn't going to break his heart. Because Maxwell knew now, after *that* kiss, if Gibson asked for a visit to the loo, despite what Maxwell's brain said, his heart and little head would say 'Hell yeah.'

He picked up the cocktail, passed one to Gibson then picked up his own and took a sip. "Here's to crazy men doing crazy things in nightclubs."

"I'll drink to that." Gibson smiled and they toasted each other. The pang in Maxwell's chest morphed into something larger, an ache making him want to bottle Gibson in a fairy jar and never let him go. The man, with his pale green eyes, freckled nose and wavy blond curls, had crept into his heart. For a while they stood at the bar observing the activity around them.

Gibson shot him a shy smile. "I know it's late but I've got nowhere to be in the morning. You said no already but that was before you went all Mr Miyagi. Do you want to go somewhere quieter with me, we could talk, get to know each other a bit more?" He fidgeted as Maxwell gazed at him.

Maxwell's brain was adamant. *He's going to break your heart. You should say no. Say no. Just like that. It's easy.*

He nodded without even realising it. His heart and little head were all too convincing.

I don't care anymore about finding 'the one.' I want him. *Even if it's only for tonight.*

"Sure. We can go to my place if you like. It's not too far." Maxwell's inner common sense hung its head in shame and despair.

Gibson beamed brightly as he took out his mobile from his waist bag. "I need to let my friends know I'm leaving. They'll be rabid they missed all the fun." He finished his drink. "They're probably in the bathroom. I think I saw them disappear before this all kicked off." He hesitated. "While I have my phone out, do you want to give me your number again? I promise I'll keep it."

Maxwell recited his number and watched Gibson key it in, all the time studying how his face scrunched up in concentration. The guy was adorable, sweet under that glossy exterior and not as confident as he looked. And he was all Maxwell's for one night.

He could live with that.

He could always start his search for true love again tomorrow.

Chapter 5

Gibson was both thankful and nervous when they got back to Maxwell's home at close to midnight. The taxi ride home had been a quiet one, neither man sharing much or talking. Once or twice Maxwell had smiled at him then turned to look absently out of the window. He looked to be regretting his decision and Gibson wasn't sure if he should call it a night. But he'd already texted Jack to let him know there was a possibility he'd only be home in the morning so he may as well see how the night played out.

Maxwell's flat was in a fairly dodgy part of the city, but it was small, cosy and looked as if a crazy Tasmanian devil had whirled through it and dislodged everything either onto the floor, or onto the top of any available surface. Gibson hung up his coat then stared around at the room, trying not to cringe over the discarded clothing, empty pizza boxes, half-filled cool-drink glasses, book stacks, piles of clothing stacked high and remnants of what looked like a nursery of dead plants and pots in the corner of the room.

Maxwell saw him looking and he chuckled. "Yeah, I'm a bit of a slob. Sorry. I don't get much time off, and I'm flying around so much I tend to leave the housekeeping for when I'm in the mood. Which is never."

"What's with the dead foliage?" Gibson waved towards the poor dried-out sticks. "It looks like a graveyard."

Maxwell laughed. "I have a tendency to kill anything green. I've been toying with the idea of getting a fish to keep me company but I'm scared it'll die too."

He walked over to the open plan area serving as a kitchen with a small cooker, hotplate and under-counter fridge. Utensils littered the countertops, and in the corner there was a random, mismatched set of crockery. On top of the cooker sat a frying pan and one small saucepan. It looked as if most of what Maxwell owned was actually out on display. Gibson hoped he wasn't some crazy hoarder person who might keep him locked up somewhere. His nerve endings tingled at that thought.

Maxwell turned to him. "Do you want anything to drink? I think I have a bottle of wine somewhere in here."

Gibson nodded. "If you have some, I'll have a glass. Thanks."

He sat down gingerly on the two-seater couch, after moving half a dozen tatty books and a box set of *Dexter* DVDs, something which made his skin prickle even more, into a neat pile on the floor. Gibson carefully laid out the pieces of Maxwell's airline uniform, currently draped across the back of the couch he wasn't sitting at.

Maxwell came over and handed him his drink. "Sorry, I don't have wine glasses, so the tumbler will have to do."

He sat down next to Gibson, leaning back against the clothing, and placed his own drink onto the side table, which was no mean feat as it was filled with *Men's Health* magazines and a snow globe of London Bridge.

For a minute there was an uncomfortable silence.

"You like your stuff around you, I see." Gibson waved a hand around the room. "It makes sense having it all to hand. You never have to wonder where you put it." He'd meant it as a joke. His own place was pristine, orderly with everything in its place, and to him this screamed chaos—but he appreciated others might not be the same.

Maxwell's face shadowed. "Sorry. I know it looks messy, but I'm not good at being tidy. You're right. I do like to see my stuff around rather than packed away."

"That wasn't a criticism, Maxwell. Only an observation." He stretched lazily, rejoicing when he saw Maxwell's eyes darken. Maxwell's heated gaze dropped to Gibson's legs, eye fucking them downwards then back upwards to Gibson's groin. The hunger on his face turned Gibson's insides to soft mush and his dick began rising in his tight shorts. A slight smile formed on Maxwell's face.

"God, you are so sexy," he murmured as he reached out and brushed the back of his hand down Gibson's smooth thigh. "The first time I saw you I knew you were going to be a handful."

"More than a handful, I hope," Gibson whispered as he set his drink down, took off his glasses and watched through blurry eyes as Maxwell's hand trailed up and down his skin. He burned with that sensual touch and wanted to get out of his shorts post haste. He had visions of his dick ripping through the fabric like one of the monsters in *Alien*.

When Maxwell's hand brushed his groin, he hissed, his breath quickening, and he couldn't help the involuntary push of his hips towards Maxwell's hand. That hand reached down and unzipped him as sienna-brown eyes focused on his. Maxwell drew a hitchy breath, realising Gibson wore nothing underneath the shorts. His tongue came out to lick his lips and Gibson lost his breath at the erotic sight.

"I couldn't wear anything under these," he whispered, throat dry. "Hey me, easy access."

Maxwell's fingers stroked his cock, rubbing his thumb over the head, and Gibson let out a soft exhale of breath as he closed his eyes and focused on the slow strokes across his sensitive skin. When something hot and wet licked at him, he moaned and opened his eyes to see Maxwell's tongue swiping slow licks up and down his cock.

"Oh…" he was breathless with the teasing assault of his most sensitive bits.

Maxwell chuckled huskily. "You taste good…I love that you shaved here." He took Gibson in, tongue slicking up and down, his mouth hollowing as he sucked Gibson's brains out. Gibson didn't want to push or be rude, but he so badly wanted to fuck Maxwell's mouth until he came.

He was no stranger to blowjobs, but the way Maxwell treated him, as if he were something precious, sent thrills down his spine and a tingling hum across his skin. Gentle fingers cradled his balls as Maxwell pleasured him, rubbing his taint, and Gibson slid further down on the couch, opening his legs and allowing his partner access to that most hidden of places. He wanted to feel a finger or two in his arse and his current position prevented it. He tugged at Maxwell's hair, urging him upwards, and the man currently feasting on him looked up. His pupils were blown, his mouth wet with pre-come and saliva. Gibson nearly came from the debauched sight.

"I need to get these off," Gibson gasped, as he stood up and pushed his shorts down his legs. For good measure he removed the rest of his clothing and stood naked before Maxwell.

"That's better," Gibson purred and pulled Maxwell to his feet. His lips found Maxwell's and he thrust his tongue inside his mouth, tasting himself on Maxwell's lips. Hands gripped his arse, and Gibson wrapped his legs around the man holding him.

"You need to get naked too," Gibson murmured as his teeth grazed Maxwell's shoulder and bit down softly. "I'm not fucking a man in a dress."

The low laugh in his ear made Gibson's groin ache.

"I'm going to have trouble doing that while you're wrapped around me like a damn octopus." Maxwell set Gibson down on the floor. "Let me get this off then. And there'll be no fucking tonight."

Gibson gasped in horror. "No fucking?" His lips formed a pout. "Don't you want me?" He'd never been refused a fuck before.

Maxwell shrugged off the tunic and slid his briefs down his legs to land on the floor. "I think *this* proves I want you." '*This*' was an impressive erection: an uncut, beautiful, upright cock Gibson drooled over. "Let's take things easy first."

He sat back on the couch and motioned to Gibson. "Get over here. On my lap."

Gibson was still a little miffed but he wasn't going to argue. He straddled Maxwell, pressing and grinding against him. Maxwell's groan of pleasure and the fact his cock was velvet-wrapped steel as they frotted like teenagers made Gibson's hole ache to be filled.

He knelt up, leveraging himself down so they were still joined but Maxwell had access to his arse. "Put your fingers in me, Max." Maxwell's pupils blackened at Gibson's use of the diminutive.

Note to self. Maxwell likes that name.

Gibson moved Max's hand to his arse. "Please, Max. I want to feel you inside me while we do this."

Max moaned. "I need lube, Gibson. I'm not doing you dry. I have some somewhere…" His hand groped around the sofa and finally he found what he was looking for.

Gibson chuckled. "There's a definite bonus to you having your stuff all over the place." He watched as Max opened the tube and squirted its contents into his hand. "Now do me. I want to see you get off like this while you have your fingers inside me."

Max stared at him, eyes unfocused. "God, the things you say…"

They kept up the momentum of rubbing against each other as Max slid cold lube against the crease of Gibson's hole. Staring into each other's eyes, Gibson cried out softly as a finger pushed into him. Every forward stroke he took in their sensual play made his senses swim and every downward movement pushed Max's finger deeper inside him. One finger became two, two became three and soon Gibson was riding those fingers like a man possessed while his cock threatened to burst.

"Oh, fuck." His movements became frenzied as Max thrust upwards harder, biting his lip as their cocks rubbed together. His fingers sparked something inside Gibson, making him cry out in pleasure. A tingle in his backside and groin heralded his orgasm.

"God, you are gorgeous," Max whispered as he found Gibson's lips and a greedy tongue filled his mouth.

With a sputtered cry and a surrendering of his body to the tremors giving him release, Gibson came all over Max's stomach and chest, fronds of come hitting his lover's jaw and lips. Max gave a deep groan and warmth flooded Gibson's nether regions in a sticky and musky-scented explosion.

Gibson collapsed against Max, aware there were still fingers up his arse. He liked the sensation of being claimed and owned by this man. This man who'd stood up for him a crowded club against another man who could have pulverised him. It was something he didn't want to analyse too much right now, as it was a little scary. He wasn't used to feeling this way.

He winced as the fingers slid out of him and Max caressed Gibson's flank with hands still sticky from lube and Gibson's own fluids. The soft stroking soothed Gibson and he closed his eyes as he lay sandwiched against Max's sticky and faintly hairy chest.

"That was epic," Max sighed. He shifted and leaned down to kiss Gibson's belly, lips lingering on his belly bar. "This is so damn sexy. So damn you."

Gibson nodded drowsily then shivered. "I'm cold…is there something wrong with your heating?"

Max scowled. "It's probably gone off again. I can't get the hang of the bloody thermostat. Budge off me, baby, let me get you warmed up."

Gibson raised an eyebrow at the 'baby' but let it go. Reluctantly he rolled onto the couch and watched Max push himself up and walk over to the control on the wall. The man had a very nice arse himself, round and tight, and…

"Oh my God, you have a tattoo!" The sight of the scorpion on Max's right hip, about three inches in length and one wide, was unexpected. Sexy, but not something he'd expect from this man who was mostly snark and witty repartee. He'd expected butterflies or God forbid, a *Kung Fu Panda*.

Max didn't reply as he fiddled with the thermostat and then walked back to the couch, half-hard dick swinging before him and showing a nice set of balls. He stopped in front of Gibson.

"Yeah," Max said, his face guarded. "A remnant from my teenage years."

Gibson stood up and traced the tattoo. "It looks like a gang tattoo," he mused. "Like one of those you'd see in some bad-arse street gang. Is that writing on there?" He leaned down and peered at it. A faint line of text mirrored the line of the scorpion's upraised tail. "*Acculeum in cauda*," he said aloud.

He stared at Maxwell. "What does it mean?"

Max opened a drawer to the side table and picked out a pack of wet wipes. He pulled the tag back, took out a handful and began wiping himself down. He handed the pack to Gibson. His eyes were distant and Gibson wondered what he'd said to cause the change in mood.

"It's Latin. It means 'the sting in the tail.'"

"The sting in the tail," Gibson repeated. He frowned. "What does it mean?"

Max shrugged. "Scorpions sting with their tails. That's about it. Nothing deeper."

"You don't have to tell me." Gibson said quietly as he wiped off the spunk from his belly. "I don't want to pry. You hardly know me well enough to share stuff." The pang in his chest as he said that made him realise how true that was.

Something is off here. I actually want to know him better. That's never happened before.

Max's eyes narrowed. "It's not that." He looked at Gibson's arms, which were goose bumped. "You're cold and it's late. Do you want to get into bed? It's warmer there."

Gibson was seeing another side to the man before him. Gone was the sexy, affable buffoon, and in its place was a wary-eyed, cautious stranger. But he was cold and bed sounded good. He didn't want to make his way home this early in the morning. And the thought of sleeping next to Max was strangely appealing. Gibson didn't do that with his pick-ups.

"I guess. Where's the bedroom?"

"You're looking at it," Max remarked drily, with a hint of the man he'd been before. "This is a poor man's flat. I'm a lowly flight attendant after all, not a dot-com geek."

Gibson frowned. "I'm a character artist, not a dot-com geek. I design computer games, do the animation and such."

Max's ears seemed to prick up as he pushed everything off the couch onto a pile on the floor and set about opening the bed out. Gibson wanted to huff in protest after all the trouble he'd taken to try and keep things neat.

"Oh? What, like *Mass Effect Three*? That's my game. James Vega kicks ass. He should be in charge of the team, not Commander Shepard."

Gibson was further confused as Max took his time organising the sheet and bed cover, throwing it on, then straightening it out carefully before fluffing the pillows. The man was a contrast to say the least. A slob in one way, and completely nitpicky another.

Gibson stifled a yawn. "The Shepard fans will kill you if they hear you say that. Mine's also third-person RPG but it's a bit different to *Mass Effect*. My guys are all assassins. The concept is a superhero squad with drag queens, gays and lesbians." He slid into the bed, wincing at the lumpiness of the mattress, and snuggled in under the duvet with a sigh of relief at being warmer. The flat was chilly. Max watched him, a faint smile on his face.

"Sounds riveting. I'd play it." He watched Gibson squirming to get comfy. "I know it's a crap bed," he murmured as he turned off the table lamp and slid in beside him. "One day I'll be able to afford a better one."

Gibson face-planted into his pillow. "Uh-huh," he said sleepily. Post-orgasmic doze was setting in. "You have to have something to aspire to, I guess."

A pair of soft lips pressed against his hair and Gibson smiled. *This is nice. I don't stay over at a guy's place ever. What does this mean?*

"'Night, Gibson. Sleep tight." The bed rocked as Max got settled and Gibson shuffled back so he was the little spoon.

An arm draped over his waist and warm breath huffed against his shoulder. "'Night,"

Gibson murmured. "Thanks for letting me stay."

Soft lips kissed his shoulder. "Thanks for staying," was the whispered reply. "Now go to sleep."

"'Kay." And with that one last word, Gibson fell asleep.

Chapter 6

The ringing of his phone and its loud rendition of Madonna's "Like a Virgin" took Maxwell out of a dream featuring him, Gibson and a bowl of cream and catapulted him into the early morning. The warm body wrapped around his was incentive enough not to answer and let it go to voice mail.

Something hard pressed against his stomach and Maxwell wanted to take the tour to discover what it might be. He pushed a strand of fair hair off Gibson's face, his heart clenching at the sight of Gibson's sleeping visage, long eyelashes against pale cheeks and lips that were slightly opened. The man sleeping beside him was beautiful. A quick peek under the covers confirmed Maxwell's suspicions—yep, one lovely, cut pink cock currently prodded him, attached to a lean, tight little body that Maxwell wanted to touch, hold and never let go. The little piercing in Gibson's belly button winked at him, inviting his mouth to taste it.

Maxwell clapped a hand against his forehead as he lay back, picking up his phone to see who had called.

"You knew this was a bad idea, arsehole," he muttered to himself. "He told you he doesn't do commitments but no, you had to take him home. And now you want to keep him."

The phone call had been from his boss, Grant. Maxwell had a horrible feeling he was going to be asked to cut short his days off and take over someone's flight. He wasn't happy to do that when he had Gibson in his bed so he declined to check his voice mail yet. It was only nine am after all. Grant could go fuck himself if he thought Maxwell was getting up earlier to go to work. Although he could use the money the extra shift would bring. Maybe then he could buy a new damned bed.

Last night had been memorable. And the 'not fucking?' Maxwell didn't think he had it in him to be inside this man and not want to own him and have his metaphorical babies. It was a level of intimacy that with anyone else might be a fuck, but with Gibson would seem to be much more. Maxwell couldn't explain it, and it pissed him off. He had no idea why he was so invested. It had been best to not go that far.

Gibson snuffled and pressed himself closer. Maxwell took a deep breath. His own morning woody was getting stiffer by the minute with the feel of the insistent press against his belly. Gibson blinked and then unfocused green eyes looked into his.

"Morning." Like a kitten, Gibson stretched and gave a deep moan of pleasure as the kinks in his body straightened out.

Maxwell wanted to moan but for an entirely different reason. "Morning." He cleared his throat because his word had come out sounding like he smoked a pack of cigarettes a day.

"I heard the phone. Do you need me to go home?" Gibson sat up, the covers pooling around his waist. Maxwell's eyes were drawn to his tight nipples and morning woody.

"No, no rush. It's my boss. I'll phone him in a little while." He needed to get out of bed. Now. Before he lunged at Gibson and pinned him down, slid inside him with all the lust and need in his being and lost his soul to a forest-eyed pixie with a belly bar.

Maxwell swung his legs out of bed and stood up. He found his underwear on the floor, slid into it and was better equipped to face the day.

"I like your tattoo," Gibson murmured as he squinted, sat back against the couch and stretched. "I know you don't like talking about it but it's awesome. Maybe I should get one," he mused thoughtfully. "A dragon, or a phoenix or something. Right here." He drew back the covers, turned onto his stomach and waved a hand at his arse. "On the small of my back. What do you think?"

Maxwell was still trying to process the round backside with its tempting pucker perched high in the air, looking as perfect as an arse could be. He cleared his throat again.

"I think it's a personal decision. I only have the one tattoo, and I wouldn't get any more. I think your skin is perfect the way it is. But, yeah, a dragon might look good if that's what you wanted. I'm going to go shower. I won't be long then you can do the same if you want."

Maxwell made his way into the tiny bathroom off his lounge-cum-bedroom-cum-kitchen and closed the door. It contained the rudimentary items, including a bath with a shower. He started the water running and pulled the faded blue curtain across. For the first time, the shabbiness of his flat hit him. As for his possessions spread all over the place, he liked to see them. Years of living on the streets and having to hide what little he'd had made him want to display them, know they were there as affirmation he'd got *stuff*. He'd never wanted to impress anyone before; no one he'd brought home had made him evaluate where he lived and what he had.

He stepped into the bath and picked up the soap as he began washing. A rush of air wafted through the room, making the curtain ripple. "Stop worrying about your place," he muttered. "It's better than sleeping in a fucking cardboard box. Better than scrounging in dumpsters trying to find food, sleeping in shop doorways or running away from guys who want to make you their bitch. You should be proud of what you have, Mooch. You made it here." He hated his street name but it reminded him of where he'd come from. He'd earned his name through his unfailing persistence trying to cajole shopkeepers and restaurant owners into giving him food that hadn't been thrown out. It had earned him a lot of slaps around the ear. He didn't want to think about the other things he'd done for food.

He finished washing, conditioned his hair, checked his pubes—he liked to keep them neat—and switched off the shower. He opened the curtain and stopped short at seeing a naked Gibson sitting on the toilet, his face pale, lips set.

"How long have you been there?" Maxwell stepped out of the shower onto the ragged bathmat and plucked a towel off the rail, wrapping it around his waist. He was glad now he hadn't beaten off in the shower. That could have been embarrassing.

"Long enough. I badly needed a pee so I didn't think you'd mind. You were so busy talking to yourself I don't think you heard me come in and take a leak." Gibson's eyes were shadowed. "You did sleep on the streets, didn't you?"

Maxwell took a smaller towel off the rail and dried his hair. A direct question deserved the direct answer. "Yes. For about eighteen months until I was sixteen. I was homeless and I lived wherever I could find a place to sleep." He'd only ever told this story to Oliver and even then not in much detail. Only the fact he'd been homeless for a while.

Gibson stared at the scorpion. "Is that when you got that?"

"No. I got it after."

"After what?"

Maxwell stared at Gibson in frustration. "After I got off the streets. To remind me." He wasn't going to say it had been done in memory of his dead boyfriend. Levi had had a fascination with scorpions.

Gibson's mouth opened and Maxwell knew he was about to ask 'remind him of what.' He huffed and rolled his eyes.

"To remind me I'm not the same person I was then. That I still carry a bite even though I might be different now, and life can still sting like a fucking scorpion."

That was the other reason for the tattoo. One he needed to remind him about where he'd come from.

"Oh." Gibson stood up. Maxwell's eyes were drawn to his semi-erect cock, the shaven groin, the pink balls hanging between his legs. There was the faint sheen down there where he'd missed a bit. Gibson was beautiful and damn sexy, and Maxwell's whole body ached with want.

Underneath the towel, he grew hard. He needed to get dressed. "Did you want to get in the shower? There's plenty of hot water still."

"Why were you on the streets in the first place?" Gibson wasn't giving up. Maxwell took a deep breath and hung the hair towel back on the rail.

"Because I ran away from the foster home I was in after I lost my family. I didn't like it. The boy I was friends with said we'd be better on the streets and I believed him. For a while, we were. He died and I was on my own."

Maxwell didn't want to think about the wasted body in their cardboard home. Holding the cold, dead body of your best friend and lover was a memory he tried to forget.

"God, Max. I'm so sorry." Gibson stroked his arm and stepped closer, his hand gripping Maxwell's arm.

Maxwell shrugged. "It was a long time ago. I got off the streets, went back to school and started over. I reinvented myself so I didn't end up like Levi."

"Levi was your friend's name?"

Maxwell nodded. "Yes. He was a bit older than me. He was a drug addict and it got the better of him."

Gibson nodded. "Was he your lover?" His green eyes searched Maxwell's face as his hand tightened.

Maxwell's throat clenched. "No." *Liar.* He wasn't sure why he'd lied about that bit. It was just too personal to admit yet. "Now can we leave this topic alone please? I'm not partial to bearing my soul so early in the morning. I haven't even had coffee yet."

Maxwell stormed out of the bathroom. He heard the shower start and heaved a sigh of relief. "God, he's a nosy little bastard." He pulled on a pair of grey sweatpants, a black tank top and went into the kitchen to put the kettle on for coffee. He had no idea how Gibson liked his—or if he even liked the stuff.

Fifteen minutes later Gibson came into the lounge, towel wrapped around his waist. He dropped it and started dressing in the clothes he'd had on the previous night. Those silver shorts slid over his pert butt and Maxwell averted his eyes. He was still half hard under his towel.

"Do you take sugar in your coffee?"

Gibson nodded. "One please. No milk, just black." The black mesh tee shirt was pulled over his head and he finger-dried his hair while Maxwell stirred the coffee.

"I'm sorry if I upset you," Gibson said as he put on his glasses and searched for his bag. "I wanted to know a bit more about you. I mean, you seem like this put-together guy—funny, cute, sexy—yet you lived rough. It's not what you'd expect."

Maxwell sighed as he came over and handed Gibson his mug. It looked like he wasn't going to get away with not telling his story. Perhaps he should get it over and done with.

"I worked hard to leave the old me—Mooch—behind. When Levi died I realised I didn't have to be on the streets anymore, so I went to a shelter. It so happened they'd been awarded a huge grant by this rich woman called Beryl Carnegie. She put a load of money into rescuing street kids. I was one of the lucky ones who managed to get help."

Gibson stared at him in wonder. "Wow, that's awesome. She must have been an incredible lady." He cupped his hands around the mug and took a sip of coffee.

Maxwell smiled sadly. "She was. Eighty years old and wanting to change the world. I met her a couple of times. She *was* awesome. That money paid for me to be checked out by a doctor, it paid to fix my teeth…they weren't good, because of my bad diet and the fact they'd been knocked out a couple of times. She even enrolled me in an evening class so I could finish my schooling."

"*Who* fucking knocked your teeth out?" Gibson said, tiger-cub fierce. Maxwell thought he looked adorable.

"Bullies, other street kids, gang members, take your pick. You were easy pickings if you were a street kid. Fair game for anyone. Including perverts and guys looking for a fuck or a blowjob." Maxwell shrugged. "You learnt to run, and you learnt to fight back. You pick up some tricks on how to stay safe and protect yourself."

His chest tightened. Those days had been dark, lonely and scary. Trying to stay out of the gangs who promised what looked like paradise—somewhere warm to sleep and food—yet wanted your life and soul in return, being asked to do unspeakable things…it hadn't been an easy life. But Maxwell had managed to rise above it. He'd done things he wasn't proud of, but he'd survived. And he had soul scars hidden under the bluster and bonhomie of Maxwell Lewis.

Gibson walked over to him and wrapped slim arms around him in a hug. "You're amazing," he whispered against Maxwell's ear. "I'm sorry you went through all that without any family around to help."

Maxwell closed his eyes, savouring the scent of soap and man even as the memories came flooding back and twisted his soul. Gibson made him want to share things. "My mum died in childbirth with me. I only had my dad and my older brother Kent and we were close." He hugged Gibson tighter. "They went on a trip to Switzerland in 2000 for the weekend. I was in school so couldn't make it. There was this huge mudslide in the Alpines and they were both killed."

Gibson made a small sound of distress. "Oh, God, that's awful. You went into foster care?"

Maxwell sighed. "Yeah. It wasn't that bad but Levi convinced me it was and we ran away. I was stupid. And by the time I realised the grass wasn't greener…" his voice tailed away "It was too late to go back. I couldn't do it. Couldn't leave Levi. He was my best friend. He needed me."

For a moment both men stood there in each other's arms and then Maxwell stepped back. There'd been enough emotional baggage unpacked. He needed caffeine.

"You want more coffee? I can use some more." He wandered to the kitchen and busied himself refreshing his cup. Gibson laid his mug down on the counter and watched Maxwell fill it up.

"What made you become a flight attendant?"

Maxwell stirred sugar into Gibson's drink. "I left school, worked various jobs, got a job in a travel agency. I loved seeing the other parts of the world. It was so far removed from where I'd been so I decided I wanted to see it too." He handed Gibson his mug. "I applied to the airline four years ago and got accepted. And here I am."

He plonked himself down on the still unmade bed-couch. "Now you know about me. What about you? Who is Gibson Henry?"

Gibson sat cross-legged on the bed as he sipped his coffee. "I'm perfectly ordinary. I design games, own a company with my best friend Jack, travel around meeting sexy flight attendants and blowing them in the loo." He grinned. "My parents are still alive and live near Edinburgh with my brother."

"And you never see the same man twice." Maxwell smiled at him but he didn't feel smiley. "And there's nothing ordinary about you."

Gibson flushed. "I'm a little commitment-phobic," he admitted. "I'm too young to settle down and I have a lot I want to do still. Jack and I want to finish designing *Camp Queen* so it can win the Croesus Gaming Award." His eyes gleamed with avarice. "It's a big award in the industry and if we get it, it could mean a lot of investment into the company so we can develop more games and grow. Perhaps even win a bigger award. We missed out on winning the Croesus with one of our previous games, *Blockshock*, when it was nominated. I want to win this time. It would be a real coup for an LGBT game to win it, and mean a lot to me personally too. It has to be the best it can be."

His face shone with hope and thoughts of obviously getting something that meant a lot to him. Maxwell hoped his dream would come true for him and one day he might get to see Gibson's expression if he actually won.

Maxwell's phone rang again, and with a pang of guilt, he realised he hadn't called Grant back yet. He answered and winced at the peeved voice of his boss.

"Thank you *so* much for answering your phone," the syrupy voice echoed down the line.

Maxwell rolled his eyes. "Sarcasm is wasted on me, you know that. I deflect it to something I can use, like, 'Oh do you remember you gave me time off and this happens to be my time-off day—one of three, if I'm not mistaken." He winked at Gibson. "Whaddya want?"

"Fiona has food poisoning. She can't make the late flight to Spain tonight unless we want her upchucking all over the passengers. I wondered if you wanted the shift and I'll make it up to you."

"Oh yeah? How?" Maxwell stood up, held the phone to his ear with his shoulder and stretched. He was gratified to see Gibson's eyes follow the movement of his tee shirt and fix on the treasure trail on his belly.

Yep. I've still got it. He wants me.

"You can still have your three days off, and you'll get a full day for the one shift tonight. That's a bargain."

In Grant terms, it was indeed a bargain. He was tight fisted with his 'in lieu' arrangements on holiday. "Okay. I'll be there later for the shift. Eight pm, yes?"

"Thanks Max." Grant sounded relieved. "I appreciate that. See you later then." He rang off and Maxwell threw his phone on the bed.

"Working tonight then?" Gibson asked. "That sucks."

Maxwell blew out his cheeks. "I could use the money, and I've nothing else planned so why not." He looked down at Gibson. "What are your plans for the weekend?"

"I've got work to do on the game today and Jack and I are going to a friend's house tonight for a get together. Tomorrow I'll be back working on *Camp Queen* again." He blew back a piece of hair that had fallen over his forehead. "More drawing. More coding. More fine tuning. It's a never-ending process but God, I love it."

The passion for his art clearly reflected on Gibson's face and envy pinged in Maxwell's chest. He loved his job, but not like this. Not with the overwhelming 'kick it to the curb' intensity showing in Gibson.

When he'd been a kid, all Maxwell had wanted to do when he grew up was be a doctor. He wanted to wear the white coat and heal people, make sure they didn't die from some stupid thing like amniotic fluid embolisms—the thing that had killed his mother when he'd been born. He knew it hadn't been his fault; his dad had told him over and over again he wasn't to blame in any way, but still. It hurt knowing his birth had killed her.

That chance had disappeared with the death of the rest of his family and instead, his path had gone a different route.

"Sounds cool. And you get to go to a party in between. Is Jack gay too?"

Gibson snorted loudly. "God, no. He's got a girlfriend, Beth. They're mad about each other. Jack and I have been buddies since secondary school." Gibson smiled fondly. "He's a bit like you, a white knight, but the straight version. Always fighting my corner and rescuing me from scrapes." His lips pursed adorably. "I seem to have a habit of getting them into them."

"And why do I believe that?" Maxwell murmured in amusement.

Gibson giggled and Maxwell fell even harder down the slippery slope of wanting to keep him. "Oh, God, I remember once this kid at school was picking on me because of my size. I mean I'm not saying I'm a lightweight or anything but I'm a computer geek for God's sake, not a fighter. Jack is a big guy. He's not fat but he's scary. We were always called Laurel and Hardy at school because of the size difference. Anyway, this guy punched me, a couple of times and Jack comes barrelling across the quadrant and punched his lights out. I swear the bullying dick flew a hundred feet through the air."

Maxwell's blood was boiling at the thought of anyone punching Gibson not once, but twice. "Jack sounds like a prince," he growled. "I'm glad you have someone like him looking out for you."

"Yeah, he's the best. He had a hernia though when he saw me in this outfit. He worries about me." Gibson smirked. "I'll cute 'em to death if anyone tried to mess with me." He leaned forward on his hands and knees and waggled his bum.

Maxwell's groin took notice of the sexy gesture and his pulse rate increased to land speed record. "Oh yes. On the scale of one to ten of cuteness, you overshoot the mark."

Gibson raised an eyebrow. "I have a tendency to do that. Overshoot." His peal of laughter made Maxwell snigger.

"God, you are incorrigible." Maxwell was getting more and more out of depth with this man. "Anyway, breakfast. Do you want some?"

Gibson shook his head in regret. "I can't. I need to get home, get on the laptop. My fingers are itchy to get some work done. Plus these damn shorts are cutting my balls in half so I need to change." He smiled up at Maxwell as he clambered off the bed. "Best I get off."

Gibson looked around the messy room, and spotted his coat. "I guess I should pop this on over the outfit so I don't get had up for indecent exposure. Or get beaten up or mugged. That wouldn't do. I'd have to call my crazy nut-kicking guy to help me out again." He chortled and as he shrugged into his coat, Maxwell's sense of loss grew stronger.

"Oh, okay. Well, thanks for last night and this morning. I enjoyed having you over."

Gibson grinned at him. "It was a pleasure. Thanks again for the whole *Karate Kid* thing at the club."

He picked up his bum bag and clipped around his waist. He reached out and framed Maxwell's face in warm hands as he kissed him. Maxwell closed his eyes and pretended, for one split second, that Gibson was his. He infused all the longing in his heart into the kiss and when they finally split apart, Gibson looked dazed.

"Great kiss. Whoever gets you one day will be one lucky guy." Those well-meaning yet careless words cut Maxwell to the quick.

He tried to smile. "Yep, one day he won't know what hit him."

Gibson flapped a hand. "Okay then. See ya around, Max. Thanks for having me."

Gibson was gone in a flash of blond hair and white teeth, leaving Maxwell with a heart emptier than it had ever been before. Gibson hadn't even bothered to give him his number. Maxwell scowled darkly. Even though he had it already, the implications rattled in his head like a loose marble. It was obvious Gibson had seen this as just a stray hook–up, and Maxwell was damned if he was going to beg for more from the man. He did have some pride left.

Chapter 7

Gibson wheeled his suitcase into his flat at midday, and heaved a sigh of relief at being home. The flight to Dublin had been an eventful one. Slotting his case in the corner of the hallway, with a promise to himself to unpack later, he went straight to the fridge and got out a beer. He opened it and took a large, thirsty swig.

"Christ, that was the flight from hell," he muttered grumpily as he slumped down at the kitchen breakfast nook on a stool. "I am never flying WeGo Air ever again."

"I don't know why you changed it in the first place, dumb arse." Jack wandered into the room, clad in sweatpants, scratching his belly and yawning. "I told you to stick with Target. They're far better." Jack yawned again and opened the fridge. He took out a half-empty bottle of orange juice and drank it down.

Gibson knew why he'd changed airlines but he wasn't going to tell Jack the real reason. Maxwell Lewis had been on his mind, creeping in like an insidious flame flicking at his heart, and he'd tried to ignore it. Cruz had noticed Gibson's man crush too and given him hell too about it. His fiery little friend had told him in no uncertain terms he was being a 'pathetic idiot' trying to avoid something his heart wanted, all uttered in Cruz' adorable Spanish accent. Gibson wasn't comfortable thinking of Max as something permanent.

"Change is good," Gibson said waspishly as he raised his beer to his lips and took another swallow. "Variety is the spice of life and all that crap."

"Yeah?" Jack grinned slyly. "It didn't have anything to do with you being hung up on that cute air steward guy you fucked then?" He sniggered as Gibson felt his face flush.

God, was he that transparent about his infatuation?

"I am so not *hung up* on him," Gibson snapped. "And we didn't fuck. He didn't want to." He heard the pique in his voice and too late he realised he'd played straight into Jack's hands. His friend was like a Venus flytrap, inviting the unaware into its inviting depths only to be devoured to the bone.

Jack nodded sagely, blue eyes twinkling. "Oh, God. The great Gibson Henry being turned down for a fuck. What *is* the world coming to?" He cackled loudly at Gibson's rude gesture. "Gib, you haven't stopped talking about Max this, Max that. Then you went all quiet, and next I knew you'd changed airlines. I knew something was up."

He walked past and ruffled and ruffled Gibson's hair, which earned Jack a glare. "He got under your skin. Admit it. Changing your flight was your way of saying you don't want to care about seeing him again when you do. You have a reputation to keep up, don't you?" His tone grew admiring. "I have to say, I've never seen you like this over one guy. He must be something else. And I want to shake his hand when I see him."

"Why?" Gibson narrowed his eyes and huffed. He thought not for the first time how well Jack knew him. He had indeed changed his flight so he didn't have to see the sultry and sexy Maxwell Lewis again. Like a dessert of something fluffy and light on the outside, but dark, spicy and tantalising when you bit into it, the man had pervaded his thoughts; those chocolate brown eyes and firm lips invading when they had no business doing so. Gibson still remembered the soft kiss pressed to his cheek in the nightclub, as if by doing it, Max could take the sting out of his slapped face and make it all better. Gibson wasn't used to such tenderness. It scared him and when he was scared, he ran.

"Because he stuck up for you and did his crazy karate thing. I want to see it." Jack's voice brought Gibson back to the present—he'd forgotten he'd even asked a question. He'd been too busy seeing a scorpion tattoo on lean haunches and the shadowed expression on Max's face when he'd talked about his past.

"Well, yeah, there was that," Gibson admitted

"And I want to meet the man who's got you all aflutter." Jack winked.

Gibson snorted. "I think you have me mixed up with someone else who actually gives a damn. You know me. I don't do repeats. Usually," he amended hastily, because he had with Max. *Damn.* And he wanted to do it again.

"You tell yourself that." Jack's knowing smile irked Gibson no end. He ignored his friend and polished off the rest of his beer. He'd had nothing to eat so it gave him a pleasant buzz.

"I'm going to shower and change then I'm going to get stuck into some work. And I'm not going to talk about him again, so there." Gibson did the adult thing and stuck his tongue out at Jack as he brushed past him to get to the bathroom. "We've got a game to get ready because next year, we're going to win the award. I don't need any permanent distractions."

Jack nodded sagely. "I hear you. Enjoy your shower." He smirked.

Gibson flounced past him, flinging his hair back as he passed. All this talk of Max had made him horny. The memory of their frenzied frotting and the feeling of Max's fingers in his arse as their cocks rubbed together was giving him a hard-on. The shower sounded like a safe place to take care of it, even if Jack knew what he was about to do.

When the water was warm enough and steam billowed out in opaque clouds into the spacious bathroom, Gibson ensured the door was locked and stepped into the glass enclosure. He loved the shower for both its size and the larger showerhead producing enough pressure to massage his head and shoulders to ease the tension in his body. There was also plenty of room to jerk off, and as he smoothed Imperial Leather shower gel all over his torso, he gave his cock a sly twist or two to get him started.

Closing his eyes, he recalled Max's lips taking his in a kiss, sparking heat in his groin; his fingers deep in his arse, finding that spot that sent shivers through him and made him plead for more. Gibson stroked his cock, fingers gripping tightly, making sure he slid his thumb over the heated head, causing him to gasp in pleasure. The warmth of the water and the fragranced steam assaulted his senses until he was dizzy with the need to come.

He lifted one leg onto the small ledge than ran on one side of the shower. As his hand tightened its grip on his dick, Gibson reached down and pushed a finger inside himself. The simple fact of having his arse filled, with the memories of Max's thrusts inside him, caused him to shudder as he worked himself faster, making one finger into two and holding back the needy groans as he synchronised his hands to both fuck himself and jerk off at the same time.

He lost his breath as water trickled into his open, panting mouth and when he finally peaked, he remembered Max's smouldering eyes gazing into his, watching him reach orgasm. Gibson's cock splattered its release onto wet tiles and was washed away.

Boneless, satiated and wondering what the hell was going on with him, Gibson finished his shower, turned off the water and wrapped a towel around his waist.

"I need to get a grip," he muttered to himself as he ran a razor over his barely-there stubble. Troubled green eyes looked at him from the mirror. "This guy is messing with my head and that's not on." He scowled at himself. "Maybe you need to get him out of your system by hooking up with someone else." There was the faint swelling of hope it could work. "I think later tonight I need to find me a club, dance and get laid. That'll solve the problem of Mr Maxwell bloody Lewis."

***

Lying in a strange bed in a puddle of cooling semen and sweat twelve hours later, after a night of tequila and some fairly dirty dancing on the floor at The Capella Club, Gibson stared at the man snoring softly beside him. Vic had been sweet enough, blowing Gibson off in the bathroom then bringing him home to his small terraced house not far from the club, but the night hadn't been anything earth shattering. Yes, they'd fucked; Vic eager and willing to be nailed as much as Gibson had been to do the nailing. It had gotten them both off but Gibson had this feeling of something *unfinished.* As if it hadn't been enough to simply have a good time. He was a little uncomfortable about the fact that as Vic had been ploughing his arse, Gibson had been thinking about Phoenix's costume design. It happened often with him when he couldn't feel an emotional connection to the man he was in bed with, but he was pretty sure when he'd been with Max, the man had been the only thing on his mind.

After they'd both got their rocks off, Vic had smiled, said, "That was good," and fallen asleep. Gibson now lay beside him in the wet patch wondering whether to catch a few z's or piss off home now. He decided on the latter.

He slunk into the bathroom, did a superficial clean-up and got dressed. When he got back to the bedroom, which smelt of sex, cigarette smoke and sweat, he gathered up his satchel and left.

His flat was dark when he got home in the early hours of the morning.

Thank God I don't have an office job to go to. Being my own boss has its perks.

He wasn't tired so he decided he'd do some work on *Camp Queen*. He did some of his best thinking in the early hours. Getting back into the familiar tasks of sketching outlines and planning his scenes made Gibson forget everything other than the task in hand.

When he heard a cough behind him, he looked up to find Beth standing in a soft towelling robe and a wry grin on her round face. Gibson liked Beth; she was good to Jack, had a wicked sense of humour and was always willing to play *Blockshock* with him. He and Jack might have developed the game but it was still a lot of fun to play as a gamer. There were still Easter eggs in the game Jack had hidden that Gibson delighted in finding.

Beth shook her head. "Gibs, it's six-thirty in the morning. Have you even been to bed yet?"

Gibson squinted at her and then at the clock on the wall. "Fuck, is it? I got in early this morning and got a little sucked in." He stretched, easing the kinks in his spine. Behind his spectacles, his eyes stung.

Beth shook her head as she moved to the kitchen. "I guess you could use coffee then. Unless you're going to try and get some sleep now?"

Gibson yawned. "Coffee first, then sleep." He smiled at Beth gratefully. "Thanks."

"You look knackered," Beth remarked. "And you pong a bit too. Had a good night then?"

Gibson flapped a hand. "So-so. And yes, I'm aware I'm not as fresh as I could be. I'll shower in a sec. I need to get some caffeine inside me first then I'll crash."

Beth chuckled as she pottered in the kitchen. "You're the only guy I know who can go to sleep on caffeine and Red Bull. If it were me, I wouldn't be able to sleep at all."

She came over and passed Gibson a steaming cup of coffee. He took it thankfully.

"It's a gift." Gibson drank hot gulps of strong coffee. "It's what keeps me going so I can get all *this* done." He waved at 'this,' his laptop and various drafts of character sketches, ideas for scenes and half-crumpled balls of paper. "Creativity is a bitch."

"I heard you had a beau," Beth remarked, staring at him over the top of her coffee cup. "Jack told me you saw this guy and now you're stuck on him."

Gibson put his cup down on the side table. "Firstly, who the hell says 'beau' anymore?" he snorted. "And secondly, I am not hung up on anyone. It was a one-night stand and won't be repeated." He wondered why that thought triggered a pang in his chest. "Anyhoo, what does your gormless fellow know? He's nothing but a big galoomp."

Beth spat out a mouthful of coffee as she laughed. "I'll let you repeat that when he's awake, shall I? He'll probably give you a wedgie."

Gibson winced, remembering the last time he'd had his underwear driven up his crack by an unrepentant Jack. "He can try," he muttered. "But seriously, what is all the sudden concern with my love life and the men I see? Have I missed the camera crew for *My Mad, Sad Life* lurking around and am I on air all of a sudden?"

My Mad, Sad Life was a current reality TV show where hidden cameras recorded roommates living together and cataloguing their chats, antics and their sometimes sexual activity. Gibson had watched it once then vowed to never do it again.

"No, dufus. We're worried about you. I mean, you flit from guy to guy like a honeybee and I guess we want to see you settled."

Gibson rolled his eyes. "God save me from happy het couples who think they have to have their gay best friend as 'settled' as they are." His tone was affectionate, and Beth sniffed.

"This guy sounded like the real deal, though. I mean, he did the Crane Kick for you."

Gibson grinned. "He did, didn't he? And he was sweet afterwards. He's funny and sexy, and oh my God, his story about living on the streets made me want to hug him better, you know?" He broke off at Beth's knowing smirk, feeling his face heat up. "What's that for?"

"You liked him," she said dreamily. "Our little boy is growing up."

Gibson scowled. "Maybe I liked him better than any of the others. That doesn't mean I want to marry him." He sniffed regally.

Even if I do have this crazy desire to call him up and see how he is. I mean, what the hell? Since when did I become potential relationship material?

Beth giggled. "Oh, Gibson. I love you can pretend to be so damn clueless. It's so adorable."

Gibson threw the lounge cushion at her. "Bite me," he snarled. "Don't you have somewhere else to be rather than harassing me so early in the morning?"

Beth delivered her parting shot as picked up the other coffee mug, presumably Jack's, and made her way back to their room. "The very fact you get all angsty about me teasing you is enough for me. I think you have a thing for this man."

With a cheeky grin, she disappeared into the hallway. Gibson sat for a few minutes, finishing his coffee and trying uncomfortably to convince himself he did not have a thing for Max, and if he never saw the man again, it wouldn't matter one jot.

Two weeks later, after not being able to stop thinking about Maxwell bloody Lewis, and having a dry spell that was driving him crazy because the men he was with weren't doing it for him anymore, Gibson broke down and sent a text.

***

Maxwell had given up on ever hearing from Gibson again. He hadn't seen him on any other flight he'd attended on since the club outing, but then he supposed Gibson wasn't some bigwig businessman who lived on aeroplanes as a second home. Also, Maxwell been working long hours and the opportunity to get together with anyone anyway had been lean. He'd even refused a blowjob in the loo a few days ago, when he'd done another flight to New York. Maxwell knew he was seriously messed up.

He was sitting with Leslie and Oliver in a bar in the middle of London when he got the text. At first Maxwell ignored it. They were deep in discussion about debating whether bare-backing was ever an option in porn scenes. Oliver ran to the belief that even if he knew the other guy's history and had his medical results shown to him to prove he was clean, he'd still not bare-back for a scene. Leslie agreed and in all truth, so did Maxwell. In his opinion, bare-backing in porn was never an option. But it was fun riling Oliver by playing devil's advocate and seeing him get all worked up about things. Since they were involved in a heated debate about the topic, he didn't want to spoil the fun by checking his texts.

Leslie shook his head, black bangs falling across his face. "I think it's two against one, Max." He grinned. "And I'm thirsty. I think we need more drinks. Come give me a hand, baby?" He cast a heated look at Oliver who cast one back.

Maxwell rolled his eyes. "We all know what that means. The two of you are going to go get off somewhere under the pretext of buying drinks. Fine, away with you. Don't be too damn long. I'm parched."

His friends stood up with alacrity and were soon halfway across the floor towards the bar—and no doubt the bathroom. Maxwell sighed as he took out his phone. He was feeling the loneliness tonight. That lonely feeling was assuaged somewhat when he saw the text message.

"Oh my God. Gibson," he murmured with growing excitement. His fingers scrabbled to open the message.

Gibson here. Hope you don't mind. Wanted to say hi.

Maxwell chuckled. *Hi. How are you?*

Ok. Wondered if you wanted to get together for a drink?

Maxwell couldn't type fast enough. This was encouraging.

Sure. When and where? I'm flying long haul this week. Back in town Monday.

Oh. I see.

Maxwell waited in anticipation for the next text. It was a long time coming.

I guess maybe we could do the Tues night? Do you know Galileo's Restaurant in Soho?

Yep. I'm with someone now who knows the owner. Want me to get us booked in?

Maxwell waited smugly. He could imagine sitting across a table from Gibson, with some fine wine, great food, candles on the table, as they stared into each other's eyes…

His romantic dream was somewhat shattered with Gibson's next text.

Oh only for drinks. Not dinner. That ok?

Maxwell scowled. Fine, if that's all he wanted, he could do that. Gibson obviously didn't see this as a 'dinner date.'

Sure. Say 8 pm then?

He was so fixated on watching his phone and waiting for the beep of a received text he didn't notice Oliver and Leslie arrive back at the table. His friend gave a low chuckle and gave him a hard punch to his arm.

Maxwell glared at him. "Stop bruising the merchandise." He glanced down at his phone. No reply.

"You had this look on your face like Santa had told you that you got that anatomically correct G.I. Joe with the nine-inch dick you always wanted." Oliver smirked. "Is there someone special on the other end of the phone?"

Leslie laughed softly and raised one immaculately plucked eyebrow in Maxwell's direction.

Maxwell flushed. "It's Gibson."

Oliver's eyes widened. "The geeky guy you're hung up on?"

Leslie slapped Oliver's arm with a snort. "Don't call him a geek. It's rude."

Oliver stared at him in confusion. "Why? It's what he is, isn't it?" He turned to Maxwell for confirmation.

Maxwell huffed. "Yes, he's a geek, but he's my geek and I'm the only one allowed to call him that. He asked me to drinks at Galileo's."

Leslie leaned forward, hand on Maxwell's arm. "Oh, I'll call Eddie, get him to ask Giddy to set you up a nice, quiet table somewhere where you guys can get to know each other. Anything special you want, tell me. I know Eddie does this fabulous beef dish—"

Maxwell leaned across and laid a finger across Leslie's lips. "Slow down, Patti Stanger. He doesn't want dinner, only drinks, so I guess we'll be sitting at the bar." He removed his finger.

Leslie looked dumbfounded. "Honestly?" he pouted. "That sucks."

Maxwell had to agree. But he'd take what he could get. "It's fine. At least he texted me." He smirked. "The boy's been thinking about me."

Oliver looked amused. "Maxwell, if I didn't know you better, I'd say you've not stopped thinking about him too. I never thought I'd see the day someone on your spreadsheet made a return entry." He winked. "Apart from me of course. I think I rated four and a half in technique." The smirk on his face made Maxwell grin.

Leslie gave a soft snort. "Do you mind? I'm right here, hello." He mock-glared at Oliver, whose face fell.

"Oh hell, sorry beautiful. I meant, you know, when you weren't in the picture, not now of course." Oliver reached over and cupped Leslie's chin. "You know you're all the man I ever want."

If it hadn't been something Maxwell himself pined for, the look of adoration between two men would have made him barf right then and there at such sweetness.

Maxwell cleared his throat. "God, you two. Stop it. You're giving me a woody. I—"

His phone pinged and he hastened to check it.

Eight pm is fine. See you then.

Maxwell knew he was busted when he looked up to see both his friends staring at him in amazement. He immediately tried to lose the goofy grin he knew he wore. But it was too late.

"Did you see your face?" Leslie said breathily. "Oh-My-God. Our Maxwell is in L-O-V-E if my romance radar has anything to say about it."

Oliver nodded his head. "Oh yes. I saw it too. My friend, you have it bad." His slow glance was assessing and if anyone saw right through him at this moment, it was Oliver.

Maxwell shrugged. "So I like the guy. Sue me."

Oliver smiled. "I like this new Maxwell. It's about time you found someone special." He waved over a waiter. "Could we have a bottle of champagne please? I think we have a little something to celebrate. My friend here found out what his heart is for."

Maxwell sighed. He was *so* never going to live this down.

Chapter 8

Maxwell waited at the bar in Galileo's for Gibson to arrive. He looked at his watch. Seven fifty-five. He'd been sitting there close on half an hour, knocking back a beer and trying to look as if he wasn't anxiously waiting for his date to show.

He loved this restaurant. The ambience was welcoming, the staff professional and friendly, and the owner of the place wasn't half bad either.

Leslie gushed about his best friend Eddie and his partner Gideon Kent, and Maxwell had to say, Gideon was very easy on the eyes. He watched in day-dreamy lust as Gideon strode around the restaurant being all bossy and macho. A polite cough brought him back down to earth. Maxwell blinked and looked into amused green eyes framed with thin black spectacles. The glasses looked different to the ones he'd seen before and he wondered how many pairs Gibson actually had.

"Am I disturbing you?" Gibson asked drily, but his eyes were amused. "I can leave if you've seen something else you'd rather have."

Maxwell knew there was no one else he'd rather have than the sexy man standing in front of him. Gibson's hair shone like spun white gold. He wore tight black jeans, with a thick belt and buckle, a tight, dove-grey shirt with a darker grey collar and open cuffs to his forearms, and black boots. The man took Maxwell's breath away and did nothing to ease the ache in his cock, an anticipatory ache he'd had since getting to the venue. The appreciative look his drinks partner gave him as he ran his eyes down Maxwell's body made his trousers feel even tighter. Maxwell thought he rocked it dressed in butt-hugging camel chinos and a white button-down shirt teamed with his dark brown leather bomber jacket.

"God, no," Maxwell said breathlessly. "No one here could possibly have anyone better than what I'm looking at." Too late he realised that probably sounded a little presumptive but Gibson didn't seem to mind. His face beamed at the compliment and his pale skin went rosy.

"Thanks," he murmured as he struggled onto a high barstool. His feet barely touched the footrest and he scowled briefly. "They always make these damn things too high for people like me. Someone should tell them we're not all six-foot monster men."

"Shall I ask them for a booster step?" Maxwell laughed at the fierce glare directed at him. "Or not. It's good to see you."

"Yeah, you too." Gibson beckoned to the bar lady. "How was the flight? Where did you go?"

"I was in New York again. Had a layover, met some old friends and now I'm back on the shorter routes."

Gibson nodded. "Cool. What can I get you to drink?"

"I'll have a screwdriver, please." Maxwell watched as Gibson gave the order to the bar lady, including a Jack Daniel's for himself.

"Are those new glasses? I don't think I've seen them before." Maxwell peered at them.

Gibson shook his head. "Nah. I have five different pairs. I like to change the frames around depending on what I'm wearing."

"You don't do contacts then?"

Gibson frowned. "Can't abide them, they make my eyes water and I get too much eye strain, especially working on a computer all the time. I have this thing about my eyes—worry about losing my sight one day—so I try and keep them happy."

Maxwell was intrigued. "Where does that fear come from?"

Gibson shrugged. "I saw this film once when I was a kid about a guy going blind and since then it's been something I worry about." He made an adorable moue. "I know it's crazy. My optometrist says my eyes are healthy, but that's me."

Maxwell huffed. "Huh." The bartender put the drinks down on the bar and Maxwell picked his up. "I was surprised to get a text from you."

"Not as surprised as I was I sent it," was the quick reply. "Jack and Cruz have been pestering me ad nauseum to get in touch, and don't even let me get started on Jack's girlfriend Beth." He rolled his eyes but Maxwell did a double take when he saw the flush staining Gibson's cheeks.

"What?" Gibson said defensively. "I told you I don't do repeats, yet here I am. What does that tell you?"

"I don't know," Maxwell said honestly. "I'm not great at reading between lines. I prefer a full-on direct approach myself. Sounds like your friends forced into you something you don't want." His chest tightened at the thought.

Gibson's eyes darkened and he licked his lips as he glanced around the restaurant. "That's what you think? I make my own mind up, Max." He grinned. "A bit like this."

He reached over and pulled Maxwell's face to his, sliding his mouth over Maxwell's willing lips and kissing him hungrily with the skill of a porn star. Maxwell wasn't quite used to this sort of display in public, especially when it wasn't even in a gay bar. As his mouth was assaulted, all he could think of dreamily was, 'God, he's a great kisser.' When Gibson released him, he stared around in a dazed stupor. The bar lady was grinning widely, her face indicating her approval.

"Was that a bit more direct?" Gibson's mouth was swollen, probably much like his own. His face was pink, the hunger in his eyes unmistakeable.

Maxwell simply nodded, dumbfounded. "As long as we don't get kicked out," he finally squeaked.

Gibson grinned. "The guy who owns this place is gay, half his friends are gay and they often indulge in a little tonsil hockey themselves at the tables. I've been here and seen it and let me tell you, it's quite a show."

"Yes, I know Gideon is gay. I know most of his friends as well, but still, he might take exception to two guys swallowing each other's tongues in his place."

Gibson snorted softly. "Better than swallowing something else in public," he murmured. "I'm rather hoping that might come later though, in private."

"Oh, God," Maxwell said faintly. "You are the wicked poster child for the sexual frustration of men everywhere, I swear."

Gibson raised two fingers to his mouth, sucked on them a couple of times, drew them out with a pop then held them in front of his mouth like the smoking barrel of a revolver. He blew on them and Maxwell truly believed he might come in his pants.

"You know Gideon then?" Gibson sipped his drink, seeming to be unaware he'd caused grievous bodily harm to Maxwell, and yet the glint in his eyes and smirk on his face indicated otherwise. "I've been here a couple of times. He seems like a nice enough guy. Sexy too."

"Not personally, only by name and conversation. I know his partner Eddie's best friend, Leslie, and I used to sleep with *his* guy."

Gibson looked confused, so Maxwell elaborated. "Leslie is now going out with my ex-fuck buddy Oliver, although you probably know him better as Nicky Starr, the porn actor."

Gibson's eyes bugged out. "You used to fuck Nicky Starr? No way, José."

"Way." Maxwell sipped his drink, taking great delight in Gibson's astonishment. "Oliver and I go way back. Obviously we don't get together anymore that way, as friends."

"Oh fuck. That's hot. Thinking of you and him…" A shudder racked Gibson's body. "Is he as good in person as he is on camera?"

"Better," Maxwell said with a smug grin. "Oliver is inventive yet he cares about his partner."

Gibson took a deep slurp of his drink. "Sweet."

"Not to harp on it, but why *did* you call me?" Maxwell was harping on it. He couldn't help himself.

Gibson rolled his eyes and threw him an exasperated glance. "You're a bull terrier, you know that? Why can't you accept I'm here and let it be?"

Maxwell shrugged. Honesty was probably the best policy. "I've no desire to invest more of myself in someone who's playing me. It's not where I want to be. Either we see each other simply as friends and that's it, or if we sleep together sometimes, it becomes something that might become more. I know it's early days and I don't want to scare you off, but I am not being a notch on someone's bedpost. Not anymore."

Gibson was quiet and Maxell wondered if he'd come on too strong.

But he was the one who contacted me, and he knew how I felt about being casual. At worst, we can maybe stay friends without benefits. It'll be tough but I'd do it.

Gibson looked up from the silent contemplation of his half-empty drink. "I liked spending time with you. I don't usually have guys on my mind afterwards, but you, I do. I thought maybe we could get to know each other better, see where this goes." He grinned. "I'm not lying when I tell you I like you, I want you, and I hope mad, animal sex is on the cards."

Maxwell's tummy squirmed in pleasant anticipation. His dick liked the idea too.

"I'm *not* looking to move fast, get married, adopt kids and move into a house together." Gibson grimaced in distaste. His fingers played with a paper napkin on the bar. He looked nervous. "That's a deal breaker. But if you're happy to take a chance and be with me when you're not gadding about the world up high, and see what happens between us, then that's a plan."

"I'm not looking for that either," Maxwell murmured. He cleared his throat. "Let's be clear. We see each other— exclusively—as and when we can?" He held his breath as he waited for the reply.

Gibson blinked. "Exclusive?" His hands stopped their fidgeting.

Maxwell's heart sank. "Yes. I mean, that's kind of how I think dating works."

"Dating?" Gibson's hands started playing with the napkin again.

Maxwell was out of his depth now. What the hell did this guy want? "Isn't that what we're going to do? Date?"

Had he completely misread the situation and made a fool of himself?

He knocked back his drink and waved to the bartender. He needed another. Gibson Henry was hard work. He gestured to their drinks. "Could we have a repeat please?"

The soft snicker from beside him made him glance round. Gibson had a grin on his face, a twinkle in his eye, and Maxwell had the distinct feeling he was missing something.

"What are you laughing at?" he muttered crossly.

"You are so gullible," Gibson chuckled. "I was yanking your chain, sexy." His hand reached up and caressed Maxwell's cheek. "I might be a bit of a slut but when I agree to *see* a guy, I'm monogamous." His eyes flashed. "Let's not call it dating yet, though. That's a big word. Let's call it seeing each other."

The warmth flooding his body was like treacle flowing through his veins and Maxwell loved it. He could live with that. For a while.

"Bitch," he sniffed as he paid the bartender. "I think this is going to be a barrel of laughs, being with you."

Gibson's face shadowed. "I can't say how it will all turn out," he warned. "But I'm happy to take it day by day, let things develop slowly…"

Maxwell reached over and covered Gibson's hand with his. "That's all I need. My social life is crap at the best of times, with my shift patterns and days off. I'll warn you it might not be ideal."

"Meh. It'll be fine. I have so much work to do I can keep myself busy twenty-four hours a day, so we're in the same boat." Gibson quirked an eyebrow. "Now can we leave the shit behind and do some serious drinking? Are you flying tomorrow?"

Maxwell shook his head. "Day off. We can get as crazy as you want…"

The evening passed in a blur of drinking, conversation and laughter and by the time the pair left Galileo's to walk off some of the effects, Maxwell was horny, drunk and desperate to take Gibson home for the night. He wasn't sure though if that's what his 'date' had planned so he went with the flow. It was when they were walking—or rather staggering—past Soho Square Gardens that he had a thought.

He pulled Gibson against the railings and pointed him towards the park. "I've always wanted to make out in a public park," he whispered. "How 'bout you?"

Gibson squinted through fogged glasses at the darkness beyond. "I'm not sure," he said doubtfully. "Haven't they got security, park keepers or whatever? And isn't it locked up?"

Maxwell shook his swimming head. "Nothing we can't handle," he scoffed. "I'm used to sneaking into parks. I lived in them when I was on the streets, remember?" He'd meant it as a light-hearted remark, but the look of sympathy on Gibson's face made him kick himself.

He'd managed to sidestep all Gibson's veiled questions. Over drinks, the man had been like a puppy worrying a stuffed toy, trying to shake the stuffing out of it. Maxwell didn't want to tell his new shiny toy about the rotten, shaming things he'd done as a homeless youth.

"Don't look at me like that," Maxwell murmured. "Those days are gone. Now come on. I can give you a leg up over the railings, and then climb over myself. If we keep to the shadows no one will see us. There's this cool garden hut in the middle I'd like to show you."

Gibson looked unconvinced. "Can't we go back to your place?"

"Come, on, spoil sport. It'll be fun." Gibson hardly had time to protest before Maxwell knelt down on the path on all fours and gestured to Gibson to climb on his back. "Up you go, leg over and onto the other side." He smirked. "Be careful of your crown jewels. I don't want them getting damaged before I've had a chance to have them in my mouth."

"Oh God," Gibson whispered as he clambered onto Maxwell's crouching form. "This is such a bad idea. I'm not used to this sort of physical activity—oomph. Fuck." The dull sound of a body hitting the ground had Maxwell standing up and peering over the fence.

"Gibson, are you okay?"

There was a rustling and an annoyed voice muttered, "Yeah, I lost my balance and fell over the fence. Tell me again this was a good idea?"

Maxwell hopped nimbly over, clearing the top with inches to spare between his groin and the spiked railing. "It was a good idea. Are you okay?"

Gibson was sucking on his hand, his face scrunched up. "No. I tore my damn hand on some bush or something. I'm injured. Carry on without me, Captain. I'll stay behind."

Maxwell laughed softly. "Give it here. Let me see."

He took Gibson's hand and peered at it. There was a nasty gash on the side of his hand, oozing blood. Maxwell reached into his back pocket and drew out a handkerchief. He wet it with spit and then applied it to the cut.

Gibson's mouth gaped open. "You carry a handkerchief? And then spit on it? What are you, my dad?"

Maxwell frowned as he dabbed at the blood. "You don't? And please, girlfriend. Enough of the dad comments. Not conducive to making out."

Gibson sniggered as he pushed his glasses up with one finger. "Maybe I have a daddy fixation."

Maxwell stopped what he was doing and stared at Gibson. "I can be your daddy," he said huskily. "Is that what you wanted to hear?"

Gibson swallowed. "Not really, but when you say it—wow. It does sound sexy."

Maxwell grinned in the darkness as he finished his doctor duties. The cut had stopped bleeding. "There you go. I'll take another look at it when we get home—mmphh."

His words were muffled by lips finding his as Gibson's tongue slid into his mouth while the Lacoste Red-scented warm man dragged Maxwell by the shirt, and pulled him closer. The handkerchief was dropped to the ground as his hands found Gibson's hips. Hardness pressed against the lower part of Maxwell's groin and he gasped with need into the mouth currently excavating his with enthusiasm.

"You drive me crazy," Gibson groaned in between kissing the crap out of him. "I love the feeling of your stubble against my skin. I don't know what it is about you that makes me feel this way. You've been in my damn head for weeks."

"I know exactly what it is about you," Maxwell managed to get out. "You're as sexy as fuck. And ditto on the head games."

Gibson's husky chuckle turned Maxwell on more and he hefted Gibson up. Slim, strong legs wrapped around his hips as Gibson rocked against him, climbed him and attacked his mouth with renewed fervour. It took some doing avoiding knocking Gibson's glasses off his face but with some practice, and some creative angling, they found out how to manage it without injury.

A bang from the street brought them both to their senses and they jumped, unlocking their mouths.

"What was that?" Gibson whispered, tightening his clutch around Maxwell's neck, his dick pressing against Maxwell's harder than before.

"Probably a car backfiring," Maxwell managed to gasp out in between heaving breaths. "We need to get out of sight of the road. I thought we'd make out a bit, not go into full-flown grinding the minute we got in here." He plucked Gibson away from him reluctantly. Gibson got his feet back on the ground.

"Come with me." Maxwell took Gibson's hand and together they walked quickly towards the old black-and-white building in the middle of the park. "Let's stand under here. It's dark, more private than where we were and hopefully no one can see us." He cast a quick glance around the park. He could hear voices coming from the far side of the park, but they didn't sound close enough to be a problem.

"You know we could have gone back to your place or mine." Gibson's fingers idly traced a path down Maxwell's chest, and for the first time, looking down at Gibson's lazy finger, Maxwell noticed his shirt was half undone. The touch of Gibson's fingers against his bare skin inflamed his senses and Maxwell drew in a deep breath.

"I know. But I've never made out in a park, and it was on my bucket list, and I want to do it with you."

Gibson's smile lit up the darkness. "*You* are a romantic, Maxwell Lewis. A big soft romantic." This kiss was softer, sweeter and Maxwell thought his legs were going to buckle beneath him. All he could do was hold Gibson, kiss him back with all the feeling he had in his soul and fall deeper into the silky web being spun around him by Gibson Henry.

Maxwell knew he was in the middle of busy London, where city noises—backfiring cars, house alarms, trundling buses, people's conversation—were paramount, yet all he could hear was the rushing in his ears and the singing in his heart as he held the man in his arms.

I am in so much trouble with this one. God help me.

Gibson finally stopped causing mayhem on Maxwell's mind and body and stepped back, face flushed, bee-stung lips wet and a look of desire on his face.

"I don't want our first real time to be in a public park." Gibson huffed and adjusted himself. "Can we go home and get into a bed? I'm pretty sticky in my underwear already."

Maxwell found his voice. "Of course, sure. Uhmm, your place or mine?"

Gibson considered. "We can go to mine if you like. Jack will probably be there but he's cool when I bring guys home."

"You do that a lot then?" Maxwell cleared his throat. "I mean, I can't judge, I've had a bit of a revolving door in my place myself."

Gibson's face was unreadable. "There've been a few. Do you want the actual number?" His voice was even.

Maxwell shook his head, panicking he'd stuffed things up. "No, of course not. Doesn't matter. Let's go to your place, then. We'll get a taxi because it's quite a trek from here back to..." his voice trailed off as he realised he *knew* where Gibson lived but didn't want him to know he knew. That information had not been gainfully come by and he didn't want to admit he'd stalked him using the passenger manifest.

"Canning Town," Gibson offered helpfully and Maxwell smiled. *Result.*

He glanced at his watch. "It's still early enough to get a taxi. Come on, let's go."

They slipped quietly along the path towards the exit and once again, Maxwell got down on his knees and Gibson once again went over, this time with no injury.

By the time they stepped out of the taxi and into the rather swanky flat Gibson and Jack shared—Maxwell admitted it was a cut above his messy place—there was a sense of awkwardness between them. The passion was still there; the sexual tension in the taxi on the drive over had been unbearable, but entering the quiet of the flat, and Gibson taking his hand and guiding him to what Maxwell presumed was his bedroom was too much like other times a man had led Maxwell to a sexual encounter.

One that hadn't meant as much to him.

Maxwell wanted this to be different.

He stopped outside Gibson's bedroom and the other man turned to him with a question in his eyes. "Are you okay? Did you change your mind?"

Maxwell shook his head. "No, of course not. I don't know what the hell's wrong with me. I guess I'm nervous?" His insides *were* jellied.

Gibson chuckled. "Nervous? Don't be daft. What is there to be nervous about?" He opened his door and beckoned Maxwell in. Gibson closed the door, switched on a bedside light, and Maxwell looked around, admiring the room, trying to get himself back in sync.

"This is trendy. Very you. Cool and classic. I especially like the picture of the muscly dude in leather and the chick in Lycra. Are they from your game—?"

Gibson reached over a soft finger and pressed it against Maxwell's lips. "Yes they are. Now shut up. You're blabbering. I think someone needs to get their clothes off." He grinned and started tugging at Maxwell's trousers.

Maxwell reached a hand down and grasped Gibson, stopping him. "Wait."

Gibson blew a strand of hair from his forehead, his expression uncertain. "What? You *are* having second thoughts, aren't you? Maybe we should have gone to your place."

Maxwell shook his head. "No, not that. Just…"

He removed Gibson's glasses, setting them down on the nearest surface, and pulled him closer, gripping his tight, round arse in hungry hands. He took his mouth in a kiss. *That* was better, he thought happily. Kissing Gibson was his favourite thing to do. The stirrings in his chinos bore testament to the fact.

Gibson moaned softly into his mouth, a sound that made Maxwell's skin prickle with heat and his cock perk up from its semi-hard state to full flagpole.

"It's not that I don't want you," Maxwell murmured in between sloppy, hot kisses. "I want you too much. I was in danger of flaring out, like the Human Torch."

"Hmmm." Gibson's tongue licked Maxwell's top lip. "I can feel how hot you are. Can I take your clothes off now? Cool you down?"

"Be my guest." Maxwell had already started pulling Gibson's shirt over his head and at the sight of pert little nipples and a smooth, toned chest he closed his eyes and imagined he was in heaven.

The impatient removal of clothes led to a few chuckles, soft sighs and breaths of awe as each man revealed the other. By the time they were both naked, any reservations Maxwell had disappeared, and it was all he could do not to jump on top of Gibson and slide into home base. His eyes ran greedily over the now supine man on the top of the bed, lying with arms raised above his head, legs splayed apart wantonly, cheeks flushed and eyes hooded with desire.

For him.

"God, Gibson," he whispered. "You are one gorgeous man."

Gibson's long, swollen cock laid against his belly as he stroked himself lazily, a sly smile on his face indicating he had no doubt as to what he was doing to Maxwell. Gibson's mouth was reddened, his cheeks pink where Maxwell's goatee had rubbed his pale skin.

"So are you. Come over here. I want you in my mouth and I need to taste that scorpion. I want to you to fuck me so hard I lose my breath." He frowned. "We are doing that tonight I take it?"

Maxwell nodded, the sight on the bed stealing his breath. "Definitely."

He crawled onto the bed, straddling Gibson's thighs then bent down to take more kisses from the sweet, willing mouth seeking his. Their cocks pressed together, skin met skin, heated and damp, and Maxwell held Gibson's hands above his head as Maxwell plundered a hot, wet cavern of tongue and lips.

Gibson ground against him, pushing his hips upwards and making soft, breathy noises. His scent stole into Maxwell's nostrils like fragranced steam in a sauna. Gibson pulled away his mouth, leaving Maxwell needy and disappointed.

"Come up here," Gibson gasped as he tugged at Maxwell's hips. "I want what you have. Feed it to me."

Maxwell needed no urging and he scooted up to straddle Gibson's chest, still holding his wrists prisoner, and then slowly, teasingly, painted his lips with the wet tip of his cock. Gibson's mouth opened as he tried to take him in. Each time Maxwell moved back, until a deep, unhappy growl from his lover made his spine tingle.

"Stop teasing me, arsehole." Gibson's body writhed beneath Maxwell's. "I need you." The plea was cut off as Maxwell pushed himself in between those swollen, pink lips and Gibson smiled around him as he took Maxwell in. His eyes closed in bliss and Maxwell could only watch in hunger and a sense of awe as his most sensitive part disappeared in and out of Gibson's talented lips.

He tried not to thrust too deep, not wanting to take liberties, but when Gibson did one particularly deep suck, causing his cheeks to hollow, Maxwell cried out, letting go of Gibson's wrists and flattening his hands against the wall instead. Gibson obviously had no qualms about Maxwell fucking his mouth; his now free hands immediately gripped Maxwell's hips and began pulling him forward, taking him deeper and deeper until Maxwell could take no ore. He wanted to come inside Gibson.

He uttered a throaty growl and pulled out, looking down at a wild-eyed, spunk-smeared Gibson as he panted and recovered his breath.

"Where's your lube and condoms?" Maxwell managed to say.

Gibson reached under the pillow next to him and shoved a tube and a condom into Maxwell's hand. Maxwell's hands trembled as he sheathed himself. The lube he opened, rubbing it over his dick, wincing as he did so because he knew the slightest touch was going to set him off.

"Do you want me on my knees?" Gibson panted. "I don't mind how you take me."

"I want you face to face." Maxwell pushed Gibson's legs apart and dribbled the lube over his hole. "I need to kiss you while I'm in you."

As he prepared the wriggling, moaning man beneath him, both kissing and twisting fingers inside him, Maxwell acknowledged this was the closest he'd been emotionally to another man. Gibson was everything he'd ever wanted.

"Enough prep already," Gibson gasped. "Do me, for God's sake."

Sliding inside a tight, heated channel, hearing Gibson's cries of both pain and pleasure, feeling his muscles tighten around him as Maxwell gained momentum and thrust in a paroxysm of want and lust—it was as if Maxwell had been waiting for this moment all his life.

For this intimate act, with this man.

Maxwell struggled to control himself from coming too soon, and he damped down the rising emotions in his body making him want to blurt out stupid things too soon. Cheesy, sentimental things like, 'I want to keep you forever. Please don't ever go away.' And, 'I think I've been waiting for you all my life.'

The dual act of fucking Gibson's mouth with his tongue and being inside him was almost more than Maxwell could bear. The smell of sex permeating the room together with the smell of sweat, the sound of their flesh slapping together and the overwhelming pleasure in his groin—Maxwell fell long and hard when he came, jettisoning into the condom with a strangled grunt. A prickling sensation flooded his skin, and there was an exquisite tightness in his groin and backside as he clenched muscles already aching from his exertion.

Gibson gave a soft cry as Maxwell collapsed on top of him and his hand moved faster as he pleasured himself, something he'd been busy doing while Maxwell was ploughing into him.

"No, let me," Maxwell gasped as he pushed those frantic hands away. He slid down and sucked Gibson's pretty cock in, sucking hard and teasing his balls and taint as he did so. Gibson's hands clenched the sheets as he muttered expletives and curses and entreaties for Maxwell to finish him, take him deep.

When Gibson cried out he was close, Maxwell moved off and watched as Gibson's spunk covered Maxwell's belly and chest. When Gibson was spent, Maxwell licked his cock clean, and then crawled up to lie beside his lover.

The two men lay replete in silence for a while, both getting their breath back. Maxwell turned to lie on his side and watch Gibson, who looked as if he was dozing. Maxwell wasn't sure what to do next. Was he expected to stay? Should he leave? He knew they'd agreed to date but how far was that being taken?

"I feel you watching me," Gibson murmured, opening his eyes. His hand came out to gently caress Maxwell's sweaty chest. "You're wondering what happens next, aren't you?"

He turned on his side to face Maxwell. Gibson's face softened. "We crawl under the covers and get some sleep," he whispered. "In the morning, maybe I'll get to taste your scorpion like I wanted to. We can go to breakfast at this little roadside cafe down the road makes the best hash browns. Then maybe we can come back here and *I* can fuck *you*." He swung his legs off the bed and stood up, motioning to Maxwell to do the same. Gibson drew back the duvet, wrinkling his nose at the mess on the top then motioned to Maxwell to get back in bed. Once they were both in, he drew the cover over them both and snuggled into Maxwell's side, resting his head in the crook of his shoulder.

"This okay?" he asked sleepily.

Maxwell couldn't answer. The simple and unexpected pleasure of having Gibson's warm body snuggled next to him like a warm puppy was playing havoc with his vocal chords. Instead, he tightened his arm around him, placed a soft kiss on the blond hair tickling his nose and settled into sleep.

Chapter 9

"Sooooo…" Then "Soooo," even louder again. Finally, "Hey, dick breath!"

Gibson looked up in irritation from his workstation to see Jack staring at him, contemplation on his face. "What? You realise you interrupted me at a critical moment when I'm drawing? What the hell is so important?" He had a bit of headache and wasn't in the best of moods.

"When do I get to meet Maxwell?" Jack leaned back in his chair, closed his laptop and slid his feet onto his desk. He slid a piece of gum into his mouth and chewed.

Gibson's temper flared. "You interrupt me to ask me that? Jack, what the hell is wrong with you?"

Jack chewed noisily, knowing how much it annoyed Gibson. His friend had a thing for pushing him lately on the subject of Max. "I want to meet the guy," Jack whined, then popped a bubble. "I mean, you've been seeing him ages now and I still haven't met the dude." He squinted fiercely. "Has the tiny Spaniard met him yet? Because, if he has, I'm challenging him to a duel. I'm your *best* best friend so I get to see this Maxwell dude first."

Gibson rolled his eyes and huffed out a breath. "No, Cruz hasn't met him. He only saw him at the club the night we met. But he and Craig have gone to South America now on a backpacking trip and I have no idea when they'll return. Some sort of sabbatical," he said gloomily. He missed Cruz but they texted every now and then when Cruz remembered to keep in touch.

"And the reason you haven't seen Max yet is because we normally come here when you're flat-out asleep in bed, and you don't get up until like, eleven o'clock in the morning, and by then he's gone. And his work roster is crazy so to be honest, I haven't even seen him much either." Gibson scowled, remembering their last fight about that specific subject.

He and Max were into their fifth week of 'seeing each other' and in that time, they'd probably been together less than the number of fingers he had.

Jack chuckled. "Oh yeah, I remember the fight you two had on the phone. You were like a little spitting kitten. Very entertaining to watch, I have to say."

Gibson grinned wryly. Yes, it had caused one bitch of an argument when Gibson had pitched a hissy fit. Gibson hadn't thought he was getting as many happy times as he should with a dedicated 'boyfriend' and it had royally pissed him off. He enjoyed his alone time, but in all honesty, he'd come to depend on Max's solid presence, his warmth and humour and his sexy body. He never thought he'd have admitted that fact. The matter had resolved itself a few days later after they'd realised they were both being wankers. The make-up sex had been awesome.

Gibson had even managed to meet Oliver Brown and his spitfire of a boyfriend Leslie a couple of times. Gibson had been awestruck at the thought of meeting *the* Nicky Starr. He'd hardly been able to get a word out, and been so tongue tied that Leslie had roared with laughter and whispered to him that Oliver was just an ordinary man, and to 'breathe, honey, breathe.'

"Where is Maxwell today then?" Jack popped another bubble.

Gibson gritted his teeth, wanting to poke his eye out with his shading pencil. "Probably up over the sea, somewhere," he muttered. "Flirting with a passenger."

He'd heard all about the stories of Max's past airline antics—the layovers with call boys on tap for discreet hotel visits, the quick shags in toilets and blowjobs in the less-populated sections of the aircraft. Gibson had even seen Max's *Sexcella* worksheet. He'd been playing a game on Max's laptop, seen the sheet, and with no respect for his man's privacy, he'd taken a peek. He'd been amused at what he'd found.

When Max had found Gibson ogling over the varying attributes of the men he'd slept with over the years, he'd quickly shut it down and moaned at him for his invasion of privacy while hastily telling him there'd been no additions since meeting Gibson.

Max's ire hadn't lasted long; honestly, all Gibson had to do was kiss him to shut him up and he was a goner. Gibson smirked at the fact he *did* have the power. And when he licked long slow trails down Max's scorpion tattoo…it drove the man crazy with lust.

"Dirty little bugger," Jack chuckled. "What are you thinking about with that look on your face?"

Gibson waved his pencil. "None of your beeswax." He hunched over his laptop, back in the land of *Camp Queen* and Phoenix.

"Sooo…"

Gibson hurled his box of paperclips at Jack on the other side of the room—it was a small room, only big enough for the two desks—and swore, "Hell, Jack, what now?"

Jack blew another gum bubble as he frowned. "You have this nasty little imp temper," he mused. "You look all sweet and tiny but inside you're nothing but an itsy, bitsy demon child."

Despite his impatience at his friend's interruptions, Gibson's mouth curved in an unwilling smile. Max had said much the same thing last week when Gibson had chucked a pair of highlighters at him. Max had made the comment about Gibson being like a cupcake with vanilla icing: sweet and pretty. Gibson thought it had emasculated him so he'd tossed his stationery. After the highlighter had hit Max on the cheek, Gibson had been relegated to being a spicy devil cake with a forked tongue. He preferred that description.

"Beth wants to cook dinner for us all here," Jack said with an injured tone. "Maybe you can ask Mr High Flyer when he's available for it."

Gibson sighed. "Fine, I'll ask him when I see him. He's flying out tonight and only back the day after. He has a layover in Venice."

No doubt he'd be getting pictures of the city, together with pictures of Max's dick, and no doubt there'd be some hot and heavy phone sex later. It was how they kept each other going. Max had suggested a Skype session, something apparently his

friend Oliver and partner Leslie did regularly, but Gibson wasn't
too sure about it.

"Is that it then?" he asked testily. "Can I get on with my
work now without you *so*-ing in my ear every couple of
minutes?"

Jack waved airily. "That's it. I wanted a plan to meet the guy
who has tamed my Gib."

Gibson turned a frosty stare on Jack. "He has *so* not tamed
me, arsehole."

*Oh yes he has. Admit it. He's become special to me in a way
I never thought I'd see.*

Gibson's mobile rang. He smiled when he saw who it was.
"Mum. Hi, how are things at home?"

His mother sighed. "Hi, darling. Things are okay here. Your
dad still isn't feeling too well; he's going for more tests. Ricky is
fine and Haggis says hello."

Haggis was the old family dog, a mix of cute and clever
mixed with collie and a bit of Dalmatian. "I'm sorry about Dad.
Do you want me to come home? Is there anything I can do?" Part
of him wanted to go home and see his workaholic father and tell
him to take it easy, and part of him hoped his mother would say
no, because he did have a load of deadlines to meet on his
gaming efforts.

"No son, that's not necessary." Doris Henry sounded tired
and Gibson wondered if he should go home anyway. "Ricky's
here, he pops in every night, so we'll be fine. We're seeing you
in next month anyway for your niece's birthday, aren't we?"

Richard's adorable daughter Chloe was turning six years old
at the start of September, and was the apple of both her father
and uncle's eye. "Yes, I'm flying up early in the morning. I'll get
a taxi to you." Max was scheduled to be on the flight, spending
the night in Edinburgh. Neither of had them had talked about him
going to meet Gibson's family. Gibson hadn't offered and Max
hadn't pushed.

His mother laughed. "Well, that'll be fine. Dad's sleeping at
the moment or I'd let him say hi. But he's been tired so best let
him catch a snooze when he can."

"Okay, Mum. Give him my love when he wakes up. Ask
him to give me a ring and we can have a father-son convo."

Doris snorted. "Convo? Is that text or game speak, Gibson? I assume you mean a conversation."

Gibson rolled his eyes at Jack. He did love his mother but she was a stickler for proper speech. "Yes, I mean a conversation."

Jack was grinning at him across the room, no doubt realising what was going on. As the favourite best friend, he too had been subjected to a few ear bashings on the proper use of language.

"Anyway, the reason I called, other than to see how my youngest son was faring, was to ask you to please bring that old Hibernian FC scarf your dad left at your place last time we visited. He swears blind he had it recently and he won't accept he didn't. He's got this bee in his bonnet about wearing it to a match in a few weeks' time."

Gibson nodded. The scarf was balled up in his cupboard somewhere—at least he hoped it was. A sudden trickle of panic set in. He hadn't seen it in a while. "Sure, I'll bring it. I can't wait to see you both again. And my gorgeous niece of course."

"Good, I'm looking forward to seeing you too, son. I'd better get off, Haggis wants walking and he's going crazy. Say hi to Jack for me and his lovely girlfriend." She paused. "Should I be saying hello to anyone special in your life, Gibson? I mean, I know you don't do relationships as such, I can't remember the last time I actually heard you talk about the same man twice. And your friend Jamie has been popping around here asking after you. He still seems very keen."

"Mum, please." Gibson was mortified at the fact his mother knew he was a player. Jamie had been a guy he'd hooked up with on his last few visits to Cramond—gay pickings were slim in the small village—but he'd been clear to Jamie that the last time had been it. Jamie had started getting a little possessive and Gibson had needed to cut him loose. Thank God Gibson had never given him his mobile number or he'd have been flooded with texts and entreating phone calls.

"Actually, there is a guy I've been involved with for a while. His name is Max, and he's cabin crew on the plane I'll be flying in on."

"Ooh." His mother's voice perked up. "Well, you'll have to bring him to visit when you're here. I'd like to meet the man who has your attention longer than a week. Right, got to go. Talk to you later." His mother rang off and Gibson put his phone down with a defeated sigh.

"Crap. Now she wants to meet him. Why didn't I keep quiet?"

Jack cocked an eyebrow. "You didn't keep quiet because you wanted to tell her that her baby boy wasn't a slut and actually had a man in his life who he didn't pick up at a club for a quickie."

"Fuck you." Gibson heaved another sigh. "I'll find some excuse not to take him. Tell them Max had to work an emergency shift or something."

Jack shifted in his chair, his face puzzled. "Why not introduce him to them? What's the harm?"

Gibson hummed. "It's complicated. I mean, this whole thing with him has moved quite fast and it's different. I like Max, a lot, but I'm not sure I want him to meet my family yet. That seems"—he struggled to find the right word—"so permanent. We're having a great time together and it's fab having a regular guy to go out with so far, but it's like chalk and cheese for me from where I was to here. I don't want to move too fast and find we don't work out after all. And he's away such a lot and that's not going to change."

I miss him when he's not around. There, I actually admitted it.

Jack nodded. "I understand, but he's good for you, Gibson. I've never seen you so settled. Or happy, bro."

Gibson blew air out of pursed lips. "Maybe I'm not ready to settle down if I don't want to take him home yet?"

Fuck. Why the hell had he said that? He *was* happy. He cared about Max and the word 'boyfriend' had *nearly* slipped out of his mouth a couple of times when he was talking about him to others, but it was all a bit scary. He'd never done the relationship thing—what if he messed it up? And he'd have his folks all over his case because once they met Max, they'd love him. Anyone would. Gibson didn't want to disappoint anyone if all fell apart.

A noise at the door made them both turn towards it. His heart sank when he saw a pale-faced Max standing there in his

cabin crew uniform and a bag slung over his shoulder. His face
was pinched, his eyes flat.

"Max. I thought you were going to Venice?" Gibson's
mouth was dry and he wondered how much Max had heard.
Judging from his body language, it had been most of it.

Max moved into the room. "The flight was cancelled. Air
traffic control problem. I thought I'd surprise you." His voice
was tight as he nodded at Jack. "You must be Jack. Good to meet
you at last. Sorry I came in unannounced. The front door wasn't
locked."

Jack nodded, glancing from Max to Gibson. "Yeah, nice to
meet you too at last. I was going out to pick up my girlfriend, so
I'd better be off." He hefted himself off his chair and hunted
around his desk for his wallet. "Gib, I'll see you later, yeah?"

Gibson swallowed past the lump in his throat and nodded.
"Sure." He knew Beth was still working so Jack wasn't going to
pick her up. He was giving him and Max space. He watched as
Jack case a sympathetic glance at him and left the office.

"How much did you hear?" Gibson stood up and walked
over to Max, who stepped back. Gibson's chest ached.

"From when you put the phone down." Max was still. "I'm
sorry you feel that way. You should have told me."

"Max—" Gibson moved again towards his lover and Max
shook his head.

"No, this isn't one of those times when you can kiss me and
make me forget stuff, Gibson. I know your tricks and it only
works when I want it to." The hurt on his face was palpable.
"I'm sorry if I moved too fast, and again, I'm sorry I'm away
such a lot. We've been through this and I thought we'd agreed to
see how things pan out over the next few months."

Gibson wanted to hug Max, drive the bleak expression from
his face. He opened his mouth to speak but Max beat him to it.
"The trouble is, I'm more invested in this whole relationship than
you. And after overhearing what I did… I knew it could happen,
so honestly," he shrugged, "it's not that much of a surprise."

Gibson wasn't going to let his observation pass
unchallenged. "Max, hear me out," he said firmly. "You have to
understand where I was coming from. This is my first time in a

real relationship and I'm scared I'm going to mess it up. And with you being away a lot, it's tough. I miss you."

Max's eyes shadowed. "Is that true?" he said quietly. "'Cos it didn't sound like it to me. It sounded like you doubt whether we should be together."

Gibson's stomach clenched. "I do bloody miss you, all the time. I get caught up in my work, but then I have a break and I remember you're not around to talk to, because you're thousands of feet in the air and I can't even text you and tell you because I know you won't see it until later and honestly, then the moment's kinda gone. I get all insecure and say stupid things like what you heard. I'm sorry."

Max still hadn't put his bag down and looked ready to run out of the door at any moment. Gibson wasn't going to let that happen. He moved closer to his lover and wrenched the bag from his hand, ignoring Max's startled look. He wrapped arms around his lover's stiff frame and buried his face in his neck. Max smelt of sweat, aftershave, curry and his own unique scent of Max.

"I'm glad you're here, honest. I like being with you. And may I tell you how damn sexy you look in your uniform?"

A soft rumble in Max's chest told Gibson he was thawing. He'd heard the same low chuckle when they lay in bed together, Gibson's ear against Max's warm body.

"And it's not that I don't *want* you to meet my family," Gibson murmured. "It's if they meet you, they'll love you, because who wouldn't, and if things go wrong, I'll never live it down and they'll make my life a misery for driving my first real relationship guy away—"

Warm lips shut him up and as he responded to the kiss, Gibson was relieved Max was still there, glad Max had understood his reservations and hadn't flown like one of his planes.

When Max finally released his lips, they stood together quietly. Gibson's nose wrinkled and he looked up into brown eyes. "Why do you smell of curry?"

"I had one before coming over here, it was pretty spicy. Sorry." Max heaved a sigh then moved to the kitchen to pour himself a glass of water. He filled the glass and turned to look at Gibson.

"Did you mean it when you said you're not ready to settle down? I won't be mad, so tell me the truth." His lips twisted in a painful smile. "Despite my high ideals about having a regular guy to see, I don't mind taking what I can get of you, whatever you want to give. It's better than not having any of you at all."

Gibson's heart tore a little at the precise moment he heard those humbling words. It looked like he'd done what he'd so not wanted to do: stuff things up. He needed to fix this.

He picked up his phone and dialled a number. Max stared at him in puzzlement.

"Gibson?" His mother sounded surprised.

"Hey Mum. I wanted to let you know Max, my *steady boyfriend*," he made sure to emphasize those words, "*will* be joining us at Chloe's birthday and he'll be staying over. We'll stay in my old room—together, if that's okay. I didn't think you'd mind."

His mother's squeal made him wince. "Oh, Gibson, that's wonderful. I can't wait to meet him. I'll get the room sorted in time, and make sure there are supplies."

A twinge of unease swept through Gibson. "What do you mean 'supplies?'"

"Well, the whole safe sex thing is important darling. I know how it is. I did the same thing for Richard when he had girlfriends to stay."

Gibson was mortified. "Mum, please say you're not going to do what I think you are. Truly. Dying here."

Doris Henry tut-tutted. "Now, Gibson, don't be coy. I'm an open-minded woman. Listen, sweetheart, I'm late for bingo. The taxi is waiting. I'll call you later in the week and see how things are going. I'm so excited to see you both." She laughed. "Oh dear, poor Jamie's going to be devastated."

The line went dead.

Gibson put down his phone and groaned. "Oh my God. My mother slays me. She wants to buy us 'supplies.'"

Max raised one eyebrow. He looked a little happier than when he'd first walked in. "You mean—"

Gibson nodded miserably. "Yes. I see condoms and lube making an appearance in my old bedside drawer." Max's snort made Gibson grin. "My mother is going to make sure she gets to know everything about you. Be afraid. Be very afraid."

Max regarded him with uncertain eyes. "I'm going to a birthday party? As your *boyfriend*?"

Gibson panicked. "Oh, crap, I guess I should have asked you first and not assumed…"

"It's fine. As long as you're sure about it all." Max's face looked happier but still unsure.

Gibson moved forward and cupped Max's cheek. "I'm sure. I've never taken anyone home before… so it means you're special. I'm sorry I fucked up and hurt you." He kissed Max's jaw softly. "Did I tell you how sexy you look in the uniform?" He stepped back, appraising Max with a leer.

Max grinned. "You did. I'm even better out of it though." He frowned a little. "Jack calls you *Gib*?" He winced as if the sound hurt him.

Gibson grinned. "He's done it forever. It's just his thing."

Max sniffed. "Not *my* thing. It sounds like some sort of hideous monkey name."

Gibson sniggered. "That's a gibbon you're thinking of, dummy."

Max pulled him close. "Whatever it is, you're my Gibson. I promise to always use your full name, unless of course I'm in the throes of passion and I call you something else. Like sexy stud-muffin."

Gibson nodded slowly. "I can live with that. Now are we going to get busy here or not?"

Gibson pushed aside his personal deadline to get some stuff over to Everett to check. Making out and making up with Max right now was far more important.

Chapter 10

Maxwell woke with a start, heart pounding and with a dry mouth. His head was foggy and aching and he needed desperately to pee. He climbed out of his lonely bed; he hadn't seen Gibson for awhile. He'd only been back half a day from the last three days' non-stop flight roster, taking on more hours to get a couple of extra days off. He shuffled to the bathroom and winced when he saw the sight that greeted him in the mirror.

His hair was in disarray, looking as if someone had taken a teasing comb to it. It stuck up all around his face, which was pale, and fuck, was that a spot? Maxwell peered through unfocused eyes at the beginnings of the blemish on his chin. His eyes looked hollow and there were dark shadows under them.

In truth, he'd not been feeling well for the past few days and the last flight to Madrid had done a number on him. It had been hectic, filled with needy, crotchety passengers, a lot of them blindingly ill and flu-like even as they tried to hide it, and he had a feeling he'd caught something off the kid in seat 18D. The child had been runny-nosed, whining and had actually sneezed in Maxwell's face when he leaned down to take his food tray away.

Maxwell's chest ached, feeling tight, and he was still struggling to breathe. He relieved himself, sloped back to bed and huddled, shivering, under the covers. He couldn't sleep; ten minutes later, he was kicking the blankets off, burning up. He gazed blearily around for his mobile then remembered it was in the lounge. He couldn't be bothered to get up and get it. He wanted to call Gibson but he didn't have the energy.

"I need to hear his voice," he mumbled as he buried back under the covers. "He'll make me feel all better..." He coughed, his chest racked with pain and he held a hand to it, willing the spell to finish. When he could finally draw a breath, he lay there, exhausted.

This sickness reminded him of one of the times he'd gotten ill on the streets. Now at least he was in a bed with access to modern medicine. Maxwell didn't have much in his cupboards because he was hardly ever sick, and he didn't keep his medicine chest stocked up because he hated taking drugs, hence why he felt so shit now.

Back then, it had only been him and Levi; Levi feeding him water as Maxwell hacked up what was left of his lungs into a dirty piece of linen that had once been a restaurant cloth napkin. Neither of them had eaten for days, Maxwell too sick and Levi scared to leave him alone in case he died while he was gone.

"You never thought of me, though, when you died, you bastard," Maxwell was delirious in a haze of fever and remaining vestiges of a long-held grief. "You made me find your cold, dead body stuffed with the crap you fed into your veins." He remembered that part of his life as if it had only just happened.

He'd crawled into the corner of the doorway recess and lifted Levi's head onto his lap as he stroked greasy hair and the cold planes of Levi's face. Levi had been his world since Maxwell had been fourteen and yes, when they'd run away together he'd been legally underage for the sixteen-year-old Levi, but that hadn't mattered to either of them. They'd been all each other had and Levi had taught him what sex was, and about caring.

He sensed a comforting presence in his room, feeling a shadow falling over him and he smiled, imagining it was his Gibson here, watching over him. Dream Gibson took hold of his heart and stroked it softly, comforting him.

"I did some terrible things on the streets for money, Gibson," Maxwell whispered as he drifted in and out of reality. "I don't want to tell you about them, because you'd hate me. I'm not proud of them but they're part of me. And I lied to you." Feverish whispers echoed in the still room as tears trickled out of his swollen eyes. "I told you Levi was only a friend. But he wasn't. He was much more than that."

Soft hands stroked his hair. "I know, baby," Gibson whispered, his voice choked.

Maxwell tried to focus on the blurred figure sitting on the side of bed. "Gibson? I'm hallucinating, aren't I?"

Something foul tasting was forced into his mouth, medicinal and disgusting. "Drink this, it'll help break your fever," was the soft reply. "I'm going to get some washcloths and try and get your temperature down. You're burning up." Warm fingers brushed away the tears on his cheek.

Maxwell smiled dreamily. Everything was all right now. Gibson was here even if he wasn't. "I like this dream," he murmured as he fell into sleep. "And I think I love you." He snorted in laughter. "No, I *know* I love you. Don't tell the real Gibson, Dream Gibson, because I don't want to scare him away."

There was the sound of a soft gasp then a light kiss was pressed to his sweating brow. He revelled in the touch.

"Sleep now," came the whisper. "I'll be here when you wake up."

"'Kay," Maxwell muttered sleepily. "Please don't go away. I don't want you to leave."

"I'm not going anywhere," Dream Gibson said. "I need you to get better. Go to sleep."

Maxwell fell into slumber with the vision of his boyfriend, his blond halo of hair shining in the dimness of the room and green eyes looking down at him with some indefinable emotion.

***

When Maxwell woke again, it was to daylight streaming into the room through half-open curtains. He blinked and struggled up to peer around him. The bedside table was cluttered with medicines and face towels and—was that a humidifier blowing steam into the air? He stared at it in bemusement. He didn't own a humidifier. The machine hissed and billowed scented clouds of eucalyptus. The time on his Lego Darth Maul clock said one pm.

"I must have been further gone than I thought," he croaked. His chest didn't feel as congested so he imagined whatever he'd been doing in his fever-driven haze had worked. He looked at the humidifier again. "Huh, even in a stupor, I'm the man."

"I doubt that," was the dry retort and Maxwell gave himself whiplash turning his head to see Gibson standing in the bedroom doorway, shoulder resting against the jamb, arms folded across his chest. When Maxwell's chest constricted this time it wasn't because he had some dreaded disease. The joy flaring through his body like strands of lightning filled it with emotion and flooded his senses.

"Gibson? When did you get here?"

Gibson came into the room and checked the humidifier water level. He added a couple more drops of oil to the heated water and swore as it spilled over onto his fingers. "About three days ago." He wrinkled his nose, wiped his hands absently on his jeans and stretched. His tee shirt rose above his waist to reveal a faint treasure trail and toned tummy. The belly bar wasn't there and Maxwell was disappointed.

Maxwell's jaw dropped. "Three days ago? I don't remember seeing you. Was this all your doing then?" He waved a hand at the bedside table and his happily steaming appliance.

Gibson nodded. "You've had a bad bout of bronchitis. I got stuff from the pharmacy, borrowed the humidifier from Jack's girlfriend Beth—he dropped it off for me—and I kept forcing medicine down you. You had nothing in your medicine cupboard." He cast an accusing stare at Maxwell. "I mean *nothing,* apart from a couple of expired condoms, an old empty tube of lube, a broken thermometer and a shower cap." He grinned. "With ducks on it."

Maxwell's face flushed beet red. "Sometimes I don't want my hair to get wet when I'm showering. Wet hair on the flight isn't something the passengers want to see."

"Yeah but ducks? Little yellow-lello ducks?" Gibson's face shone with mirth. "You must look so cute. I was tempted to put it on while you slept and take a picture. Jack was all for it too. He wanted to share it on Facebook."

Maxwell gasped. "You didn't, did you? Because that would be the height of cruelty…"

Gibson sat down on the bed and reached out and brushed sweaty hair from Maxwell's forehead. "No, I didn't. And I threw out the old condoms and crap. Hope you don't mind. I didn't want you taking risks."

"You fed me medicines? I hate taking that stuff. That's why I don't have it at home. What did you give me?"

"It was only paracetamol and some Day Nurse. You needed to break your fever, Max."

Maxwell narrowed his eyes. "You've been here all the time? Did I say anything stupid when I was so out of it?"

Gibson's eyes darkened. "Nah, nothing. Do you feel better?"

Maxwell might have just woken up but he wasn't stupid. He *had* said something, obviously, from the quick change of subject and the wary look on Gibson's face. But for the life of him he could hardly recall anything of the last three days apart from some memories of Levi still lingering in his brain and a vague recollection of Dream Gibson being in the room.

"I smell rank otherwise I'd hug you and give you a kiss for looking after me," he said. "I don't believe you've been here three days and done all this." He gestured at the room. "Thanks."

Gibson shrugged. "That's what boyfriends are for. I took the ravish key and opened up." He grinned. The 'ravish key' was the spare key Maxwell kept hidden in a secret place outside his front door in case Gibson got the yen to come over and 'ravish' him in the middle of the night. It was a fantasy of Maxwell's and not one Gibson had played into yet although he hoped one day it would come to fruition. "I brought my laptop over and worked when you were sleeping. The joys of being my own boss and being able to work from anywhere."

"Crap. I don't suppose I called work to tell them I was ill."

"No, I did. I remember you mentioned Grant was your boss so I found his number in your phone and called him. He said get better and don't come back until you're well because he can't have you spreading the germs to the passengers and crew. Nice guy though. He was worried about you."

Maxwell frowned. "You found his name in my phone? It's password protected."

Gibson rolled his eyes. "It's swipe protected and honestly, an L swipe to unlock? It took me two tries and I was in."

Maxwell narrowed his eyes. "You're a bloody computer hacker." He grinned. "Can you top up my bank account for me?"

Gibson sighed. "I'm not a hacker. Not much anyway. A ten-year-old could get in your phone. You're not the most security conscious of people, babe. Remember I got into your *Sexcella* sheet? The unprotected one, which should have some sort of password on it, given what was in there. I mean, a man's dick size is personal *and* confidential information." He shivered theatrically and cast Maxwell a sly glance.

A frisson of discomfort slid down Maxwell's spine. "You looked at it again?" He realised Gibson had called him 'babe' a moment ago and it threw his train of thought. He liked the endearment. He thought Gibson might have called him it before but his memory was fuzzy.

Gibson glared at him. "No, idiot. You asked me not to, didn't you? I don't break my promises." His beautiful lips curled in a kitten snarl and Maxwell wanted to kiss him. For being there when he'd been sick, for taking care of him like no else ever had since Levi had died, for being the best boyfriend a man could be. But he could taste his own breath and he had no desire to inflict it upon Gibson.

"Let me get up, have a shower and brush my teeth then I can apologise properly to you for that remark," Maxwell promised and was gratified when Gibson's face creased in a smile.

"Fine. Be careful when you stand up. Last time I took you to the loo you nearly fell down."

Maxwell blinked. "What? You've been taking me to the toilet?" He started to hyperventilate. "Fuck, how embarrassing. For what, number ones, number twos? Oh crap, this is bad."

By now Gibson was giggling and Maxwell's heart reached out and sucked the man deeper into it than he thought possible.

"Crass, Max. No number twos. I did have to hold it while you peed because you couldn't see straight and I didn't fancy cleaning piss off the walls." His face grew thoughtful. "You might need to take a laxative. You haven't *been* since I got here. But then you've hardly been eating anything other than those energy drinks I've been giving you. And soup."

Maxwell stared at him, face flaming, horrified at the talk of his potentially non-performing bowels.

Gibson cracked up. "Oh my God, your face. It's a perfectly natural thing, you know."

Maxwell huffed haughtily. "Not in my book. That kind of talk gets relegated to conversations about lady 'things' blocking up the toilet and eyeless dolls roaming homes looking for someone to kill. I don't like either of them." He swung his legs out of bed, feeling lightheaded. "Whoa. I see what you mean. You might have to help me to the bathroom."

Gibson helped him stand up and together they made their way to the shower. Gibson made Maxwell sit on the closed lid of the toilet while he brushed his teeth over the basin, then got the shower started, removed Maxwell's boxers and helped him in over the side of the bath. Maxwell's legs were wobbly, and his head a little fuzzy, but the sound of the water, its heat and the spicy smell of the shower gel as Gibson poured copious amounts over his shoulders was heaven.

"There," Gibson said huskily, watching as Maxwell massaged his scalp with shampoo and water. "I'll leave you to it. I bought fresh clothes and put them on the basin. Let me know if you need anything." He moved to draw the shower curtain and Maxwell reached out a wet hand and gripped his hand.

"You can join me if you like. Make sure I don't slip and fall down. That would be the boy-friendly thing to do."

He watched desire flash in Gibson's eyes as he bit his bottom lip. "I don't know, you've not been well, maybe you shouldn't overdo it."

Maxwell growled. "Gibson, get your clothes off and get in here right now. I'm strong enough to do what I want to do to you." He stroked himself softly and watched Gibson's pupils dilate.

His lover swiftly shrugged off his tee shirt, slid his jeans down over his hips, together with his tight blue briefs and stepped into the shower. Water cascaded over them both in the enclosed space as Maxwell drew the curtain.

"That's better," he murmured as he pulled Gibson to him, his lover's head fitting perfectly under his chin. Maxwell slid his hands down Gibson's flanks, pressing their groins together. "Right where you belong."

The soft groan leaving Gibson's lips was taken by Maxwell's mouth. Gibson tasted like spice and apple and Maxwell couldn't get enough.

"Why do you taste so good?" he managed between frantic, long, open-mouthed kisses.

"It's spicy chai tea," Gibson murmured as his hand caressed Maxwell's cock, teasing strokes threatening to blow Maxwell's mind. "Now shut up and kiss me."

To Maxwell, the slow, intimate sexual ballet taking place in a bathtub behind a faded shower curtain was worthy of a scene not out of a porn movie, but rather one of those sensual avant-garde films he'd watched in the past. He'd seen a few and never failed to get turned on by the slow, sensuous grinds of bodies against each other, tongues flicking softly then eating each other's mouths with groins and cocks pressing together, slick skin against skin as two men made love slowly, lovingly as droplets of water caressed eager bodies.

He wished he had a film camera in here, so he could play it back because he was sure the sinuous strokes of Gibson's firm torso against his and his hands encircling both of their cocks as he stroked them off was worthy of another watch…and another. His lover may have smaller hands than him but he knew how to use them to bring Maxwell to the peak.

When he finally cried out into Gibson's open mouth, his body convulsing with pleasure and skin tingling with sensory overload as he orgasmed, he took satisfaction in seeing Gibson doing the same. Their combined essences dripped down bellies and legs to be washed away in the water. The two men stood together, panting and replete, Gibson's slick wet head pressed into Maxwell's shoulder as his hands gripped Maxwell's arse, pulling him closer.

"That was what I needed," Maxwell gasped as he brushed wet hair from his eyes. "*You* were all I needed to feel better."

Gibson was quiet and Maxwell looked down at him. "You okay?"

His lover stood back, taking some shower gel to wash off the remains of their release from his body. "Yes, fine." He sounded a little uncertain. "You were something. I like it when we go slowly." His hands reached up and cupped Maxwell's cheeks. "Now we should get washed up and get out of here. You need to eat something, get your strength back for another one of these." He waved down in between their now clean bodies and grinned as he stepped out of the shower and took a towel off the rack. He wrapped it around his waist and left the bathroom.

Maxwell stayed where he was and shaved. Then, water wrinkled and feeling like a new man, he got dressed and went to find Gibson. He had something on his mind and Maxwell was determined to find out what.

He found Gibson on the couch, computer on his lap, surrounded by sketchpads, crumpled wads of paper in one neat pile at the foot of the couch and a coffee cup—one of the three Maxwell owned. An open container of Chinese food and what looked like the remains of three packs of sandwiches were stacked neatly side by side on the small side table.

Maxwell waved at the tidy debris. "This is what kept you going while you were here?" Something different caught his eye and he gasped. "You cleaned up some of my stuff."

Some of his worldly possessions had either disappeared, or been packed neatly in piles on the rickety dining room table. Horror of horrors, they might even be stored in cupboards.

Gibson looked guilty. "Sorry. I can't work in chaos, so I tidied up a bit. I'll mess it up again before I go, I promise." He cast a jaded eye around the now mostly empty room. "Although I have to say it looks better like this. I also threw out the dead plants."

Maxwell opened his mouth then shut it again. "What? But they might have lived, gone through a birth of re-growth!"

Gibson shook his head in amusement "Max, they were dead. D-E-A-D. There was no coming back for those poor critters. Best to let them go in peace and with some dignity."

Maxwell huffed. "I guess I'm lucky I didn't have a fish. Poor thing might have found itself flushed down the toilet."

He'd meant it as a joke but Gibson's face shadowed. "I'm sorry if I overstepped the mark. I was trying to help."

Maxwell's stomach clenched. "No, I was joking. I don't mind at all. God, I'm crap at this whole thing. My excuse is I was at death's door and I'm still recovering." He'd haul his stuff out when Gibson left.

He knelt down beside Gibson and peered at his laptop. "Whatcha doin'?" His fingers traced slow circles on Gibson's leg.

"I'm doing some animation." Gibson's eyes lit up eagerly. "I've got Phoenix how I want him, I think, and now I'm playing around with movements and simulations."

Maxwell stared at the complicated mess on the screen. It looked hellishly complicated to him but as he watched Gibson's slim fingers fly over his keyboard, creating incredible actions on screen, he was awed.

"Wow, you're a clever little fella, aren't you? That is awesome."

Gibson beamed. "I love it. I also do a lot of the design for the backgrounds and the environments." His tongue stuck out the corner of his mouth as the rather stylish figure on screen— Maxwell presumed it was Phoenix—leapt over what looked like a sleeping toad princess on the ground then performed a double somersault.

"What the hell is the thing lying down?" Maxwell muttered as he peered at the screen.

Gibson smirked. "*She's* called Rhea Lipstick. She's a drag queen with a nasty temper. You don't want to wake her up. She'll literally cut your balls off."

Maxwell gaped. "Hell, you're making up Mrs Bobbitt games here?" He clutched his testicles in sympathy.

Gibson snickered. "Feeling a little tender, Max?" He reached out and brushed Maxwell's crotch.

Maxwell wanted to purr in pleasure. "Keep that up and I'll make sure you're *more* than a little tender," he murmured.

Gibson grinned. "Promises, promises," he murmured, then went back to his game.

"What is the plan then with *Camp Queen*? How long do you think it will take you to finish it? You said something once about entering it into some competition?" Maxwell watched as Gibson blew a strand from his face and frowned.

"We've been working on this for the best part of two years, using every resource we have to help, and I'm hoping we have it finished by Christmas, for launch in about February next year. We might get entered in the Quasar or Gaymz Choice competition this year if someone nominates us. Then submissions for the Croesus Gaming Award take place next year in May." He scowled. "We missed the Quasar win this year by a couple of points...we came second. Which was good, don't get me wrong, but I want to be first."

"What do you get if you win?" Maxwell asked, fascinated. This was a side of a business he'd never thought about before. To him, the games were simply there to be played.

His lover smiled. "Monetary value-wise it's not great. Winner gets 5,000 pounds." Maxwell thought that was a damn good amount in his estimation. He could do a lot with that kind of money.

Gibson's eyes gleamed. "But the year after we launch, we want to enter the British Academy Game Awards. That's going to be the big one. And winning the Croesus next year will give us some respectability." He sighed. "The current games we have going bring in enough money for Jack and me to run our business and pay for the development of the new games." He looked uncomfortable. "Jack put quite a bit of money into Anomaly when we started up and he's virtually paid back but I want him back where he started.

"We're neither of us rich, but we earn a salary and the revenues pay for our flat and living expenses. Winning a big award will give us the boost we need to fund other games, pay for the freelancers we use and allow us to run the company." He grimaced. "I don't even want to think about not making it and having to go back to a nine-to-five job selling suit shirts or burgers. I'm over all that having–a-boss shit."

Maxwell had spent his entire life managing every single penny he earned to best advantage. He lived on a diet of canned food, soups, noodles, one-pound ready meals and didn't smoke or drink unless he was out socialising. Cabin crew wasn't the best-paid job in the world, although it had other perks. To him, being able to work where you lived and answer to no one sounded like a dream. A pipe dream for him though. He couldn't write, draw, was not musical and although he wasn't bad on the technology side—being able to fix things and understand how they worked—he had no transferable skills he could use to start his own business. He was a little in awe of Gibson and his obvious intelligence and creativity.

"How did you get into doing this anyway?" He watched as Gibson's fingers did miraculous things to the character on his screen.

Gibson didn't answer for a while and Maxwell sat patiently. He knew first-hand how his lover got so absorbed in what he was doing to the exclusion of everything else—even him. Gibson was entranced, busily typing something into one of the online forums he was always chatting in. Something to do with networking and problem-solving.

He stroked Gibson's thigh, but it still didn't seem to detract his boyfriend from his steadfast concentration. Maxwell sighed, a deep, heavy sigh echoing in the room. When it didn't get the reaction he wanted, he did it again, squeezing Gibson's leg tightly. This time Gibson glanced at him.

"Sorry, did you say something?"

Maxwell wanted to roll his eyes but refrained. "I asked how you got into this line of work."

Gibson shrugged. "I've been doing it since I was a kid. I was a geek at school and did all the computer science and IT things I possibly could. When I left school, I took a gap year, worked here and there then did a BA Hons in game design for three years in Manchester. Jack and I started Anomaly Media while we were at uni together and it evolved to what it is now."

"You lived in Manchester? Where, at the university?"

Gibson shook his head, brow furrowed as he studied something back on his screen. "No, we lived in Manchester not far from the University. I didn't need uni digs, and I was able to live at home. Mum and Dad paid my tuition so I didn't have student loans when I left. They only moved to Cramond after I finished my degree. I moved down to London then with Jack."

Maxwell couldn't help feeling a little narked even though he knew it was daft. While he'd been living on the streets turning tricks then clawing his way back into civilisation through a series of deadbeat jobs to support himself until he'd finally found his niche in becoming a flight attendant, Gibson had his own life all planned out, with a supportive family and loving parents.

What the hell do I have to show for my life? What do I have to offer someone like him who's going places? I couldn't even save Levi. He loved his drug dealer more than he loved me. How can this man ever want someone like me?

He moved away from interrupting Gibson as he worked, to sit cross-legged on the floor beside him, staring absently out of the window at the sky outside. His throat ached a bit as he thought about what he'd missed out on. He thought he'd grown content with his lot, but this new relationship had thrown things his way he believed he'd gotten over. He hunched forward, wrapping his arms around his knees as he tried to suppress the welling of emotion inside. He blamed the fact he'd been sick and his resistance was low for his present state of mind.

"Max, are you okay?" Gibson's voice was worried and Maxwell heard him get off the couch and come to kneel beside him. "Are you feeling sick again?"

Maxwell took a deep mental breath and turned to flash a smile at his concerned lover. "No, everything is fine. I wanted to let you get on in peace." He wanted to talk but didn't quite trust himself yet. Perhaps later might be better when he didn't feel as vulnerable.

Gibson's eyes narrowed. "Don't lie to me," he said softly and reached out and stroked Maxwell's cheek. "Your face says otherwise. Was it something I said?"

"Of course not. I enjoy hearing about you. I'm proud of you for achieving so much."

Gibson studied his face intently and Maxwell flushed. "What? I know I've been sick and not looking my best but stop staring at me like I've grown a mole or something."

Gibson didn't look convinced. "No mole. I thought maybe you'd remembered—" His mobile rung and he gave Maxwell one final scrutinising glance and went to answer it.

"Mum, this is a surprise. I wasn't expecting a call—"

Maxwell stood up and stretched, staring out the window into the street below. He was still out of sorts but tried to push those feelings away. He had a gorgeous boyfriend, a job he enjoyed even if it was getting on his tits a bit with the long hours, and a roof over his head. He needed to count his blessings rather than find new insecurities to torment himself with. In fact, he'd been planning on having a conversation with his company to see if there were any ground crew jobs going. The idea of not being up in the air all the time and spending more time with Gibson was appealing, especially after their last fight. He made a mental note to speak to Grant about it once he got back to work.

He turned to Gibson to tell him, only to find him huddled on the floor, back against the wall, his face white and eyes looking as if they'd seen the devil himself.

"Baby, what's wrong?" He hurried over to him. Gibson's hands clutched the phone on his lap and the quacking noise emanating from it sounded panicked. Maxwell squatted down beside him.

"Gibson, talk to me." His heart clenched in panic. Gibson simply stared at him and Maxwell recognised his expression; he was no stranger to shock. He prised the phone from his lover's cold and trembling hands and lifted it to his ear.

"Hello, this is Maxwell, Gibson's boyfriend. He's upset, what did you say to him?"

"Maxwell." The woman's voice sounded strained. "This is Doris Henry. Gibson's mum?"

"Oh, sorry." Maxwell stammered. "I didn't mean to be rude. I was worried about him."

Because he's fucking comatose on the floor and I can't bear the stricken look in his eyes.

"He's had some bad news," Doris said softly, a quaver in her voice. "His dad—Cliff—passed away this morning." Her voice broke but she carried on. "He had what we think was a stroke and it's all rather stressful here. I needed to tell him but I don't know how much he heard. He disappeared on me."

Maxwell stared down at Gibson's pale figure and his heart ached for his pain. "I'm so sorry," he said, feeling the words were inadequate but not knowing what else to say. "I'll take care of him, I promise. He's safe with me. Is there anything else I can do?"

"Look after my boy for me, please." The sniffles on the other end of the phone were breaking Maxwell's heart. "He and his dad were very close and he didn't get the chance to say goodbye. He's going to be devastated. Please take care of him. I'll call him later when I know more about what's happening. I know he'll want to come up here. Can you help him organise things?"

"Of course," Maxwell promised. He stared down at the blank face below him. "I'll put your number in my phone and send you a text then you'll have my number too. Mrs Henry?"

The soft sobs continued. "Thank you. I have to go, the doctor's here. Tell Gibson I'll call him later. Tell him I love him." The phone went dead. Maxwell put it down on the side table and sat down beside Gibson. He reached out and tried to pull him into an embrace. Gibson was still and unresponsive.

"Come here, love. God, I hate you're going through this." He finally got Gibson in his arms, face pressed against his chest. Gibson still hadn't said anything. "Your mum told me to tell you she loves you and she'll call you later." He got a half nod.

Gibson spoke. "I never gave him back his scarf."

Maxwell frowned. "What?"

Gibson sat up and got to his feet. He stared down at Maxwell, green eyes blank and a frozen look on his face. "He wanted his scarf back and I hadn't looked for it yet. He'll need it. I need to go home." He picked up his phone and went to the couch, where he started packing all his PC stuff into his laptop bag. Maxwell stood up and joined him. He knew the scarf wasn't needed now but he'd do anything to help Gibson get through this.

"I'll take you home. I'll get us a taxi. You're in no state for the train. We'll look for the scarf when we get you home."

Gibson nodded again jerkily as he stuffed clothing into a holdall. He stared around blankly, and spotted his laptop. He fingers moved across the keyboard, saving and shutting down his open applications, and then it too was relegated to the depths of his laptop bag.

Maxwell wished Gibson would cry, give way to whatever emotions were swirling in his head, but it didn't seem forthcoming.

Gibson stared around at the room. "Is the taxi coming?"

Maxwell fetched his phone, which sat on the dining table. "Shit, not yet. Bear with me. Let me get someone."

He made a quick call and arranged a taxi for ten minutes' time. Gibson was already at the door, holdall in one hand, laptop bag in the other. Maxwell reached out for the holdall and took it.

"Let me help you." He saw Gibson's jacket lying over the back of the couch and picked it up, along with his own brown bomber jacket.

Within a few minutes, they were downstairs, standing in the cool morning air as they waited for the taxi. Gibson had said nothing more. He stood still and silent, a look of what Maxwell could only call *nothing* on his face. Maxwell noticed his fingers tapping nervously at his side and reached over to hold those cold ones in his warm hands. Gibson's fingers stilled and a soft sigh escaped his lips.

"I'm here," Maxwell murmured. "Whatever you need."

When the taxi arrived, they got in and the short distance to Gibson's flat was done in silence. As they entered the flat, Jack sat at the dining room table and his face lit up when he saw them come in.

"Gibson, my man! I must say the dude behind you looks much better than when I last saw him. Maxwell, how are you feeling?"

Maxwell muttered a greeting as he dropped the holdall in the entrance and watched as Gibson struggled to say something.

Jack looked at him, confusion on his face. "Gib, what's wrong?"

Gibson's voice was flat as he put down his bag and moved past Jack towards his bedroom. "My dad's dead. I need to find his scarf." He disappeared into the hallway.

Jack's mouth gaped open and pity and sadness played across his face. "Jesus, what happened?"

Maxwell repeated what Mrs Henry had told him and Jack passed a hand over a stubbled chin. "This is gonna kill him." He realised what he'd said and went beet red. "I meant—"

Maxwell nodded as he gave a tired sigh. "I know what you mean. And it's true. He's been virtually catatonic since his mum called earlier. He's not dealing well at all." He cocked an eyebrow at a still shocked Jack. "Do you know what this thing is about the bloody scarf?"

Jack nodded. "Last time his mum called, Gib told me he needed to find it to take home for his dad. It's a football scarf his dad left here when he was here last time." He cast a worried glance towards the hallway. "I can't believe Cliff's gone, that's awful. He was like family to me."

"I'm sorry he told you the news like that." Maxwell placed a comforting hand on Jack's shoulder. "This must be a shock for you too."

"It is." Jack ran a hand through his unruly hair. "I suppose I'd better go try talk to him."

Maxwell snorted. "Good luck with that. I've been trying for the past hour. Maybe you'll have more success."

Jack shrugged. "Maybe." He turned and left the room.

An irrational flare of jealousy struck as Maxwell considered perhaps Gibson might turn to Jack for comfort instead of him. They had been friends since they were teenagers after all.

And isn't it all about Gibson feeling better and not my own stupid insecurities? Of course it is. Stop being such a twat.

And when Jack came back five minutes later muttering Gibson was a stubborn ass and needed his butt kicked, Maxwell couldn't help feel a little happier. He knew it was wrong. But he was only human.

"He's turning his damn cupboard inside out looking for that scarf and he doesn't want help," Jack growled but his eyes were a little red. "Least not from me. I think you should go mash some sense into him."

Maxwell sighed. "I'll try." He remembered he'd been supposed to text Gibson's mother. "Crap. I need to get his phone off him anyway so I can text his mum. Let me enter the den of doom and see whether I emerge alive."

They grinned awkwardly at each other. Jack looked sad and Maxwell flashed a sympathetic look at him as he left. When he got to Gibson's bedroom, he was stunned at the sight greeting his eyes. A closet full of clothes and underwear had vomited all over Gibson's normally neat room. The bed was filled with stacks of jeans, shirts, jackets and assorted boxers, briefs and some items Maxwell thought looked interesting but realised now wasn't the time to investigate further.

At first, he couldn't see Gibson. The wardrobe doors were open, the space inside empty like Mother Hubbard's cupboard. From somewhere beyond the piled clamour of fashion on the bed was the noise of quiet, heart-rending sobbing. The sound struck him to his core. Maxwell didn't know how many more times his man was going to cause his heart to ache and his eyes to prickle with tears. Since he'd met Gibson, his inner hormonal teenage girl was on high alert.

He stepped over yet more jackets, coats and tee shirts, went around to the other side of the bed and found Gibson, face streaked with tears, sitting on the floor, a tattered old green and white scarf twisting in his hands. Red-rimmed, puffy eyes behind fogged-up spectacles stared up at him glassily as Maxwell sat down beside him.

"You found it," Maxwell whispered. His hand reached out and clasped fidgeting fingers in his. They were ice cold.

"It was right in the back of my cupboard," Gibson's voice was choked. "I'm not a football fan, so when my dad left it I chucked it in there. I always meant to get it out and give it back to him because he loved this scarf." Green eyes glistened with tears. "Now I'll never get to do that, Max."

His body shook as he broke down and Maxwell drew him closer, feeling warm tears soak his tee shirt. He murmured soothing noises and stroked Gibson's back, his hair, anywhere Maxwell could so Gibson could feel he was there. Maxwell cursed whatever deity controlled the motherfucking universe causing this pain and grief. He knew full well how it felt to have the people you loved the most die on you.

"Let it all out, baby," he muttered into Gibson's hair. "I'm not going anywhere."

He held the shaking, weeping man in his arms until he stilled, only the occasional hiccup and tremor wracking his body.

"I didn't get to see him before he died," Gibson finally sniffled. "I should have gone up there when I heard he was sick. Everyone thought it was the flu or something, no one thought anything was serious." His voice choked up.

Maxwell reached over and picked up an old tee shirt and dried Gibson's face gently, wiping away traces of tears and snot from his face. Gibson had seen Maxwell at his worst and he could do the same for him. He kissed Gibson's head. "Don't blame yourself for not being there. I know that's trite and easier said than done, but take it from somebody who knows. These things happen and there's nothing you can do about it."

Jack walked into the room, eyes searching, face worried. "Hey, sport," he said softly as he came over. "Are you okay?"

"I'm fine, thank you, but I'm not sure about my man." Maxwell quipped and was gratified when his reply caused a slight snort from Gibson. Jack sighed and sat down, Gibson now sandwiched between them.

"I'm sorry I blurted it out the way I did when I came in. It was cruel. I know you liked my dad too." Gibson looked up, shame on his face.

Jack reached over and chucked his chin. "Don't worry, you were upset, I get that. I'm sorry, Gib. Your dad was legend."

"Yes he was," Gibson replied, still clutching the scarf as he snuggled against Maxwell. The three men sat in silence for a while and then Maxwell grimaced.

"Gibson, can I have your phone please? I promised your mum I'd text her my number so I need hers."

Gibson shuffled and plucked his phone from his jeans pocket. He unlocked the screen and handed it over. Maxwell scrolled down and sent himself a message with Mrs Henry's number. In the lounge, his phone beeped. He wrested out of Gibson's grip and stood up.

"Be back in a min. Let me get it done before I forget."

When he got to his phone, he quickly sent Gibson's mother a text introducing himself then put his phone in his pocket in case she called. When he got back into the bedroom, Jack and Gibson were busy putting all the clothes back into cupboards and on shelves. The scarf was laid lovingly on Gibson's pillow.

Maxwell joined in and once the room was clear of abandoned fashion, he reached out and drew his lover into a hug. "Are you hungry? I can order your favourite pizza if you like. A Mighty Meaty. Like me." He smirked, hoping the old joke would make Gibson smile.

Jack groaned. "Enough, already. I don't need to hear your disgusting innuendos about how big your dicks are. I get enough of that from Gibson. Like what he said to me the other night when I threatened to rip his tongue out." He stopped abruptly as Maxwell grinned. Jack didn't know him well enough yet or he would never have made the remark.

Maxwell sniggered. "Wow, who knew your friends were so violent, Gibson?" He turned. "I happen to love your tongue. It has so many uses. Like when you wrap it around my—"

Jack made a disgusted noise like 'Gah' and fled the room.

"Ice cream cone. I was going to say ice cream cone, you dirty-minded dog." Maxwell said in an injured tone. He supposed the wide grin on his face didn't lend credence to his lie.

"God, Max, you are bad." Gibson's watery smile was a panacea to Maxwell's tender heart.

"Yep, I have that badge already. And what did you say to him the other night anyway?"

Gibson grinned fleetingly. "I asked him how I was going to rim guys without my tongue."

"Oh, God," Maxwell's dick gave a sly, happy nod at the thought. It was one of his favourite things to have done to him so a Gibson without his tongue was inconceivable.

Crap. I need to stop thinking about sex. My boyfriend has lost his father, you animal.

"Jack seems like a cool guy. I like him."

Gibson nodded. "He's a peach. He and Beth are the best. She's funny and keeps him in line. I love her to bits."

How about me? Do you maybe love me a little? God, I'm such a needy bastard.

"Do you need to call your mum back now you're feeling a little better or do you want to wait until she calls you?"

Gibson's face shadowed. "I need to get home to help Mum and Ricky with all the arrangements." His face set stubbornly. "I'm not letting them do everything on their own. I'll take a look at flights and get up there soon as I can."

Maxwell shook his head. "Leave it. I'll do it for you. I used to work in travel. I'll get you sorted. Maybe I can even reschedule some of my flights and go with you earlier." He'd call Grant to see what he could do to get whatever shifts he had changed. They'd originally only been due to fly out to Chloe's birthday next week. Maxwell wished with all his heart fate had given Gibson those extra days to at least see his dad one last time.

Gibson flashed him a grateful smile. "Thanks, I appreciate that. My head's all messed up. I want to sleep for a bit. I'm actually not hungry much after all." He looked longingly at his bed.

"Get in there and wallow for a bit. I'll go sort stuff out and come check on you in a little while. We'll get that pizza later then."

Gibson needed no urging and soon he was naked, his body sliding under his duvet. He clutched the scarf in his hands. His face was still pale, his eyes swollen. Maxwell wanted to undress and lie beside him, cuddle him until all the hurt went away. But he had work to do getting Gibson to what remained of his family.

Chapter 11

Gibson stared out of the plane window, seeing little and not in the mood to appreciate the beauty of the clouds and sea below. His brain hadn't functioned properly since he'd learnt of his father's death. Well, that, plus Max's fevered mutterings when he'd been sick. Gibson was still processing that unguarded conversation about the things he'd done on the streets and the words 'I think I love you.' He had a heavy feeling in the pit of his stomach he knew what Max might tell him what he'd done to survive when he was homeless.

And Gibson wouldn't judge him if it was what he thought it was.

But the worry had taken a backseat in the face of his dad's death; he could only manage one momentous event at a time. When he was stronger, he'd ask Max about 'those things' and tell him they didn't matter.

Beside him Max shifted, his longer legs trying to find comfort in the crowded aeroplane. "I'm more used to being out there than in here," he moaned as he shuffled his backside on the seat and waved a hand at the cabin crew. One of them rolled her eyes and Gibson snorted softly in agreement. The crew had been attentive to them and were a pleasant bunch. One of them had even commiserated with Gibson on landing the 'Maxwell fish,' but she'd said it with a gleam in her eye and a fond smile. It appeared everyone loved Max.

Gibson smiled faintly. "Stop complaining. We're nearly there." He idly fingered the green and white scarf around his neck. He checked his laptop bag was still under his seat and gave a sigh of relief. He didn't know whether he'd get in any game development while he was away but he didn't travel anywhere without his laptop.

Max had pulled in every favour he could to get them on the earliest flight to Edinburgh a day later. Gibson still didn't know how he'd managed it.

When he'd asked, Max had jokingly told him he'd threatened to release some rather risqué pictures of his boss, Grant, to his wife that Max had taken at a rather drunken stopover one night in Naples. Gibson still wasn't sure if Max had been serious. Sometimes he couldn't tell.

There was one thing worrying him. He'd overheard Max agreeing to take unpaid time off to accompany him back to his family. Max could ill afford that.

"Tell me again you didn't have to sell your soul to come with me this week?" He turned to look at Max who stopped fidgeting and stared back. "I mean, you'd been sick, then this—did you have the leave due?"

Max frowned. "I told you. It's fine. We get to use my airline discount to save some money. Driving us up wasn't an option because my decrepit Punto wouldn't have made it. And hiring one would have cost a small fortune. Stop worrying. It'll be extra for the taxi fare to your house."

Gibson sighed. "Sorry. I'm on edge I guess." He turned to stare out the window again. A warm hand reached out and caressed his cheek. He looked back into his lover's warm brown eyes.

"Gibson, I know the funeral is only in a couple of weeks but I think I'm more useful to you now as support. I'm sorry I can't be there with you but I'll never get the time off." Max's face crinkled in a look of guilt.

Gibson leaned over and kissed Max's lips, not caring who saw it. "I appreciate it, honest. Seeing my mum and brother is going to kill me, and *not* seeing my dad." He tried to get past the lump in his throat as tears threatened. "I'll be able to face it better if you're there with me this time around."

The intercom crackled and the captain announced they were preparing to land. As Gibson pushed his tray up and handed over the remnants of the food he hadn't yet eaten—he had no appetite—he was thankful for Max's reassuring presence beside him. In a short time, the man had become someone special, someone beloved. It scared the crap out of Gibson.

First things first. Dealing with his father's death was going to be tough enough.

***

When he stepped up to the front door of the small, honeysuckle-festooned cottage in a lane set back among fields and cows, the impending family reunion was everything Gibson had both dreaded and looked forward to.

His mother's pale, grief-stricken face set with a brave smile and his brother Richard's bear hug as he held Gibson tightly and whispered he was glad to see him all conspired to make Gibson a gibbering wreck.

The mongrel greeting Gibson with such excitement had him in tears as he knelt down and buried his face in the thick fur. When he stood up, his face surely a mess, the three family members stood, in a group hug, crying, comforting each other and murmuring words of love and support. It was only when his mother finally released him and he could draw a breath that he realised Max was still standing awkwardly on the doorstep with a dog sniffing at his crotch.

Gibson wiped his eyes and nose on the sleeve of his tee shirt and motioned to a Max who looked ready to turn and run like a hound. He guessed Max wasn't used to loud, emotional displays of affection or family antics.

"Haggis, leave Max alone. Mum, Ricky, this is my boyfriend, Max Lewis. He'll be staying a few days with me."

If Gibson hadn't been so emotional he might have laughed at the panicked expression on his lover's face was he was enfolded into Doris Henry's big arms, his face pressed against a soft bosom.

"Max, lovely to meet you, child, even under the circumstances. I've heard nothing about you so I look forward to getting to know you." Max looked spooked, his eyes widening. He cast a panicked glance at Gibson who took pity on him.

"God, Mum, please let him go, before you kill him with kindness from those boobs of yours."

His mother tut-tutted but released the man currently looking as if he was being consumed with motherly affection. Doris's eyes widened when she finally noticed what Gibson wore around his neck. She reached out and touched the scarf with reverence.

"You found it," she breathed. "I don't believe it..." She burst into tears again as Gibson took the scarf off and wrapped it around her neck as once again he and his brother comforted their mother.

It was Ricky's turn to say hello. He held a hand out to Max and nodded, but there was speculation in his blue eyes. The sort that said, 'You hurt my little brother and I'll pluck out your eyes and feed them to you.'

If Gibson hadn't been feeling so raw he might have found it funny. Instead he watched as Max shook hands and murmured pleasantries and consolations. They were all ushered through to a big, warm farmhouse kitchen filled with various plates containing cakes, foil-wrapped secrets and various pastries dotting brightly coloured platters.

Doris gave a shrug. "The neighbours have been around, taking care of us. They're good souls but the doorbell hasn't stopped ringing."

His mother sounded exhausted and Gibson leaned in and gave her another hug. "It's going to be okay," he whispered as his throat clogged up. "We'll all get through this. Dad wouldn't want us falling apart."

His mum nodded. "I know, Gibson. I miss him so much."

"Me too," Gibson managed. She didn't need to know how much he'd fallen apart since her phone call or how Max had pulled him up from his doldrums more than once. "Maybe when we're sitting down I can hear the rest of the story and what happened. I know I've been putting it off but I want to know the whole story."

Doris nodded and moved away to pick up the kettle and fill it up. "I'll make us some tea then we can have a sit down. Go get your stuff out the car, love, and take it up to your room. We can have tea in the drawing room."

An hour later, curled up on the couch with Haggis and Max on either side of him, Gibson knew everything more he needed to know about his father's death. It was simple. It hadn't been a stroke. Cliff Henry had been over working, unwell from a bout of flu, which had debilitated him, and then he suffered a pulmonary embolism. Tragically, nothing could have been done and he was dead by the time the ambulance got him to the hospital.

Gibson noticed Max's reaction when his mother confirmed it had been an embolism. He'd drawn in a breath, a shadow of pain crossing his face.

That means something to him.

Gibson reached out and touched Max's hand. Sienna coloured eyes regarded him with darkness in their depths.

"Babe, are you okay?" Gibson asked in concern.

Max nodded jerkily. "Yeah. It's..." He cleared his throat. "The same thing happened to my mother. An embolism."

"Oh I'm sorry to hear that, Max," Doris Henry said softly. "This must bring back bad memories for you then."

Max shook his head. "She died in childbirth. With me. I never knew her." He fidgeted with his hands. Gibson reached out and laid a comforting hand on Max's arm. Even though Gibson knew this already, his heart still ached for what Max must be going through reliving the circumstances of his birth.

Doris leaned over and clasped Max's hand in sympathy. "Do you have other family?"

Gibson saw the wariness creeping into Max's face. He wanted to ask his mother not to go down that road in case it led to well-meaning questions about his past. Max would no doubt be mortified if Gibson's family found about his street past.

"No. They're dead too. I have no family." Max rolled a shoulder as if it was hurting. "It's only me." The finality in his tone was a warning to anyone not to pursue the topic.

"And me," Gibson said, rubbing his thumb over Max's hand. "Remember? Blond, sexy fabulous cute guy you picked up on a plane?"

Richard snorted and Doris laughed. "That's how you met? Sounds like a great story."

Both Max and Gibson flushed. That wasn't a story they were sharing anytime soon. Gibson had a feeling that to his mother and brother, a blowjob and jack-off in a bathroom stall was not the stuff of true romance.

"But he *is* all of those things," Max murmured, looking at Gibson with an expression that made him want to run up to his room with Max right now and have his way with him.

Gibson's mother smiled. "Oh my," she said softly. "I think you made a good choice here, son. I like him."

Gibson heaved a sigh of relief later that night when he and Max were finally alone in his room. It wasn't late, only eight o'clock, but he'd seen his mother flagging, and Richard had wanted to get back to his own family a few miles down the road. They'd all been overwhelmed and decided an early night was the best idea. Tomorrow they'd go over the final funeral and cremation arrangements, the songs being sung and the eulogies and then hopefully things would be in place to say a final goodbye.

Gibson snickered when he opened his bedside drawer and saw the items in there. "Mum's been busy." He held up a string of about twelve condoms, large and medium sizes, and snorted again. "You're only here three nights. What does she think we're going to do—fuck like bunnies?" He held up the mid-size bottle of lube. "Bubble-gum flavoured. I've not tasted it before." His face shadowed. "I'm not sure I'm up for much, though."

Max leaned over and hugged him. "Being here by your side is enough for me. I want you to try to get some sleep tonight. You haven't been lately."

Gibson watched in fascination as Max laid out his clothes in piles. Underwear. Tee shirts. Jeans and sweatpants. Multi-coloured columns of varying sizes and textures making short stacks leaning like the Tower of Pisa.

"You know that's a chest of drawers, right?" he remarked. "You can actually put the stuff *inside* the drawers."

Max nodded. "I know. I like it this way." He continued unpacking, one final short pile containing two thin pullovers. Warmth flooded Gibson as he observed his quirky man. He didn't understand the need inside Max to have his things close to hand and on display, but he appreciated he needed to. Gibson stepped up and wrapped his arms around Max's waist.

"Have I told you how much I'm thankful you're here with me?" he whispered against Max's tee shirt. Gibson pressed his ear to Max's back, listening to the faint heartbeat.

Max's arms reached backwards, encircling him as he leaned back into Gibson. "You have, but I like hearing it," was the quiet reply.

"You ground me," Gibson whispered as he closed his eyes to the steady throb of the heart beneath his ear. "Make me strong so I believe I can get through this. You help me forget for a while."

And wasn't that the truth. He'd gone from Gibson the Unbeliever to Gibson the Fallen with this man. The sense of belonging to someone, along with the knowledge he too possessed something he wanted and needed, was a revelation.

Max twisted around to face him. His eyes shone; whether it was moisture or the soft light in the room reflecting off his dark pupils, Gibson wasn't sure. He didn't care because Max was kissing him, sweet, gentle kisses with a warm wet tongue and lips tasting of tea and shortcake biscuits.

As they stood there, pressed against each other, mouths exploring and breaths feeding each other's passion, Gibson wondered fleetingly if Max would ever be one hundred percent conscious and tell him again he loved him. He wanted to be sure; he didn't want those words to have been fuelled only by fever and paracetamol.

Later, lying cuddled up beside Max after a satisfying session of nothing more than stroking each other to release, both of them breathless between moaning gasps uttered in the darkness of his bedroom, Gibson wondered if he'd ever say the words back if they were said to him.

***

The next morning when Gibson and Max came downstairs at eight-thirty, there was a full cooked breakfast on the table. His mother looked tired and strained.

Gibson scolded her. "Mum, you didn't have to get up early to make breakfast. Max and I would have had cereal or something."

He poured coffee for him and tea for Maxwell as his boyfriend stood uncertainly at Gibson's side

Doris flapped a dishtowel in their direction. "I couldn't sleep, so I got up to cook. It gave me something useful to do." She scurried around the kitchen putting bacon, fried tomato and eggs together with slices of fried bread onto white plates. "Sit, Maxwell. You're a guest in my house. The least I can do is feed you boys."

Breakfast was a sombre affair. Haggis scrounged scraps, which Gibson fed him guiltily off his plate, hoping his mother didn't see, and Max ate his toast, not saying much. It was clear he was uncomfortable with the whole family environment. Gibson's ex-fuck buddy Jamie knocked on the door as they were drying up dishes, and rushed in to embrace Gibson with a wet, smacking kiss with a hint of tongue then murmured with a soft Scottish lilt, "God, I'm so sorry about your dad." Max didn't look charmed. His eyes smouldered, his lips curled and the look of venom he threw Jamie's way would have killed an entire army in their tracks.

Gibson hadn't been prepared for the welcome and he hastily extricated himself from the body pressed against his, determinedly removed the groping hands on his arse and glared at Jamie.

"Shit, Jamie, stop mauling me in front of my boyfriend."

Jamie's not-so-innocent blue eyes under his droopy fringe of brown hair widened as he looked comically at Gibson then at the snarling Max. Gibson shivered in delight seeing possessiveness in Max's eyes. He knew he shouldn't feel this way but it turned him on.

"Oh, I'm sorry, Gibson. I didn't know."

"Yes you did," Doris Henry said. "I told you about him, Jamie. You're taking a chance." She smiled faintly as she turned to the sink and plunged her hands into the soapy bubbles.

"Well, I forgot." Jamie's lips pursed into a moue of displeasure as he stared appraisingly at Max. "This is the new guy? Huh." He didn't sound impressed.

Gibson suddenly wanted to snort in laughter at the look crossing Max's face, a look of indignation and dislike. Gibson needed to head this off at the pass. He crossed to Max and rose on his toes, reaching up to place a soft kiss on Max's tight lips.

"Max, this is Jamie. He's an—" He struggled for the right word. Ex didn't seem the right word for mutual blowjobs and jerk-offs. Fuck buddy would be frowned upon by his mother, although technically it was the right term.

"Friend," he said lamely. "Jamie, this is Max. My *boyfriend*." He made sure to enunciate the words. Max's face relaxed a little but he still looked at Jamie as if he was dog dirt on his shoe. Gibson held tightly to Max's hand.

"Whatever." Jamie waved a dismissive hand in Max's direction. "Gibson, I'm so sorry about your dad, my lovely. Is there anything I can do?"

Gibson shook his head, his throat clenching at the concern in Jamie's voice. "No, but thank you. Not unless you can bring him back."

The younger man's round face softened. "I wish I could, baby. I wish I could." Gibson winced as Max's hand tightened around his at the endearment.

Jamie looked at Doris. "Mrs H, you look tired. Can I do the washing up for you? You take a seat and I'll finish up while these guys dry up." He gently pushed her out of the way and took over. Doris rolled her eyes at Gibson and moved away to sit at the kitchen table. Gibson wondered how much of a visitor Jamie had been to his home while he'd been gone. He and his mother appeared comfortable with each other. The same couldn't be said about Max. He finished drying up in silence then muttered something about having a phone call to make and disappeared out into the garden.

Gibson glared at Jamie. "You've upset him," he accused. His heart was already heavy with grief and the last thing he wanted was his rock rolling away downhill. "You shouldn't have kissed me. We're not an item anymore, remember?"

Jamie stared at him wide eyed. "I'm sorry, Gibson. I suppose I got carried away. He seems a little…standoffish. Are you sure he's right for you?"

Gibson scowled at him fiercely. "He's perfect for me." And how true were those words. Gibson had never expected to say them, especially not so soon after starting a relationship. "He's not used to family; he's been on his own fending for himself since he was fourteen years old and he's learnt to hide himself away from people."

Gibson's mother drew in a horrified breath. "Alone since he was fourteen? What happened?"

He had no desire to tell anything of what he knew of Mooch's dark tale. That was Max's story to tell should he ever want to, and even Gibson was waiting for it. "He lost his whole family and went to foster care. But he's amazing, Mum. He's warm, he's funny and he looks after me. I lo—like him. And he likes me."

He loves me in fact. Gibson held the thought close to him.

Jamie looked shame faced. "Okay, well, I'm sorry. I miss you. But I guess I need to get over it."

Gibson nodded. "He's special, Jamie. I need to go see how he's doing. Mum, you okay?"

Doris waved a hand. "Go find your fella, Gibson. We'll be fine." She grinned faintly. "Jamie, have I told you about that young man at the youth centre, who thinks you're cute? His name is Dennis…"

As his mother did her gay matchmaking, Gibson left Jamie expressing horror at the thought of dating a man called Dennis and hurried off to find Max. He found him leaning on the old white picket fence, staring out across the grey expanse of the sea, as the wind blew his hair across his face and turned his cheeks ruddy. Gibson thought he'd never seen a more heart-stopping sight.

"You okay?" Gibson asked softly. "I'm sorry about Jamie. He can get a bit much."

Max shrugged. "Not your fault. This is your home, your family and your past. I'm a guest."

A pang snapped through Gibson's chest like a rubber band being launched inside him. "Max, you're my boyfriend. My family is yours. What's wrong?"

Max cleared his throat. "I guess I'm not used to family things. It's been such a long time I don't know how to act. Like offering to do the dishes for your mum. Jamie didn't even hesitate about it, but it didn't even occur to me…"

Gibson reached up and framed Max's face in his hands. "Stop it. No one expects anything of you. Being here for me is enough." He pulled him closer, feeling Max's body respond to his closeness as they stood together in the garden trading tender, gentle kisses.

Max sighed into his mouth, whispers of tea-scented breath and toothpaste. Part of Gibson wanted to hear Max say those words again, those ones he'd uttered in the dim, medicinal depths of his bedroom. The other part of him still worried about what might happen if he did.

They drew apart, mouths swollen, eyes darkened with the knowledge that perhaps later they'd be able to fulfil their need for each other again in the privacy of Gibson's room.

"Are you doing okay?" Max reached and brushed a strand of hair from Gibson's face. "This is about you, not me. I want to try and make you feel better, not the other way around."

Gibson nodded at the reminder of why he was home. "I feel pretty raw inside, but I need to be strong for my mum. She might look strong but she's fragile, I can tell. She and my dad were close. They were married thirty years, and now he's gone."

Max drew him closer, a comforting, strong presence he fell into, closing his eyes as he breathed in Max's scent. They stood for a while, simply feeding each other with spoonfuls of solidarity and familiarity.

"I'm sorry I can't talk about my past much," Max murmured sadly. "It's not something I want to share. It's sordid."

Gibson snuggled in. "I don't know much about it either," he said gently. "I know you were on the streets with someone called Levi who you obviously loved, and he died. I know how you ended up there and I've picked up things here and there. That's about it."

Max drew a deep breath. "I don't want to tell you about the stuff I did then," he muttered. "I don't want to see disgust in your eyes."

Gibson hugged him. Max had said as much when he'd been fevered and sick. "I could never be that man. I wouldn't judge you. I *want* to hear it. Max, baby, that's what boyfriends do. They listen."

There was silence. When Max spoke again his voice was pained. "Levi and I were lovers. He showed me the ropes. We ran away together because he told me it would be better. And for a while it was. Then he got hooked on drugs, and it spiralled down from there. Sometimes he was so out of it, I had to find the money to help us survive." Max shuddered. "I found I could get easy money for food and shelter being a rent boy on the streets."

Gibson moved and looked up into shadowed eyes. "I suspected as much," he said, lifting a hand to touch Max's cheek. "And listen when I tell you I don't care. You did what you needed to do. To keep you and Levi alive."

Max laughed harshly. "I was lucky I didn't pick up any diseases, but I always insisted on condoms. I guess it paid off." His eyes grew distant. "I sat down next to Levi for over an hour before I realised he was dead." His voice choked. "I even kicked him to try wake him up for fuck's sakes. The cops arrived and carted us both off, to a shelter. I was dehydrated, starving, malnourished and full of lice. At the shelter they sorted me out." His tone grew soft. "There was this policeman, the one who found us. He was so damn kind. He had a sixteen-year-old kid at home so he could empathise, I guess. I fell apart, and he was there for me. It kills that I never knew his name, to say thank you afterwards. I tried to track him down but couldn't find him." He sighed heavily. "I buried Levi and then turned my life around."

Gibson traced the lone tear trickling down Max's cheek. "I don't care what you did back then. I think you did good, babe. I mean look at you now." His own eyes stung. "I'm so glad you made it through. I can't imagine not having you in this world."

They stood together in a fierce embrace, staring out at the windswept sea. Later in the night when Max slid inside him with a soft sigh and a kiss, offering Gibson everything he needed and wanted, Gibson wondered how he'd ever existed without this man.

Chapter 12

The flight home a few days later was lonely, unwelcomed and too soon. Maxwell was glad he'd managed to organise that he worked on the return flight and it was hectically busy. It kept his mind off seeing Gibson's slim figure and pale face standing at the gate as he'd waved goodbye to the taxi taking Maxwell to the airport. Laying himself raw and spilling his guts had unsettled Maxwell, but it had been a long time coming, and it had been time for Gibson to know more.

His feelings about Jamie being there instead of him were enough to make him a little bitter. He trusted Gibson but not Jamie. The situation rankled and burned in his gut. The only shining light was Jack and Beth were coming up to attend the funeral. Maxwell was confident they'd be there for Gibson when he couldn't be.

Home. When he walked in around eleven pm, his flat appeared empty. Gibson's red and white jersey lay on the couch, no doubt left there after a frantic session making out when they'd divested themselves of clothes, eager to be with each other. A pair of Gibson's worn trainers lay under the coffee table, the ones he used to go walking in when they decided to go down to the river and watch the container ships pass by. They bought fish and chips while sitting and imagining what the cargo was and where the ships were headed.

Everywhere Maxwell turned there was a reminder of Gibson. Crumpled up pieces of paper in the waste bin was evidence of perceived failed renderings of Gibson's creativity, at least according to him. Maxwell though they were incredible. His lover had an artistic talent for drawing that blew Maxwell's mind.

Books were stacked neatly on the sideboard, instead of being sprawled across the room. His possessions were tidied up and packed away and Maxwell simply hadn't bothered to take them out again to their original position. The need to display the things he owned wasn't as important to him anymore. He had something more valuable now than stuff.

He unpacked, had a shower, changed into comfortable clothes and made himself noodles. He pulled out his bed, switched on the television and watched Nigella creating some fabulous dish but he didn't quite take it all in. His mind was still in Scotland with a man dealing with his father's death and trying to be strong for his family.

He picked up his phone and sent Gibson a text.

Hey baby. Got home safely. How you doing? xxoo

He watched Nigella folding some concoction of meats into pastry as he waited impatiently for a reply. It came ten minutes later.

Glad you're safe. Miss you already tho. I'm doing okay. xx
Wish I was there. I feel crap coming home without you. House is empty. No sexy Gibson driving me crazy.

Haha. Giving you a rest from my crazy. There was an emoticon of a smiley face rolling his eyes.

I like your crazy. How's your mum? Maxwell wanted to ask about whether Jamie was still hanging around but he didn't want to seem needy or insecure—even though he knew he was.

Holding up. She's tough. Her friends are rallying around. My uncle is here. He flew in from Wales earlier today. We're all good.

Maxwell experienced the familiar pang of longing to be there with a family that rallied around in tough times. His phone pinged again.

Got a message from Cruz. He's still in Rio, not coming back still for a while. I think they're planning on moving over there.

Maxwell knew Gibson missed his friend. He still hadn't met the man properly other than at the club.

The next text lifted his spirits.

Jamie left today too. He's gone back home, he's going on holiday tomorrow with his brother to Ibiza.

Maxwell sighed with relief. He could afford to be magnanimous now.

Oh I wasn't worried about him. Ibiza sounds cool. Maybe one day we'll get there together? Partying, drinking cocktails, sex on the beach?

Firstly - liar with a capital L Secondly are you talking about the drink or something else?

Maxwell scowled. He'd been rumbled. He chose to ignore the liar remark.

Both of them. He found a gif of someone—one of the Three Stooges, he thought—raising bushy eyebrows over and over again in a suggestive fashion and sent it.

Lol, I thought so. You are such a bad boy.

"You have no idea," Maxwell murmured with a satisfied smile. He lay back on the couch and propped a cushion under his head as he got comfortable. Maybe a little sexting would take Gibson's mind off things for a little while.

Are you in bed?

Yeah…?

What are you wearing? Maxwell sniggered.

I wish it was you. Instead I'd have to say the little black thong you like.

Maxwell groaned. He did love Gibson's little thong, which showed his pert arse to perfection but he doubted he was wearing it to bed. The little bastard was messing with him.

Oh? All I'm wearing is my hand on my cock.

It was no lie. Maxwell was already stroking himself as he arranged his phone on the pillow next to him, waiting for the next text. His dick was already hard and thinking of Gibson in the thong was making it harder.

There was a delay before his boyfriend replied.

Do you wish it was my hand on your cock instead? Like this?

Maxwell moaned as he released his cock to read the full text. It had been accompanied with a picture of a cherished item he recognised, a familiar hand wrapped around it teasingly.

He hastily sent a quick text back with hands sticky with his own pre-come. He'd have to clean his screen later.

God, you are sexy and such a bitch tease. Now I have to jerk off, so I'll be a while.

Take your time. I'm busy this side too, thinking of you being inside me. Feeling you fill me with your gorgeous cock.

Maxwell closed his eyes and his back arched as he thrust upwards into his hand, thinking of Gibson doing the same thing miles away. He smelt Gibson on the pillows still, saw his green eyes in his memory, experienced the warmth of his skin against his as he trembled and bucked beneath him, needy and wanton, his muscles clenching around Maxwell's cock as he orgasmed.

Maxwell gave a cry of release as his own fluids spilled over his hands onto the cover, leaving him gasping and spent. For a few minutes he lay there, drowsy and replete. His phone beeped again.

God. I wish you were here. I came like a freight train thinking of you.

Maxwell wiped his hands on his ever available wet wipes and picked up his phone.

Me too. Want you here so badly to fall asleep beside. Miss you so much already.

He wanted so badly to write the words he wanted to say but it wasn't fair to do that to Gibson right now. He had enough going on in his life without an "I love you" being sprung on him when he was at his most vulnerable.

His phone beeped again.

Knackered now. Need to sleep. Me and mum going to the funeral home tomorrow to finalise arrangements. I'll call you tomorrow night xx

K. Sleep tight lover. Speak tomorrow. Can't wait. ♥

Maxwell put down his phone and sighed ruefully as he regarded the sticky mess across his belly and duvet. Time to clean up then hit the sack and dream about tender green eyes staring into his.

***

A week later, Maxwell went into work—he'd been putting in as many hours as he could while Gibson was away—but Maxwell wasn't flying this time. He had an interview with the manager of the ground crew at London City. He was a little nervous.

Benjamin Sibonga had a body built like a rugby forward and was reputed to be a hardnosed, tough, but fair man. He was well respected by both his crew and the airport personnel alike, and his cheery Ugandan visage was always apparent as he wandered the airport like a man on a mission to ensure everything was running well. Maxwell left the interview nearly two hours later, drained, sweating and feeling as if he was one of the unfortunates at the bottom of the scrum in Benjamin's rugby team. The *interrogation*, as Maxwell grumpily called it, had been gruelling and tiring. The walk around the airport in his guided tour had been a fast-paced, no-holds-barred look at what went on down on the ground.

Maxwell knew working as ground crew would be vastly different to being in the air— helping to guide the aircraft into the gate, loading and unloading luggage from the plane, preparing the paperwork and fuel requirements for the pilot, and embarking and disembarking passengers onto the aircraft. It was all hectic, physical work. But it was more stable and less hours than flying, and he got to go home each day with no lengthy stay-overs or days away from home. Despite his love of being in the air, Maxwell loved the idea of coming home to Gibson, being able to spend more time with him, perhaps even plan a trip to Ibiza or somewhere else.

He had to wait a few days for the rest of the interviews to be concluded then Benjamin had promised to call him to let him know one way or another. Gibson would be home in a week's time and Maxwell hoped to be able to give him some good news. At least, he hoped Gibson would see it as good news.

Before he'd left for Scotland, worried he'd made the wrong call about changing jobs, Maxwell had called Oliver about it. His friend had been supportive.

"Max, you care about this guy. Being together a bit more can only be good for your relationship. Besides, the money's better too, isn't it?"

Maxwell sighed as he held his mobile phone to his ear with one hand. "Yeah, a little better. But what if he doesn't want to see me more? I mean, Gibson is used to so much more. He's actually *going* places, and here I am working at an airport and eking out a living."

I was a homeless rent boy with a deceased drug addict for a partner. Could he accept that?

"Stop it." Oliver's voice was fierce. "You had a tough time and you dragged yourself up. You've never told me exactly what happened when you were a kid and I don't need to know. The man I know now is not a nobody, Max. He's a tough, strong man who deserves more. Don't for fuck's sake be like me and try to push away the best thing that ever happened to you. It'll make you miserable. Gibson makes you happy. Stick with him."

"I know," Maxwell had whispered. "But when I finally tell him all the things I did back then, to keep alive, what if he hates me for it? What if I disgust him, Ollie?" It was the closest he'd ever come to telling anyone else what he'd been all that time ago. He closed his eyes as he'd waited for Oliver's reply.

When it came his friend's voice was heavy with compassion. "Baby, whatever you did to survive when you were a kid, he'll understand. From what I've seen, Gibson is very into you. I doubt he'll be put off by your sordid stories of days past. Trust me."

Maxwell was humbled by Oliver's understanding. "I hope so." He took a deep breath. "I love him, Oliver. I never thought I'd say that to anyone." *Not since Levi.*

Oliver's voice had a smile in it when he next spoke. "I'd never have guessed from the goo-goo eyes you made at him when we had dinner together. Leslie said he was already planning which wedding suit to wear to the Big Day. A Debussy of course."

Maxwell scowled. "Bite me, buster. I do so not make goo-goo eyes at people."

His friend laughed loudly. "You keep telling yourself that. I know what I saw."

Maxwell smiled as he rung off as he remembered the dinner conversation. Oliver had been right.

Maxwell took another sip of his tea then his eyes were drawn to a news story on the television about drugs. He turned up the volume.

"The young woman who was arrested in Indonesia a month ago on charges of drug trafficking is now facing the death penalty. She was allegedly found with over ten pounds of heroin in her possession when she was searched at the airport. Her parents have started a campaign to get her freed but at this stage it is unlikely that will happen."

He turned down the volume as he muttered angrily. "People go into countries known for having the death penalty for drugs, taking their stuff in and then when they get caught they expect to be treated differently? Don't do that kind of thing in the first place, lady. Can't do the time, don't do the crime."

When Levi had died, the post mortem that had been done had discovered he'd been subjected to some *very bad shit*. Shit that had been cut with every nasty thing imaginable and caused Levi's heart to stop, his throat to swell up and vomit to gush from his mouth. It was why Maxwell hated the smell and look of puke even now.

Once he'd been strong enough, he'd gone back on the streets, trying to find the dealer who sold the bad shit to Levi—to no avail. It was probably best because Maxwell didn't know what he would have done had he found the bastard. Back then his values had been skewed, his psyche fucked up and his ethics dubious. Beating some low-life dealer to death in a back alley as retribution for the death of the man he'd loved might not have been a stretch.

"And that is the one thing I *never* want to tell Gibson," he murmured as he stuck a lasagne ready meal in the microwave. "It's too much. I don't want him to feel he has to sleep with one eye open in case the psycho side of me comes calling."

When his phone rang four days later with a familiar number, Maxwell closed his eyes and hoped it was good news.

"Maxwell? It's Benjamin here. How are you?"

He crossed his fingers. "Fine, thank you. It's good to hear from you."

Benjamin gave a great belly laugh. "Of course it is. Especially when you hear my news. You are on the team, my friend. Your personal references checked out, and Grant says he'll be unhappy to lose you but I couldn't get a better employee."

Maxwell had been ready to do his personal Gilda Gray shimmy when he'd heard 'you are on the team' but hearing his future boss say his last boss thought he was worth it made him want to add a little break dancing into his moves. "Oh that's awesome news, thank you so much. You won't be sorry."

"I'd better not be," Benjamin growled. "Everyone wants to work on my team because we are the best and look after each other. I turned down a lot of applications to give you this job, so I will expect you to work hard and be part of the family."

Maxwell grinned. "Not a problem. I think I can do that. I'm truly pleased." And he was. He knew he'd miss flying but being with Gibson more than made up for it. As long as Gibson thought so too.

After he put the phone down and did his little dance around the room, he fell onto the couch in a contemplative mood. He started his new job in a month's time, with a generous increase in salary and benefits. He might even be able to start that savings account he'd always wanted if he was clever; then perhaps next year he and Gibson could go on holiday somewhere.

"Beach, sea, blue skies, cocktails, sex and more sex," he sighed as he dreamed about the future. "Gibson in a speedo, a white one, all wet…" That thought was leading to sensations he'd have to deal with, but right now his stomach was rumbling and he needed to eat. Warding off a hard-on at the thought of his beautiful man in wet beachwear, Maxwell took himself off to the Turkish diner down the road for a celebratory meal. After a plate of alinazik, a bellyful of sweet syrupy baklava and more than a few of small glasses of raki, Maxwell was merry and satiated. He staggered back to his flat inebriated and happy, where he continued to think of Gibson in his wet Speedos. He fell asleep contented, spent and eager for Gibson to come home so he could share the news and have the real thing in his bed.

***

Coming home a few days after the funeral was bittersweet. One part of Gibson wanted to stay with his mother and brother as the closest links he had to his dad; the other half was eager to see Max again, to crawl into bed beside him and be held as if he was precious. Gibson always knew he could count on Max to make him feel that way. He'd done a lot of thinking while standing watching his father's coffin enter the flaming furnace consigning him to ashes.

He'd resigned himself to the fact Max was more than a passing phase. The past two weeks, not seeing him and needing him, had brought that home. Seeing the vulnerability when Max told him about his past had near broken Gibson's heart.

After Gibson got home that evening, he unpacked his bags and put his laptop away, thankful he'd managed to get a little work done while he'd been gone. He showered then changed into some of his sexiest clothing—his favourite Andrew Christian thong, tight black jeans making his arse perky and a soft, loose-fitting silk shirt that clung to his body—and made his way to Max's flat.

Max wasn't there; his flight was apparently on its way back from Venice and would be landing within the next hour. Gibson let himself into the flat with the ravish key and settled down to wait for Max's return.

His phone rang and he answered it. "Jack, hi. Sorry, you weren't home when I got in and I've come straight out to see Max."

Jack's voice always lifted Gibson's spirits. "No worries, munchkin. I was over at Beth's, her dog's been ill and he needed to go the vet again. I helped her get him there and it took bloody ages." His voice softened. "You okay? It was a grand funeral, Gibson. You gave your dad a real send off. Beth and I were glad we were there."

"Me too," Gibson said quietly. "It made things easier. Thanks."

"Always, sport, you know that." Jack's tone grew aggrieved. "The flight home the day after was shit though. We hit some damn thunderstorm and the plane was shaking side to side like a rag doll in a terrier's mouth. Beth was petrified, and I have to say I needed new knickers too."

Gibson snickered. Jack wasn't fond of flying. "Aww, diddums. You big baby. It was a bit of turbulence."

"Turbulence?" Jack's voice rose. "I was thrown about like a damn piece of ice in a cocktail shaker. I don't know how Maxwell does it all the time."

Gibson snorted. "He told me once about this time a passenger had an epileptic fit in the middle of a huge storm, and there was some old woman who kept standing up and telling everyone the world was ending and they were all going to die. She was trying to drive the devil out of the poor guy jerking in the aisle. They had to forcibly restrain her and belt her into another seat with an air steward holding onto her while they dealt with it all. The other passengers were getting pretty scared."

Jack gasped. "Oh hell, that sounds awful. I guess you need your wits about you to manage that sort of thing. Maxwell strikes me as someone who's pretty put together though."

Gibson smiled. *Unless he has a bad hair day.* "Yeah, he's a rock. I'm sitting waiting for him to get home."

There was a grin in Jack's voice when he spoke. "No doubt you're going to jump his bones the minute he walks in the door? I smelt the cologne in your room. It was your getting laid one."

Gibson sniffed haughtily. "Are you referring to my Paco Rabanne *Invictus*? Any man would want to bone another one after smelling it."

Jack cackled. "Sorry, not me. I'm immune to your charms. Now give me a lady dressed in *Paris* and I could say the same thing. I love the scent."

Gibson groaned. He knew Jack sprung a hard-on for the fragrance. He'd been with him last Christmas when they'd trawled every department store in the world looking for the right perfume to buy Beth. *Paris* had eventually made the grade.

Jack chuckled. "Anyway, let me go and let you get it on with your man. I assume this means you won't be home tonight?"

Gibson nodded smugly. "You assume correctly. It's been a while and if I don't have sex tonight, my balls will explode and paint the walls."

There was silence on the other side. "Nice…thanks for sharing that image."

Gibson giggled and was mortified at the sound. He never giggled. "Pleasure. Oh and when I get home tomorrow we can have a catch up on where we are with the game and speak to Emmett and the others. I'm done my side but it will be good to have a pow-wow. I know I've been a bit distracted lately."

"You got it. And stop beating yourself up about not being around. We'll get *Camp Queen* finished in time, I promise. See you tomorrow, Gib. Say hello to Maxwell for me."

Jack rang off and Gibson put the phone down in a spare space on one of the crowded side tables. He'd managed to get Max to start packing some stuff away but some areas he didn't like to see touched. This side table was one. It currently held an old lamp, shining refracted light through a crinkled lamp shade, a battered copy of the book *Moby Dick*, a leather belt rolled into a ball, a tarnished silver chain with a grinning skull, which Gibson knew had been Levi's, and an old gold locket containing pictures of Max's family—his mum, dad and brother. Max wore the silver chain sometimes, normally when he went out but not at work.

Max had gone into a total panic one time when the jewellery items had disappeared. Gibson still felt guilty about putting them away in the side drawer thinking the small items would be safer there and hadn't wanted to tell Max what he'd done. When he'd had the chance, he'd retrieved the items and placed them on the floor under the sofa. When he'd *found* them triumphantly a few minutes later, he'd thought Max was going to cry with relief. Since then, this table stayed strictly untouched. It was obvious these things held great personal value.

He sat, texting Cruz to find out what was new. He and Craig were still travelling somewhere in South America, currently on a private island, having the time of their lives and it looked like they'd be there for a while still. Gibson was happy for his friend but he missed his vibrant personality and warm hugs. And when he heard the front door open nearly two hours later, after the over indulgence of some Ferrero Rochers and a half a pint of strawberry cider he'd found in the kitchen, Gibson was more than ready to welcome Max home. He was tired of watching endless episodes of *CSI*, which was all there was on the television worth watching as Max didn't have Sky, Now TV or Netflix. Max was frugal with his money, not surprising given his past.

Gibson launched himself into Max's arms as he came into the lounge. Gibson wrapped his legs around Max, latched onto his neck and proceeded to kiss him to death. Max appeared startled at first but soon got into the mood and before long, they were both panting, gasping messes on the couch, half dressed and more than ready to take it further.

"This is some welcome," Max managed to get out in between evading Gibson's tongue. "Did ya miss me then?"

Gibson sunk his teeth into Max's throat, eliciting a cry of pain. "Can't you tell? Plus I'm high on chocolate and cider—never a good combination."

"Oh I think I like this combination," Max gasped as he fumbled with Gibson's jeans. "I can't say the same about this damn zipper though."

Gibson flung himself back on the couch as he unzipped and pushed his jeans down his legs. He smiled slyly at the heat appearing in Max's eyes and the sultry gaze down at his groin. Soon Gibson was naked apart from the clingy white thong he wore.

"You..." Max's voice choked up. "I can't believe you're wearing that."

Gibson frowned. "Why, don't you like it?"

Max was having trouble breathing. "Oh I like it very much. I had this fantasy of you a while ago in a white Speedo, coming out the pool all wet, and I could see everything...and here you are now, dressed in that. It's a dream come true."

"Not quite true," Gibson smirked. He leapt up and went to the kitchen. Taking a large bottle of water from the fridge—not too cold as the fridge didn't work well—he unscrewed the cap and took a long swig of water, letting it dribble down his chin onto his bare chest. Max's dark eyes stared at him in lust.

Gibson gave the bottle to Max and lay back on the couch. "First, you get your clothes off," Gibson murmured. "Then you pour this all over me, right here..." He palmed his cock and groin suggestively and a frisson of delight sprinkled his skin like a warm breeze at the look of greed on Max's face.

"God," Max said faintly as he stood up and divested himself of all his clothes. "You are such a fucking tease." His brow furrowed. "Shouldn't we put a towel or something down though, so the couch doesn't get too wet? I mean we have to sleep on it tonight."

Gibson made an impatient gesture. "God, babe, whatever. Wet me so you can fuck me please. I'm dying here." Trust his anal-retentive partner—he sniggered—to think about something clean-freaky at a time like this.

Max scowled and went over to the sideboard. He opened the door and took out a spare towel then came back. "Lift up," he instructed. Gibson rolled his eyes but did what he was told. Once the towel was down, Max knelt before him with the open bottle and leaned in.

"And for the record, I'm not *fucking* you," he whispered.

Gibson's mouth opened in an indignant protest—hadn't they been here before, what was wrong with the man?—but was muffled by the soft press of lips against his.

Max released his mouth, leaned back and positioned the water above Gibson. "I'm making *love* to you."

The first drops of water fell onto Gibson's groin and he took in a breath. The water was cool, thank God, or his cock might have shrivelled to nothing. Although from the intense expression on Max's face, the quickening of his breath and the dilation of his pupils, Gibson had a feeling he'd have no problem getting to full mast again. And when Max filled his mouth with water and leaned down to douse it on Gibson's cock at the same time he mouthed it through the wet fabric, Gibson knew he'd have no problem sustaining his erection. God, he could come from this sensuous water play alone.

By the time Max had wet him with both his mouth and by pouring from the bottle, until Gibson's front was soaked and his cock and balls pushed pinkly through the delicate white fabric, Gibson's hole was aching to be filled and possessed by something other than the fingers currently pressing insistently inside him.

Max was hard, his cock bobbing as he leaned in and out, delivering this particular form of water torture. The look of rapture on his face turned Gibson on like nothing else. He was being worshipped and adored, and it was a heady feeling.

"You look so damn sexy lying there. My very own wet dream." Max poured what was left in the bottle onto Gibson's cock and then sat back, gazing at him with eyes drinking him into their depths.

"Please," Gibson mewled. "I need more than your fingers inside me."

Max opened a condom and sheathed himself. "Do you ever want to reverse things more?" he asked huskily as his fingers ran trails through the wetness on Gibson's belly. "Because you know if you do, that's fine with me. I don't mind either."

"I thought you liked topping?" Gibson said; the thought of making love to Max was appealing. Gibson was a bottom at heart, but with Max, he enjoyed being inside him.

"I do. But for you, I'd do anything and enjoy it. You know that, baby."

Gibson considered then shook his head. "Not tonight. Tonight I want *you* to take *me*. I want to do you again, but not tonight."

Max chuckled sexily. "That's more than all right with me." He finished dripping the rest of the water lazily onto Gibson's stomach and chest, leaning down and lapping the moisture pooling in his belly button.

Gibson moaned. "I'm ready to fucking explode here and I want to do that with you filling me up. Stop teasing."

Max grinned and took Gibson's mouth in a cool, wet kiss as he fulfilled Gibson's basest desire and slid into him. Eyes the colour of autumn leaves stared into his intently as between them, they fulfilled each other's need for one another. Gibson closed his eyes and fell into the sensation of being owned, of being seduced and being…loved.

Slow, steady thrusts of Max's hips, coupled with his own needy movements to meet the slick skin of his lover's groin, made Gibson smile dreamily as his fingers gripped firm buttocks and urged Max deeper.

There was no need for words. Soft sighs and groans were the only sounds permeating the dark recesses of the room and Gibson moaned softly as his climax built. He managed to groan out a word.

"Fuck…" He shuddered as he came, warm streams of sticky come coating them both as his arse clenched tighter. Max gave a strangled groan and murmured Gibson's name. His body stiffened and he gave one last, slow push of his hips then he buried his face in Gibson's neck. Teeth nipped the sensitive skin of Gibson's throat and he let out a small cry of pain and satisfaction.

"Are you eating me, Max? 'Cos that's what it feels like."

Max lifted his head, hooded eyes filled with emotion staring down into his. "I want to bloody consume you," he whispered as he moved away. "Any way I can. God, honey. You turn me into an animal."

Gibson nodded in drowsy satisfaction. "Hooray me." He reached out a languid hand. "Now give me those damn wet wipes and let me clean myself off. I'm all sticky and I want to curl up beside you and go to sleep."

Max handed him the ever-present wipes and they cleaned themselves up and then crawled under the duvet. Gibson snuggled into Max's right side and gave a contented sigh.

"I missed you so much and this is the best way to spend the night. I love being with you."

"Me too," Max said softly against his hair. "I wish I could have been there for you when you had the funeral."

Gibson trailed fingers across Max's damp, wipe-fragranced stomach. "It was fine, lover. Stop beating yourself up about it. You're here now. *You're* all that matters." He closed his eyes and burrowed deeper into the duvet and Max's body.

Max gave a soft sigh and pressed a kiss against the top of his head. "I'm glad you feel that way. I was going to tell you about this tomorrow but I think now is the right time." Max shifted and Gibson heard him take a deep breath. "I'm transferring to ground crew in a few weeks. I got the job."

At first, it didn't register. Gibson heard the words 'transfer' and 'ground crew' in his head and satiated as he was with sexual release, he didn't quite process it. Once the penny dropped and he realised what Max had said, he shot upright, covers falling from his body.

"What? When did this all happen?"

Max shrugged and turned on his side to face him. "I had my interview a while ago and they decided I was a good fit their team. While I'll be working different shifts, night and day, at least I won't be on stay-overs and flying around the country. I'll be home more often." His voice faltered. "Is that okay? I mean, I thought you'd be pleased, because you always say you don't see me enough…"

The vulnerability in that voice made Gibson's chest ache. "Of course it's okay with me. You know that. But are you sure? I mean you loved flying, and I'd hate to take that away from you."

"I love you more," Max blurted and Gibson lost his breath. He stared down at Max, not quite sure what to say. They looked at each other and then Max sighed.

"Sorry, I didn't mean to make you uncomfortable." He lay back, throwing his arm across his eyes. "It slipped out. Fuck."

Gibson lay back too, hands clasped under his head as he contemplated the ceiling and the enormity of the words he'd heard. Had wanted to hear. They weren't unexpected—after all Maxwell had told him so before—but hearing them in the warmth of the bed they'd made love in without a fever in sight was a little scary. Another emotion warmed him too, though: joy.

"Say something." Max's voice was tight. "Anything."

"I'm thinking," Gibson countered. "I want to say the right thing."

"If you have to think about it, then maybe there's nothing to say." Max muttered huffily.

Gibson sat up and glared at Max, a surge of affection making his words less critical. "Stop being such a douche." He pulled off the covers and watched as Max removed his arm and watched him from narrowed eyes. Slowly, Gibson leaned over and traced the outline of Max's tattoo with his tongue. In between teasing licks, he carried on his conversation.

"You know, it's not the first time you've told me that." Max stiffened and Gibson grinned as he placed soft kisses across Max's stomach. "And I'm a Cancer. We like to think about things before blurting them out, not like you Scorpios who say whatever's on your mind, whenever." His eyes widened. "Oh my God, I realised you're a Scorpio and have a scorpion tattoo? How radical is that?" He could almost see Max's eyes roll at those words. "Is that why you chose a scorpion?" Gibson asked curiously.

Max growled. "No. And what do you mean you've heard those words before?" Gibson noted with delight Max made no move to stop the slow exploration of his body.

"Well, when you were sick, and I was looking after you, you told me then. Of course you thought you were talking to Dream Gibson at the time…" He bit the flesh on Max's stomach and he let out a yelp.

"I knew it." Max sat up, and Gibson moved back. "I knew there was something you were hiding afterwards. Why didn't you say anything? And what exactly *did* I say?"

Gibson smirked. "You told me not to tell Real Gibson. That you didn't want to scare me away. And look, lo and behold. I'm still here."

"So you are." Max's voice was thoughtful. "Did I let any other gems of wisdom loose while I was feverish and my boyfriend was taking advantage of the situation?" His voice was more relaxed and a little teasing. The tension had disappeared from Max's body as Gibson nibbled his ear and nodded.

"Uh-huh. You told me you liked to dress up in a furry suit and pretend to be a squirrel. Oh and I think the words 'sucking my nuts' was mentioned a couple of times..." He shrieked as Max pushed him back onto the bed, a slow smile forming on his face.

"You lying little rotter. I said no such thing." Max growled. Gibson had poked the bear now and a merciless tickling ensued, leaving Gibson gasping for breath and giggling uncontrollably. He was particularly susceptible to having his ribs tickled.

Soon, he was breathless, lying beneath Max's hard body—in every sense of the word—staring up into his face. It was a definite *moment*.

In the stillness of the room there was only each other, and Gibson could hear the steady beat of his own heart. His arms were pinned above his head as Max lay across him. He was waiting for something. Gibson didn't want to disappoint him.

"You love me, then?" he breathed and watched in delight as Max's eyes dilated and his nostrils flared. The answer, when it came, was simple.

"You know I do."

"Oh, okay. I guess it's a good thing I love you back then." Gibson reached up and encircled his Max's neck with strong arms, drawing him in for kiss. Max made a small sound and then Gibson was lost in the slippery warmth of the eager tongue in his mouth, the hands running through his hair and the insistent press of a hard body against his. When they finally drew apart for breath, both men were panting and, if Gibson's body was anything to go by, both were once again very turned on.

However, this wasn't about making love right now. It was about sharing, about the future.

"You're the best thing to ever happen to me," Gibson said softly as he rested his head on Max's chest. "I never thought I'd see it, but you enchanted me the minute you did that whole *Karate Kid* thing in the club. I didn't realise it then."

Max laughed. "You sound like someone from a cheesy romance novel." He reached over and moved a damp tendril of hair from Gibson's cheek. "I fell for you the minute I saw you on the plane."

Gibson groaned mock theatrically. "Oh, God, listen to us. Please tell me we aren't always going to be this damn soppy. I think I might throw up." But his tone was teasing. And when Max disappeared under the covers and took him in his warm and eager mouth, Gibson arched his back and gladly gave in to being cherished.

Chapter 13

Maxwell sighed happily and finished licking runny ice cream off his fingers. Life had settled into some sort of normality after Gibson's return from Scotland. The last two months had been interesting to say the least.

He'd learnt Gibson had a nasty streak when interrupted too many times from his game design. Maxwell had made the mistake a few weeks ago of distracting him not once, not twice, but three times during a particularly complicated 3-D rendering 'thingy' he was doing. The subsequent potty-mouth invectives coming from lips he'd kissed not too long ago had horrified Maxwell. The broken house phone lying in pieces in the rubbish bin had borne testament to Gibson's temper as he'd had hurled it at the wall. And Maxwell thought *he* was the one with the bad temper. Huh.

When he'd mentioned it to Jack one evening as they'd swapped stories about the creatively endowed but fiery virago currently in his living room on a conference call with some hairy dude called Everett, Jack had laughed loudly and sympathised. Apparently he'd been on the receiving end of Gibson's hissy fits more than once.

Maxwell had also found out said Everett was a former fuck buddy and was coming over for the Quasar Game Conference to be held in a weeks' time. He'd made a mental note to not let Chewy, as Jack had named Everett, go anywhere near his boyfriend on his own. Maxwell was planning on going to the Con too, even if the outpouring of geekiness he expected to encounter killed him. Gibson could get his geek on with the best of them, something else Maxwell had discovered.

Jack wandered in, munching on something looking like a cross between half a cow and a loaf of bread. It was the biggest burger Maxwell had ever seen, oozing mustard and tomato sauce down Jack's chin. Maxwell was always in awe of Jack's appetite and the kitchen at his and Gibson's flat was always stocked with the most amazing variety of foods and snacks.

"He still busy with Hairy Boy?" Jack took a bit bite of his burger. "They get on the phone and they talk for hours. Best settle in for the long haul, buddy."

Maxwell sighed. "Is he always like this? So intense when he gets his teeth into something?"

Jack nodded and cheerfully wiped a splodge of mustard off his lip and sucked it. "Yep. Gibson is a perfectionist when it comes to his gaming. He drives me crazy." He grinned fondly. "But he's a consummate professional and there's no one I'd rather do this whole business thing with."

Maxwell wiped his sticky fingers on his jeans. "The game is nearly finished then? Gibson was saying it'll be ready for next year, maybe a little earlier than February."

Jack's eyes shone. "Yeah. We've come along great these last couple of months." He prodded Maxwell slyly in the ribs. "Thanks to you."

"Me?" Maxwell was surprised. "What did I do?"

"You've kept him happy, Max," Jack said softly. "Taken his mind off his dad's death, looked after him and made sure he ate properly. He's lapping it up and it's the happiest I've seen him. You're good for him."

Maxwell's body flushed with happy warmth. "Oh. Thanks, that means a lot." Surely, he had never felt more content. Coming home to Gibson curled up on the sofa bed, reading or on his laptop, or coming over here to Gibson's house and being part of a close-knit circle that included Jack and Beth, whom he liked, was like being part of a family. And when they went to visit Gibson's family in Scotland, he was made to feel welcome too. It was eons away from his previous life as a travelling salesman of his sexual wares and high-flying cabin attendant.

"How's the new job going?" Jack asked with a squint. "Gibson says you're enjoying it."

Maxwell nodded. "It's great. Hard work, and sometimes the early morning shifts piss me off, but at least I'm home much more and we can organise a weekend together now, or time away. It was a good move."

"Good stuff, sport. Glad it all worked out for you." Jack glanced at his watch. "I need to go meet Beth. She's got drinks with her work colleagues and I'm meeting up with her at the pub. Tell Gibson I said goodbye and I'll be home later. If not, I'll text him."

Maxwell nodded. "Will do. Tell Beth I said hi and have a good time."

Jack grinned. "Yes, spending the evening with a bunch of dentists and dental nurses sounds like a dream come true. Hopefully Beth still has her uniform on. I love seeing her like that." He snickered dirtily.

Maxwell chuckled. "Go get 'em, Tiger. I like a man in uniform myself."

"Yummy, so do I." Gibson wandered through then, flashing a wicked smile at Maxwell. "In fact, baby, perhaps you can put on your old crew uniform and we can do a bit of role play, give Jack some ideas for what he can do with Beth?"

Jack's jaw dropped.

Gibson continued with a sultry look at Maxwell, whose trousers grew tighter with every word Gibson uttered. "I'm thinking bad-tempered passenger on a flight who needs to be given a little slapping to discipline him. Or maybe a big bad flight attendant who's in need of an attitude adjustment…" He struck a pose, pointing at Maxwell dramatically. "On your knees, boy and suck my dick!"

Jack's face was pink. Maxwell was amazed; Jack was so put together in most ways, but mention sex—especially gay sex— and he was reduced to a blushing adolescent. Maxwell took pity on the flustered Jack.

"Yeah, Gibson, I don't think that's helping. Stop teasing him."

Jack glowered at Gibson and shot a thankful glance at Maxwell. "What he said. I'm off. I'll let you know whether I come home or stay over at Beth's. See you guys later." He disappeared then returned a few seconds later with a mutter to pick up the bag he'd left in his hasty departure.

Maxwell shook his head in amusement as he watched Jack scurry out the flat. "You are such a little bitch sometimes. You live to make that man feel uncomfortable, I swear."

Gibson shrugged and bit into an apple he'd taken from the fruit bowl on the table. "He's used to it by now. He's so vanilla and shy about sex. Sometimes I like to shock him."

"You finished your conversation with Chewy early. Jack said you two would be on the phone for hours." Maxwell slumped down on the couch and Gibson sat next to him, still munching his apple.

"We got everything sewn up earlier than we thought. I'm seeing him next week at the Con anyway so we can chat then." He frowned. "And please don't call Ev *Chewy* when you see him. He has a thing about it. He's not a fan."

Maxwell cleared his throat. "You and he had something going then?"

Gibson rolled his eyes. "We were fuck buddies, Max, nothing serious. And he knows I have a serious fellow now so this won't be another Jamie scenario, I promise." He moved to straddle Maxwell's lap and bit off another large piece of apple. His mouth approached Maxwell's and Maxwell opened obediently as Gibson fed it to him from his mouth. Gibson smiled in approval as he chewed the sweet fruit.

"Good boy," he crooned. Maxwell shuddered in anticipation as he realised what role play Gibson was acting out. He got his confirmation a minute later when Gibson lifted Maxwell's shirt over his head.

"Now, sweet slave boy, it's time to give the master his reward," Gibson whispered sultrily. As another piece of apple was pushed into his mouth, followed by a wriggle of Gibson's arse against his cock, Maxwell surrendered.

***

Wall to wall geek. Maxwell wasn't sure what the collective noun was for a bunch of them gathered together at a gaming conference, but he thought perhaps a google of geeks might be a good term. Maybe even a nerd herd. He sniggered and Gibson looked over at him through his new thin, sexy, black-framed glasses and raised an eyebrow.

"What's so funny?" Gibson asked with a pout. His eyes darted around the venue like a fish in a bowl. He'd been on tenterhooks about today for the past week, both at seeing Everett and taking part in the convention set in the middle of London on a cold and overcast November day.

"Oh, nothing," Maxwell said airily. "Checking out the atmosphere, immersing myself in the rush of geekiness flowing towards me." He flapped a hand, feigning a swoon. "I'm feeling quite faint with it all."

Gibson scowled but his eyes smiled. "Don't be a dickhead."

He looked delectable in dark blue chinos, an open, long-sleeved white shirt with a darker blue string necktie strung loosely around his neck and a brocade waistcoat, in shades of grey and bronze. Maxwell wanted to eat him all up.

Gibson's brow creased in an adorable frown. "I'm looking for Ev; he said he'd be here by now but I haven't seen him yet…" His voice trailed off as he peered around the room.

Maxwell sighed. He'd been preparing to meet the man Jack—who'd been with them earlier but disappeared into the crowd—called Chewbacca. Gibson appeared to think of the world of Everett from Canada, and Maxwell wanted to make sure he followed suit. There was a small niggling jot of jealousy lurking in his soul but he'd manfully tried to suppress it.

"I'm sure he's around, isn't he, like seven feet tall and hairy? He should be easy to spot…" His own voice tailed off as Gibson's eyes flashed dangerously.

"You've been listening to Jack, haven't you? I'm going to kill him."

Maxwell decided wisely to keep quiet and not cast any further aspersions on Everett. He sighed and resigned himself to being dragged through the teeming crowd of men and women all talking about things Max couldn't even pronounce. He was out of his depth. He was pushed, pulled, jostled and had his feet stood on half a dozen times before Gibson gave a loud, joyful cry and let go of Maxwell to literally jump into the arms of a man standing amongst a group of earnestly gesticulating geeks.

"Ev, I've been looking for you everywhere, you bastard. It's so good to see you." Gibson's enthusiastic greeting didn't escape Maxwell and he noted sourly that 'Ev' certainly didn't seem to mind being mauled by a sexy blond dynamo. He waited patiently though until Gibson had finished hugging and kissing the man on the cheek thankfully and then turned to him, eyes sparkling.

Truth be told, Maxwell was a little disappointed. Jack had built up this picture of—well, a comical, Chewbacca type of character—and Everett Talbot, while hairy, wasn't true to the image at all. Ev was a six-foot, broad-shouldered, good-looking man of about thirty, with a thick beard, dark, thick, rusty-coloured hair and yes, hairy arms and chest that showed though his polo shirt. It resembled a safari hunter's lion trophy hanging on a wall.

He was a bear and Maxwell didn't want to think of his man and this one together because it made him way twitchy.

He smiled politely when Gibson introduced them.

"Ev, this is my boyfriend, Max. He works for London City Airport, but he used to be cabin crew. He gave it up so he could spend more time with me." He cast an adoring glance at Maxwell who basked in those words. "Max, this is my friend *Everett*." His tone held a warning and Maxwell gave a little sigh. He'd better not upset the apple cart and call the man Chewy after such an adoring look from his lover. He wanted more of them.

"Hi, Everett, great to meet you." Maxwell squawked as he held out his hand, expecting it to be shaken and instead found himself with a mouthful of burly chest as Everett hugged him like the proverbial bear.

"Hey, Maxwell, great to meet you at last. I've heard so much about you from this little tyke I feel I know you already." Everett's voice echoed in Maxwell's ear as he tried to extricate himself from the vice grip he was encompassed in. Finally breaking free and running a hand over his hair to make sure it was okay, Maxwell nodded.

"Oh, he's talked about me to you?" His natural sense of smugness lurked close to the surface as he considered the import of those words. "What did he say?"

Everett laughed, a loud belly laugh, and everyone turned around to stare at him, despite the hub of the arena. "God, he doesn't stop. It's Max this, Max that. I can't wait for Max to get home so I can bone him, yada, yada, yada."

"Really…?" Max drawled, watching Gibson's face go pink. "How interesting…"

"Yeah, enough bromancing and spilling my secrets, you big hairy bastard." Gibson punched Everett on the arm but it was like a gnat swatting—well, a bear. Maxwell was still affronted at the fact Gibson got to call Ev something hairy when he'd been warned off it.

Gibson became all bossy, something Maxwell loved to watch. "We've got some stuff to talk about, Ev, so maybe we can grab a coffee and find a spot at Coffee Dork, and you can tell me about those improvements you made to the program."

"Coffee Dork? That's a real place?" Maxwell said faintly. He was overloaded with nerd-dom and it was starting to hurt. He liked playing games as much as the next man but this was too much.

"It's a proper franchise, Max," Gibson said with a long, suffering roll of his eyes. "I'm gonna take Ev over there, we'll have a quick talk and I'll come and find you later. Maybe we can meet in a couple of hours over there by the giant locust thingie. I think it's supposed be Locula, the vampire locust from *Green Scream*." He waved towards a ceiling-high green monstrosity in one corner with waving antenna and what looked like a sound booth on its back. People were actually climbing rope ladders to get up to it. Maxwell looked at the vampire locust then back at Gibson who stood there, tapping his foot impatiently.

"You call a couple of hours a quick conversation?" Maxwell said in dismay and pique. What the hell was he supposed to do for two hours on his own?

Jack appeared beside him as if by magic, cackled and shoved him in the back. "I told you they talk for ages when they get together. Come on buddy, I'll look after you. I'll find you something to occupy your time. Gib, Chew—" Jack bit off the word as Gibson stared daggers at him. "Ev, see you both later."

Maxwell didn't even have time to say goodbye before he was hauled for time immemorial through the seething mass of humanity. He finally finished up somewhere he knew he'd like and he wanted to kiss Jack for introducing it to him. The bar was called Pablo's. Maxwell heaved a sigh of relief when he and Jack found a spare table and chairs and sat down. It was lunchtime after all and Maxwell could do with a beer. Jack winked and went off to order them as Maxwell sat back with a sigh and took out his mobile. He might as well catch up on the world of Twitter and Facebook while he was here.

Three beers and two and a half hours later, and there was still no sign of Gibson. Maxwell was feeling a little woozy and he needed fresh air. Jack had been a consummate host, keeping him company in between visiting certain exhibits—obviously, he wasn't as big on this exhibition as Gibson was—but Maxwell needed some space. And peace and quiet. The constant chatter and noise in the hall was fraying his sanity.

"I'm going to go outside, get some air," Maxwell said to Jack as he stood up.

Jack nodded. "Cool. I'll tell Gibson where you are when he gets back. I'm going to stay here and try get to the next level of this game." He looked up. "It's probably raining. You might need an umbrella."

"*If* he gets back," Maxwell muttered. "And I don't have a brolly." Thoughts of him and Everett had been flitting through his mind, and while he trusted Gibson, his insecurity was bleeding through.

"He'll be back," Jack said confidently. "Stop being such a worry wart. He gets a bit distracted."

"Okay. Well, let him know where I am and I'll hopefully see him in a bit, not too wet." Maxwell picked up his jacket, drained his beer and stopped to take a pee on his way out. After a veritable mission getting to the entrance, he finally made his way out into the overcast, drizzling climes of the city.

"Great," he grumbled. "Bloody raining again." It had in all truth only been raining for two days, which by British standards wasn't bad, but he was in a bit of a mood. He'd known Gibson had things to do, but he was missing him. And the fact Everett had *his* Gibson wasn't making it any better.

"Oh grow up, you stupid git," he told himself as he stood, shivering with the cold breeze despite his thick, wool-lined denim jacket. "Stop being such a misery guts." Scolding himself for his stupidity made him feel a little better.

He took a few deep breaths of the rain-scented air as he watched the denizens of the capital walking past in Macintoshes and coats, huddled underneath umbrellas. His eyes noticed a figure huddled in a shop front two doors down and his heart sank. One thing Maxwell couldn't do was resist giving something to the homeless people who lined the streets. It was the least he could do. He usually gave food, coffee or warm clothing but he had none of those things at the moment and nowhere to buy them. It would have to be money.

He opened his wallet, took out two five-pound notes and walked over to the figure sitting in the corner, hidden by a blanket already spattered with rain. He squatted down in front of them, not too close, knowing from experience sudden moves could startle some of the street kids. That alone could cause all manner of mayhem, perhaps even a knife in the ribs.

He'd been there and done it himself before, threatened someone with a sharpened skiv he'd made from a plastic knife taken from a McDonald's. The well-meaning man had taken him by surprise after he'd had to fight off a john who hadn't wanted to pay for the blowjob he'd given him in the alley. Maxwell had already suffered a black eye and a kick to the nuts as a result of that escapade and he hadn't wanted any more abuse. Needless to say, the well-wisher had beat a hasty retreat, but he had left the sandwich he'd bought behind.

"Hey," Maxwell said softly.

The figure stirred and muttered and Maxwell crinkled the pound notes in his hand. "I don't want to leave this here. I'd like to make sure it gets put somewhere safe. Can I slip it under your sleeping bag cover?" Levi had hated anyone touching any of his stuff and had a tendency to become a little violent when he thought someone was trying to take something away from him.

The figure mumbled something and lifted the cover away from the face. Maxwell saw an old woman with pale, grey, stringy hair and dulled blue eyes. Her face was weathered, the familiar signs of crack and alcohol abuse staining her features.

Maxwell knew people looked at the homeless and thought all they'd do was go buy drugs and booze with the money they'd been given. But even drug addicts needed food and warm clothes, and when he and Levi had been together, the money had been spent in equal parts in putting food in their bellies and finding shelter. Maxwell had refused to use it to keep Levi in drugs. That had been money Levi had to find himself. It had been a catch-22, and one Maxwell had battled every day. Until the day he'd woken up and discovered he no longer had to worry about Levi.

"You can give it to me," the woman said hoarsely and Maxwell pressed the money into her grimy hand. Her eyes squinted at him and he stood up, not expecting a thank you. He turned to go back to the shelter of the game venue.

"Mooch?"

His body went stiff, and it wasn't with the cold air blowing down the street. His throat closed up and the blood rush to his head made him feel faint. He swung around slowly and faced the woman who had the gleam of recognition in her eyes and a slight smile on her face.

"It is you. I'd know those brown eyes and chin anywhere." She shook off her blanket and stumbled to her feet. "Don't you recognise me? It's LouLou."

Maxwell's teenage past came flooding back in a cacophony of memories, both wanted and unwanted. LouLou had been one of Levi's dealers. She and Levi had had a special bond that went beyond the simple supply and demand relationship. The pair had been like family, with Levi going to her when he'd had words with Maxwell, or wanted to be alone.

Three weeks before Levi had died, LouLou had disappeared and Levi had got agitated about it. She'd never shown up again, and Maxwell thought she'd simply moved on—or worse, died and been carted away. Levi had gone back to their old meeting place, a shop corner in the dregs of town, but he'd never found her again. Levi had been truly devastated by her loss. Until the day he died, when he'd come back from meeting another one of his dealers, and he'd appeared a little more upbeat. Maxwell had never found out why, despite his prodding and then—well, then it had been too late. Levi had died and Maxwell was left alone.

"LouLou. Of course I remember you." Maxwell was shocked. Eleven years ago she'd been a woman who admittedly looked rough but a lot better than she did now. The years and no doubt the drug abuse had taken its toll on her body to the point he hadn't recognised her.

She nodded eagerly. "You look so different, so grown up. You got off the streets then?"

Maxwell nodded. "Yes, I managed to move on when Levi died. You remember Levi?"

Her eyes slid away from his and she nodded jerkily as she stared at the ground. "Of course, he was a good lad. I was so sorry he died. I told him not to, but he still did." The words made no sense.

Maxwell frowned. "Told him not to what?"

She looked at him then her gaze faltered again. "He found me. I'd been away, in a shelter. I'd been sick. But he came looking for me for his stuff, and I gave him some. But it wasn't good." Her drug-addled brain was no doubt confused but the chill down Maxwell's spine grew colder.

"Wait—are you telling me you gave Levi the shit that killed him that night?" The freezing chill was no doubt melting now from the burning anger stabbing his gut.

When she opened her mouth and the words spewed forth it was as if she was unburdening her soul and Maxwell was her avenging angel.

"He'd always trusted me. And I told him it wasn't good stuff, that I got it from someone I didn't trust. But he said he needed it and I let him take it. I needed the money. He said he'd chance it." She slumped against the wall, her face twisted in guilt. "I never meant to kill him. When I heard the news I knew I'd have to disappear for a while, in case the cops came looking for me." She wailed in despair. "I'm sorry, Mooch. He was a good lad. I know you loved him. He loved you something fierce, he did."

Maxwell could barely focus with the remembered grief and the heat of rage threatening to immolate him. "You fucking bitch." His venomous tone made her shrink back in fear, clutching the wall. "He trusted you and you fucking murdered him."

He heard his suppressed street roots growing like greedy grasping tendrils through his mind and body. "He vomited to death and I found him cold and lifeless. Because of you and your bad shit he put in his veins, I was left alone!"

LouLou shook her head in panic. "I'm sorry, lad. I didn't mean to hurt him." She cowered against the wall.

"Max." Gibson's voice echoed in the dull throbbing of Maxwell's mind. "Baby, calm down. She's an old lady, you're scaring her."

Maxwell snarled as he swung round. "I'd never hurt her, Gibson. That's not who I am. You need to back off though. This is my business, not yours."

Oh, God, listen to me. I've turned back into Mooch. I can't be him. I can't.

Gibson's face was pale, his glasses speckled with rain, his slight form shivering in the cold. "Anything upsetting you is my business, Max." His face was grim but determined and Maxwell had never loved him more. But this moment wasn't about love. This moment was about hate and despair and rage at every shitty thing he'd ever been forced to do to survive, brought back by the sight of a woman on a pavement, the woman cowering before him.

"Leave this alone. She killed Levi, for God's sake!" Maxwell spat.

Gibson stepped forward, his face filled with compassion and love. "I heard what she said. I didn't want to interrupt, because I thought you needed this. To find out what happened all those years ago. But it's not going to bring him back. Levi has gone, Max. But you still have me. I'll help you through this." He stepped forward, arms open as if to take Maxwell into them, and Maxwell lost it.

He shoved Gibson away violently, needing space, wanting nothing more than to run, to get away. Gibson cried out but Maxwell needed solitude, somewhere to lick old wounds suddenly torn open. He turned, feet pounding the wet pavement as he escaped. He wanted to be anywhere other than back there, in that moment.

Maxwell wasn't as fit as he used to be, and his breath came in heaving gasps as he pushed and shoved his way through the people going places. It was only when he stopped for breath and spied an alleyway, with a large dumpster in it, and a plethora of cardboard boxes, that he finally stopped running and slumped down onto the cardboard, back against the wall, as he fingered the silver chain around his neck. Levi's chain.

Gibson's face swam in his vision and he clung to that loving visage as he sat in the cold alleyway until everything went dark and he remembered no more.

Chapter 14

I'm fine. Leave me alone for a bit. Don't come over. I'll call you soon. I'm sorry about everything. So damn sorry.

Gibson sat on his couch, curled into the corner as he huddled under his duvet. He'd stared at the text countless times in the last two days. It was the last message he'd had from Max since he'd ran off into the darkness, leaving Gibson with a scared, guilt-ridden homeless woman and a nasty, deep gash on his temple and a swollen right eye where he'd hit the wall after Max had shoved him.

Jack had been incandescent with rage when he came to his friend's aid after his panicked phone call. Max had been called every name under the sun as Jack had taken Gibson to the first aid room to have his wound dressed. Jack had thought he needed stitches but Gibson had firmly disagreed. He hadn't wanted any more fuss made.

His chest ached both from seeing his lover's pain and at being rejected. He'd had to spill the beans on Max's past to Jack to explain why he'd lost it, and while sympathetic to Max's grief and past history, Jack had growled angrily there was no excuse. Gibson had agreed, but he'd quietly argued with Jack it had been accidental.

He knew deep in his bones that Max would never hurt him on purpose.

LouLou had packed up her bundle of meagre belongings and scarpered. Gibson had watched her go through blurry streams of blood running into his eyes and a headache of note. His glasses had also been damaged in the meeting with the wall, and they'd now been resigned to the bin.

Gibson had wallowed in his own misery the past few days. Jack and Beth had been there for him, insisting on staying every minute with him to ensure he didn't have a concussion.

Gibson knew Jack had texted Max with a terse, uncomplimentary message about how he'd hurt Gibson and he was a complete dick. Max had replied then, as Gibson's previous texts had gone unanswered.

He stared morosely into the depths of the couch, seeing nothing and wondering how things had gone so terribly wrong that night. He'd gone outside searching for Max only to find him shaking with temper and looking very un-Max like. The soft, sweet, funny man Gibson knew and loved had turned into a tough, feral ruffian intent on hurt. Mooch was back. Gibson had heard the conversation, and his stomach had gripped with dread. He'd had to intervene.

"Not that I helped the situation at all," he murmured now to himself. He sighed and reached over for his sketchpad. He'd had little appetite to work on *Camp Queen*, which was nearly complete. He had a few minor touch-ups to do before they sent it their beta testers. Instead he'd started idly drawing his and Max's story in graphic form as a means of staying close and reliving their relationship.

He smiled softly at the images before him in his white drawing pad. They were black and white pencil renderings of Max's famous crane kick in the club; Gibson falling over the fence, hurting his hand and Max with his handkerchief, kissing it better. There was even the scene with the heaped clothes on the bed while Gibson sobbed in Max's arms on the floor.

A soft touch on his shoulder made him look up. Beth stood there, holding out a cup of tea. "Here, drink this." She handed the mug to him and he nodded his thanks. She sat down beside him and her eyes widened.

"Wow, these are incredible," she breathed as she looked at the drawings. "You are so damn talented. I wish I could draw like you."

"Yeah, well I might not have the real thing but I have this." Gibson traced a picture of Max lightly with his finger. "I wish he'd come over so we can talk, you know? I don't know what's going on in his mind anymore."

"Sweetie, he's hurting too, I know he is. That man adores you. It's on his face every time he looks at you. Yes, he's being an arsehole, but he discovered something that threw him for a loop." She sighed. "It didn't give him the right to do what he did and not talk to you now, but I think he'll come around. Be patient."

She flipped the sketchpad and her face softened at the picture of Max sitting beneath a tree with Gibson seated between his legs, leaning back against his chest. "That's beautiful," she murmured. "You two look so good together. That's how I know things are going to be okay."

Gibson stared at the picture wistfully. "We went to Sherwood Forest for the weekend and pretended we were Robin Hood and his Merry Man. It was a great weekend."

Beth sat up, her eyes brightening. "Gibson, why don't you make this into a comic? If Maxwell sees these pictures, he'll have to know you love him. It'll remind him of all the good times. Maybe it will bring him to his stupid senses."

Gibson raised his eyebrows. "Seriously?"

Beth smiled. "I'll take it over and drop it off for you because I guess you don't want to go to his place yet." She grimaced. "Don't ask Jack to do it. He's so mad with Maxwell, he'll probably punch him."

Gibson considered the suggestion. The more he thought about it, the more he liked the idea. Max couldn't possibly ignore the fact they were important to each other if he saw these pictures. He grinned at Beth, feeling hopeful. "I'll do it," he said decisively. "I have all the software already to make the storyboard, and the right paper, and my hot shot printer-scanner. I'm sure I can make some sort of a graphic comic out of all this. Great idea, Beth."

Half a day later he still hadn't heard from Max, but Gibson had a beautiful colour comic ready to go, and he put it in an envelope with a brief note he hoped wasn't too soppy.

Wanted you to have this to remind you of our time together. Please talk to me. I love you.

Beth left him with a soft kiss to his forehead and a promise to deliver it to Max's door. And if he wasn't in, then she'd leave it in his mailbox.

A day later Gibson was ready to climb the walls. Beth had assured him she'd left the envelope in his letterbox, yet Max still hadn't called him. Now Gibson sat in the dark, again under his treasured duvet, the soft strains of classical gaming music playing on the sound dock on the sideboard and wondered if it was finally over. He'd even called Max to ask him if he got his comic. Nothing. It had gone straight to voice mail. Texts remained unanswered.

Gibson hadn't been sleeping. He'd cried himself to sleep more than once, and he was beginning to doubt he'd ever hear from Max again.

Beth and Jack had gone out an hour ago to a film première and Gibson was alone. He fingered the healing scar on his temple and winced. It was still livid and tender, and his eye was a little swollen with some yellow bruising. He reached across to the side table and picked up his well- worn copy of the extra comic he'd made for himself. It was an unhealthy obsession, flicking through the pages, reminding himself of past events.

He'd done some further work on *Camp Queen* but his heart wasn't in it. That irked him; his passion for something had been relegated to an activity he did because he had to. Max had replaced Gibson's love for his art and it both thrilled and frustrated him. He was a lover first and an artist second now. He hadn't even told his mother or brother yet about Max not speaking to him. If his mother thought he was heartbroken she'd never give up bugging him, especially so soon after his father's death.

There was a soft knock on the door. His heart leapt but he daren't hope. After all, it could simply be the neighbour who kept coming around asking for all manner of things to borrow—a screwdriver, a cup of ice, a triple-A battery. Gibson pushed the duvet off and padded to the door in his socks. His dress sense lately ran to warm tee shirts and baggy sweatpants and he didn't care what he looked like right now. Cruz would have a hissy fit at the current state of affairs. But Cruz was now in Rio de Janeiro with Craig, living the good life.

He slipped the safety chain on in case a serial killer stood outside then opened the door. He lost his breath.

Max stood there, hair mussed and curly, dark shadows under eyes, which were dull and lifeless. His face was pinched, his usual cheery demeanour lacking, but it was the hesitancy and wariness in those brown eyes that made Gibson want to cry. Max looked as if he never expected anything good to happen to him ever again.

"Max." Gibson closed the door briefly and took off the chain. When he opened it again, Max's eyes were drawn to the bruise around his eye and he paled, visibly upset.

"God, your face. I never meant to hurt you—please believe me. I got scared and pushed you away, but I didn't do it to hurt you."

"I know it was an accident," Gibson said quietly. He gestured inside. "Do you want to come in?"

Max nodded and hitched his rucksack tighter onto his shoulder. Gibson stood aside as Max entered, then closed the door and padded back into the lounge, sitting down on the couch and drawing his duvet around him like a safety blanket.

Max stared around the room nervously, then sat down in the easy chair, his rucksack on his lap. His fingers fidgeted with the straps.

"Jack's not here," Gibson said tiredly. "He and Beth went out. You're not going to get beaten up. I wouldn't let him touch you anyway."

"That's more than I deserve," Max said quietly.

"Bullshit," snapped Gibson angrily. "Where the hell have you been? Wallowing in self-pity? It hasn't been a picnic for me either, you know."

Max sagged down in the chair and closed his eyes as he passed a hand over his hair. "I know. God help me, I know. Jack told me what I'd done to you, your beautiful face and I was ashamed. I couldn't bring myself to face you."

Gibson snorted. "And you thought by ignoring me it would make things better?"

There was silence.

"I hated myself for losing control like that," Max said finally. "It took me back to the time I was on the streets, trying to stay alive and out of trouble." He laughed harshly. "I thought it was all behind me until I saw LouLou again. Finding out it was her who gave Levi the drugs sparked something inside and I lost it." He gulped. "And I hurt you too. I—" he took a deep shuddering breath, the anguish on his face breaking Gibson's heart. "I hurt the one person that means the most to me."

Gibson closed his eyes briefly, his throat clenching as the ache in his chest magnified. "I'm not so sure about that." He shifted and clutched the duvet. "I can't compete with a dead man, Max. I can't. I know it was a long time ago but you have these memories I can't replace and I doubt I ever will."

Max stared at him wide eyed. "What?" He put his rucksack down on the floor and knelt down in front of Gibson, as if in supplication. "Baby, you aren't competition for Levi. You never were. There is no comparison. I never loved Levi like I do you." He raised his hands helplessly. "I realised something these past few days. Levi and I only had each other. We protected one other, looked out for each other. It was a relationship born of necessity. I loved him and I always will. But it wasn't like what I have with you."

"What do you mean?" Gibson asked, hope flaring in his chest that perhaps things weren't too late to be fixed.

"I mean I have this amazing guy, this clever, funny, sexy man who makes me feel indestructible, who loves me for everything I am and never judges. I have this man who makes me feel like I'm the most special person in the world, and I fucked it up. And do you know what he still did?"

Gibson waited, not sure what he was supposed to say. Max reached inside his bag and brought out a now tattered copy of the comic.

"He made me this. He drew all the places we'd been, all the things we'd done, good and bad, and he sent it to me with a note saying he loved me." Max's eyes shone with tears and Gibson was ready to bawl too. "It was the singular most incredible moment of my life when I saw this gift and knew he still loved me despite me being a prick. I cried for a whole day, every time I saw it. I even took it to bed with me because I couldn't bear being parted from it. It made me feel close to you."

"I thought you didn't like it," Gibson whispered. "It took you so long to get here."

Max reached up and cupped his face in shaking hands. "I needed to pull myself together so I could come here tonight and tell you this. I needed a little time to get my head straight." His voice choked up. "I love you so much, baby. I thought I'd lost you." He stood up and motioned to Gibson to lift the duvet. He sat down next to him and pulled it back over them both.

"I thought I'd failed Levi when he died. I'd always looked out for him, kept him safe, even though he was the older one. Finding out I couldn't have saved him—it hurt. These past few days I realised he died because of the drugs he took, not because I let him down. The feelings I have for you are more than anything I felt for him. You are my world, Gibson Henry, and I'm going to spend my time proving it to you, if you'll still have me."

He leaned in and removed Gibson's glasses, laying them gently on the side table. He kissed Gibson's swollen eye, then the ugly gash on his temple. "Battle scars *I* put there," he murmured sadly. "I'm so sorry. What can I do to make it up to you?"

Gibson stared into those brown eyes he loved, falling into their depths, and whispered, "Kiss me, you idiot. It's been ages."

The words had hardly left his lips when he was pushed back against the couch arm and Max's mouth found his. He'd expected frantic, frenzied kissing born of need but instead found himself subjected to a tender and loving embrace as Max worshipped his mouth. Halfway through the kiss, Gibson felt wetness on Max's cheek and opened his eyes to see a solitary tear trickling down Max's face. His heart stuttered, tightening with emotion, and he pulled away and softly traced the stain on Max's skin.

"It's okay, Max. We're fine, I promise."

Max nodded and slid his hands beneath Gibson's baggy tee shirt. "Take me to bed, Gibson." He gave a watery smile. "I'd hate Jack to come home and find us naked together, it'll blow his mind. And I don't need any excuse for him to kick me out."

Gibson chuckled softly. "Yeah, that would drive him over the edge. And he won't be kicking you out. Come on then." He pushed Max away and struggled to his feet, dragging the duvet off and trailing it behind him as he walked to the bedroom. He switched on the light and threw a stray red shirt over the top to create a sexy ambience. It didn't take him long throw the cover back on the bed and start undressing. Luckily his room was toasty warm thanks to the central heating. Max followed him and stood in the doorway.

Gibson looked at him as he took his glasses off, then his shirt and plonked it on the chair. "You okay?"

Max stared at him from shadowed eyes. "I want you to undress me."

Gibson's body thrummed with delight. *That* thought sent a rush of blood to his dick. In the past, Max had always ripped his own clothes off in haste and the thought of slowly disrobing the man in front of him was heady.

"Sounds good to me." He pushed his trousers off his hips and stepped out of his briefs, leaving him nude and evidently ready for action. Max looked at his groin and licked his lips. The little movement sent Gibson into a tailspin.

"Christ, Max, stop looking at me like that," he said breathily. "You're going to make me come."

"Not before you take off my clothes and make love to me," Max murmured softly. "Make me yours completely. I need this."

Gibson walked over to him as Max regarded him with eyes shaded chocolate with desire, biting his bottom lip.

There was no need for words as Gibson lovingly, gently disrobed Max. First to go was the polo shirt. Max lifted his arms and blew out a soft exhalation of breath as the shirt was pulled over his head. Gibson sucked on the rosy nipples left bare and smiled around them at Max's moan.

Next, while still sucking on the needy buds of flesh, Gibson unzipped Max's jeans and pushed them down over his hips. Gibson teasingly caressed the erection beneath the silk of Max's boxers.

"God, Gibson, you are killing me." Max's body was tense, his hands wrapped around Gibson's waist.

Gibson ignored him, simply went down on his knees and mouthed the thick cock he found, revelling in his lover's hiss of need. The silk fabric was spotted with wetness and Gibson took great delight in slowly sliding them down Max's legs to fall in a whispery heap on the floor.

Max's cock sprung up, and Gibson hummed a happy sound as he took it in. Max gave a stifled cry and grasped Gibson's head, winding his fingers through his hair. Gibson had no problem being pushed down or further onto what he had in his mouth. He rather enjoyed it, loved the rough treatment and a man fucking his mouth. Especially if that man was Max.

"Not too much," Max gasped. "Want to come when you're inside me, not like this."

Gibson finished licking a long swathe up the outside of Maxwell's dick then looked up. "You want me to fuck you?"

"No," Max said, sounding a bit irritated. "I want you to make love to me. I need to be yours completely tonight."

Gibson's own cock perked up. "Get onto the bed." Gibson kissed the tip of Max's prick and stood up, going over to the side table to take out condoms and lube. Max moved onto the bed and watched as Gibson bounded onto the mattress and slid in beside him.

Gibson waved the lube mischievously. "I guess lube is your friend, then? It's been a while since I've been in you."

Maxwell nodded, eyes heated. His fingers closed around Gibson's cock, squeezing it and Gibson let out a squeak.

"Shut up and do this." Max lay back and widened his legs in invitation.

Gibson didn't need further urging. He picked up the lube, opened the tube and dribbled it onto his fingers. He covered Max's body with his own, finding his lips, and as they ravaged each other's mouths, he slid slick fingers inside Max. He loved the fact he had a squirming, moaning man underneath him as he opened him up, making sure to find the spot inside that made his man buck beneath him and cry out.

And when the time came to slide inside Max, cock sheathed and gasping at the perfect fit of them together, Gibson was ready. Max's hoarse entreaties to go deeper, to move, to take him spurred him on to obedience and soon there was nothing but the perfect rhythm of two men moving together.

Sweat, wet, heated skin, scented musk and fevered kisses was all it took for Gibson to reach his peak and explode inside the hot, tight channel of his lover. Max's strong legs were wrapped around Gibson's waist as Max stared up at Gibson with swollen lips and hooded eyes. Max pumped his own cock a few times and then he too was climaxing in a spill of sticky essence, coating their bellies and chests.

Gibson slumped on top of Max with a groan. "Oh, God, that was incredible. We are *so* doing that again soon. I don't know why I don't do it more." He slid off to lie beside Max on the bed, as he tried to draw a breath. He plucked the filled condom off his dick, tied a knot in it then placed it on the bedside table. Normally he'd throw spent ones on the ground but if Max stood on it in the middle of the night, he'd never hear the end of it.

Max was quiet and Gibson turned, propping himself up on one elbow, and gazed at him. "Are you okay?"

Max reached up and caressed his jawline. "Awesome. That was amazeballs."

Gibson cackled. "Amazeballs? Now who's the geek?"

Max grinned. "There's no doubt about who's the geek in this relationship, lover. You wear that badge with honour and pride." He sat up and kissed Gibson's eye gently, then the healing scar on the side of his face. "Thank you for not kicking me to the curb."

"Now why would I do that?" Gibson murmured as he snuggled into Max's side. "I love you. People in love forgive each other. What's a little smack against a wall between friends?"

Max winced and Gibson backpedalled. "That was a joke. Bad taste, sorry."

They lay in silence for a while then Max shifted. "I need to clean this stuff off before it itches. Where's your wipes?"

Gibson huffed. "In the bathroom. God, you are such a neat freak."

Max sniffed as he got out of bed. "Forgive me for not wanting to stick to the sheets."

He padded naked to the door and opened it. It was with a sense of surprise when Gibson heard a loud shout of "Oh, for fuck's sake put some damn clothes on!" as Max came scurrying back into the bedroom and slammed the door.

Max stood stock still in the room, face scarlet, as laughter welled in Gibson.

"Jack came home early, huh?" Gibson sniggered and then the floodgates released and before he knew it, he was rolling on the bed howling with mirth. Tears rolled down his cheeks as Max stared at him indignantly.

"Fuck, he saw me in the altogether, and so did Beth," Max sputtered as he quickly pulled on his sweatpants. "I thought they'd gone out?"

"So did I," Gibson managed to get out in between laughter. "Something must have gone wrong. Oh, God, your face, you looked like a rabbit running from a fox."

"You are such a little bitch," Max huffed. "How am I supposed to go out there now? Not to mention Jack wants to kill me."

Gibson finally managed to stop laughing, but held his aching sides as he got out of bed. He peered around myopically for his pants and slid them on. "I'll go find out what's going on, shall I? You can sit here and cower in bed, you big sissy."

He nimbly sidestepped a slap to his behind and opened the door to escape into the hallway. Jack's bedroom light was on and he knocked on the door then barged in. "I thought you two were out for the night? Sorry you got an eyeful of Max's junk, but *I'm* rather partial to it."

Jack's face was scarlet as he sat beside Beth, who was pale and lying on Jack's bed. "Beth got one of her migraines so I brought her home." He flashed an ill-tempered stare at Gibson. "What's he doing here?" He flushed. "I mean, I can guess what you were doing but are you two an item again?"

Gibson pursed his lips. "Yes, we're all good now. He was looking for the wipes to clean himself up when he ran into you."

Beth sniggered. Jack looked uncomfortable.

"Oh joy. TMI, Gib," he muttered as he gently brushed hair off Beth's cheek. "Are you saying I can't give him a good kick now for what he did to you?"

Beth slapped Jack on the arm. "That's exactly what it means, you big bully." She smiled wanly at Gibson. "I'm glad you got back together. That makes me happy." Her face went a little green and Gibson was concerned at the pallor of her face. "Jack, I think I'm going to be sick. Could you get me the rubbish bin because I don't think I'll make it to the bathroom?"

Jack was up in a flash and handing her the small wastepaper bin. She retched and leaned into it, obscuring her face. Jack held her long hair away from her face.

"What can I do?" Gibson asked feeling useless. "Can I make tea or something?"

Jack shook his head. "Nah, she needs to get it all up and then lie down in a dark room." He cast a fond glance at Beth. "I'll be with her, we'll be fine. You go back to your naked antics." He scowled. "And tell Maxwell from me if he hurts you again all bets are off."

"Yes, dear," Gibson said snarkily. "Do you want me to tell him he's grounded too? Or put him on the naughty step?" His face grew thoughtful. "I rather like the idea of grounding him on the naughty step...or should that be grinding?"

He chuckled at Jack's death stare and blew a kiss at Beth. "Hope you feel better, my lovely. I'll see you both in the morning. I have a scaredy-cat fella to go harass. Nighty night."

Beth laughed softly. "By the way, Gibson? Max *does* have nice junk."

Jack glared at her as Gibson sniggered and left the two alone.

He remembered to stop by the bathroom on his way and fetch the wipes.

Chapter 15

Maxwell leaned back in the posh chair he sat on around a beautifully dressed table filled with chatting, enthusiastic people. He and Gibson were in Manchester for the weekend at what Gibson jokingly called the 'semi-prestigious' gaming award event called the British Gaymz Choice Awards. Gibson had told him smugly it was *the event* for the design and production of LGBT games—and where gay gamers gathered. He'd subsequently sniggered at the clever use of alliteration.

Maxwell had no idea there was actually a gay gaming community, and Gibson had seriously informed him sometimes it became tiresome to trawl beneath the anti-gay slurs in some other forums. Years ago, an LGBT group decided in order to have their technical questions answered, and converse with like-minded individuals, having their own forum was the way to go. The best reason for Maxwell currently sitting surrounded by a bunch of people talking about things he couldn't hope to understand, was that *Camp Queen* had been nominated in one of the categories; Most Anticipated Game of 2016.

Maxwell had been loftily informed that the online forums talked amongst themselves and held a vote on what game they were looking forward to. Gibson and Jack's game was on the list. Maxwell had known Anomaly Media was popular and their games were well received, but finding out Gibson and Jack were two of the hottest properties in the gaming community had floored Maxwell. Both men played it down with a sense of humbleness.

Maxwell watched as Gibson leaned over to the man sitting next to him and laughed at something he said. Maxwell couldn't hear much—the noise level was deafening—so he smiled and stared around him. He'd never been one for big events like this, where the cutlery shone under bright lights, huge bouquets of flowers festooned the table and everyone wore a monkey suit. It was all exceptionally Christmassy, with only one week to go before Christmas Day.

They were spending a few days up in Manchester after the event, visiting Canal Street, taking in a couple of shows and generally winding down from the events of the past six months.

Things had been getting better between them every day and Maxwell thanked whatever mythical gaming gods lived above that he still had Gibson in his life.

He cast an appraising glance at Gibson who looked edibly sexy tonight in his tuxedo with its Chinese lapels, a black and white polka-dot bowtie wrapped around a crisp, white shirt, which moulded to his toned body. Maxwell was looking forward to peeling it off later tonight in the hotel.

He wriggled uncomfortably in his new suit, and cursed the slow creep of his briefs under the tight trousers. Gibson had taken him shopping and insisted this one fitted perfectly, but Maxwell was finding it a little constrictive. He had seen the appreciative gleam in Gibson's eyes when he'd come out of the bedroom suitably attired. Maxwell had the smug feeling he'd be getting lucky tonight.

Gibson turned to him and winked, placing a warm hand on his. "Okay, Max?"

Maxwell huffed. "You mean apart from not understanding a word anyone is saying and having my knickers trying to eat my arse? Oh yes, I'm cool." He grinned as Gibson chuckled.

Gibson moved closer and lowered his voice, staring at Maxwell over the top of his spectacles. It was an action that never failed to turn Maxwell on; it was such a sultry move. Especially when it was accompanied with a lick of pink, ripe lips. "You tell those knickers it's my arse to eat and I fully intend doing that later."

Maxwell's trousers grew even tighter and he gulped. "Bitch. You've made me spring a hard-on."

Gibson's sultry laugh again made Maxwell's cock swell. He opened his mouth to no doubt say something equally as saucy when the microphone on the stage echoed and the compère, some famous gaming multi-millionaire called Alex de Clair, cleared his throat.

"Ladies and gentlemen, your attention please. I trust you've all enjoyed the delicious food, got yourselves a drink or two and enjoyed the evening so far. We're ready to begin the ceremony now so please make sure mobile phones and tablets and the like are switched off, or muted, so we can respect the entrants and the wonderful presentations we're about to see. A huge amount of hard work has gone into the evening, and the nominees deserve our full attention. Thank you."

The lights dimmed as everyone sat back to enjoy the show. Jack and Beth slipped in to their seats beside them; they'd been at another table talking to someone they knew.

"Here goes nothing," Jack said, as he loosened his bow tie. "No matter what happens, short shit, we did good. We're going to rock with this game next year."

"I know we will." Gibson shot him a fond glance as they fist bumped. "I'm nervous though."

Beth reached over and placed her hands on both Jack and Gibson's arms. "You two are champs," she murmured softly. "My heroes."

The performance began. Maxwell had to admit it was worthy of being classed in the same category as the Royal Variety Performance. There were famous musicians performing, actors he'd seen in some of the movie blockbusters, and various scantily clad men and women dancing on stage. It was professional and entertaining, and when a well-known comedian came on stage, Maxwell laughed until tears ran down his face.

And, of course, in between were the things they'd come to see—the gaming community's games of the future. Maxwell was bowled over by the quality and attention to detail in them, and marvelled at the creativity involved. He stole a glance at an enraptured Gibson, whose eyes shone as he watched the fruits of his peers' labours.

When *Camp Queen* was shown as a nominee, and there were snippets of the game on the enormous screens on stage, Maxwell could find no words. He'd seen bits of it on Gibson's laptop, and been privy to some of the detail in the game. Seeing it in full screen in public with everyone ooh-ing and aah-ing and realising this was Gibson's work—and Jack's too of course, and poxy Everett, but in his mind mostly Gibson's creation—stunned Maxwell into silence. Tears pricked his eyes at the sheer scope of the game and he blinked them away furiously, dabbing surreptitiously at them with his pristine, starched napkin.

Maxwell loved his comic book with a passion because Gibson had made it especially for him. Yet this game unfolding before his eyes was simply more proof his lover was a genius. He'd never been so proud of him. Later he had a special gift of his own for Gibson for Christmas. Maxwell warmed thinking of what lay in his shoulder bag.

He held Gibson's hand tightly as he smiled softly at him, and they watched the category nominees finish. He closed his eyes and prayed for probably the first time in his life to a god he didn't believe in, as well as every other fate he knew, for Gibson to win.

When the introduction was over, Gibson's tightening of hands alerted Maxwell he was as nervous as he was. Beth whispered to Jack soft words of support and encouragement.

"You're amazing and I love you," Maxwell whispered to Gibson. "No matter what happens, to me you won hands down."

Gibson smiled, his eyes a little teary at those words and he nodded. "Thanks, baby."

There was the usual anticipation before Alex de Clair opened the envelope and kept the audience waiting.

"It seems we have a winner," he said in his lilting Irish tone. "I have to say I probably agree with this decision, even though I'm not supposed to take sides. But I've been watching this little company go from strength to strength and marvelling at the attention to detail and amazing game play produced by them. They are truly a force to be reckoned with in the gaming world, and I see big things ahead for them." He paused dramatically.

Gibson squirmed beside him. "For fuck's sake get on with it," he muttered as Jack nodded his agreement. "Tell us already."

"And the winner is…" There was another pregnant pause and Gibson squawked again in protest. "Anomaly Media for *Camp Queen*!"

Beth's shriek made Maxwell's ears bleed but he didn't care. All he cared about was looking at the stunned expression on

Gibson's face at the fact their game had won Most Anticipated Game of 2016.

"Oh my God," his lover said faintly as he sat there, gob smacked. Jack was equally as blindsided. "We won?"

"Yes, honey, you won." Maxwell punched Gibson in the shoulder. "Now go and up there and get your award."

Beth was pushing Jack out of his seat too, and both of them watched as Gibson and Jack made their way to the stage. They both looked shell-shocked.

"Oh, God, Maxwell, isn't this awesome?" Beth said dreamily as she gazed after them. "It's a dream come true for them both to win an award like this."

Maxwell nodded and clasped her hand as they watched their respective partners ascend the stage and stand beside Alex. There was some conversation between them and hugs as the award was handed over. Jack looked uncomfortable being in the spotlight and pushed Gibson forward to accept it.

Alex grinned at their obvious discomposure. "Congratulations guys for this achievement. I meant what I said. I've had my eye on you boys for a while and this is a real achievement for you both. You should be very proud. I'll be talking to you both about your future plans."

He handed the microphone over to Gibson, who took it wildly and glanced out at the audience. He pushed his glasses up with his index finger, and Maxwell smiled at that familiar gesture.

"Uhmm, this is a huge surprise. I mean, a *huge* surprise." His voice tailed off and Maxwell wanted to run up and stand beside him, tell him to milk this opportunity because he so deserved it. "I think I speak for both myself and Jack when I say we are absolutely honoured and thrilled to have won. I'm not used to giving speeches so I hope I don't say the wrong thing, but there are so many people to thank, I'd be here all night if I did." There was an appreciative chuckle from the audience. Jack fidgeted beside Gibson, looking as if he wished he was anywhere but the stage.

Beth giggled. "He looks so gormless up there. He hates this sort of attention. But oh my, he's my man and I am so damn proud of him."

"I hear you, sister," Maxwell murmured. "Our men are awesome."

Gibson found his second wind. "The guys I want to thank know who they are, and believe me, I'll be contacting each and every one of them after this show to tell them how grateful I am to have them as colleagues on this project. Jack"—he turned to his friend who was pink cheeked at being singled out—"Jack has been the best business partner and collaborator ever and he deserves a round of applause." The room exploded with clapping as poor Jack blushed scarlet and mumbled something. Maxwell thought ruefully Beth's hands were going to catch fire at the rate she was clapping.

The room grew quieter and Gibson stood further towards the front of the stage. "There is one special person I want to thank out there. Someone who held me together and gave me the encouragement and support and love I needed to get through some tough times."

Maxwell closed his eyes briefly. Surely Gibson wasn't going to…

"His name is Max, and he's my boyfriend. He's been there for me and now that I have an audience, I'm going to take the opportunity to tell him how much he means to me. Max, baby, I love you. Thanks for helping us make this happen." He held up the award to a fierce round of cat calls, hoots and more clapping. Maxwell's heart swelled so much with love he thought he might burst.

"He's killing me here," he muttered and Beth laughed and punched his arm.

"That was so sweet," she said dreamily. "He is so romantic."

Gibson turned and said something to Jack, who scowled fiercely and shook his head. Gibson muttered something. Jack capitulated and took the microphone, looking ill at ease. Beside Maxwell, Beth drew a breath and leaned forward expectantly.

"Uh, yeah, I'd like to thank everyone too, what he said." Jack jerked a thumb at a grinning Gibson. "And also tell my girlfriend Beth I love her too and she's the best thing that ever happened to me." He hurriedly passed the microphone back to Alex.

Beth was sniffling now, and Maxwell passed her his napkin.

"Ladies and gentleman, another round of applause for Gibson Henry and Jack Cunningham from Anomaly Media!" Alex de Clair beamed at the audience as Gibson and Jack exited the stage.

Maxwell couldn't wait to congratulate Gibson in a more intimate and up-close–and-personal way, but he supposed he'd better stick to a hug and a kiss for now.

Maxwell stood up as Gibson reached the table and pulled him into his arms. He held him tightly, nuzzling his soft hair. "Thanks for what you said up there," he said, half choking on emotion.

Gibson pulled back and kissed him softly. "I meant every word," he murmured, his eyes shining. "You're my rock, Max. I never thought I'd say that to anyone." He held up the award. "This means a lot to me, but you? You're everything."

The next kiss they shared was not as gentle and Maxwell vaguely heard cat calls and whistles from the crowd as he was thoroughly mauled. He wasn't complaining though. When Gibson finally released him, Maxwell was dazed. Jack and Beth beamed beside them.

Jack spoke excitedly. "Did you hear what Alex de Claire said up there? He wants to talk us about the future. What do you think it means?" he asked excitedly.

Gibson shrugged. "Not sure, but it sounds like we have some fun times ahead."

Maxwell reached into his bag. "I have something for you too," he stammered to Gibson. "I was going to give you this later but now seems the right time." He pulled out a crumpled pile of A4 paper, tied into a roll with bright red, green and white ribbons, with a multi-coloured glitter bow perched on one side.

Gibson stared at the present. "This looks interesting," he murmured as he took it and began unravelling the strands. Maxwell confessed wryly to himself he may have gone to town a bit on the ribbons.

Once the wrapping had been relegated to a pile of colour on the table, Gibson rolled the sheet open.

"What the hell is it?" Jack peered over Gibson's shoulder curiously, Beth beside him. Maxwell saw Gibson's eyes widen and grow bright as he looked up at Maxwell.

Gibson grinned, the joy in his eyes hard to miss. "The perfect end to a perfect evening," he announced.

He laid the sheet down on the table. It was a copy of Maxwell's *Sexcella* Worksheet, set with a smiling picture of Gibson in the middle and '*Stuff #5, he's my #10*' written in one corner of the photo. There was another comment at the top of the document: "TO BE DELETED–NO FURTHER USE" written in big black letters.

Gibson looked gob smacked. "Max, you're crazy, you know that?" His eyes were filled with love. "This is such an awesome present, thank you."

"I still don't get it," Jack grumbled, squinting at the sheet. "I mean what the…oh. Shit, Maxwell, you kept *this* sort of detail?"

His face screwed up in embarrassment and Beth giggled. "Sweetheart, you'll need to bleach your eyes if you read any more."

Gibson drew Maxwell into a deep, passionate clinch and for the moment, Maxwell heard and saw nothing more. When Gibson released him, Maxwell was rock hard and ready to roll.

"Not fair," he squawked, making sure his dinner jacket still covered his groin. "We need to go home right now."

Gibson laughed. "Later. Right now, I want to celebrate with you, catch a dance or two on the floor and then we're going to back to the hotel so I can bonk your brains out." He winked and Maxwell's groin grew hotter. He liked the idea.

The sound of Frankie Goes to Hollywood's "Relax" blared into the room and Maxwell grabbed Gibson's hand to drag him onto the dance floor. As they gyrated to one of his favourite tunes, and he watched Gibson's blond hair fall into his eyes, his spectacles steam up, and his beloved face crease in a smile as they stared into each other's eyes, Maxwell knew he'd got exactly what he wanted for Christmas.

DAMAGED GOODS

Jax crept into Clay and Tate's story in Feat of Clay *and demanded his own book. Such an incredible soul deserved to find his own happiness. It's not easy being him in a world that often demands perfection in every way, especially physically. Every day there are people being made to feel less than simply because they don't meet this image.*

This book is dedicated to everyone who's different in any way, who's ever been discriminated against because of what they look like or where they come from.

You are all worth it.

Never forget that YOU matter.

ACKNOWLEDGMENTS

As always, to my readers and the people who enjoy my books. Without you, there would be no Jax. No Dare. No Men of London. And to my wonderful beta readers—thank you from the bottom of my heart for making the book better.

AUTHOR NOTE

In order to try and get into Jax's situation, I downloaded some NVDA software and then sat at my dining room table with my eyes partly blindfolded so I could get a feel for what it was like to be him. I'm very shortsighted, so it wasn't that tough, but that NVDA software is something. I'll bet it takes a while to get used to. I was busy doing this and noticed the room was really quiet. I peered out from my blindfold to find my family standing there staring at me with some trepidation. I said, "I'm seeing what it's like to be sort of blind," and my husband rolled his eyes and went into the kitchen to make coffee. The things we do as authors to get our research right. :)

Also, I contacted the Irish Travellers Association here in London to get some information, and they were very helpful. It's a tough one, living in a country where "pikies" as they are known (a derogatory word) are lumped together as all being thieving, drunken, aggressive scum. Popular reality TV programmes that propagate this don't help either. It's worth remembering that, as always, the myth isn't always the truth, and that in every community there are good and bad elements. I've tried to portray a bit of both in this book, to be realistic, but with the leaning toward Travellers being the same as everyone else—families trying to make the best out of a situation.

DAMAGED GOODS

Chapter 1

Jax was being watched and it wasn't the first time. He sensed eyes on his back; *someone* was out there in the ever-present shadows. He took out his EarPods, switched off the music and laid his iPod down beside him on the blanket. He turned around again and glared through his prescription sunglasses at the spot in the garden where he believed his mysterious observer to be. Jax couldn't see clearly that far away, given the state of his eyes; distance was a blur and he did his best work close up. His scowls obviously hadn't deterred his watcher. He opened his mouth to snarl out a challenge to whoever was lurking in the shadows then shut it promptly when a loud hail drew his attention.

"Jax? Where are you?" A voice echoed from the back porch of the rambling Victorian red brick house he lived in. It was a large, three-storey affair situated on a leafy street in Camden. Jax turned from where he knelt planting gladioli corms and squinted in the direction of the voice.

"In the garden, Randy," he called, sitting back on his haunches. Jax had been out here over an hour trying to prepare the bed for an influx of what he hoped would be beautiful flowers. He knew he'd probably planted a couple of the corms upside down; sometimes it was hard to differentiate between the top and bottom. He gave a mental shrug. The bulbs would either grow or they wouldn't. He rather liked the idea of someone down under in Australia having a flower bursting through. He gave a soft chuckle at his silliness and stood up, stretching as he did.

The sensation of eyes on him seemed to disappear and he frowned. Whoever it was must have left, flown like the proverbial bird. He wondered what the hell was so fascinating about him that someone had to spy. It had been a few times now he'd noticed his spine tingling.

He stretched again, scratching his belly absently.

"God, you have dried mud everywhere, my lad." A chuckle sounded in his ear as Randy, his boss, quasi-father figure and owner of the halfway house, Castaways, where Jax lived, leaned in to brush errant streaks of dirt off Jax's front and back. Randy mimicked a West Country accent with his next words. "You look a right farm boy. Especially in that damn hat."

The wide-brimmed straw hat Jax wore was his favourite. It had the dual purpose of keeping the sun off his face and bright light out of his sensitive eyes. It also made him look like a character from *The Adventures of Huckleberry Finn*. All he needed was the "Aw, shucks" piece of straw in his mouth.

Jax grinned as the blurry figure of Randall Pierce shifted into clearer view. The portly, short man and his wife Jen held a special place in his heart. Three years ago, at age fifteen, Jax had come to Castaways as a damaged and insecure young teenager and had stayed on ever since. It was his home now, together with the other much younger boys and girls who each had their own reasons for being there.

The familiar scent of Old Spice gave Randy away every time. Jax tilted up his chin, looking out from beneath his sunglasses with slightly narrowed eyes. For some reason no one had ever been able to explain, it helped him see better when he did that. He stared at the other man, making out familiar bearded features and warm brown eyes.

The pang of longing for the days when he'd taken his full sight for granted whipped through him, but resolutely he pushed it back into the depths where it belonged.

There was no place in Jax's life for regrets and self-commiseration.

"I've only got a few bulbs to go." He gestured at the bucket beside him with the last remaining corms. "Hopefully we'll get a gorgeous display when they all decide to bloom."

"You've done a great job, lad." Randy punched him lightly on the arm. "Jen sent me out to find you. She says there's lunch for you in the house. Toasted ham, cheese and marmite, your favourite." Randy's lips twisted in distaste. "I really don't know how you can eat that marmite stuff. It's terrible."

Jax laughed. "Hey, don't knock it. Haven't you ever had any marmite tea when you're feeling sick? It's the best pick-me-upper."

Randy made a face. "Ugh. No thanks. Go on with you, inside and clean up. You haven't eaten today, have you?" He tutted.

Jax shook his head in amusement. "I'm eighteen, Randy, not one of the little kids who needs supervising." He'd turned eighteen five months ago, in October, and it had been a milestone for him. Now legally an adult, he was able to manage his own affairs, including now having a say in the trust fund his father had set up for him.

Jax batted Randy on the chest playfully. He and Jen tended to protect him too much sometimes. It was fantastic knowing good people cared about him, but occasionally it made him feel a little stifled.

Randy looked shamefaced. "Yeah, sorry. I forget sometimes. I'm so used to that young kid from three years ago."

Jax smiled. "Don't apologise. I understand. You're used to mothering the younger ones." He turned to go then swung around. "Have you seen anyone strange around here lately? I've had this really weird feeling someone is watching me from over there." He gestured towards the wooded area on the garden boundary.

Randy looked over in the same direction with a frown. "Nope. Must be your Spidey senses kicking in. I've not noticed anyone over there, and no one's come to the house who shouldn't have. Maybe you have an admirer," he said slyly.

Jax gave a harsh laugh. "Oh, that must be it. Someone fancies damaged goods." He rolled his eyes, choosing to ignore Randy's irritated snort.

***

He *wasn't* stalking his fantasy. He *wasn't*.

Dare clamped his lips together mutinously as he hunkered down behind a towering oak. The tree lay on the outskirts, in the garden of a large Georgian house. From a distance, Dare watched as the beautiful blond man he'd been *observing,* thank you very much, tenderly placed what looked like flower bulbs in the rich soil. The man—whom Dare had first called Angel, though he now knew his name was Jax thanks to the younger kids playing in the garden yelling to him—leaned over. His pert jean-encased backside pushed out into the air and Dare swallowed, mesmerised by the enticing sight. A pang of guilt washed over his skin at the sneaking knowledge that yes, he could actually be deemed a stalker.

"I've only watched him a few times," Dare murmured under his breath. "It's not like I'm some pervert checking through the windows. I mean, the guy is in plain sight and there's no boundary fence, so why shouldn't I look? Anyone would. God, he's gorgeous. A flawed angel with those blond curls and blue eyes."

His wistful voice echoed in the quiet of the forest surrounding the large house called Castaways. It was some sort of place for homeless kids, Dare thought. He'd found this vantage point by accident one day when he'd been out gathering bits of greenery for his boss, Sally, an eccentric seventy-year-old woman who owned the sweet shop he'd managed for the past three years.

Some weeks ago, Sally had decided she wanted to display certain wildflowers in their place of work. She was also heavily into aromatherapy at the moment, so she sent Dare out each week to pick new blossoms and plants to further her ambitions to be a "flower child," as Dare teasingly called it. He hadn't minded. It had become a pleasant routine to take the short tube ride to Camden to perform what Sally loftily called his "ecological duties." This secluded part of the woods around the area was the best place she knew of to find the flowers. Dare had caught sight of the beautiful man in the garden tending to a bunch of what looked like unruly kids, and now, having seen his Angel, Sally could send him out every day and Dare wouldn't mind.

"But that *would* make me a stalker," he said to himself. "So I'm not one now—yet." He huffed and ducked back behind a bush as Jax turned to stare fixedly in his direction from underneath his wide-brimmed straw hat, an item Dare found rather endearing.

How the hell does he do that? It's as if he knows I'm here. Must be because he doesn't see all that well. Maybe his other senses are enhanced, like Daredevil.

Jax's stare from behind dark glasses was disquieting to say the least. The first week Dare had spotted his mysterious stranger, Jax hadn't been wearing his hat or glasses. His porcelain skin had appeared blotted with small flecks as the sun shone upon him.

Underneath puckered eyelids, Dare knew Jax's eyes were pale blue. The previous week, Jax had ambled over, dangerously close to Dare's hiding place, to retrieve a ball one of the kids had thrown. Dare had held his breath, hoping not to be seen. But the man had gotten close enough for Dare to notice the colour of the sky reflected in Jax's eyes.

Up close Jax was a tarnished beauty; a vision of blond, pale sexiness and innocence. Dare had been captivated. He'd picked up that his man-crush didn't see well. That was obvious from Jax's cautious gait and careful steps when he walked. He never participated in any of the real rough and tumble with the younger children.

On a previous occasion, Dare had heard Jax jokingly tell one of the kids that he'd be the easy winner in a game of Blind's Man Bluff. The fact Jax had been hurt somehow made Dare's heart ache in his chest. He wondered if it been due to a car accident.

Dare heard a man call out and Jax turned and shouted a response as he stood up and stretched. Dare lost his breath as he ducked behind the tree. Jax's long, slim arms reached towards the sky as his tee shirt drew up over his belly, revealing an expanse of creamy pale skin and a tight stomach. Dare closed his eyes, willing his groin to cool down.

"Look at you, you *are* a damn pervert," he muttered. "Lusting after a guy you'll never have. He's probably straight anyway, or got a boyfriend. I need to get laid. It's been too long."

His insides squirmed at the reason for his current lack of sexual activity other than his own hand. The last man he'd been with over two months ago had crushed him and left him feeling wary and more than a little nervous about trusting anyone.

Dare renewed his observation and then sighed as Jax and the other man, named Randy, made their way up to the house.

Time to make the journey back to the shop with his small bag of wildflowers and grasses. Sally would be waiting impatiently, tut-tutting at his tardiness. Dare grinned sheepishly to himself as he gathered his tote bag stuffed with foliage. He'd been gone longer than expected thanks to Jax.

Sally was going to clip Dare's ear when he got back.

***

"Jackson Grady, don't you talk about yourself like that. I won't have it, son. You're one helluva catch for the right ma—person."

Jax noticed the quick correction. He felt sure Randy had been about to say man, but as Jax hadn't really told anyone yet what the hell his sexual preference was, Randy had played it safe. Jax knew Randy had his own suspicions about the way Jax leaned.

His sex life to date had been relegated to a quick, chaste kiss with a girl at fifteen—something he'd not enjoyed—and since then, nada, nothing. Just his imagination and his right hand. He'd never even French kissed anyone. He believed he had a thing for men rather than the ladies; his early school years ogling his school mates' torsos and their dangly bits in gym class and showers, plus his current gay porn stash, attested to that. However, back then, Jax had hugged that fact tightly to himself, for fear of reprisals closer to home.

Now what he *needed* was the chance to test out his theory with a real, live human being of the willing male persuasion.

Jax huffed. "Oh yes, I'm quite the catch." He tried not to sound bitter but didn't think he was succeeding. "Let's drop this topic, shall we? I'm not in the mood to talk about it." He leaned down and picked up his iPod off the blanket on the grass. Nodding at Randy, Jax shoved the EarPods back in and turned up the volume.

He picked up his gardening tools and placed them in the straw basket Jen had given him to use. When he'd finished cleaning up, he turned to look at Randy, who was still standing there with an exasperated expression. Jax knew that his churlish display of angst was unwarranted.

He'd never been on a date, never had any level of intimacy with another human being, male or female. He was an amateur in the dating and relationship department and it sucked. He wanted what his friends Tate and Clay had—a significant other to spend time with and laugh, support and hopefully have sex with. Jax didn't see that in his future. Who the hell would want him, looking as he did?

At the thought of Tate and Clay's tempestuous, passionate relationship, Jax's chest constricted. There were two men who deserved each other. God knows they'd fought hard enough to get where they were, but oh, how he envied them.

He became aware of pudgy, impatient fingers snapping in front of his face as the music of Evanescence swelled to a crescendo in his ears. Resignedly, he hefted the basket onto one arm and removed one of his EarPods to hear what Randy was saying.

"That's bloody better, young man. God, you can be an irritating little sod."

Randy's tone of affection belied his harsh words.

Despite himself, Jax grinned. "I'm a teenager, old man. It's just how we roll."

"Yes, well," Randy muttered. "No excuse for rudeness. Now are you going up to the house to eat that damn sandwich or shall I tell Jen to chuck it in the bin?"

Suddenly Jax was famished and the thought of iced peach tea and a sandwich got his taste buds salivating. "Keep your pants on. I'll go eat the damn sandwich."

The two men grinned at each other and for the hundredth time Jax blessed his lucky stars he'd been fortunate to find a place at Castaways with Randy and Jen. When Jax had left the hospital, he hadn't been ready to live on his own, despite the money he'd inherited. He'd been on his own then, his entire family gone.

Another regret he pushed down into the depths of his personal no-fly zone.

Randy smiled happily. "Good. I could do with a cuppa myself and another one of those pork-and-pickle monstrosities Jen makes. Come on. I'll bring up the empty seed cartons for recycling, and you take the basket. Make sure you wash those tools off before you put them in the shed. You know how Jen hates mud all over her stuff."

Jax rolled his eyes. "Yes, oh slave driver." He mock bowed as he chuckled at Randy's low growl. "I shall do as I am told. I am but a mere serf doing Master's bidding."

"I get the feeling you rather like that idea," Randy murmured slyly. "I know you've been watching those films on your computer, the ones with the cute slave boys and the sexy overlords. What's it called? *Arabian Knights* or something?"

Jax's fair skin prickled with heat from his blush and he thought he'd go up in flames from embarrassment. So much for thinking he'd been keeping his obsession a secret. *Arabian Knights* was indeed a show he was fixated on, a contemporary, sexy Scheherazade-type tale with a mostly male cast and a real *Game of Thrones* feel—another show he was addicted to. It cemented for him the interest he had in men, given the times he'd wanked off in bed to the memories of both shows. It took Jax a long time getting through one episode, as his eyes grew tired and sore from the strain of watching, but he wouldn't give it up for anything.

"God, dude, have you been spying on me?" The best defence was a quick, indignant offence. "Is nothing private anymore?" He huffed and turned to go up the house.

Randy gave a loud snort of laughter as he followed. "Kid, I pay the bills for the PRIMA satellite channel subscription and I can't help notice the breakdown of what's been watched when they send me the bill. You're the only other adult in the house who has access to the over-eighteen ones."

Jax turned in consternation. "Oh God, does it cost you more money? I thought it was all part of the free channels? Sorry, I'll pay my bit if you need it—"

Randy laid a warm finger on Jax's lips. "Relax. It's not charged out. They simply like to let me know what's been watched—all part of their marketing strategy. Stop worrying."

Jax pursed his lips and blew out warm air. "Oh cool. I thought—" his voice tailed off and he decided Randy didn't need to know anything at all about Jax's privately paid-for subscriptions to certain *educational* TV channels on his wide-screen computer. His PC was his own domain where he lived vicariously through others and got a bit of training on what to do should he ever find himself fortunate enough to have a man in his room or his bed.

Jax wasn't keen on the whole arse-sex thing—it looked painful—but he certainly wanted the feel of another man's hand on his cock, or a little frottage. Or—and his heart raced—a blowjob. Or being rimmed. Any of this was Jax's idea of losing his stupid virginity.

He trudged up towards the house, grimacing at the soft squelching of mud under green grass, mud which he knew was currently attaching itself to his nearly new Nike trainers.

Truth be told, he was glad to be out of the sunshine of the cool March day. His sunglasses nipped at the bridge of his nose, the hat made his hairline sweat and itch, and not for the first time, he cursed the fact he had to wear them both. A hot shower and some soothing eye drops would go a long way towards making his ultra-sensitive and aching eyes feel better. Then perhaps he could work on his PC for a while.

Back in the house, Jax gulped and gobbled down the tea and sandwich then gratefully escaped to his room for his own one-on-one time. Once he'd had a refreshing shower, he contemplated going downstairs to the drawing room and practicing scales on the piano. Following some encouragement from his friend Clay, Jax had recently taken it up again after a long hiatus. He enjoyed tinkling on the piano and making the little kids sing along to silly songs like "Old McDonald." It was a great way to get his rusty skills oiled.

Once his degree had been achieved and his stint as a student was over, perhaps he might even consider taking formal lessons again.

With a martyred sigh, he decided his studying needed to come first. His A-level distance psychology course was both a joy and a trial. The joy: He was fascinated with the study of the human mind and psyche. The trial: He had to curtail his efforts on focusing on his screen, and also use his rather expensive, customised NVDA software that allowed him to navigate his system without too much eye strain. Using this special programme helped him immeasurably.

His first task, however, was opening up his laptop and checking his mail.

Jax grinned when he noticed an email from Tate, Clay's boyfriend. Tate didn't do Facebook or social media; he had an inherent distrust of it given his background as a policeman and undercover agent. He preferred email, so Jax was often subject to terse messages with links to useful studying references, quirky news articles and occasionally a random link to either art exhibitions or street graffiti pictures. Oh, and anything to do with Banksy. Tate had a particular fetish for the street artist, having even tried once to find out who he was—to no avail. Jax had no doubt that Clay would have been able to track the artist down had he wanted to. The man, with his ex-Special Forces background, had the uncanny knack of getting people out into the open.

Jax put on his glasses and squinted at Tate's email, not wanting to use the software to read it out in case it was something rude or contained swearing, something Tate was partial to sending. Last time Jax had opened a link from Tate about some US comedian, Jen had been passing by Jax's open door. She'd almost dropped the load of washing after hearing the filthy invective coming out of Jax's speakers, uttered in a flat, robotic voice. It *had* been rather disturbing.

The current email message was decisive and to the point, like Tate himself.

Thought you might enjoy this, I pissed myself laughing.

Jax thought the YouTube video looked harmless enough and he turned up the volume. A minute later he was chortling like a kid at the spoof interview of a supposed Banksy in his hometown in Rata, Spain.

He was still chuckling when he packed up his study books and went to bed, blurry eyed but pleasantly tired that night.

Chapter 2

Dare perched precariously on the top of a wooden ladder as he restocked shelves. He loved working in the quirky sweet shop called Bon Bon Bizarre, selling all the strangest sweets Sally could find. Weird sweets with names like Spermies, meatball bubble gum or bacon candy—anything that sounded disgusting—were eagerly snapped up by her and placed in the brightly coloured jars, on sturdy wooden shelves, in glass-fronted cabinets. It was a busy, surprisingly profitable and popular shop.

He growled at the jar of flesh-coloured bubble gum he held. His ear still stung from the pudgy finger that had flicked it on his return to work.

"Like her bloody slave, I am. I ought to report her to a tribunal or something." His stomach growled in sympathy, reminding him he hadn't had much to eat today. "That woman is a menace. I don't know why I work here." He smiled slightly, knowing his boss was in earshot.

A hand lightly tapped his backside. "You work here because I pay you well, feed you occasionally and let you stay above my shop virtually rent free." The dry tones of the woman standing below him made Dare look down.

A short, rotund woman with frizzy silver hair stood peering up at him from over the tops of her huge pink glasses. She was dressed in a bright-coloured floppy blouse and black stretch pants. "And because no one else will put up with your surliness."

"I'm not surly," Dare muttered as he clambered down from the ladder. Sally Busby barely made it up to his chest; his six-foot-three frame dwarfed his employer. "I'm just not feeling particularly friendly at the moment."

"Surly," Sally trilled as she darted around arranging flowers in the small confines of the shop. She resembled a brightly coloured hummingbird—albeit a wide one. "You're grumpy because I gave you grief for ogling your man-crush too long and made you clean out the stock room." She snickered. "I never thought I'd see a man of your size scared of spiders."

"Everyone's scared of spiders." Dare glared at her. "And he's not my man-crush." He didn't even flinch at that damn lie. "God, why did I ever tell you about him?" He knew why.

It had been an unguarded moment; he and Sally had finished off a bottle or two of wine together and he'd confessed his admiration of the blond beauty of Camden between Irish drinking songs and a rousing chorus of 'Hakuna Matata' from *The Lion King*. At one time it had been his little brother Kean's favourite film and Dare had seen it more times than he cared to remember.

Sally opened the till, took out a five-pound note and tucked it into her bra in a display of shamelessness. Dare winced at seeing freckled white cleavage—and was that a damned nipple?

Sally noticed it. "You might be gay, lovie, but believe me, you've had boobs in your mouth before. I'm sure your mother breastfed you."

Dare's face went alarmingly hot. "Sally, for God's sake. I don't want to think about that. And how am I supposed to balance the till if you keep dipping into it?"

Sally rolled her eyes. "Don't I always leave you a note?" She scribbled on a blue Post-it and put it in the till with a flourish. "There. All squared off." She stuck her tongue out at him.

Dare shook his head in affection as he put the ladder away in the back room, keeping a wary eye out for arachnids intent on harm.

The shop, located in Swiss Cottage, was small and compact, and sometimes he felt a little claustrophobic. He was a big, stocky man with broad shoulders, the proverbial giant next to the diminutive, rounded Sally who was barely five foot two in heels.

"I'm just popping next door to get us a coffee," Sally announced as she bustled past him. "Only another hour to go and then you can go upstairs and jerk off to your wet dream of a man."

Dare didn't even deign to reply to that one. He merely sniffed disdainfully as his face flushed with heat. He turned his attention instead to making sure the jars on the shelf labelled Scarylicious Sweeties were all facing the right way.

Gobstoppers like human eyeballs stared back at him. Sally's soft laugh echoed in the empty shop as she left, no doubt to go bombard Tony, the cute but faux Italian next door at the coffee shop, with details of both Dare's man obsession and her own recent antics learning the saxophone.

He dreaded the promise Sally had made to give him a rendition of 'Ain't No Sunshine' one day. Merely thinking of it gave him the chills. He'd heard her practicing a couple of times and—well, he had to admit she wasn't particularly talented.

She wasn't wrong, though. He probably *would j*ack off later thinking of the unobtainable Jax.

There was a soft knock at the shop door and Dare turned from wiping down a shelf and grinned when he saw who it was. His best friend Rob stood there, making a silly face at him through the glass.

Rob worked as a cashier in the bank down the street and they'd often enjoy a beer together at the local pub. He gestured to Rob to come in, and his friend pushed open the door and sauntered into the shop. Brown eyes stared at him from below a shock of dark red hair.

"Evening, mate. You all closed up, ready to have a pint?" Rob peered around him. "Where's Sally? Gone home already?" He perched his bum down on a high-topped stool and leaned an elbow on the counter. Rob was tall and gangly and fancied himself a lady's man of note.

Dare shook his head. "She went next door to get us coffee. Probably still chatting up Tony. I'll need to wait for her to get back before I leave."

Rob nodded as he picked up a jar of Pickle Popping Candy, opened it and shoved some into his mouth. His face immediately twisted with what Dare knew to be the after effects of lemon, lime and some secret manufacturer ingredient that puckered the mouth and made the eyes water. Dare thought it might be hellfire and brimstone because that's what he imagined it tasted like. He'd made the same mistake and would never do it again

He watched curiously as Rob's face went pink as he gasped for breath.

Finally, with streaming eyes and a curse, Rob was able to speak again.

"Jesus, Dare, what the hell? That stuff is shite. It almost sucked my insides up through my mouth."

Dare screwed the lid back on the jar with a satisfied chuckle. "That's what you get when you come in here without so much as a qualm and steal sweets you know nothing about. How many times have I told you, you can't just help yourself to things?"

"Who the hell buys that crap?" Rob grimaced as he tried to clear the taste from his mouth, looking for all the world like a dog trying to rid itself of hair it had eaten.

"The kids love it. It's one of the best sellers. They dare each other to eat it and then see how long they can last out. Some of them have incredible staying power."

The shop door opened again and Sally entered bearing polystyrene cups. "I thought I saw you, Robert, so I got an extra one. Salted caramel latte if I recall?"

Rob nodded eagerly. "Yum. Thanks, Sal." He grimaced. "It will take that awful taste out of my mouth." He waved at Dare. "I thought I'd take my mate here for a pint after work. He can tell me again about the sexy stud he's been stalking."

"I am not stalking him. Fuck you." Dare glowered at a smirking Rob.

"Language, young man, language." Sally passed Dare one of the cups. "It doesn't become you or me. Yes, Rob, I've heard about this young man Dare's been spying on when he's supposed to be picking flowers."

Dare took an angry slurp of his coffee and yelped when it burnt his lip. "Sorry about the cursing. It slipped out because of my arse-idiot friend here."

"You need to get laid," Rob said. His eyes shone with sympathy. "It's time to get back in the saddle. I bet you haven't had a good screw in ages." He snarled. "Because of that tosser Michael, you've been running scared."

Rob's words struck a chord with Dare. "I'm over Michael." His words sounded uncertain even to him.

Rob snorted. "Yeah, right. You're still smarting over that fucker, and it's time you concentrated on moving on. Maybe with angel boy?"

Dare scowled. "I don't even know if he's gay. Anyway, I don't want to spook him. He's like, you know, quite innocent. Not like me." His tone was bitter.

Sally's face softened. "Dare, sweetie, just because you've had a bad experience with a man doesn't make you an idiot or a patsy. It makes you human. Michael was a man who wanted both bits of his cake—the wife at home *and* the hot young man-lover. His loss, my lad."

A familiar pang of shame and hurt assailed Dare and he took a deep breath, trying to quell the emotions hidden deep down inside. Michael had been his world for six months and in a blink of an eye, just before Christmas, it had all ceased.

"Enough hashing up the past." Rob nudged Dare's arm. "I know I'm straight but take me to that gay club you like and we can find you a man. That'll make you forget blondie for a while and that douchebag Michael." He winked slyly. "There's often ladies at these clubs nowadays as part of the whole 'gay man with his straight-lady harem' thing. They might appreciate a man who loves their assets as much as you do a pair of balls and a co—"

Dare reached out and placed a large hand over Rob's mouth. "Shut it."

Sally watched in amusement. "Well, finish up your coffee and get off then. I'm going to be on my way home in a few minutes anyway."

Sally lived with her husband, two French poodles, a parakeet and a ferret in a large house a block away. The flat above the shop wasn't quite suitable for her menagerie of animals or stay-overs by her adored grandchildren.

Dare had been pleased about that. It gave him a home other than a large but crowded caravan in the Travellers' site where his own family lived on the outskirts of London. He loved his parents and ten-year-old Kean, but being with them every day would have driven him crazy. Kean didn't really respect the fifteen-year age gap between him and Dare, always whining to be included in Dare's social life, which wasn't great but not suitable for a young boy.

"So," Rob drawled as he cast appraising eyes over Dare's body. "Go upstairs and get into a sexy cut-off tee shirt that shows off all those tats you have. Put on some tighter jeans so you can wiggle your arse and attract a man in that weird gay mating dance you do. Then we can get off to Innuendo."

"You're looking far too forward to this," Dare said dryly as he raised one eyebrow. "Are you *sure* you aren't a closet homo? I know we've had this discussion before…"

Rob grinned. "Oh I'm sure. I like pus—" He swallowed his words as Sally's gimlet eyes observed him frostily. "The ladies. I like the ladies."

Dare snickered as he left the shop front and made his way up the narrow stairs to his two-bedroomed flat. He knew it was no good arguing with Rob once he'd made his mind up. Plus, it would be a good distraction to go to a club, dance and maybe take someone home and fuck them senseless. Rob was right. It had been a while.

After he'd showered and changed, Dare picked up his leather jacket and stuffed a couple of packets of lube and some condoms in one of the pockets. His wallet went in his jeans back pocket. He shook his head in amusement. "Shit. I'm being pretty hopeful, aren't I?"

He heaved a sigh as he glanced around the room, made sure it looked tidy enough in case he brought anyone home. His sheets were clean and he had supplies, so in his mind he was all set.

Now all he had to do was find a man. A slim, blond man with the face of an angel who could make his dirty fantasies come true.

Well, a guy could hope.

Chapter 3

Jax stood fidgeting in the queue as he waited for his turn to be served. The music shop was busy; it was lunch hour at the shopping mall he liked to visit not too far from Castaways. Jax wasn't fond of tube travel and crowds, although he managed to get around on his own—albeit slower than anyone else. His days out needed planning and careful consideration to the most viable routes for his lack of sight but it was a challenge he always prided himself on taking.

As a treat to himself, Jax had come down to the music shop to snap up a copy of the new CD of his favourite band, Alterego. It was early afternoon and he was anxious to get home and listen to it.

Someone behind knocked into him and Jax turned quickly. A kid in a hoodie muttered a 'Sorry 'bout that' and moved away.

Jax smiled. "No problem," he murmured as he turned back to face the harassed cashier now serving him. He paid for his CD, put his wallet back into his jacket pocket and made his way past the crowd out into the mall. As he walked carefully across the packed concourse of the centre, someone jostled him again. Startled, Jax dropped his treasured CD. Before he could bend down to retrieve it, a hand swooped down and plucked it from the ground. Jax opened his mouth to say 'Thank you' and lost his breath gazing into the face of the stranger before him.

The man was dressed in what looked like a dark track suit and he was stunning. Quite a few years older than Jax, he was well built with broad shoulders and ink-black, curly mid-length hair with lighter streaks. Blue eyes stared at Jax with a mixture of interest and a flicker of apprehension. There was some other emotion in them too, but Jax wasn't sure what it was yet.

The stranger held out the CD. "Here you go." He cleared his throat and stared at Jax.

Jax could have swooned at the vague Irish lilt of that deep voice and he swallowed, trying to find words—any words. "Ermm," he finally squeaked out as he felt his face blush.

Oh God, way to go, champ. It hadn't been the most eloquent of replies. He tried again. "I mean, thanks for picking it up."

The man grinned. "No problem. I like the band too, so it would be a pity if you lost your CD."

For a moment they stood regarding each other, and Jax shuffled his feet. "Well, thanks again. I guess I should be off home." The warm smell of sandalwood and sweat drifted into his nostrils. The man smelt tantalising, and Jax wanted to get closer, to inhale the aroma of sexy male into his body.

The dark stranger nodded. "It was a pleasure, honest." He cocked his head, seeming to make a decision, and then cleared his throat uncertainly. "Tell me, do you drink coffee, or tea?"

Jax blinked at him. "Do I—well, yes, of course. Who doesn't?"

The other man held out his hand. "By the way, my name is Dare. Pleased to meet you." His eyebrows lifted in enquiry.

Jax clasped the strong hand in his. "My name is Jax. Short for Jackson."

Dare smiled. "Well, Jax, short for Jackson, can I buy you a coffee? We can sit and talk about Alterego and what you think of their latest track, 'Pyromania.' I'm quite partial to it myself."

It was then Jax panicked. He'd been engaged in conversation by one of the sexiest men he'd ever seen and it was blowing his mind. His heart was racing and his palms were sweaty and he had no idea what to do next.

Dare obviously saw his panic and he smiled reassuringly. "I'm sorry if I've startled you. I was just trying to be friendly." He looked a little disconcerted. "Perhaps this wasn't a good idea. I'm sorry."

Jax shook his head vehemently. "No, it was a great idea. It's just, uhhm, I really need to get home." *So I can breathe.* "Perhaps we can have coffee another time, if I see you around?" He gestured vaguely around him. "I'm sure we'll bump into each other here again."

Dare's face shadowed and he nodded. "Of course. We can talk music another time. Safe travels home, Jax. And enjoy your new CD."

He gave a faint smile and moved away into the teeming mass of people and was soon lost to sight.

Jax was still flabbergasted someone had actually asked him to have coffee. Whatever Dare's reason to extend the invitation, through Jax's own nervousness and insecurity, he'd just lost whatever opportunity he had to find out.

"Stupid, stupid," he berated himself as he crossed the road as he made his way to the tube station. "You just don't think. You might never have another chance to talk to him again. I mean, it's not that you visit the mall that often, you idiot. Christ, what the hell is wrong with me?"

His missed opportunity still rankled that night when he went to bed and dreamt of Dare.

***

Two nights later, Jax awoke from a deep sleep, but he had no idea what had woken him up. His eyes blinked open and he lay under the cover, his heart thudding. He slowly became aware of his surroundings and gave a soft, annoyed sigh as he lifted his watch closer to his eyes. The illuminated dial shone brightly. Half past midnight. He'd fallen asleep on the couch again.

The last thing he remembered was listening in the dark to an audio book on his iPod and snuggling under one of the kids' blankets that had been left lying around. Everyone had gone to bed already by the time Jax had gotten comfortable. It was his favourite time of night, that solitude in the lounge when everyone disappeared and the fire burned in the grate.

Now the room was cold, but not so silent. Somewhere behind the back of the couch, there was a soft footfall. It probably wouldn't have been heard by anyone else, but over time, his compromised eyesight had heightened his other senses, and he had learnt to make good use of them.

He held his breath, wondering whether it was one of the kids sneaking around to steal a midnight snack from the kitchen across the hall. But the steps sounded quite a bit heavier than a child's, so he didn't think so. He smelt the scent of a strangely familiar male cologne in the air.

There's a damn burglar in the house and I'm thinking he smells good.

There was a soft, muffled expletive and Jax's spine tingled. He had two choices. Remain still and let whoever it was hopefully go on his way, or call out and let the person know Jax was there. He considered the options. Burglars didn't usually steal things in the middle of the night wearing what Jax thought was an expensive aftershave. He might have impaired vision, but he had a healthy shout on him. No doubt Randy would come running if Jax cried out for help.

He needed to challenge this fucker. He wasn't about to let some dipshit steal Randy and Jen's worldly possessions. They worked too hard for them.

Jax stood up and quietly sidled over to the fireplace to pick up the poker from the urn at the side of the hearth. It would make him feel better to have it in his hands when he challenged the potential burglar.

"Who's there?" he called out. He hated the slight quaver in his voice, not wanting to appear defenceless to a potential burglar. "I can hear you, so no use hiding. Just tell me what you want here. Or get the fuck out of my home."

He wouldn't tip his hand, telling the burglar he had a weapon. Let the bastard find out for himself, Jax thought grimly. The scuffling noise stopped and now all he could hear was someone's steady breathing.

Jax stood straight and tall, hoping he looked intimidating in the dim light, where no one could see he wasn't superhero material.

A quiet voice echoed from the darkness. "I'm not here to rob you or hurt anyone. I hope I didn't scare you." The voice sounded familiar and Jax frowned, trying to place it.

"I'm not scared." He gripped the poker tighter. "Who the hell are you and what are you doing here?" He let out the breath he hadn't known he was holding and scowled, reaching down to fumble for the table lamp. He switched it on and the room flooded with warm light. Jax momentarily closed his eyes, trying to adjust to it. When he opened them, a large, blurred figure stood by the door to the hallway. It was half open and Jax guessed the man had been trying to make a clean break away from whatever he'd been doing in the house.

Jax stepped around the huddled blanket on the floor and made his way closer to the other man.

If he was going to hurt me, he'd have done it already.

"Are you going to tell me what the hell you're doing in this house?" he demanded. Something propelled him forward; he didn't feel nervous anymore, simply curious. As Jax got closer, he squinted at the stranger, trying to see him more clearly.

"I came to return something." The other man's even tone sent a shiver through Jax's body. "Something that was taken from you that didn't belong where it was."

Now Jax was sure he knew the person behind the voice. It surely couldn't be who he thought it was, could it? He moved, closing the distance until he could see more clearly. The sight that greeted his eyes took his breath away.

God, it is Dare from the mall. Crap, he's one sexy beast. Even if he might be a serial killer.

Jax waved the poker at Dare. "What the fuck are you doing here?"

Dare huffed. "It's a long story." He eyed the poker dubiously. "Really, a poker? That's your weapon of choice?"

Jax snorted. "I can clobber you with it if you try anything. Come on, dude. Tell me what the hell is going on. Are you that desperate to have coffee with me?"

Dare laughed, a little shakily. "'Dude?' You love that word. It's pretty cute when you say it. And yes, I'm definitely partial to having coffee with you one way or another. But this wasn't quite what I had planned."

Jax blinked. His eyes felt gritty and sore and he had gunk bunging up one corner of his left eye. He reached up and rubbed it away softly. "How do you know I use the word 'dude' often?"

Dare gave a deep, indrawn breath. There was silence. Jax got the impression Dare had revealed something he wasn't supposed to.

Jax grew impatient. "Are you going to tell me anything anytime soon? Because if not, I'll call out for the owner of the house and he can call the cops, then we'll get the story—"

"No, no police." For the first time Dare sounded panicked. "God, you're so damn feisty."

Jax got the impression that wasn't a problem for this man from his admiring tone. His groin warmed more. Now his dick was standing at half-mast and it was the last thing he needed if he did have to call on Randy.

I'm getting a hard-on for someone who broke into the house. Could shit get any weirder?

"So, what's the story, Mr Dark and Sexy? Do you actually have one or are you just an opportunistic burglar making something up?"

The chuckle that emanated from Dare's mouth was low, and yes, still damn sexy.

"Really? You think I'm dark and sexy?" Dare's face twisted into a grin. "I'm
flattered. You're something yourself."

Jax went on the offensive. "Do you always hit on people whose houses you break into? What are you, like, the Flirty Burglar or something?"

Really? This god of a man thinks I'm something? And honestly—the Flirty Burglar. Face palm.

Now Dare gave a loud, deep-bellied laugh. "No, not everyone. You're special." He sighed. "I went recently to visit a friend. Someone I know back home."

Jax didn't miss the hesitation on the word 'friend.'

Dare continued. "I noticed they had something that belonged to you. They'd, shall we say, *misappropriated* it, and I knew it belonged to you. I wanted to return it. So I came in through the French door there—which wasn't locked by the way, you guys really need to more careful—and put it back over there." He gestured to the sideboard table. "That's it. No mystery."

Jax went over to the sideboard and gasped when he saw what lay there. "The pocket watch my dad gave me. I thought I'd lost it." He swung around to see Dare pass a hand over through his hair, a guilty look on his face.

"How did your 'friend' come by this? And how did you know it was mine?" Jax picked up the gold watch. It was a treasured possession, and he'd been distraught when it had disappeared a couple of days ago. He'd thought he'd lost it at the mall; that perhaps it had dropped out of his pocket when he'd reached for his wallet. It went everywhere with him. It was all he had left of his father.

Dare looked ill at ease. "It was taken from your pocket when you were out at the shopping centre that day I saw you. And your initials are on it." He sounded guarded.

Jax frowned. "How did you know it was mine? You didn't know my name before that day."

Dare fidgeted. "I *did* know your name was Jackson. And I knew you'd lost a pocket watch. I found this one with *Jackson* engraved on it and put two and two together. Plus, I asked my bro—my friend where he got it and he told me it was a blond guy with…" he hesitated. "…some scars on his face. And you're pretty hard to mistake."

Jax's blood chilled. "Oh yeah, that's right," he said stonily. "I'm half blind and scarred, so hard to miss." There came the familiar ache in his chest, one of frustration and loss. "That gave your 'friend' the right to steal it from me?"

Dare's eyes widened and he stepped forward, once again closing the distance between him and Jax. "No, you're getting this all wrong. I mean, you're gorgeous, and when he said it was the blond man with the glasses, I knew it could only be you."

Jax was speechless. Both from having Dare so near and from his words. "Gorgeous?" he said faintly. He knew focusing on the fact someone thought he was attractive was not really the point here when something had been stolen from him and was being returned in the middle of the night. He wanted to pursue this angle a little.

"Yeah." Dare murmured, looking uncomfortable. "To me anyway." He swallowed. "I've, er, I've kind of noticed you a little sometimes, when I run errands for a friend. You and I cross paths from afar. But it's only been a few times," he said hastily. "I mean I'm not a stalker or anything. Cross my heart. I'd never do that to anyone."

The penny dropped. "It's you," Jax gasped. "You're the one who's been lurking in the shrubbery outside the garden." His mouth dropped open. "So if you've been spying on me, you probably knew what my name was when we met at the mall the other day."

Jax wasn't sure whether to be flattered or weirded out. He thought he was a little of both.

Dare snorted. "Guilty as charged." He squirmed. "I'm sorry. You probably want to hit me for checking you out. I'm gay, just so you know. But you're probably not, so just don't take this wrong. I just appreciate a sexy guy. It's how I'm wired. When I saw you at the mall, I thought it would be a great chance to maybe sit and talk to you. Get to know you a little more. That's why I wanted to have coffee with you." He shrugged, clearly ill at ease.

"Wow, dude. That's just..." Jax shook his head. "That's *so* not cool."

God, that is so cool. He was sexy to this man? Inside, the warmth of being appreciated and admired blossomed like a fierce blush. He'd never had that happen before. Not unless you counted the graffiti artist he'd met with Tate and Clay ages ago when they'd gone to the abandoned swimming baths.

Dare's face was crestfallen at Jax's words, and beneath the tanned skin Jax was sure the man was blushing at his confession. Jax wasn't going to let him off the hook that easily by admitting he thought he fancied guys too.

"So you've been watching me? Why? Just because you liked the look of me?"

Tate and Clay wouldn't like this turn of events so Jax resolved not to tell them. He'd get a hundred and one rapid-fire questions from both of them as to Dare's intentions, his background and his jockstrap size.

Knowing Tate and Clay, they would probably hunt Dare down if they thought he was a threat to Jax. There was a fine line between what Dare had done and actually being stalked, but Jax felt he wasn't at risk. There was something innately trustworthy about the man standing in front of him. And he'd returned Jax's treasured pocket watch.

Dare looked uncomfortable. "I guess. I was in the garden the other day when you noticed the watch was missing. And before that I've heard the little kids call you Jax and your dad call you Jackson." He smiled. "He was mad at you that day and he used your full name. I get the full-name thing when my mum's cross with me as well."

Jax turned the pocket watch in his hands, letting the chain trail through his fingers. He noticed his 'Why' hadn't been answered yet. "Randy isn't my dad. My dad's dead." The familiar grief flooded his mind and he pushed it back. "Randy runs this shelter." He stared at Dare fiercely, chin tilted. "The shelter for people who don't have anywhere else to go. The misfits."

Dare's face shadowed. "Sorry. I didn't know what your situation was and I didn't want to presume."

Jax hadn't wanted to sound like a petulant child and he felt ashamed. "Randy and Jen are great and I love it here. It's my home now." It suddenly struck him as outlandish he was standing there spilling his guts to a man who had admittedly snuck into his home. "Anyway, thanks for returning my watch. Tell your brother not to steal stuff from people anymore. It could get him into trouble."

Dare's eyes darkened as he realised Jax had rumbled to who his 'friend' was. "I apologise for him. He's only ten and he's not a bad kid, just an opportunist. I was with him at the mall that day when we met. I try to be a good role model for him but I'm not around much." He shrugged. "I guess I'm not a great example, doing this." He waved a hand around the room, discomfort on his face. "But I didn't want to get him into trouble by marching up to the front door to bring it back. My type of, of…people aren't kindly seen by the powers that be."

Jax snorted, wondering what Dare's 'type of people' was. "Well, at least you took the trouble to return something precious to someone who missed it. That's a pretty good move in my book. Even if you did break in to do it."

An indignant look crossed Dare's face. "I didn't really 'break in' if the door was unlocked." He swept a black curl off his cheek and blew out his cheeks like a hamster. It was possibly the cutest thing Jax had ever seen—and he loved small animals.

The two men looked at each other and shared a secret smile. Jax's heart leapt like a jack-in-the-box springing from its confinement.

"So what did you mean, your type of people?" he asked curiously.

Dare shifted uncomfortably. "I'm part of an Irish Traveller family. They live in a settlement just outside the city." His voice deepened. "I have my own place though."

Jax could have guessed about the Irish connection from Dare's black hair and blue eyes. He was pure Irish fantasy in person. And then there was the sexy accent. Dare seemed nervous talking about his family, yet there had been a hint of pride when he spoke about his own place.

"That sounds pretty cool," Jax said softly.

Dare shrugged. "People have pre-conceived notions about Travellers. They see most of us as dirty, thieving gypsies and tend to ostracise us. There's a lot of prejudice out there. We're not all the same and of course there are good and bad elements in the community, but that could apply anywhere. Most of us work jobs and live normal lives, like everyone else. We're not the stereotype dressed in rags dancing around campfires." His voice was passionate and Jax had no doubt this was a touchy subject.

Dare took a deep breath. "I'm sorry. I didn't mean to preach. I get carried away sometimes."

Jax found Dare fascinating. "I understand prejudice. I see it every day when I go about my own business and people think I'm stupid or slow because I don't see so well. Sometimes, people have preconceived notions that don't match reality. It's how we deal with them that gets us past it."

Dare's eyes widened. "That was… really profound."

Jax chuckled, Dare's admiration warming his heart. "So, your family. They live at this Traveller site?"

Dare nodded. "Yeah, in a caravan. Not the quaint gypsy type—more of a huge static trailer with all the mod cons. Mum, Da and my brother Kean. He's ten and a real handful. Sometimes he gets caught up in stuff he shouldn't. The Traveller community is pretty insular. They have their own ideas of what's right and wrong. Their own laws. It's not easy for a kid to grow up like that. Luckily he has some positive influences in my mum and Da." He lifted his hands, palms up. "And me, I hope."

Jax's voice was wistful. "I get it, honestly. I understand peer pressure. And that's cool. Having proper family, I mean."

Dare stared at him. "Can I ask what happened to your...your eyes? I know we've only just met, but I'd like to know." His voice held nothing but concern, and his gaze never wavered.

Jax wanted to see Dare's eye colour, so he moved closer. "Family trouble," he said curtly. "My stepbrother decided it would be fun to beat me half to death then throw chemicals in my face." He waved demonstratively. "This was the result."

Dare's eyes focused on him intently. Up close, he was even more stunning than Jax had believed.

Oh God, he has the darkest, most beautiful blue eyes I've ever seen. And there's silver in his hair. That is damn sexy.

Dare stepped forward, closing the gap between them. Jax flinched and gripped the poker. Instinctively he knew Dare would never do anything to hurt him; he didn't know how he knew that.

"God, I'm so sorry that happened to you," Dare breathed softly, and those blue eyes filled with an unexpected flash of pain. Dare's hand came up as if to touch Jax's face, and he drew in a sharp breath as Dare's hand dropped back to his side.

Jax wished it hadn't. Feeling someone else's warm hand on his damaged skin, another man's hand on him—he was faint with wanting it. Wanting someone warm to curl beside in his bed, skin that met his and lips that took his own was a fantasy he'd dreamed of for so long. And this was the closest he'd ever been to a man he found attractive.

He supposed wryly the feeling in his groin was proof he liked guys.

I don't even know this man other than he's as hot as hell and the sexiest thing I've ever seen. God, back off, you idiot. Why the hell would he want me, even if he says he thinks I'm cute?

"I'm sorry. I shouldn't have invaded your personal space like that." Dare turned to leave, his posture awkward. "I think I should go. If you're okay with it, we can pretend this never happened. Again, I'm sorry my brother took your watch. And I'll stop...noticing you, I promise." His lips twisted in a wry grin. "Although I guess that helped get you your watch back, didn't it?"

Jax watched with a dry mouth as Dare moved towards the glass doors at the front of the sitting room. Oh God, it was now or never. He might not get another chance like this one.

"Dare, wait."

Dare stopped and turned back, one eyebrow quirked in question.

"I, uhm, I think I might like guys too." Jax stammered.

A second eyebrow shot up to meet the other one. "You *think*?"

Jax scowled at the incredulity in Dare's tone. "Well, yeah I do, I mean, it *seems* to be my thing, but I've never really—" He was damned if he was going to admit to another man he was a virgin. He flapped a hand vaguely. "You know?"

Dare nodded, looking hesitant. "I guess."

Jax closed his eyes, feeling mortified. That hadn't quite gone the way he'd planned it in his head. He sounded like a gormless idiot. Dare's next words took all his reservations and blew them into the water like a submarine torpedo.

"Are you seeing anyone?" Dare shifted awkwardly, his eyes looking down at the floor.

"Seeing anyone?"

Dare's lips curved sinfully. "Yes, you know, like have you got a significant other, male or female if you're, you know, not sure."

Jax pulled a face. "No, girls aren't my thing."

Dare grinned, his face alight with suppressed mischief. Jax was enchanted. "And you only *think* you're attracted to guys? That's a pretty telling statement right there."

Jax swallowed. He'd have to level with Dare and risk being laughed at. "I've never, you know, had the chance to test any face-to-face theories about liking guys. I only know what happens to me when I watch stuff online. You know, guy stuff."

His face burned and he closed his aching eyes, not wanting to see any derision reflected on Dare's face at the fact that he watched gay porn and got turned on. Instead, he got a waft of mint-scented breath on his face, and when he opened his eyes, Dare was right there, gaze searching.

Jax tilted his chin to see better. A soft exhale of air and a sudden hitch in Dare's breathing signalled Dare had probably taken the gesture as an invitation to kiss him.

"Yes," Jax whispered, and then warm, soft lips touched his.

He moaned softly and closed his eyes. His fingers unclenched and the poker dropped to the carpet with a plop.

"God," Dare murmured against his lips. "You're killing me here." The kiss grew fiercer and for a moment, Jax thought he might get his first French kiss.

He groaned in disappointment when those lips left his and all he was left with was a dick in his pants that throbbed incessantly and needed release.

"*You* are worth waiting for," Dare whispered raggedly as he stepped away. Jax had felt the hardness of Dare's cock against his and knew he was equally turned on.

"Why did you stop?" His chest heaved as he opened his eyes and struggled to focus.

Dare laughed. "I'm not rushing anything with you. To be honest, I can't believe we just did that and you didn't swing that poker at me." He glanced down at the metal object on the floor.

Jax reached down and touched himself. "I can. You just...feel right." All his instincts screamed he could trust this man.

Dare drew in a breath and Jax felt a sense of satisfaction that he had this effect on his dark intruder.

"If you're not seeing anyone, then maybe we can go out sometime. On a date. Get that coffee we talked about." Dare cleared his throat and scuffed his feet on the floor.

Jax's heart filled with some emotion he'd never thought to feel again. Hope.

"Yeah, if you really want to," he managed to get out. "I'd like that."

Oh God. Everyone is going to kill me for this decision. Solution: Don't tell anyone.

"This is so damn weird," Jax muttered. "Making a date with a man I don't know, one who broke into my house to return stolen goods."

Dare grinned. "I thought we'd ascertained that I didn't break in? And anyway—" he took a deep breath. "One of my friends took me on a stupid speed-dating session once. It was bloody awful. I mean, you see someone for five minutes then go off with them, to their home, a restaurant, wherever. That seems a lot more risky to me than we're doing now. I mean, you have met me before for a whole minute and a half. And until a few moments ago, you had a deadly weapon in your hand in case you didn't like the look of me." He smirked. "That was more than I got when I sat across the table on that dating thing with a man who stunk of BO and had a distinct leer in his eyes."

Jax nodded thoughtfully. "I s'pose so." It did make a twisted kind of sense.

Dare chuckled, and then, like his name, daringly leaned in and kissed Jax's cheek. "I definitely want to have that date," Dare murmured. "Would you have any objection to giving me your mobile number? Then I'll call you and we'll set it up. I just need to check my work schedule, see when I can get some time off."

Jax quoted his mobile number. He sure as hell wasn't going to show this gorgeous man the specially equipped phone he needed to use. His Doro phone, a well-meant present from Randy and Jen on a previous birthday, was an expensive gadget and made his life so much easier, but it wasn't particularly pretty like some smart phones. He really wanted one of *those*. Nowadays they did anything he might need and more, but he didn't want to offend Randy and Jen by acquiring a sexier phone.

Dare fiddled with his mobile and Jax's phone buzzed.

"I sent you a text, so now you have my number," Dare said. "And I should be going now before you change your mind and call the cops about the crazy man in your house." His face creased in a soft smile. "'Night, Jax. Good meeting you again, even if under strange circumstances. I hope we can speak soon." He slid out the French doors into the night and Jax stood there, still befuddled by the night's events.

He'd just agreed to a date with a potential stalker and a man who'd slipped into his home unannounced. A man about whom he knew nothing.

But he still hadn't been French kissed.

"Ungh," he muttered in frustration as he ascended the stairs to his bedroom. "Tate would so kill me. Best keep this a secret."

He jerked off thinking of Dare's deep blue eyes and warm smile and was just dropping off into a fantasy-induced sleep when his phone buzzed, indicating a text. Sleepily, he played it back, listening to the text message. The polite American voice he'd chosen for the app and the words made him smile dreamily.

Can't wait for our date. Sleep tight. Dare.

Jax fell asleep with those words of promise echoing in his ears.

Chapter 4

The bright light of morning brought sense to Jax's fevered night dreams of sweaty, sensual sex and the heady feeling of being wanted by another man. He'd woken up feeling warm and fuzzy and made his way to the shower, where reality had set in with a vengeance.

What the fuck had he been thinking? He'd made a date with a man who had crept into his home. Not only that, but a man looking like Dare—older, wiser, more experienced, who could have his pick of men, and was never going to be satisfied with the likes of Jax.

He burned with embarrassment. He'd made a real fool of himself last night. Yes, he'd liked being kissed—it had been incredible—but going on a date? Perhaps getting even further and having sex of some sort with Dare? That was just a pipe dream.

He wrapped a towel around his waist and sat down on the bed, his heart heavy as he gnawed at his bottom lip. Then, making a decision, he picked up his phone and requested Dare's number. Once retrieved, he spoke into his phone softly, knowing the words would translate to text.

I don't think we should go out. Thanks anyway for asking me. Jax.

He hit send and stood up, eyes prickling.

When he went down the stairs for breakfast, Jen smiled at him from where she stood arranging flowers on the sideboard. "Morning, Jax."

Jax nodded a greeting. "Morning, guys." He seated himself at the table and pushed his dark glasses up his nose. He didn't wear them all that often inside but he wanted the anonymity today. The glasses shielded him. He placed his mobile on the table and tried to ignore it. He couldn't stop the little hope inside him that Dare might text back and try and make him change him mind. He wouldn't of course, but still…

Two of the other children were finishing their morning cereal and toast. Damien waved at him and spoke through a mouthful of Rice Krispies. "Hi Jax."

He nodded absently. "Morning, squirt. And don't talk with your mouth full. It's rude."

Damien heaved a big sigh and went on chewing. Jax squinted and reached carefully for the jug of orange juice on the table. The times he'd knocked it over because his depth perception was off were numerous, and he had no desire to make a mess this morning. It might just make him boil in frustration. He poured the juice into the glass at his place setting, feeling Jen watching him.

"You okay, honey? You sound a bit upset." Jen had a sixth sense when it came to all of them; she was loving and caring, but Jax didn't feel like getting into a conversation right now. He shrugged as he helped himself to a slice of buttered toast and spread jam on it.

"Yeah, I'm fine." He wasn't hungry but he forced the toast down. "Just had a late night, studying." He sensed Jen staring at him.

"Jax, you shouldn't be up so late," she scolded. "You did a lot of studying yesterday. You need to make sure you give those eyes a rest."

And there's the reason I shouldn't get involved with anyone. Everyone wants to baby me. Smother me with caring. Like I'm a damn child.

Before Jax could reply, Krispin piped up from the other side of the table. "I heard noises down here late last night but I didn't get up. I was scared."

Jax went cold. "What sort of noises, buddy?"

Krispin sniffed. "Just voices from the lounge. I thought one was you. I didn't know the other man."

Jax forced a laugh. "You must have been dreaming. Maybe someone left the telly on. There was no one here that I know of."

"Maybe." Krispin sounded unsure. "I really thought you were talking to someone." He lost interest and started flicking bits of Rice Krispies at Damien.

Jax stayed silent and finished eating, draining his breakfast drink. His mobile pinged and his heart leapt. He daren't open it as it was still set to speech mode and the message would be read out. He couldn't risk anyone hearing it if Dare was texting him back.

"What are your plans for today? It's Saturday, so I hope you're doing something fun rather than studying." Jen finished arranging the flowers and moved over to the window to fuss with one of the curtains.

"I'm going to see Tate and Clay later. I'm catching the tube. On my own." Jax hadn't meant his tone to be so hard but it came out that way anyway. Both Randy and Jen disliked it when he took the tube by himself. To be fair, it was a bit of a mission but the station wasn't far, and if he took it slowly and was careful, he could make it alone. It took him twice as long as everyone else but that was a small price to pay for his independence.

I have to start somewhere. I can't live here forever. I need to think about Clay and Tate's offer.

Both Clay and Tate had told him he could have the small annexe on the side of Clay's house that he currently used as an office. There was even a small bathroom attached to the room, so Jax would be pretty self-sufficient. The idea appealed immensely, but he worried about leaving Randy and Jen. They relied on him to do odd jobs, help out with the kids and be an older brother to a lot of the seriously abused and traumatised children. Jax wasn't sure he could, or should, take that away from them—even if they could use his room to house more kids like him and the others. He knew his days at Castaways were numbered and it was probably time to start thinking about moving out and moving on.

That was a decision for another day and it both scared and exhilarated him.

"Oh. Okay then." Jen sounded uncertain. "Well, be careful how you go. And let me know when you leave their house later so I know when to expect you back. Krispin, stop flicking cereal at Damien. I expect you to clean it up after breakfast."

Jax sighed. He knew Jen was simply being a concerned almost-parent, but it still frustrated him that he was expected to check in all the time. "Fine. I'll text you when I'm ready to leave." He stood up, desperate to listen to his incoming message. "I need to get ready, and I've a few things to do still. I'll see you later. Have a good day, lads, and Krispin, help clear up your mess, okay?"

Krispin murmured his sulky agreement as Jax left the room for the quiet solitude of his bedroom. Sitting on the bed, Jax stared at his phone then played back the text from Dare.

Something happen for you to change your mind? Are you okay? D.

Jax closed his eyes before sending a text back.

I just don't think it's a good idea. Two different worlds and all that crap. Best not to get involved with each other.

He threw his phone on the bed and went to find his favourite hoodie, buried beneath a pile of dirty washing in his laundry basket. He insisted on doing his own washing—there was no way he'd let Jen see his semen-stained underwear from his nightly activities—and he'd been lax in that department lately. He was lucky he *had* any clean underwear in his cupboard.

Jax had just finished shrugging into the hoodie and putting some hair product on his curls to tame them a little when his phone rang. His caller ID announced in soft tones it was Dare. In a quandary as to whether to answer it, Jax bit his lip. It stopped before he could make a decision. For a few seconds there was silence then it rang again. Still Dare.

With an exasperated huff, Jax answered testily. "Yes?" He sat down on the bed.

There was a chuckle on the other end. "You're not a morning person then, I take it?" Dare's voice with its soft lilt was teasing and Jax almost melted but decided to stand firm.

"I don't mind mornings. Why are you calling?"

"I wanted to find out why you changed your mind about our date. I thought we hit it off quite well." Dare's voice was even but there was a trace of something—hurt?—in it.

Jax squirmed. It was one thing sending a text, another thing having the person you'd just fobbed off on the other side of the phone. "Yeah, I just don't think it's going to work. I mean, we're so different, you know?"

Dare was quiet, only the sound of him breathing echoing down the line. "How do you mean, different? I'm a bloke, you're a bloke. We're not that different age-wise—I'm twenty-five, by the way—and we obviously have chemistry from that kiss last night. What's so different about us?"

Jax cleared his throat. "We just are." He lay back on the bed and stared at his booted feet.

Dare snorted. "You mean because you can't see all that well and have some facial scarring, you think no one could find you attractive, don't you? That you're no real catch for anyone."

As that was exactly what Jax thought, he couldn't refute the statement. His mouth dried up and he didn't know what to say.

"Do you really think I'm that shallow?" Now there was real hurt in Dare's voice and an element of disappointment. Dare's voice softened. "For what it's worth, I think you are the hottest, sexiest guy I've ever laid eyes on. I see under that exterior, into what's beneath. And *you* are beautiful. I know that without even getting to know you better."

Jax's chest ached as he considered Dare's words. "How can you know that? I mean, look at me. I'm just a student, I live in a halfway house, I'm not, like..." his voice trailed off. "You can do better for yourself."

"Don't talk crap. I want *you*." Dare's voice shook slightly. "What you went through, what you do at that halfway house with the kids. I've seen you, remember? You're like this, this...hero they all look up to. You're so damn strong and brave. And I want a chance to get to know you, even if it doesn't work out." He laughed raggedly. "I know that sounds weird and I don't want to come on too strong and be that crazy stalker guy. If you say not to call you anymore, you have my word I won't ever do it again. I promise you'll never see me again."

That thought panicked Jax more than the thought of a date. "You really think I'm hot and sexy?" he whispered.

"Baby, I do." The endearment threw Jax and made him all warm inside as his lips lifted in a smile. "Like you can't believe."

Jax gave a soft laugh. "You're as hot as shit too. You have this whole bad-boy thing going for you. The only thing that could make me fancy you more would be if you had tattoos everywhere."

"Then I guess it's good for us both that I do." Dare sounded amused but Jax was more taken with the fact his dark stranger had tats.

"Oh God. Kill me now." His groin was once again growing heated. He ran a hand across the front of his jeans, pressing down his hardening dick then stopped in mortification at realising what he was doing, almost masturbating to a man's voice on the phone. "Where are they?"

"My tattoos? On my arms and one on my hip. And across my shoulders. Maybe one day you'll get to see them up close and personal. That means we need a date first." Dare sounded smug.

Jax's jeans were growing tighter by the minute. "That's pretty sneaky, doing that to a guy." He knew he had a silly grin on his face and all his reservations about meeting this strange man called Dare had flown straight out of the window.

"So how about it? Are we still on for that date?"

Jax took a deep breath. He could no more resist the lure of seeing Dare again than he could a promise by an eminent surgeon to restore his full sight.

I owe it to myself to give it a try.

"Yes, okay. Let's do it. I'm sorry I'm messing you around, I—"

Dare interrupted him. "You're scared. I understand that. So let's try one date and see how it goes. We'll make it a public place so you feel comfortable. And feel free to tell anyone where you're going and who you're with. I want you to feel safe. What kind of food do you like?"

"I eat mostly anything, but not Chinese."

It's too finicky with all that rice and I end up with it all down my front. Not the right tone to set on a first date. And chopsticks slay me. And he's right. I do need to tell someone where I'm going.

"I'm a steak and potatoes man myself. I know a really great restaurant where we can sit and chill and get to know each other. I have a car too, so I can pick you up. Shall we say next Friday night, around seven thirty pm?" Dare sounded pleased with himself.

Jax grinned. "Yeah, that sounds like a plan. At least you know where I live."

Dare's soft laugh sent a thrill of feeling through Jax's body. "There's that. Okay, I'll see you then." There was a shout and Dare spoke hurriedly. "I have to go. The boss is looking for me. See you next week. Bye, gorgeous." The phone went dead.

Jax sat on his bed with what he imagined was a goofy expression on his face. He still wasn't sure how the turnabout to go out on a date had come up but he was glad he'd given in.

And it was just one date.

With a man-god with sexy tattoos.

Friday couldn't come soon enough.

***

"Who is this guy and what does he do? Have you got his details so I can run him? And just what kind of a name is Dare anyway? Sounds a bit suspect to me. And you say he's seven years older than you? Is he some sort of pervert looking to score with an eighteen-year-old?"

Tate Williams narrowed his eyes as he gave Jax the gimlet stare no doubt perfected from hours of interrogating actual bona fide suspects in horrific cases. Jax didn't think it was suited to interrogating eighteen-year-olds about potential first-time dates.

"What the hell?" he snapped. "His name is like yours, arsehole. Four letters and ending in e. And like hell are you running any checks on him. Forget that lame-ass idea." He scowled at Tate. "And I'm halfway to nineteen, fuck you very much, and no, he's not a damn pervert. Must you always think the worst of people?"

"You gonna kiss him with that potty mouth?" Tate's brow furrowed but his eyes gleamed with amusement. "Clay, baby, what do you think?"

He turned to the large frame of the man seated in the arm chair beside him.

Clay Mortimer ran a hand through his silver-streaked dark hair, a grin crossing his handsome face. "I think you two are going to be the death of me, is what I think. You're like kids when you get together." He gave a deep laugh. "It's entertaining to watch though." He cast a fond yet exasperated glance at his boyfriend. "Tate, you can't run any checks on this poor guy, you'll likely scare the man away. Stop being such a doom monger. Jax seems pretty taken with him, and so far, Dare sounds like a decent guy. He wants Jax to feel comfortable on this date, that's obvious."

Jax flushed. "He's okay. I mean, well, more than okay. He's pretty hot."

Hot wasn't the word. Scorching was more like it. Dare, with his curling, unruly, thick black hair streaked with silver, was Jax's wet dream.

"Aww." Tate ruffled Jax's hair. "Our little lad is growing up, Clay." He waggled his eyebrows suggestively. "Do we have to have the birds and the bees talk now?"

"Fuck. You," Jax retorted. He felt his skin flame. He knew Tate was teasing him—he wouldn't be Tate if he didn't—but Jax's insecurities at his lack of experience did rankle.

Tate leaned over and laid a warm hand on Jax's. "I'm kidding, Baby Bird," he said. "I know you have this in hand." Tate knew better than anyone about Jax's vulnerability. Jax squirmed every time he remembered that angst-driven teen conversation in his room months ago.

'Baby Bird' was a reference to Jax's code name. They all had one; it was part and parcel of being taken into a family of tough cops and investigators, where trouble could flare at any minute. Tate had chosen all their names. Jax was Baby Bird, Clay was Clayzilla—something that caused Clay to squirm uncomfortably and Tate's wide grin to surface every time it was mentioned (Jax was eaten with curiosity to find out why, but could guess)—and Tate was simply Graffiti. In an emergency, that's how they'd be referred to.

Clay shook his head as he settled back in his chair next to Jax and crossed elegantly trousered legs. Even off duty from the investigative agency he ran, Jax thought Clay looked like a GQ model.

Clay steepled his fingers as he regarded Jax. "Are you going anywhere nice? Galileo's perhaps?"

Jax had forgotten about Clay and Tate's favourite restaurant. It was probably a little too romantic for his first date with Dare, though. "No, we're going to some steak restaurant he knows. Maybe Galileo's might be a second or third date choice. If we get that far." He sighed moodily.

"If he doesn't want a second date, he's going to be the one missing out." Clay's warm, confident voice was like a soothing balm to Jax's fragile and bruised soul.

Jax sniffed. "We'll see. It's early days yet." He fiddled with the cord on his hoodie.

"So you met him at the park when you were with the kids?" Tate's eyes were appraising. "What's his job then?"

Jax shook his head, hoping the eagle-eyed Tate or Clay wouldn't see through his lie about their meeting up. "I have no idea. We didn't talk much about that. I know he has a little brother, though, and a mum he visits."

He wasn't about to tell anyone the real story of how they'd met or that Dare's brother was a thief. That would make both his friends nervous. Although "friends" wasn't really the word to describe his relationship with Clay and Tate.

Having met at Castaways nearly a year ago, Jax and Tate had formed an immediate bond. Tate was like a big brother. With Tate had come Clay. Strong, dependable and the voice of reason to Tate's sporadic displays of temper and moodiness, Clay was the quasi-father figure Jax missed dearly.

Clay and Tate were inseparable, devoted to each other, and Jax had no doubt both of them would lay down their lives for each other—and for him. He never ceased to marvel at the way he'd become part of this unlikely trio. It had been the best thing ever to happen to him since joining Castaways with Randy and Jen.

"Have you given any thought to moving in here yet?" Clay regarded Jax thoughtfully. "If you're going to find yourself a boyfriend, you're going to need some privacy, and you're not going to get it where you are."

Jax knew it took a lot for Clay to make that offer. He'd feared his and Tate's lifestyles might put Jax in some sort of danger. From what Tate had said, it had been the same outlook he and Clay had fought about before, nearly leading to them breaking up.

Apparently Tate had once again managed to convince Clay that Jax would be safe enough and not to mollycoddle him.

Jax sighed. "I've discussed it with Randy and Jen. They both tell me they're quite okay with me leaving even though they'll miss me. I'm just not sure I can do it."

"You know the offer is always open." Tate stood up and stretched. "I know it's tough striking out on your own. But you won't be alone. You'll have us."

Clay stood up. "I'm going to get a drink. Jax, do you want anything? A beer, glass of wine? I'm not sure what eighteen-year-olds are drinking nowadays."

"Got any WKD?" Jax liked the Red one.

Clay looked disconcerted. "No, I don't think so. What the hell is that?"

"Never mind. I'll have a beer, thanks."

The rest of the afternoon was spent getting slightly tipsy and enjoying the company of two men who really knew how to keep a person entertained with their banter and dirty talk. When it came time for Jax to be on his way, he wasn't happy. He needed to make it home in the daylight, as darkness was always an extra trial for him.

When he was ready to go, Clay and Tate hugged him.

"Safe travels home," Clay said. "Think about that moving-in situation. And let me know how your date goes." He looked as if he wanted to ask more but stopped himself. Tate had no qualms.

"Text me the venue you're going to," Tate flapped a large hand. "And maybe send me a picture of the guy so I know who to kill if he hurts you."

Jax punched Tate hard in the arm. "Forget it. I'm a big boy. I don't need a damn babysitter. And Tate, if I feel anyone following me or lurking around, I shall know it's you or one of your flunkies spying on me. You know I have this sixth sense. So just don't do it."

Tate's eyes widened in mock horror. "I'm hurt. As if I'd do that." His eyes narrowed and Jax knew Tate actually been thinking about it.

"Tate, leave him alone." Clay motioned to his lover, who scowled. "This is for him to do." He smiled at Jax. "I promise you my man won't interfere. Go get him, tiger."

Tate didn't look happy but he knew when he was out-voted. He waggled a finger at Jax. "Fine. Just text me when you get back from your date, so I know you're home. Otherwise I won't sleep."

Jax sighed. He supposed he could do that. It was actually nice being cared about like this although he'd never admit it. "Fine, Mr Fussy Pants. I'll do that."

Tate nodded then leaned over to kiss Clay. "I'm going to the gym. I fancy a swim. I've got some tight muscles I need loosening up." He smirked. "And when I get home I know another muscle that'll need relieving."

Clay groaned. "God, don't. We have company, you animal."

Jax put his hands over his ears. "Oh God, strike me deaf as well as blind," he joked. "Rick's told me the story about finding the two of you in flagrante delicto and I don't think we need a repeat performance."

Rick was Tate's policeman nephew and had been subjected to the tableau of Clay and Tate getting busy one day when he'd come over unannounced. He swore he'd been traumatised forever. Jax had snorted with laughter at the tale.

Tate winked. "It'd be better than all that gay porn you watch. My man is hot in person." He kissed Clay again, this time a dirty, open-mouthed kiss that left Jax reeling with the passion of it.

God, he wanted to be kissed like that. He hoped Dare would be the one to do it, and soon.

Tate uttered a sultry laugh as he swaggered out of the door, Jax close on his heels. He waved at Tate as his friend sauntered down the street towards the gym at the end of the road. Jax plugged his EarPods into his phone, turned up the volume and made his way to the tube station and home.

Chapter 5

Monday morning. Dare hummed happily as he restocked yet more shelves with boxes of Fantasy Fizzers, Gunky Gumballs and Disgusting Doo-doo. He winced at some of the names.

"There is no way I'd eat this crap," he muttered. "Probably kill me." He peered suspiciously at a box of something called Salty Sailors and snickered. They were little cracker biscuits in the shape of sailors.

"I could *so* do something with that. Loads of images of sailors and seamen coming to mind…"

A sharp flick to his nether regions made him look around. Sally stood there, peering at him once again over the top of her glasses. "That sounds rather as if you have something on your mind." Her eyes sparkled wickedly. "Thinking of that young man you've been spying on?"

Dare hadn't told anyone else about his visit to Jax's house and risqué date-making skills, and he wasn't about to start now. "Maybe. A man can dream, can't he?"

"Indeed he can, handsome." Sally cocked her head to one side like a curious little bird. "Are you ever planning on making your presence known and finding out whether he swings your way?"

Dare couldn't look at her. Sally had an uncanny knack for ferreting out untruths and his face was an open book most of the time. He crouched down and pretended to be straightening boxes on the bottom shelf.

"I can't exactly run out of the undergrowth screaming, 'I've been watching you and I want to know if you're a homosexual like me,' can I? I'd get bloody arrested," he muttered. "And there doesn't really seem to be any other opportunity to get him alone.

He doesn't go out much." That much was true but he crossed his fingers anyway, hoping Sally wouldn't notice.

"But you were humming, all happy like, which you haven't done in a while, and that leads me to believe, young man, that something has happened that you're not telling me about." Sally wagged a finger in Dare's direction. "I'll wangle it out of you, mark my words. Secrets do not elude Sally for long." She smirked. "I'm just popping out to get some milk. We've run out." Sally disappeared out into the buzzing street of morning shoppers.

Dare rolled his eyes. God save him from nosy bosses and well-meaning friends. Rob had said much the same thing last night when they'd gone to see a film. Dare had found it awkward keeping his secret; he held the fact Jax was going out with him close to his heart like a pressed rose.

When Jax had sent him that text cancelling their outing, he'd wanted to swear a blue streak. He'd realised Jax was scared and hoped he'd be able to salvage it. It had luckily all worked out for the best. So far. Jax was skittish and Dare knew anything could happen between now and their date.

The one thing Dare couldn't come to terms with was the way Jax had been maimed by someone he knew—a family member.

"If I ever find the fucker, I'll kill him," Dare murmured as he unpacked more boxes and placed their contents in jars, buckets and on shelves. "How anyone can do that to someone is beyond me. Especially to *him*."

Dare's mobile went off and hoping it was Jax, his spirit momentarily lifted out of the darkness he'd been in. It wasn't. A spark of alarm pierced him.

"Kean, is everything okay?" Dare rarely got calls from his little brother. "Shouldn't you be in school?"

His brother sniffed. "I've been sick today, D. Got the runs something awful. I exploded all over the bathroom this morning."

Dare winced at the image that conjured up. "Okay. Great visual there, Snoopy. Where's Mum and Da?" When Kean was about eighteen months old he refused to go anywhere without his favourite Snoopy toy.

"Don't call me that stupid name, you know I hate it," Kean grumbled. "Mum's here, baking and Da's gone out. I don't know where, not work though. He didn't have a job on today."

Dare sighed. Their father had probably gone to the bookies, the pub, anywhere but home.

Patrick Rowan was a hardworking man, operating a gardening and DIY business most of the week, if jobs came his way. He expected his sons to take care of themselves and their mother. He was a man not suited to being stuck in a caravan, however spacious, with a sick child.

Occasionally Kean helped their dad out when he did gardening jobs, enjoying being treated like an equal. It was amazing how Kean managed to charm himself into the good books of the women Patrick Rowan worked for. They thought it was adorable having a kid tagging along and helping Da.

His little brother was quite an accomplished con artist, something Dare didn't want to think about too much. It boded of a future criminal career choice, one he hoped to deter by being a good role model.

"So what's up then?" he asked.

"I was bored. I haven't seen you in a while. I wanted to talk to you." Kean huffed but Dare heard the undercurrent of need in his voice. Not for the first time he felt guilty that he'd moved away from the Irish Traveller site they'd lived in for many years.

The Traveller community he'd lived in was close knit, looking after their own, but it had become a place he'd found stifling in its insularity. It was why Dare had left when he could, even though he missed his parents. He hoped one day Kean might be inspired to do the same and find his own path.

There was also being gay. Most of the community had been accepting, including his folks, but, like anywhere, there'd been a few elements that had given him hell and made his life miserable. He'd been glad to leave them behind, especially the brutish Sammy Coulter. Sammy had been a bully of note, and he and Dare had butted heads more than once.

"I know, buddy. I've been busy working and stuff. And fixing your mistakes."

Dare grinned, knowing he'd get a reaction to that one. He'd taken Kean to the mall to buy some new comic he wanted and had noticed his little brother shadowing Jax. Kean was preternaturally adept at spotting things of value in people's hand and pockets, which meant Dare had to keep a close eye on his younger sibling.

He'd thought the boy just enjoyed scouting people, but when they got home Dare noticed the glint from the pocket watch in Kean's hand as he admired it. Dare's heart had sunk. He'd seen Jax glancing at the watch more than a few times and knew it had to hold special meaning—really, who used a pocket watch these days?

When Dare confiscated the watch, he read Kean the riot act—for all the good it did—then set out to restore the wrong that had been done to Jax.

The concept of not taking other people's property hadn't quite sunk into Kean's brain well enough yet. He was a work in progress but Dare had faith. He also knew his mother would have slapped Kean silly had she found out about his transgression. Hence the secret had been kept between the brothers with the threat of Dare telling their mum if Kean did something stupid again.

"Yes, I know I was stupid about the damned watch. You told me so the other day, like, ten times." Kean's voice grew curious. "So did you manage to give it back okay? Is he happy he's got it?"

"Yeah, I managed to sneak it in. And when I saw him with it, he looked really pleased. It meant a lot to him."

"Cool. So when am I going to see you again? I've got a new comic I want to show you—a limited-edition Spiderman." Kean had a thing for graphic novels and used all his money to buy them.

At least, that's what Dare hoped, and that somewhere a book shop wasn't missing a rare edition snuck out under cover of a baggy sweatshirt. He'd kill Kean if he found out he'd been stealing *again*.

"I'll try make it over this weekend to see you all. Maybe Saturday. I have a date Friday." Dare regretted saying the words even as he said them.

Kean's tone brightened. "A date? With your angel guy?"

Dare passed a hand over his eyes and huffed gently. "Yes. His name is Jax, though. Not angel guy."

"Whatever. The guy you're stuck on. Are you gonna have butt sex with him?"

Dare's mouth fell open. "Jesus, Kean, what the hell? You don't get to ask me questions like that."

He almost heard Kean shrug on the other side of the phone. "Take a chill pill, big guy. I was only asking. I know about this stuff, you know. Guys and girls. I mean, I have a gay big brother. I need to know how it works in case *I* get a case of the gay cooties."

Dare was out of his depth and a little annoyed. "The gay cooties?"

I can't believe I'm having this conversation with my ten-year-old brother.

Kean laughed. "Yeah, you know, if I turn out to be gay too. At least then I have a heads up on what it's all about."

Dare sat down on a stool, his legs refusing to stay firm. "Are you—do you think you might be gay?"

"Nah, I like girls too much. I just wanted to cover all the bases."

"I see," Dare said faintly. Maybe he *had* been gone too long from home and the kid needed some guidance. Maybe he should move back. "You'd tell me if you decided, you know, you liked guys, wouldn't you? You wouldn't hide it from me. Or Mum and Da."

"They seem all right with you, so I guess they'd be fine with me too. But honest, like I said, I like girls. I kissed Rhianna Kent the other day and she told me I was a good kisser. She made me hard."

"Oh Jesus," Dare whispered, face flaming. "Kean, do they teach you sex education at school?"

Kean snorted loudly. "Oh yeah, that stupid stuff about where babies come from, and condoms and AIDS and stuff? They teach us but, honest, Big-D, I know about this stuff. I have the internet."

And there it was. Dare decided he needed to move back right now and put his little brother on the straight and narrow if he was learning about sex on the internet at the tender age of ten.

"Kean, I swear to God, if you are watching anything you shouldn't be I'm going to break your neck. Aren't there parental controls on the internet at home?" He was sure he'd set them up when his mum had originally had broadband installed. She'd not known anything about Wi-Fi or internet, and he'd gone over to show her what it was all about.

Maria Sarah Rowan was adept at homemaking and bringing up her sons with a fairly decent outlook on life, but technology was so not her thing. She'd once completely fried a new microwave by putting tinfoil containers in it.

"Big brother, take it easy. I'm not watching porn or anything. Pinkie swear. But I watch *Queer as Folk* and *Murder in the First*. I've seen people making out on screen, guys and girls."

Dare willed his rapid heartbeat to slow down. "Okay. Actually, not okay, because I'm pretty sure both of those shows are after the watershed when you should be in bed. I guess that's not happening too. The going-to-bed thing."

There was a loud bray of amusement down the phone. "I'm ten, not five. My bedtime is about eleven. I—oh hang on, Mum's here. She wants to speak to you."

There was a clatter and then a soft voice echoed in Dare's ear. His mother had a slight Irish accent, brought on more by exposure to her husband's broader one than from actually being Irish.

Maria Rowan was English by birth but Dare's parents had been together since they were teenagers. "Kildare Patrick Rowan, when are you going to come visit your mother? You're always off, gadding about, and not taking any time to visit your poor family."

Dare licked his lips and tried to make excuses. "I've been busy, Mum, I was just saying to Snoopy I'll come over this weekend and visit. I'll bring you some of your favourite Wee Beastie Babies from the shop." His mother was fond of the aptly named jelly babies that took on the shapes and forms of numerous monsters and evil creatures and oozed sweet red sticky blood when bitten into. It was a gift guaranteed to delight her.

"Oh, you're too good to me, son. Make sure you come over then, and bring me my treats. Or else I might have to come find you instead." The threat was there, faint but unmistakeable.

"Your brother wants to say goodbye, so here he is. See you Saturday, *mo Mhac*." The phone was handed over.

"So, we'll see you this weekend?" Kean's voice was animated. "I have this new shot to show you. Da put a new hoop up for me, and I'm getting really good at it. We can play a game of Dodgems."

Dare groaned softly. Dodgems was some lame-arse game his brother had put together, like dodge-ball but using apples off the tree that grew in the Traveller encampment. His larger size made him fair game for his gleeful brother who was a slippery otter when it came to evading the hardened missiles being lobbed back at him. Dare would bear bruises for a week.

"We'll see. Now go back to bed, be good for Mum and maybe read a damn book instead of watching telly. Get some culture into that deprived soul of yours."

"Yeah I could do that, I s'pose." Kean's voice brightened. "Mum's got her Kindle. I can read that book everyone's talking about, *Fifty Shades* or something? See you Saturday, bro." And with a wicked chuckle, Kean disconnected.

Dare shook his head wearily. His little brother knew how to push all his buttons. He fervently hoped Kean had been joking about reading that book. He finished unpacking the new stock and went to the back room to make himself a cup of calming green tea.

Chapter 6

Date night was as nerve-wracking as Dare had expected. He hadn't managed to keep it the secret he'd hoped it would be. The minute Sally had seen him spruced up as she was leaving the store, she'd inveigled the truth out of him. He'd no doubt the next time Rob came into the shop for more unpaid-for treats, he'd be told the full story. Dare was resigned to the fact his dating life was now open scrutiny for the pair.

It had been a while since he'd been out on a date. Since Michael had left, Dare hadn't had a relationship, a proper date or anything meaningful. His sex life had been relegated to an occasional hook-up somewhere, a quick satisfying of the carnal urges and a lot of his own handiwork.

Tonight, though, wasn't about getting in Jax's pants. Tonight was about getting to know each other and finding out who was this beautiful man behind the vulnerable and damaged façade. Dare knew instinctively his date wasn't very experienced in the whole dating-mating game. He'd have to tread carefully so he didn't scare Jax away.

"Just keep it in your trousers," Dare muttered as he parked his battered and weather-beaten Ford Focus under the dim glow of a street light. He'd been lucky to find parking not too far from the house. "I want him like Beyoncé wants her seasoned chicken, but this needs to go slow."

He mounted the steps and knocked on the door then pulled the bell pull for good measure. Inside the house, a bell tinkled. A few minutes elapsed and Dare was ready to knock again when suddenly the door opened. Reflected in the warm light of the hallway, Jax stood looking like…well, a sensuous angel.

Dare's good intentions of keeping this date to one of platonic and meaningful communication went to hell. Framed in the doorway, dressed in tight black jeans fastened with a belt with a silver buckle, a form-fitting bottle green button-up shirt with a Mandarin collar, and dark, well-worn black boots, Jax looked edible and downright sinful.

A tailored black jacket covered his slim frame and he'd left his wavy blond hair loose, framing small ears. Dare was sure there was a sheen of lip gloss on those oh-so-kissable lips.

Jax's pale skin glowed under the porch light and Dare didn't take notice of Jax's scarring or wrinkled eyelids. Not that he'd really thought about those flecks of tarnished silver being anything other than what made Jax who he was.

The tightness in Dare's trousers was unbearable and he was glad his long, sweeping greatcoat covered his groin. Mostly. He cleared his throat and stared into pale blue, disturbing eyes as Jax lifted his chin and regarded him. A faint smirk swept across Jax's face and Dare lost his breath.

The little bastard knows exactly what effect he's having on me. He's planned this.

"Evening, Dare," Jax said. "Are we ready to go, or do you need to come in and use the bathroom or something?" Again, there was the teasing lift of soft lips.

The little shit! He's toying with me.

"No, I'm fine. Unless I need to meet anyone else in the house, introduce myself so they know who I am?"

Jax frowned and stared at him fiercely. "Not necessary. I'm not going to the damn prom and need someone to check out my date. I've told whoever needs to know."

Ha. My kitten has claws. I like that.

Dare shrugged. "Okay then. Let's get off. The car is just a few spaces down." He wanted to ask whether Jax needed an arm to grab onto, as he was walking in the dark, but wasn't sure how to do that without getting another laser stare. He needn't have worried.

Regally, Jax motioned Dare aside, then, holding onto the balustrade carefully, he stepped gingerly down the concrete steps towards the pavement. Dare noticed Jax's white knuckles gripping the railing but stood back, giving the other man his space, but remained ready to catch him if he fell.

Soon Jax stood on the pavement and Dare didn't miss the small grin of satisfaction, fleeting but there. His chest warmed at that defiant gesture.

He led the way, walking slowly, keeping a step ahead of Jax but an eye on his careful gait and measured, purposeful footsteps. Once or twice, Dare noticed him falter, and the desire to take Jax's arm and help was a temptation he didn't think he could refuse, but did.

He was awed at Jax's determination to prove he could be independent, be a normal date even though his bad vision must have made it difficult to navigate the cracked pavement in the deepening shadows of the night.

When they reached the car, Dare unlocked it with the remote and went around to open Jax's door.

"I can open it," Jax said haughtily, hand outstretched to stop him.

Dare rolled his eyes. "I'd do it for anyone I'd asked out on a date. It's manners, not babying." He ignored Jax's huff and the door squeaked open. "Sorry, it needs a bit of oil. This door jams a bit. It's an old banger, this one. In you get."

Jax harrumphed but got into the car. Dare closed the door and grinned to himself as he went around the front to his side. This man was going to be a real challenge, and he was definitely up for it.

Dare pulled on his safety belt and waited for his date to do the same. Jax struggled with getting the belt into the clip at the side of the seat. Dare didn't want to tell him the fastening was a little damaged and he might battle with it. He waited patiently for a minute, listening to Jax's soft swearing as he persevered and finally decided it had gone far enough. They could be here all night at this rate.

He reached over and put his hand over Jax's. The feel of the warm hand under his own was heady. Dare wanted to stroke, touch and lift it to his lips to kiss it.

"Let me help," he muttered and slid the belt into the clip. "It's a tricky one. Everyone has trouble with it."

Jax's frustrated sigh was warm on Dare's face. "Don't patronise me," he snapped, folding his arms across his chest.

Dare snorted loudly. "Stop being such a damn drama queen. Like I said, it's busted and people struggle with it. It's not just you, sunshine."

He chuckled at Jax's annoyed huff and started the car.

"It's not far," Dare said as he drove into the street. "About ten minutes away. Are you hungry?"

"Yeah." Jax stared ahead of him. "I could do with a nice piece of meat."

Dare nearly swerved into a cyclist. Jax laughed softly.

"Christ, is this how it's going to be then?" Dare smiled as he checked the cyclist out in his rear view mirror. "You making terrible innuendos and giving me a heart attack? And then there's the way you look tonight. Really nice." He winced at that description. Surely he could have come up with something better. Apparently Jax thought so too.

"Nice? Candy is 'nice.' Flowers are 'nice.' Is that the best you can do?" Jax teased as he settled into his seat.

Dare reached over and touched Jax's hand gently then put his own back on the steering wheel. "Stunning," he said. "Completely stunning. Is that better?"

"Yeah," Jax whispered. "Much better." He threw a grin at Dare. "You look very hot yourself. I love those pants on you. Very trendy, and they fit like a glove."

Dare had worn his best pair of dark beige tapered linen trousers, teamed with a soft, long-sleeved white shirt and his well-worn dark brown greatcoat with upturned collar. He'd agonised over what to wear for nearly an hour before settling on this ensemble. He was pleased Jax approved.

Jax reached into his jacket pocket. He withdrew a packet of gum and proffered it. "Fancy a stick?"

Dare nodded. "Thanks."

Jax took the gum out of the packet, unwrapped it and then brought his hand up to Dare's mouth. "Open," he said huskily.

With a dick that wouldn't stay down, Dare obeyed. Soft, warm fingers brushed his lips as Jax slid the gum into his mouth. Dare lost his breath as his heart pounded crazily.

"Oh dear God," he said faintly. "*You* are going to be the death of me."

"Funny, someone else said that to me recently." Jax sat back in the seat, seeming pleased with himself. Dare felt an irrational flare of jealousy flood his body. He hoped it hadn't been another potential boyfriend.

The rest of the drive passed in companionable silence, and Dare was grateful for that. When they got to the restaurant and parked the car in the small, crowded car park, Jax was out of the car before Dare could come around and open it. He laughed softly to himself.

Together they made their way across the brightly lit courtyard and into the warmth of the venue. Dare had asked for a quiet, private area so they could talk undisturbed as they got to know each other. When they were shown to a small, cosy table for two in the dimly lit recess of the restaurant, he couldn't help noticing Jax's fleeting look of disappointment. It was swiftly gone and Dare wondered what was wrong.

The waiter seated them with an elegant wave of his hand and a practiced smile and procured the drinks menu. He left them in peace with the quiet assurance he'd be back in a few minutes to take their order.

Jax didn't look at his menu. "I know what I'm having to drink," he said softly. "A glass of white wine, whatever the house one is, will be fine for me." He drew out a pair of burgundy spectacles and put them on his nose. Dare wanted to eat him up at the cuteness of it, though at the same time a wave of guilt flushed over him. He hadn't thought about Jax possibly not being able to see all that well in the dim light.

"Sorry, Jax." Dare reached over and touched Jax's arm. "I didn't think you might need more light to see the menu. Would you like to move somewhere brighter?"

Jax looked up, his gaze guarded. "I'm fine." He looked down at his menu again.

Dare shook his head. "No, you're not. Something's wrong. Tell me what it is."

Jax swallowed and looked up with such a vulnerable expression it made Dare want to fold him in his arms and kiss the hurt away.

"I thought"—Jax took a deep breath—"I thought maybe you wanted us to sit here out of the way in the dark because you don't really want to be seen with me like this." He waved a hand at his face. "But it's fine if we sit here. I don't mind—"

Dare had heard enough. With a low snarl, he stood up, marched round to Jax and then crouched down beside him. Aware that some of the other diners looked on curiously, he ignored them as Jax stared down in surprise and with some trepidation.

"I'm only going to say this once." Dare laid a hand on Jax's thigh to steady himself. "I sat us here because I wanted somewhere quiet to have you to myself. I didn't want to share you tonight. And let me tell you, Dylan O'Brien himself could walk through that door right now and I wouldn't give a fig because I'm with you, the most gorgeous man in this restaurant tonight. No bullshit, just the truth. So stop thinking you have nothing to offer because in my eyes, you have everything anyone could want."

He stood up, leaned down and pressed a soft kiss to the top of Jax's head then went back to his seat. The woman at the next table threw him a warm smile. Jax shuffled in his seat but Dare saw the dawning joy cross his pale face.

"Okay," Jax murmured with a pleased smile. "I get it. Stop the whole being insecure thing and enjoy the evening."

Dare nodded. "You got it." He perused his menu. "You decided what you fancy to eat yet?"

They took their time to decide and when the waiter appeared, they passed on their order and he swished away again.

"So." Jax leaned across the table, a grin on his face. "You have a thing for Dylan O'Brien? You like the cute guy with glasses look? You seem to have a type."

Dare shrugged. "I do, a bit. Not always though. I'm an equal-opportunity man. I like my men in all sorts of shapes and sizes."

"Uh-huh. Equal opportunity, hey? Does that apply to anything else? Like, in the bedroom." Jax's expression looked positively devilish in the soft light.

And we're back to flirting and driving me crazy.

"Depends on the guy. I've been known to indulge in a lot of things."

Jax's tongue came out and he licked his lips. Dare's good intentions were diminishing with each passing minute under the sultry gaze levelled at him. Jax might have damaged eyes but he managed to use them well enough to convey his intent.

"Have you been single long?" The question was innocently asked but Dare had no doubt it was said so Jax could satisfy himself that he wasn't involved with anyone else.

"A couple of months. I got rid of my last boyfriend because he cheated."

"Oh, that sucks. Bastard." Jax made a face as if he'd bitten into a lemon. "I hate it when someone thinks they can do that and destroy people's lives."

"Has anyone ever done that to you? You sound as if you have some personal experience." Dare asked. The waiter arrived with their drinks and they stayed silent while he put them on the table then left.

Jax sat back in his chair and fiddled with his napkin. The sexy, teasing man had disappeared. "No, not me. I've never had a boyfriend or anything like that. My comment was directed more at my parents' relationship. My dad was seeing a woman behind her husband's back after my mum died. This woman finally left the guy to marry my father. Her ex-husband fell apart and went through a bad time. I didn't really approve of the underhandedness of their affair, but it was my dad. I couldn't really tell him what to do." Jax shrugged. "Sylvia and I never really got on." His expression shadowed and he took his glasses off, as if he'd remembered he'd had them on, and laid them on the table.

Dare sat forward and took Jax's hand in his. "You said it was your stepbrother who attacked you—was that her son?"

Jax was silent for a few long moments. When he spoke it was weary resignation. "Yes. Terry was eighteen when it all went down, but he'd never liked me. He was a bully and enjoyed picking on me. Dad was so busy travelling, he wasn't around much to see it." He took a healthy sip of his wine. "Then it all went to shit, and Dad died a couple of months later when I was in hospital. My stepmother sold up and left for God knows where and Terry was in jail so I was on my own. I went to live with Randy and Jen at Castaways. I met Randy at the hospital and really liked him and what he was doing. They offered me a place to stay while I completed my studies and I took it."

Dare marvelled that there was no bitterness in Jax's voice, merely a matter-of-factness unusual in someone only eighteen years old. Jax had experienced so much tragedy in his life, came out of it an orphan and yet still shone like a beacon.

Dare's thumb stroked slow circles on Jax's hand. "I'm not even going to say anything trite about all the stuff you just unloaded. My life hasn't been perfect but shit, it's a picnic compared to what you've been through. What about your friends? Where were they when all this went down?"

Jax fiddled with some spilt salt on the table. "I had a few, but when it all happened, they kind of dropped off my social calendar." He gave a short, sharp laugh. "My then-best friend Dane moved to Dorset with his family, and the other guys I knew from school didn't bother coming around much. We just lost touch.

"Tell me about yourself." Jax closed his hand over Dare's. "Who is Dare? Is that your real name?"

At that moment their food arrived, and once again they waited until the waiter left. Dare tucked into his medium-rare rib eye steak while Jax ate his fillet covered with pepper sauce.

"My full name is Kildare, so everyone calls me Dare. Kildare Patrick Rowan. I was born here in England as was my mum. Da's Irish, though. A fourth-generation Traveller, maybe more. He came over here as a boy and he's been here in England ever since. He met my mum when he was thirteen and that was it for him, he says. It was love at first sight."

Jax's voice was wistful. "That's a cool story. I like romantic endings." He smiled. "So what kind of job do you have?"

Dare swallowed a mouthful of steak. "I manage a sweet shop. It's called Bon Bon Bizarre. I enjoy it. It's a great place to work."

Jax blinked. "A sweet shop? That's different." He put his knife and fork down and stared at Dare in apparent fascination. "Is it, like, a huge chain store?"

Dare shook his head. "No, it's a tiny, old-fashioned store in Swiss Cottage run by my boss Sally, who's a character and a half. I live in the flat above the shop and manage the front of store, the takings, the health and safety inspections, managing stock, all the running of the shop really. Sally does the counter work too but it's tough on her. She has arthritis in her knees so she does the books and all the marketing stuff rather than standing around."

Jax's tone grew sly. "You sell lollipops, gobstoppers, all sorts of sucking sweets then? I'll have to buy some. I'm a real fan of sucking things."

Dare groaned at the image of those beautiful pink lips pursed around his cock. "God, you never give up trying to get me going, do you? I thought you said you'd never had a boyfriend—"

He stopped at Jax's stricken expression.

I am so fucking stupid. Way to point out that the guy's inexperienced and make him feel a fool.

Jax's face was set. "No, I'm afraid I haven't. But I've practiced on a dildo before. Does that count?" He didn't let Dare apologise. "I haven't exactly had many opportunities to suck *real* guys off, but I'm pretty sure I'd like it if I did." He looked down at the table, his fingers nervously tracing patterns he probably couldn't see on the tablecloth amidst the flickering tea light shadows.

Dare's stomach roiled with regret. "I didn't mean anything by that remark. I'm sorry it upset you."

Jax said nothing, just kept tracing circles with shaking fingers.

Dare reached over and stilled that trembling hand. "I *love* the fact you're new to all this. It's such a privilege for me to be here with you, for you to trust me. I want this date to be special. Can we just get back to trading stories about each other? I'll even tell you the one about the time I threw up on the London Eye, and the time Sally had to rescue me from a spider. I'm not fond of spiders, by the way, so you'll need to be the tough one in this relationship and catch them for me. I do nothing but scream like a girl if I see one."

His confessional spew seemed to be having the desired result; Jax was smiling faintly, his fingers under Dare's reaching out to trace a slow lick of flame down the inside of his wrist.

A few seconds passed before Jax spoke again. "So you're a big scaredy-cat when it comes to spiders? You'd never tell that from looking at you. You're so…big. And brawny."

Jax removed his hands from Dare's and lifted his wine glass to take another sip.

Dare sat back. "So I'm told. But a spider could kick my arse any day. It's a childhood phobia—but not started by spiders." He took a slurp of his beer as Jax gazed at him in interest, waiting for the rest of the story.

"I was born in Cornwall and there were these caves down by the sea that me and my friends played hide and seek in. One day I was trying to hide and my leg got trapped. My friends ran for help but while I was stuck in the sand, these little sand crabs came out and crawled all over me. There were dozens of them." He shivered, remembering the scrape of crab claws and their slow, deliberate moves across his skin.

"To this day anything like a crab, a spider, a beetle, freaks me out. I can't stand the feel of their legs on my skin."

Jax raised his wine glass towards Dare and pushed his now empty plate to one side. "Good to know. Message to self. Don't ever let crawly things come anywhere near Kildare Patrick Rowan." He laughed self-deprecatingly. "Not that I'd be able to see them much, so you might have to keep a good watch out for yourself."

Dare leaned forward, his curiosity piqued. "Just how well do you see?" he asked softly. "What does the world look like to Jackson Grady?"

Jax toyed with the stem of his wine glass. "Like I'm seeing things through a slight heat haze." He stared down at the table. "When Terry threw the chemicals in my face, my eyes were closed. But of course having corrosive liquid tossed in your face makes you open them."

He fell silent and Dare waited, fury rising in his chest at what had happened. "The stuff hit my eyes and burned them. I was lucky; my eyelids protected my eyes from the initial splash. Our housekeeper at the time found me and washed my eyes out with milk. That helped minimise the damage. I was lucky, actually. It could have been worse." He shrugged and sipped his wine. "I function like an extremely short-sighted person most of the time, with help. It just takes me more effort. And there *are* some things that I can't do anymore."

Dare wanted to pull Jax close and never let him go.

Jax cleared his throat. "I've gotten used to it. I see better close up, and it helps if I do this." Jax lifted his chin and his blue eyes narrowed and focused on Dare. "But further out, it's a bit of a blur, and I need to concentrate and focus harder."

"And your glasses help?" Dare gestured to the spectacles lying on the table.

"They help reduce glare, make things a little better vision-wise when I need to see further. I have prescription sunglasses when I'm out in the open. My eyes get tired easily. I have to be careful not to strain them too much." Jax sighed heavily.

"It's why Randy and Jen keep such a close eye on me when I study. I do a mix of sight work and NVDA—visual desktop assistance where stuff gets spoken out, like my mobile over there does with messages and stuff." He motioned to his phone lying on the table. "So I don't damage my eyes more. I don't really need the Braille stuff, although I've been taught a bit because there's always the chance I could still go completely blind." His voice quavered a little, and Dare's heart broke.

Jax ran a hand through his hair, leaving it mussed. "I just want to be normal sometimes, you know? Not have to think about how I read, how much TV to watch. I used to play computer games. I don't anymore. The movements and flickers of colour hurt my eyes. Films at the cinema tax my eyes a bit too much."

"You listen to audio books? Radio programmes then?" Dare would buy a whole library of audio books if it made Jax happy.

Jax nodded. "Yeah, *anything* I can do that doesn't mean taxing my vision, I do. I don't want a white stick and a guide dog, so I have to look after my eyes. Even though it pisses me off." He made an adorable moue and it took all Dare's powers of resistance not to move to his side, pull him up and kiss him.

"What are you studying?" Dare's flawed angel was amazing; studying even when he couldn't see properly.

Jax leaned over eagerly. "My A levels in psychology through distance learning. It's how I got my GCSEs. I chose this course of study because one day I want to open my own counselling halfway house and help abused kids like the ones at Castaways."

Dare was impressed but felt inadequate. The closest he'd ever got to studying had been in secondary school, which he'd left when he was sixteen with a few *meh* GCSEs and nothing else. It made him feel small, knowing Jax was doing all this with a visual impairment to boot.

Dare loved his work at the sweet shop but it wasn't quite the same as Jax's future plans.

"You have quite an ambition there," Dare said. "That's a big goal, and a costly one. But I have no doubt you'll do it. You're incredible."

Jax's face flushed and he smiled. "Thanks. It's a long way away, but I have a plan to make it happen when I'm twenty-one. So I have time still."

Dare wondered what the significance of being twenty-one was. He didn't get a chance to ask because the waiter arrived to take away their empty plates and give them the dessert menu. They declined desserts, asking for coffees instead.

The rest of the evening passed in pleasant getting-to-know-you conversation, the typical give and take of anecdotal information that helped them to learn a little more about each other. Dare now knew Jax was extremely partial to piano music, having played when he was younger, that he had a friend who was into graffiti and that Jax had a thing for Ryan Reynolds. Well, who wouldn't?

Dare didn't want the evening to end. He didn't want to go home to an empty flat, and he didn't want to leave Jax.

Over coffee, Jax had gotten even more daring in his flirting and Dare didn't think his poor dick could last much longer. Especially when Jax's foot had somehow found its way up Dare's inner thigh and began to artfully stroke. Up and down. A little further up then down. He had carefully but deliberately crossed his legs, alleviating the delightful but torturous friction. Jax had flashed a wicked grin, holding all sorts of promise.

Oh, how Dare wanted so much more, but tonight wasn't the time to get it.

From early in the evening, he'd had no doubt what Jax's expectations were, and Dare wasn't quite sure how to let his date down without a fight, or destroying his confidence. He knew he was in a pickle but he was determined to stick to his guns. Jax needed nurturing into the relationship, and sex was something that would have to wait for a while or as long as Dare could hold out, which he guessed wryly wouldn't be long.

Chapter 7

After dinner they sat in the car, their bodies' warmth and their somewhat laboured breathing misting the inside of the windows. When Dare reached out to turn the key in the ignition, Jax laid a hand on his arm. "Don't. Not yet." His husky voice held a faint tremor.

Dare stared at him in the darkness and swallowed. "Why not?"

Blemished eyes stared into Dare's soul. "Because I want you to kiss me first. Full on, like we're in a porn film." Jax leaned closer, his plump, wet lips parting slightly. He removed his glasses and put them in his jacket pocket.

Dare squirmed, his groin inflamed with want and need. "Jax, I want to take this slow. I don't want to fuck up anything we might have going. I want more of this."

Jax nodded with hooded eyes. "Me too. And just to make things crystal clear before we go any further—a meeting of your dick and my arse? Not going to happen. Maybe never. But I know there are other things we can do. Kissing is one of them." He reached up a warm hand to cup Dare's jaw. "So kiss me. Please."

Dare's spirits lifted. To be honest, anal sex wasn't something he'd participated in too often, even though he enjoyed it. He could live without it. Hearing Jax be so definite about how he thought things might play out took some of the pressure off. And fuck yes, Dare could kiss this wanting man, and show him what it felt like to be desired for the first time in his life.

He shifted closer and took Jax's face in his hands. He bent his head and, as their lips touched, magic sparked.

Jax tasted of coffee and something spicy, no doubt the pepper sauce he'd eaten earlier, and his mouth was eager, searching, his lips opening beneath Dare's, allowing him access.

Beneath closed eyes, Dare heard moaning. He deftly slid his tongue against Jax's questing one, holding back from eating Jax alive in a sexual kissing frenzy. Dare wanted to devour the man in his arms, consume him piece by piece until nothing was left. Jax's small gasps of pleasure turned him on beyond what he could bear as the other man's hands reached out to Dare's waist and gripped him fiercely, pulling him closer.

Jax was warmth and light and the scent of Dare's possible future. Dare knew he was being stupid—he'd only just barely gotten to know the man behind the fantasy—but something in his soul accepted that this was exactly the way it was supposed to be. Which both exhilarated and terrified him. Jax was only just beginning to find his sexuality and might not want him forever.

And Jax might need more than Dare could ever offer.

When Dare pulled away, reluctant but needing to breathe, Jax moaned. "Where are you going? I haven't finished with you yet." He reached out his strong hands to draw Dare closer and Dare shook his head with a breathy chuckle.

"Take it easy, Mr Ravenous. I needed to draw breath. Look at the car. The windows are all fogged up. A copper will be stopping soon and rapping on the window to tell us to move on." He meant it as a joke so when at that exact moment there was a rap on Dare's window, they both gasped with horror, holding their breath and staring wide eyed at each other.

"You think that's the police?" Jax squeaked, face creased in panic. "Oh God, are we going to be arrested?"

"No, not arrested." Dare muttered. "It's a damn restaurant car park. They can't do that." He hoped he was right. He opened his window and stared out at the grinning face of a young woman, in her late twenties, with pink and green hair.

"Hi there! I'm sorry to be so rude, but we've just arrived here, and my girlfriend and I can't find parking. I saw you get into the car." She smiled wickedly. "Then the windows started steaming up. Monica dared me to come over here and find out whether you intended leaving so we could have your space or whether you were, like, going to rock the universe some more. In which case we'll drive around the block again and try and find somewhere else to park." She giggled.

Dare was speechless. He was about to open his mouth when Jax leaned over and stared out of the window with a smirk on his face.

"I guess we could take this elsewhere," he said. His hand squeezed Dare's thigh. "I can take him home and have my way with him, I guess."

"God, you two are damn cute. My name's Rachel, by the way." She waved a hand over to a VW Beetle idling further down the car park. "Give us a minute, Mon, they're going now," she shouted out. A headlight flashed in return.

"Pleased to meet you, Rachel," Dare said faintly. "Um, okay, we'll get going so you and your girlfriend can park. Enjoy your dinner."

Rachel nodded. "Sure will. And you two enjoy the rest of your evening." The smirk on her face left Dare in no doubt as to what she expected them to be doing later.

Face flushing, Dare started the car and reversed out as Rachel waved goodbye to them.

Jax laughed loudly. "That was classic. She had no shame, did she? I mean, what if we'd been naked and getting it on right here in the car? Would you have opened the window then?"

Dare frowned. "Of course not. I would have made sure we were decent before then."

"So, where are we going now then? I seem to have a problem that I think we should take care of. I hope you do too." Jax tried for teasing but Dare heard the undercurrent of uncertainty in his voice.

"I'm taking you home," Dare murmured.

God, I want to throw you down on a bed, kiss you from head to toe and show you everything *there is to know about being with a man. Everything. But I need to pace this, so I don't scare you off.*

Jax's face darkened. "I'm not a fucking child. I think I can cope with more than what we've done tonight."

Dare sighed. "You think I want to stop this here? God, you have no bloody idea what I want to do to you." He manoeuvred around a slow car and drove a little faster as the traffic thinned.

"Then do it." Jax's tone was steel. He sat staring ahead, lips thinned. "I'm not fragile. I'm not going to break."

Dare swallowed. "I know you're tough. I just want it to be special."

Jax softened. "It *is* special, to me. Tonight was amazing. Having someone take me out, kiss me like you did—it was awesome. More than awesome. Mind blowing." Jax huffed. "So what now? I go home with a huge boner and beat off in bed or the shower, like usual? Is that the plan?" He was like a sulky kid.

Dare couldn't help snorting with amusement. "That's *my* plan for tonight. It's our first date. Let's not rush it."

Jax sat in stony silence on the drive home. Dare tried to make conversation but all he got were monosyllabic replies and grunts. He sighed. He remembered how he'd been at that age, horny and hormonal, so he could sympathise with Jax.

When they reached Castaways, Dare got out of the car to open his door. By the time he'd got around to the passenger side, Jax had already climbed out and stood hugging himself as he glared mutinously from underneath the dim street light.

Dare would have laughed at the sight if he hadn't thought it would get him a thump, or a kick to the groin. "Well, I had a great time," he said. "Thank you for coming to dinner with me."

Jax snorted. "I had a good time too, I s'pose."

The petulance in his tone once again made Dare want to grin. Instead he stilled his face and continued to stare, noting the flush that crossed Jax's cheeks at the scrutiny.

"Thanks for buying me dinner. I still think you should come inside and we should finish this." Jax waved at his groin. Dare glanced down and smiled at the hard evidence he saw pushing against Jax's tight trousers.

"No doubt," Dare remarked softly. "And it's not because I don't want to, I promise. But I don't want to be that first-date-bonk-guy with you."

"God save me from the ethics of a gentleman," Jax muttered under his breath. "Fine. But you need to know I'm going to be thinking of you when I'm jacking off later."

It was Dare's turn to snort. "Ditto. I'll be doing the same." He followed Jax up the steps to the front door, waiting to see him safely in. At the door, he hesitated. "Are you going to punch me if I try and kiss you goodnight?"

Jax's face grew still. "I'd bloody well punch you if you didn't," he growled and reached out to pull Dare's lips down to his waiting ones.

Dare fell under Jax's spell even more at the touch of that fevered, hungry mouth against his and the tongue that pushed its eager way inside his mouth. He grasped Jax's backside, pulling them closer as they made out. When things got too hot to handle, and Dare was in danger of coming in his pants, he pulled away, lips sore and still feeling Jax's urgent need on his mouth.

"I don't think I can take much more of that without making a fool of myself," Dare said huskily. From the look on Jax's face, he felt the same. His beautiful face was dazed, eyes hooded and lips swollen and wet.

"'Night, Jax. Sweet dreams. I'll call you tomorrow, and maybe we can make a plan for another date?"

Jax nodded. "'Kay. Night, Dare. Thanks again for the night out." A brief smile crossed his face then he slotted his front door key into the lock, opened the door and vanished inside.

Dare stood there, eyes closed, breathing in the residual fragrance of the man he wanted more than anyone else in his life.

Chapter 8

Wednesday, Jax had navigated his way to the sweet shop to visit Dare and have lunch with his irresistible hunk. It had been a few days since their last date and Jax couldn't wait to inhale Dare's scent. To feel those skilful lips brushing over his waiting mouth. To enjoy the grip of those strong hands when they grabbed Jax's hips.

These thoughts had consumed Jax's every waking moment.

They'd seen each other a few time times since their first date, talked on the phone, texted, but it was never enough.

In the days in between, somehow Jax had gotten in a bit of studying, but truly, his mind drifted to Dare every third moment. Those fathomless blue eyes, that unruly tug-on-me hair, those incredibly broad shoulders…Yeah, Jax was totally crushing on Dare.

Standing in the overstocked store, Jax recalled the sweet shops he'd been in when he was younger. He'd spent time choosing a carefully selected item with his parents or running into a favourite shop to spend the last bit of his pocket money.

They'd been special places where a boy could marvel at the colours of gumballs on display, or gaze wide-eyed at the treasure on offer behind glass cabinets. As he'd grown older, the enchantment had evaporated and his sweet shop of old had been replaced by the latest mobile phone shop, or funky fashion store.

Watching Dare at work in the oddly named shop called Bon Bon Bizarre, Jax felt some of the old childhood magic returning. The shop was an eclectic collection of everything he remembered as a lad, looking for all the world like something out of a fairy tale. It was the epitome of a child's imagination of a sweet shop: bright, quirky and filled with colour.

Jax squinted closely at labels on glass jars as his eyes tried to make out scrawling, chaotic text like something with legs had been dipped in ink and then journeyed across a white label.

"Acid Wriggle Worms," he finally pronounced. He snorted in laughter. "Aptly named. Who the hell writes these labels anyway? It's worse than my doctor's writing, all wiggly and uneven."

Dare chuckled, his deep baritone rumbling down from his perch high up on a ladder, where he removed jars off the shelf to dust. "That's Sally's. I can't read it either half the time. I'm surprised the kids can, but they seem to have this knack of it."

Jax tilted his head as far back as he could to get a better view of the man on the ladder in front of him. Jax watched in appreciation as Dare stretched up to pluck a dusty box off the top shelf, his painted-on jeans tightening around his perfect arse, giving Jax an extremely pleasant and tantalising view. The man had a backside tight enough to bounce gumballs off. And those legs: strong, muscled thighs led down to shaped calves.

Dare wiped down the shelves then lovingly restored the box to its rightful place. Jax bit back a smile at the deference with which Dare treated both the shop and its contents. He seemed comfortable here, a man at ease among the trappings of childhood and fantasy. He was respectful to the customers, treating them all as if they were all gold.

There had been one special-needs child in the shop who'd taken close to half an hour to choose a tube of sherbet. Dare had waited patiently, helping the boy with his choices, and when he had finally decided, Dare had wrapped it in a shiny packet and presented it as if the jewels of the Orient had been in there.

Having managed a lot of distressed and needy children at Castaways, Jax lost a little piece of his heart when he saw the deference and care Dare had employed with the child. Actually, the losing-the-heart thing happened each time Jax saw Dare in action.

Two giggling young ladies in their mid-teens came into the shop—again. It was the third time they'd cruised through since Jax had been there. They cast sly, admiring glances up at Dare on the ladder, which caused Jax to scowl fiercely.

"Hi Dare," one of them called out, drawling his name. Spidery eyelashes fluttered with practiced perfection. Jax wanted to snarl at the sex kittens to leave his man alone.

"Hi again, Nadia, hi Lacey. Back for more?" Dare grinned. One of them glanced at Jax sympathetically—she'd done the same thing the previous times she and her friend had come in and he'd ignored it—then she simpered up at Dare.

"Yes, you can never have enough Sucky Sour Sizzlers," she giggled as her friend busied herself picking up boxes of various sorts from the cabinet. They were placed on the counter and then both girls waited expectantly for Dare to dismount the ladder and go behind the till.

Sucky Sour Sizzlers? Really? That was her angle?

Jax huffed angrily as Dare charmed the pants off them once again and gave them a cheeky smile. The girl closest to Jax—it wasn't hard for her to be very near, given the compact nature of the shop—hadn't stopped stealing glances at him and finally he'd had enough. He wasn't a fucking one-man freak show.

"What?" he snapped. "Do I have something on my face?"

Her mouth opened and she fidgeted uncomfortably. "Oh no, I'm sorry. It's nothing, honestly."

"Then stop staring at me," he said through gritted teeth.

"Jax," Dare said gently. "I'm sure Nadia wasn't being rude. Calm down, baby."

The two girls swung their heads towards Dare so fast Jax thought they'd given themselves whiplash. His immediate reaction was a flash of sly satisfaction at the fact Dare had said such a thing in front of them.

"Wait, are you two, like, boyfriends?" one of them—Lacey, Jax presumed—squealed loudly. Jax winced at the high-pitched sound as he waited for Dare to answer. After all, he'd started it by being so damn nice to them.

Dare darted a glance at Jax and swallowed. Jax raised an eyebrow in his direction. In truth, he was as nervous as all hell for the answer.

"Uhm, yes, we're sort of seeing each other," Dare managed weakly.

"Oh my God." Nadia fanned herself with her hand. "Why the hell are all the cute ones gay?"

Jax rolled his eyes. As if he hadn't heard *that* one before. There should be a pop song written called "The Straight Girl Mantra." He knew he was being a bitch but Nadia staring at his damaged face had really pissed him off.

Dare grinned, seeming a bit surer of himself now. "I have the cutest one in the box."

As cheesy as that sounded, Jax liked it. He sauntered over to Dare and placed a hard, possessive kiss on his lips. "No, *I* do," he said and flicked a triumphant stare at the two girls. Beside him, Dare laughed softly.

"Am I running a social circle here, young man?" A woman's voice interrupted the standoff. "Dare, am I paying you to flirt with the customers and make out with your boyfriend?"

Jax panicked, swivelling around to see the short, tubby form of a woman standing behind him. She'd obviously snuck in through the back. He was nervous at the idea of meeting Dare's boss, as that was no doubt who this brightly dressed woman was.

Dare laughed loudly. "No, ma'am, you do not." He wiggled his eyebrows at the two girls. "Ladies, if that's all, then I need to get back to work before Boss Lady Sally here helps me sing soprano."

"Damn right, honey," Sally muttered. "I'm in the mood to squeeze *something*. Have we got a stress ball handy?"

Dare reached under the counter and tossed a green rubber ball to Sally, who caught it deftly. "Here you go. What's rattled your cage?"

Nadia and Lacey threw a startled glance at Sally, who smiled politely back. They left the shop with a backwards longing stare at Dare, who waved cheerily at them.

Sally sidled up to Jax and peered at him from beneath gold-rimmed spectacles. "I see you have a stunner here, Dare," she said approvingly. "Every bit as handsome as you said he was."

Jax felt his cheeks blush beet red. 'Stunner' wasn't any way he'd ever describe himself. Sally hadn't even commented on his scars, or ruined eyes.

Sally chortled. "Oh would you look at that. The man is adorably shy." She reached out a soft hand. "Sally Busby, my love, owner of this establishment. Pleased to meet you at last. You're a real improvement on the last one." She sniffed.

Jax shook her hand. "Jackson Grady," he blurted out. "Nice to meet you too."

Dare loomed protectively over Jax, his hip almost touching his. "So why are you in such a mood?" Dare enquired of his boss.

Sally huffed and opened the till. She took out a few notes and Jax turned to look at Dare as he puffed out an irritated sigh.

"Bloody husband is driving me crazy. He decided this morning he wanted to adopt another dog without even telling me. So now I have something that looks as if it would fit through the eye of a needle, it's so damn skinny. It's a whippet." She grimaced. "I'm not fond of them but Christopher insists if he hadn't rescued it today it would have been put down."

Jax wondered why Dare was staring fiercely at his boss.

Sally noticed and rolled brown eyes. "Oh for God's sake, you are such a damn brute."

Jax watched in confusion as she scribbled on the back of someone's old receipt and opened the till to pop it inside.

"There. Happier?" she growled.

Dare nodded. "Much." He flashed a smile at Jax. "Sal has this habit of forgetting to leave me a note when she takes money out of the till. Then it takes me forever to balance the damn thing."

Jax nodded. "Oh. I see." He turned to Sally. "You must trust him a lot to do that." He cleared his throat. "I mean, not that he's untrustworthy or anything, but money management is really important, and this is your business…" He tailed off, aware that he was floundering a bit.

Sally's face softened. "He's been with me a long time, and I trust your young man with my business. Dare has been a wonderful asset to me."

Now it was Dare's turn to be embarrassed. Jax stared, fascinated. He hadn't thought Dare could get flustered. His sexy 'boyfriend' seemed at a loss for words.

"I'm not, really, I mean, I like it here, so I do my best."

Sally patted his cheek. "You do a sterling job, darling. Now let me leave you to get on with things. I have some work to do in the office, so if you need me, that's where I'll be." She turned to Jax. "Lovely to meet you, Jackson. You look after my young employee here, and treat him well, and we'll always stay friends."

She winked and bustled off into the back room.

Dare reached out and pulled Jax into his arms, burying his face in Jax's hair. "She's gone," he murmured softly. "So I can kiss you properly now, to say thank you for protecting my virtue from those two harpies."

Jax opened his mouth to say that if the irresistible hunk hadn't flirted with them, he wouldn't have had to be such a bitch. His mouth couldn't form the words, though, as Dare's tongue greedily invaded it. Jax closed his eyes, relishing the velvet feel and the taste of toffee.

When he was released, Jax stepped back and fingered Dare's jaw. "Why did she say I was an improvement on the last?" He was feeling rather narked at the thought that Dare had had someone else special in his life before Jax. He snickered a bit at that thought. Before Jax equated to BJ.

Dare sighed. "His name was Michael Cowan. He's the cheater I told you about at dinner. We were together six months. I split up with him when I found out he was married. To a woman."

Jax's eyes bugged out. "No way," he exclaimed. "A woman? What the hell was he playing at?"

"He liked to play both sides of the street, but neglected to tell me about the whole I'm-married thing," Dare said grimly. "I only found out because one day flowers arrived at my flat from him addressed to Ginny. There'd been a mix-up at his florist with the address."

"Oh my God, so you kicked him out of your life?" Jax was happy cheating Michael wasn't around, but his tender heart hurt at the thought Dare had been cuckolded like that.

"I did, but not before I decked him one." He smirked. "I haven't seen him since." Dare reached out and pulled Jax into his arms. "Enough about that piece of crap. I have you now, and you are *so* much better in every way."

He lowered his mouth for a kiss.

Jax thought dreamily that he could stand here all afternoon doing this. In Dare's arms, in a sweet shop smelling of vanilla, spice and banana, and with Dare's hard body pressing against his, causing Jax's skin to tingle and his groin to ache pleasantly.

This was worth his interminable waiting for that someone he'd dreamed about. He only hoped it would last a little bit longer and lead to more than they'd done so far. The thought of being completely naked and doing more daring things with the man of his dreams was the cherry at the top of Jax's fantasy-filled milkshake.

A cherry that definitely needing popping.

Chapter 9

Three days later, Jax was more than ready to fulfil some of his fantasies. He had butterflies in his belly, sweaty palms and a dry mouth and he wondered if everyone felt this way when they were waiting to see what the night would bring with a prospective lover.

It was the first time he'd been in Dare's flat above the shop. He navigated his way around the small room, which had an eclectic mix of décor. Mismatched cushions were sprawled across the beige fabric couch, their autumn colours giving a warmth to the room. On one wall was a simple print of a seascape, on another the picture of two horses grazing in a green field. It was comfortable and welcoming and Jax instantly felt at home despite his nervousness.

The flat was open plan, with a small kitchen leading off the lounge. The kitchen held an impressive assortment of gadgets and implements. It looked like Dare enjoyed cooking and that boded well since Jax wasn't a great chef. To the left, a closed door led to Dare's bedroom, where he had gone to change out of his work clothes.

Trying to distract himself from the vision of a half-dressed Dare, Jax picked up a small wooden box on the side table, marvelling at the intricate detail of the carving. He wasn't usually so nosy but the box intrigued him. He opened it to find a battered silver coin nestled in faded blue velvet.

He heard the bedroom door open and hastily put the box down. His butterflies increased a thousand-fold when Dare came out of the bedroom and leaned in to kiss him softly on the cheek.

"Sorry I was so long," Dare murmured. "I wanted to look good for you."

"Oh my God," Jax said faintly as his cock plumped and his groin heated up at the rate of an atomic explosion.

Dare was one gorgeous man. He wore a dark blue cut-off tee with 'Beast Mode' emblazoned in white on the front. It hugged his broad, sculpted torso, and just met a pair of black, skin-tight jeans.

It was the tattoos that made Jax salivate, now revealed in all their glory. He'd only ever seen occasional glimpses of them as Dare mostly wore long sleeves in the shop. He'd said he felt uncomfortable showing his ink in Sally's place of business.

Dare's muscled right bicep bore the winding tattoo of a black panther; its tail wound around his upper arm like a bracelet, its head taking up most of his forearm. His other forearm was similarly marked with a grey salamander in a similar position; its flicking tongue encircled his wrist.

Dare grinned. "You like my tats then?" He flexed his arm, making the panther move sinuously and Jax thought he'd come right there on the spot.

"Uhmm, yes," he managed to get out. "But I want to know what the ones look like underneath."

Dare's eyes darkened. "You'll find out later," he promised with a wink.

Jax swallowed. "How much later?"

Dare cupped Jax's chin with a warm hand. "After we've eaten. I thought we'd have pizza."

"I don't want anything to eat. I want you." Jax moved over to Dare and slid his hands under Dare's tee shirt. "I think I've waited long enough to see those tattoos."

Dare stopped Jax going any further. "Patience," he murmured. "I'm hungry. I haven't eaten much today."

Jax was instantly mortified. "Sorry," he stammered. "I'm being selfish. I ate earlier so I didn't think—"

Dare placed a soft finger across his mouth. "It's fine. Don't worry about it. I ordered already." He raised one eyebrow. "You're a fan of pepperoni, right? I got that and a Hawaiian. I love pineapple. They'll be here in about thirty minutes."

He moved away into the kitchen. "Do you want something to drink? A beer, a soft drink?"

Jax shook his head. He was too wound up to drink anything and alcohol would just dull his senses. He was a lightweight when it came to booze. "Naw, I'm okay, thanks. You go ahead, though."

Dare gestured towards the couch. "Sit. Make yourself comfortable." He went to the fridge and took out a beer, popping the cap and taking a long, satisfied gulp, his Adam's apple bobbing as he drank.

Jax sat down at one end of the couch, watching something typically mundane become a full-blown sensuous act. He wanted to lick down that expanse of flesh, trace it with his tongue and place quick butterfly kisses on Dare's skin. He wanted it so badly, and he wanted it now.

A sudden thought made him panic.

On every date Dare keeps putting me off. Perhaps he doesn't want me after all. Perhaps what I have on offer isn't enough for him and he just wants to be friends.

His face must have given away his musings because Dare frowned and sat down beside him. He put his beer down on the side table.

"Jax, you okay?"

Jax forced a smile. "Yeah. I guess I am a little hungry after all."

An hour later, the pizza was mostly devoured and Jax was surprised to see he'd had his fair share.

Dare leaned back on the couch and rubbed his stomach. "Now I'm full. You have enough?"

Jax nodded as he finished his last mouthful of pizza. Dare took the empty boxes to the kitchen then came back and sat next to him.

Jax motioned towards the little box he'd opened earlier. "That's an interesting piece. Does it have some special meaning?"

Dare smiled and picked it up. "It belonged to my Da. It was his Da's, and his Da before him. It's a silver good luck charm, which goes to the eldest son on their twenty-first birthday. It's supposed to bring a long and prosperous life." He opened it and showed Jax the coin he'd already seen. "Apparently it was a coin thrown out by some rich aristocrat all those years ago. One of the

Traveller horses drawing a cart stood on it and flattened it. My great- great-however-many Grand Da picked it up and as he did, a stone that was thrown at his head and would probably have killed him if it had hit him, missed. So it was counted as being lucky and it's been in the family ever since."

"Why did someone throw a rock at your granddad?" Jax fingered the coin, twirling it in his long fingers.

Dare shrugged. "He was a dirty gypsy in a town full of rich people. Whoever threw it was making a social statement I guess. Get out of town, you dirty varmint type of thing." His voice was even but Jax sensed a trace of bitterness.

He reached out and trailed his fingers down Dare's cheek. "Fuck those idiots who tar everyone with the same brush and judge others like that. I happen to like my beautiful Irish Traveller."

The expression that crossed Dare's face was tender and Jax thought surely no one could look at someone like that without having feelings for them.

Dare reached out and drew him into his arms, running fingers through Jax's hair. Jax snuggled into Dare's shoulder.

"This okay?" Dare asked quietly and Jax nodded, his eyes closed as he breathed in Dare's scent, revelling in warm, strong arms around him. He daren't speak; he was too full with emotion. He'd dreamt of this for too long and now that he had it he never wanted to let it go.

Dare kissed the top of Jax's head and Jax couldn't help making a sound like a cat purring. His man stilled, and Jax looked up from his comfortable snuggle.

Dare's eyes were heated, his lips parted and the look of desire on his face left Jax breathless. Slowly, Jax leaned in and traced Dare's bottom lip with his tongue. Dare tasted of beer and pineapple and sex.

This time it was Dare's turn to make a noise. It was halfway between a pant and a groan and it turned Jax on more than he'd ever imagined a sound could do.

"God, you are the sexiest creature on God's earth," Dare whispered. Then Jax couldn't think anymore as Dare's mouth plundered his, their lips grinding together as Dare pushed him back onto the couch.

Dare's hard body covered Jax's, pressing him down with his weight. His hard cock ground against Jax's, and Jax couldn't help rutting upwards, trying to find relief, anything to assuage the ache and burning need in his groin.

"Please," he whimpered into Dare's mouth. "Please touch me."

Dare's pupils were black, rimmed with thin dark blue, and he nodded. His fingers reached down and unzipped Jax's jeans. He hesitated. Jax was unwilling to simply be an inactive participant in the seduction; he needed to feel Dare's own heated flesh in his hand. Perhaps if he made the first move into virgin territory…

He unzipped Dare, reached into Dare's boxers and took his cock in hand, then watched Dare fall apart.

"God," Dare choked out. Then Jax cried out as his own cock was grasped in strong and callused fingers, and they began to jerk each other off.

Jax had no doubt he wouldn't last long. All his fantasies of having another man touch him this way, the visions of the young *Arabian Nights* lads in the film he watched as their lovers pleasured them—this was where it all led up to. Warm flesh against flesh, breath ghosting goose-pimpled skin, the scent of musk and sweat and the taste of the man currently sending him into the stratosphere.

He couldn't get enough; his libido was in overdrive, his heart filled with feelings he'd thought he'd never experience. Joy and happiness mixed to make a potent brew of emotion that welled up through the pores on his skin and into the air like fragrant, needy bubbles of satisfaction.

His fingers slid up and down the velvety steel heat that was Dare. As Jax stroked and slid his fingers over the tip of Dare's cock, Dare mirrored his movements. It was as if they worked as one, their passionate strokes of needy hands mixed with wet, greedy tongues, and nips and sucks against hot, sweaty skin promising final release.

They were made for each other, fitting together like two pieces of smooth, finely crafted wood. Like the beautiful trinket box with its precious sliver of metal encased inside.

Jax had never felt so complete in his whole life.

"Oh God, you are something," Dare panted in Jax's ear as he bucked beneath him. "I'm not going to hold out much longer. I'm gonna blow."

"Then do it," Jax whispered as he thrust his tongue into Dare's ear. "Spill into my hands, let me see what you look like when you come."

He'd never thought of himself as having the ability to talk dirty, but it seemed Dare liked it. Dare gave a guttural cry, his body shuddering as hot fluid covered Jax's hand. The feel and smell of his lover's release was *his* trigger to find his own climax, and for the first time in his life, he orgasmed in another man's hand.

It was better than he'd ever dreamt. It was euphoria and triumph mixed with a healthy dose of satisfaction.

He was definitely no longer a virgin.

They lay together on the couch in the hazy comfort of post sex, both too sated to move.

"Epic," Jax finally managed, opening half-lidded eyes to see Dare slumped dreamily beside him. "Better than I ever thought it could be."

He placed a soft kiss to Dare's swollen lips.

"I was right," Dare murmured. "You *were* worth waiting for."

Jax preened and trailed come-covered fingers through the sticky mess on Dare's stomach. Watching Dare's eyes, he raised fingers to his mouth and sucked them.

"I've never tasted another man before. I'm glad you're my first," he whispered. Dare's come was sweet mixed with a strange taste. Jax liked it. He wanted more. So he took it, revelling in the expressions of wonder and affection on Dare's face.

"God, baby, the things you say." Dare's voice was husky, and Jax loved the endearment. Another first.

"Do you realise we just had sex without taking all of our clothes off?" Jax murmured sleepily. "Next time perhaps we can get more naked."

Dare snorted softly. "My underwear is pretty sticky. Perhaps we should get cleaned up. I can loan you some clean jocks to slip into if you want." He didn't sound all that bothered about getting clean.

Jax shook his head. He knew it was stupid but he wanted to lie in his semen-laden briefs a little longer. It was a badge of honour he wore proudly.

"Maybe later," he said, his words muffled against Dare's shoulder. A sudden thought struck him and Jax sat up. "I haven't seen *all* your tattoos yet. Will you show them to me?"

Dare stood up, reached down and lifted his shirt over his head, his gaze into Jax's eyes unwavering. Jax licked his lips. The sight of Dare's naked chest was a study in beauty. Dark, curling hair on his body led down the treasure trail into jeans still unzipped, silk boxers crusted with his come.

Jax's eyes widened as Dare slid his hands down his flanks, stroking the circle of roses and thorns on his hip teasingly with his thumb. Then Dare slowly did a teasing pirouette, his tattoos and strong, muscled body spotlighted by the dim side lamp.

"Oh," Jax whispered, leaning forward, his eyes filled with wonder. In the muted light, and still suffused with the intimate moment they'd shared, the dragon tattoo with its wings outstretched as it spread across Dare's shoulders and back overwhelmed Jax.

It was a study in sensuality, Dare's body a canvas for its majesty and detail.

Jax sighed in pleasure. "My God, I'll never get tired of seeing your body. It's beautiful."

"So are you," Dare murmured as he sat back down next to Jax. "Now if I recall you said something about *both* of us getting more naked." He motioned to Jax to lift his arms and then slipped his shirt off.

The look of awe on Dare's face when he saw Jax's torso for the first time was heady. Jax wasn't muscled like him, and his skin was pale and freckled, but he was toned and didn't think he was too bad looking.

"God, baby, you are stunning," Dare breathed, his eyes drinking Jax in. "I want to taste those nipples, and map every damn freckle on your body..." His fingers traced a path around one of those nipples and Jax squirmed.

"Ooh, someone's ticklish there," Dare teased and proceeded to drive Jax crazy with his tongue. Jax lay back and let Dare worship his body any way he wanted, the same way Jax planned to do in return.

That dragon tattoo was certainly going to be thoroughly explored.

***

"That man is driving me fucking crazy." Jax threw his rucksack on his bed and moodily threw himself after it. "Two weeks we've been seeing each other and we're not much further on than we were before. What the hell is his problem?"

Jax had been studying like mad for a mock exam one of his online tutors was delivering next week. Work with the kids at Castaways took up time as well, so spare time for them both was limited. The times when the new lovers were able to get together were the hours Jax looked forward to the most. Like the recent visit to the local fair.

From his pillow, he picked up the foot-high blue and yellow Minion—'Kevin'—Dare had won at a fairground attraction a few days ago. Jax held the stuffed doll out in front of him. Kevin stared back with a goofy grin and no concern at all in his shiny eyes.

Dare had been quite the master marksman and the poor little yellow ducks slipping by at the back of the fairground stall had stood no chance against his deliberate shots.

When Dare had presented Kevin to Jax, with a low bow and a snort of laughter, at first he had been mortified. Then a group of youngsters had shouted encouragement and trilled wolf whistles, and he'd been browbeaten into accepting. Now Kevin had a place of honour on his bed. Dare had won it especially for him, and Jax had become attached to the stupid thing. Much as he was becoming attached to Dare, both emotionally and physically— although the limitations on how far they had gone worried and frustrated Jax.

Despite their seven-year age gap, Jax felt he was mature, given what he'd been through. He and Dare had shared interests in things like finding stupid things on YouTube to watch and following certain bands they both enjoyed, like Muse. They also had common goals in supporting causes trying to rid the world of prejudice and discrimination. And *finally*—Jax had found someone else who liked Marmite.

He was slowly losing his heart to Dare, and it scared him witless. He'd never experienced this sort of emotion for anyone before. It was why he'd not told Dare about his trust fund—about the pile of money waiting for him when he turned twenty-one. Jax wanted to hold Dare's interest all on his own, and while he didn't think Dare was the sort who would find the money to be his most attractive feature, he didn't want to risk it. He knew he didn't have that much to offer, but he wanted what he had *now* to be enough. Even if it was only for a short while.

An innocently beaming Kevin was the focus of his frustration for things not moving along fast enough in the sex department. Jax scowled at the toy, who stared blithely back.

"I know I said I'm not keen on the whole anal sex thing, but shit, there's other stuff we could do. He's being such a damn gentleman."

Jax contemplated punching Kevin in the face, pretending Kevin was Dare, but he decided the Minion didn't deserve that. Instead he satisfied himself by tossing Kevin down beside him. The stuffed toy fell face down on the bed. That sight made Jax even more unhappy.

"Sure, you can lay there with your arse in the air hoping he'll rim you. But will he? No way. Uggh. That man is going to kill me." He punched his pillow and laid back, hands behind his head as he stared up at the blurred white ceiling.

In his defence, he was an eighteen-year-old guy full of raging hormones, wanting to finally explore his sexuality after a damn long drought of absolutely fucking nothing. He wanted to feel Dare's mouth on his cock. Dare's tongue inside him. Feel the stroke of cock against cock, naked, sweaty, panting sex and frotting that would blow his brains out when he came.

But Dare still hadn't progressed things past mutual hand jobs. And kissing. Lots of kissing.

The thoughts being mulled over in his fevered brain were interrupted when there was a knock at his door.

"Come in," he called out, grateful for the distraction of convincing himself he wasn't even worth a blow job. There was no reply. The knock came again. Jax got off the bed and went to open it. He saw the pale face of little seven-year-old Cathy peering round the door. He beckoned her in gently.

He had an open-door policy with all the kids in the house, provided they respected his privacy and knocked first. They often dropped in to chat. He had learnt some sign language, not enough to have a proper conversation with Cathy like Randy and Jen did, but enough to communicate. Jax thought guiltily he really should do better at learning more of it. Luckily she read lips. He didn't think he'd ever heard her try to say anything.

Jax spoke slowly, making sure his lips formed the words as best he could. "Hey there, what's up? Come and sit with me a while."

He plonked himself down on one side of the bed, leaving plenty of room for Cathy to come in and park her slight body on the top of his bedspread. She sat down, her eyes immediately straying to Kevin. Her hands reached out as if to pick him up, then she hastily pulled them away, but not before Jax had seen the look of longing on her face.

He grinned at her. "My friend got that at the fair. Want to play with him?"

She regarded him with big brown eyes then nodded. Jax passed Kevin over to her and she surveyed the Minion thoughtfully.

She signed something and he sighed in frustration as he looked at her "I'm sorry, sweetie, can you do that again? It takes me time to see what you're trying to say."

She did it again and he nodded. "Yes, it was good of my friend to give it to me."

She signed again and Jax chuckled. "Oh, I see where this is going. If I'm *your* friend, I'd give Kevin to you?" The underlying reason for Cathy's visit became clear.

Cathy's eyes sparkled and she nodded eagerly.

He pretended to think about it. "Well, he is pretty special to me. I mean, you shouldn't normally give away things other people give to you as gifts."

Cathy's face fell and she hugged Kevin closer.

Jax leaned over. Cathy watched his mouth avidly. "I think my friend would understand why Kevin should be yours. You're a special little girl and I think you and Kevin would take good care of each other. You keep him, Cath. He's all yours."

At Jax's words, Cathy's face lit up. She beamed and poor Kevin got squashed between them as she bounded up onto her knees to hug Jax tightly. Little arms wrapped around his neck.

He hugged her back then chuckled. He pushed her away gently to speak. "Hey, I think Kevin is struggling to breathe. Let's check he's okay, shall we?"

Cathy nodded and offered him Kevin. Jax pretended to listen to the toy's heart, and then nodded gravely. "He's fit and healthy, little ma'am. I think he needs some garden time, along with his owner, so why don't you go show the other kids? I can hear them playing out the back."

Cathy threw him another dazzling smile and dashed out of the room. He stood up and squinted out of his window into the backyard. A few moments later, he saw Cathy's blurred figure run excitedly into the group of playing children, holding Kevin aloft like a trophy. The others gathered around her and it looked as if they were happy for her.

His mobile pinged with an incoming call. Dare.

Jax answered. "Hey. I was just thinking about you. In a totally non-sexual way of course, as we all know grown men don't do that sort of thing."

I might as well push it while I can.

Dare's chuckle made Jax's body shimmer with delight and his skin prickle.

"Is that so? Well, then, perhaps I should keep my plans for tonight to myself. God knows I'd hate to disappoint you when you're having those non-sexual thoughts."

Jax panicked.

Was tonight the night? Have I just stuffed this up for myself?

"What plans? I thought you were going to see your family tonight?"

"I was. My Da called, said he'd got some unexpected free tickets to Ripley's in the West End. Kean's been dying to go to, so Da's taking him and Mum out. I said I'd go over and see them next week instead." Dare cleared his throat. "With you, if you want to go. I think it's about time you met the menace who is my little brother. And saw where I was brought up."

Jax was speechless. "You want to take me to meet your family?" His insides glowed with warmth. He'd never been introduced to anyone's family before in this way. "Wow, okay. If you're sure."

"I'm sure. I know it's early days yet, and I don't want to scare you off. It's not so much to meet the family—more to see where I'm from. Give you some insight into the world I grew up in." Dare went silent.

Jax blinked, trying to ease one eye, which felt sticky. He hoped he wasn't getting another infection, something he was prone to. The last thing he wanted was to have a swollen, leaking eye when he met Dare tonight. "No, it'll be good to meet them and see where you lived when you were a kid yourself."

"Great." Dare sounded relieved. "So, about tonight…" The words hung in the air suggestively. "Do you fancy having takeout at my place? I'll swing by, pick you up, we can maybe listen to some music and order Chinese or something." He hesitated. "Do you want to maybe stay over?"

The loaded question hung like a balloon in the air, and Jax gulped.

Oh God, tonight was *the night.*

"Sure." He finally squeaked out then closed his eyes in mortification. "Sounds like a plan."

"I'll pick you up at seven-thirty then. See you tonight."

The line went dead, and Jax put the phone down, feeling nervous and excited. He needed to double check the internet, see what the hell he needed to do to prepare himself for every eventuality.

Whatever was about to happen, he wanted this night to be just perfect.

Chapter 10

As much as he loved pizza, listening to the rock bands Palace and Birdskulls and snuggling up to Dare on the couch, Jax loved the thought of being in his man's bed naked, with their heated bodies pressed together, much better. To this end, he cultivated his plan of the slow seduction with the same determination that had got him through multiple hospital operations and overcoming his loss of sight.

Relentless was his middle name. He knew deep in his bones there was no way Dare could resist him tonight. Truthfully, he had the sneaky feeling Dare had anticipated it. The only problem was, as much as Jax was teasing Dare, Dare was doing the same to him.

There were the soft brushes to his arm when Dare leaned over to adjust the blanket they huddled under. Brief touches of Dare's leg to his own as they shifted on the couch. Dare idly fiddling with his hair, sending skitters of shivery delight across Jax's sensitive skin. Jax trailing fingers over Dare's biceps, mapping out the tattoo, causing Dare to shudder and close his eyes in pleasure. Hell, whispering his lips against Dare's neck and bare shoulder where his shirt had pulled aside made Jax ache with pure lust.

"So, this is how it's going to be, huh?" Dare murmured as he kissed his way from the pulse in Jax's throat to the spot under his ear where Jax was über sensitive. "You're going to drive me crazy with all your seduction techniques and hope I give in?"

Jax nodded and sucked hickeys onto Dare's delicious skin, that spot on his bare shoulder where his shirt had been pulled away. Jax was proud of the fact he'd ripped Dare's shirt open with such force two of the top buttons had popped off. He loved marking his man where no one else could see but Jax.

"Uh-huh," he said, his voice muffled. "I have my wiles, you know."

"Don't I," Dare said with a soft expletive as Jax sucked harder. "You keep that up, you're going to reach bone. God, you're like a sexy blond vampire."

Jax lifted his head, staring into Dare's flushed face. "I could eat you," he whispered in what he hoped was his most sultry voice. "Suck you here…" he nipped Dare's throat, eliciting a low cry of pain, "or here." Jax moved down to open Dare's shirt further and sucked his pectoral muscle. "And of course, here." He palmed Dare's hardened cock and then pressed against it with nimble fingers.

Dare hissed and reared up. "I've had about enough of this," he growled. Jax felt the flush of triumph that Dare had been the one to break first. "Come here, straddle my lap, you teasing little bastard. I give in. I can't resist you."

Jax climbed into Dare's lap, grinding into his crotch as he leaned down to pillage Dare's mouth with pent-up sexual need. From the sounds Dare was making, and the look in Dare's blown-up pupils, he was definitely in control.

"I knew you'd kill me this way," Dare gasped as his hand brushed the front of Jax's crotch, stroking the hard outline of the cock underneath the trousers. "You are just too hot."

Jax drew in a breath and pushed into Dare's hand. "I want to feel your naked skin on me." The words spilt from lips yearning to be kissed again. He was desperate. He imagined himself debauched with hair falling over his eyes, his lips wet from where he'd licked them…

"Baby, let's make it to the bed at least," Dare managed to get out.

Several frustrating and sexually charged minutes later, with Dare hell-bent on driving Jax crazy with soft kisses, sly touches and whispers of the dirty things he wanted to happen, they got up and went to the bedroom. Before the door swung closed, Jax lunged forward and thrust his tongue in Dare's mouth while fumbling to undo the zipper on trousers that were keeping him from his target—Dare's cock.

"Want this," he panted as his lips bit Dare's. "God, please let's get the edge off and touch each other properly. Cock against cock. I'm going to fucking explode if you don't and I want to feel you holding me when I do." He pulled his shirt over his head and let it drop.

Dare wasted no time unbuckling Jax's belt, unzipping the skin-tight jeans and sliding them off. Jax had gone commando in preparation for just this.

Dare groaned huskily. "God, what you do to me," he breathed. He moved away and quickly stripped, his cock bouncing up against his stomach, freed from its tight navy blue briefs.

Jax's breath once again caught at the sight and the intricate tattoos decorating Dare's body, badges of sheer sensuality. He wanted to lick and bite every talented stroke of the tattooist's pen, follow the trail on Dare's hip round to his dick and suck him in.

"You are so damned sexy," Jax gasped as Dare pushed him back on the bed and covered his writhing body.

He gasped at the first feel of another man's cock against his. It was better than he'd ever dreamed. Dare's impressive cock was silk over steel, rubbing against him, bringing his body to a place he never knew existed. Every synapse in his brain flared in pleasure and his skin tingled as he hardened more than he'd ever imagined possible. He thought he might burst out of his own skin. Wonderful, incredible, orgasm-inducing friction teased his cock with steady motions of slippery, hot flesh.

He moaned, frantically pushing against the heat of the shaft teasing his. His throaty sounds of pleasure and lust echoed in the room and he relished every animalistic sound.

"Oh God, yes," he panted, the scenes behind his closed lids beatific with pleasure. "Never stop doing that. Never."

"You had this all planned out, didn't you?" Dare whispered in jagged breaths as his cock kept up its relentless assault against Jax's own. "You—little—bastard."

Jax opened his eyes as Dare's voice faltered to see Dare's lids fluttering closed and sheer pleasure spread over his face as he moved. Jax's blood heated and pooled in his groin. He'd become quite adept at giving Dare pleasure, at anticipating what he needed to do to get to Dare to make those sexy noises.

As they rubbed together, he bit Dare's shoulder, then licked the mark he'd left. Dare groaned on cue, and delicious thrills of awareness and gratification coursed through Jax at those sounds and the clear evidence in his hands of Dare's arousal.

The smell of sex and male sweat permeated the air, making Jax's head swim with the heady, pungent odours. He whimpered in Dare's ear, whispering jagged promises of things he wanted to do interspersed with entreaties to pump him harder, make him come, not to hold back.

Mouths melding as they met each other's movements, their locomotive desperation would not be derailed. Jax couldn't hold off any longer; he gave a choking cry and his body trembled as hot spurts jerked from his aching balls, coating them both with the relief of Jax's release. His orgasm brought Dare to the same point of no return, and he grunted, face creasing in ecstasy as they collapsed in each other's arms, chests heaving, bellies and groins slippery with their combined come.

It had been quick, intense and as hot as fuck.

"God," Dare breathed huskily. "That was epic but over far too soon. I knew I'd blow the minute my cock touched yours. I've been dreaming about this for weeks."

Jax closed his eyes and breathed in Dare's scent. "Yeah," he murmured. "Me too. You do something to me. I can't even describe it." He shifted to see Dare. "We could have been doing this a long time ago, you know. I tried my best."

"I know, but I wanted to make sure it was the right time." Dare snorted. "I think this was definitely the right time. I couldn't have gone on much longer without doing more than we had."

They were quiet. Jax's thoughts tumbled in his head like the steady whirr of a washing machine, rolling round and around in the drum.

"Why me? I mean, you must have access to a lot of male booty. Look at you. You're, like, this wet dream." Jax's insecurities had suddenly kicked in. "I understand if you've changed your mind about the sleepover. It's just, I've never woken up with someone before in the morning. I kind of thought it would be nice. But it's cool if you don't want to, I can just leave. I mean—"

His rambling was cut off by Dare's hot mouth and swirling tongue. Jax melted, feeling certain he belonged right here, flush against Dare's warm, hard body.

When they parted and he saw Dare's swollen, wet lips and the look of bliss on his face, Jax's heart leapt.

"You're the one I want so you're staying with me," Dare murmured. "I do have to be up early in the morning, so I'll probably sneak out before you wake up. I have to be in the shop at seven-thirty. I promised Sally I'd open up in the morning to catch the before-school kids."

Dare reached over and flicked on the bedside light. The room flooded with a warm light. He fumbled with his bedside drawer. "Here, you might want to wipe that spunk off yourself." He handed Jax a pack of wet wipes, taking a couple himself. Jax nodded as he absentmindedly cleaned his hands and groin, and then wasted no time in executing the rest of his plan to have more of Dare's bare skin against his own.

Jax wriggled onto his stomach and arched his body languidly, knowing his backside had been toned by years of swimming and gym work.

The hitch in Dare's breath made Jax snicker.

"God." Dare's voice was filled with awe. "You are gorgeous. Like a thoroughbred colt, all long legs and that arse, fuck…" He broke off. Jax turned his head to watch Dare stare greedily at his backside.

"Glad you like it." Jax smirked as he wiggled his bum, pushing it up into the air.

Dare looked as if he was trying to hold back his amusement.

"You're a little shit." Dare smirked as he lay watching Jax from the other side of the bed. "I have a feeling you're going to be my downfall."

Dare twirled himself back into bed, his naked, warm, smooth body a miracle. Jax thought he'd died and gone to heaven when Dare reached out and pulled him against his chest.

Up this close, Dare's eyes were darkened, his expression tender. "Jax, I truly believe you've completely put me under your spell," he whispered. "It's insane."

Jax's heart ached, and he felt a headiness he'd never experienced before. No one had ever said his name with that tone of reverence, looked at him with that glowing worship or look of longing in their eyes. It made him feel like a god, ten feet tall, and his dick felt the same way. It was already pushing forward, eager to conquer. He reached out and touched Dare's lips, fingers lingering.

"I want to taste those tats, do more things to you. And you to me."

He was empowered with his success in seduction tonight but he wanted more. A blow job perhaps, even the feel of Dare's fingers at his entrance, soft touches over that most sacred of places—and he definitely wanted a rim job.

Dare looked at him and shook his head. "I made a promise to myself to take this slow." He reached over and touched Jax's cheek softly. "There was no way I could keep my hands off you altogether tonight. I needed to feel your body against mine without clothing. You are too damn alluring."

Jax's mouth fell open and he frowned with displeasure at being denied. "Are you fucking serious?" he snarled, disappointment welling in his chest.

"Deadly serious," Dare said. "I need to get some Zs. Early to rise and all that crap. Now go to sleep." He kissed each of Jax's damaged eyelids and then stole a quick peck on the mouth for good measure.

"Jesus." Jax pouted, his temper flaring. "God save me from valiant knights out to protect the innocence of the young virgin. Is that how you see me? As someone to be protected? Because I can tell you right fucking now—"

Again his words were cut off by the insistent pressure of Dare's lips against his. Jax moaned. It seemed his man had this apparent magical ability to shut him up simply by kissing him so he couldn't think straight.

And when the hell did I start thinking of Dare as my *man?*

When the need and lust had been satiated through kissing—for the moment—Dare leaned away and pulled Jax's body to him then pulled the covers over them.

"Hopefully we'll have lots of nights like this one," Dare murmured softly. "I'm happy you're here with me, right now, like this. It means a lot to me."

Jax didn't have a reply to that. He was partial to curling up along the hard, masculine body beside him. He grumbled under his breath and felt Dare's grin against his hair.

In truth, never in his wildest dreams had Jax imagined this turn of events so soon, and it was still a dream to him, so much so he actually pinched himself and hissed at the sting.

Dare's forestalling more sexy play didn't stop Jax's lips and tongue from slyly tracing the lines of the salamander on Dare's left arm. Then Jax licked leisurely along one strong bicep, ending with a kiss on Dare's shoulder. With his hand still tangled in Jax's hair, Dare's steady breathing soon echoed in Jax's ears as his lover fell asleep.

Jax basked in the warmth of Dare's body, the scent of his hair and the rise and fall of his soft breath. Despite the aching discomfort in his groin, he thought dreamily heaven really *did* exist.

Chapter 11

Dare took a deep breath and scrambled out of his car. Jax was already fumbling for his door handle and finally they stood together outside, gazing at the scene spread out before them.

Rows of modern caravans dotted here and there with the brightly coloured and quaint sight of old-fashioned horse-drawn wagons in between greeted them as they stood at the entrance to the Traveller site on the outskirts of London.

"Erm, I can only see big colourful shapes, but are those proper gypsy caravans in there?" Jax's face was a picture of wonder as he took out his glasses and perched them on his nose. He looked adorable. "Does that mean there are horses somewhere?"

Dare grimaced. "Mum and Da prefer the term Traveller wagon themselves, as do a lot of our people. The word 'gypsy' tends to bring bad connotations with it, so we don't really use that term anymore. And yes, there are horses on site, over in one of the other fields."

Jax breathed out in awe. "Wow. Okay, take me to see them up close and personal later. I want to see them properly. I love horses."

Dare smiled. "My folks' caravan is further down. It's one of the newer ones with all the mod cons, more suitable for family life. Follow me. Be careful of the terrain, though, it's uneven and there are probably rabbit holes. There's a lot of them around here."

"Bunnies too?" Jax teased. "Wow, you really know how to treat a guy."

Dare chuckled. "I have my moments." As they walked, he watched out of the corner of his eye, ready to support Jax if he stumbled navigating his way carefully over the ground.

The last few days they hadn't seen much of each other. Jax had been away for two days at some one-on-one study lesson in Wembley. He had exams in summer next year and Jax being Jax, he was determined not to let his impairment get the better of him.

Dare had never known he could miss someone so much. Yes, there was texting and phone calls but not being able to see Jax, even briefly, had been like he was a child having his favourite thing taken away. Not for the first time, he felt apprehension and fear at investing so much in Jax. He was only eighteen—although Jax would protest he was eighteen and a half, the half meaning a lot to him—and still new to the whole world of dating and sex.

Dare wasn't sure he'd hold a younger, newly minted gay man's interest once he knew what was on offer out there in the big gay world. And Dare didn't have much to offer. He worked in a sweet shop, even if it was a respectable job, and he didn't even own a house. His folks lived in a caravan on a Traveller site, and while he wasn't ashamed of the fact—he was who he was—it made him wonder if it would be enough for someone else, especially Jax with his big plans to change the world one day.

All Dare could promise himself was to enjoy the time he had, initiate Jax gently into the delights of relationships and sex, and hope his own heart didn't get too broken if it finished.

He reached a hand out as Jax faltered on the slope, seeming to lose his balance, and then breathed a sigh of relief and withdrew his hand when Jax righted himself with a curse.

"You weren't kidding about the damn holes in the ground," Jax muttered as he avoided a rotting tree stump prodding up through the grass. "If I didn't know any better I'd say you'd brought me to a poxy obstacle course."

"Oh, you figured that out? Clever lad." Dare grinned as Jax gave him the finger. "Ouch, be careful. I might bite that off for you."

"Having it in your mouth would be nice," Jax murmured *sotto voce*. "Or maybe I could stick it somewhere else if you'd prefer? Somewhere warmer and tighter?" The suggestive tone and dirty words brought heat to Dare's face.

"Hell, don't start that now. I don't want to meet my folks with a boner."

Jax flashed a dirty smile at him and snorted.

Dare knew Jax's sexual frustration well because he felt the same thing himself. The past few weeks, keeping his cool and not pouncing on Jax at every opportunity and showing him everything he wanted to know had been a tough job.

Jax was impatient and demanding, sensuous and insatiable. The frotting and mutual hand jobs had been the sum total of their activity to date. They hadn't graduated to blow jobs or much finger play yet. Quite intentionally, Dare had delayed this, with the sure feeling that once he tasted Jax, the other man would forever, unconditionally own him.

Dare didn't think he could taste Jax and not want more. It was an illogical and stupid fear but he couldn't rid himself of it. He'd already fallen hard, but this was his last remnant of sanity left in a world that had become infatuated with the man beside him.

"Cat got your tongue?" Jax murmured as Dare stopped outside his parents' huge caravan. The steps up to the dwelling were surrounded by potted plants, containers of herbs and his mother's favourite blooms of the season lay in long wooden troughs, petunias in a riot of colour. He had to admit the entrance looked festive and welcoming.

"It's been a while since I've been home," Dare confessed as he motioned Jax up the wooden steps and stood protectively behind him. "And it's the first time I've ever brought anyone here."

Jax's face flushed as he turned to stare down at Dare on the lower step, and Dare's chest ached to see the pleasure reflected there at that statement. "You've never brought a guy home to see your family before—not even your ex?"

Dare shook his head as he reached up and knocked on the door. "Never. Michael wouldn't have been seen dead here."

Jax scowled as they waited for the door to open. "He sounds like a complete douchebag."

Dare had to agree. He moved up to stand beside Jax as the door opened and the large frame of his father filled the doorway.

"Kildare, good to see you." Patrick Rowan stepped back. Dare entered first and was pulled into a fierce hug that threatened to crush his bones. "It's been too long, son. We missed you." His Irish lilt was as strong as ever.

"Me too, Da." Dare gasped when he was let go. "I'm sorry it's taken so long. Work and stuff, you know."

Patrick grinned down at them both. Dare noticed Jax looking a little nervous.

"Aye, I see that. This is the stuff you've been busy with then?" He waved at Jax, who swallowed and offered Dare a worried glance.

Dare laughed. "Yes, Da, this is my 'stuff.' His name is Jax."

Dare's father reached out a callused, large hand and clasped Jax's in his. "Pleased to meet you, son. Kildare's told us nothing about you so it'll be nice to find out a few things."

"Pleasure, sir, thanks for having me." Jax dropped his hand awkwardly and Dare grinned at the slight wince. His father had a pretty tight grip.

"Come on in. Your mother is in the kitchen, and Kean is watching the telly. Some rubbish he has a fancy for." Patrick shook his head ruefully. "Gone are the days when kids used to entertain themselves outside like I did. Nowadays it's all bloody telly, iPhones, MP fives and shit like that."

"MP four, Da," Dare murmured with a chuckle. "An MP five is a submachine gun."

"What the fuck ever." Patrick grinned and gestured to Jax to move ahead into a spacious lounge. The thirty-five-foot caravan boasted a lot of room, with three bedrooms, a full bathroom and homey kitchen. Dare had grown up in similar versions, admittedly smaller, until Kean had arrived. Then his father had needed to invest in something more family oriented.

Dare's mother bustled out of the kitchen and squealed in delight. "Dare, my darling, look at you! You look so well. I think this young man is good for you." Dare suffered his mother's tight hugs and kisses to his cheek and then she turned to Jax, who stood looking a little wide-eyed. Patrick Rowan went into the lounge and sat in his armchair.

Maria's eyes softened as she approached Jax. "It's an honour to meet you, love. You're a breath of fresh air after that last bastard Dare was seeing. He couldn't even be bothered to come visit us."

Jax nodded. "I heard about him. He was very much a bastard, I agree. I mean, who would ever want to give *him* up?" He waved a hand at Dare.

Dare saw that with that little gesture and few words his mother was smitten, much like him. It also cemented Jax deeper into Dare's heart.

Just then Kean ran through from another room and tackled Dare with a whoop. "Hey, Big-D! Nice of you to come visit at last." Dare found himself pummelled to the floor as his mother sighed heavily and stepped over him and his brother.

"Jax, come with me to the lounge. We can all sit in there while these two get reacquainted."

Dare caught a glimpse of Jax's face as his mother ushered him along. It was one of longing—wistfulness crossed with sadness. Then he had no time to think on what that was about as Kean sat on top of him and tickled him unmercifully in the ribs.

Kean's brown eyes sparkled wickedly, his freckled face evil. Dare knew something was coming, something he wasn't going to like. He struggled, trying to get up. "Get off me, you little brat. Let me up. I'm not one of your bloody playmates."

Kean shook his head and reached into his pocket, pulling something out. He held it in front of Dare's face. "I found something you might like down at the river yesterday. Look at this."

The terrified shriek that left Dare's lips at the sight of the large spider dangling from Kean's left hand was not manly. It was in fact probably the most awful sound ever but Dare didn't care. All he wanted was to get the hell out of the way out of the devil child holding him captive and away from the horror in front of him.

"Kean, get the fuck off me, you little shit. Let me up, and get that thing the hell away from me. I swear, I'll slap you stupid if you don't."

Kean cackled and stayed where he was. It was only when Maria Rowan came to Dare's rescue and dealt the younger boy a sharp clip to the back of his head with a newspaper that Kean made a move, no doubt to avoid another whack.

"Jeez, Mum, fine. I'll get off the big scaredy-cat. It's not real anyway." He slid away to stand safely out of reach and stuck a tongue out at his brother.

"Leave your brother be," Dare's mother said. "You know how he hates spiders."

From the lounge Dare heard the sound of unrestrained laughter as he scrambled to his feet, throwing a ferocious glare at Kean and a furtive glance at the spider in his hand. "I'll get you back for that, you little wanker."

"Kildare Patrick Rowan, language," his mother admonished.

Dare rolled his eyes. First Sally, now his mother. What was it with these women and his swearing? He dusted himself down, giving Kean the stink eye, and fixed his mussed-up hair. Then he tried to enter the lounge with as much dignity as he could. The sight of both Jax and his dad sitting there with tears rolling down their cheeks didn't make his mood any better.

"So I don't like spiders. Sue me," he growled as he plopped down beside a clearly delighted Jax.

"Oh God, that was precious," Jax said, wiping his eyes, his face pink. He looked at the wetness on his hands with surprise. "I can't normally cry this much but my God, that was epic and it was so worth the aftershock. My big bad Dare terrified by an itsy-bitsy toy spider."

Dare wasn't sure whether to be affronted by Jax's amusement or thrilled that he thought of him as 'his big bad Dare.'

"I told you I don't like them," he said sulkily.

Jax kissed his own fingers then laid them against Dare's lips. "It was adorable," Jax murmured. "I haven't laughed like that in a long time."

Dare frowned. "What do you mean, 'the aftershock'? What happens when you cry too much?"

Jax sighed. "My eyes don't cope too well with it. They get really sore afterwards and it can lead to infections."

Dare's stomach plummeted at the thought that, for Jax, something as simple and normal as crying could hurt him.

Jax leaned over and pressed Dare's cheek softly with fingers that were warm and fleeting. "Take that worried look off your face," he murmured. "It's no big deal."

Patrick had been observing the two men with keen scrutiny, eyes going from one to the other. He leaned forward, his face set.

"Who did that to you, Jax?" he asked, face grave.

"My stepbrother," Jax replied. "This was the result of a drug and alcohol-fuelled night out."

"That doesn't make it right, lad," Dare's father said gently. "What happened to him?"

"He was sent to prison. He's still there, due out in a couple of years' time." Jax's voice was quiet but Dare saw the apprehension. He sucked in a breath. This was the first time he'd heard that Jax's attacker would be getting out of prison.

Patrick nodded. "Where he belongs, then, for now." He looked at his son. "And when he gets out, you'll have my Dare looking out for you, no doubt."

Dare frowned. "Da, that's a long way away. We don't know what's going to happen between now and then so let's not go that far down the road."

Patrick smiled. "Oh, you'll be there, son. I don't doubt it." His appraising glance slid between Dare and Jax and he nodded to himself then sat back in his chair.

Dare was a little nonplussed at having that synopsis of their future together declared and looked over at Jax who looked just as dumbfounded. Kean came into the room and sat down in front of the couch. He stared at Jax curiously and Jax stared back evenly. Dare's hands grew clammy. He hoped Kean wasn't going to ask about butt sex. He'd kill the little bugger if he did.

Maria bustled into the room bearing a tray of mugs filled with steaming tea and a plate heaped full of what Dare knew were homemade chocolate-chip brownies. His favourite.

"Tuck in, boys." Maria sat down on the floor between her husband's legs and Patrick put a hand on her shoulder. Dare smiled at that. It had always been his mother's favourite place and she'd fiercely defended the fact when other women had sneeringly called it a submissive gesture. He'd thought his mother's exact words to them had been 'Fuck off and leave me be. I'll damn well sit where I like and if you think that's submissive, you're a damn idiot.'

They helped themselves to tea and brownies and when Kean opened his mouth to speak, Dare held his breath.

"Are you Dare's boyfriend?" Kean squinted up at Jax.

Jax didn't hesitate. "Yep."

Kean pursed his lips. "What happened to your face? Did you know Dare was spying on you and called you his angel?"

Dare scowled. "Kean—"

Jax laughed. "Yes, I know now he was watching me. No, I didn't know he called me his angel, but I do now. As for my face—" he reached over and took Dare's hand. "My stepbrother did it because he was a mean bully. That's about it really."

Kean frowned. "Your own brother did that to you? What a tosser."

Patrick leaned over and flicked Kean's ear, causing him to yowl. "Language, boy. You're only ten."

Jax chuckled. "Yes, he was. But it's over now and in the past."

Kean shifted uncomfortably and his eyes flicked to his parents then back at Jax. "Did Dare tell you anything about me?"

Dare knew what his brother was asking—did Jax know he'd been the one to steal his pocket watch? He waited with bated breath for Jax to answer.

"Yep." Jax took another cookie off the plate. "He said he had this cool little brother who sometimes needed a kick up the arse but that underneath he was a good guy. You're lucky to have him. Just like I am." Jax munched on his brownie, a beatific smile creasing his face. "These are really good, Mrs Rowan. The best ever." And that was the extent of anything to do with the theft of the watch. Dare had no doubt no more would ever be said. His Jax was a forgiving soul indeed.

"Call me Maria," Dare's mother said. "And thank you. It's my grandmother's recipe."

"So, Jax," Patrick was relaxed in his chair but his blue eyes—just like Dare's—watched keenly. "What has my son told you about his family? And about his background?"

Jax sat forward. "He's told me about where he comes from, and some things about the Traveller community in general. I did a bit of research of my own too. I had no idea there were organisations that work with you to try and get people to accept more of what you stand for. It was quite an eye opener." He sighed. "I'm just sorry people see the need to pigeonhole everything and put it into nice, acceptable boxes."

Patrick nodded. "Aye, it's been an uphill battle for years. But I'm not going to lecture you now about why we deserve to be left in peace." He grinned, looking like an older, gruffer Dare. "Today's a social visit, eh? My son introducing me to his young man."

"Yes, sir." Jax smiled back at Patrick. Dare could already see acceptance in his father's eyes.

"We even have our language, you know," Kean piped up. "I can't speak it, but it's called Gammon. Like the pig." He sniggered and his father clipped his ear.

"Don't disrespect the language, young lad," Patrick admonished, but his tone was fond.

Dare watched Jax soak up all the Traveller trivia he was given like a sponge and marvelled at how Jax entranced his parents like he'd never seen anyone do before. It was plain they approved of him.

When Dare's parents left with Kean an hour and a half later to go for a walk—no doubt planned—Jax sat back with a sigh. "Your folks are incredible. And your brother. Oh my God. He's the most precocious kid I've ever met, and I've met a few. I like him."

Dare leaned over and wiped a crumb of chocolate off Jax's mouth. "I'm lucky to have my family. I'm glad you appreciate them."

Jax's eyes narrowed. "So, tell me, *Big-D*." Dare's brow furrowed at that use of his brother's nickname. "How did you get that name? I mean, I can hazard a guess but I'd like to hear it from your own lips." Jax gave a wicked smile.

Dare reached over and pulled him closer. "Never you mind," he murmured against Jax's lips before he claimed them for his own.

After a heavy necking session where Dare kept one ear open for the sound of his family's return, Jax lay back, looking well kissed and satisfied.

Dare desperately needed to go to the loo. He wasn't sure how he'd manage it with the current hard-on he had but he'd have to give it a valiant try or wet his jeans. "I need to take a piss," he announced as he stood up to go to the bathroom.

"I'm going to get a bit of fresh air," Jax called after him. "See what's happening outside."

It took Dare quite a while to get his dick under control so he could pee. It involved some creative manoeuvring and contortions to hit the toilet without missing. As it was, he had to clean up after himself a little.

When he came out of the bathroom, red-faced and swearing from the exertion, Jax wasn't back. Dare searched; there was no sight of him outside the caravan and it was getting duskier.

Dare walked around, greeting people he knew, smiling at children kicking balls around and even stopping to say hello to one or two dogs. The community seemed much the same as when he'd left—close knit, sometimes guarded, but still welcoming and friendly. It was only when he rounded a caravan not far from his parents' that this concept was put sorely to the test. He thought Jax might have gone to the nearby field to look at the horses and he'd been right; Jax was there, but not enjoying the horses.

At first, Dare didn't believe what he was seeing. A man, one he recognised, had a pale-faced Jax by the throat against a tree. His other arm was pressed against Jax's chest as he jeered at him.

Red film coated Dare's eyes and a simmering fury rose at the spectacle playing out before him. He strode towards them, with every intention of causing mayhem.

Jax bore a bruise on his cheek; his mouth was split, with blood oozing from the nasty cut, but it was the fear and resignation on Jax's face that made Dare's chest tight and his pulse race.

"Sammy Coulter, let him go before I fucking kill you," he roared as he drew closer.

Sammy turned slightly, his mouth twisting in a sneer. "Oh look, another damn faggot," he spat. "Butt buddies unite, is that it? Is this yours then?" He released Jax's chest and gestured dismissively at him. "I mean, look at it. Couldn't you do any better than a freak like this?"

When Jax's eyes closed in apparent defeat, Dare's heart broke. He lost it and, with a fierce cry, launched himself at a surprised Sammy, who seemed unprepared for the ferocity of his attack.

"He is not an *it*, you fucking moron." He punched Sammy low in the kidneys and felt a primal satisfaction at Sammy's cry of pain as Sammy released Jax and doubled over. Jax slid down against the tree, coughing and retching.

Rage infused Dare and he bunched his fists in case Sammy decided to fight back. A firm hand gripped Dare's shoulder tightly.

"Enough, son." Patrick Rowan's voice was commanding, and Dare knew better than to disobey. "You've proven your point."

Panting heavily, Dare debated the merits of a good kick to Sammy's groin. The warning glance of his father put paid to that idea.

"Take Jax and go back to your mother. I asked her to take Kean home so you and I can sort this between us. She'll fix your young man for you." Patrick stared down at the snivelling Sammy, dislike apparent in his father's eyes. "I'll take this one home to his da and tell him just what an arsehole he's been. Richard will sort him out." Richard Coulter was a tough, rough man but fair. Dare had no doubt Sammy would be punished in some form or another.

Dare went to his lover, who was still crumpled at the foot of the tree, face still, lips tight. "Come on, baby," he whispered. "Let's get you cleaned up."

He helped Jax up, wincing at the look of pain on Jax's face as Jax got to his feet. It looked like Sammy had got in a few body blows.

Dare supported Jax as they made their way back to the caravan amidst curious and sympathetic stares from others in the campsite. It wasn't the fact Jax was hurt physically that scared Dare the most; it was that he was quiet and emotionless. His flawed eyes were shadowed and there was no life in them. At the foot of the caravan stairs, Dare stopped and cradled Jax's face in his hands. Jax looked up blankly, his bottom lip puffy. He was shaking, his hands ice cold.

"Jax, everything is going to be okay. Please don't let one stupid bastard spoil today."

There was no reaction, not even a flicker of eyelashes. Dare pulled Jax's face towards him and placed a tender kiss on his undamaged cheek. "Please," Dare whispered. "Please don't disappear on me. Stay with me, sweetheart."

He helped Jax up the stairs into the caravan and called for his mother. Maria came out of the bedroom and gave a gasp of horror.

"Oh dear God. That bloody bully Sammy. Bring Jax into the kitchen, son. I'll get the medical kit out."

Kean stared at Jax, his face falling. "Is he okay?" he stuttered. "I saw Sammy hit him." His bottom lip trembled.

Dare nodded. "He will be." God, he hoped so. "Can you go find me a blanket from your room and take it to the couch for Jax?"

Kean nodded and sped off.

Jax was soon settled on a stool in the kitchen, as Maria busied herself cleaning up the cuts and applying arnica gel to the bruises. Dare stood, his hand protectively on Jax's shoulder, watching helplessly as his mother tended to Jax, who was still shivering but seemed more aware of his surroundings and Dare.

"Da's taken Sammy to his da for him to sort him out." Dare watched as Maria expertly applied soothing gel to Jax's reddened throat.

"What the little bastard deserves," Maria snarled as she gently motioned for Jax to lift his tee shirt. Dare was almost sick when he saw the livid bruise on Jax's torso.

Maria applied gel to that too, smiling as Jax flinched. "There, my sweet. I know it's cold but it'll do you well. Right, let's get that shirt down and you go sit with Dare in the lounge. I'm going to make you a cup of tea. You're in shock, even if you don't know it yet."

"This incident was a trigger. Jax was beaten before, when his stepbrother got hold of him." Dare said dully as he helped Jax off the stool. "Beaten so badly, he was in hospital. I never wanted this to happen to you again." He whispered to Jax. "I should have watched out for you better." His voice cracked.

Jax drew a deep, shuddering breath and looked at Dare. "Not your fault," he said huskily.

Maria nodded and laid a comforting arm on her son's. "These things will happen no matter what we do, son. Don't blame yourself. Now go on with you both. I'll bring some tea in a minute."

When Dare took Jax through to the room, Kean was waiting there, wide-eyed. The blanket was spread carefully across the couch and Dare ruffled his brother's hair as he passed.

"Thanks, squirt."

He lifted the blanket and motioned to Jax to sit on the couch. Once Jax was settled, Dare sat next to him and pulled the blanket over them both. He wrapped an arm around Jax and kissed him on the head. "Cuddling is one of my favourite pastimes," Dare murmured against soft hair. Jax gave a tired sigh and huddled closer.

Kean came over and held something out to Jax. It was his treasured Darth Vader action figure. "Do you want to keep this for a while?" he asked shyly. "It always brings me good luck."

Jax took the toy and for the first time since being assaulted by Sammy, his face lit up and he spoke.

"Thank you," he replied, and Dare noticed his throat must still have been hurting from the timbre of his voice. "I'll hold on to it for a little while, but I'll give it back before I leave." Jax's fleeting smile gave Dare hope. His throat clogged with emotion at Kean's gesture.

"Thanks, little bro. That's a sweet thing to do." Dare's eyes prickled.

Kean shrugged. "He's your boyfriend. And I like him. He's pretty cool." He patted the blanket and left the room.

"He's a great kid," Jax whispered. "Like his big brother." His voice caught. "This was nothing to do with you, you know that, right? It was just a shitty thing that happened."

Dare was about to reply when Patrick appeared. "You got a moment, Kildare?"

Dare squeezed Jax's hand and got to his feet to join his father.

Patrick motioned him to the side. "Sammy's dad will take care of things," he said. "Hopefully that young man will learn a valuable lesson about not being a damn bully." He searched Dare's face. "I've never seen you like this. Are you falling in love, son?"

Dare sighed and turned to look at Jax huddled on the couch, pale and unmoving. "No, Da," he murmured softly. "I think I've already landed."

Chapter 12

The journey home was quiet, fraught with Jax's own sense of hopelessness and what he knew was Dare's helplessness at not being able to make things better. Dare drove with Jax's hand tucked firmly under his on the gear knob, seeming to want to infuse Jax with comfort and the knowledge that everything was all right.

Jax wasn't sure of that. Old wounds and fears had spoilt the day for everyone.

When Patrick and Maria had hugged him, murmuring soothing words, Jax had wanted to bawl his eyes out at their concern. He'd returned Kean's figurine to him despite the young boy's assurance he could do without it. He'd asked Kean to keep it safe for him until next time. Throughout the drive back to London, Jax didn't speak; he stared out of the window at things he couldn't see since his glasses had been broken when Sammy punched him in the face. Now he'd need to get new ones. Dare had said he'd go around to Castaways tomorrow and collect his spare pair.

Jax hadn't wanted to go to his own home. He didn't want the kids seeing him like this; it would scare them. When Dare had asked if he wanted to stay over for a few days, he'd accepted gratefully. He'd called home and spoken to Jen, telling her what happened. He'd finished the conversation explaining why he was going to be staying at Dare's, promising to call back to give her an update.

Dare's flat was cold when they got in. Dare switched the heating on and turned to Jax. "If you like, I'll run you a bath and you can soak for a while. Then I'll spread some more of that gel stuff Mum gave me on your injuries."

Jax nodded slightly and let himself be led to the bathroom.

"You need help undressing or can you manage?" Dare asked.

Jax stared at him. "I can manage to undress myself," he said tersely.

I might be fucking useless at defending myself but I can take my damn clothes off on my own.

Dare inclined his head. "Okay then." He turned on the taps and poured a generous helping of bath salts and bubbles into the water. He turned to Jax. "I'll check on you in a while. I'm going to see what we can have for dinner."

Once he was nude, Jax slid into the generous bathtub and sank down beneath the scented, bubbled waters. As the warmth soothed him, his body began to shake. He wrapped his arms around his knees, trying to stop the trembling. Idiot tears fell. He'd never felt so damn useless in his life trying to defend himself against someone he couldn't overcome. He'd shown himself as a coward, someone unable to defend himself. How could Dare possibly want someone like him? Dare was so strong, so fierce. He'd landed one punch to Sammy and that had been it.

Jax had been watching the horses, trying to coax one across to him, when someone had kicked him violently in the back. Stunned, he'd jolted forward, his glasses falling off and onto the ground below. He had heard rather than seen them crack, breaking as his assailant had stepped on them.

"Fucking little fairy freak," the voice had hissed as its owner wrestled Jax to the ground and held his arms behind his back. "I saw you come in with that other faggot. You his bed warmer, then, you little bitch?"

Jax had tried to fight back, to turn around so he could land a good kick to the man's balls and disable him that way, but his assailant had been too strong. Instead, he'd found himself lifted to his feet, swung around and slammed against the tree, knocking the breath out of him. Then an arm had been pressed against his throat as invectives spewed forth in a never-ending vitriol filled with hate and filth.

Jax had zoned out. Memories of being beaten, kicked, spat on and threatened by his stepbrother Terry had come flooding back, filling him with icy terror that it was happening again and that this time he wouldn't make it. Part of him thought that might be best; another part of him thought about Dare, and how they still had so much to explore. That had been the catalyst that told him he needed to fight, overcome this attack. He'd been garnering his courage to do something, anything to get out of the situation when he'd heard Dare's voice. Feelings of both shame and relief had flooded him.

"I'm nothing but a fucking victim," Jax mumbled to himself as the bath water grew cold and his tears fell. "A freak that nobody else wants. Sammy was right."

He was more upset about the fact he felt like this rather than the pain of his injuries. He prided himself on being strong, but this incident appeared to have broken him. Again.

He was startled by a loud, angry growl as Dare knelt down beside him and warm hands pulled his face up from his chest. Jax's sight was clouded by tears and swelling, but he could still make out Dare's angry face as Dare glared with concerned dark eyes, clad only in tight boxer shorts and no shirt, his tattoos a frieze of blurred beauty.

"Stop talking about yourself like that." Dare's voice was fierce, possessive. "You're not a damn freak and you're certainly not a victim. Don't let that stupid wanker make you feel bad about yourself. And as for nobody wanting you, that's a fucking lie. Those kids at the halfway house want you. Your crazy psycho friends Tate and Clay want you."

At that Jax gave a small snort of choked laughter. He'd told Dare all about the couple and their jobs and Dare was more than a little apprehensive about meeting them one day.

"*I* want you." Dare's voice deepened and Jax's groin thrilled to the sound. "You have no idea how much. I wanted to kill that bastard for what he did to you. Lucky my dad was there, because I might have lost it, seeing you like that. I didn't want to be like Terry and Sammy, someone who can't control himself, but hell, I saw red."

Jax sniffled and wiped his nose. His jaw dropped when Dare stepped into the bath with a giant splash and sat down with his back against the taps. His knees came up as he made room for Jax between his legs. "Come over here," Dare muttered. "Let me take care of you."

Jax's cock was already swelling beneath the water and those words simply made him harder. He stood up, water droplets flowing down his body like fragranced rivers leading to a bubbled surface.

Dare glanced at him and gave a soft grin. "*Wash* you, I mean. Save that for later."

Jax gave a watery smile. "Promise?" He settled back into the water, his back against Dare's slightly furred chest. Water splashed over the side of the bath, soaking the bathmat. For good measure he wriggled his arse against the wet fabric of Dare's boxers, the sound of his lover's hiss making him feel much better.

Dare brushed wet hair away from Jax's cheek and kissed it softly. "Let's get you cleaned up and then into bed." His husky voice sent shivers down Jax's spine. "I think tonight I need to show you just how much somebody wants you. How much you drive a man crazy."

Oh God. Does that mean tonight we get to do more? He still wants me, even though I'm spineless?

Jax leaned his head back and looked up at Dare. Dare's eyes were black, the look of sheer need on his face turning Jax's insides to a pile of slush as realisation dawned.

He really does want me.

Suddenly the bad events of the day released their tight grasp on his psyche and all Jax could see was Dare. No doubt that was the intended distraction. Affection for the not-so-subtle ploy and something else washed over Jax, and he swallowed, not wanting to acknowledge it right now. Surely this emotion he felt was too soon? Although at this stage, he'd take what he could get of the man in front of him staring at him with heated eyes.

"Hurry up and wash me, then," Jax whispered as his fingers trailed down Dare's arm, raising goose bumps on that wet flesh. "Then show me. I need this. Need you."

Dare wasted no time. Before Jax knew it, he was washed, dried and standing by the bath with a towel wrapped around his waist. Dare stood beside him, prominent bulge straining the fabric of his wet underwear. Jax's dick tented his towel and he was ready to pass out with hunger for the man regarding him with darkened eyes and a distinct look of desire on his face.

"Go through to the bedroom." Dare's voice was gruff. "Get comfortable. I'll be along in a minute." Jax nodded and left the bathroom.

Dare's bedroom was warm and cosy, dimly lit by an art deco lamp with a red shade standing on the chest of drawers. Jax draped his damp towel on the top of the chest then slid beneath the bed covers. He shivered as the crisp linen hit his cooling skin.

"Don't worry, you won't be cold for long." Dare stood looking down, a smile on his face. Jax's breath caught when he saw Dare had lost the wet boxers and was naked, his cock standing to attention against his belly. "I have a plan to keep you warm, skin to skin. It's the best way."

"Oh God," Jax said faintly, longing suffusing his body. His own hard-on was becoming distinctly needy. "Hurry up then because honestly, I don't think I can wait."

Dare's nostrils flared and he pulled back the covers and without any further warning, his hardened body covered Jax's, his insistent cock pressing against Jax's belly. Jax managed to take in a deep, gut-churning breath before his mouth was taken in an assault worthy of a clan of stealthy ninjas.

He was vaguely aware of Dare pulling the covers over them as Dare ground himself closer, small gasps of pleasure leaving Dare's mouth in between wet, devouring kisses that left Jax weak and moaning.

"Never doubt a man could want you," Dare whispered when he finally let Jax breathe again. "Look at you. You're perfect."

Jax closed his eyes as soft kisses flitted across the scars on his face, and a hot mouth traced the contours of his eyes.

"You are the sexiest creature I've ever met. Brave, strong— so damned determined. That's what I see when I look at you. Not a coward or a freak." Dare's words filled Jax with warmth and light.

Dare turned his attention to Jax's throat, lips trailing down…and down. Jax hadn't realised he wasn't breathing as Dare's mouth found the soft hair of his sparse treasure trail and followed it; it was only when Dare's heated velvet mouth surrounded his cock that Jax took in a deep gulp of air and then exhaled with a loud, exhilarated cry that he was sure the neighbours would hear.

He'd dreamt of this moment for so long: having Dare's lips wrapped around him. Now it was happening, it was better than he'd ever dreamed of. "Oh my G-God," Jax stammered, senses reeling, hands scrabbling at the bed covers, clutching them in ecstasy. "Don't we need a condom for this? Is it safe?"

Dare stopped the slow licks up the base of the cock and raised his head. His lips were swollen, his face filled with dreamy satisfaction. "You're *my* virgin, love. It's safe. Just lay back and enjoy it. Come in my mouth. I need it. Need you."

Jax squirmed and wriggled as Dare's mouth closed over him once more. Strong suction made him whimper, his toes curled and his fingers let go of the bedcovers to wrap themselves in Dare's thick hair. His backside left the bed as fingers gently rubbed the strip of skin between his balls and arse. Jax was sure he was going to pass out from the pleasure.

"Jesus, Dare. How can you make me feel like this? Is this how it always is?"

Again Dare raised his head but not before giving one final swirl to the tip of Jax's cock. "No. This is because it's you and me. This is special."

Dare continued the intense pleasuring, and slowly Jax gave in to the rising swell of incredible sensation currently filling every pore on his skin with heat and tingles. He gripped Dare's hair tightly, babbling nonsense in between pants of elation as the sensations grew deeper. His hips pushed up against Dare's talented mouth as he spread his legs wide, offering himself like a whore.

Dare chuckled, the sound reverberating against Jax's cock. A sly finger slid imperceptibly over Jax's arsehole, fleeting but causing Jax to cry out as Dare did it again. No penetration, just the touch of a callused finger against that most sensitive of places.

Jax's head swam. He frantically humped Dare's mouth, shouting in triumph as he came, wanting to be swallowed whole by the wicked mouth of the man currently taking him to such giddy heights. His body spasms finally stopped, and he lay splayed weakly on his back with his hand across his eyes. His brow was sweaty, his chest rising and falling in great heaves.

He'd never come so hard in his whole life; he'd erupted like a damn volcano.

The sound of Dare removing his mouth, the 'pop' as he lifted his head and grinned at Jax was enough to make him as gooey inside as his limbs felt.

Dare moved up Jax's body, kissing him as he went, until his tongue, wet and slick with Jax's essences, covered Jax's mouth. Jax sucked Dare's tongue, wanting to taste himself.

"Your turn," he whispered after. "Do you want me to do the same?"

Dare shook his head, and Jax felt a spurt of disappointment. It was short-lived as Dare pushed himself onto his elbows and gazed down at him.

"Lie down onto your stomach. I want to give you something else you've been wanting."

Jax did as he was told, his legs trembling, his belly fluttering with anticipation.

"Now get up on your knees and show me that beautiful arse," Dare whispered.

Jax whimpered, but again, he did as he was told. He knew he could trust his lover not to do anything Jax wasn't ready for. And if it was what he thought might go down, he was more than ready for it.

"I want to taste you. Right here." Dare pressed a finger to Jax's hole, and Jax cried out softly at the touch. "I want to show you exactly how much I want you. All of you."

Jax closed his eyes, his face scrunched up into the pillows, and he gripped the fabric tightly as the heat and wetness of Dare's tongue began to lave at his entrance.

Dare pulled open his cheeks, kissing the skin in between then returning to lick long, wet stripes from Jax's taint to his hole. Jax couldn't help but push his backside back into Dare's questing mouth and tongue. When he felt Dare's tongue slip inside his hole for the first time, he couldn't speak. Slippery, hot and hungry, the sensation of that muscle inside him made his knees weak. The stress and pain of the day had disappeared, leaving only the feeling of being cherished and worshiped.

"God, oh God," Jax finally managed to chant in a frenzy of babble. "That feels... I can't..."

"Don't come yet," Dare said huskily. "I have something else in mind when you do that." He thrust his tongue into Jax deeper than before, then withdrew and gave one last slow lick.

Don't fucking come? What the hell? I need to so badly, Oh God, that feels absolutely fucking amazing.

He cried out in frustration when Dare's tongue stopped its torture. He lay, a gibbering wreck, surrounded by a scrunched-up sheet and thumped-in pillows filled with his sweat.

Dare chuckled softly. "Lie on your side, now love. I want to rub myself in between those beautiful arse cheeks of yours, if that's okay? I won't go inside you, I promise."

Jax's heart stammered a faster beat, a staccato pop song as opposed to the overwhelming rock ballad he'd just experienced. He bit his lip. "Is it…" he stuttered.

Dare smiled down at him and brushed a damp lock of hair from Jax's forehead. "This type of frottage is classed as safe sex. I know you don't have to believe me, but I'm clean, and I would never put you at risk. I'll wear a condom if that's what you want."

Jax stared into Dare's warm eyes then nodded and turned onto his side. He'd read all about this sort of thing on the web and believed it was true, but he'd wanted to make sure from Dare himself. "No condom," he murmured. "It's fine. I want to feel you."

His belly was already clenching in anticipation of feeling Dare's beautiful cock rubbing against him after his tongue had been inside. He moaned softly as Dare pulled Jax's arse towards his groin. His face flushed with heat at the thought of this intimate act being played out behind him.

"Relax, and enjoy," Dare whispered against his ear, with a soft lick of tongue against Jax's lobe. "Just do what feels right. There are no rules." There was the sound of something being torn—Jax assumed it was a packet of lube, although he was sure he still had enough of Dare's spit as lubricant down there—then fluid-covered fingers coated the skin between his cheeks.

He hissed. "Shit, that's cold."

Dare laughed, the sound sexy and teasing. "Need just a little of this your first time. Because once I get started I won't be able to stop."

The hard, velvety feel of Dare's cock slipping between Jax's cheeks was enough to make him to gasp. The slick, hot member being pressed against his already sensitive skin, the thought of another man's cock being in that most private of places, was enough to make him hyperventilate.

"Easy, baby, breathe slowly." Dare's amused voice echoed in Jax's ear, along with a hiss of satisfaction as Dare rubbed himself against Jax's crease, his thrusts becoming stronger with each movement. "Push back if you like, tighten those gorgeous arse cheeks, whatever feels comfortable. It won't take much for me to blow, I promise. I'm nearly there anyway."

Jax couldn't get any words out. Instead, he sighed, panted, pushed back against the insistent sleek dick causing friction in the most delightful of places. He was already hard and wanting, and he reached down to take care of himself...and found his eager hand covered with Dare's strong one, helping him stroke his cock.

Dare's teeth lightly scraped Jax's shoulder as Dare moved faster. They found a rhythm that worked, and Jax closed his eyes as he revelled in the feel of Dare behind him, hot breath in his ear, deep grunts and sighs turning him into a basket case of lust and want.

"Oh fuck, I'm going to..."

Dare's groan sent shivers across Jax's skin, as their hands moved faster on Jax's cock. Dare gave a strangled grunt, and Jax found the sensation of being rubbed against sadly gone as Dare pulled away.

"I don't want to come too close," Dare gasped as hot fluid coated the back of Jax's thighs and arse. "Your first time. Want to make sure you're comfortable with all this."

Jax wasn't sure if he cared at that point, as his cock exploded for the second time that night. It wasn't as intense but still caused his skin to prickle and his body to flush with heat. He arched back into Dare's groin, hearing his lover's moan as their bodies collided.

"Hell." Dare's rueful voice cut through the sounds of heavy breathing and panting. "I wish I was eighteen again and could come twice in a short time like you did. It takes me a bit more time to recover for a second round."

Jax smiled and wriggled against Dare's groin. His backside was sticky, his crack a little sensitive. "Yeah? Well, you are an old man after all."

He yowled as sharp teeth bit his neck.

"I'll old man you, little brat." Dare wrapped a warm arm around Jax's waist. "You want to clean up or stay like this?"

Jax shuffled closer. "Stay like this," he said sleepily. "It's perfect. Feeling you behind me, your come on my body—it couldn't get any better." He was satiated, happy, the events of the day a distant memory. He'd had what he termed proper sex for the first time and

It. Had. Been. Awesome.

He couldn't wait to do it all again.

Soon.

Dare chuckled. "Oh, it can get better, honey. Just wait and see. This was just an appetiser."

Jax shivered in delight at the promise in Dare's husky voice. "I look forward to the main course. Perhaps next time I can taste you, have your cock in my mouth. And I really love the way you taste." He pushed his bottom against the heated groin behind him. "Love having you here, your tongue and my arse up close and personal."

"Jesus." Dare croaked. "Warn a guy before you say dirty things like that, will you? I stand corrected. I think I might manage a second round sooner than I thought."

Feeling Dare's now semi-hard cock pressed against his sticky cheeks, Jax grinned. "Hold that thought. I don't think I can come again tonight. Maybe later…"

Jax turned and stared into Dare's eyes. They were dark, warm, and the look on Dare's face as he gazed back made Jax feel warm and fuzzy. No one had ever looked at him that way before.

He leaned in, closing his eyes, and kissed Dare, a soft, lingering, breathy kiss that promised more than simply sex. "Thank you. For giving me this. I needed it." He ran fingers tenderly down Dare's jawline. "And thanks for making me wait for it all. It was so worth it. I know I was an impatient git."

Dare drew him closer and tucked Jax's head against his chest, fingers strumming down his spine gently. "I'll always try and give you what you need. And all you have to do is ask if I don't."

Jax closed his eyes, listening to Dare's steady heartbeat, relishing the strong arms wrapped around him. He never wanted this moment to end. He prayed that Dare wouldn't get tired of him, wouldn't become bored with a flawed, sometimes insecure young man with baggage.

He comforted himself with thinking that whatever the future held, he'd always have this moment, even if he might have his heart broken in the process.

Chapter 13

Jax was perched on the stool behind the counter of Bon Bon Bizarre, watching Dare clean the windows outside the shop. It seemed his lover was truly a jack of all trades, and nothing was too much for him.

Jax squinted through his new glasses as his man expertly swiped down the wet windows with a squeegee then leaned in and peered at the glass with a frown. Dare obviously wasn't happy with his work, because he cleaned it again. Jax shook his head in amusement. In the six weeks they'd been seeing each other, he'd learnt three things about Dare. One, that the man was a perfectionist and took his job seriously. Two, that he was a hot, sexy and inventive lover who never failed to rock Jax's world. Having an older and more experienced boyfriend was definitely a plus. Three, that Dare's friend Rob was a crazy bastard.

They'd had dinner together a few nights ago and Rob had been as entertaining as hell. Jax had really liked the laconic, wise-cracking redhead, and he was glad Dare had someone like him as a friend. They'd all arranged to get together for drinks in a few days' time.

Jax sighed and looked down at the textbook in front of him. He'd popped over to have lunch with Dare and been convinced to stay longer. He'd thought he might as well study while Dare was playing window cleaner. He looked down at his book and tried to focus on the page in front of him.

Origins of psychology: Wundt, introspection and the emergence of psychology as a science.

He sighed again. He loved his subject but he'd rather be with Dare right now, doing something far naughtier. The thought made him smile.

"Huh. I guess that smile means you're enjoying having a boyfriend? And that you're getting some?" The familiar voice held sly laughter.

Jax looked up, startled. Tate stood before the counter, a smirk a mile wide on his handsome face. He regarded Jax over a pair of aviator sunglasses, arms folded across his broad chest. Dressed in dark black chinos and a tight, dark blue tee shirt, over which he wore a leather jacket, he was the epitome of bad-boy chic.

Jax stared back at him haughtily. "You surmised that from me just smiling?" He couldn't help the grin passing over his face, and Tate laughed loudly.

"I was right though. Is that him, then?" He jerked a thumb towards Dare outside—a Dare who was now standing stock still, and from what Jax could vaguely make out, glaring into the shop through the window.

"Yep. That would be he. The master of the Mr Muscle window cleaner." He laughed. "What the hell are you doing here anyway? Spying on me?" He'd deliberately been keeping Dare from Clay and Tate for fear they'd interrogate, or far worse, waterboard him to find out his intentions. It seemed Jax's luck at keeping them all apart was about to run out.

"Oh, Clay and I were running some errands around here. We thought we'd pop in, say hello, maybe meet the man at long last."

Jax narrowed his eyes. "You didn't know I'd be here though. So were you going to 'pop in' just to give him the once over, check him out?"

Tate pretended to look shocked. "Baby Bird, are you suggesting I'd do something so devious? I'm hurt." He laid a hand over his chest but sniggered when Jax scowled.

"We both know you are. And stop calling me that. So where's Clay?"

Tate snorted. "Fighting with a parking attendant. She wanted to give him a parking ticket for parking in a loading zone. He was arguing that he has his permit which allows him to do whatever the fuck he likes. It was a battle of wills but I think it's safe to say he'll be the winner. That's Clay." The note of pride in Tate's voice at his partner was evident. "He'll be here in a moment, unless he shoots her. In which case I'll be bailing him out of jail again in a little while."

Jax shook his head. "I don't know anyone else who can make jokes about things like that and actually mean them." He frowned. "What do you mean 'again'?"

Dare walked into the shop, bucket and squeegee in hand and walked over behind the counter to stand by Jax. "Hey, baby," he said. "Everything okay?" His voice was wary.

Jax nodded. "Yeah. Dare, this is Tate. I've told you about him."

Beside him, Dare relaxed. "Oh." He put the bucket down on the floor and went over to Tate, holding out his hand. "Pleased to meet you. Jax has told me a lot about you and your partner."

"Really?" Tate drawled. "Because Baby Bird here has told me damn all nothing about you." He peered over his glasses. "In fact, one would think he'd been trying to avoid introducing us. So we decided to make our own appointment to view."

Jax had no doubt both Tate and Clay already knew everything about Dare that they needed to know. It was simply the way they rolled, and he'd resigned himself to that fact. Frankly he was surprised they'd waited this long to make an appearance.

Clay Mortimer growled as he strode into the shop. "Fucking officious, power-hungry bitch. Tate, honey, I nearly shot a government employee. Think I can get away with it?" He flashed a grin at Jax. "Hi there."

As always, Jax was impressed by the sheer presence of the man. Dressed in a dark designer suit, with a white shirt open at the neck and a navy blue tie dangling loosely from the collar, Clay looked as if he was the poster boy for sexy, hot as fuck Businessman of the Year.

Jax was gratified to see Dare's eyes widen as he stared from one hot man to the other. He smirked. Jax did have rather hunky friends; he was the first to admit.

"Oh shit," Dare breathed. "Are you just being social or is something wrong? I mean, Jax tells me you two are pretty busy doing whatever it is you do, and I know that's kind of dangerous from what he tells me, so is there a problem? Oh God, is the sweet shop laundering money or something? I mean—"

Both Clay and Tate's eyes had widened in surprise at Dare's nervous outpouring of what Jax could only term drivel. Jax gave a laugh and leaned over to silence him with a deep kiss. God, his man was adorable. Jax withdrew his lips and smirked.

"Remember those times you tell me to breathe? Well, now it's my turn. I'm sure these two"—he turned and glared at Clay and Tate, who looked a little sheepish—"are only here to say hi and scope you out. I doubt Sally is some crazy kingpin criminal who's sending funds used to buy candy to villains all over the world."

Dare went scarlet. "Yeah, I know. I'm being an idiot, sorry. It's just I'm a bit nervous meeting these guys, you know?"

Jax sniffed. "Tate watches the Muppets and Clay loves to listen to Barbra Streisand. Believe me, they're nothing more than sweet, fluffy teddy bears."

Tate let out an indignant huff. "Hey, the Muppets are sheer genius. Don't diss my show, Baby Bird."

Dare chuckled. "Baby Bird? You keep calling him that. What's the meaning behind it?"

Clay waved a hand. "Our jobs, as you say, tend to be a little on the wild side. Jax comes over to stay sometimes and we each have a code name in case of an emergency. That's his call sign. Because he's small and cute."

Jax pursed his lips. It was time to play his ace in retaliation for being described as 'small and cute.'

"Oh, I found out why you're called Clayzilla," Jax said slyly. "Tate told me the other night when he'd had one beer too many. It's because you have a huge—"

Clay leaned over and placed a large, tanned hand on Jax's mouth. "I have a gun," he murmured silkily. "I *will* use it if you finish that sentence." He turned and bore gimlet eyes at a grinning, unconcerned Tate. "And *you* will pay for divulging that secret," he warned.

"I can't wait for my punishment," Tate murmured, the sudden flare of heat in his eyes at Clay turning Jax's groin warm and his dick hard. He didn't even want to think about what that might mean. Well, he did, but not right now.

There was a tangible sense of sexual tension in the air, shattered when Dare cleared his throat uncomfortably. "So, not that this isn't nice, but I really have to get back to work. Is there something else I can do for you both?"

Tate and Clay looked at each other, then together, as if synchronised, they turned to scrutinise Dare with intent stares. Dare fidgeted and Jax placed a hand on his arm in support. He knew his friends were taking Dare's measure and he hoped they liked what they saw. Not that it would make him change his mind or anything, but because he respected them both and wanted them to like his boyfriend.

After what seemed like ages, Clay nodded. "He'll do," he mouthed at Jax, who relaxed, not realising he'd been holding his breath.

Tate narrowed his eyes then moved forward and clapped Dare on the back. "Yeah, he's got moxie," he said in a fake American accent, and then he smiled. "I guess Baby Bird did good with this one." The smile didn't falter as he leaned menacingly towards Dare. "But you do anything to harm Jax and you and I will be having a different conversation."

Dare's mouth fell open and he glanced at Clay and Tate nervously. "I'm not going to do anything to hurt him," he said softly. "He means a lot to me."

Clay flicked Tate on the back of his head, causing his partner to swear. "Stop scaring Jax's boyfriend. Hell, you're such a damn bully." His face softened as he looked at Dare. "You look after him and treat him right. That's all we can ask. He's been through a lot." He turned to Tate, who was rubbing the back of his head and throwing dirty looks at Clay.

"Come on." Clay smirked. "Let's go see if that damned parking bitch has given me a ticket after all. If she has, I swear, I'm going to run her over with my car when I leave."

Clay reached out and enfolded Jax in a hug before Tate did the same.

"See you soon, Baby—Jax." Tate gave Jax an appraising glance. "And let me know about the whole moving-in thing. You said you were going to think about it. The offer still stands. I imagine you and Mr Muscle here need some privacy." He smirked as he turned tail and left the shop, Clay behind him.

Jax was trying to hold back a fit of honest-to-God giggles at the bemused look on Dare's face. "So what do you think of the guys?" Jax said finally.

Dare gazed back at him. "I think they're scary but hot as fuck. Not as hot as you," he amended hastily, "but jeepers. They are something, aren't they? And does Tate always use weird names for people? I mean, I like Mr Muscle, don't get me wrong, but he sounds like he's sizing me up for some covert operation."

Jax shrugged. "That's the way they blow. And I happen to think the description fits. And they've been so damned good to me, listening to my tales of woe." He smiled twistedly.

Dare cleared his throat. "Do you know that you've never really told *me* all the details of what happened to you that night? When do you think you'll be ready to tell me everything? I mean, Tate and Clay probably know more than I do." His tone was matter-of-fact but Jax heard the undercurrent of frustration at being excluded.

He sighed. He'd told Dare a few bits of his story but not much detail. They simply didn't talk about it. He hadn't wanted to taint their budding relationship with his sad tale of violence and abuse.

Now was probably the time.

Jax took Dare's hand in his. "I guess you should know the full story." He took a deep breath. "That night I was home alone, doing mundane things like sorting out washing and doing dishes. Dad was away. Sylvia, my stepmother, was at some charity ball. Terry was out, I never knew where he went." Jax shivered. "He was always a damn bully, doing things to try get me into trouble with Sylvia, breaking my stuff, leaking pens onto my new shirts…" His voice tailed off. "I never knew what I did to make him hate me so much, and whenever I asked him, he hit me. So I stopped asking. It's why when I thought I was different and liked guys, I never told anyone. He would have made things worse."

Dare's eyes were wide and he grasped Jax's hand tightly. "I was packing his washing away into his cupboards for Sylvia and he came into his bedroom and found me there. I knew he was on something by the dilated pupils and the smell of booze coming off him."

Jax shuddered. "He went mental. He tackled me to the floor, kicked me in the face over and over again. I heard my cheekbones and other bones fracture. I felt like I had broken my insides after he'd finished kicking me. When he disappeared, I thought, thank God, he's gone, but I couldn't move. Then he came back and hell got even worse."

Dare gasped in horror. "Oh God. Come here, love." He pulled Jax in and wrapped strong arms around him. "This isn't for you," he whispered against Jax's hair. "This is for me. I need to feel you close right now."

Jax closed his eyes against Dare's broad chest as the memories of that night flooded back like a waking nightmare. "Thank God for Lucy, our housekeeper. She came back unexpectedly. Terry was wrecking stuff in the yard, hitting Dad's other car with a baseball bat. Lucy managed to get inside, lock the house and she called the police. She poured milk in my eyes and that may have saved what vision I have now. She's an angel."

His voice caught and he took a moment to compose himself. "The last time I saw Terry was in court. I'd only been out of hospital a few weeks and they asked me go and give my story for the prosecution. I was in a wheelchair because I couldn't stand for long periods. My stepmother sat glaring at me the whole time, as if it had been my fault. I didn't wait to hear his side of the story. I couldn't sit there and listen to him justify what he'd done. I've never found that out, and I don't want to hear it." Jax drew a shuddering breath. "I said my bit, Lucy verified my story, and then my lawyer took me back home. Later they told me the verdict had been quick. After they recorded a guilty verdict I just put it behind me and got on with my life. I didn't have any other choice."

Jax blinked back tears. Dare's warm breath touched his cheek. "Then a few months later I went to the clinic for skin grafts and special eye treatment and while I was in there, Dad had a heart attack and died. I never got to say goodbye to him. I never got to tell him I thought I was gay, or had feelings for men. I think he would have understood, but Terry stole that from me too."

He tried to speak past the lump in his throat, remembering the deep sense of loss. "I couldn't even attend the funeral. I got out of the clinic, found Sylvia had sold and packed everything up and left. Everyone had gone. I was all that was left. Even Lucy had been let go and sent away. I never saw her again. I tried to find her but…" he shrugged.

Dare gave a strangled groan. "I can't stand to think of what you went through. Is that when you decided to stay at Castaways?"

Jax's face relaxed. "Yeah. I met Randy at the hospital a couple of times when he came to visit some of the kids. We struck it up really well and kept in touch. I heard he had an empty room there and asked if I could take it. The rest is history."

Dare kissed the top of Jax's head. "And now you have me. I promise I'll never go anywhere. Well, not unless you want me to."

Jax sighed against his chest. "No chance of that happening."

Dare murmured into Jax's hair. "Thanks for telling me. I can feel your heart beating so damn fast. It wasn't easy telling me, was it?"

Jax shook his head, breathing in Dare's beloved scent. "No. I didn't want to taint what we had with my stupid story. I'm glad I told you now, though."

Dare's hug grew stronger. "Your story isn't stupid." He frowned. "What was all that about you moving in with them? You haven't mentioned that before."

A group of school kids came into the shop and Dare moved away. He watched them warily, moving back behind the counter again.

Jax sighed and rubbed the back of his neck. He had a headache starting. "Castaways is getting busier, more kids needing care than ever before. And I'm there, perfectly able, taking up space." He grinned wryly. "Well, you know what I mean. My large room alone could be used to create two smaller ones and then two kids who really need help could stay there. I know Randy has a waiting list, and me not being there will mean a huge difference to a kid in need." He sighed. "I really need to consider it."

Dare nodded. "Sounds like something you've been thinking about then?" He cast a quick glance at one of the kids who was fingering a pile of sweets. Jax knew that shoplifting was a real problem for Dare and Sally, sweets being something easy to pop in a school blazer pocket.

"Seriously thinking about it. And now I have you—well, it makes more sense privacy wise." He smirked at Dare's heated look at him. "It will give us more space, because their place has this annexe Clay uses as an office. He's already put a small en-suite bathroom in, just in case, and it already has its own entrance."

The other alternative was buying his own place and drawing down on his trust fund. He knew his dad's lawyer, Matthew, would agree to release the money. Jax didn't think he was ready for that yet though, and he didn't want to tell Dare about his trust fund right now. Deep down he thought he knew Dare wouldn't simply stay with him because of it but it still niggled in the back of his insecure mind. He had no intention of throwing any spanners in the works yet. The story of his ordeal was enough for one day.

"Sounds like a dream come true," Dare agreed as he moved around the counter to take payment from one of the kids for a pile of Pukey Pastilles. "What's holding you back?"

Jax waited until the kid had paid and he and the others had left the shop. "I guess the kids, being there for them. Randy and Jen rely on me too. But I also know they've been talking about needing more room for needier kids but won't push me out. It's a bit of a catch twenty-two for us both really. Me being there to help out or not being there so they have more room. Not to mention they're my family and we'll miss each other."

Dare came to the front of the counter and pulled Jax into an embrace. "Anyone would miss you if you weren't around," he murmured, lips pressed against Jax's hair. They stood there for a moment, Jax pressed against Dare's body, smelling the familiar spicy fragrance of his aftershave, and loving the heat from the hard body pressed against his. When Dare moved away, Jax huffed in annoyance.

Dare grinned at that, glanced at his watch and smiled. "Time to start locking up and getting home," he murmured. "We can continue the cuddling upstairs."

Jax felt better at that thought. "I think maybe we order some takeout, go upstairs and get settled in for the night. Does that sound like a plan?"

Dare's lips sought his. "I think that's a hell of a plan," he whispered just before he took Jax's mouth in a deep kiss.

Jax closed his eyes blissfully. Life didn't really get much better than this.

Chapter 14

Jax loved these rare moments when Castaways was quiet and peaceful. It was normally a barrage of sound, children shouting, balls bouncing on the landing, running feet and the hustle and bustle of Randy and Jen as they moved around. Today, however, the kids had gone with Jen to the zoo to celebrate Damien's eighth birthday. It was a treat indeed on a sunny June day, and one that had been eagerly anticipated by the children as well as Randy and Jax. Randy was happy to be left alone at the house; he apparently had myriad little jobs to do, which he could get to with no kids to distract him. Jax had been spending a lot of time with Dare in the last few weeks, talking and having delicious monkey sex, and he was behind his own personal schedule for study work. He'd had to make it up to keep on track, and having some peace and quiet always helped his study routine.

He was taking a well-earned break lying on his bed, closing his sore, aching eyes and trying to make his brain stop working for a while. Suddenly there was a loud knock on his door and he heard Randy's voice.

"Jax, are you in your room, lad?"

He opened his bleary eyes. God, he was really paying the price for his marathon study session. He'd only meant to close his eyes for half an hour before hitting the books again. He felt his watch. Shit, it was two o'clock.

"Yeah, I'm here." He yawned and sat up in shock as his bedroom door flew open.

Thank God I have trousers on. What the hell?

No one ever came into his room without first being told they could. It was an unwritten rule in the household because with his eyesight, it prepared him for who might be there in front of him.

Not to mention he needed privacy now and then, especially when he 'thought of' Dare.

Randy barrelled in. "I was calling you, didn't get a reply. I was worried."

"I fell asleep, didn't hear you." Jax frowned. "What's up?"

Randy stood at the foot of the bed, his face pale, a look of concern on his face.

Jax sat up and ran a hand through his mussed hair. "What's going on?" He reached for his glasses and slid them on, his eyes still feeling gritty. "Why are you acting so weird?"

Randy's face closed ranks. "Nothing you need to worry about," he said tightly. "I just wanted to make sure you were okay, that's all."

The slow burn of frustration started in Jax's chest. "Oh yeah, like this whole thing is not going to make me curious," he scoffed. "Something's put a rocket up your arse, Randy, or you wouldn't have just burst in here like that." He got off the bed and slid on his tee shirt. "Why were you so worried about me?"

Randy clenched his fists. "You didn't answer me." His face was evasive.

Jax lost it. He had the headache from hell. Eye strain was a bitch. "Bullshit." He clenched his fists. "I'm not a kid, Randy. You need to tell me what the hell is going on."

"Fine," Randy said. "I got some bad news a few minutes ago from the solicitor that handled your case. Plus one of the kids also said they'd seen someone lurking around at the gate a couple of times yesterday. The man disappeared both times when Jen went out to speak to him. On its own, it's nothing suspicious but now…" his voice tailed off.

Jax stared at him, stomach dropping. "What news?"

Randy's face twisted unhappily. "It looks like Terrence was released from prison two weeks ago. He got paroled, something which was unexpected. He's only been inside three or so years. Nobody expected him to get out yet."

Jax sank down on the bed, feeling nauseous. "Oh God. You think it was him at the gate? He was supposed to be inside for at least five years. They promised me." His hands clasped the bedside covers, memories taking over as he pondered what this might mean. Randy watched him with alarm and sat down next to him on the bed. He pulled Jax close, warm hands stroking his back, as he murmured soft words of support.

The soft, slow circles on Jax's taut back muscles helped, and soon he felt a little better. His breathing evened. "You really think it's Terry hanging around?"

"I don't know, lad. Perhaps we're just being paranoid."

Jax went cold. "I can't go through that again," he whispered.

Randy hugged him fiercely. "I'll kill the little tosser myself before he lays another hand on you. Come on, let's go downstairs and make you some tea. That'll put things right." He stood up.

Jax gestured to him. "I'll come down in a minute. I need to just sort myself out first."

Randy nodded and left his room. Jax stood, staring vacantly into the mirror above his desk. This changed everything. If Terry was out and maybe coming for him, he couldn't stay at Castaways. The kids here had seen enough violence and abuse in their short lives. At the trial, Terry had apparently said he would come for Jax when he was released. It seemed liked he'd made good on that promise.

No cup of tea was going to make this whole situation ever come right.

The day passed in a blur of anxious glances cast his way and whispered conversations between Randy and Jen on the other end of the phone. Randy had called Tate to tell him, and of course Tate had then called Jax.

"Don't worry, Baby Bird, we got your back."

"I know." Jax hated that they had to have this conversation,

"I spoke with Jen and Randy, and they agree—it's time you move in with us."

In his bones, Jax knew it was time for him to leave and let other kids take his place. This whole Terry thing was simply the catalyst. "I'll call when I've settled on what to do."

"Make it fast, Jax." Tate rung off without another word.

Later, when Jax escaped to the darkened recess of his room and lay under his duvet, listening to music, he thought the plan through. The decision whether to move out of his home had been made for him. He wasn't willing to risk bringing a personal fight to Castaways. He texted Tate and told him he'd move in with him and Clay. Tate's response was unequivocal.

Good news. Don't sweat this. We're here for you. I'll make the arrangements.

That deed done, Jax considered his options. One of them wasn't running scared. Yes, he *was* scared but he was damned if he'd let Terry dictate his actions, other than the move. That was all Jax was prepared to relinquish control of. He needed to be tough to show Dare he could take care of himself.

"You're not having me this time, you bastard," Jax muttered as he lay on his bed and squeezed his favourite stress ball, a joke present someone had got him of a man's arse in a thong. At least he hoped it was a man's. Fondling a lady bum just felt wrong. "I might have fallen to pieces when that douchebag beat me up at Dare's place, but that's not happening again to me. Fucking ever."

Finally, Jax called Dare. He'd put off imparting the bad news long enough; Dare deserved to know what was going on.

The sound of that familiar voice was bittersweet. "Hey, gorgeous." There was the sound of rustling in the background. "You were lucky, you caught me on a break eating my sandwich. What's up?"

"Hi. I'm glad you're eating something. I know you get busy."

"Yeah. It's just ham and tomato but I'm famished. A good sarnie and a cup of coffee. What more could a boy want? Unless you were here. Then my day would be perfect."

Jax took a deep breath. "I wish I wasn't about to spoil your lunch, but—but I have some bad news."

Dare's voice became urgent. "What bad news? Are you okay?"

"Yes, I'm fine." Jax hesitated, his throat dry. "I got told today Terry is out of prison. Randy thinks he's been hanging around this place."

"Oh shit. Are you holding up okay? You know I'd never let anyone harm you, right?" Dare's voice grew fierce. "If I have to beat the shit out of this guy myself, I will. He's not getting anywhere near you."

Jax chuckled. "I know you would. But it won't come to that. I'm not running scared from this arsehole. But I have told Tate I'll move in. I don't want anything bad happening at Castaways, and besides, it's time to give up my room to kids who really need it now." His tone steeled. "I'm not letting Terry get the better of me. Tate's already said he'll give me some self-defence lessons when I move, which is apparently Friday, by the way. Those guys move fast."

"Oh, that's only two days away." Dare sounded impressed. "Okay then. I can live with having you safe and sound with them sooner rather than later. I like the idea of those two looking out for you."

Jax felt a prickle of irritation at what he thought was condescension in Dare's voice. "Dare, I don't need anyone looking out for me. I know you worry about me, but honest, I can deal with this. I know I kind of lost my shit when we were at your parents' place, but that's not going to happen again. I'm not being a victim anymore."

Maybe that way I get to keep you.

There was silence.

"Sorry," Dare said softly. "I didn't mean to imply you couldn't take care of yourself."

Jax sighed. He was being such a drama queen. "No, it's okay. I'm just a little stressed. I know you mean well. I'm just being a bitch."

Dare's soft snort echoed down the phone. "Yeah, but you're my bitch."

Jax smiled at that. "You know it."

They chatted for a few more minutes, Dare promising to call Jax again once he got off work. The Terrence issue was skirted around but Jax knew Dare would have more to say on it. And no doubt Clay and Tate would when they picked him and his stuff up on Friday.

"God, how am I going to say goodbye to these kids?" Jax put his mobile down after he finished his call and stood staring unseeingly down into the garden. "It's going to kill me."

He knew he'd miss Randy and Jen like mad. They'd done so much for him. Castaways had been his home for over three years now. On the plus side, his new home wasn't too far away, and he'd no doubt be able to come over anytime he wanted.

Jax heaved a deep sigh. Life was forever changing for one damn reason or another. He smiled ruefully as he thought about the old adage, "The only constant in life is change."

Some changes, like Dare, were for the better. Others were as a result of circumstances or decisions.

All Jax could hope was that he was making the right ones.

***

Friday came around sooner than expected. Dare joined Jax early that morning, having taken an unexpected day off to help him move. Jax thought resignedly it was more to keep an eye on there being no rogue Terrys lurking around the premises than an altruistic gesture to help him pack. Together, they packed up Jax's things into boxes then fitted what they could into Dare's car.

Both Clay and Tate arrived around mid-morning, driving a large pick-up truck with a canopy. Apparently it had been borrowed from the police impound lot and had previously been used for smuggling drugs. Jax didn't even want to know how his friends had organised it.

The truck was big enough to get his bed and various white goods in, as well as most of the larger boxes. Jax was amazed at the amount of crap he seemed to have collected in the last few years, having forgotten he still had stuff stored in the basement of Castaways. He couldn't even remember what was in the boxes, but he was looking forward to opening them later. It would be a bit of a trip to the past for him, no doubt, and he hoped there would be no nasty surprises in them.

Clay organised with military precision, being bossily supervised by Tate. The parting with the kids and the people Jax had come think of as family didn't go as well. While Tate and Clay finished loading his things, Jax and Dare stood in the lounge, surrounded by a sea of sad little faces, some already sprouting tears.

Jax had hugged each one of his kids, and his heart was aching at having to leave. Seeing Damien sniffle, large, fat drops rolling down his cheeks, was the last straw. Jax gripped Dare's hand tightly as he crouched down beside the young boy. Dare had been his rock during this move, and Jax thanked God that he was there now, supportive as always.

"I'm not going far, Dami," he tried to console the boy even as his throat clogged up. "I'm only a little way away, and I'll come back as much as I can, I promise."

"I don't understand why you have to leave." Damien's eyes were round and tearful. "Have we done something wrong?"

Jax blinked back his own tears as he enfolded Damien in his arms. Beside him, Randy and Jen looked on, faces pale and miserable.

"No, you guys haven't done anything wrong. I love you all so much. It's just that—" Jax swallowed and sniffed as his nose blocked up. He couldn't get the words out.

Dare let go of Jax's hand and knelt down beside him, looking into his eyes. "Let me try."

In his visits to Castaways, Dare had inveigled himself into the kids' lives with ease, his compassionate and easy-going nature something they grown to like. Dare wouldn't mention the imminent threats as a factor, so Jax wondered what his lover would say to give the kids comfort.

"You know what things were like when you came here the first time?" Dare asked Damien softly. "How you felt, all scared and not knowing what was going to happen to you?"

The boy stared at Dare with wide eyes. He nodded.

Dare nodded back. He carried on. "Then, when you realised you'd found a safe place to be, and things got better, and you had all this"—he waved a hand toward Jax, Randy, Jen and the other children sitting quietly on the side lines, watching—"you felt better, yes? Because you had another family to take care of you?"

Damien nodded again and wiped away a tear from his cheek. Dare smiled too and took out a tissue from his jeans pocket. He pressed it into Damien's hand.

"Well, think of two other boys and girls just like that, all scared and not knowing what's going to happen to them. If Jax moves out, not too far away, then that means two other children just like you, all confused and alone, can come here and be taken care of. And you, Damien, you can help them settle in and show them the ropes."

Jax swallowed at the explanation, at the compassion shining from Dare's face as he tried to soothe the child's fears. Jax had never loved Dare more than at this moment. And Jax knew, without a shadow of a doubt, that he did love Dare. The momentous realisation flooded his chest with warmth at the same time as his stomach clenched with what it could mean for them both.

Clay and Tate had come into the room, and through vision blurred by tired eyes and tears, Jax saw them standing by the doorway, no doubt calm and watchful as they observed the scene before them.

Dare reached out and took Damien's hand in his. "You can all help these other kids not to be afraid anymore. And Jax moving out... Sometimes adults have to make some tough decisions, ones that might make them sad. I mean, look at him. He's just as unhappy as you, doing this. But he knows it's the right thing to do, so those other children can have a chance at a normal life, like you got to have." Dare stood up and looked at the little faces looking up at him. "So you all need to be brave, and I promise you we'll come visit as much as we can. Is that a deal?"

Damien regarded Dare with huge, soulful brown eyes. Then he sniffed again and nodded. He blew his nose loudly with the tissue, and Krispin broke the sense of sadness permeating the air with a loud snigger.

"Boogers, Dami. I can see your boogers!"

The children erupted into sniggers of laughter, and Dare grinned as he reached over and took Jax's hand again. "Right, we need to get on our way now but we'll be back soon. Isn't that right?"

Dare turned to him with a grin, and Jax was sure that everything he felt for Dare was reflected on his face. Dare's grin faltered and he took a hitch of breath. His dark eyes searched Jax's as his fingers tightened around Jax's hand.

"Yes," Jax said. "We'll come visit."

Jax moved over to Randy and Jen to be enveloped in a fierce bear hug from them both. "Thank you for everything you've done for me," he whispered against their necks, now wet with his tears. "I can't tell you how much I love you both. You took in a broken teen and made him whole again."

Randy's voice was choked when he spoke. "You're an inspiration, young Jax, and we've been blessed to know you. Come back soon and see us, you hear? And bring that big softy of a boyfriend with you. He's so right for you, my boy. I'm happy you found him."

Jen placed a soft kiss on Jax's cheek. Her eyes were wet and shiny. "What he said, my lovely. You've been such a part of this home and family; it's tough to see you go. The only thing keeping me together is knowing you're not far and you'll be back."

They stood back as Jax returned to Dare's side.

"Are we ready to go then?"

Tate's quiet, steadying voice grounded Jax, who took a deep and shuddering breath. "As much as I can be." He moved to the table, picked up his rucksack and slung it over his shoulder as he waved at the children gathered around. "Guys, I'll see you soon, yeah? Look after each other, and be good for Randy and Jen. Krispin, no more tricks with the cling film, okay? Randy won't appreciate another pair of trousers getting pee all over them with the splash back. Cathy, look after Kevin for me. He's going to need some love."

Jax strode over to where Clay and Tate stood and nodded. "Let's go, guys. I'm ready." Behind him, Dare placed a comforting hand on the small of his back and Jax left the room without looking back.

He didn't fancy breaking down again.

It was time to let go.

Chapter 15

Dare huffed out a breath and regarded Jax's new abode with envious eyes. It looked like Clay and Tate had spared no expense in making Jax feel welcome in their home. Dare's own little flat paled in comparison to this spacious, minimally decorated room. It was masculine, in shades of burgundy and cream, and splashes of colour adorned the walls in the form of various graffiti-splodged canvases.

He leaned in to stare at one with the initials TW in the corner then inspected them all and noticed the same initials on each picture. He'd been well aware of Tate's predilection towards despoiling certain walls and doors at his favourite haunts, but this was something even grander.

"Huh," he mused as he scratched the build-up of stubble on his chin; he hadn't shaved for a couple of days as Jax seemed to like the scratch of it against his fair skin, so Dare thought it could stay—for now. It would get too itchy, though, and he'd have to shave. "Looks like Tate is more than just a pretty face. These pictures are epic."

"Pretty face? Me?" Tate's amused voice cut through Dare's reverie and he flushed at being caught out. "Glad you like it. It's the only one I have."

Dare waved a hand at the paintings awkwardly. "These are really cool. You're talented."

Tate shrugged as he dumped a large box on the floor. "It's a hobby. One I have besides pissing Clay off." He grinned. "*That's* my favourite hobby." He pressed his lips together, looking uncertain. "You think Jax likes his room? I wasn't sure what he liked, so thought this might do for a start. He can change stuff if he wants…"

"Jax fucking *loves* this room!" Jax stumbled in with a bundle of clothes in his arms and almost fell onto the king-size bed in the middle of the room as he dropped tee shirts, jeans and various other items onto it. "It's perfect. Tate. Thank you so much."

His face was pink from the exertion of moving boxes and bringing stuff in up the stone stairs leading up to the house. Dare thought he looked adorable, with his flushed skin and blond hair falling over his eyes.

Jax had insisted on helping them unpack the car. Although it took him a little longer to navigate the steps outside and he couldn't carry as much as he needed a hand free in case he fell. He'd been a stubborn little bastard, refusing any help.

"That's the final load," Jax huffed as he brushed hair from his face. "All my shit is now officially *inda* house." He squinted around him, his chin tilting in that familiar gesture Dare loved. It showed off the sexy line of Jax's throat, a place Dare loved to kiss and nibble on.

Jax grinned widely. "And do you know what a luxury it is having my own bathroom? I've never had that before, always had to share with everyone else. It's going to be heaven having a bath all by myself, without anyone disturbing me, knocking and whining that they have to pee." He gave a wicked snort. "Well, maybe not quite by myself. I fully intend dragging you into that bath with me." He gestured a hand at Dare.

Dare's blood heated up. "It's certainly big enough," he murmured and for a moment he forgot Tate was standing there, the promise on Jax's face hard to ignore. "Maybe we can test drive it tonight. You can drive."

Jax's nostrils flared. "Is that the bath you're talking about or something else?" They stared at each other and Dare stopped breathing for a few seconds, he was so turned on. They used the term 'test drive' usually for a night of passionate cock-on-arse-cheeks action.

Tate cleared his throat loudly. "I'm *so* happy you two have a plan to screw each other's brains out," he said in amusement. "I'll leave you alone to work stuff out. This room has become rather hot. I need to cool myself off." He smirked at them and left, making a point of closing the door behind him.

The minute Tate disappeared, Jax strode over to Dare and pushed him onto the bed. Dare toppled backwards, and his mouth fell open as Jax leapt onto the bed and straddled him, looking down with lust in those blue eyes beneath their flawed eyelids. Dare wasn't quite sure what the hell was going on, but he liked it. A dominant Jax was a real aphrodisiac.

"So," Jax growled silkily. "You want my cock against your arse later?"

Dare reached up a hand and traced the line of Jax's jaw. "I was talking about the bath originally, but I like your version better."

Jax's breathing stilled and his fingers beat a soft tattoo on Dare's chest as he leaned forward. "Excellent," Jax purred, the tantalising hint of peppermint caressing Dare's face and scenting his nostrils. "I look forward to it."

Dare pulled Jax's face down to his. "Thinking of you having me later always makes me hot as fucking hell," he whispered, and Jax whimpered as Dare crushed their mouths together.

Jax fisted his shirt and ground his crotch against Dare's in a frenzy of need and urgency. Dare lost himself in Jax's scent, in the feel of his lover's lips as they tried to consume him, in the sounds Jax made as their tongues duelled, the whole sensation driving Dare crazy. Dare wanted to wear Jax against his body like a warm tee shirt, to feel Jax's heat and passion warm his heart and brush against sensitive skin until he could no longer bear it. He thought he might explode from feeling too much. He'd never experienced such emotion in his life before.

I love him, Dare thought dimly as the assault on his body and senses continued. I am so far gone and I don't ever want to let him go.

Along with that realisation, which to be honest wasn't all that surprising, came the gut-wrenching thought that when he fell from heaven, he would fall hard and spiral to earth in a never-ending twist of hurt and loss. Because surely this couldn't last?

When Jax reached inside Dare's now open jeans, took him in hand then wrapped a hot, wet mouth around his cock, Dare let his insecurities go and gloried in the *now*. He pushed the future to a distant place in his mind and slammed the door shut. *Now* was all he had and he'd sure as hell would enjoy it while it lasted.

Later, they lay satiated and sleepily on top of the bed, both of them half dozing. Dare drifted between wakefulness and a pleasant dream of himself and Jax naked and horny on a sunny beach somewhere with turquoise waters and cocktails.

Jax was curled against him like a kitten, and he murmured something against Dare's neck. Dare turned to him and smiled at the sight of Jax's face, peaceful and content.

"Did you say something?" Dare murmured as he reached over and drew Jax's briefs up over his now flaccid dick. He tucked it in then zipped up Jax's jeans. "You look like a debauched, dirty angel lying here next to me. Best get this put away so it can rest until later."

Jax chuckled sleepily. "Yeah, have you seen yourself? I've been eying out your cock wondering whether to suck it again or let sleeping dogs lie." He swallowed, his face flushing with desire.

Dare's pants and boxers were pushed down to his knees. Both he and Jax watched idly as Dare's semi-hard cock made its approval known of Jax's suggestions.

"I'm not stopping you," Dare murmured.

Jax ran light fingers down Dare's stomach, smiling slyly when Dare's cock jumped. "You're a greedy bastard, aren't you?" Jax sighed regretfully as he tucked Dare back in with the same care shown to him. "I think maybe we should get up and be sociable. Clay and Tate no doubt know what we've been up to, but it is nearly dinner time. I guess I should go see if they need any help. We can hold on for the big finale until later." His nose scrunched up. "I'm no big shakes at cooking, but I can get by with a little help from my friends." He smirked at Dare's snort. "I make a mean egg and chips, and I can do toasted sandwiches as well."

"You're a regular Jamie Oliver," Dare remarked drily as he levered himself off the bed and stretched. "I need to pee anyway. I'll get cleaned up then yeah, I guess we should go say hi." In truth he felt rather bad at having moved Jax in and immediately taken him to bed. Christening his new bed was one thing, but it did seem a little rude.

When Jax and Dare went through to the large sitting room, with its wide windows looking out into the garden, Clay was sitting at the table in the adjoining conservatory, peering intently at his laptop. He looked up when they came in, a gleam lighting up his dark eyes.

"Well, well, well," he remarked laconically. "Nice of you two to make an appearance. We were wondering whether you'd hunkered down for the rest of the day."

Jax sniffed. "It's only afternoon," he said airily as he plucked an apple from the fruit bowl and bit into it. "We could only have been gone an hour or so."

Dare shifted uncomfortably. "Actually, it was more like three hours. I think we fell asleep."

Jax stopped biting into the apple and frowned. "Really? Oh crap."

Dare turned to Clay. "Sorry about that," he said softly. "It was rather rude of us to just disappear."

Clay gave him an appraising glance. "Don't sweat it. I understand hormones, and all that." He stood up and narrowed his eyes. "Tate and I don't have a lot of housekeeping rules in this household, but I'm going to tell you what we *do* have."

Dare nodded and Jax rolled his eyes. Dare nudged him with an elbow. "Stop being a brat."

Clay smiled. "Jax, you need to keep your own room fairly clean. We have a housekeeper because Tate and I are away a lot and we need someone to keep things going. She'll do most of the tidying up, change sheets, washing and such but we expect you to not create chaos." Clay raised his brow.

"On the days she's not here, which are Thursday to Sunday, you wash your own dishes and clean up your own mess. Do your own washing if you have something you desperately need. And next is the most important rule of all." He paused and Jax and Dare waited expectantly. "If Tate or I ever invoke any code name, or tell you guys to leave the house, or run or fucking get down on the floor and play dead, you do it. Without question." Clay's voice was tempered steel. "We don't anticipate anything happening but it works to play safe. Got it?"

Dare nodded, feeling a little intimidated. Jax seemed to be feeling the same because he grasped Dare's hand tightly.

Clay nodded grimly. "Good. Jax, you know your code name already, *Baby Bird*." Jax made a *pffft* noise and looked disgusted.

Once again the eye roll was evidenced and Dare wanted to laugh, but dared not. He was still in awe of Clay. He'd heard the man had a thousand ways to kill you and he didn't want to risk experiencing one of them.

"You have a code name too, Dare, seeing as how I think you'll be spending a lot of time here." Clay stopped as a wicked grin crept across his face. "You will be known as *Candyman*."

Jax had just taken a bite of his apple and at Clay's words, he spluttered and the piece of apple went flying out of his mouth and onto the floor.

Dare snickered. He rather liked that name.

"No fucking fair!" Jax spat out, with a venomous look at Clay. "How come he gets a cool name and I get one that makes me sound as if I'm five years old?"

Clay raised an eyebrow. "If the shoe fits..." He burst into loud laughter as Jax hissed and gave him another dirty look.

Clay moved over to Jax and laid a large hand on his arm. "Tate chose that name for you. To him it means more than just what the words mean. You know what he went through last year with everything, and what happened with that young girl he met. Calling you Baby Bird is just his way of showing you how much he cares. He wants to protect you like he couldn't do with Lily." He shrugged. "We can change it if you'd like. Anything in mind?"

Jax was silent. Dare could almost see the wheels turning in his boyfriend's head. Dare had heard a little about Lily the homeless girl and how it had messed Tate up, finding her dead in an alleyway.

"No, it's fine," Jax muttered, the scowl fading. He bent down to retrieve the piece of apple then placed the fruit fragment in a nearby plant pot. "I guess it'll do." A brief smile flitted across his face. "Does that mean I can look in the mirror now and say, 'Candyman, Candyman, Candyman'? Which one of you do you think will appear?"

Dare shuddered. He'd hated that film; it had scared the bejesus out of him. "Don't you bloody dare do that," he said. "The last thing we need is some psycho serial killer in the bathroom."

"Ah, Dare's scared," Jax teased. "Do you really believe in that crap?"

Dare didn't answer because honestly, he wasn't really sure.

Jax cackled loudly. "My big bad boyfriend is scared of a horror movie *and* spiders," he retorted. "Clay, can we make sure we have no arachnids in the house? Dare screams like a girl when he sees them. I'm the one who has to remove them out into the garden."

Dare wanted to kill Jax. He had indeed been called upon a few times to rid Dare's home and the shop of super creepy, hairy-assed spiders. Dare wasn't proud of the fact but it was a given there was no way he'd go near them.

Clay shook his head in amusement. "Perhaps we should teach Dare to use a gun. He can shoot them." He smiled and moved back over to his laptop and sat down in his chair. "I've got some work to catch up on before Monday. Tate will be back later; he had an errand to run. Jax, dinner tonight is on Tate. He's making some fancy pasta dish which is apparently healthier for me." Clay smiled ruefully. "He's trying to cut down my weekly intake of Big Macs. Pasta is okay, but it's not a hamburger."

Dare wanted to chuckle at the wistful tone of Clay's voice. The man didn't look as if he had a spare ounce of fat and his body was fit, solid and drool worthy. Jax poked Dare in the ribs.

"Stop perving," he said slyly.

Dare poked him back, embarrassed at being caught out. A tickled fight ensued, with both of them giggling like children. When they finally stopped, out of breath, Clay was rolling his eyes at them.

"God save me," he muttered to himself. "Tate, baby, what the hell have we done? We've taken on a damn kindergarten."

When he glanced at Dare and winked, Dare breathed a sigh of relief. It appeared he was passing muster all round at squiring Jax.

"Soooo," Jax drawled, staring at Dare from lowered lashes. Dare knew that look and his groin flared with heat. "Dare and I are going to start unpacking some of the stuff that was put in the basement. I've got boxes down there I've never looked in for years and it's about time I sorted it out. We'll be down there if you need us."

"No sex in the basement," Clay growled after them as Jax dragged Dare towards the basement door. "That's a sacred place. We have special work stuff down there and I don't need to wipe your spunk off it when we want to use it."

"Ha, old timer," Jax said as he opened the cellar door and peered down the narrow steps. "Condoms, Clay. Catches most of that mess. I'll have to give you a couple." He fell into peals of laughter as Clay made to get up.

Jax clutched Dare's arm. "Babe, quickly, you go first. Then if I fall, I have something decent to land on. Hurry, before Clay gets over here."

Dare found himself being pushed unceremoniously down the steps into the darkened cellar. He held on to the wooden railing and walked, hearing Jax's steps behind him. It was dark and silent and rather spooky. He went slowly, ready to help if Jax got into difficulties.

When he got to the bottom, he fumbled for a switch. He found it and clicked it on. Light flooded the basement and he gasped.

Shit. This isn't like any basement I've ever seen.

Huge was one word. Impeccable another. Spreading over what looked like the whole bottom of the house, the room was clean, with white shelving and cupboards, computer equipment and a huge safe in the corner. Somewhere a generator hummed and it was airy and cool. There was a table on one side, surrounded by three chairs and a variety of maps and paraphernalia. A larger leather screen sheltered more computer equipment and desktop PCs.

"Wow." Dare waited for Jax to step onto the solid concrete floor and then moved around, inspecting what he saw. "This is a surprise. This place is radical. I could live down here myself."

Jax squinted around him. "It's like some sort of war room. You know, like you see in the movies. I expect a geeky dude to pop out from behind those screens, or out of a cupboard."

Together they moved around marvelling at the myriad different items they found.

"I wonder if there are weapons in this safe," Dare muttered as he stared at it and fingered the dial.

Jax shrugged. "Probably a whole damn arsenal in there if I know those two. Unless it's where they keep their kinky sex toys."

Both of them sniggered and looked at each other mischievously.

"So these must be *your* boxes." Dare stopped and gazed at Jax uncertainly. "There aren't a lot of them." He brushed his hand over the three large boxes. "Have you got any anywhere else?"

Dare didn't think this could be the sum total of a vibrant young man like Jax.

Jax's face shadowed. "Everything I managed to keep is here," he said softly as his fingers drifted over the brown surface of the boxes. "The rest was packed up when Dad died and moved out to wherever my stepmother went. She took it all. I was still in the hospital." He took a deep breath. "I didn't have much say in it at the time. My dad's lawyer made sure I got the stuff from my bedroom."

Dare hated seeing the bleak expression on Jax's face. His man was warmth and light and love. This Jax looked vulnerable and stricken. Dare reached out and pulled Jax into a fierce embrace. He sighed softly, allowing himself to be cherished.

Dare nuzzled Jax's soft hair, breathing in its coconut fragrance. "God, I hate that you went through that. Have you got nothing else of your family's then? Just these boxes?"

Jax stiffened in Dare's arms then pulled away. His face was guarded and Dare frowned.

What the hell? Why does he look like I said something wrong?

"Jax. Are you okay? Did I say something?" Dare asked, perplexed.

Jax shook his head, eyes haunted. "No, you didn't. It's just," he bit his bottom lip nervously. "My dad did leave me something else when he passed away." He seemed ill at ease.

Dare took Jax's hand in his. "Well, that's good, isn't it? You have something of his to remember him by."

Jax gave a short laugh. "It's not really a thing, Dare. It's more of a—" He seemed to be struggling with finding words.

"It's a bank account. A trust fund to be exact." He pursed his lips together and seemed to be waiting for Dare to say something.

"Oh." Dare was lost. "Okay then, that's good though isn't it? Why are you being so weird about it?"

Privately he was a little floored hearing Jax had a trust fund yet had lived simply at Castaways. Perhaps it wasn't *that* kind of trust fund. The ones that allowed spoilt rich kids to buy yachts, the latest designer fashion and party the nights away in places all around the globe. He didn't think Jax would be one of those brats anyway.

Jax couldn't seem to look Dare in the eye. "I get it when I'm twenty-one but I have access to it now, through the same lawyer who helped me get these boxes." He waved at his possessions. "Matthew has been very good at releasing funds when I need them so I can study, and help Randy and Jen with Castaways."

He darted a swift look at Dare, who was bemused. Dare wasn't quite sure why Jax was so uncomfortable. He had to know Dare wasn't into him because of any money he might have, because Dare hadn't known about it.

Dare tried again. "So, that's a good thing, helping the guys out. It's a cool gesture."

Panic flared on Jax's face. "Oh God, you can't tell them, please. They don't know I give them money towards the upkeep of Castaways. Randy would pitch a fit if he knew."

Dare began to see what Jax's worry was. "Ah, I see. You're an anonymous donor then?" He reached over and pulled Jax into him, kissing his cheek with lips that wanted to do more but for now were happy to be as they were. "That's admirable. So are you."

Jax's hands fidgeted at Dare's waist, as he clutched Dare's decidedly sweaty tee shirt anxiously. "I didn't want them to know, or they'd feel crap about taking my money. It's not as if I'd miss it anyway, what with it—" Jax broke off and pressed his lips together. His fingers fidgeted at Dare's side.

"What with it…?" Dare prompted gently. "Don't leave me hanging here."

Hell, it was like trying to get a kid to tell him where his tummy hurt, or what he wanted for dinner. Kean was just as evasive sometimes. Dare waited patiently, his fingers stroking slow, deliberate trails down Jax's spine.

Finally, Jax muttered, "What with it being, like, a shit load of money and I'll never use it all up in a million years."

"So why didn't you want to tell me?" Dare asked. "Are you worried I'll judge you because you're rich, or only stay with you because I know you've got money in the bank when you reach twenty-one?" He was joking but, when Jax stayed quiet, Dare felt sick.

Then Jax's ruined eyes lifted to stare into Dare's. "I just thought..." he took a deep breath. "I mean, I don't have such a lot to offer, and I was worried stupidly it might be the clincher, you know? Even though deep down I knew it was stupid, that you would never—"

Dare's temper flared and he moved away from Jax and glared at him.

Jax stared back uncertainly. "I'm sorry. I didn't mean to upset you. Me and my big mouth—"

"You think I'd cement what we have because I find out you have money?" Dare's voice was cold. His chest ached and his stomach roiled with despair that Jax could think that. "*That's* how much you think of me?"

Jax reached out desperately, gripping his bicep. "No," he said desperately. "I'm sorry."

Dare shook the hand off his arm. "I can't believe it." His throat closed up. "Here I am thinking we had something special when all along you've put off telling me about this in case I'm a fucking money grub." He laughed harshly, and Jax's anguished face paled. "I might be the son of a Traveller family who live in a caravan," he spat out, "but I'd never take advantage of you that way. Never."

His eyes stung with tears. He needed to get out of there before he said something he shouldn't. Something like: *I'm in love with you, you bastard. I don't care if you don't have a penny. I just want you.*

He swung around and started up the stairs. Turning, he saw Jax, face white, lips trembling. Those incredible blue eyes were full of fear.

Dare shook his head. "I just need to go and calm down so I don't say something I regret. I'll ask Clay to come down and help you up the stairs. Don't try doing it yourself."

"Dare, please," Jax whispered.

The sight of his lover's stricken face broke Dare's heart, but he shook his head again, willing the lump in his throat to disappear. "I'll call you later. Just give me a while, okay? We can get into sorting out your stuff when I come back." Then he clumped up the stairs, almost ran past a stunned Clay and managed to mutter a strangled, "Thanks. Could you please go down and help Jax up the stairs? I don't want him hurting himself," before making his way out the front door.

Once out in the bright sunshine, Dare stopped and waited until his nausea passed. He knew he'd probably overreacted, but he needed to be alone.

***

Jax stood in the basement, his heart pounding and the need to be sick overwhelming him. He was cold; his head felt as if it were stuffed with cotton wool and he thought he'd never feel happy again.

I've insulted him. Why the hell did I say that?

He'd thought it was time to let Dare know about the money, but he really hadn't handled it well. At least Dare had said *when* he came back, not *if*.

Hot tears tickled behind Jax's eyes. A firm hand grasped his shoulder, and Clay's worried face came into sight.

"Jax, let's go upstairs, buddy. You can tell me what the hell happened."

Five minutes later, sitting in the armchair in Clay's office, as the older man regarded him worriedly from across his desk, Jax was still numb.

"So what happened? Things were going well and then poof, Dare stormed up here like a dozen horny drag queens were trying to get their hands on him."

"I fucked up," Jax whispered, as he sat staring down at his lap. "I'm no good at this relationship stuff."

Clay snorted in sympathy. "I'm thirty-seven years old and I still fuck up at 'this relationship stuff.' Tell me what went down," he demanded.

Jax summarised what had gone down and felt drained once he'd finished.

Clay stared at him thoughtfully. "I can see why he's a bit pissed off," he muttered softly. "But like you said, this is new to you, this whole boyfriend thing, being in a relationship. And your man isn't the sort to bear a grudge," Clay murmured. "He'll come around. Give him a while to think about it and simmer down. I bet he'll call you."

Jax sniffed. "What if he doesn't? What if he thinks he can do better?"

Clay gave an exasperated sigh. "The guy would have to have rocks in his head if he thinks he can do better than you. And... he's pretty far gone, you know." Clay's tone softened. "The way he looks at you, treats you—that's a man who really cares about you, who'll forgive and forget. You're only eighteen, Jax, and that mouth of yours'll get you into trouble sometimes." He smiled. "Dare will realise that fact sooner or later and he'll call."

"Are you sure?" Hope flared in Jax's chest as he stared at Clay's calm face. "Because I think I love him."

Clay's face shadowed. "I can't tell you it will last forever," he said. "But you look at him with the same feeling I used to have about Tate when I was your age." He grinned fleetingly. "And look as us now. I can't get rid of the man."

He stood up, came around to Jax's side and pressed a comforting hand on his shoulder. "And if Dare doesn't come around, I can always send Graffiti around to make him see sense."

Despite the pain in his heart, Jax sniggered. "Yeah, that should do it. No one can refuse Tate anything."

Clay's nostrils flared. "Ain't that the truth."

Later, in his new bedroom, curled into his duvet with a cup of hot chocolate and his phone close by, Jax tried to summon the last vestiges of hope that Dare cared enough to do what he'd said he'd do, and call.

Jax sent a text: *I'm sorry I fucked up, I didn't mean to insult you. Please can we talk? I can't lose you. xx*

He fell asleep with his phone clutched in his hand, hoping that the next morning might bring better news or a message.

At this point, he'd take anything he could.

Chapter 16

Pain. Crippling, breath-stealing pain that ravaged his body. Jax clutched at his belly; the feeling of something loose inside him overwhelming. His throat was clogged with the taste of metal and blood rushed through his ears. He retched, bile and blood leaking from his mouth. He tried valiantly to pull himself to his feet to escape, but each time he tried, he shuddered in agony, hearing the crunch of bone.

For one heart-stopping moment, he believed his ordeal to be over. Then he heard footsteps pounding on the hardwood floor. He whimpered as dread and panic flooded his body.

"Little bastard, teach you to fuck with me." Terry's crazed roar echoed around the bedroom and Jax curled up into a ball, crying out as his stomach and back exploded in further suffering.

"Terry, please," he whispered. "Please don't."

Despite the ache in his throat, he screamed as stinging, acrid-smelling liquid hit his face. Instinctively, his eyes flicked open but he shut them rapidly again as something stung his eyeballs. That low buzz of pain soon became a shrieking crescendo. Before long, he was gasping in fear and scrabbling at eyes with fingers covered in blood.

Oh God, please let this stop, *was his last thought as agony took him and sailed him away into another place, a place where the torment ceased. Vaguely, somewhere, as he succumbed to darkness, he heard a woman's anguished scream ring through the house.*

"Jax, wake up. For Christ's sake, come on back to me, Baby Bird." Tate's worried voice penetrated Jax's psyche. He opened his eyes and blinked blearily at the distorted figure in front of him. His heart pounded, his eyes stung and all he could do was lie in the twisted depths of his bedding and will his pulse to stop racing.

"You were having a nightmare, screaming like a bloody seagull. Are you okay now?"

Tate's warm fingers brushed away wetness from his face and Jax took a deep gulp of air. "Yes," he whispered, as Tate's concerned face swum into clearer focus. "I'm fine."

"Hell, I thought you were being murdered in your sleep. Clay was ready to get the gun out and shoot the fucker."

Another blurred figure stood at the door, watchful and alert. "You good?" was all Clay asked as he loomed in silhouette against the hall light.

Jax nodded again. "Yeah. Just a nightmare."

Tate turned to look at Clay. "Go back to bed, baby. You've got a flight in a couple of hours. I'll handle this."

The figure in the doorway nodded. "You know where I am if you need me, either of you." Clay disappeared.

Tate stared down at Jax, his face creased in a frown. "Same nightmare as always?" he asked.

Jax nodded. "I haven't had it for ages. Looks like I'm losing it again." His voice trembled and Tate shook his head.

"Clay told me you got upset today. Things tend to have a habit of coming back when you're stressed. Believe me, I know. Remember though, it's all in your head. No one's going to hurt you." Tate's voice was fierce. Jax let the concern and affection wash over him like a warm blanket. He blinked sleepily.

"Go back to sleep," Tate murmured. "Try at least." He stood up. "Tomorrow things will be better. Dare's going to get in touch and it will be like your little lovers' spat never happened." His teeth flashed in a white grin. "Again, believe me, I've been there. So listen to the wisdom that is Tate Williams, aka the Love Guru."

Jax managed a tired chuckle. "Yeah, right." His pulse was steadier now, his heart not threatening to jump out of his aching chest. "Thanks, Tate. For being here, you and Clay."

"No worries. Sleep tight."

Tate left the room and closed the door behind him. The hall light went out. Jax's room was once again flooded in darkness. Jax pulled the duvet over his head and tried to get back to sleep.

After a restless night, he woke the next morning to a robotic voice in his ear.

"Got your message. I'll swing by after work. We can talk."

There were no endearments, but Jax took it as a good sign that there was still a chance to mend things. He spent the day trying to get on top of some sadly delayed studying and finally fell asleep on his bed, surrounded by papers and textbooks. He was awoken that night around seven o'clock by the doorbell. He switched on the bedside light and tried to finger-comb his hair into something more fetching than the sparrow's nest he thought he likely had on top.

Jax's heart thrummed and his palms were sweaty. He opened his bedroom door and listened to the low voices from the kitchen. It sounded like Tate, Clay and Dare were having a conversation, seemingly about the merits of ground coffee versus instant. At Dare's low laugh, shivers coursed through Jax. He heard footsteps coming towards his room and quickly shut the door and leapt back on the bed. He opened one of study books and sat there with it on his lap, trying to look casual.

There was a soft knock at the door and Jax lay back, shrouded among his pillows. Perhaps he'd give the impression he was relaxed and nonchalant, rather than the truth that his insides churned and his mouth was dry.

"Come in," he called out. Dare entered and Jax recognised his unique scent, warm and spicy notes of sandalwood meeting sweaty, sexy man. The fragrance rushed to his head, making him giddy, and he peered over at Dare.

"Hi. I'm glad you came over."

Dare sat down on the bed, the mattress shifting down. "I said I would, didn't I?"

There was an uncomfortable silence. Dare motioned at the textbook. "You been studying?"

Jax nodded airily. "Yes, catching up. This one"—he picked up the textbook and squinted at it, the words like blurred smudges on the pages—"this one is particularly tough going."

"No doubt." Dare's voice held the hint of amusement. "I see you've learned a new skill."

Jax blinked. "What skill?"

Dare grinned faintly. "Reading upside down." He reached out and took the textbook from Jax, adjusting it. "There. That should make it easier for you. And put your glasses on when you read." His eyes shone in the dim light, dark and warm.

Jax frowned, his ploy at trying to be cool and collected discovered. "You think you're so clever." There was no heat in his words though and he swallowed. "I'm really glad you're here. I'm so damn sorry I said what I did to you about the damn trust fund. It's my own damn insecurities making me stupid about this stuff."

Dare watched him intently, hands dangling between his thighs as he hunched forward on the bed.

Jax forged on. "I mean, I can't believe I have a guy like you, you know? Someone who's gorgeous and sexy and whole. Someone who could have anyone he wanted. I know you're a decent man, Dare. The best man I've ever met. So for me to imply the trust fund would make any difference to the way you saw me was reprehensible. And I apologise."

He leaned forward and laid a hand on Dare's thigh. "Can you forgive me?" He held his breath as Dare's other hand came up and covered his.

"You don't think I'm insecure about this too? About what we have?" Dare shook his head in frustration. "God knows I've thought about it often enough. I'm your first gay experience, the first relationship you've had. You're sexy, intelligent and a beautiful soul. What have I got to offer you beyond anything we do now? One day you might wake up and think, I'm only eighteen, I need to experience more than this one man." Dare's voice was husky. "And I would never hold you back from that if that's what you wanted. I'd have to let you go, so you could experiment." His voice caught. "It would kill me but I'd do it if that's what you wanted."

Jax's mouth dropped open. He'd never imagined Dare could feel this way. He always seemed so put together.

"But I don't want anyone else," he whispered. "I only want you."

Dare huffed. "You're eighteen, do you really know—"

Dare was stopped by the rough press of Jax's hand against his mouth as his temper flared.

"Don't you fucking dare say I'm too young, that I don't know what I want." Jax bit out fiercely. "I've been taking care of myself since I was fifteen and taking care of other kids too. I've been managing my own trust fund with Matthew, my lawyer, and making decisions around it. I've been studying, making my own way, so one day I can have a proper career doing what I love. I made my own decisions in hospital to have skin grafts and go through surgical procedures you don't even want to know about because they'd make your toes curl."

His voice choked up. "I've watched everything and everyone I love be taken away from me, and had to live with the fact I'm damaged goods and that I'll be lucky if a man ever wanted me."

Dare stared at him, his face cast like bronze in the dim light of the room. He was holding his breath, eyes wide. He looked stunned by Jax's passionate confession and he wasn't finished. "Then I found a man and fell in love and I'm damned if I'm going to let anyone take him away from me. That includes my own stupid mouth and insecurities. So, Kildare Patrick Rowan, you'd better be prepared to have me in your life for a lot longer than you think I might be, because I have no fucking intention of letting you go anywhere."

Jax stopped speaking, his breathing ragged. Dare simply stared and Jax wondered if he'd gone too far.

Then Dare chuckled and leaned in and placed his forehead against Jax's. Jax went a little squinty-eyed. Warm hands came up to frame his face.

"You are *so* hot when you get feisty like that," Dare whispered, and Jax closed his eyes as Dare's lips moved down to trace his jawline. "But I *never* want to hear you refer to yourself as damaged goods again. You have a fondness for that phrase and I hate it. I'll tan your backside until you can't sit down."

Jax had to say that didn't appear to be much of a threat to him right now with Dare's lips moving down his chin to kiss the curve of his throat. The thought of Dare's hand on his rear, spanking him, was a complete turn-on. "And most important, did I hear you say you fell in love with someone?"

Jax's eyes stayed closed as Dare licked his way along his throat and down to his collarbone. "Uh-huh. With this sexy, infuriating guy they call Candyman, which is a lame-arse name but it fits, because he's sweet and he works in a sweet—"

Jax's lips were effectively sealed and there was a soft, eager tongue in his mouth. He whimpered like a puppy and grabbed Dare's neck, pulling him closer. Jax lay splayed back on the bed, Dare's hard body covering his. There was the gentle thrust of hips against hips, groin against groin and hands that sought each other's skin as if grabbing onto life buoys floating on the vast expanse of sea.

When they came up for air, they were gasping, and Jax's groin was aflame, his dick pressing against his jeans. From the feel of the hard-on pressing against him, Dare had the same problem.

"You drive me crazy," Dare growled. "But I don't want this to be just about sex right now." He sat up, pressing his cock down with the heel of his hand. Jax stared at him, lips sore and swollen, his brain buzzing. He was torn between finishing what they'd started and hearing what Dare had to say.

Dare took a deep, shuddering breath and moved away. Jax couldn't help feeling smug at the intentional distancing. It didn't help that the devil on his shoulder whispered dirty things in his ear, entreating him to take advantage of Dare's state. Huh, go figure that the angel was nowhere to be seen.

"I need to tell you this," Dare murmured. "I was upset about what you said yesterday, but when I'd had time to calm down I understood why you kept it from me. Jax, I don't care if you don't have a damn penny to your name. I—" Dare stuttered on the words. "I love the man in front of me, the one who shines so brightly he blinds me. The one who has my heart in the palm of his hands. The man who owns me."

Jax pushed a lock of damp, dark hair from Dare's cheek and stared into his anxious eyes. "My Irish poet," he whispered as he pressed feather-soft kisses to Dare's eyelids, cheek and lips. "Is that your way of telling me you love me too?"

Dare's pupils were blown, black eyes staring into Jax's soul. "Completely," he avowed softly. "You had me under your spell the first time I saw you at Castaways."

Jax pushed Dare down onto the bed and straddled his lean hips. "So can we have make-up sex now? And I can lick all your tattoos?"

Dare blew out a puff of irritation. "No, I keep telling you. It's making love with us, not sex. And yes." Dare's eyes drank Jax in greedily. "It's time to make up. Lick away."

It only took a few fluid movements to arrange themselves in a sixty-nine position, and even less time to draw down each other's zippers and fill each other's eager mouths. And when light exploded in Jax's brain and his cock found release in the wicked and talented mouth of his poet, Jax knew his heart had found a home.

Chapter 17

Life had settled into a melange of passion, comfort, and being constantly delighted by Jax's inventiveness and wickedness creating havoc in Dare's usually ordered world. Jax had taken to having a boyfriend like a *Happy Feet* penguin enjoyed dancing. Sometimes Dare blushed at the things he was expected to do and the places he was expected to do them. For Jax, no place was sacred. Employing the skills he'd acquired—blowjobs, rimming (a particular favourite of Jax's, both giving and receiving) or mutual frottage—he made sure one or both of them came any place he took a fancy to. Dare hoped Clay and Tate would never find out what was done in their sex-prohibited basement one crazy evening when Dare and Jax had too much to drink while unpacking boxes. If the chair had a voice, it would no doubt be talking to a therapist now. Or it would have combusted with the level of heat generated by two horny male bodies. Dare's tats were a particular fetish, and Jax took great delight in driving Dare crazy with his imaginative tongue and fingers. The dragon on his shoulder was Jax's favourite; Dare still bore the bite marks of their latest frenzied passion.

Dare grinned as he tallied up receipts and scribbled IOUs from Sally. The basement romp had definitely been a night to remember. His boyfriend had a *very* flexible body—and an insatiable dick.

A cough behind him made him turn. The shop had been quiet today, despite it being the July school holidays. The air that blew in from the street outside was warm and scented with the fragrance of hot dogs and burgers from the vendor across the street.

Rob stood smirking at him, arms folded as he leaned against the door jamb. "Hell, you had such a sappy look on your face then. I take it life with the gorgeous Jax is agreeing with you?" Rob stepped into the shop. "It's been, what, three and a half months you've been going out now. When's the wedding?"

Dare shook his head. "No plans for that just yet. We're taking things one day at a time."

Rob smirked as he plucked a gobstopper from an open jar and popped it into his mouth. "You said yet," he managed to garble around the large candy. "Does that mean it's something you might do one day?" His eyes bulged as the heat from the Devil's Dick gobstopper—off the '18+ Only' shelf set higher up—made its presence known. These particular sweets had a strong cinnamon flavour, which grew stronger with each layer that dissolved. Dare had seen tougher men than Rob brought to their knees by the unmasking of the sweet's intensity.

Dare allowed a satisfied chuckle as Rob flapped a panicked hand at his mouth. "You know you have dick in your mouth, right?" Dare offered slyly and saw Rob's eyes widen.

"Bastard!" Rob hissed as he tried to disgorge the sweet from his obviously inflamed mouth. "This is fucking vile. Ugh." He managed at last to spit the candy out and both men watched as it shot out, landed on the floor and rolled slowly to a stop at the tapping foot of Sally. Her narrowed eyes were currently focused on Rob's reddening face as he tried to expunge the taste in his mouth with his sleeve.

"I think Dare has told you before to be careful about what you put in that big mouth of yours," she remarked drily as she prodded the gobstopper back to Rob with one pointed foot. "He has some experience in that regard whereas you—not. Now pick that gooey thing up off my clean floor and chuck it."

Rob bent down with a mutter and plucked up the offending item. He threw it into the rubbish bin. "Cursed, foul thing," he hissed. "Be gone with you."

Dare laughed loudly. "It was your own damn fault." He turned to finish reviewing the paperwork in front of him.

Sally moved behind the counter and sat on the stool. She took out a folder from under the counter and began sorting through it. "I hate preparing for taxes," she muttered. "Bloody sharks want to take every hard-earned penny."

Dare smirked at Rob. "Best keep out of Sally's way," he grinned. "She gets all tetchy when she's doing expenses and crap."

Rob scowled as he picked up a packet of Bat Boogers and peered at it in interest. He placed it back on the shelf. "So where's golden boy?"

Dare frowned. "If you mean Jax, he's due here in a little while. He had a meeting with his accountant this morning and he said he'd swing by afterwards. I've got the afternoon off and we're going to an art exhibition. Something called Blind Art. It's one of these tactile and audio-descriptive events."

Rob raised his eyebrows. "Sounds interesting. I didn't even know they did stuff like that."

Dare hadn't either. He and Jax were always trying to think of things they could do apart from clubbing that didn't impact Jax's vision too much. Cinema was a no-go because Jax's eyes grew tired quickly and they had to sit so close to the screen it was uncomfortable for them both. Theatres and museums were much the same problem apart from special museum exhibits that encouraged the other senses. Dare tried not to make a big deal of it because Jax was already insecure about Dare not being able to enjoy *normal* sorts of things together. Dare couldn't give a hoot. As long as he had Jax he didn't care what the hell he did.

Rob's brow furrowed. "He has an accountant?"

Dare didn't want to elaborate too much on this one given its sensitivity. "His dad left him some money when he passed away. He needs someone to manage it for him." He'd never asked Jax just exactly how much money he had. It wasn't something he cared to know, and the subject had never been brought up by either of them since their argument.

Rob nodded. "Cool. Well, not cool his dad died but that he left him some money. Anyway, are the two of you up for a party tonight after your art exhibition?"

Dare shook his head as he stacked packets. "Nope. Jax has a study night tonight. He has some tutor coming over to the house to help him with something he's struggling with. I'm going over to have dinner with my family. So sorry, mate, you're on your own."

Rob looked crestfallen. "Crap. I'm meeting this new girl at this party and I wanted you to be my wingman."

Dare snorted. "Since when are you worried about meeting a new lady?" He knelt down to clean the bottom shelves and move around the stock.

"This one is a bit special," Rob said sheepishly. "We've been Whatsapping and tonight we get to meet for the first time. She seems really great."

Dare sat back on his haunches and regarded Rob carefully. "Is this that Antonella person you've been enthusing about? The legal aid lawyer?"

"Yeah." Rob seemed a little nervous. "She's really clever and funny, and I don't want to cock it up."

Dare stood up, wincing as his back muscles complained. "Just be your usual charming self and you'll be fine. I mean, who wouldn't love the Robster?"

Rob rolled his shoulders and sighed. "I guess. I *am* pretty awesome."

Sally made a rude noise. Both men stared at her. She squinted at them from above her glasses. "What? I just realised I spent nearly fifty pounds on bloody cleaning fluids this year. I mean, what the hell? I need to figure out a cheaper way to keep this place clean."

Sally went back to her mutterings and Rob and Dare glanced at each other in amusement. Half an hour later, Rob finally left to go back to work. He seemed to be able to take exceptionally long lunch breaks.

When Jax arrived earlier than planned, he looked shamefaced. "I've left the tickets for the art show at Castaways," he confessed. "I popped in earlier to see the kids and left my man bag in the entrance. We'll need to pop past and fetch them. It's not too far out of our way anyway."

Dare kissed him hello. "Not to worry. I'm due to finish in half an hour then we can get off."

Sally waved them away. "Oh, go on with you both. I'll hold the fort. You lads go and enjoy your afternoon." She sighed, a mock put-upon sound. "I'll manage the bratty kids and elderly shoplifters all on my own."

Dare laughed as he kissed her cheek. "You love it. Queen of all she surveys and all that." He held out his hand to Jax. "Come on, sexy, let's go fetch the tickets. It'll be nice to see the kids again and say a quick hi. It's been a while since I saw them."

Fifteen minutes and a tube ride later and they were walking hand in hand up the leafy Camden street towards the Castaways house. Jax seemed content, and Dare caught him glancing sideways at him more than once as they walked.

"What is it?" Dare asked. "Do I have something stuck on my face?" He reached up a hand and wiped his chin in case he had leftover brown sauce on it from his sausage sandwich that morning.

Jax chuckled. "No, babe. It's just this." He lifted their joined hands. "The fact I have you and that we can do this in public is just..." He shrugged. "I never thought I'd have it, is all. I still have to pinch myself when I see you and remember you're mine."

Those words sent a thrill through Dare. He loved thinking of himself as Jax's. "Oh yeah," he murmured. "I'm yours all right. It's a pity we both have our own plans tonight or I'd show you just how much that rings true."

Jax gave a sultry laugh. "Talking of rings, you mean I could *own* you again? You've become a bit of a rimming slut, sweetheart." He squeezed Dare's hand and gave a dirty smirk.

Dare grinned. "I guess."

They were chatting as they reached the gates at Castaways, and Dare noticed a man standing beside the hedge framing the gate. Dare paid no attention to him as there was a bus stop close by. The man was probably trying to find some shade from the hot July sun.

As he reached out to open the gate to go up the steps, the man stepped forward. "Jax? Can I talk to you?"

Jax stiffened and Dare sensed the fight or flight response. Flight seemed to lose out as Jax's hand reached out and tightened around Dare's, his fingernails digging into Dare's palms.

"God, Dare." The pain in Jax's voice turned Dare's veins to ice and he stared at the man approaching them.

Without even thinking, Dare positioned himself in front of Jax. "Can I help you?" he asked gruffly. Dare's gut told him who this was but he daren't vocalise the name for fear it might make the apparition true and give it life.

The man standing in front of him was in his mid-twenties, stocky and at least six foot four. Muscles bulged through his cut-off tee shirt, and intricate tendrils of tattoos adorned each arm. His short, bristle-cut hair was dark and his eyes above the dark shadows of his face were shadowed, haunted.

Beside Dare, Jax gripped his hand tighter and slid closer. He was trembling, his face stark white, and although there was fear in his gaze, there was also hate.

The man swallowed, shifting on his feet like a boxer. "My name is Terry Afton. I'm Jax's stepbrother." His voice caught. "I was the one who did that to him." He gestured with a shaky hand towards Jax's face. "I need to speak to him, if that's okay with you both. I can see you're a couple."

Jax's hand loosened in Dare's and he stepped forward.

"Fuck. You," he spat, and Dare saw vehement spittle fly from Jax's lips. "I have nothing to say to you, so fuck off back to the hole you crept out of." He clasped Dare's hand again. "Come on, let's go. We have a show to catch. This piece of shit needs to disappear." He pulled Dare towards the gate, and pushed the latch to open it. The gates swung open with a creak.

"Jax, please. Wait." Terry stepped closer, one hand reached out entreatingly.

Dare turned and shook his head. "Don't get any closer to him," he growled. "I will smack you one. He doesn't want to speak to you, so leave him alone. And if you come near him again I'll call the police. I'm sure you're out on bail and this is probably violating your parole. In fact, maybe I should do that anyway. How the hell did you find him in the first place?"

Jax tugged at Dare fiercely, making him mount the steps with him. A couple of lampposts down, Dare noticed another man leaning against one. He appeared watchful, wearing a dark grey hoodie with a baseball cap pulled down over his face. Perhaps he was a friend of Terry's, there in support? Dare didn't have time to ponder on it because Jax was muttering anxiously beside him.

"Come on, let's go." Jax's fingers tightened in Dare's.

Terry's body slumped, his whole demeanour one of defeat. "That's true, but I don't care." His eyes closed briefly. "I needed to tell my stepbrother I'm sorry for what I did. I've spent the last few years regretting every moment of it. If that sends me back to prison, then so be it. It's where I belong anyway."

Jax snorted loudly but ceased pulling Dare up the steps. "Is that supposed to make me feel sorry for you? Some shitty sob story about how tough you had it in prison? Well, it won't work on me. Fuck off, Terry."

His words were tough but his body shook and his voice hitched. Jax was not as put together as he wanted to appear. Part of Dare wanted to shepherd his man into the welcome confines of Castaways and leave Terry on the doorstep. The other part wondered whether this was the closure Jax needed at last to put his ordeal behind him.

Dare was happy to play mediator because, if it helped in any way, it was worth donning the role. He could always kick Terry's arse later.

He stopped Jax's ascent, moving to stand on the same step. Dare grasped Jax's chin in his hands and turned him face forward. Jax's ruined blue eyes were wet, darkened with emotion, his face as pale as spoilt milk. He stared up, lips trembling, his Adam's apple bobbing, the pulse in his jaw throbbing insistently.

"Are you sure?" Dare asked softly. "I'll support whatever you want to do but do you perhaps need to hear what Terry has to say? It won't make things better but it might close that door that's always open a chink in your head. The one that wonders why this happened to you and where the rest of your old family are. Aren't you a little curious to find out why he'd risk having his parole revoked just to speak to you?"

Jax's lack of response gave Dare heart that perhaps he was doing the right thing. Jax's breathing was uneven. By his sides, his hands flexed open and shut constantly.

Dare persevered. "I'm here with you, love, so nothing is going to happen to you. I'll beat the shit out of him first." He glared at Terry, whose face was lit up with hope.

"He's right." Terry's voice wavered. "My counsellor told me I had to try amends somehow. She meant write a letter, I think, but this works better for me. I borrowed money from Mom to hire a private detective to track you down, Jax. I told her it was for a deposit on a flat. I've been trying to pluck up the courage to approach you for weeks."

Jax turned and stared down at Terry, his body stiff. "Don't ever call me Jax again." His voice was deadly. "*You* can fucking call me Jackson. You might have a twelve-step programme of some sort you have to do, now that you're an out-of-prison loser, but I'm damned if you get to call me by the same name my friends and real family do."

Dare had never been so proud of Jax or more in love with him than he was at that moment. Hearing that fierce battle cry, seeing the determination of spirit and the quiet ferocity made him tingle. His man was an awesome force to be reckoned with.

Terry nodded. "I deserve that." He fidgeted awkwardly. "So, do you want to talk here or...?" He waved a hand in the direction of the house.

"Oh hell to the no. You don't get to go in there. That was my home. We do this? You speak out here." Jax was uncompromising and he began to make his way down the steps again. Dare stood back, letting him do it on his own. The last thing he wanted to do was show Terry Jax needed any help. Jax would be mortified.

Dare followed Jax down the stairs and stood beside him, waiting, just being there in case he was needed. The man in the hoodie under the lamppost stood watching. Dare wasn't sure if he should go over and find out who the fuck he was.

He was jolted out of his paranoia as Jax squared up, tilted his chin up in defiance and growled. "So speak to me. I don't have all day."

Terry stared at Jax, and Dare saw the man was struggling with his emotions. When Terry started speaking it was as if a flood of words was being unleashed, an unstoppable force of pent-up guilt, regrets and recriminations.

"I came home that night boozed up and drugged to the eyeballs. I walked into my room and saw you there with that washing, packing it away. The great Christopher Grady's son, the boy who could do no wrong. Being all domestic and doing what he was told, the perfect son." Terry's voice was a monotone.

"I envied you and your father. He loved you so much and mine was a drunken rich tosser who'd left my mother when I was two years old and didn't even bother seeing me again. Your dad really didn't care for me. I knew that. I tried so hard to impress him but nothing seemed to work. So when I saw you, I just snapped." Terry's voice quavered. "I let it get control of me, the booze, the coke. The other stuff. I wanted to destroy something your father loved because he didn't love me, and you were conveniently there. I don't even remember all of it."

Jax was statue still, blond hair blowing in the slight breeze, eyes focused on his stepbrother. Dare could hardly breathe himself, the story sordid yet compelling.

"Afterwards, when the police took me away, I zoned out. I was horrified by what I'd done but there was no way I could take it back." Terry swallowed, fingers grasping at the skin on his arms, pulling it until it was pink and swollen. "I told my lawyer to have me sent to prison for what I'd done. My mother tried to fight it, to make me cop a plea of temporary insanity because of the drugs. I knew I couldn't do that. I deserved to go to prison."

Terry laughed harshly. Still Jax had said nothing, just gazed at Terry, his expression implacable. Dare brushed his thumb over Jax's fingers, feeling them twitch.

"Problem is that attitude is what got me out early. I didn't want parole. I wanted to stay inside as long as the sentence warrants. My parole officer and the prison psychologist fought for me, saying I was sorry, that I'd been rehabilitated. That I regretted what I'd done. I didn't have a choice in the matter and they let me out early."

Terry stopped, looking drained. "So I got out. My therapist told me I had to try and make amends with you, but not to make contact." He gave a twisted smile. "So you can report me if you want. I'm ready to go back inside."

Jax left the safe arena of Dare's body and stepped forward. "Where's your mother?" he asked quietly. "Where's Sylvia?"

Terry shrugged. "Somewhere in the south of France, I think. I haven't seen her since I got out a month ago. We've Skyped and she's sent me a ticket to join her at her and her posh bloke's fancy villa." His face shadowed. "Despite everything, I was sorry to hear of your dad's death, Jackson. You have to believe me."

He moved towards Jax and Dare stepped in front of him. "Careful," he warned.

Terry stopped and then smiled. "Your boyfriend seems crazy about you. I used to be, you know, a bit of a dick about things like this but not anymore. Prison changes you. You see things. I'm glad you found someone."

"No thanks to you." Jax's voice was a whiplash crack. "I've heard your story now, Terry. Is that all you wanted to tell me?"

Terry's eyes widened. "I wanted to tell you I was sorry. That I hate myself for doing that to you. I needed to make restitution with you. I need you to say you forgive me. And if you can, perhaps I can be in your life again, keep trying to make things right." His tone was hopeful. "I'll do whatever I can to prove it."

Jax was breathing heavily, eyes narrowed, lips thinned. Dare placed a hand on the small of his back, spreading his palm against his thin shirt, letting him know he was there.

"I don't need you," Jax said. "I have Dare now, and other friends. People who care about me and help me through things. I have a new family now, Terry, and you're not part of it."

Terry stared at him with pain in his eyes.

Jax reached out and took Dare's hand then looked back at Terry. "You're lucky. You still have a parent, a mother who loves you despite what and who you are. I suggest you take that ticket and get on a plane and start over. You have to live with what you've done. I've come to terms with my lot and I'm stronger now than I was."

He lifted his chin, strength emanating from the tilt of his jaw. "I forgive you, Terry, if that's what you need to move on. Take that fucking second chance you've been given and use it. But I never want to see you again. Stay out of my life. Next time we won't be so generous in not telling the cops you violated parole."

He turned to Dare and brushed a trembling hand across Dare's cheek. "Take me inside, please," Jax whispered. "Before I fall apart in front of him."

Dare needed no further instruction. Tenderly, he wrapped one arm around Jax's now shaking shoulders and started up the stairs. Behind them, Terry called out.

"I'm sorry, Jackson. I'll stay away if that's what you want. You'll never see me again, I promise."

Dare turned back to watch Terry leave, noticing that the man at the lamppost had disappeared. It must have simply been a curious onlooker observing the drama being played out in the quiet London street. Dare brought his attention back to Jax, pushed the front door open and got them both inside then watched as his boyfriend broke down in his arms.

Jax's quiet sobbing broke Dare's heart and all he could do was clutch his shuddering body close and let him finish.

There was a scuffling sound from the kitchen and Jen appeared, wiping floury hands on an apron. Her face flooded with concern when she saw the two of them. "My goodness, what's happened?" Her hands reached out to run through Jax's hair and Jax turned to her and pulled her into the hug.

Dare's throat was choked at being so enfolded. Jen's sweetly perfumed hair tickled his nose and he wrinkled it, valiantly trying to stop a sneeze. "We met Terry outside. He came to tell Jax he was sorry. It all got a little emotional. Bottom line, Terry's gone and I doubt we'll be seeing him again."

"Oh my sweet boy," Jen kissed Jax's wet cheek. "Let it all out, my love. We've got you."

Dare sneezed loudly and both Jax and Jen jumped almost a foot in the air.

"I'm sorry," Dare said. "That was such bad timing. Talk about ruining the moment."

Jax gave a watery chuckle. "No, it was great timing. I need to stop blubbering and man up."

Dare gripped Jax's face fiercely as Jen moved away to watch them. "Don't say that. What you did out there—God, you were so brave. I am so damn proud of you."

"Really?" Jax sniffed as he wiped his eyes and nose with a tissue Jen handed to him. "I was a bit of a badass, wasn't I?"

Dare nodded. "You were incredible handling it the way you did." He pulled Jax close and squeezed him tight. "I love you."

"Love you too." Jax's voice was muffled as he was pressed close to Dare's heart. "But I need to breathe, baby."

Dare laughed and let Jax go. They stood staring at each other, Jax's eyes shining with love. Dare's chest swelled with emotion.

"We've still got time to make that art exhibition," he said huskily. "Grab the tickets and let's get going. I'll treat you to a late lunch at that place you love so much afterwards."

Jax's face lit up. "Rainforest Café? I love that place. Makes me feel like a kid again." His eyes searched around the hallway. "Where's my bag gone? I'm sure I left it here."

Jen sighed. "It's in the lounge. Where you left it."

Jax grinned and kissed Jen's cheek. "Thanks." He motioned at Dare. "I'll just go get it, then we can go."

He scooted off and Dare heard a cacophony of hoots and cheerful hellos as the kids playing around the house spotted him. Jax's pleased exclamations at seeing them all made Dare sigh in resignation. At this rate they'd never get to the exhibition.

Jen came over and placed a soft hand on Dare's cheek. "Thank you," she murmured. "For making him so happy. I'm so pleased he has you. And I'm glad he's made his peace with Terry and that there's going to be no trouble. That little bastard doesn't deserve it, but our Jax has always been a forgiving soul."

Dare looked into the drawing room at Jax tickling and teasing one of the kids as they giggled like crazy.

"No, thank *you* for looking after him," he said softly. "I'm the lucky one. Thanks for keeping him safe and making him the man he is today. He's the most extraordinary person I know."

Jen gave a sigh. "He is unique," she admitted. Compassionate eyes looked into his. "It's not all going to be easy, you know. He's a moody soul, and he still has some issues to work through. But I'd say seeing how you say he handled Terry today, he's getting there."

"Yeah. He is. And don't worry. I've seen his bitchy side firsthand." Dare grinned. "I'm in for the long haul, so I think I can take it. The rest of him is worth it."

Jax came in, beaming and clutching his satchel. "Got it. We can go."

Jen pulled Jax in for a hug. "Enjoy yourselves. Come visit soon. It's the school holidays now and the kids would love to see you again."

"I promise," Jax agreed. "I told them maybe we'd take a trip to the zoo. Dare here can play chaperone to us all." He winked at

Dare, who wasn't sure how he felt about playing that role to a bunch of zealous, boisterous children. Including Jax.

"Don't I get a say in this?" Dare asked with a pout. "Are you trying to make my hair greyer?"

Jax reached up and twisted a strand of Dare's silver-laced black hair in his fingers. "I love the look, it's as sexy as hell. And I promise I'll make it up to you somehow." His wicked smirk left Dare in no doubt as to how he intended to make up.

Dare was sold. "Fine," he grumbled half-heartedly, even as his dick perked up in his jeans at the thought of Jax giving him happy times. "But I refuse to go anywhere near the insect section, if they have one. You're on your own with that one."

"My big bad dude is afraid of spiders, Jen," Jax crowed as he hefted his bag over his shoulder. "Like, girl-screamy scared."

Dare opened his mouth to say it had only been once—well, maybe twice—but when he saw the naughty glint in Jax's eyes he sighed ruefully. Why encourage his boyfriend? Best to accept it and move on.

"Come on," he huffed. "Let's get a move on. At this rate I'll not be seeing my folks for dinner and you'll not be seeing your tutor." He turned to Jen. "I'm sure we'll see you soon. Say hi to Randy for me, will you?"

Jax said his goodbyes and soon the two of them were out in the afternoon sunshine, as they walked to the tube station.

Jax's mobile rung and he answered. "Tate, hi. Yes, I'm fine, why?" His face scrunched up in disbelief. "You did what? Really?" Jax stopped. "I can't believe you were following Terry."

The man against the lamppost made perfect sense now. Dare grinned. God bless two crazy motherfucking Special Forces operatives or whatever they were, looking out for his man. He needed to send them a bottle of whisky or two to say thanks. Maybe a few Big Macs for Clay.

Jax stared at him. "You knew about this?" His face darkened.

Dare shook his head vehemently. God forbid Jax thought everyone was protecting him and he didn't know about it. Dare didn't have any intention of being the focus of any Jax's ire. "No, I didn't know anything. I did see someone lurking around in the area and wondered what he was up to. I thought he was just a nosey parker." He smirked. "I'm observant but I didn't know it was Tate. Sue me."

Jax scowled and turned his attention back to Tate. "So how long has this been going on? This protection racket?" His face grew fiercer. "Whaddya mean it doesn't matter? Of course it does—"

He stopped as Tate's voice grew louder. Dare could almost make out what Tate was saying, but not quite. For the first time Dare saw Jax speechless. He simply nodded every now and then as he listened to whatever Tate was saying.

Finally, lips pursing mutinously, Jax muttered, "I guess so, and thank you. But it's all good now. Yeah, see you later in the week. Say hi to Clayzilla for me." He disconnected the call and glared at Dare, who wore a wide grin.

"What?" Dare said innocently. "Did you get your arse reamed and not in a good way?"

Jax punched him in the arm. Hard. "Shut up." He grasped Dare's hand as they continued walking. "They had someone on Terry right from the get-go. Tate said he didn't think he was a threat but they weren't taking any chances. Apparently the regular spy dude told Tate Terry was on his way over here and Tate insisted on taking over."

Jax's face pinked up. "Tate said he was proud of me for facing Terry down. He sounded like he was going to bawl. I swear I heard him getting all choked up." He grinned. "Big softy." He frowned darkly. "Then he told me to shut the fuck up and just accept they'd always be looking out for me. After both of us."

Dare squeezed his hand. "We have good friends," he said. "I'm glad they care about you. Makes my job easier." He stopped, thinking that sentence would piss Jax off.

Instead of a protest that Jax could take care of himself, Dare got a kiss. A soft, gentle kiss as Jax framed his cheeks in cold hands and pressed warm lips against his. Dare lost himself in the moment. He didn't care that he was on a public street, or that PDA might attract the wrong attention. This was Jax.

When Jax pulled away, his blue eyes gleamed with amusement. "I'm not rising to that bait," he murmured. His hand lightly brushed Dare's crotch. "However, if you want *me* to start teasing, I know a few things to make you hot and bothered."

He sniggered and walked away, swinging his arse and beckoning Dare along with a crook of his finger.

Dare shook his head ruefully. "Note to self," he muttered as he followed the sexy backside in front of him. "You are never going to win with this one."

In all truth, Dare was content with his lot. Life as he knew it was pretty damn good.

Chapter 18

Jax couldn't see a thing. Literally. The black velvet bag over his head smelt of perfume and he wondered where Dare had got it from. He stumbled and heard Dare's laughing voice as a strong arm reached out and gripped his arm.

"Steady, baby. Just take it slow. I've got you."

Jax trod carefully over uneven ground. His new Skechers were going to get full of grass stains and mud from the smell of it. They were obviously in a field somewhere. Jax smelt the scent of hedgerows, briny water and damp grass, which crackled underfoot with frost. He shivered. His suede and lamb's wool jacket kept the chill out mostly, but he was still cold.

"Thank fuck for that. Where the hell are we going?"

Dare snorted. "Nice try. I told you. It's your second birthday surprise."

Jax huffed then wrinkled his nose when the fabric of the bag was sucked against his nose. "Some birthday surprise. You stick a bag on my head and tell me to get in the car. You're lucky I trust you."

It had indeed taken Dare a little convincing to get Jax to put the bag on. Having to be completely blind for a while had scared the hell out of him. Dare had apologised profusely, saying he was sorry that he hadn't thought about it. The look of abject misery on Dare's face when he thought he'd been careless had made Jax's heart ache. No one cared about him more than Dare.

Jax had graciously acquiesced to being effectively blindfolded, but with the stipulations that Dare would not leave his side and that Dare would touch him all the time so he knew he was there. It was partly fear at being in the dark and partly a need to feel Dare's hands all over him. Jax was particularly horny tonight.

The drive to wherever they were had taken only fifteen minutes and Jax sat back and daydreamed, using his time to think of the all ways he was going to make Dare give him a special birthday treat later in bed. Those fantasies had led to an uncomfortable tightness in his pants, a hard-on that still pressed against his tight blue jeans.

"Nearly there," Dare murmured. "Just a few more steps."

"Ugh." Jax's nose was assailed by a familiar stench. "Dare, is that horse shit I smell? Dude, if my new trainers get any of that crap on them, I am going to make you lick it off." He tried to hold his breath as Dare chuckled.

"It's horse shit, but you're nowhere near it. We're just downwind, that's all. And really—make me lick it off? That's disgusting."

"No more than having my new shoes coated in shit," Jax grumbled.

The Skechers and his new jacket had been a birthday present from Clay and Tate. Dare had bought Jax a new mobile smart phone, one that apparently did everything he'd need and had special software installed by the vendor. Jax had fallen instantly in love with it. He had also been thrilled with his new man satchel from Dare, a beautiful leather piece with plenty of pockets and zips.

"There's a lot of things I'd lick off *you*, sweetheart, but that isn't one of them." Dare's hand crept down and squeezed Jax's arse, causing his dick to go into a tailspin. "Maybe later I'll prove that."

"Oh God," Jax groaned. "Really? I can't see a fucking thing and you're giving me a boner now?"

Dare's husky chuckle did nothing to alleviate said boner. However, the loud un-Dare-like snort from somewhere in front of Jax and a whinny did help him take his mind off it.

"Is that a horse? Dare, why are we in a field with horses?" Jax felt a prickle of alarm. What the hell was going on?

"Hold your horses, baby." Dare sniggered. "Just stay still a minute while I get this off your head. You won't be able to see much 'cos it's dark but I hope you see what you need to." His voice was uncertain. "I hope you like your birthday surprise."

The hood was removed and Jax blinked owlishly, trying to focus. Dare softly perched Jax's glasses on his nose, and Jax blinked again as he slowly got what vision he had back. He gasped in wonder.

Directly in front of him, fireflies danced on the ground, leading up wooden steps. Jax tilted his chin, gazing up to the top and took a deep, delighted breath.

The fireflies weren't flittering insects but tiny tea lights that lit a pathway up the steps to an old gypsy caravan, door open, welcoming them in. It was brightly coloured in rich hues of red and green and blue. Somewhere inside it, more fireflies flickered. The scent of pine and sandalwood drifted down the stairs.

Jax turned to Dare. "Where are we?" he breathed. "It's like something out of a fairy tale." He wanted to pounce on Dare, hug him, kiss him and tell him how much he loved it, but he couldn't speak anymore, his heart too filled with love.

Dare shifted. "It's a field owned by a family friend. They let me borrow their caravan, and I set it all up here. Monk and Elder," he waved to the front of the caravan, "the horses, they're ours for the night too. So I can take you for a ride across the field in the caravan later—if you want to, of course."

"Oh God." Jax wasn't sure whether to laugh or cry; he wanted to do both.

Dare frowned and moved over to him. "Are you okay? I thought you'd like this, you always said you loved the look of these caravans. And you like horses, right?"

Jax stepped forward—he risked a quick glance down to make sure he wasn't heading into horse shit, a man still had his pride—and pulled Dare's mouth to his fiercely. He wanted to consume Dare, eat him, possess him like nothing before. He tried to show Dare just how much love he felt through his kiss, and when he released his boyfriend he was smiling but dazed.

"Dare, I love it. It must have taken you ages to set this up. It's perfect. My God, no one has ever done anything like this for me. I mean, a caravan, horses, all this…" Jax waved a hand. "It's perfect. Thank you, baby. This is the most awesome birthday present ever. And you know how I love my new shoes. And my phone."

Dare's face lit up amidst the flickers of candles. "I wanted to do something different." He tugged at Jax's hand. "Come inside. Let me show you what else I have planned."

"I hope it's nasty," Jax murmured as he carefully mounted the rickety wooden steps behind Dare. "Because I'm in the mood for nasty."

At the top of the stairs Dare turned and grinned down at him. "Nasty is most definitely on the cards. Later though. Right now, we have food to eat. Ta-dah!"

He released Jax's hands and waved inside the caravan with a flourish. Jax's jaw dropped as he peered inside. The caravan was small but compact and cosy. The flickering tea lights lent a romantic ambience. A blanket was spread on the narrow floor, with a bottle of something chilling in a metal bucket, and various plates scattered across it. They were currently covered with tinfoil and Jax imagined they contained food. He squinted around, trying to make things out.

Dare smiled. "This is a Bowtop caravan. It's rounded like a barrel and the one most Travellers would have. There are other kinds but Miriam and Lance own this one—my folk's neighbours." He gestured to the side. "On the left there's a small wood-burning stove, and here are the cupboards. And of course at the back, across the caravan and off the floor is the bed. It pulls out to be a double but isn't quite made for anyone taller than about six foot. Like me. So we may be a bit squashed later but it'll be worth it."

Jax moved inside, peering at the ornate carvings and decoration. "It's stunning," he breathed reverently. "I've seen them in pictures, but this is the first time I've ever been in one. It's gorgeous." His stomach growled and they both laughed.

Dare pressed down on Jax's shoulder. "Sit down, and we'll have something to eat. I've got all sorts under the tinfoil—smoked salmon, pâté, chicken, olives, those little sundew things stuffed with cheese that you like, and there's champagne in the ice bucket."

Jax sank to the floor and pulled a cushion under his backside. "This is amazing. The best birthday I've ever had."

Dare crouched down in front of him. "I'm glad," he murmured. "I wanted it to be special." He sat down next to Jax and began to take the covering off the plates. Soon they were both tucking in and sipping champagne.

Jax was feeling pleasantly lightheaded when Dare leaned over and gave him a champagne and smoked salmon flavoured kiss. "Time for your other birthday present," Dare murmured.

Jax giggled. He actually giggled. The champagne must be more potent than he'd thought. "You?" he suggested sultrily. "I'd like that."

Dare's eyes heated up and his jaw clenched. "Oh I am definitely on the birthday gift list," he whispered into Jax's ear, giving it a swift kiss. "But first, I need you to meet the lads."

"The lads?" Jax squinted around. "Have we got visitors?"

Dare pulled Jax to his feet and Jax stumbled, a wave of intoxicated dizziness washing over him. He found himself pressed against his Irish poet, front to front, and for a moment all time stopped.

This moment, this one singular time, would be etched in his memory bank like a lithograph. In a split-second flash of awareness, Jax realised that this moment was the one he'd been waiting for all his life: to be loved, cherished and looked at like Dare was looking at him now, with an expression of pure love mixed with desire. The gypsy caravan, the twinkling lights, the soft harrumphs of the horses as they stood waiting to be put to their purpose, and the smell of Dare's body, a mix of sweat, spice and cotton candy—there would never be another moment just like this.

"But there will be more moments," Jax whispered to himself as he laid claim to Dare's lips. "Lots of them, just as special. Promise me moments, Dare. That's all I want from you."

Dare stared down at him with hooded eyes filled with such emotion Jax wished he could bottle it and keep it close. "Jax, I promise you moments, my love. Always."

Jax nodded, satisfied. Dare never lied. "Whoever the lads are, they can wait. I need you right now."

Their undressing was a ballet of sensuous movements performed awkwardly in the confines of a narrow space. It didn't matter that the leftover food was scattered across the floor or the ice bucket overturned to spill what remained of the chilled water. Neither cared, their focus on the frantic pulling of clothing and clicking of teeth against each other's. Lips greedily sought more as the chill October night crept in like a thief and turned heated skin to goose bumps.

All that mattered was finally being one on the raised bed, which after one swift pull from Dare, had turned it into something comfier.

Jax cried out in ecstasy as Dare covered his flushed and sensitive body, taking Jax's mouth with passion and need. Jax's head swam, but it wasn't from the champagne. It was from being so completely possessed. It was from the hard thrusting of one cock against another.

Dare's breath taunted Jax's skin with heady pleasure as his mouth sucked and marked it until he thought he might die from the sensation. Talented fingers ghosted flaming trails across Jax's arse, Dare's soft caresses at Jax's rim making him surge upwards like a storm in need of breaking out into the wild open spaces. They'd done a little finger play before and Dare's fingers had been inside Jax, but this was like nothing Jax had ever experienced. The feeling of those urgent presses, the crooking of Dare's finger against that most sensitive spot caused Jax to whimper shamelessly and beg for release.

And when release came, hot, musky-scented fluid coated their hands and bellies with the force of their combined orgasms and shouted triumphs. The passionate storm passed and in its wake was left trembling limbs and heaving chests.

Jax's legs were wrapped around Dare, keeping him close. He couldn't move. Dare's sweating body warmed him against the night breeze wafting in through the still open door.

"I think we might have scared the horses with our shouting," Dare finally managed with a kiss to Jax's damp brow. "The lads."

"Oh, they're the lads. I did wonder." Jax was drowsy, satiated and wanted nothing more than to lie here with Dare for the rest of his life. "Pleased to meet you, lads."

Dare huffed. "They'll want more than that, babe. A carrot or two at least." He moved away from Jax, who gave a soft protest. "I need to move. My arse is cold."

Jax waved a dreamy hand. "We can't have that. I need that arse warm and happy for me later. For when we do this again."

Dare lay on his back, staring up at the ceiling only a little way above. He was too tall for the bed. Jax's legs almost touched the end, and he was a little shorter so Dare's knees were slightly open and crooked. Jax curled up next to him, flinging his arm over Dare's waist to keep himself on the raised bed. His backside was sticking out into the air as it was. This bed wasn't really made for two grown men.

Jax nibbled Dare's nipple, loving the sound he made. "I like your fingers inside me." He hesitated. "Does it bother you that we don't, you know, do anal?"

Dare stroked a gentle finger down the side of Jax's jaw. "Not one bit. What I get of you is enough for me."

Jax persisted. "But you'd like that, right?"

Dare laughed softly. "I would. The thought of being inside you would be heaven. But you need to be ready." He shrugged. "Not every relationship needs both guys to like it. We have it good just the way we are now and that's okay by me."

They lay in silence for a while. Jax had so much he wanted to say but he wasn't sure how to start. He took a deep breath and sat up to stare into Dare's fathomless dark eyes.

"So what happens next?" He trailed come-dried fingers down Dare's torso then whorled Dare's chest hair in small circles. The words came out of his heart in a flurry, like small pebbles rolling down a mountain.

"I mean, I'm still living with Clay and Tate and I need to be there until I graduate and get my degree and can find a job of some kind until I set up my business. Not that I need a job. My trust fund meets my needs adequately enough, but I refuse to rely on that. It's too soon to move in together, but we could I guess, if you'll have me, 'cos I can pay my way, I promise."

He saw Dare was looking at him with laughter in his eyes but Jax needed to get this off his chest before he exploded. He'd given a lot of thought to things over the past couple of weeks. "And I don't really know what your future plans are. Are you going to stay at Bon Bon Bizarre, like, forever, or have you another career plan in mind?"

Please God, I need him to stay. I need him to tell me it's going to all work out.

Dare shut Jax up by pressing urgent lips to his, taking his mouth in a gesture of possession and love, and Jax swam in the heady scent of that sensation. When he was released, he raised a hand to his lips, imbued with a heat that wouldn't stop burning.

"Oh," he said softly. "That was…" Words refused to form and all he could do was stare at the man in front of him who was rocking his world.

Dare kissed his forehead. "You think too much, love," he murmured. "It all gets stockpiled inside of you and then when you release it, it's like a damn cannon going off. You've been pondering on all this stuff for a while, haven't you?"

Jax nodded. Dare trailed soft lips down his throat and Jax closed his eyes in supplication.

Dare kissed Jax's ear sloppily. "I think you should stay with Clay and Tate for a while. Not because I don't want you living with me, but because I think Tate will kill me if I move you out after you've just moved in." He smiled. "And there's something I was waiting to tell you on your birthday which might impact any decision we make on moving in together sometime. Good news I hope." He looked uncertain.

Jax stroked tousled locks of hair out of Dare's eyes. "Go on," he prompted.

Dare cleared his throat. "Sally told me she wants to retire. Her arthritis is getting worse and, as much as she loves the shop, being there every day is getting too much for her. She and her husband Ben want to take a cruise too, some two-month thing they've been thinking about."

He sat up awkwardly, the flickering lights showcasing a body that Jax wanted to lick, worship and adore for the rest of his life. Dare pulled Jax up, his back pressed against Dare's chest, and he wrapped warm arms around Jax as he nuzzled his hair.

"Our shop is profitable, plus Sally has money behind her, and she's planning on opening another branch down in Devon. A friend of hers is going to run it in the interim. Sally and Ben own properties down there and she thinks she has the right spot for it."

"*Our* shop?" Jax teased. "Go on, I can tell there's more."

"She's given me full managerial control of the shop here and"—Dare paused—"Made me a forty percent shareholder in Bon Bon Bizarre. Including all the shops she plans on opening. She won't take any money from me, says she'll get her piece out of the back end of the profits." Dare grinned. "I own part of a business, Jax. Can you believe that?"

His voice was wondrous and Jax's heart leapt with joy. It was better news than he'd expected. He struggled free of Dare's arms and turned to kneel between his legs, hands framing Dare's face. His head bumped the top of the caravan.

"Baby, that's awesome news. My God, it's the best news I could get for my birthday. My boyfriend is a businessman now." He kissed Dare fiercely. "I'm so damn proud of you."

Dare grinned. "Yeah, it's a bit scary, I've never done the whole enchilada before but I've got this amazingly clever boyfriend and I'm hoping he'll steer me straight if I need it." Jax leaned in and kissed Dare soundly.

"Yum." Dare stroked Jax's arm. "So I'm thinking, I'll stay over the shop until everything gets settled and I'm up to speed with what I need to do, and then..." Dare brushed a hand down Jax's cheek. "Sally said we can decide whether I want to manage the London shop or the one in Devon. It's an option, depending on how we feel about it when it all pans out. It could be a while but..."

Warm hands stroked Jax's back and he practically purred in satisfaction. "Then perhaps we can decide where we want to live. Together."

Jax snuggled in. "I'd like that. Living by the sea side sounds intriguing, and I know you were born out that way. Our friends and family are here, though, so I guess we'll have to tackle that when we get there." Jax sighed in contentment and snuggled back in against Dare's body. It was good to have options. He'd never really thought he'd have them before he'd met the man in his arms.

Everything was coming together. Jax could see their future. He was never letting Dare go. Wild wolves would have to rip him from Jax's dead fingers before he'd release his man.

After a while of lazing in Dare's arms Jax sighed. "Didn't you say we could go for a ride around the field with the lads?"

Dare sat up quickly. "Yes." It was clear this was something he really wanted to do. "I didn't want to disturb you, though, you looked so peaceful."

Jax trailed lips down Dare's shoulder. "I'd love to meet your friends. Shall we get dressed and do this then?"

Dare looked down between them doubtfully. "We're a bit messy. Did you want to clean up or something? I've got wet wipes in the bag somewhere."

Jax shook his head. "Yeah, wipes will do." He brushed a lock of hair from Dare's eye. "I want to see you handle the horses and sit beside you up on the front. See my sexy Irish Travelling man be all macho."

Dare lifted an arm like Popeye, trying to look rough, tough and manly and Jax snorted with laughter. "God, you are adorable. And may I say that bicep is a work of art?" He pulled it in for a kiss on the tattoo. "Now let me get off this damn bed and then you can follow me down."

Jax jumped nimbly to the floor and snickered as Dare tried to untangle his longer limbs and broader shoulders from the confines of the bed to do the same.

Soon they were both clean and dressed and out in the cool night air. It was close to ten o'clock. Dare held Jax's arm, guiding him as they moved around to the front of the caravan where the two large horses stood patiently, nostrils blowing plumes of steam into the air.

Jax stroked the nose of the one closest to him. "What kind of horses are they? They're so big but they look gentle."

Dare stroked the mane of the other horse. "Monk and Elder here are Coloured Cobs." He shrugged. "Gypsy Cobs if you like. They're strong, brave, have great temperaments and are the real gentlemen among horses. My dad used to have a couple. As kids we were always riding them and looking after them. I don't get a chance to do that much anymore." His tone was wistful. Jax made a promise to himself there and then to buy Dare a horse for his birthday in February. He'd figure out the details on where to keep it later. He was sure Dare's mother would have an idea or two.

Dare motioned up. "Come on, up with you onto the front seat. They're all reined up already and ready to go. We won't go far, just around the field."

Excitement thrummed through his body as Jax climbed up onto the seat with Dare's help. He shifted his backside onto the solid wooden seat plank and watched as Dare sprung nimbly up and faffed with the reins.

Dare made some strange noises, gave a few commands and before Jax knew it, he was actually riding in a genuine gypsy caravan. He wanted to yell in delight but didn't want to spook the horses.

The caravan bobbed across lush fields, the horses snorting and chuffing softly. Jax looked at Dare. He seemed in his element here, standing up and talking softly to the animals leading them along.

Jax reached out and squeezed Dare's strong thigh. "Thank you," he said. "This has been one of the best nights of my life." He hesitated. "In fact, every 'best night of my life' memory I have is with you."

Dare's smile lit up the darkness. "My claim to fame," he murmured as he guided the horse in a slow, steady clop across the field. "I can say the same, Jax. Every single thing I count as good in my life has you in it."

Dare stopped the horses and sat down next to Jax, drawing him close. "See up there?" he gestured at the night sky and its glittery sparkles. The moon was full, a tie-dyed sphere of grey and white. "You're like that to me. A shining star that never gives up. It keeps burning, bringing hope to people."

Jax's eyes filled with tears. "That's because I love you."

Dare kissed the top of his head. "I love you too. Happy birthday, baby. I hope we get to spend a lot more of them together."

Jax nodded confidently. "Oh, we will. I'm not letting you go anywhere. You're my Irish Cob. My beautiful poet."

They gazed at each other, smiles on their faces.

"Are we having a moment?" Dare teased softly.

Jax looked at Dare, his chest swelling with adoration for the man he called his own. "Yes, we're having a moment. Now kiss me."

So Dare did.

HARD CLIMATE

To the gorgeous and talented Adam Lambert, for giving me the music to write by and for being the inspiration for Leslie, if people didn't know already. I know you won't ever get to see this dedication, but hey, it's worth saying. We all have our muses of music. You're mine.

ACKNOWLEDGMENTS

As always, I need to thank the people that know who there are for whom nothing is too much trouble: observations, support, excellent beta reading skills, and the genuine willingness to help no matter what. And for always being there for me.

At Boroughs, there's my wonderful editor Michelle Klayman to thank, who makes each one of my stories the best it can be and does so much to try keep one of her writers sane. Of course, you've all seen my fabulous covers, and the man to thank for these is Chris Keeslar, whose genius makes my covers pop and people go 'Oooh!'

I'd like to say a huge thanks to the people at one of the Brain Tumour charities—the charity doesn't want to be named—who gave me invaluable assistance while writing this book. Charities like this one, which work behind the scenes, trying to make people's lives better, make all the difference.

I'm not really a tree hugger. I understand the way the world works and that sometimes things have to be done to preserve a way of life, because sometimes there is no alternative. Yet sometimes there are, and that's when people like Mango keep us steady and focused. They try to keep the balance between chaos and progress, and I have a true respect for all of them out there.

There are so many more I could thank but then that would become a book in itself. So, if I haven't mentioned you, know you are still loved.

HARD CLIMATE

Chapter 1

A violent headache woke Ryan Bishop, the pain stabbing insistently with the vicious claws of a panther. He'd gone to bed with it and been plagued by troubled dreams that were now fathomless and forgotten.

Wide awake and knowing he'd not get back to sleep, he pushed back the covers. That small movement, plus his heavy head, made him want to upchuck over the side of the bed. He stood, dizzy and nauseated, then stumbled to the bathroom, where, a few moments later, he was brutally ill. His legs gave out and he crumpled to the tiled floor, clasping onto the porcelain seat as he vomited his guts out.

"Holy shit," he groaned, throat raw from his efforts. "Maybe it was those damn oysters we had last night." He and his good friend Lenny James had gone to a quiet but popular oyster bar in Covent Garden.

Ryan wondered whether this was punishment for overindulging on seafood and a bottle of shared wine. Based on his limited alcohol intake, he didn't think he deserved this god-awful headache. The pressure behind his eyes threatened to expel them from his head.

He wiped his mouth with tissue paper and stood, wishing he hadn't as his head exploded yet again. He swore, went over to the basin and winced when he saw the man in the mirror staring back at him. *That* man had cracked, dry, pale lips, his chalk white face surrounded by auburn curls matted around his small but slightly pointed ears. Bloodshot and bleary blue eyes blinked back at him.

Ryan groaned. "God. I look fucking awful." He reached for his toothbrush and plastered toothpaste over it. He brushed his teeth and tongue, trying to rid himself of the lingering bitter taste, and swore never to drink again.

Half an hour later, after taking some painkillers, he felt more human. He showered, dressed in a comfortable yet trendy tracksuit and went into the kitchen to call Lenny to see if he felt ill too. As he waited for his friend to answer, Ryan made one of his special protein shakes containing milk, banana, whey protein, a dash of honey and various multivitamins. It worked to alleviate the aftereffects of drinking. He badly wanted a smoke but he was trying to give it up. The nicotine patches were making him bitchy and irritable—more so than usual—and he wasn't sure what was worse, the effects of smoking or the constant mood swings.

"Morning, sunshine." Ryan winced at Lenny's cheerful voice as spots danced a polka before his eyes. "You're up earlier than I expected."

Ryan squinted at his wall clock, the display fuzzy. It was only ten a.m., so yes, by his standards he was up early on his treasured day off.

"Couldn't sleep," he groaned as he sipped his shake. "Woke up with the fucking hangover from hell and puked everything up. I wondered if it might've been a bad oyster?"

Lenny snorted and Ryan pulled the phone away from his oh so delicate brain.

"Bad oyster at Sonny's? You are joking, right? He'd kill you if he heard you say anything bad about the food at his restaurant. I ate from the same batch and I'm fine."

"Yeah, well maybe you have a cast-iron stomach or something. I didn't think I drank much either." Ryan took another sip of his shake, the headache receding a little.

"You didn't. We finished about one and a half bottles, child's play for us." Lenny's voice grew concerned. "Could be you're coming down with something. Stomach flu maybe?"

Ryan nodded, glad his head no longer threatened to fall off his shoulders and roll on the floor, as if he were an aristocrat during the French Revolution. "I suppose I could have caught something from the club. There was a stag group there a couple of nights ago. One of them looked a little under the weather. He was coughing and spluttering." He heaved a sigh. "Shit, I feel awful. I'm going back to bed I think. Try to sleep it off a bit."

"Sounds like a plan," Lenny agreed. "Brook and I are going to the theatre today with his folks." He sounded nervous. "They have this box at the Valedictorian. It's some play Brook has wanted to see for a while."

Ryan chuckled. He knew how neurotic his friend got around Brook's stately Kenyan, and oh so refined, diplomat parents. "Well, enjoy. It's a pity my show finished a few weeks ago. You could have brought them to see it."

"Yes, it's damned inconsiderate of those financial backers to decide they'd had enough of a run with your show. I loved *Come to Bed, Baby*. It was a classic and you were perfect for the part. Lucky you have a fancy drama degree from university. And we all know you don't need any encouragement to be a damn drama queen."

Ryan grinned. That was certainly true. "Well, it's not every day you get a chance to play a drag queen character named after your own night club. Delilah Delish was tailor-made for me. I know I did a lot of soul-searching about taking the part but I couldn't refuse Monty's offer."

Monty Franks was a well-known producer and playwright in Ryan's circle of friends. Ryan had jumped at the opportunity to tour with the play occasionally and perform his role at the theatre four times a week.

"Ten months was a good run and I only committed to eight anyway, so the extra two months were a bonus for Monty. I enjoyed every minute, but to be honest, I'm pleased to have more of my time back to manage the nightclub full time. It was draining jumping between the two. Kyle covered the club for me while I was on my drama queen sabbatical, but it's time to take back the reins." Kyle Tripper was Ryan's extremely capable front of house manager at Club Delish.

Ryan yawned. "And besides you know Laverne loves getting up on stage with me at the club and strutting her stuff with Delilah." Lenny's cross-dressing alter ego, fashion designer Laverne Debussy-Smith, was more than happy to accommodate Ryan's impromptu drag queen shows at Club Delish for the amusement of the patrons.

The delighted snort from the other end of the phone made Ryan smile. Lenny was so damn happy nowadays since he'd found his soulmate. The sexy Brook Hunter was Lenny's raison d'être, a beautiful man with an even more beautiful smile. Brook accepted both Lenny and Laverne with all the enthusiasm the man could muster. Ryan was glad Lenny had his happy-ever-after although Ryan did miss him in his bed. They'd been exceptionally compatible fuck buddies.

Lenny sniggered. "Oh God, I can see Brook's folks watching you flounce about on stage in your tight, slutty dresses, making all those filthy innuendoes you revel in. I think Brook's toes would have curled at the thought of taking them to see it, although me personally, I think they'd have enjoyed themselves." His voice became softer. "Have you heard from Mango yet?"

Ryan's headache came back with a force. "No," he snapped. "That bastard hasn't called me in over a month. Not since he left me a little note on my pillow saying 'Got to go, be in touch soon.' So fuck him. I hope he's in some primitive village being devoured by cannibals. They can eat his dick first, while he's still conscious. That'd teach him."

There was silence at the other end of the phone. It probably wasn't a surprise to Lenny that Ryan's on-off bed partner and, unfortunately, the love of his life, Mango Munroe, had gone AWOL. Mango was the reason Ryan was finding it so hard to quit smoking. The man drove him to a packet of cigarettes for solace like nothing else.

"Hell." Lenny's voice was hesitant. "I still can't believe he fucked off like that. I mean, the guy is crazy about you, I'm sure of it. But he's damn commitment-phobic."

Ryan laughed harshly. His heartache joined up with his headache and he wanted nothing more than to curl up in bed under his feather duvet. "You said it, honey. That man likes to have his cake and eat it too. We all know he struts into town to have his turn at my cute tushy and, once he's sampled the goods, he fucks off elsewhere. And I'm the incredibly stupid, naïve sucker who lets him do it. It's been two years, Lenny. I'm not waiting for him any longer. He can kiss my perky arse."

"I'm sure he does regularly, Ry." Lenny's voice was dry but sympathetic. "And this isn't the first time we've had this conversation, love. Maybe it's time to move on and find a man you deserve and who can give back what you give. You're one hell of a catch, Ryan Bishop. Don't let anyone tell you otherwise."

Ryan drained his shake and put the glass down on the countertop. He stared out the window at the street below. Two floors down, Soho bustled about its business, not knowing that Ryan's heart was breaking in a flat above Club Delish.

"I'm ready to move on, Lenny. I didn't tell you last night because I wasn't sure I was going to take it further. Speaking to you now made me realise I need to." Ryan took a deep breath. "I met this paramedic guy called Eric. He came into the club a while ago to take one of my patrons to hospital after the guy had a heart attack. Eric is hot *and* funny. We've been talking and he's been hinting for ages he'd like to take me out. You're right. I need to forget fucking Mango. In every way. I'm tired of fighting lost causes."

Ryan blinked one eye, which seemed to have lost focus. It took a moment before his vision cleared. "Anyway, I still feel like shit so I'm going back to bed. I'll keep you updated on the Eric situation. Have fun at the theatre with your man and his folks."

"I will," Lenny promised. "Hope you feel better. Text me tonight, let me know how you're doing. And stay focused with the whole not smoking thing. I'm proud of you for making it this far, so don't waiver. Speak soon." The line went dead.

Ryan sighed and trudged back to bed. He climbed in under his duvet without even getting undressed. He lay staring at the ceiling for a while, thinking about Mango and craving a smoke again.

"I hope wherever you are, you bastard, you're having a shit time," Ryan muttered. "You don't deserve any better. And when you come back? Don't come knocking on my bloody door. 'Cause this"—he ran a hand down his body— "is closed for fucking business."

***

Cat shit. He was up to his ankles in fucking cat shit.

Manning 'Mango' Munroe stood in the assembly hall of a small school in the middle of someplace he'd dubbed Rural Bumfuck. His eyes watered, his nose streamed and the smell seeping into his nostrils was acrid.

He stared around in disbelief, trying not to gag. "You have *got* to be fucking kidding me," he muttered, as he wiped his eyes.

Next to him, his friend Teddy was looking similarly gobsmacked and affected. "I know it's been empty a while but how much shit can thirty-odd feral cats generate?" His nose wrinkled at the vile smell wafting up from the stained floor tiles.

Mango narrowed his streaming eyes as a tatty cat slinked across the floor in front of him. "This is fucking ridiculous." He squinted down at his shoes. "These trainers are ruined."

To be fair they'd only cost a tenner at Primark but still.

"Maybe they have a damn cat signal like the dogs in *One Hundred and One Dalmatians* and this is their nightclub." Teddy cleared his throat. "I know the council wants to reopen this place but can you imagine any of your kids going here with all this crap? Even when it's cleaned out—yuck." He waved his water gun in distaste.

"Yeah, I'm never having kids, so wrong question." Mango looked over pointedly at Teddy's wife Della, another member of their cat-defence party. "But I guess you'll know that feeling soon enough."

Della was six months pregnant. When the smell had hit them as they walked in, both Mango and Teddy had tried to talk her out of staying, given her condition, but she'd been as stubborn as hell insisting she was helping them. Della, however, had been clever enough to wear a mask, scented with rose water, over her mouth and nose. Both Mango and Teddy had declined her offer.

Mango sighed. He knew when to give in to common sense, at least when he was involved in the job. Other times, not so much. "Hand over the damn mask," he said in resignation as he held out a hand towards Teddy. "I know you shoved them in your pocket. I'm man enough now to say I need it."

Teddy reached into the pocket of his hi-vis jacket and took out two masks. Mango put one on and Teddy did the same.

"Well if the twat of a council employee hadn't decided to play the fucking cat whisperer and gotten all scratched up and mauled for his trouble, we wouldn't be here trying to stop the exterminators," Teddy growled from behind his face covering

Mango nodded. It hadn't taken much prompting for Eco Drive Dynamics—the outfit they were currently helping out—to get wind of the fact that a whole population of feral cats was to be wiped out next week. The council hadn't taken kindly to one of their own being attacked by "dirty, disease-driven vermin," as they'd put it.

Mango sighed. "EDD is a fucking fancy name for a bunch of ex-university students and their rich, elderly patrons who've got more money than sense. But I couldn't get out of this—I owed Mick one. This whole event reeks of desperation from codgers who've got an axe to grind with the local council." He grinned. "Not to mention Mick is banging the head honcho of the money behind EDD. Lady Kitty Salisbury. I think she has some clout up high."

"Mango!" Mick Pleasant—CEO of EDD and banger of the aptly named Kitty—shouted across the cold, filthy floor. "Are you ready to go? The council guys are approaching; we need to be ready for them."

Mick shooed away a cat lurking a few feet away. The animals were mostly contained in the two rooms but various hues and mottled colours of feline still circled the assembly area. They appeared to be as wary of the humans as the humans were of them.

Mango glanced down at the primed and loaded giant water gun he held. He glanced across at his friends who held similar weapons.

They looked as uncomfortable as he did. Teddy still had a 'what the fuck am I doing here?' expression on his face and Della—well, she scowled and gave them both a filthy 'this is so not what we signed up for' look.

Mango sighed. This wasn't exactly his ideal way of fighting for the cause either but he'd said he'd help so…here he was. He was a man of his word, if nothing else.

When he replied, he hoped Mick could hear him through the mask. "Yeah, ready. Those suits won't know what hit them." This was said literally and metaphorically; the three people approaching them with an air of false bravado and trepidation wore shiny grey suits with white shirts. One of them, a man in his fifties, carried a clipboard. The others, another man and a woman, followed closely behind him. Befitting sensible council employees, they all followed health and safety rules and wore masks.

Mango grinned wolfishly despite his reservations. Fuckers were going to be squawking soon enough by the time he'd finished with them. Not to mention frozen. The low December temperatures outside were barely above zero.

The man carrying the clipboard cast wary glances at the few cats circling the enclosed area. He reached Mango and raised one bushy eyebrow. Mango was fixated by a long, stray hair on one of the eyebrows, which curled out of sync and looked as if it was trying to escape.

"You're going to intimidate me with a water gun?" Behind the mask, the other man's voice was muffled but sneering. "Perhaps you should go home to your kids, lad, and give them back their toys. You're not going to stop us."

"We're here to defend the cats' honour and preserve life as they know it,' Mick shouted from across the room.

Mango winced. He hated Mick's idealistic phrases, reeking of pretentiousness. He pulled his gaze from the potential escapee eyebrow and focused on the man's clipboard.

"Well, bully you," the other male councillor said. "They're damn cats for God's sake. They're vermin and we're within our rights as the owners of this school to get rid of them."

"Yes, but there are other ways to fix this situation," Mango argued. "We can potentially rehouse some of them. Neuter the younger male ones and send some of them to the animal control shelter. The local one has already agreed to help us take them in. It might be more expensive and time consuming but it's the humane way. And yeah, a lot of them will be euthanised but at least some of them will have a fighting chance."

"The operative word there being 'expensive,'" the female councillor scoffed. "We have a budget, you know. We can't kowtow to every nutter who comes along wanting to make a PETA statement. You people make me sick."

Mango snapped. He'd hoped they might see sense but there was obviously no other way to resolve this. He wanted to get home, wash the stench of cat pee off him and indulge in a pint of Guinness.

He raised his weapon, aimed and fired.

A stream of yellow liquid shot from Mango's water gun, hitting the clipboard carrying man full on the mouth. He sputtered and staggered backwards, moving the mask away from his lips as he tried to wipe off the liquid. At the same time, Della and Teddy launched their assault and the three council employees shrieked as jets of diluted Tesco's Value apple juice shot forth and soaked them to the skin.

"Oh my God, you're shooting piss at us," one of the men yelled as he tried to avoid the stream.

Mango cackled. "Yep." He aimed at the woman trying to hide behind her colleague. "I wasn't hauling out my actual pecker to do it in these temperatures. It would have fallen off and I don't give up my dick for anyone."

Well, apart from a sexy, cute, frustrating nightclub owner who has eyes of lapis lazuli and an arse like a peach I want to feast on.

Now wasn't the time to be thinking of his long-term lover Ryan Bishop. Too much thinking of his man drove Mango crazy. And right now he had a war to fight.

Regrettably, the battle was over sooner than anyone expected. Forty minutes later, Mango was pulled forcibly out of the school by two grim-faced policemen, one of whose face and uniform now bore the fruits of Mango's labours with his water gun.

Mango hadn't meant to blast the copper. It was only because one of the sneaky, cowardly council people had ducked that PC Plod had gotten the full wrath of an apple juice bullet.

Mick, Della and Teddy stood by, restrained from coming to Mango's aid by a number of other black uniforms. Mango was glad; Della was in no shape to be thrown into a police cell. Teddy would have fought tooth and nail to protect his wife and future child from incarceration and it would have done none of them any good.

Mango, however, was used to being thrown in jail. It was an occupational hazard. He'd never spent real time inside though, as some believed. That was an urban legend he quite enjoyed playing up.

He ripped off his mask and threw it on the filthy ground, calling out to his crew as he was escorted to the police car outside. "Call Ryan and let him know I might need him to bail me out. Don't come near the police station. I don't want anyone detaining you or Della." Ryan had Mango's emergency credit card under lock and key and was often called upon to provide bail money or similar emergency funds. "The bastard will probably mouth off but tell him he needs to listen and pay any fines. Fucking pronto too, tell him."

That last comment was valid. It wouldn't be the first time Ryan had let Mango languish in a prison cell for a couple of days out of some sort of petty vengeance for him being in trouble again. He might be a gorgeous and sexy bit of goods but Ryan had a nasty streak when he was pissed off.

***

Mango was in a foul temper. It had been nearly fifteen hours since he'd been hauled off to the local police station in Rural Bumfuck. He still wasn't sure exactly what village he was in; he had a bad memory for place names. All he knew was it started with Meadow and was somewhere in Norfolk.

He'd been fortunate. The police officer who'd been drenched by what had since been established *wasn't* urine had calmed down by the time Mango got back to the picturesque but small police station. Sergeant Merrow had locked Mango in a room with a chair and a table after allowing him his phone call. Mango had phoned Ryan but there'd been no answer. The sergeant had smirked the whole way through the one-sided conversation, including the message left, which had simply been, "Get me the fuck out of this hellhole."

Mango slurped down the now cold coffee he'd been given and sat tight. Luckily it appeared no charges were being filed. He *was* pissed off at having to be claimed as if he were a pawned item. It didn't look as if Ryan had been sympathetic to Mango's message considering how long Mango had now been incarcerated.

"That man needs a spanking," Mango muttered as he stood up and stretched. His knees creaked and he winced. "It's been a while since I gave him one." That thought made his groin ache and he scowled. The last thing he needed now was a boner. "He'd better bloody get here soon before I start gnawing through the walls like a fucking beaver."

An hour later Mango was seriously contemplating his rodent escape plan. It was only the sudden unlocking of the door and appearance of a grinning Sergeant Merrow that saved Mango's teeth and fingers.

"Your friend paid the fine." Merrow smirked as he leaned against the door. "He's a feisty one, isn't he? And I think perhaps you might be in a spot of bother when you get home, mate. He wasn't happy with you at all. No, not at all."

"Yeah, so what else is new," Mango muttered as he shrugged into his worn suede jacket. The small room had been hot and stuffy and he stunk of sweat, crap and apples. "Ryan is always pissed off with me for something."

"No, he wasn't particularly complimentary," Merrow agreed as his eyes crinkled in amusement. "I think 'overgrown schoolboy,' 'damned fucking tosser' and, my personal favourite, 'deluded fuckwad cocksucker,' formed most of the conversation."

Mango stood before the policeman and glared. "That's all? Practically fucking terms of endearment coming from him. I've heard worse. So I'm free to go now?"

Sergeant Merrow nodded. "Yes. Although if it were me, I'd be staying here where it's nice and safe." He chuckled loudly.

Mango shrugged. He rather liked the sergeant.

"I like living dangerously." Mango held out a hand. "Thanks for not making a big deal out of this. I'm sorry you got blasted with apple juice. It was those officious council bastards I wanted to get a point across to."

Sergeant Merrow grasped Mango's hand and shook it. Mango winced as his fingers were crushed. The policeman had one hell of a grip.

"Those officious council bastards pay my salary, so I have to defend them. And between you and me, mate, we need the school opened. The kids need somewhere to go and for the people who live here, a bunch of cats shouldn't come before them." Keen eyes observed Mango who had sympathy now for errant schoolboys being chastised by the headmaster. "I think your ploy worked though. I understand the parties are at least talking about alternatives to killing the poor furry blighters. Maybe you can arrange with them to come to a compromise?"

Despite Mango's activism, he was always willing to hear the other side's story. "That's all we wanted in the first place and they refused to listen." He nodded. "I'm sure there's an easier way to fix this."

Sergeant Merrow nodded. "Good. I'd hate to see you in here again because next time, I might not go so easy on you."

Mango grunted as he passed the policeman and started towards the exit. "Oh and it's a clowder of cats by the way. Not a bunch."

Smirking at having the last word, Mango didn't notice the person lunging towards him. He heaved an "oof" as said person wrapped warm arms around him and hugged tightly. A protruding belly pushed against him and Mango wriggled uncomfortably. It felt weird.

"There you are. We were getting worried about you. Ryan called and said you'd be getting out soon and might need a lift." Della Wick stepped back and stared at Mango from under a swathe of blonde hair. Her brown eyes were concerned. "You okay, no one hurt you? 'Cos if they did, we can claim police brutality—"

Mango flapped a hand in irritation. "Don't be daft. This isn't damn *Luther*. The cops were fine with me. I want to get home and have a shower. I reek of cat shit."

Della narrowed her eyes and stared at him. "Someone's in a mood."

Mango sighed and gave her shoulder a pat. He wasn't one for displays of affection, something which was part of his problem with Ryan. With all his friends too and Della and Teddy were among the best. They'd known each other for over ten years. "Sorry. I've been cooped up in that shithole for hours and I'm knackered. I think Ryan might chop off my balls too while I'm asleep, providing we see each other again soon. He's pissed off with me."

Della chortled. "Oh boy, is he ever. You should have heard him on the phone to me."

Mango growled. "Yeah, I've heard some of the choice phrases he used to describe me. But I don't get it. You guys were there too and he's not mad with you. What's so special about me?"

Della reached out and punched Mango's arm. "*We* didn't run off for nearly a month without telling our partner where we were going or keeping in touch. *We* weren't the ones who called said partner and asked once again to be bailed out of a bad situation. You know you only call Ryan when it's convenient, Mango. It's not the first time we've had this conversation."

Her tone was exasperated and Mango scowled. "Ryan isn't my *partner*. He's a guy I fuck when I have the need. I don't owe him any explanations. He knows I travel around a lot."

Deep down inside he knew the words were hollow and untrue. Ryan was far more than a fuck buddy but he wasn't ready to admit it yet. That way, Mango couldn't hurt him. Past experience had taught him it was best not to let people get attached.

Della smiled, her eyes pitying. "You keep telling yourself that, idiot. Everyone knows he means more to you than you show. But hey, you stick your stubborn head in the proverbial cat shit and hope it doesn't choke you."

She flapped a hand towards the car park. "Come on, I'll drive you back to the hotel. Everyone's waiting there. It seems we might have a solution to the problem."

"Oh? What would that be?" Mango followed Della to the minivan. "I believe our little sit-in worked, according to the bobby in the police station."

Della nodded as she opened the car door and clambered in clumsily, cursing when her stomach got in the way. "God, I'll be glad to get this little bugger out of me."

Mango grinned as he got into the passenger seat. "I'm glad I'm a bloke. It might be fun sticking in it but getting something out?" He shook his head. "I don't envy you women. I'm in awe of you though."

The car started and they began the drive back to the bed-and-breakfast they'd been staying in while plotting their protest.

Mango sat back and enjoyed being chauffeured. "So some compromise has been reached?"

Della nodded. "Apparently our little escapade came to the attention of some council bigwig who was unaware her staff had planned to murder a shitload of mummy and daddy cats and their babies. She's insisted we find another way around it—like having a specialist team come in and take them to the animal shelter we spoke about. It'll cost more and take more time but it will make everyone happier." She snickered. "Apart from the councillors currently having their arses reamed by Mrs. Bigwig for not doing the 'right thing.'"

"Huh." Mango couldn't argue with the result. "Kudos to the council bigwig."

"Mick's meeting with her now. Councillor Gwyneth Merrow is going to be a local celebrity in animal conservation circles by noon today, methinks."

Mango felt his mouth spread in a wide grin. "Merrow, huh?"

Thank you, Sergeant. I had no doubt you contributed to this turn of affairs. I don't believe in coincidence.

He cleared his throat as Della expertly navigated bucolic country lanes and avoided cyclists and hikers on the side of the road. The area was teeming with them.

"So, you spoke to Ryan? How was he?" Mango cast a quick glance at his friend.

Della snorted loudly. "He's a filthy-mouthed diva who wants your balls on a platter is what he is. I've never heard him so angry, and believe me, I've heard him mad at you before. But this time, methinks he's had enough."

Mango's alarm grew. "Why, what did he say?"

Della looked at him, her face prim. "I'm a lady, I can't repeat half the things he called you. There was a lot of fucking, buggering and other nasty words involved. Oh, and something about a cannibal and your cock, I forget the exact words he used. It didn't sound as if it was a pleasant experience anyway."

"Crap." Mango stared out of the windscreen at the curved road ahead. "Sounds like I'm in a load of trouble." He missed most of Della's quiet murmur but it sounded suspiciously like, "Serves you fucking right."

A surge of guilt swept over him. Ryan *didn't* deserve Mango's shoddy treatment. To be the man left behind when Mango was off on what Ryan had laughingly called "his crusades" had to suck. "His crusades" had started out as a term of affection between them and had now metamorphosed into more of a curse.

"So, anyway, he told me he's got some hot date next week with some sexy paramedic. Mm. Got to love a man in uniform." Della's words cast a chill down Mango's spine.

"He what? He has an actual date? Not a hook up?" His stomach clenched at the thought of Ryan getting involved with someone else.

Della shrugged. "He's tired of waiting, my friend. You can't blame him. That man only had eyes for you." She flapped a hand. "And now you've kept him hanging on far too long. The man has needs." She narrowed her eyes. "And Ryan doesn't do casual fucks, despite what you might think. He waits for you to come around to your senses and see him."

"He sleeps with Lenny," Mango snapped. "They're as tight as two budgies on a perch."

Della sniffed. "He hasn't done Lenny since *he* found true love with his gorgeous Brook fella. And before, it was pretty random between the two of them anyway. Ryan was travelling around with the show and depending on your dick when it was around, to keep him happy he played with Lenny. So it's only been you, I think, and that hasn't happened much given your predilection for running off without telling him."

"How the fuck do you know all this?" Mango demanded. "Are you his new best friend or what?"

That should be my *fucking role.*

Della cast him a pitying look as she pulled into a parking spot in front of the small bed-and-breakfast they were staying in. She switched off the engine and opened the door, struggling to get out of the car. "We're on Facebook. He messages me on WhatsApp. We chat. Which is more than you bloody do." She slammed the door and Mango grunted. He hauled himself out of the car and glared at Della over the roof of the car.

"I hate social networks crap. And we have an open relationship. He can fuck who he wants." Those last words stung like hell, soured the taste in his mouth and Mango scowled. It looked as if a man in uniform could be the next one to enjoy the fruits of Ryan's lithe and oh so sexy body and soft lips and vanilla scented skin. Mango's skin crawled at the thought. He hadn't minded Lenny so much, but anyone else... Well, he knew he had no choice given their agreement, but he didn't have to like it.

What the hell am I doing letting someone else take him away from me? Christ, I need to sort out this clusterfuck of a relationship before I end up losing him. Fuck, no way I can handle that.

God, he was such a hypocrite.

Mango had his own set of rules when it came to satisfying his carnal needs when he and Ryan were apart. Quick, impersonal blow jobs only. He'd never stayed in another man's bed other than Ryan's, didn't get into kissing and certainly never went the whole hog. His arse was reserved for Ryan and Ryan alone. He knew he was fucked up but he did have some decency reserved deep down in his psyche.

Della shook her head pityingly. "It's not about the physical, dolt head. It's about what he needs emotionally. And there, you big jerk, is where you're missing the plot."

Mango knew he wasn't. He knew the plot well; he simply chose not to follow it. In his heart, he knew Ryan *was* the only man Mango had ever considered giving it all up for and committing to. In moments of loneliness, fighting his way through a rain forest or standing on the prow of a ship saving seals, Mango truly believed Ryan was all he ever wanted.

But I can't tell him. It's unfair to make a person hope one person is ever enough for them.

His own family drama sprung unbidden into his mind and Mango's gut seized. He wouldn't take the chance of that particular tragedy ever happening again. He swallowed hard as he stared out at the scenery beyond. He clenched his hands in front of him to stop them fidgeting. Memories flooded his soul and he pushed them deep down where they belonged. The past could not be undone.

Ryan Bishop was a good man, a man worthy of something so much more than their bursts of togetherness but Mango wasn't sure how to give it to him.

He followed a waddling Della up the path into the bed-and-breakfast and guessed he'd spend the rest of the day and night in the little country hotel, then head home tomorrow to his flat in Camden. He had a burning need to make a plan to go eat humble pie and visit Ryan. It sounded as if there were some bridges to be mended—again.

The thought that Mango might have irrevocably fucked things up between them made him nauseous. When he reached his hotel room, he wanted nothing more than a shower to wash off the cat shit stench and gather his thoughts. He had a man to appease and win back.

And knowing Ryan Bishop, he wasn't going to make it easy.

Chapter 2

"You have *got* to be fucking kidding me."

Ryan gulped down the remains of his Heavenly Hawaiian Kona Coffee and stormed over to his front door. He was as pissed off that he'd wasted a mouthful of expensive and exclusive coffee as he was with Mango, who stood at the entrance to his building being an insistent pest.

After the first buzz of the doorbell, Ryan had checked the security camera to determine who his visitor was. When he'd seen it was Mango, he'd ignored the bastard. Mango obviously didn't have the keys he'd been given for Ryan's flat and Club Delish in case of emergencies.

The buzzer had gone again. And again. Each time Mango lay on the bell longer than before. The fourth time it sounded, Ryan was ready to commit murder. The overwhelming desire to punch Mango's lights out was, however, accompanied with an instant body tingle at the sight of his lover. Ryan knew this moment had been coming but he still wasn't prepared for what he needed to do.

He flung the door open and put his hands on his hips. "You've got a fucking nerve," he growled as Mango smiled hesitantly at him.

"Sorry for the buzzing and knocking." Mango waved a tanned hand. "I didn't have my keys with me."

Ryan's temper got the better of him. "It's been six fucking weeks. Haven't you got a whale to save or a bat to protect? Maybe visiting a whole rain forest of pygmy dwarves and their habitat? I know I have nothing here that might pique your eco-warrior interest so you may as well piss off." Part of Ryan hoped

Mango might do as he was told and postpone the pain for another day.

"Hello to you too, babe." Mango raised one eyebrow. Ryan had to admit each time he did that it was as sexy as hell. And Mango knew it. "Pygmy dwarves?" Mango drawled, with amusement. "I had that particular excursion a few months ago, remember?"

"Don't call me babe." Mango's smile faltered as Ryan took the comment and ran with it. "And I remember the whole pygmy dwarves scenario *very* well. It was the night you left me at dinner sitting alone like some pathetic man waiting for his date because you had an urgent plane to catch."

Mango looked a little abashed but Ryan hadn't finished. He waggled his index finger in Mango's face. "Oh, wait, I remember now, the pathetic man waiting for a date *was* me. Because his date-to-be decided he had more important places to go." Ryan took a deep breath, willing his ever-fiery drama queen to stay on the down-low. The throb in his temples signalled a low-grade headache coming on.

Mango held out a hand in a 'whoa, stop' gesture. "Ryan, I explained about that. The only plane out to the North Congo was the one I had to catch. They'd grounded a whole load because of some rainstorm coming in. It was the only way to get in and out of the conservation area." He grinned faintly. "And for the record, you call them pygmies, not pygmy dwarves."

Carefully constructed break-up plan forgotten, Ryan's temper combusted at Mango's teasing. "What-the-fuck-ever," he exploded and slammed the door right in Mango's face. He only wished Mango's nose had been closer so he could have had the pleasure of hearing it break.

The knocking started as Ryan stalked into the kitchen to calm down and pour himself another cup of coffee from his cherished Fracino Bambino coffee machine. Ryan was aware he had two noteworthy vices—Mango and good coffee. Three, if you counted his favourite singer, young teen sensation Callum Webster, who was currently crooning his way through melodies on Ryan's fabulous sound system. Despite the fact Ryan was thirty years old, cute young, gay Callum was all it took for Ryan to sigh dreamily and melt like a teenage girl.

Five minutes later, try as he could, Ryan couldn't turn a deaf ear to the intermittent tap of knuckles against his front door. He closed his eyes and took a deliberate sip of his drink. Then he managed a deep breath and went back to open the door gently because if he pushed it open the way he wanted to, he'd possibly take it off its hinges. Ryan folded his arms across his chest as he waited for Mango to speak.

"Jesus, Ryan. Could you at least invite me in so we can talk about this?" Mango's nostrils flared and he ran a hand through hair Ryan noticed had grown longer. He rather liked the tousled, hippy look. He also liked the neatly clipped beard framing Mango's delectable mouth.

Mango's watchful dark eyes regarded Ryan with an expression he wasn't sure he could name. Mango's eyes had always fascinated Ryan. So dark brown as to appear black, they were as sexy as fuck when Mango came inside him.

Ryan took a deep breath. Back off, he admonished himself silently. You're not supposed to care what he's feeling, remember? Whether it was regret or resignation in Mango's eyes, it didn't matter. *It's all bullshit. And this bullshit will be over soon.* Ryan's heart thudded and he was sure anyone within a few feet could hear its distress.

Mango did an exasperated half turn in the corridor and swung back around to face Ryan again. One muscled arm waved a hand in the air. "For fuck's sake. Do I need to beg? Fine, I'll do it. Please may I come into your home, Ryan, so we can talk some more and clear the air?"

Ryan regarded this burly man who had his heart, then acquiesced and waved Mango inside. What he needed to say should be done indoors. Because afterwards Ryan would no doubt fall apart. "Be my guest. Please, come in."

He got a kick out of seeing Mango's lips tighten and his hands clench at the sarcasm. *Screw you. You're in the wrong here not me so don't give me attitude.*

Ryan walked through the open plan lounge dining room and into his kitchen. He took another sip of his coffee, making a point not to offer Mango anything. "So, how did your birthday go? *I* spent the thirty-first of December dining with a rather splendid older man I met at the club. Afterwards I brought him back here and fucked his brains out. What kind of present did *you* get for your special day?" His tone was mocking and the ache in his chest grew as Mango's face paled.

Mango had told Ryan months ago they'd celebrate Mango's thirty-fourth birthday in style as they'd missed celebrating the previous one together. Ryan had made plans for them to go away to somewhere warm with beaches and sea. Then Mango had disappeared on one of his missions and Ryan's dream of a luxury getaway with the man he loved had vanished.

"Jesus, Ryan." Had Ryan imagined the flash of pain in Mango's eyes? It had flitted across his face too, Ryan was sure but it was gone in an instant. "I was in Norfolk with Della and Teddy, on a job. I didn't even think about my damn birthday."

"Obviously not," Ryan drawled as he went into the lounge and flung himself onto his plush leather couch. He curled up in one corner, bit a nail nervously and regarded Mango.

Ryan cast a yearning eye around the room for his cigarettes but remembered he'd locked them away in the sideboard in his bedroom. "Or else you would have remembered we were supposed to go away over Christmas and this year we were doing something special for your birthday." He shrugged. "No matter. I enjoyed your birthday on my own." He grinned but he didn't feel happy. "Well, not quite on my own," he clarified with a lick of his lips. "I was with Adam. He took me to the Callum Webster concert. You know, the singer I lust after and have been trying to get you to see? I decided to treat myself and we went together."

Mango's eyes darkened. A jolt of realisation punched Ryan in the gut. Mango wasn't happy with the scenario Ryan had painted. His "throw it out there" comment about Adam, aimed at taunting Mango, had hit a nerve.

What the hell was *that* all about? Mango had made it quite clear he wasn't ever going to commit and they were both free to muck around. So why was Ryan's fake story making Mango look as if he wanted to be ill?

Ryan had indeed brought Adam Lazarus back to his flat but the fucking out of brains hadn't happened. Ryan's heart simply wasn't in it. He had never wanted an open relationship in the first place.

Since June last year, he hadn't even had Lenny to scratch his itches anymore. To be fair, it had been as far as Ryan had been prepared to take screwing around with other men. When Mango wasn't around to meet his needs, Ryan had grown used to beating off in the shower, watching porn and jacking off as he thought about Mango. He wasn't about to make Mango feel better by telling him though. The bastard deserved to think Ryan was off ploughing any guy's arse he could find. And being ploughed in return.

Mango's eyes widened. "Oh shit, I did say we'd do something special, didn't I? God, I'm so sorry. We were going somewhere, weren't we?"

Ryan nodded. "That was the plan. A friend of mine has this villa in Madeira and I'd arranged the flights for your birthday. Don't worry, I got the money back as soon as I realised you'd skipped out on me." The bitterness in his voice was evident. "I should never have tried to plan anything ahead of time anyway. I'd have been better off getting you your own personal travelling bail bondsman or whatever they're called because, let's face it, you only call me when you need something."

Ryan knew he was being whiny but he didn't care. He'd gotten Mango out of jail one last time. Now he needed to be strong and kick the man to the curb. Life needed to move on.

Mango sat on the couch next to him and leaned forward, elbows on his knees as he stared down at the floor. "I'm sorry," he said gruffly. "I had no one else to call. You have my emergency card here."

Ryan got up silently and walked over to an armoire in the corner of the room. He pulled down the beautifully crafted wooden top, took out an envelope and walked back to Mango.

"Here. I don't want to be custodian of the funds anymore. You need to find someone else to get you out of shit. I'm over it. I'm sure one of your other bitches will do it." Inside he winced. Delilah Delish was making her dislike of the current situation known. His inner diva was coming out, acidic, sarcastic and hurtful.

Mango's eyes widened. "What? I don't have other *bitches*, Ryan. And please don't insult yourself like that. You know it's not what you are to me."

Ryan's throat clogged up. "That's the problem. I don't know what I am to you. Am I a hole to fill when you need it? Your backup when you need getting out of trouble? I'm not doing it any longer. It's been two years and I'm done waiting for someone who can't give me more. We're over. Done."

His eyes pricked with tears but he blinked them back. His head ached, he felt sick and all he wanted to do was huddle under the covers of his soft and welcoming duvet and cry until he felt nothing. He seemed to be sobbing a lot lately.

Mango stood up, his face shocked. "Ryan, please, let's talk about this. I know I've been an idiot but surely we can fix this?"

Ryan shook his head fiercely. His head was pounding and he needed to lie down. "No, not this time. I have a date next week with a man who wants to be with me, a man who for some reason thinks I'm someone special. Eric can give me what you won't, and I need to take a chance or I'll end up as an old, sad queen on a sofa with a couple of cats to keep me company. If I'm going to try and have something with another man, you need to be out of the picture completely."

His voice faltered. "You're too much temptation, Mango and I can't resist you. Never have been able to. Even now I want you." *I love you.* "So please, take your card and leave. If I find anything else of yours lying around, I'll pack it up and ask Brook to bring it by." Lenny's boyfriend lived across the hall from Mango.

Ryan walked over to the front door and opened it. "I think we've said as much as we need. I'd like you to leave now. Oh, and give Brook your keys back. You won't need them anymore."

Mango's face tightened and he moved towards Ryan, reaching out a hand. "Ryan—"

"Don't touch me." Ryan knew if Mango did, his resolution to do this would crumble. "Please just leave. And don't come around to the club for a while. I mean a long while. Until I'm over you."

Mango's face was white, his lips trembling. Disbelief and guilt coated his face and the pulse in his throat throbbed wildly. Ryan steeled his heart and waited for Mango to go. This wasn't the first time they'd had this discussion or performed this pas de deux.

It was, however, the first time Ryan had truly meant it all.

Finally, Mango gave a curt nod. "This isn't over, Ryan," he said softly, his voice thick. "I'm not giving you up. I know I'm a bastard and I haven't given you what you need but I can change given time."

Despite his earlier warning about no touching, Ryan couldn't resist it.

One last time.

He stepped forward, eyes brimming, and cradled Mango's face in his hands. He kissed Mango gently on the lips, relishing this final taste of the man, feeling Mango's warm breath against his mouth.

"It's over," Ryan whispered. "Please don't be cruel and keep in touch. Let's make this a clean break. It's the only way I'll cope with it." Then he pushed Mango out the door, closed it and sank down against it onto the floor as his tears fell in sheets of salty grief.

***

"He did what?"

A week later, Teddy stared at Mango across the small table in the pub around the corner from Mango's flat in Camden. "He broke up with you? God, I'm sorry, mate. Are you okay? You look like crap. I guess all the travelling to save the world finally got to him." He squinted. "He has a point though. You have been a douche."

Mango scowled as he fingered the peeling cardboard beer mat. "And with such a vote of confidence, my day is truly made." He threw the beer mat back on the table where it skittered across the sticky, scratched surface and fell onto the floor. He picked up another one. "I don't know why I came out with you. I should go back to bloody work. Yes, he broke up with me. As in, he doesn't want to see me. He won't return my calls, my texts and refuses to let me into the flat to talk. The only news I'm getting is from his friend Brook and those paltry bits require thumbscrews."

In the last week, Mango had ignored everything Ryan had said about not keeping in touch, determined to wear him down through texts and phone calls and show him things could be different. He needed to see Ryan and, well, work his way through what he wanted, no, *needed* to say. The fact Ryan thought he was simply a hole for Mango to fill had cut him to the core, made him more ashamed than he cared to admit. That was not how he felt about Ryan and knowing he thought that way hurt deeply.

However, Brook Hunter was indeed the sole imparter of information at the moment, as far as Ryan was concerned. Brook had knocked on Mango's door one night and silently handed him a jacket. It had been one Ryan had taken, saying he loved wearing it when Mango wasn't around because it smelt of him. In return, Brook had gotten Mango's keys, something which still made Mango feel sick.

He threw the now shredded beer mat onto the table. "All I've been able to get out of Brook so far is Ryan is fine. Lenny is helping him through and I should stay away from Club Delish for a while. Lenny apparently has a plan to kick me in the balls when he sees me next. Laverne plans on castrating me, so the rumour goes." He scowled. "For the past week I've been quietly sneaking into the back of the club. I'm friends with the bouncers and they haven't been specifically told I'm persona non grata. If they have, the obviously feel sorry for me because they let me in."

It was tough; he hadn't been sleeping or eating properly, his concentration was suffering. He was too busy worrying about Ryan and his date with Eric. It seemed Della had been wrong about Ryan's abstinence given the whole Adam story. That alone made him jealous and he wanted to track this Adam down and punch the guy's lights out.

And now Ryan was looking at actually dating someone else.

"All Brook says is give Ryan time." Mango toyed with his napkin. "I asked him whether it worried him Ryan goes to Lenny all the time when he needs support? I mean, they used to be— you know. Fucking." Mango shredded the napkin. "Brook looked at me as if I was an idiot and said he trusts Lenny."

He'd been lucky Brook hadn't decked him one for asking such a question.

Teddy frowned at him disapprovingly. "If Lenny's what Ryan needs to get over you, so be it. As a friend of course." He leaned over and poked Mango in the chest with a big, strong finger. "You fucked up. I never understood the whole open relationship thing. The part I don't get is you profess to care for Ryan but disappear without telling him and only call him when you need a 'Get Out of Jail Free' card. That, my friend, is selfish."

"So what do I do? I'm going mad not being able to see him. I need to tell him I'm sorry and fix this." Mango remembered something. "Oh, wait, maybe I should go down to the theatre and see if I can get hold of him there, backstage after his show. I think I still have my pass somewhere on me." Mango scrabbled in his wallet and only stopped when Teddy laid a firm hand on his. His face was stern.

"Mango, this is exactly what Ryan is talking about. His show finished last year—on the fifteen December. The backers pulled out and decided to close it. Ryan's managing the club full time now. Christ, don't you know anything that's going on in Ryan's life? Even I knew that much." Teddy shook his head.

Mango supposed the answer to Teddy's loaded question was a resounding no. He'd been too busy fighting causes to keep track of Ryan's life. Causes were important, critical, but they had cost him Ryan. He said as much to Teddy, who leaned back and regarded Mango with a faint look of disgust. It was sobering. Teddy had never looked at him that way before.

"Mate, your man didn't kick you out because of what you do. It's because of what you *didn't* do. You didn't involve him, share stuff with him. You work with this idea you have he'll always be there for you when you need him but when he needs you, you do a piss-poor job of being there. He's a convenience for you." He slurped down his beer as Mango glared.

"You've been talking far too much with your wife." Mango took a handful of peanuts from the glass bowl on the table and crunched down on them. "She and Ryan have been fucking Facebooking and twittering and shit. And Ryan is *not* a convenience."

No, Ryan Bishop had gotten under Mango's skin like a damn leech in the jungle and Mango was having the devil of a time prying him out. He'd never said the L word but Mango felt sure what he was feeling right now was the loss of it. *Fuck.*

Teddy heaved a long-suffering sigh. "It's tweeting not twittering and yes, I talk to my wife. Maybe you should take a leaf out of our book and do the same. It might give you some insight into what Ryan's all about."

"That's not going to happen if I can't even get him to talk to me," Mango growled. "He's a stubborn little bastard and when he makes his mind up about something, it's damned difficult to get him to change it."

Teddy shifted his heavy bulk in the creaking wooden chair. Mango was almost afraid something was going to give. Teddy wiped a hand across his mouth, removing the foam moustache from his beer. "Well, we have nothing more coming up with idiot group EDD. I mean, the last jaunt was a fucking joke." Subject officially changed. "I care about cats as much as the next person but it was a small local protest and not something we should ever have been involved in."

"Yeah." Mango grunted moodily. "I owed them a favour and said we'd help out. But I'm getting too old for this shit. Starting to lose the passion a bit, you know?" He frowned. "I've been thinking about applying for a job at United University. The teaching one." United University London, or UUL, was on the outskirts of the city and was a small but rapidly growing specialist place of learning.

Teddy leaned back and whistled softly. "Whew, mate, that's a turn up for the books. I never thought you'd consider a desk job. You *must* be missing Ryan." He eyed Mango appraisingly. "It was one helluva sweet deal if I remember. Gives you a chance to use those fancy degrees you have and get paid handsomely for it too. Everyone wants a piece of the Mango Monroe arse." He grinned.

Mango had a BSc (Hons) in Ecology and Wildlife Conservation, a PhD in Biodiversity Conservation and Applied Ecology plus a host of others letters attached to his name. He'd studied at Bournemouth University as a young man and over the years he'd been sought after for lectures, workshops and case studies. Part of his worldwide travel involved talking about what he did to others interested in the field.

Mango fiddled with his now empty beer glass. "They've said I should go for the position there as a Lecturer in Ecology and Global Change." He made air quotes with his fingers. "Damn fancy title and I guess it's something to think about, although I still have to do the whole interview crap. And maybe, just maybe, I can see Ryan and tell him about it. See if it changes his mind about not having me around."

Teddy leaned forward. "You never talk about what made you the way you are," he observed softly. "You hate being tied down and more than once you've mentioned you can't commit to one man because it's not the way you roll." He raised one eyebrow. "I've never been able to get through to you. I see it all the time, even with me and Della and I think we're as good as friends as any. You back off and keep your distance. Do you want to talk about it? Because I'm here if you do."

Angry conversations, wild sobbing and visions of red soaked bedsheets and an empty, white face leapt into Mango's head, along with a smell he'd tried to forget for so long. He clenched his fingers into his palm, trying to still the guilt and fear that rose unbidden in his head.

"It's the way I'm built, I suppose. I came out of the arsehole mould, obviously." Mango's lame attempt at a joke didn't fool Teddy. His friend's green eyes narrowed and a look of compassion fluttered over his face.

"Well, you know where we are if you ever want to talk. Della and I are here for you. Because, honestly, Mango, if you can't commit to Ryan or at least try, there's no point in trying to salvage anything. It's not fair to either of you. So think long and hard about things, my friend, and decide. Don't take too long. That man of yours is something else and someone will snap him up. If they haven't already."

And with Teddy's earth-shattering parting shot, and a reminder of Ryan's date with paramedic Eric, Mango's belly churned as his friend motioned the waiter over for another round of beers.

***

Mango woke with a start, sweating and gulping in air. His chest heaved and as he sat up, the covers pooled around his waist. He gripped them tightly in clammy fingers.

"Fuck. Double fuck." He took a few deep breaths, his eyes adjusting to the darkness. Once his racing heart had calmed, he lay back against the headboard and closed his eyes.

More unwanted memories had pummelled him in his sleep. Mango swallowed bile and swung his legs out of the bed. He padded over to the bathroom in his boxers, took a piss, then went to stare out of the window into the street below.

All he could see reflected in the grimy glass was the last scene in his head, scarlet, gleaming swashes of silk on a wooden floor, ungainly white limbs sprawled on a mottled bedspread and a hand that hung limply off the bed.

He swore and pressed his damp forehead against the glass. "That was a long time ago," he murmured. "Why the hell won't you let me be, Mum? You have to fuck up my life even more *now*?"

Mango wasn't given to introspection because he didn't see the point. Things were what they were and there was no changing the past. He'd learnt that the hard way. Yet standing there half naked, the images of red and white violence still burned in his brain, he wondered, for the millionth time, whether he could have done anything else to try and erase his past from his psyche. Forgive himself the guilt he felt each day in not being able to stop what had happened. He had a whole lot of 'what ifs' and 'if onlys' in the carrier bag of his memory and sometimes the bag rattled loudly and deafened him.

A year of therapy when he was a boy had taken its toll. He'd only done it at the insistence of others who believed he needed help.

"And a lot of fucking good it did me," he growled at the reflection in the mirror, a tousled haired, fierce looking man with a furrowed brow. "Talking about my problems never solved them, just brought them home even more." He pursed his lips and shook his head. "And now, the nightmares are back. It's all bloody Ryan's fault. If he hadn't chucked me out, I wouldn't be having them."

Even as he said the words, he realised how ludicrous the accusation against his ex-lover was. It was Mango's own insecurities and neuroses that had cost him Ryan. And now he had to decide how to face them to try and give Ryan what he needed.

Because Mango needed Ryan, badly, and if baring his soul was the only way to get him back, then Mango knew he had to find the balls to do it.

"Put on your big boy pants, you pussy," he muttered to the man in the window. "It's time to rock and roll. If you have any intention of keeping your man, you'd better fix this shit storm you've caused."

He hitched up onto the wide windowsill and glanced at his watch. Five a.m. He might as well watch the sun come up and the world come alive. There'd be no more sleep for him now. He had a plan to make.

Chapter 3

Club Delish was packed solid and there was the heady smell of sweat and booze in the air. There were drag queens—the club had always attracted its fair share because of Ryan's West End show and his occasional Delilah Delish performances—twinks, bears, men in designer suits, jeans-clad hippies, goths and leather daddies. As always, the audience was an eclectic mix, a smorgasbord of testosterone.

"My darlings, you know we love spending time with you but it's past my bedtime and this lady needs her sleep to look this good." Laverne Debussy-Smith passed a hand down her splendidly clad body and winked at the audience. There were catcalls, jeers and whoops of appreciation. "And the gorgeous Delilah needs to get her beauty sleep too, although to be fair, that bitch needs very little. It's a fucking shame someone can look so good without trying."

Ryan stood across the stage from Laverne, clad in his royal blue satin dress, which clung to his every ridge and curve. This was the last show he and Laverne would be doing for a while in their respective roles. Lenny was flying to Europe on holiday for a couple of weeks with Brook.

In truth, Ryan wasn't feeling well. His monster headache was back, he was dizzy and he wanted nothing more than to get off the four-inch heels he was wearing, have a bath and collapse into bed. A little bit of his favourite singer might not go amiss either. Of course, having Mango in his bed would do the trick too.

Ryan sighed. Mango had been a relentless bastard with his texting and calling and Ryan missed him so fucking much. Everywhere he went reminded him of Mango. Every song playing on the radio, every happy couple he saw on the street—Ryan wanted so badly to have it all with Mango.

He'd almost been tempted to return his ex-boyfriend's calls since he'd chucked him out. Ryan had resisted so far but he wasn't sure how much longer he could do it despite his blue balls.

His date with Eric had gone well but the sexual spark hadn't been there and Ryan had regretfully declined another one. Eric had been understanding, gently saying Ryan was obviously still smitten with his ex and he thought it best if they were friends rather than anything else. So any imagined relief Ryan had thought he'd be getting from another human being had pretty much been fucked up.

The conversation he and Lenny had had earlier in the change room echoed in his head.

"So are you back in the dating pool now, then?" Lenny had asked with a waggle of his eyebrows. "Is being Mango-less working for you?"

Ryan had scowled. "Let me tell you something. Dating again sucks. Grindr is not my fucking friend and I'm tired of faceless dick pics." He'd rolled his eyes. "I swear that man has spoilt me for anyone else. I can't seem to make a connection with any of the guys I've met."

In truth, Ryan hadn't really been trying that hard. He'd formed a profile on various dating apps in the hopes of getting over his ex but it simply wasn't working. The truth was, he didn't want another man. He wanted Mango. And wasn't that a damned joke. He'd chucked away the only man to ever really mean anything to him.

Go Team Ryan, he'd thought bitterly as he finished his makeup. Standing up for your principles truly sucked.

A roar from the audience brought him back to the present.

He sighed as he minced across the stage waggling his arse. Time to wrap this up so he could get away. He was halfway across when his head swam and his eyes went out of focus.

What the fuck?

In the hazy distance he saw Laverne striding towards him and heard her cry of concern. He felt himself falling, heard the roar of the crowd below and somewhere in the distance he was sure he heard Mango's roar of panic. Then the side of Ryan's face smashed into something hard and wooden and he heard no more.

***

"Ryan, talk to me. Wake up, love. Can you hear me?"

Ryan knew he had to be either hallucinating or brain damaged. There was no way in hell Mango was here and had called him "love." Ryan opened one sticky eye and peered blearily out into a pair of burnt sienna eyes gazing at him. Well, four eyes actually. Ryan appeared to have a problem focusing and two identical faces swam in his vision.

Mango's face was anxious, his curly golden brown hair falling in front of his face as he leaned forward into Ryan's sphere of vision.

"Ouch," Ryan muttered as he struggled to sit up. He was in the large, plush armchair in his and Laverne's shared dressing room. "What the hell? My face hurts. Did somebody hit me? Because if they did, I swear, get me up and I'll smack them back—"

His words were cut off by a finger pressed against his lips. He blinked and stared into Mango's now clearer visage.

"Nobody hit you, you little diva." Mango's voice was like honey and Ryan drank it in. "You fell on stage and landed facedown. It's swollen and bruised but you'll live. Nothing broken as far as we can tell."

Mango removed his finger and Ryan groaned.

"I face-planted in front of the whole audience? Way to go. I'm mortified." He collapsed back on the chair with a scowl and squinted at Mango. "What are you doing here? I thought you weren't coming to the club for a while—I banned you, remember?"

Mango looked uncomfortable. "Yeah, 'bout that. I might not have listened."

Ryan narrowed his eyes. "Bastard. I should have known better than to trust you to respect my wishes."

"Respect your wishes? Ryan, babe, you sound like you're planning your funeral." Mango snorted in amusement. His eyes gleamed and Ryan wanted to punch the smirk off his face.

Instead Ryan glared. "Where's Laverne?" He fingered the gash on his head. "Where's my wig? You took it off—is it okay?"

Ryan's red-haired wig was his pride and joy and it had cost the producers of the show a fortune. They'd let him keep it, along with most of his wardrobe, when the show had closed. Ryan looked after his wig better than he thought he would a small child.

"Your damn wig is safe. I put it on the polystyrene head over there in the corner. Your shoes are in the closet." Mango jutted a finger towards the recess. "After we got you in here, Laverne went off to explain to the masses you were fine. They were going a bit crazy out there, wanting to cram the stage and help. She needed to pacify them."

"Oh." A wash of warmth flooded Ryan knowing his patrons cared enough to storm the stage. "Maybe I should go out there and tell them myself."

He started to stand up and Mango pushed him down.

"Sit," he instructed. "Laverne told me to keep you here by any means necessary." His face creased in a grin. "And we both know I have a number of ways to keep you horizontal. Or, in this case, resting nicely."

Ryan huffed. Despite his head pounding and the side of his face stinging with what felt like carpet burn, his groin took notice of Mango's innuendo. The memories of being pushed roughly onto a bed, clothes ripped off and lying there naked while Mango worked his magic came flooding back. They'd always been compatible in bed and outside of it, when they had managed to be together—well, when Mango managed to stay around.

"Ooh," Ryan said snarkily. "Promises, promises."

They stared at each other with heated gazes, then Mango chuckled. "I take it you're feeling better." He frowned. "I want to know why you fell in the first place. Have you been feeling all right?"

Ryan sighed. "I've been having some headaches and I've stopped smoking, or been trying to. And these nicotine patches drive me crazy. For all I know it's their evil chemicals bleeding into my body making me worse. Maybe I should give them up and go back to smoking?" He eyed Mango hopefully.

God the man looked good. Tight worn blue jeans, a soft, white, button-down cotton shirt with sleeves rucked up to his elbows, and battered tan hiking boots completed his relaxed ensemble. He looked as if he could be the decadent poster boy for a fashion shoot in a special *GQ for Hikers and Outdoorsman* issue.

Mango shook his head firmly. "Oh no, there's nothing you can do to your body that's worse than that damn smoking. I don't believe you've given it up—how long now?"

"About two months."

Mango had never liked Ryan's smoking. Mango treated his body well, eating healthy foods and yes, he had the occasional joint or two, and Ryan had tempted him to eat pizza a few times but that was about it. Mango also frequented his local gym whenever he got the chance. The conservationist and eco freak applied the same stringent principles to his body. Leave it natural and look after it.

Ryan didn't hold the same idealistic views. He was blessed with good genes, kept himself fit dancing and doing his own gym routine at home when he fancied and hated any other exercise unless they were sexual calisthenics in bed.

"And oh my God, is the boy a bitch about it." Laverne swept into the room, a vision of blonde hair, gleaming pale pink lipstick and the latest Doreen Vanquois frock—a masterpiece of pearl chiffon and silk. "Until you've seen him in a hissy fit about not being able to light up, spitting his discontent like a llama, you ain't seen nothing." She heaved a deep sigh, her bosom heaving, then she reached up to remove her wig and hairnet.

Lenny James's tangled blond hair was revealed and he grinned at them both. "God, that's better. As much as I'm trying to grow my own hair so as not to have wear the damned thing anymore, it's driving me crazy. It gets everywhere." He pursed pink lips and blew a strand off his face. "Anyhoo, boys, to the matter in hand. Ryan, what the hell happened out there? Are you eating?" He gave Ryan the once over with a critical eye. "You've lost weight. No surprises why." He narrowed aqua coloured eyes at Mango in disapproval, then looked back at Ryan. "But you've not been well for a while with these headaches and dizzy spells. When are you going to go and see the doctor?"

Mango stared at Ryan in concern. "Not been well for a while? How long is a while?"

Ryan got to his feet, pushing away Mango's restraining arm. He was fed up being mollycoddled. He smoothed the creases out of his dress, sighing in frustration as he saw them.

"Enough already, you guys. Yes, I had a fainting spell. Yes, I've lost a bit of weight. But I'm fine. It's probably the patches." He walked over to the dressing table and picked up a half-empty box of scented face wipes. Ryan peered into the mirror and winced at the sight. The right side of his face was swollen and red, a few scratches streaked with dried blood. He sniffed in resignation and began cleaning his face.

"Normally when people give up smoking they put weight on," Mango said quietly. "Lenny's right—you've lost a bit."

Ryan decided he'd had his fill of being clucked over. "Why do you care? We're not together anymore." He ignored Mango's hiss of breath and Lenny's exasperated sigh.

Ryan's hands trembled as he wiped crusted blood off his temple. "If you'd done as I'd asked and kept away, you've never have known about any of this. So you can be on your way now and not worry about me. That ship sailed when I kicked you out three weeks ago." In the mirror he saw the pained expression on Mango's face. Ryan swallowed and carried on removing his makeup.

"You know I've been trying to get in touch with you for ages to talk to you about this whole 'kicking me out' thing." Mango moved up behind him, his face twisted. His hair swung around his face, giving Mango the appearance of a lion with a tangled dark honey mane. "Don't talk like there's nothing left between us. That's a fucking lie and you know it."

Ryan could see Mango wasn't going to give up. Part of him rejoiced, the other half quailed.

Lenny made a rude sound. "Boys, boys, let's calm down, shall we? Mango, I thought Ryan and I were the drama queens." He shooed Mango away and clasped Ryan's shoulder. "Chicken, I know you're hurting."

Ryan rolled his eyes and finished cleaning. He turned to stare into Lenny's eyes.

Lenny carried on. "You two sound as if you have some unfinished business. Ryan, will you allow me to ask Mango to see you upstairs and get you settled? It would take a weight off my mind and let me get on with finishing up here tonight. I'm worried you might have a concussion but I know you won't let me get a doctor to see you."

Ryan pressed his lips together. He wasn't sure it was a good idea and from the glint in Lenny's eyes, it seemed he was trying to play matchmaker. Ryan had also been horny for days and seeing Mango, albeit under these circumstances, was sending Ryan into a hormonal tailspin. He groaned inwardly. That was a cop-out excuse. He wanted Mango—wanted some of him even if it was just for tonight. Yes, it went against one of the main reasons he'd broken up with the man in the first place. But...

"I'm not sure. I'll be fine on my own. Promise." Ryan's words were unconvincing even to himself.

Lenny raised one pale, perfectly plucked eyebrow. "Forgive me, but you look like shit. I'm not certain that's true."

Mango moved into Ryan's personal space and lifted his hand to tenderly pick something off Ryan's cheek. "You missed a spot."

Ryan's breath caught at being near enough to smell the familiar scent of Mango once again—Christian Dior's Fahrenheit, Mango's all-time favourite. Yearning crept through Ryan's body like a thief in the night—silent, deadly and with stealth, which meant it would do what it needed and leave without a trace. Except there would be consequences. In the morning Mango would leave and once again Ryan would be alone and wishing for something—and someone—he couldn't have.

Mango's voice grew husky. "Ryan, listen to me. I've had time to think since we've been apart. There are things I need to tell you—changes I'd like to make. I want to prove to you I can be your guy—the one you need. But it will be a slow process and you need to be patient a little longer. Can we at least talk about this when you're feeling better?"

There were the words Ryan had waited two years to hear. Yet, hearing them now when he was vulnerable and his head throbbed, they were welcome but now wasn't the right time for a discussion. He sighed. He didn't want to be alone tonight.

"Fine, you can be my bloody nursemaid if it'll make him happy." Ryan jerked a thumb in the direction of Lenny, who beamed in sly satisfaction at getting his way. "That's it though."

Ryan grabbed his crotch and scowled at Mango. "Don't think you're getting a slice of *this* pie tonight, honey, because it isn't on the menu." Ryan wasn't convinced he meant those words but still, they needed saying.

Mango gave a growl of laughter. "God, you slay me. I didn't even think about it. I want you to be okay."

Lenny poked Mango hard in the chest. "You, Mr Arsehole, take him upstairs, get him settled and stay with him please. He can sleep and you can check on him now and then."

"Hey. Enough with the arsehole comments. I might know I'm one but I don't need everyone else telling me so." Mango frowned. "I thought people with concussion shouldn't fall asleep?" He cocked an eyebrow at Lenny who sighed.

"Old wives' tale," Lenny remarked. "As long as Ryan is talking, able to walk and doesn't have dilated pupils—and I checked earlier, he doesn't—he can sleep. If any of those things happen, Ryan, you're going to the damned hospital. And don't fucking argue with me," Lenny warned as Ryan opened his mouth. "It's non-negotiable."

Ryan pinched his lips together in pique. "Shit, fine then. Honestly, you two are a couple of pussies fussing over a kitten." He stalked to the door, hearing the sniggers behind him and turned and said, "So are you coming up to tuck me in?"

He walked out the door and to the stairs that led up to his flat above the club. Mango followed, after muttering something to Lenny. Halfway down the narrow corridor, Ryan was light-headed but he was determined not to show any sign of weakness to the man behind him. He wanted to get the dress off and into some comfy sweats and a tee shirt.

He stumbled as he reached the bottom step of the narrow flight of stairs leading up to his place. Mango made an exasperated sound, and the next thing Ryan knew he was being scooped up in brawny arms and held in Mango's firm grip, resembling a woman about to cross the threshold.

Ryan squawked in disbelief. "Put me the fuck down, you big baboon." He struggled, the fabric of his dress proving slippery as he fought his way out.

Mango held tight, a wicked grin on his face. "I thought I was a pussy? No can do. I'm not taking a chance on you diving headfirst down the stairs and bruising more of your beautiful face. Or breaking something." Mango began to climb the steps. "So hold on and enjoy the ride."

Ryan had no choice but to do as he was told. In truth, he liked the feeling of being back in Mango's arms and felt his heart beat steadily, almost in cadence with his strides up the steps. Ryan closed his eyes, suddenly weary, feeling the soft exhalation of Mango's peppermint-scented breath against his face. Churning within were emotions that what worried him. Mango had always been a drug and being without him the last couple of weeks had been hell. Now he was here and Ryan had the horrible suspicion he might fall under his spell...again.

And he was horny. That never boded well.

"So is the flat unlocked?" Mango strode up the stairs with ease, scarcely out of breath even though he carried a five-foot-eleven, one-hundred-and-sixty-pound man dressed in satin.

"What?" Ryan stared into quizzical brown eyes.

"Well, you made me give my keys back, so I need to know whether the door is open or whether I need to put you down while you unlock it." Mango's voice was even but Ryan heard the censure in it.

"Oh. It's open. I don't lock it much, you know that." The key had only been for those times when Ryan had gone away and Mango or someone else had been watering his plants.

"Good," Mango huffed as he reached the top of the stairs and reached out awkwardly for the handle. "Because I'm knackered. You're not as light as you look even with the weight loss."

"Bite me," Ryan said tightly. *Bastard. He knows how sensitive I am about my damn weight.*

Mango chuckled. He pushed the door open, staggered inside and across the room and deposited Ryan on the living room couch.

He lay back and glared at Mango. "Now I'm dumped like a sack of potatoes?" Ryan closed his eyes. "Wow, whoever said romance was dead."

"You okay?" The sofa sagged as Mango sat down and brushed his fingers through Ryan's unruly curls. "Need a pain killer or something? Some Calmettes?"

"No, arsehole. I need to get out of this dress, have a shower and get into bed." Ryan swung his legs over onto the floor and stood up. "And I mean a shower as in, 'on my own and don't come in.'"

Mango shrugged. "Suit yourself. I promise to be a good boy." He wandered into the kitchen and opened the fridge. He was a veteran at late night snack preparation. Many times in the past he'd come back to bed with a monster sandwich filled with anything he could find in the fridge. He liked to eat healthy but a snack after sex was his downfall. Ryan had always made sure he'd kept whole wheat bread, plenty of salad and fresh cold meats from the corner deli; a habit he still respected.

Ryan showered alone, half gratified Mango didn't try to sneak in and surprise him, and half disappointed that he didn't. When Ryan wandered into the lounge, clad in his comfy sweatpants, and nothing else, he found Mango sprawled over the couch, reading a magazine and feasting on what resembled a haystack made of bread.

"I see you made yourself at home," Ryan remarked acerbically as he poured a glass of ice water. He was irked to see Mango had a large glass of orange juice on the coffee table and hadn't even offered to get Ryan anything.

"Yeah." Mango idly flicked the page of the magazine. "Carrying your arse up the stairs gave me an appetite."

Ryan snorted inelegantly. "No one asked you to do that. I could have made it on my own."

Mango sniffed as his eyes travelled from Ryan's face down his body, lingering on his bare chest, smiling slowly as he focused on Ryan's groin and back up to his eyes.

Ryan's throat was dry, his heart thudded in his chest and beneath his sweat pants his cock plumped up like collagen-filled lips. Mango stood, throwing the magazine down on the sofa. His eyes never left Ryan's as he prowled towards him, a lion stalking his prey.

"You clean up nicely." Mango's voice was husky. Ryan's eyes dropped to his ex-lover's groin, the distinct outline of an erection evident against his thigh. "But I think I've told you this before."

Mango reached out and touched the side of Ryan's face gently. "You're going to have a heck of a bruise," he murmured. "I'll have to kiss it better." He reached over and swept his lips over Ryan's aching jaw.

Ryan couldn't help it, he closed his eyes, the intimate contact more than he could bear. He cursed himself for being so weak. He knew exactly where this was going and he wanted it, craved it. He could no more resist Mango than a thirsty tree root seeking out life-giving water.

A soft, needy sound escaped from Ryan's lips and Mango hissed out a breath. "God, I missed you." He trailed hungry lips down Ryan's throat, stopping to lick the pulse throbbing there. "I've been a miserable bastard these past few weeks. Even Teddy told me to fuck off and get a grip. When you fell down on stage—my damn heart near stopped."

Ryan tipped his head back so Mango could get to more of his throat, his shoulder, his everything. He knew he was a pushover but at this stage he didn't care. His cock ached, his jaw ached, his heart ached, and all he wanted to do was lose himself for a while and forget how they had left things between them.

"It's nothing. I'm fine."

Mango's lips took one of Ryan's nipples in his heated mouth and Ryan moaned, his hands coming up to grasp Mango's hair.

"Oh God, you bastard, you know how I love that." Mango's sly palming of Ryan's cock made him harden more, those talented fingers ghosting over what Ryan felt sure was about to rip out of his sweats. It had been a while.

Ryan found himself being lifted, Mango's strong arms under his backside. Ryan's legs found one of their favourite spots— around Mango's waist. His head swept down to claim Mango's mouth fiercely, a hard, insistent press of lips and tongue as he was walked down the corridor into the bedroom, a hot, sloppy, needy meeting of mouths.

Mango laid Ryan on the bed and climbed atop him, straddling him. His eyes, burnt embers with glints of flame, stared down hungrily as his fingers ran down Ryan's bare chest.

Ryan, who was sprawled boneless beneath him, begging to be taken, tried to make some token protest but his heart and his body weren't in it. "This is not what I had planned when we came up here—"

His words were cut off as his sweatpants were removed in one swift tug. His cock sprung up, free at last, and Mango grinned down, lips swollen and pink.

"Liar. You knew exactly what was going to happen when I got you up here. Admit it. You still want me."

Ryan didn't have time to answer because an eager tongue slid alongside his, ravaging his mouth. Mango's still-clad body shifted and the feel of the denim against Ryan's groin and sensitive cock was too much to bear.

"Jesus, get your damn clothes off. I need to feel skin. But leave your shirt on. You know I like you half clothed when you fuck me." Ryan panted out his commands in between gasps of pleasure as Mango stroked his cock.

"I haven't been gone that long that I'd forgotten that little fact, Ry." Mango stood on the bed above Ryan and swiftly removed his jeans and boxers. His cock stood up against his toned and tanned belly, his balls hanging before Ryan in a display of wantonness. Then, one by one, Mango undid the buttons of his shirt. When he finished the shirt hung loose around his taut body, framing his broad shoulders and Ryan lost his breath at the sheer sensuality of the man staring down at him. Plus he called him Ry, something Mango said only when they fucked, and it made Ryan even harder and more desperate.

God, I am such a pushover. A needy bastard who needs his Mango fix. There is no hope for me.

Mango knelt down on the bed. "You always look like heaven," he whispered as his lips grazed Ryan's cock. His shirt brushed Ryan's heated, sensitive skin and the sensation made him gasp.

"Such a damn sexy man," Mango whispered, "and I don't know why I treat you like I do. Because this, here, what we have—it's special."

Ryan tried to breathe as Mango licked the tip of Ryan's dick, his tongue pressing against the underside.

"So special you run off all the time?" Ryan's voice was ragged. "Leave me with a note?"

Mango looked up, and the expression on his face was one Ryan hadn't seen before, complete vulnerability mixed with guilt.

"I'm a prick," Mango said, his hand sliding up and down Ryan's cock with firm strokes. "I want to make it up to you. Can we talk about it later? Because right now, I have this overwhelming need to taste you."

Ryan's hips left the bed as Mango took him in his mouth. Ryan's strangled moan of pleasure made Mango chuckle. That vibration around his cock sent Ryan's head spinning in a kaleidoscope of vibrant colours and dizzy somersaults.

Mango was adept at blow jobs. He had a sinful mouth, no inhibitions and a distinct desire to consume Ryan and make sure nothing remained. All Ryan could do right now was hold on for the ride, welcome his climax and not scream like a banshee when it took him and he emptied his balls in spasms of sheer joy, straight into Mango's willing, dirty mouth. When he pushed his fingers deep into Ryan's arse—Ryan hadn't even heard him open the lube—it guaranteed Ryan shot his load, his balls and brains completely blown to smithereens.

Glistening with sweat, his arse aching from Mango's fingers and feeling completely taken, Ryan lay back, chest heaving with the force of Mango's sensual assault.

He crawled up Ryan's body, moving his arms and pinning them above his head with a strong hand. Mango's other hand moved down and motioned to Ryan's to bring his legs up. Ryan followed the silent instruction, their sexual dance coming back with full force.

"Ready?" Mango whispered. "I can't wait to be inside you. Tell me it's okay."

Ryan reached up and traced Mango's lips with his finger. "It's okay. You're back where you belong, for now."

Mango's eyes softened and he sat back and sheathed himself. That was something else Ryan wanted so badly. No condoms and the feel of pure skin inside him. Given their supposedly open relationship though, even if one-sided at the moment, Ryan wasn't about to take any chances.

Then Mango moved over Ryan's eager body, took his lips in a searing kiss, and pushed in. Ryan cried out against Mango's mouth as he was filled. This familiar feeling of having Mango inside him, of being possessed, was one he'd missed.

All Ryan wanted to do was live in the moment—*this* moment.

With the steady thrusts into his body, their harsh breathing, the wet kisses and the smell of semen and sweat—Ryan was home with the man he loved. Fuck everything else tonight because this was all that mattered. This closeness, this dance of sensuality and sex, the slap of flesh on flesh was the drug fuelling Ryan's senses and he needed it.

Mango gave a harsh cry as Ryan wrapped his legs tighter around him and Mango collapsed, his breath tickling Ryan's throat. For a moment they lay together, satiated, sticky with sweat and stuck together.

Then Ryan drifted into a satisfied sleep and dreamt of being with Mango where he belonged. Reality and the fact he'd been a needy, deluded idiot—again—was a subject he'd tackle tomorrow.

***

The next morning Mango woke to find Ryan staring at him, a serious look on his face. Mango grinned sleepily. His good mood at finding himself back in Ryan's bed was shattered when Ryan spoke wearily.

"This shouldn't have happened." Ryan swung his legs over the side of the bed and stood up. "I knew it was a bad idea for you to come up here last night but I couldn't help myself. I'm a weak, pathetic man when it comes to you."

Mango sat up. The covers pooled around his waist and he shook his head fiercely.

His stomach roiled.

I have to give him something. Anything, to make him see how I feel about him.

"Don't talk shit. We have chemistry. And an emotional connection."

Ryan laughed harshly. "Really? Nothing has changed. You're still Mr Gung Ho off anywhere in the world on a whim and I don't see it changing anytime soon. And we're both looking at having other partners because you won't commit to anything. The crap in your past you never talk to me about keeps you distant. And I was serious about breaking up with you, and now I've gone and fucked it up for myself as well." He gave a disgusted snort. "Show me your body and your dick and I'm gone. How fucking shallow am I?" He made to move to the bathroom and Mango sat up and grasped his arm.

"You're wrong. I told you I wanted to change and I still mean to." He ached at the thought Ryan might walk out on him a second time.

Ryan sighed softly, yet on his face, Mango saw resignation and yearning. "I wish that were true. We've gone this route before, remember? It ended up with me being a wuss and sobbing in Lenny's arms." Ryan smiled sadly. "As much as I'd like to believe you've changed, I'm not sure I could again."

He turned and Mango got out of the bed, desperate to make Ryan see he was serious. Time to do that soul baring. He stood in front of his startled lover and clasped his face in his hands. "I'm so fucking serious about you that I've decided to go for an interview for a lecturer position at United University so I can be here for you."

Mango was gratified to see Ryan's jaw drop.

"You what?" Ryan gasped. "Are you kidding me?" A faint gleam of hope glinted in his eyes and Mango rejoiced at the faint promise.

"No, I'm not joking. I've got some trips and functions coming up though and I'm going to have to do them as I've already committed. If I got this position the university would expect me to take on a couple of trips too, as it helps my profile to be seen out and about. But they'll be minimal."

He became aware they were both standing naked and shivering in the room and he tugged Ryan back onto the bed. Ryan gave a startled shout as he ended up on top of Mango, who clasped Ryan's arse, holding him tight so he couldn't escape. "It means I'll not be away as much."

Ryan stared down into his eyes. "Will it mean no more open relationship? We'll be exclusive?" His tone was wary.

Mango's chest tightened, the thought of being exclusive, being someone's 'everything' scared him and brought back bad memories. His momentary hesitation made an already skittish Ryan snarl and struggle out of Mango's grip. He leapt from the bed and sneered down.

"I fucking thought so. Nothing has changed, has it, arsehole? Now get the fuck out of my bed and out the door. I've had enough." He stormed off and into the bathroom, slamming the door. It locked shut with a click.

Mango blinked. Well, that hadn't gone the way he'd thought. A burning sense of outrage assailed him. He stood up, pulled on his jeans, strode over the door and banged on it angrily.

"Hey, you don't get to do this to me, Ryan. I'm trying here and it would be nice if you gave me a chance to finish my fucking story."

The response from behind the bathroom door was the slamming of what Mango thought was the bathroom cabinet. Knowing he was playing with fire but not caring anymore, he yelled, "Come out here and face me like a man and stop pitching a hissy fit, you bloody drama queen pussy."

He drew a sharp breath at the frigid silence. Ryan felt strongly about insults to his masculinity. When he was Delilah Delish, he dealt with them, accepted and even invited them, but when he was Ryan, it was the one thing that pissed him off.

The door flung open and Mango found himself being pummelled by a fiery bundle of naked, wiry strength delivering some truly dirty insults. He put up his arms, trying to ward off the smacks and blows, and tried not laugh in the process. That would have been sheer suicide, but God, Ryan was cute and awesome when he got like this.

"Cock-sucking, ass-licking, miserable, bat-loving son of a bitch," Ryan spat. "I am so not having a bloody hissy fit, you bastard." These last two words were punctuated with some vicious jabs to Mango's balls.

He narrowly avoided injury as he dodged, stifling a chuckle. "Oh yeah, you're Mr Cool. Would you please stop trying to drive my nuts through my stomach and calm down and listen to me?" He gripped Ryan's hands tightly, holding them down at his sides. Ryan's eyes were stormy but Mango didn't think it was all anger. There was passion and need in those blue depths too.

"Ryan, honest, I know I've been a damn will-o'-the-wisp in the past but I'm trying to make things different. Please, could you sit down and listen to me?"

Ryan's lips thinned but he nodded and sat on the bed, his arms crossed over his chest.

Mango took a deep breath and sat in front of him, legs crossed as he stared into Ryan's wary eyes. He tried hard not to focus on the fact his lover still had no clothes on. Ryan's lips twitched a little when he realised Mango was trying valiantly not to stare at him. The faint almost smirk gave Mango hope.

"I put in an application about a week ago to the university," Mango said. "They were pretty impressed with my CV but they've had a couple of people apply so they're trying to put together interview times and shit. It will probably take place abroad but they're not sure yet."

"What made you decide you wanted to do that?" Ryan lifted his chin in the stubborn gesture Mango knew so well. "I mean for two years you've not wanted to be tied down and now all of a sudden you have this change of heart?"

Mango shrugged. "This last stupid eco event, ending up in jail again and you having to bail me out, Della telling me what a prick I'd been, Teddy saying much the same—I knew they had a point." He took a deep breath. "Then you breaking up with me— it didn't feel right, damn it. We're good together—always have been. I couldn't bear the thought of not being with you anymore. Being shut out of your life because I was a prat."

Ryan lifted his legs to sit cross-legged on the bed and Mango's eyes couldn't help but be drawn to the sight of his naked groin.

"Do you think perhaps you could put some pants on?" Mango growled. "It's pretty distracting seeing your cock and balls right there in my face."

Ryan sniggered. "I thought you liked my cock and balls in your face."

"Well, yeah, normally," Mango threw back. "I thought we were having a serious chat here though?"

Ryan rolled his eyes and flapped a hand. "Fine, I'll put on some damn underwear."

He stood up and sauntered over to the dresser. Bending down so his arse was displayed in all its glory, he opened the drawer, reached in, bent down and stepped into the tight red satin thong he'd taken out. It was one of Mango's favourites, displaying Ryan's delectable assets with little left to the imagination.

Ryan plonked himself back down on the bed and raised an eyebrow. "Better?"

Mango scowled. "You can be a real bastard."

Ryan nodded. "I try." The sly gleam in his eyes made Mango want to throw Ryan back on the bed and rip the damn thing off his body. He held back his caveman impulses manfully.

"So, you were saying"—Ryan ran a hand down Mango's jaw—"you're a prick and you decided to make things up to me. Go on. I'm liking the direction this is taking so far."

Mango took a deep breath. "I've been hesitating on commitment because I'm fucking scared, okay? Being someone else's everything, being *that* person for someone—let's say I've seen it not turn out so well in my own life and it wasn't pretty."

Ryan glared at him. "How the hell would I know, Mango? You never talk to me about the past or the things I think you went through when you were a kid, even though I've asked." Ryan's chest rose and fell with frustration. "Over two years we've been together and you've never let me in."

Mango ran a hand through his hair as he huffed out a breath. "I know. It's, you know, it's hard for me to talk about this stuff. Even though I want to."

Ryan's eyes softened, his anger dissipating. "I know, you're the original strong, silent type. But if we're going to have any chance moving forward in a relationship, you're going to have start trusting me with some of the gory details."

Mango winced at Ryan's unfortunate turn of phrase. Gory details was spot on. "Let me see if I can explain things a bit."

"Well, that'll be a first," Ryan muttered. He titled his head expectantly.

Mango's throat was tight. He'd never told anyone this story before and he wasn't sure he could fill in all the blanks.

"I find it tough having someone be reliant on me. Not reliant I suppose, but someone who expects me to be there for them all the time. To have someone worried sick because I don't come home one night, or I'm late." He swallowed as bright blue eyes regarded him steadily. "It always seemed easier to be a someone no one expected to be there because then there were no expectations. Do I sound crazy?"

Ryan leaned back, a frown on his place. "It sounds as if it's a lonely place to be. Sad too. We all have that worry when we love someone. Christ Mango, what the hell happened to you? Is it the reason why you've never committed to the thought of an 'us'?"

Mango nodded. "It was easier to pretend what we had was transitional, something not set in stone. That way I could never hurt you in the same way my dad hurt my mother, even though it was unintentional and not his fault."

Ryan made a startled sound and Mango heart thudded as he fidgeted.

God, let me not make a hash of this. I hope he understands.

"Something happened with your parents." Ryan's tone was matter of fact. "They made you this way."

Mango took Ryan's hand in his, stroking the back softly. This was the tough part of his story.

"My dad was a geologist. He worked with an international consortium. His job took him all over the world and he was rarely home. When he was, it was good and we spent some great times together. Then he'd go off again for weeks at a time, with an occasional phone call. My mum..." He sighed. "My mum suffered from depression for most of my life. I never realised what it was until afterwards. She'd stay in her bed, rarely go out, except for when she took me to a film or the museum, rare days when she seemed happy. I was pretty self-sufficient. When my dad came home, it made things better. But they'd argue constantly. My dad tried to tell my mum it was his job to put a roof over our head."

Ryan reached a hand up to cup Mango's cheek, his eyes filled with concern. "He was trying to provide for his family. It can't have been easy for him either."

Mango nodded. "He was torn between giving us a life and saving for me to go to University, because it was something he wanted desperately for me. I'd always wanted to do the work I do now. He encouraged it. Mum wanted it for me too but she didn't like how it was being earned for us, with him being away so much."

Mango smiled as a memory surfaced. "She used to tell me he was her Fred Astaire and she was his Ginger. That they belonged together and she never wanted to be apart from him. She said she wanted him at her side always. At the time her words were romantic to a young boy. When I grew older, I realised it was perhaps a sign of mental instability. My mum was a needy person. She constantly needed reassuring and people around her telling her she was valued. Including me."

Ryan's fingers ran a comforting trail down Mango's arm. "That's a lot for a little kid to be responsible for."

Mango shrugged. "You make do, don't you? You try and keep the peace and do what you can. Until the day you can't."

Familiar feelings of loss and panic washed over his body like the cooling caress of a gentle breeze. "When I was ten I came home from school one day. The house was quiet. Too quiet. Normally my mum would fill it with people when dad wasn't home. Ladies from the local WI, knitting groups, book clubs— anything she could do to take the silence away. That day there was nothing *but* silence." His eyes prickled. The memory of that silence and the events that unfolded afterwards seemed like it happened yesterday.

Ryan gave a comforting tug to his arm. "I'm here," he murmured. "And if you want to stop this story anytime, I'm good. I don't want to push you, sweetheart."

Mango's throat was dry, the memories of one of the worst days of his young life seeping from his damaged psyche like dribbles from a leaking dam. "I need to tell you this. It's time." He took a deep breath, noticing his hands shaking. "That day, the only one I saw when I got home was my dog Monty. He was a terrier I'd had since I was about five years old. He was quiet too.

Not his usual bouncy self." Mango shut his eyes, seeing the whole scene playing out again before his eyes. "I did some stuff, chatted to my best friend Andy. We were close, spent a lot of time together. Then I realised it was dark, and late. I went looking for mum, thinking she'd overslept. I was used to her sleeping during the day, it was another sign of her depression." He drew a deep sigh. "I knocked on her door. She didn't reply so I went in." Here his voice faltered and Ryan tightly gripped both of Mango's hands in his. "When I went in, all I could see was red. Red everywhere, on the bed and on the floor. And the coppery smell of blood."

Ryan drew a deep breath, his face paling.

Mango swallowed again, trying to moisten his dry throat. "She'd cut her wrists, the right way, vertically. She'd made sure she wouldn't stand a chance. I didn't know a human being had so much blood in them."

Ryan's shocked exclamation of "Jesus, baby," accompanied his blue eyes welling with tears.

"I remember screaming and screaming. I don't remember much else. A neighbour heard me, came over and found us. I was sitting on the bed beside her, covered in blood, holding onto her hand. The neighbour took me back to her place after she called the police. When my dad got home, he was devastated. He asked my aunt Joan to come to fetch me and take me to her house in Torquay. I had to answer some police questions but afterwards I went with Joan."

He heaved a juddering breath. "I remember her face. It looked so damn sad, her eyes open and staring at me. I vomited up everything there in the bedroom and sat in a pile of my own puke. I couldn't move."

Mango's chest ached, a deep seeded pain that grew in intensity as he continued. "I wondered if I'd come in to her room sooner if I'd have been able to save her. My dad told me nothing I could have done would have helped but I still wondered. I was so wrapped up in my own stuff I didn't realise my mother was killing herself in the room down the hall."

His voice faltered and tears blurred his vision.

"Oh, God, I'm so sorry," Ryan whispered, his voice choked. "You were only ten years old, love. Just a kid. You can't blame yourself. Christ, I can't believe you had to experience that sort of trauma so young." He reached over and pulled Mango to him, hugging him tightly. Soft lips pressed against Mango's cheek in a comforting kiss.

Mango had a feeling of weightlessness, as if a balloon filled with something heavy that had been tethered to him was now drifting off into the stratosphere. Sharing his story had been easier than he'd thought. Especially telling it to Ryan, who was wrapping him up in comforting arms, while murmuring strangled words into Mango's ear about how he was there for him and he was so glad Mango had finally unburdened himself.

"I wish it had been the end of it." Mango cleared his throat and started again. "We travelled up for the funeral and afterwards I went back to Torquay. My dad had stuff he needed to sort out." He swallowed. "A couple of weeks later, my dad was due to pick me up from my aunt's place and take me home."

Mango's heart ached. In his mind, he still saw the bright sunshine outside as he sat waiting for his father on the beach outside Aunt Joan's home, watching the waves washing onto the shore. He even remembered the seagulls swooping down to pluck whatever it was seagulls plucked from the sea.

"He never made it. On the way down, he went off the road. The car rolled a few times and finally stopped in a field. The ambulance got there but he was dead at the scene."

Ryan gave a distressed cry. Tears rolled down his beautiful, pale cheeks, staining them with Mango's past. He hadn't wanted to cause this sort of sadness in his soft-hearted and overly emotional lover. It was why he'd tried to keep it inside, so the pain was his and his alone.

"It's okay," Mango whispered as Ryan sobbed in his arms. "It was a long time ago. I was ten years old. Joan was a great role model and she became my surrogate parent, brought me up. I got over it."

"You *never* got over it." Ryan's tear-streaked face came up from wetting Mango's chest and he stared at him out of red-rimmed eyes. "You might have gotten over their deaths but you've been carrying the residue of those events around with you ever since, affecting the way you live your life."

Mango untangled himself from Ryan's arms and went to fetch him a tissue from the box on top of the chest of drawers. He certainly couldn't argue with Ryan's insightful observation. It was something he'd known for a long time.

Mango had never seen his friend Andy again either. They'd messaged each other occasionally but eventually the friendship had fizzled. Mango still wondered what had happened to his first boy crush. Because, of course, now that he was older, he recognised the feelings he'd had for Andy back then as being the start of him recognizing his sexual makeup. At the time the fondness he'd felt for the cheeky, blond haired young boy he'd put down to being lonely and needing a friend.

He handed Ryan some tissues and sat down. "Yes, I suppose. It made me promise myself I'd never give anyone the power to hurt me like Dad did Mum but more importantly, I never wanted to become a special someone to anyone. It's a huge responsibility, having someone care for you so much that they'd kill themselves over you. My mum left a note saying she couldn't live without my dad."

The pang in Mango's chest twanged, a rubber band being pulled back and released. "I wasn't so important for her to stay alive for, apparently. My aunt tried to tell me it wasn't anything to do with me, it was the depression making my mum that way. But still." He shrugged as Ryan blew his nose loudly. "As for my dad—I always thought he felt the same about my mum. That he'd rather have driven off the road and died to be with her than be with me."

Ryan shook his head vehemently. "What did the inquest reveal? That he did it deliberately?"

Mango stood up, pacing the room. "No, it was classed it as an accident, pure and simple. Dad had a blow-out. But I always wondered."

Ryan jumped up and clasped Mango's face in his hands. "Never think either of them didn't want you," he said fiercely. "Your mum was ill and she couldn't cope. Your dad was on his way to fetch you and you need to believe they both wanted you, baby. Like I do." He nuzzled into Mango's neck and for a while, they were silent, simply enjoying each other's nearness.

"Please tell me your aunt Joan is still alive." Ryan snuffled against Mango's neck. "I couldn't bear it if there was a sad story there too."

Mango laughed hollowly. "She's alive but she's in a home. Alzheimer's got to her. She's in her seventies now, and she's still down in Torquay. I visit now and then but she doesn't recognise me and it upsets her when I visit, so I don't go very often." He felt a twinge of guilt and sadness.

"Fuck," Ryan said, his voice broken. "Everyone you loved is gone."

Not everyone, Mango thought. It was too soon to tell Ryan though. This wasn't the right time.

Ryan leaned in and kissed Mango on the lips, a fleeting caress of comfort. "So is this why you push everyone away? You don't want to get close in case you lose them or you hurt them and they end up like your mum?"

Mango muttered into his boyfriend's fragranced throat. "Yeah, I guess." He moved back and looked at Ryan. "But I know I need to get over it if I want to keep you. I'm planning on being around a lot more if I get this teaching job, and yes, of course I want us to be exclusive."

Ryan's breath warmed Mango's throat. He looked up, blue eyes serious. "Thing is, the exclusive thing is easy enough for me." Ryan sighed. "Since Lenny, I've not had anyone else. Only you when you were around. The rest of the time—my flesh jack, vibrator and hands were my best pals. I'm not cut out for senseless sex without there being anything else. Those days are long gone." He made a deprecating moue.

Mango stood back in surprise and regarded Ryan with narrowed eyes. "What about the guy Adam you mentioned, the one you went out with on my birthday? You said you fucked his brains out."

Ryan shrugged. "I lied. We had a great dinner, watched Callum perform—boy is fine, by the way—Adam had a drink here and went home." He grinned slyly.

Mango couldn't believe it. "You conniving bastard," he murmured affectionately.

Ryan's eyes shone with mirth.

"All this time I've been thinking of you having a good time with other men and you're telling me you weren't?" The relief Mango felt was overwhelming. He also felt a little guilty about the things *he'd* done. The anonymous blow jobs, hand jobs and rutting against another man until he got off.

Ryan reached up and traced the contour of his jawline. "That look tells me you weren't as celibate as I was," he muttered. "I can't judge you for what you did when we were apart. You made the rules clear up front and I chose to follow them, albeit grudgingly. But not anymore. I s'pose I have to forgive you for being a douche based on your heartbreaker of a story." His eyes softened. "I wish we'd had this conversation sooner. It would have made things so much easier for me to understand things."

Mango puffed out a breath of air. "I need you to know something else too."

He framed Ryan's face with his hands and stared into his earnest blue eyes. "I've never spent the night in another man's bed since we got together. I didn't even kiss them. That always belonged to you and you only. Oh yeah, and I know the gossip around the club and the whole perception people have of me tootling off to have sex with guys." His voice grew fierce. "But I can promise, hand on heart, I have *never* tainted your club that way. It would have been so wrong to do *anything* in Club Delish that wasn't with you."

Ryan's eyes grew wide. "So all the times I saw you 'tootling' off backstage or into back alleys was nothing nefarious? I mean, you're a man slut institution at the club."

Mango grinned softly. "I got a reputation by going out for a joint, or a chat with one of the guys there. That's all it was, I swear. Have you ever had one of your guys come up and brag about what I did to them or them to me?"

Ryan shook his head and scowled. "No. I thought it was because I was the boss and they knew I'd probably kick their arses one dark night out of spite."

Mango laughed. "It's because nothing ever happened. Sure, guys tried it on, tried to steal a kiss, shove their hands down my pants, but I always refused. Club Delish is sacred, Ryan. It's yours." His face darkened. "I've never had anything but casual blow jobs or hand jobs and such with someone else, anywhere.

There was one time, at the club, this gorgeous young twink wouldn't leave me alone. He was willing but I couldn't do it."

Ryan looked hurt. "If I was right there, why the fuck wasn't I the one you were taking home?"

Mango sighed. "It was all part of my plan to keep my distance, not get too attached. It seemed like the right idea at the time." He hesitated. "My childhood story was a difficult one to tell, you know? I've never told it to anyone before. And I'm sorry it took so long." He hesitated. "It doesn't mean I was right running off last time and not telling you where I was going. I'm sorry about leaving a stupid damned note. I deserve to have my nuts kicked in."

Ryan kissed him, a deep, sultry meeting of lips, tongues and teeth that made Mango's head explode and his dick harden.

"I have plans for those nuts later, so I don't want them damaged." Ryan released Mango's mouth and grinned as he licked his lips salaciously. "Right now, my gorgeous, sexy bastard, we've both bared our souls enough for one morning. You are all mine and I'll scratch out the eyes of anyone, man or woman, who tries to take you away." His sultry voice made Mango's cock perk up even more. Ryan's warm fingers sliding into Mango's pants and stroking him made it even happier.

"So now I think I need to take what's mine and enjoy it. Cement this relationship so to speak. So get your arse on my bed, and spread 'em. It's time for me to take charge."

Mango wasted no time in obeying Ryan's command. Before Mango knew it, he was flat on his back with a gorgeous, passionate man riding him as if his life depended upon it, the red thong long abandoned to the floor.

Mango could truthfully say he'd nowhere else he'd rather be.

Chapter 4

Ryan sat in the doctor's waiting room, nervous as hell. He killed time flicking through the pages of a glossy *GQ* magazine. He was unable to focus on the hunky, suit-clad men and turned to stare absently out into the small courtyard beyond the glass. Outside the late afternoon sun shone and on a wooden bench, a nurse sat smoking a cigarette.

Ryan sighed. He hadn't felt like a smoke for ages, the craving reduced to his occasional look of longing at someone else as they enjoyed their cigarette. And he hadn't been wearing the nicotine patches lately, thinking they were the reason he felt like shit. Ryan supposed he should be thankful for small mercies that the craving had disappeared.

The thought of his boyfriend made Ryan smile dreamily. Each day Ryan was feeling more optimistic about his future with Mango. In the past few weeks, their relationship had progressed to one of semi-normalcy.

Well, as normal as one could be with a partner like Mango.

He'd no sooner come back from some demonstration against global warming in Stuttgart than he'd gone away again three days later to Scotland for some conference against tainted water springs. Each time though he'd forewarned Ryan and made sure he knew about it. Mango didn't ask permission—neither of them wanted a relationship that was constrictive—but he was being more open and collaborative.

It wasn't all glitter and sparkly shoes. Ryan and Mango were both too stubborn and independent, but the few flare-ups they'd had since seeing more of each other was more than made up for by the sizzling make-up sex. As did the "I've missed you so much" sex when Mango returned.

Because of the club and Ryan's early starts and late nights, they tended to spend more time at Ryan's flat than Mango's. Mango had practically moved in. His clothes littered Ryan's floor. Mango was an untidy bastard and his toothbrush and razor were the only things that stayed in their own spot in Ryan's bathroom. Ryan hadn't been sure whether he should ask Mango yet whether he wanted to move in permanently and rent out his own flat. He didn't want to spook the man. Things may be better between them but moving in indicated a whole new level of commitment.

Mango had been granted an interview for the university job and now he waited for them to set a date. It was all looking really positive.

On the nights he found himself alone, Ryan had consoled himself with meeting Eric for dinner or coffee. Eric had become an occasional friend and good company, although his eyes hid a sadness he'd yet to share with Ryan. The man had secrets of his own.

"Mr Bishop, please would you come through?" The nurse beckoned Ryan over into his GP's surgery and said the words Ryan had heard a thousand times before in films of many genres. "The doctor will see you now."

Ryan tried not to snigger at the phrase as he followed the trim figure of the woman through the door. She smiled at him and left him alone with his childhood doctor, Christopher Patel. Christopher was a friend of his mother.

"Ryan. Good to see you. Well, not good, because you're in a doctor's room but you get what I mean." Christopher beamed at Ryan who smiled back.

"It's good to see you too." Ryan sat down gingerly on the chair beside the doctor's desk. Last night he and Mango had overindulged with a variety of implements and toys and Ryan felt a little fragile this morning. Sometimes lube didn't make up for enthusiasm and a boyfriend who loved his job as the one pounding Ryan's arse—multiple times.

"How are your folks—your mother?" Christopher sounded apologetic. "I haven't spoken to her for a while. They were in Corfu for a couple of months, weren't they? Is your dad still playing at concerts?"

Ryan nodded. Corfu was one of his parents' favourite getaway destinations and they spent about half the year there. Ryan had actually been born on Corfu, during one of his father's concerts. His father was a sought-after classical pianist; his mother a semiretired clinical psychologist who travelled with him.

"Yes, they're still there. Between you and me, I'm not sure they're coming back." He rolled his eyes. "Dad's thinking of retiring himself but we'll see how it goes. We all know he can't keep his fingers off a piano."

Christopher's face crinkled in a grin. "Don't I know it. Your mother tells me the same thing." He leaned forward, looking serious. "So, tell me why you're here. What's up?"

Ryan sighed. He hadn't made the decision to come seek medical advice lightly. However, he was still having headaches and feeling dizzy, and sometimes he needed to focus on things to see them. He'd also noticed his legs growing weak when he danced or strutted across the stage.

As he proceeded to give his summary of ills, Christopher nodded and made notes on his tablet. Ryan had his blood pressure taken, his ears, nose and throat checked, and myriad other tests.

Finally, Christopher sat down with a sigh, a frown of concern on his face.

Ryan regarded him uneasily.

"It could be nothing. It could be something." Christopher looked uncomfortable. "I'm sorry to be so obtuse. It could be something as simple as vertigo triggered by diet or low blood sugar because you haven't been eating as well." He checked his notes and hummed. "I want to refer you to a colleague for a second opinion, to rule out anything more serious. After I've consulted with them, if there's still no obvious cause, the next step could be referral to a neurologist who'll possibly schedule an MRI scan to see why you're having headaches when you've no history of them." Christopher cocked his head to one side. "Are you still not smoking?"

Ryan nodded. "I've abstained. The patches helped but I don't use them anymore. I thought perhaps they might be the reason for the trouble I'm having?"

Christopher huffed. "It's doubtful. I'd suggest we get another doctor appointment set up and we can take it from there."

Feathers of fear fluttered in Ryan's chest. He'd always been so healthy, hardly ever needing to go to the doctor and the whole idea of seeing a specialist to find out what was going on in his brain terrified him. His hands trembled and he clasped them between his knees. Christopher seemed to notice his agitation. He reached out and placed a gentle hand on Ryan's arm.

"I'd like to say don't worry but I know you—you're a worrier. Try not to let it get to you too much though as it may make things worse."

Ryan nodded. "Thanks. So you'll let me know a date?" He stood.

Christopher nodded. "You'll get a letter confirming the appointment. Obviously, try to keep it if they do get you in because doctor's appointments are like hen's teeth." He fumbled in his desk drawer. "In the meantime, here's an information sheet for things that could trigger vertigo. I'd suggest you have a read and avoid the foodstuffs and drinks on here as a precaution. We can check on your progress at your next check-up."

"Thanks, Christopher. I'll keep the appointment when I get one and take a look at the sheet," Ryan promised fervently. "I appreciate everything."

He left the surgery feeling in two minds about things. He was glad he'd been to see the doctor but he was also worried about the diagnosis. Ryan sighed. He'd have to be patient and wait and see. He also decided he wasn't going to tell Mango or his folks about any of it either. There was no point in making any of them worry unless there was something to worry about. Which, hopefully, wouldn't be the case.

When he got back to his club, Ryan's front of house manager, Kyle Tripper, met him at the door with a frosted glass of something and a wink. "Afternoon, boss. I thought you might appreciate a Cucumber Punch when you arrived." He passed over a cold glass filled with the grape juice and lemonade drink, garnished with slices of lemon and cucumber.

Ryan took it gratefully. Kyle's mocktails and cocktails were legendary. His background had been as both a cocktail waiter and croupier in some fancy place in Las Vegas until he'd split up with his boyfriend and come back to the UK, where he'd been born. Mario, his ex, had been a dancer but Kyle didn't talk about him much.

Ryan had the feeling there was a real story there but he wasn't going to push. He'd been glad to bring the purple haired, quirky younger man on board as manager when he'd had the chance three years ago. He was good with numbers, dexterous with a deck of cards to the point of genius and tough but fair. The staff loved him almost as much as they did Ryan.

Later, Ryan was working in his office on the upper level, where glass fronted windows looked out over the dance floor, when there was a soft knock at the door. Ryan looked up and smiled at the man standing there.

"Eric. This is a surprise." He stood up and went over to give his friend a hug.

Eric Kirby was a six-foot-plus mass of muscle, with a shy smile and a mess of dark strawberry blond hair, coupled with green eyes the colour of jade. He was a striking figure, and in his paramedic uniform, he looked even better. He might only be Ryan's friend but Ryan wasn't bloody dead. He could appreciate the assets of a mega-attractive man.

Eric embraced him back and stood back. "I finished my shift, thought I'd see if you fancy a drink. Is Mango away or is he home at the moment?" There was no malice in his voice, simply curiosity. Eric was one of the gentlest men Ryan had ever met. It was probably the reason they hadn't clicked on a sexual level. Ryan liked a bit of rough with his sex and he didn't think Eric was the type.

Ryan shook his head. "Mango, bless him, is currently on a train, no doubt spitting blood. He went up to Manchester this morning for a meeting and someone threw themselves in front of the tracks. He wasn't hurt but cocked things up royally. All the trains are delayed and Mango's having trouble getting home." Ryan grinned at the ranting text he'd got a few hours ago before he'd gone to see his doctor. It had been curt and dirty as Mango lambasted those unfortunate individuals causing mayhem on the British rail tracks.

Eric glanced at Ryan and frowned. "Are you okay? You look a little pale." He moved closer and scrutinised Ryan's face.

Ryan blinked at the unexpected concern, while piqued he wasn't presenting his best side to the hunky man in front of him. "I'm fine." He dismissed Eric's concerns with a flap of his hand. "I have Mango in my life. He gives me grey hair and turns me pale with frustration."

Eric chuckled. "Diva. You have no grey hair and look as good as always. You're a little paler is all." He moved back, seeming a little awkward at being so close. "So, are you in the mood for a quick one?"

Ryan raised an eyebrow in mischief and Eric laughed, even as a flush stained his cheeks. "I meant a quick drink."

"Oh I know what you meant," Ryan drawled. "Sure, let me get my coat and we can pop down to the local. I'm in the mood for a Raging Bull."

Now it was Eric's turn to blink. "What the hell is that?"

Ryan smiled wickedly. "Tequila, black Sambuca and coffee liqueur. You should try one. It puts hair on your chest." He winked. "Not that you need it."

Ryan thought Eric's blush was cute. Eric wasn't overly hairy but he had a nice smattering on his chest from what Ryan had seen though the open neck of his shirt.

"Sounds interesting. I might have to try one."

Ryan swung around and went to the coat rack. "Let me get my jacket and we can pop off. Kyle can manage without me. It's my night off anyway."

"I didn't think you ever had a real night off, boss." Kyle leaned into the doorway, his violet eyes sparkling. "The only time I see you leave this place nowadays is when you and your crazy boyfriend go off to do the dirty." He grinned and came into the office. "Sorry to interrupt but I've got those papers you were waiting for. The lawyer delivered them earlier, and I know you'd want to keep them somewhere safe to read tonight."

Ryan huffed a breath of relief. "Thank God they've arrived. I've been on fucking tenterhooks waiting to have them in my hot little hands. Let me at 'em."

He'd recently upped his mortgage on the building, taking out some extra capital to do renovations. Deep Purple, the sex bathroom, as he'd nicknamed it, needed a revamp as did the bar itself. Plus, he wanted to create a small, intimate bistro in the rear of the building where people could have private functions. It had been a tough negotiation with the bank but he'd triumphed. He'd sold his soul a little bit more.

Ryan couldn't help noticing Eric give Kyle an unobtrusive once-over. And if he wasn't mistaken, the scrutiny was returned. Ryan smiled inwardly.

Well, well, well. That's…unexpected.

Ryan wondered if perhaps this might be something he could pursue for the two men currently casting covert glances each other's way. Ryan rather fancied himself as a matchmaker.

"You two haven't met yet, have you?" Ryan waved an airy hand. "Eric, meet Kyle. He's my second-in-command and this place wouldn't run without him. He kept it going for me while I was performing in the play. Kyle, Eric is a friend of mine. He's the paramedic—"

"Who helped the guy who had the heart attack a while ago." Kyle finished his sentence with a smile. "Of course I remember him. Who could forget a hunky man in uniform saving someone's life?" He stepped forward and held out a hand.

Eric took it, looking a little hesitant. Ryan smirked.

Kyle, with his deep purple, spiked hairdo, mascara and guy liner circling violet eyes and numerous piercings, was a little overwhelming. He had the forceful personality to match his appearance.

"Uhm, yeah, hi," Eric said shyly as Kyle took his hand. "Pleased to meet you, Kyle."

"Oh, the pleasure's all mine, believe me," Kyle drawled and Ryan bit back a laugh as Eric's eyes widened. "So you're going for a drink together?" He cocked an eyebrow at Ryan. "Mango away saving the world or is he swinging by later?"

"He's stuck on a train, trying to get home. No doubt I'll see him tonight." Ryan shrugged himself into his jacket. "Maybe one night when you're not working you can join us?"

Kyle grinned. "I'd love to. Maybe one day when my slave driver of a boss gives me time off."

Ryan laughed. "Maybe I'll be the one working next time and you and Eric here can get acquainted. It's always good to make new friends."

Kyle hooted loudly. "Oh my God, you are so damn obvious, boss. You, my friend, are no *shadkhan*."

Ryan stared at him. "What the hell are you talking about?"

"It's a Jewish matchmaker," Eric said softly, his face pink.

Kyle's eyes narrowed. "I've never met anyone who knew the term before. Are you Jewish?"

Eric shook his head. "My partner is. Work partner," he clarified hastily. "He's always talking about how his grandmother, his *bubbeh*, is trying to set him up with someone using a *shadkhan*." He grinned. "Aaron's trying hard to resist because he says he'll find his own damn woman."

Kyle looked at him speculatively. "I'm Jewish too. Not devout"—he waved a hand with its blue painted nails in their direction—"but I was brought up in the faith as a kid. Now I'm not into religion at all. It's a complete waste of time." His tone hardened and his eyes darkened.

It wasn't the first time in the past eighteen months Ryan had heard the sentiment from Kyle. He'd guessed there was a story behind it. Ryan sighed. God, did everyone have something in their past they couldn't let go of? Why couldn't life simply be fun and fair for everyone?

"Anyway, I'd better let you guys get off. See you later, boss. Eric, nice meeting you. Maybe one day we'll all get drunk together." Kyle turned and left the office.

Eric cleared his throat and turned to Ryan. "I have to ask. Is that his real eye colour? Because they are amazing and they match his hair."

Ryan chuckled. "Contacts. I've never seen Kyle's real eyes. Stunning, isn't he?"

"Were you trying to, you know, match-make?" Eric's eyes crinkled in amusement. "Don't you think I can find my own dates? I know *we* didn't work out but it doesn't mean I'm a lost cause." His tone was teasing.

Ryan laughed. "I have no doubt. No, I was trying to include him, he's a great guy." He crossed his fingers at his lie and rubbed at his forehead, frowning at the sudden ache. "Right, shall we get going? I'm liking the idea of a Raging Bull better with every passing minute."

It was more like three Raging Bulls and half a bottle of wine later.

Eric had asked him how Mango had gotten his name and Ryan had sat back, ready to spew forth the story Mango had told him one night, as they'd been lying in bed after a lazy evening of sex.

"So how the hell did you get the name Mango?" Ryan had asked. "Are you named after a fruit? I mean, I know you are a fruit and all but it seems a little too obvious."

Mango had turned and glared as Ryan snorted with laughter.

"I am not named after the fucking fruit," Mango growled. "And like no one's ever asked me that before."

Ryan managed to contain his amusement at his lover's disgusted expression and waited. Mango pushed the bed sheet aside and scratched his stomach absently. Ryan's attention had been drawn to his half hard dick but he nobly averted his eyes and prompted Mango to finish. "So?" he drawled. "Tell me all about it."

Mango huffed. "In 2005 I was in Rwanda with an eco team. We were looking at elements of biodiversity and conservation of the tropical forests. We were in some little village in the middle of nowhere—"

Ryan interrupted him, eyes wide. "Wasn't it a conflict zone? Weren't you in danger?" He'd seen the graphic images and news reports and was aware the civil war in the country had torn it violently apart.

Mango shrugged. "Yeah, it wasn't ideal. We had armed patrols, curfews, safety lectures. But it needed to be done. I was only twenty-five, full of piss and vinegar and thought I'd be okay." His face shadowed. "It wasn't fucking pleasant though. Some terrible things happened there." He refocused on what he'd been saying. "So, at the same time we were there, Médecins Sans Frontières was as well. They were dealing out HIV and AIDS advice, treatments and vaccines for some of the other diseases."

Ryan leaned over and snuggled into Mango's side. "Sounds as if it's a busy little village," he remarked.

Mango grinned. "Yeah. There was this little wizened old woman, about four feet high and probably about ninety years old. The doctors wanted to give her a shot of something for something, I can't remember what. She kept refusing and they were tearing their hair out. She'd been pretty friendly to me previously so I thought I'd try convince her. So I went over to her with the injection in my hand, trying to tell her she needed it because it would help her."

He chuckled. "This tiny four-foot woman picked up a damn battered old pot and threw it at me, saying 'Man, go. Man, go.' over and over again, shouting and trying to chase me away. She was petrified of the needle. My team thought it was hilarious and from that point on I was known as Mango. It stuck like crap to a blanket and I could never get rid of it." He scowled. "So it was nothing to do with the bloody fruit."

Ryan was snickering at the story. "Oh, such a classic tale. Pity you won't ever have any grandkids to tell it to."

Mango had already made it clear he wasn't the paternal or grandpa type. Ryan wasn't concerned. He had no plans to have kids himself.

"I guess you can put it on your tombstone though." Ryan struck a dramatic pose, rising to his knees on the bed and flinging up one arm. "Here lies Manning Munroe, known as Mango because he was chased by a little old lady—ouch."

Mango had tackled naked Ryan to the bed and covered his body with his.

"So damn funny you are," he'd said huskily in Ryan's ear. "I'll show you fruity." And Mango had proceeded to drive Ryan wild with the use of some strawberry lube and his cock.

It had been a fun night to remember. Ryan left out the last bit in the telling, thinking Eric didn't need to know the intimate details. Eric was chortling, fit to bust a gut, and Ryan was pleased he'd managed to deliver the story even though he'd heard himself slurring a bit during the telling.

Later that night Ryan staggered home, Eric at his side in not much better condition. They staggered up the steps to the flat, arm in arm. Ryan fumbled with the keys to open the door.

His vision was blurred, his head pounded and all he wanted to do was visit the porcelain god, be sick and go to bed. As Ryan fumbled with the lock, the door swung open to reveal a tousled-haired Mango staring down at him.

God, even half asleep my man is sexy as fuck.

"Baby, you're home," Ryan slurred. "I'm home too, did you notice?" He reached up and tweaked Mango's nose. Mango sighed and looked at Eric.

"You guys enjoyed yourselves, I take it." His voice was noncommittal but even in his drunken state Ryan noticed the narrowing of Mango's eyes as he observed Eric hanging on to Ryan's arm.

Oooh, was Mango jealous?

Ryan liked that idea.

Eric chuckled drunkenly. "He was on a roll tonight. And he's cute when he's drunk, but I thought I'd better bring him home before the bartender decided to steal him." He let go and leaned against the wall.

Mango scowled. "Oh yeah? Babe, were you flirting again?" His tone was wry and Ryan didn't miss the eye roll as Mango reached out and hauled him towards him.

"He was sexy," Ryan protested. "And he gave me free drinks. Eric, are you coming in? Perhaps you should stay over." He turned to stare at his friend. Two friends in fact. Ryan squinted, trying to clear his vision.

"I'm sure Eric would rather get home than watch your drunken arse all night," Mango murmured. His eyes were guarded.

Eric shook his head and laughed. "I'll be fine, I'm only five minutes away. I'm not as drunk as you are. I'll leave you in Mango's capable hands." He laughed. "Such a great name. Loved the story. Ryan, I'm sure he'll take care of you. Shit, we're both going to have one heck of a headache in the morning."

"Already have one," Ryan muttered as the room swum and he clung to Mango's strong bicep. "Ooh, you been working out again, sexy? I think you need to show me those muscles you've been hiding. All of them, including the one in your—"

"There'll be no showing of any of my muscles tonight, you deviant. I think it's time for a remedy, then bed. Come on. Eric, thanks for bringing him home. I owe you one." Mango extended a hand and Eric shook it.

"That's what friends do," he slurred. "Night Ryan, I hope you don't feel too bad in the morning. Thanks for tonight."

Ryan waved a hand. "Night, gorgeous. Safe journey home and remember what I told you about Kyle. Go get him, tiger."

Eric laughed again and clunked down the stairs. Ryan found himself manhandled to the kitchen and plonked down on a kitchen stool.

"Sit there, and don't fall off," Mango said as he busied himself with opening cupboards and the fridge. "I'm going to make you a drink that will rehydrate you and hopefully alleviate any hangover you'll have in the morning."

Ryan made a face. "Erggh. Not that crap you stick in a blender, which has raw eggs and vegetable shit in it. I'm not drinking it." He clamped his lips firmly shut and glared at Mango.

"Yes you will." Mango took out the blender and loaded what Ryan could only call most of the contents of his fridge into it. "Even if I have to force feed it to you." He turned to the kitchen counter and put the top on the blender.

Ryan wrinkled his nose. "Oh God, you have a feeding fetish. I'm not into stuffing, babe, not unless it's me being stuffed with the gorgeous dick you keep in your pants."

Mango's shoulders shook with what Ryan imagined was silent laughter. Then the air was rent with the ear splitting sound of grinding and whirring. Ryan felt ill at the noise and he pressed a hand to his mouth.

"I'm going to barf," he managed to get out and promptly threw up all over the kitchen floor.

Later, when he'd been hustled to the bathroom, washed and bundled into bed, he lay cuddled under the duvet listening to the sound of Mango cleaning up in the kitchen. He'd argued he could clean up his own vomit but Mango hadn't listened. The upside to Ryan's spewing-up was he hadn't been made to drink Mango's special blend of hell. As Ryan drifted into sleep, the feeling of being cared for and kept safe made him all fuzzy and happy.

Life seemed to have taken a turn for the better.

***

"Boss, I need you. We have a problem."

Ryan groaned loudly as Kyle barrelled into his office in a panic. Kyle was normally the king of unflappable but the look on his face now didn't bode well.

"What is it?" Ryan looked up from where he'd been sneaking a quick doze on his desk—well, okay not quick, from the time on his watch he'd been napping for about an hour—and winced when the bright artificial light hit his eyes. He was still suffering with the hangover from hell from last night.

"It's almost midnight," Ryan mumbled. He'd been working most of the day taking care of the endless cycle of catering orders, business plans, expenses and bill paying and ensuring the website and social media stuff. Life as a nightclub owner wasn't all glamour.

Kyle nodded. "It is indeed. Mango not around tonight?"

Ryan shook his head. "No, he's got some fancy dinner with Ted and Della. He's staying over at the hotel tonight."

Outside, the steady bass of music blared.

Kyle pursed glossed lips. "I got you. Anyway, sorry to wake you but…it's Deep Purple. A fight broke out earlier. Greg and Rufus got it sorted, but…" His voice tailed off.

Ryan was mortified. A fight had broken out in his club and his staff had had to deal with it themselves because he'd over indulged the night before? That simply wasn't acceptable.

"Why didn't anyone call me?" he snapped as he stood up and steadied himself with a hand on his desk. "Who was fighting?"

"You needed the sleep and our bouncers are big boys. We handled it, it's what you pay us good money for." Kyle sniggered. "Although from the looks of you, you could do with a bit more rest." He leaned in and peered at Ryan's eyes. "Wow. I've never seen that particular level of bloodshot before."

"Yes, well, we all have our crosses to bear," Ryan said snarkily. "So tell me—who was fighting and what's the problem?"

"Friends of Jelly Driscoll. One of them got into it with his boyfriend at the door. Started slapping him around. Rufus managed to subdue them but we are left with a bit of a…situation."

Ryan groaned. Jelly Driscoll, so called because of his rather round jelly belly, was usually respectful of the club, as were his friends. However, when he'd had one drink too many, he'd been known to cause trouble with his sidekick, his petite Chinese boyfriend Casey.

"Fuck. Where are they now?"

"Rick kicked them both out, said not to come back. It's what they left in the damn bathroom that's the problem."

Should Kyle look so amused considering they had an issue? What the heck is going on?

Ryan narrowed his eyes. "Show me."

He followed Kyle out of the office and across the dance floor towards Deep Purple. The strobe lights hurt his eyes and the continuous beat of the music throbbed in his head.

People danced around him, touching him, calling him by name and greeting him. He ducked his head, nodded and smiled and breathed a sigh of relief when he followed Kyle's slim form towards the bathroom. Two of his bouncers guarded the doors, which were closed.

They both grinned at him when they saw him.

"Evening Mr Bishop." Greg was a Tom Hardy look-alike, all muscle and bald head. No matter what he did, Ryan couldn't get him to call him by his first name.

The other one, Rufus, bared shark-like teeth in Ryan's direction. He was one of Club Delish's oldest-serving bouncers.

"Ryan, you're not going to believe what those two got up to in there. We didn't want anyone else going in and adding to the mess, so we thought we'd stand guard for a bit till we figure out what to do. I think both of them were on something, because honest, mate, I've never seen anything like it. And I've seen a lot." His Aussie twang was spiced with laughter.

One thing Ryan didn't tolerate was open drug use at Club Delish. They had a zero tolerance policy if people were caught using anything and his staff policed it as best they could. Realistically there was no way on earth you could stop it altogether, especially on the dance floor where mouths slid against mouths and anything could get passed along.

"Let me see," Ryan said resignedly. "Open the damn door."

Rufus swung the door open and motioned for Ryan to go ahead. Kyle followed close behind. Ryan stepped into Deep Purple and his jaw dropped.

"What the fuck? What did those crazy motherfuckers do to my club? I'll fucking kill them."

He stared around the despoiled walls of the bathroom in horror and fury. Beside him, Kyle, Greg and Rufus waited.

Kyle nodded. "I thought you might pitch a fit. It's why I told Greg he'd better get rid of them ASAP before you got loose on them. Because the last thing we need is the headline, "Owner of local gay nightclub cuts balls off local patrons.""

The pastel and purple coloured walls were a riot of other colours and startling images. Half a dozen cans of spray paint lay littering the grey tiled floor, where splashes of colour dotted the surface. Ryan moved forward, speechless. The tight feeling in his chest threatened to implode and he swallowed down his anger.

"Those fuckers drew cocks and balls on my walls with *spray paint*?" Wherever one looked, badly drawn upright dicks and heavy balls garnished the walls in a riot of colour. They'd even drawn on the cubicle doors.

"And Christ, is that supposed to be some sort of artistic mural?" *That* was a rendition of one man fucking another. Despite its childlike graphic and obvious lack of talent, it was still detailed enough to recognise what it was. A slight man knelt on the ground while another rather larger man drove into him from behind. Above the picture—and Ryan hesitated to call it even that—the words "Jelly loves Casey" were emblazoned in bold letters.

Ryan swung around, eyes blazing. "*This* is how you guys protect my fucking club? Allowing these arseholes in here to do this?" He spat out the words and saw Greg's face darken but he said nothing. He glanced at Rufus who stood stock-still, arms folder across his chest. Ryan knew the minute the words had left his lips he was being unfair—Rufus and Greg were the best bouncers he'd ever employed—but his indignation and fiery temper were getting the best of him.

Ryan's head was ready to explode. He rubbed his temple, willing the pain in there to subside. Damn hangover was doing a number on him.

Kyle stepped forward, placing a strong hand on Ryan's arm. "Ryan, it wasn't their fault. Jelly told a couple of his mates to cause a diversion inside the club entrance, hence the fight, and both of these guys"—he waved at the stoic bouncers—"were helping resolve it. One of Casey's scarily big mates stood by the door and stopped people coming in, telling everyone Deep Purple was closed because of a burst water pipe. Then the arseholes got busy in here while everyone was otherwise occupied."

"Who stopped them?" Ryan snapped out.

Rufus held up a hand. "I did, boss. I finished up with Greg at the door, came back here to check things." He smiled slightly. "The big-ass dude Casey had on the door didn't last long once he saw me coming back. He hightailed it pretty quickly. I came in and saw this shit. I called Kyle and he went to find you."

Ryan's guilt increased. While he'd been sleeping it off his staff had been dealing with a bad situation and he'd lambasted them for it. He heaved a shuddering sigh. "Sorry, guys. I didn't mean to go off on you. You did the best you could."

"That's all right, Mr Bishop." Greg grinned at him. "I know how you feel about your club. We'll get this sorted though, don't you worry. We'll make sure Jelly and Casey pay for the damages."

Ryan nodded in resignation. "I'm insured for this sort of thing but the policy excess is pretty steep. Let's see what the quotes for the damage are. And here I am borrowing money from the bank to do this damn place up. It'll be needed now. Jesus."

He cast a jaded eye around the bathroom and sighed. "Okay. Let's tell everyone this is off limits and they'll have to use the other bathrooms. Make sure you tell everyone to keep the sex shit out of there so paying patrons who need to can take a leak. I know that's asking a lot but do your best to keep it to a minimum. It's not like I haven't enjoyed a blowjob or a quick shag in there myself." He gave a wry smile.

Kyle nudged him gently on the shoulder. "I've already spoken to our insurance broker. He'll file a claim first thing

Monday morning and we'll get the ball rolling. Leave it with me."

Ryan wanted to hug him. Kyle, however, was a bit funny about close contact and Ryan thought it best not to.

"Thanks, I appreciate the help. I'll be in the office if anyone needs me. Some last minute things to do and I'll be off to bed."

Usually Kyle locked up in the early hours of the morning, although Ryan did take over occasionally to give him a break. Ryan's manager insisted it was what Ryan employed and paid him for, taking the late night shifts. He'd murmured he'd nowhere else to be anyway. Ryan hadn't ever seen him with a significant other; Kyle was circumspect about his private life.

Kyle nodded. "Okay. Get some sleep, boss. Why not leave the paperwork for another time? You look a bit washed-out."

Ryan glared at him. "Washed-out? Just what a guy needs to hear."

Kyle smirked. "Stop pouting. You've got a couple of days off now until the club reopens on Tuesday. So get some damn rest."

Ryan scowled. "I'm not pouting," he said sulkily. *Oh shit. He so was.*

He left his more than capable team dealing with the detritus of the evening and wearily made his way to bed. When he climbed under the duvet and closed his eyes, his one ardent wish was that Mango was there beside him, his warm body cradling Ryan's. With a pleasant memory on his mind, Ryan fell into the dark recesses of sleep.

***

Mango let himself into Ryan's flat around eight thirty a.m. Sunday morning. After a quick and early breakfast, he'd hailed a taxi and got home as fast as he could. He tried to be as quiet as possible entering the bedroom, not wanting to wake Ryan up. What Mango found there took his breath away.

Ryan had always been the sexiest man Mango had ever known. The duvet was pushed away, revealing a lithe, nude body sprawled across the bed. Seeing Ryan now, lying half on his stomach, one arm outstretched as if reaching for the alarm clock on the bedside table, made Mango wanted to pounce on him.

One slim, almost hairless leg was drawn up to Ryan's stomach, giving Mango an enticing look at what lay between Ryan's legs. His auburn curls were spread across a cream brocade pillow, framing delightful, slightly pointy ears—ears that sometimes made Ryan self-conscious, but Mango thought were as cute as hell.

He moved around to the side of the bed, watching the rise and fall of Ryan's chest and seeing his lush lips part and exhale. The ache in Mango's chest intensified, an ache of longing, wanting and possessing. The need in his groin was overwhelming.

God, he wanted Ryan so badly. Mango had never met another man he'd had such a physical and emotional connection to. He was fucking terrified of it. How he could have ever thought he'd be able to keep this man at bay, push him away and pretend he didn't matter was now becoming apparent as a fool's errand.

Ryan murmured and shifted in his sleep, his out-flung arm drawing into his chest as he curled his fist and brought it against his body. He looked beautifully vulnerable lying there, a sleeping kitten, but Mango knew beneath his innocent façade was a tiger—his tiger. One who bit, clawed and scratched, yet purred softly when shown affection and made to feel as if he mattered.

Quietly, Mango disrobed and left his dinner party clothes in a heap on the floor. He climbed in behind Ryan and pulled the duvet over them, then yanked Ryan into his arms. Ryan gave a soft, contented sigh and snuggled back. The feel of warm arse against Mango's groin was bliss and when Ryan wriggled, his intent evident, Mango grinned and planted a soft kiss on the back of Ryan's neck as his cock lengthened and pressed into Ryan's crease.

"We'd better hurry up and get this morning fuck over with before my boyfriend gets home," Ryan murmured, his voice tinged with amusement. "He could be home anytime soon."

Mango licked a trail down Ryan's neck and felt him shiver. Mango's fingers traced small circles on Ryan's taut belly, slowly and tantalisingly moving down.

"Then I guess we'd better hurry up," he whispered as he pushed his tongue inside the delicious crevice of Ryan's ear. Ryan gave a small whimper and pressed even closer against Mango. "I've heard he's not a particularly nice man to cross and if he comes home and finds me sticking it to his boyfriend, he might do me harm."

"Oh, he'll do you harm," said Ryan breathlessly as he shamelessly rubbed his now slippery cheeks up and down Mango's wet cock. "And God knows what he'd do to me."

Mango stopped teasing the inside of Ryan's ear. "What would he do to you? Tell me. I'd like to hear how he'd punish you."

Ryan's breathing was hoarse and Mango ran his fingers lightly along the velvet flesh of Ryan's dick, his thumb digging lightly into his slit. Ryan made a sound of need and pleasure and Mango's breathing sped up.

"He'd tell me to get to my hands and knees and get ready for his gorgeous cock," Ryan panted, and his face turned so Mango could capture those beautiful lips in a wet, possessive kiss. He lived for Ryan's kisses. They were hot, passionate and knew no boundaries and Ryan gave everything he had when taking his mouth.

Ryan continued his erotic expectations of what Mango would do. "Then he'd push his fingers inside me, tease me with them like the bastard he is. He knows I like more than a couple of fingers inside me."

"Would he put his fist in you?" Mango asked, the thought making him harder than he'd thought possible. They'd talked about it before but so far it hadn't happened. It wasn't something Mango had done to anyone before but the idea turned him on.

Ryan's breath deepened. "God," he said, his voice ragged. "I'm not sure. One day I'd like him to try it, not quite yet."

Mango bit Ryan's shoulder and Ryan shuddered and a deep groan echoed in the quiet of the bedroom as Mango slid his fingers along Ryan's crease, circling his hole. "What else would he do? Slap this beautiful arse of yours until you were pink and stinging? Fuck you?" He slid two fingers inside and found a nub of flesh. He rubbed it and Ryan squirmed, a rush of breath leaving his mouth.

"Oh, God, yes," Ryan gasped. Mango slid in another and moved them around, loving how responsive Ryan was to every movement. His arse pushed against Mango's fingers, urging him deeper. Mango obliged, his own cock sliding along Ryan's flesh wherever he could find friction.

"I need more." Ryan pushed the duvet back and got onto his hands and knees. Then he arched his back, pushing a ripe, toned backside up and inviting Mango in.

Ryan's eyes were wild as they looked back at Mango, the need and lust undoing him. "Once he'd opened me up, he'd use his tongue. Fuck me deep with it, drive me crazy, drive into me with his cock. He'd probably slap my arse too. He likes to cause me a little bit of pain."

Mango tried not to hyperventilate as he got to his knees and moved behind Ryan.

"He sounds like quite the animal, this boyfriend of yours." God, Mango was so rock hard he thought he'd come from the conversation alone. "Perhaps I should leave now and let him do you as you so graphically described." Mango positioned himself between Ryan's legs, parting his cheeks. The sight that greeted his eyes was one he wanted repeated over and over again. He'd never tire of it.

Mango leaned in and wet Ryan's hole, pushing his tongue in ever so slightly. He loved the taste of Ryan, the special flavour of soap, musk and man coated his tongue and drove him crazy.

Ryan went wild. He pushed back, and Mango chuckled at the desperate gesture.

"God, don't make me have to beg," Ryan gasped. "Do me deep with your tongue. Then fuck me before he gets here."

Mango needed no further urging. He had a feeling if the dirty talk went on much longer both of them would blow their loads too soon and he very much wanted to fuck Ryan first.

He continued to assault Ryan's entrance with spit and fluid from Mango's own leaking cock. When he thought Ryan had had enough of his tongue and lips, Mango slicked them both up with lube. Then, at Ryan's desperate and breathless urging to fuck him, Mango slid home.

He thanked God there was no need for condoms now. It was one of the most affirming contributions either of them had made to their current relationship. There was something to be said for monogamy and regular testing.

Ryan cried out and tightened around him as Mango plunged deep. Being inside his lover was one of his favourite places. Tight, heated muscles gripped his dick as the friction of flesh against flesh caused spirals of pleasure to whirl across Mango's groin and the rest of his body.

Mango gripped Ryan's hip with one hand, as his other rose and fell in sharp slaps against the firm flesh of Ryan's arse. The sound of the slap mirrored Ryan's cries as he begged for more, begged for Mango to hit him harder.

When Ryan's skin was a beautiful shade of pink, Mango reached around and took hold of Ryan's rigid cock. With each thrust, he stroked and jerked Ryan, and when he heard shuddering sobs from his boyfriend that he was about to come, Mango gave one last stroke. He rejoiced in Ryan's strangled cry of ecstasy as warm fluid coated Mango's hand and arm.

It didn't take long after for him to reach his climax. Mango spilled inside Ryan as Ryan's muscles clenched around him and forced out every drop in his balls.

His body spent, Mango wrapped his arms around Ryan's chest, holding him close as he collapsed backwards to sit open legged on the bed. Ryan followed willingly, Mango still inside him. Ryan's languorous arms reached around to draw Mango's lips to his and take his mouth in a post coital kiss.

"God, you are epic," Ryan said dreamily, lips wet and swollen. "I'm glad my boyfriend didn't come home. I don't think he could have done it any better."

Mango laughed wearily and nuzzled Ryan's sweaty neck. "Glad to hear it. Maybe I can give him some pointers."

Ryan moved, and Mango's dick slipped free. Ryan twisted to face him and reached out and cupped Mango's face in warm hands.

"I think I might keep you instead," he said huskily.

Then he pressed his hot and nubile body against Mango once again and ravished Mango's already sensitive lips with his own ferocious mouth. As he was pushed back onto the bed, with Ryan stuck like Velcro to his body, Mango closed his eyes and surrendered to the feeling of being irrevocably owned.

Chapter 5

It couldn't be true. Ryan refused to believe it. He gazed at his neurologist in horror, the words the man had uttered still echoing in his disbelieving mind.

"You think I might have a fucking growth in my head?" The words sounded strange and he couldn't help swearing. Ryan gripped the desk tightly, trying to anchor himself in reality because this whole scenario had to be a bad dream. He hadn't expected this when he'd come for yet another medical appointment in the past couple of weeks. His doctors hadn't been able to determine the cause of his current condition, so he'd been referred to the neurologist. The man had been thorough and had prodded, poked and checked him for the past forty minutes before telling him he was through.

Doctor Trin nodded compassionately. "An MRI will show us exactly what we are dealing with and I'll be booking an appointment for you as soon as possible. At this stage I can't say exactly what's going on in there. But the symptoms and the things you've been experiencing sound like it might be a possibility."

Ryan sat back in the plastic chair, dazed. "I never thought— I didn't think it would be something so serious. Eye strain perhaps, maybe a trapped nerve—I never thought it could be a growth. Shit, this is—" Words failed him and he ran a nervous, trembling hand through his hair. "So what happens now? I go for this MRI and if you find anything, you open up my brain?" He was aware his voice was almost a shriek.

Doctor Trin smiled, his placid face soothing. "Mr Bishop, I've seen a lot of cases and most of them are treatable with surgery. I can't say much more until we do the MRI, see if what I suspect is true. If so, we need to determine where the growth is and whether it can be removed. That, however, is thinking too far ahead. First we need to see what we are dealing with."

Ryan's heart beat faster. "What if it's cancerous? What happens after that?" His hands were cold and clammy and he wanted to throw up.

Doctor Trin shook his head. "We will do this one step at a time, yes? First we see what is going on. Then we tackle the rest of it." His eyes softened. "Mr Bishop, I can assure you, we will deal with each problem, if there are any, as it arises. I know it sounds as if I'm making light when I tell you to try not to worry but at this point there's no need to think the worst—so try not to worry unduly."

He pulled his pad towards him and popped a pair of black-rimmed spectacles on his nose. "I will make an appointment for the MRI as soon as I can, and once we have a result, we will determine next steps between us. I promise to keep you informed every step of the way and I will not sugar coat anything. You will have my best and most professional prognosis and treatment options and together, we will get you through this, yes? The fact you have given up smoking is good too." He smiled wryly. "Although I imagine the desire to smoke right now is fairly prevalent."

Ryan nodded numbly. "I could manage a cigarette right now. It's a shock, you know. I'm hardly ever ill and now this."

Doctor Trin pursed his lips. "You have family to talk to, to share this with? I would recommend you talk to people who care for you, so they can help keep you positive and share the burden." His voice grew firm. "Do not shoulder this on your own, you need to speak to people you love about it."

Ryan swallowed. There was no way he was sharing this with anyone yet, not until he knew exactly what he was facing. His parents were in blissful ignorance, still in Corfu and likely never returning. And his relationship with Mango over the past couple of weeks might have improved, but news like this would still freak Mango out, given what had happened to his parents. He'd suffered enough tragedy—Ryan wasn't giving him this sort of stress as well.

Mango had an important interview coming up and he needed to be on top form. From what Ryan had been told, it was a fierce and competitive race for a prestigious job and Ryan needed Mango to win.

So he lied. "Yeah, I will. So, you'll let me know when I need this MRI?"

He left the doctor's surgery, shell-shocked and disbelieving. He couldn't face going back to his club yet. One look at his face and anyone would know there was something wrong. Ryan needed to ponder, think about things on his own.

He called Kyle to tell him he might be a bit late getting back from his business appointment and made his way down to the Wentworth Street Market. The quaint and busy street set with market stalls and bric-a-brac was a favourite. Ryan ambled aimlessly, haggling with one merchant to purchase an old vintage waistcoat, and arguing amiably with another vendor for a hat for Mango; an Indiana Jones–type Ryan thought Mango would look sexy in.

To stop himself from giving in to having a smoke, he treated himself to a bagel loaded with cream cheese and salmon, washed it down with a bottle of Snapple and chatted jovially to the market vendors, one of whom convinced him to buy a beautiful pair of matching antique rose gold men's rings. Ryan loved the two different sizes. They'd obviously been specially made as a matching set. One was perfect for his ring finger, the other would probably fit Mango's larger one. Ryan thought perhaps one day they might work for a special occasion. It seemed odd to plan for the future now that there was a question as to whether he might have one. The rings nestling in his pocket were his own affirmation he was going to be okay.

All in all, he managed to convince himself life was normal and there wasn't the threat of something dark and invasive hanging over his head—more like inside his head. It was all a big misunderstanding, he assured himself. They weren't going to find any crafty little buggers growing in his noggin.

Ryan was still trying to convince himself when later in the night he got home to a cold and empty bed. He'd been expecting Mango to be there, warm, willing and ready to cuddle up to. The flat was lonely without Mango's comfortable presence. Ryan realised he hadn't checked his mobile phone messages. He sat down on the side of the bed and scrolled through them. Mango's was message number three.

"Babe, I'm not coming over tonight. Got an early start in the morning to this shindig in Scotland so I need my sleep. And we both know if I come over there, we won't be getting much of it." The smile in Mango's voice was welcome but Ryan would rather he be here in person. He'd forgotten Mango had this trip up north to some climate control conference. Yet another trip encroaching on their time together. Ever since Mango had decided to apply for the university job, he'd been spending more time away trying to fit in existing obligations he had, obligations he'd admitted shamefacedly to Ryan he'd forgotten about. It appeared everyone wanted a piece of him while they could still get it.

Ryan understood but he wasn't happy about it. His one solace was Mango might soon be more home-based and Ryan was looking forward to that reality if it happened.

The message carried on. "My flight is at four a.m. tomorrow morning, and I'll be back on the weekend sometime. Sleep tight and I'll call you once I get to Argyll. Speak soon." There was a slight delay before the next text, which was, "Love you. Bye."

Despite his frustration at not having Mango tonight, his "love you" brought tears to Ryan's already aching eyes. He and Mango didn't say those words often to each other. Hearing his more reserved boyfriend say them now when Ryan felt so vulnerable was bittersweet. Ryan listened to the rest of his messages, then lay back on the bed, fully clothed. He kicked off his shoes and laid an arm across his eyes. He doubted he'd get much sleep tonight.

***

The Thai restaurant across the street from the club was jam packed with patrons and Ryan's head ached from the constant noise and chatter as he sat at the table, toying with his napkin. It had been almost a week since his neurology appointment and he still couldn't stop thinking about it. His neurologist had scheduled Ryan's MRI in record time and he wasn't sure whether that was a good or bad sign.

His mantra, however, had become: It's not a problem. There won't be anything wrong. This is only a formality.

Mango had gotten back from Argyll on the weekend with some stomach bug and had spent most of his few days home in bed. Luckily he was better now, but it had been touch and go as to whether Ryan would smother the big oaf with a pillow. His boyfriend was a terribly needy and grumpy patient.

While nursing his man, whom Ryan had exasperatedly named Fluzilla, Ryan had tried not to let his anxiety about the upcoming MRI appointment show at work and with his friends.

"Hey, are you okay? You look a little distracted." Eric's soft voice catapulted Ryan back to reality, and he blinked, staring into Eric's worried eyes.

Ryan nodded, trying to force a smile. "Yeah, I'm sorry, I was wool gathering. I promise you it's not the company being boring." He reached across and laid a hand on Eric's warm one, who clasped it with a friendly grin.

"Glad to hear it. You looked pretty far away. Everything okay?"

Ryan nodded again. "Fine. I—"

"So this is where you got to. I've been looking for you." The curt tone surprised Ryan and he turned to look up at Mango, who stood by the table with a scowl on his face. Mango's eyes were focused on Ryan's hand, still clasped in Eric's. To say he looked displeased would have been putting it mildly.

"Oh, hey." Ryan stood up to give Mango a quick kiss on the cheek. "Eric thought I needed a bit of lunchtime cheer, so I left Kyle managing the club and entertaining the customers with his card tricks. I swear the man has magic hands. I rather fancied some Pad Thai and it's two-for-one Wednesday."

"Mango. Good to see you." Eric stood up and clasped Mango's hand firmly. "Are you going to join us?" He gestured to the spare chair.

Mango grunted. "No thanks. I'm on my way to the airport, wanted to see Ryan before I left. Took me some time to track him down though." He dropped his hand. He appeared to be in a damn bad mood. Well, fucking snap. Ryan was mad now too.

"Airport? You've only been back a few days from Scotland, and you've been ill the whole time. So what trip is this? You didn't tell me about it." Ryan's heart dropped and he sat back down in his chair, as did an uncomfortable looking Eric, who picked up his drink and took a quick gulp.

Mango continued to loom with a dissatisfied expression on his face. "Yeah, well, it's unexpected to me too. I'm not fucking happy about it. One of the delegates for the Ecological Challenge conference in Oslo had a car accident and he can't make it. The CEO of the company organising the conference called me earlier and requested I take his place as one of the keynote speakers."

He scowled. "It's more blackmail, to be honest. More of a demand than a request. I owed them an appearance, and Randolph is collecting. Apparently I signed a contract last year, which gives him one more event to push me into. I'm not prepared or anything near it, so I'm going to have get it done on the plane."

He ran a hand through his already mussed hair. "I hate being unprepared. And to cap it all off, I lost my damn wallet this morning. Had to jump through so many bureaucratic hoops to get all my cards cancelled and get the bank to rush a new one through so I can take it with me. So it's been a shitty bloody day all round."

Try my life, Ryan thought as he suppressed his temper. It's no fucking bed of roses at the moment either.

No sooner had the thought formed than it was pushed guiltily to the back of his mind. It had been *his* decision not to tell Mango or anyone about what he was going through so Ryan couldn't blame them for not understanding his emotional state. The fact he had his MRI appointment on Friday was worsening his already dark mood.

"So this company can call you up and you jump on a plane?" Ryan stared down at the tablecloth, his insides churning. He'd been looking forward to tonight, having planned dinner and some decidedly raunchy activities to take his mind off his current situation. "Wow. I wish I had the same pull they appear to have."

Mango snorted. "It doesn't look as if you'd miss me much anyway." He stared pointedly at Eric.

Ryan started and gave a harsh laugh. "Oh, for God's sake. Eric and I were simply trying to enjoy lunch together. At least after this I go back to the club and my flat, I don't get on a plane to fucking Oslo." He clenched his hands, fingernails biting into flesh. "So how long are you away this time?"

Before Mango could reply, Eric spoke quietly. "I assure you, Mango, Ryan and I are only friends. You needn't worry about anything going on between us."

Mango regarded Eric thoughtfully, nodded and then looked back at Ryan. "In answer to your question, I'll be away a couple of days. I'll probably fly back Sunday if I can get a flight. The event finishes on Saturday night and there's some damn gala dinner evening I need to attend as well."

"Oh well," Ryan remarked caustically. "Pack the tux and have a good time why don't you? Have a glass of champers on me."

Oh God, I'm being a diva again. I can't seem to help it lately.

Even Eric looked a bit taken aback by Ryan's vitriolic response. He stood up, the napkin on his lap falling to the floor.

"I'm going to go the bathroom," he murmured. "Leave you guys to have your conversation without an audience." He strode off in the direction of the back of the restaurant, leaving Ryan and Mango staring at each other.

Mango was the first to shuffle and look discomfited. He sat down in the empty chair next to the one Eric had vacated.

"Ryan, I know this is unexpected. And I'm sorry about being in such a shitty mood." Mango glanced at his watch. "I need to do this and get Randolph off my back. My plane leaves later tonight and I have a ton of stuff to do still, so I need to make a move. But I don't want to leave on bad terms."

Ryan was weary of arguing and wanted nothing more than to finish this particular conversation, get back to the club and perhaps have a stiff whisky. "Then go," he muttered, flapping his hand in a 'shoo away' gesture. "I'll expect you when I see you. We'll talk when you get back." His voice hardened. "And to be clear—I'm not fucking Eric. So get the message in your head and stop being catty about it. He doesn't deserve it."

Mango looked startled but had the grace to flush. "Fine," he acquiesced gruffly. "I'm sorry. Tell Eric I apologise because I need to go." He got to his feet. "I'll text you when I land." His voice rose in a question, his eyes hopeful.

Ryan shrugged. He wasn't letting Mango off easily.

"Fine. Have a good flight." He reached out and picked up his drink, taking a sip from it as he watched the restaurant for signs of Eric's return. Mango gave an exasperated sigh and the last thing Ryan felt was the soft caress of Mango's hand on his shoulder, coupled with a kiss to the top of his head. Then Mango was gone leaving Ryan to finish his lunch with Eric.

Ryan watched Mango walk away, the whisky looking to be a better idea with ever step Mango took.

***

Rain lashed against the glass and the streets of London were grey and sodden. Ryan sat in the wide bay window of his flat, sipping his coffee. He was dressed in an old comfortable tracksuit, arms wrapped around knees curled up to his chest. He observed the drenched commuters below, thinking how the umbrellas of all hues and colours dotted the streets below like bottle tops.

In his ears, the husky tones of his favourite tunes kept him mellow. He watched as raindrops ran quickly down the window, as if in a race to get to the bottom.

The real dark blot on the current landscape had been attending his MRI appointment a couple of days ago and waiting for the results. The specialist had said it could take some time to get the results and Ryan would need to be patient. His mantra was an ever-present companion.

It's not a problem. There won't be anything wrong. This is only a formality.

He'd been careful to avoid the foods and drinks on the list the doctor had given him but to be honest, nothing much had changed. It was another thing for him to worry about. He'd hoped desperately his symptoms might have cleared and been attributed to potential vertigo.

Ryan shivered, the coolness of the window chilling him, despite the double glazing. It was his day off and Monday had dawned in typical fuck you fashion with what appeared to be the British equivalent of a monsoon.

He stared up at the dark skies and closed his eyes, praying fervently Mango would be fine. He'd boarded his plane earlier to fly home from his unexpected trip. It had turned out to be longer than anticipated, as the Sunday flights had been fully booked.

Mango had been in constant touch during his time away with texts and WhatsApp messages. The texts had started from Heathrow and Mango had kept up a barrage of comments from sitting in the airport terminal up until he'd left Oslo a few hours ago.

Ryan had been amused by the messages commenting on the appearance of Mango's fellow attendees at the conference—*Jesus would you look at this guy? He looks like Chuck Norris on crack* came with an accompanying picture that certainly bore Mango's words out—to touchy feely messages like: *Hey baby, what are you wearing right now?* and *Missing you, can't wait to get home.*

Ryan had responded with his usual snark. *I'm wearing nothing right now, too busy jerking off. Want me to send you a picture?* and *Oh, so you're going to stay home this time for a while?*

Mango's response to the latter one had been a GIF of a snarling kitten slashing its claws. Ryan had smirked when he'd seen it. Sometimes it paid to remind his lover what Ryan was capable of.

He'd wanted to be catty in return and tell Mango that Eric was more than happy to keep Ryan company, but even he'd thought it would be pushing things a little too far.

He had enjoyed the full frontal picture Mango had taken in his bathroom shortly before he'd dressed to attend his gala dinner. All Mango had been wearing had been his bow tie.

Ryan had referred to the image countless times in his boyfriend's absence.

Now all that remained was the make-up sex. He didn't plan on being easy though. Mango would have to work for it.

He was roused from his musings by a knock on the door. He looked over at it and frowned. Mango had a key so it couldn't be him. Perhaps it was someone from the club. It would have to be an emergency to bother Ryan on a Monday. His days off were holy, not to be interrupted unless all hell broke loose.

He sighed and unpeeled himself from the window seat. He glanced down at himself. He was wearing an old tracksuit but it was his Dolce & Gabbana so he supposed he'd look presentable enough opening the door. He hoped fervently it wasn't Kyle with any bad news about the club.

Please don't let there be any more cock and ball drawings on my walls. Or blocked up toilets, sour beer deliveries or dislocated shoulders from hefting the kegs.

When he opened the door he was greeted by a sodden Mango bearing a bunch of blue flowers. Both Mango and the bouquet looked a little bedraggled. The flowers were a stunning blue, appearing to be orchids of some sort.

Ryan's heart beat a little faster. "Don't you have your key?" He stood aside to let Mango pass. The heady scent of the bouquet wafted past Ryan.

"I packed my keys in my damn suitcase and said damn suitcase has gone missing. I had to file a lost baggage claim." Mango shook his head, his dark hair wet and tousled. Drops of water flew everywhere and Ryan was reminded of a dog shaking itself. Mango dropped his shoulder bag onto the floor and grinned, reaching out to offer Ryan the flowers.

"These are for you. A little wet but I thought they matched your eyes. They're blue dendrod—something or the other. Blue orchids, the florist called them."

Ryan was gobsmacked. Flowers matching his eyes? Mango had to be on something. Such a romantic gesture was unheard of. Ryan took the bouquet and smelled them deeply before placing them on the side table in the hallway.

He didn't even have time to breathe out a "thank you" or "who are you and what the fuck have you done with my boyfriend?" before he was pushed back against the wall. Mango's mouth found his in a blistering and filthy kiss, his stubble grazing Ryan's skin. He moaned at the sensation. His cock grew excited at being so roughly treated. He had a bit of a kink for it and Mango never failed to disappoint. He'd also forgotten he was supposed to be playing hard to get. Having your lover's hardened cock and greedy mouth pressed against you tended to eradicate rational thought.

"You were such a moody bastard with your texts," Mango breathed into his ear. "I've brought you flowers. Now I get to do

465

this to you." He reached inside Ryan's trousers and palmed Ryan's rapidly growing cock.

The squeak coming out of Ryan's mouth was unmanly, but hell, he was aroused. His sweatpants were yanked down to his knees, along with his briefs, and Mango dropped to his knees, sucking Ryan in.

Mango's hungry, wet, hot mouth swallowed Ryan whole and at the same time Mango's fingers slid between Ryan's legs and fingered his taint.

"Oh God," Ryan said faintly as he looked down at the dark head bobbing on his aching dick. Mango's hair had fallen over his eyes, which were half closed in a state of bliss as he sucked Ryan off with an expertise born of practice. It was one of Mango's special abilities, and one he prided himself on. If there was an official cock-sucking award ribbon, Ryan could safely say Mango would be the proud winner.

His mouth withdrew, causing Ryan to give a gasp of disappointment.

"Did I hear you say I should win an award?" Mango's lips were swollen, wet, and the dirty grin he threw Ryan made his dick jump.

"Did I say that aloud?" Ryan groaned at the sudden chill of having a wet cock and no warm mouth to keep it heated. "Yeah, I mean, if the shoe fits, you know. You'd get my award. Now could you shut the fuck up and finish the job?"

Mango chuckled sultrily. "And *there's* the man I know and love." He gripped Ryan's hips tighter, sliding his hands around to the cheeks of Ryan's arse and kneading them firmly. Then once again Ryan's cock was enveloped in wet sloppy heat, tightening friction and a tongue that knew exactly how to make Ryan squirm.

He slapped his hands against the wall, closing his eyes as he was deep-throated to a depth a submarine would have been proud of. His own gag reflex didn't extend to this level of proficiency.

Ryan cried out when a finger circled his hole, teasing him with a steady pressure but not entering. He heaved a shuddering breath. "Jesus, I need you deeper. Own me."

Mango laughed around Ryan's cock, the vibration teetering Ryan on the edge of sanity as he felt his climax build.

"No lube on hand." Mango's muffled words sunk into Ryan's heated brain. "Not doing you dry. Later, in the shower, I'll fuck you through the wall, I promise."

Beneath Ryan, Mango shifted, reaching down to undo his jeans zipper. One hand reached inside his pants and pushed them down his hips. With a muffled and satisfied groan, Mango jacked himself off in time to his steady sucks and licks on Ryan's cock.

That sight alone triggered Ryan's orgasm and he shuddered as he came into Mango's greedy and willing mouth. Mango sucked him dry and was still licking the come from his lips when he leaned back, eyes half closed, lips parted and shot his own release all over Ryan's thighs and stomach.

The sight of those white ropes slathering his body, and Mango's look of bliss as he stared up into Ryan's eyes when he came, was a sight Ryan would never tire of. For one brief moment, Mango was raw and exposed and Ryan loved seeing him this way.

Mango stood, his eyes hooded, mouth red, swollen and wet and leaned in to kiss Ryan. This time, the kiss was gentle, tender and he lost himself in it. The slow glide of tongue against tongue and Mango's hands resting possessively on his waist banished all other thought and fears from his mind.

Finally, they drew apart, staring into each other's eyes.

Mango smiled warmly. "Well, what a great welcome home," he murmured, brushing a stray curl from Ryan's eyes. "I'll have to bring you flowers more often. It's good to be back." He pulled up his jeans and zipped them, then pulled up Ryan's sweatpants for him.

Ryan grimaced. He was sticky and now his treasured tracksuit was full of come. Personally, he'd have showered first. He found his voice and raised an eyebrow in Mango's direction. "If I recall, I didn't have much choice. You thrust a bunch of flowers into my hands and went down on me." He sniffed, but grinned. "Good to have you home. I missed you. Even though you called me a moody bastard."

Mango chuckled and peeled himself away from Ryan. "Sometimes the Delilah in you shoots to the surface. I love it though. Makes my life interesting." He regarded Ryan steadily, his gaze fond.

Ryan harrumphed. "Delilah is never far away, boyfriend, and you'd be good to remember. The woman will cut off your balls in your sleep without fluttering a false eyelash." He grinned at Mango's sudden look of discomfort and pressed back against him, fingers trailing down his bristly cheek. "You haven't shaved for a while. I like it."

Mango reached up and fingered his chin. "It's been a rough few days. Shaving wasn't a priority." His eyes grew heated. "Besides, I know you love it when I'm all prickly. It turns you on."

Ryan could still feel the burn on his skin where Mango's stubble had scraped him. His dick plumped up a little and Mango grinned filthily.

"Ready again so soon? What say we take this to bed?" He didn't stop to listen to Ryan's reply; he simply headed towards the room in question.

Ryan picked up the blue flowers, smiling goofily at the fact Mango had bought him flowers for the first time in their relationship. He placed the blooms in a vase, filled it with water and put them on the dining room table. Then he followed Mango into the bedroom.

Later that night, curled in bed, sleepy after a boisterous bout of dirty sex, shower calisthenics that made his body ache and a robust pounding that made him scared to sit on his arse for a while, Ryan debated drowsily whether to tell Mango about his current medical issue.

When he heard Mango's soft snores, he snuggled in closer against his lover's warm body, and Ryan decided to leave it for another day.

He'd do it when the time was right. And the time wasn't now.

Chapter 6

"So, we'll see you tomorrow in Madrid?" The woman's Spanish-accented voice over the phone sounded brisk and sure of itself.

Mango sighed and leaned back in his dining room chair. He'd come over to his own place to fetch some more clothes for the week ahead and do some washing. Ryan's machine scared him with its myriad buttons and blinking lights. He hadn't caught the woman's name when she'd called fifteen minutes ago and subjected him to a gruelling telephone interview, asking questions he was sure he'd already answered in his CV.

"Ermm, is there possibly another day we can do this? I mean, it's pretty short notice and I'm not sure there are any flights out to Spain for a meeting tomorrow afternoon."

He stared out of his flat window at the clear skies beyond. Mango had been aware there could be an interview this week but neither he nor Ryan had anticipated it being so quick in the making.

Mango had another problem closer to home. Ryan had been off his game the last couple of weeks. Sure, he had tried to pretend nothing was wrong but Mango knew something was up. He'd planned on taking Ryan out for a quiet dinner tonight to get to the bottom of whatever was bothering him. Kyle had already been let in on the plans and promised to hold the fort. Mango guessed he'd have to call and put it off now.

The voice, when it replied, was dry with a hint of steel. "Mr Monroe, this position is highly sought after. We have two other potential candidates for the role. I do believe it is in your best interests to make the interview with Professor Spencer tomorrow. I need to ensure everyone in his diary is able to make the meetings and not waste his time. He is a busy man." Her voice became condescending. "And I can assure you there are flights out here constantly, so I'm sure you'll have no trouble getting here."

Christ, Mango hated the secretarial gatekeepers who believed they were God's gift to their bosses. His first response was to tell her to go fuck herself, but common sense reinstated itself. He and Ryan had both agreed the position he was going for was the best of a few he'd looked at, both salary-wise and job-wise and he couldn't afford to let it slip by. It would only be a day or two and he could come back and interrogate Ryan about what was bothering him.

Mango swallowed his pride and grunted an affirmation. "I'll be there tomorrow at three p.m." His irritation grew at the fact he now had to organise a flight, pack and leave Ryan in his current state of whatever the fuck was bothering him.

"Good. Text me or call when you arrive in the country and I can let Professor know you're here." The woman sounded smugly satisfied and Mango wanted to reach through the phone and wrap his hands around her neck to choke the condescension out of her.

He clenched his teeth together. "I'll try get an early flight and be there with plenty of time."

"You do that, Mr Monroe," said the crisp voice. "See you tomorrow." The phone went dead.

"Fuck you." Mango stuffed his phone back in his pocket and scowled. "Condescending cow."

He felt a little better after cursing at her.

"Who's a cow?"

Mango swung around at the familiar voice and smiled. Ryan's dark hair was windswept and tousled, his blue eyes wide. He wore a tight pair of black jeans and a deep bronze shirt overlaid with a brocade waistcoat. His treasured Armani jacket was clutched in one hand and he carried a Marks & Spencer carrier bag in the other. He looked edible as hell.

"Glad to see you're using the key I gave you," Mango teased as he stood up and went to hug Ryan. Ryan felt lighter somehow, less substantial. "Babe, you need fattening up. You're fading away."

Ryan pulled away and pouted. "That's a wonderful way to boost a man's confidence." He mock scowled. "I'm not eating as much, I guess. But I'm fine, honest." He slung his jacket down on the couch back. The shadow in his eyes belied his words.

Mango reached out and put a hand over Ryan's. He thought he'd try again. "I've had this feeling something's bothering you. Care to tell me about it?"

Ryan clattered around in the kitchen, and for a moment Mango thought he was being ignored. Then Ryan spoke quickly.

"It's everything going on at the club, you know? The new mortgage, the worries about affording the repayments even though I need the extra capital to improve the club, the damn repairs to the bathroom because those arseholes wrecked it." Ryan's voice was fierce. "I guess I haven't been taking care of myself." He reached out and caressed Mango's jaw. "I will though. Starting with this." He held up the carrier bag. "I bought us lunch. Chicken cacciatore, fresh asparagus, Caesar salad and chocolate mousse for dessert. Thank God for the special deals."

Ryan disappeared into Mango's kitchen and Mango followed him, still not quite satisfied with Ryan's reply but not wanting to push it.

"Do you need any help?" He watched as Ryan unpacked the bags.

Ryan shook his head and shooed him away. "Nope, I'm fine. You go relax, finish your washing or whatever and look sexy. I'll tell you when I'm done." He pulled out a bowl and a couple of plates from the cupboard.

Mango stood there, uncertain. "Actually, I need to get on the laptop and check out flights." He took a deep breath. "Don't freak out but I've got a final interview tomorrow for the university lecturer job I mentioned to you. The only problem is it's in Spain tomorrow afternoon. The professor doing the final interviews is on sabbatical there for a few months and this is the only opening he has for a while."

Ryan stood stock-still, then swung around to face him. He smiled and Mango was sure he hadn't imagined the fleeting look of despair preceding it.

What the hell is going on with him? Something's up, I know it. If I push him though, he'll clam up completely.

"Oh, wonderful news. You're going to ace the fucking interview, I know it." Mango was hugged and kissed and Ryan drew back and regarded him with shining eyes. "You'd better get started on looking for a flight. I'd hate you to miss this opportunity." He flashed a quick smile and turned back to the kitchen counter where he began preparing the food.

"Ryan, are you sure everything is okay?" Mango came up behind him and laid a hand on his shoulder. "You've been a bit preoccupied the last few weeks and it doesn't feel like club shit. You don't seem yourself. Talk to me, love."

Ryan continued setting out their lunch. "Of course I'm fine. Like I said, it's been a bit stressful." He turned and ripped open the bag of salad, loading it into the bowl.

"Are you sure?" Mango persisted. "Because I'm not."

Ryan swung around. "Mango, stop fussing." His tone was even. "This is a fabulous opportunity for you and nothing is more important than you getting there to sunny Spain, all relaxed and ready to kill in your interview. Now, shoo. Go find your flight and let me get lunch sorted." His tone brooked no argument and Mango sighed. He knew when Ryan got like this there wasn't much more Mango could do if he didn't want a hissy fit and to end up arguing. And that was the last thing he wanted today.

"Okay," he finally agreed, turning and making his way back to his laptop on the dining table. "But when I get back, I'm taking you to dinner and I'm going to spoil you, make sure you get some meat on those bones. Then perhaps we can have fun with another sort of bone."

"Subtle," Ryan said drily. "Very subtle."

Mango sniggered as he sat down and drew his computer towards him.

***

A day later, sitting in the swanky Caray restaurant in the Gran Melia Hotel in central Madrid, Mango fidgeted impatiently as he waited for Professor Spencer to make his appearance. He hated wearing a suit but Ryan had picked out the outfit and insisted it was "power dressing" for success.

Of course the suit was a Debussy and fit Mango as if it had been moulded from his frame. It was a gift Ryan had given him for Valentine's Day, along with a red rose and some inventive sex.

Mango was early; he'd arrived a few hours ago and killed time wandering around the beautiful city. He'd also been quite surprised the demon from hell secretary had been fairly accommodating. Wonders would never cease.

Now he sat with his second espresso and waited. He'd texted Ryan earlier to tell him he'd touched down and sent him a picture of the hotel. There'd been no reply yet but he supposed Ryan was probably at the club, up to his eyeballs in work.

Mango still wasn't comfortable with Ryan's explanation yesterday. The sex they'd shared last night had been softer, gentler, as if Ryan needed reassurance of some kind. Mango had been happy to give it, enjoying the slower session as much as Ryan had. Afterwards, lying with Ryan nestled in his arms, Mango resolved, come hell or high water, to get to the bottom of what was troubling his man when he got home.

"Mr Munroe?" The soft English voice at his shoulder made Mango stand up to see a tall, stooped man staring at him. He was in his mid-sixties, Mango guessed, with tanned skin and bright brown eyes.

Mango nodded. "Yes, sir. Professor Spencer?"

The older man nodded as he shook Mango's outstretched hand, then waved him back down into his seat. "Yes indeed. Pleased to meet you at last. Call me George. I've heard a lot about you from colleagues and people in the know. I've been looking forward to our chat. Thank you for making it over to Spain at such short notice." He shrugged apologetically. "I'm on sabbatical but still pressing issues need my attention and I fly to Zurich tomorrow for a couple of days."

An hour later Mango was feeling a lot more relaxed. He and George seemed to have hit it off. Mango was about to answer yet another discerning question from the man opposite him when his phone rang. Mango's face grew warm. The cardinal rule of interviews and he'd fucked it up by not switching his phone to silent.

"I'm so sorry about this, I forgot to switch it off. Do you mind if I switch it off now?" Mango reached across the table and picked up his phone as it stuttered madly on the glass table.

The professor stared at him and gave an indulgent nod. "Please. Go ahead."

Mango frowned when he picked it up. Why the hell was *Lenny* calling him? He wasn't even aware Lenny had this number. A shiver of cold ice slid down Mango's spine and he warred with himself, wanting to answer yet not wanting to stuff up his interview. His concern won out.

"Profess—George, I'm so terribly sorry. Would you mind if I saw what this was all about? It's from someone I wouldn't expect to have called unless there was a problem at home."

Spencer frowned but he didn't seem upset. "Of course." He sighed heavily. "Young people and your gadgets. I don't understand the allure myself."

Mango stood up and hit the answer button, moving away for some privacy. "Lenny, what the hell? Didn't you hear from my ring tone I was abroad? I'm in Spain in an interview."

When Lenny spoke, his voice was tired and flat. "Sorry, Mango. I needed to get hold of you urgently. Ryan collapsed earlier this morning. He was at the club and Kyle found him in his office. He's at University College Hospital."

Mango's stomach plummeted and he felt the threads of panic unravel in his chest. "Is he okay now? I mean, what the hell happened?"

"There's something he hasn't been telling us." Lenny sighed heavily. "Ryan's been seeing a doctor and a specialist for a while apparently. Those headaches and things he's been having are more than he let on. His doctor won't tell me anything else yet, only says he thinks perhaps Ryan had some sort of panic attack earlier. He won't tell me why. Ryan's still sleeping it off. As soon as he's awake, they say they'll discuss it with him before they can tell us anything."

Mango had to sit down. He sank into his chair, seeing Professor Spencer stare at him anxiously.

"Why the hell didn't he tell me? And why are you the one calling me anyway—how come his doctor isn't?" Mango sat forward in agitation.

"Kyle had his doctor's number on file at the club and Ryan still had me down as an emergency contact." Lenny's voice was apologetic. "Seems he hadn't updated it to you yet."

"But I don't understand," Mango whispered. "Why keep this to himself? I need to come home and be with him. I'll be on the next plane out of here."

"I thought you might feel that way. I bought you a ticket already, the earliest one I could get a seat on. You're on the seven p.m. flight. I figured it would give you enough time to wrap up and get to the airport."

Mango nodded. "Thanks, Lenny, you're a saviour. When Ryan wakes up tell him I'm on my way and I'm going to tan his hide for keeping this from me." His voice shook and he blinked back tears. "Tell him I love him, please, if you get to see him. And I'm coming home. I should never have left him in the first place. I knew something was wrong."

"Don't kick yourself too much for this one, my friend. We all knew something was off but decided to let him be and tell us in his own time. In hindsight...meh, it didn't work." Lenny's voice grew steelier. "Next time we'll make sure we damn well hold him down and force it out of him. He can fucking go as high on the Diva-con scale as he likes but it won't help him." Lenny heaved a sigh. "I'll pass on your message and see you later. He's in good hands. I know you'll worry but we're here for him until you get here. Safe travels, my friend." Lenny ended the call.

Mango was cold, the sliver of ice down his spine turning into an iceberg. His mouth was dry. Ryan was sick and he hadn't told him. Didn't he trust Mango to be there for him...no matter what?

"Mango, I couldn't help but overhear you have some trouble at home, son. You're as white as a ghost." The professor touched his arm in concern, brow furrowed in worry.

Mango nodded, unable to find words. "My boyfriend has been rushed to hospital. I'm so sorry, I need to get home. Our friend booked me a flight at seven p.m." He looked at his watch and closed his eyes. "It's only a few hours to go, so I need to get to the airport."

The older man smiled kindly. "I agree, you need to get home to your family. I'll order you a taxi. You go fetch your bag."

Mango stared at him dazedly. "I'm sorry about this. Perhaps we can reschedule?"

Spencer shook his head firmly. "Not now. I'll get in touch with you at a later stage when everything has settled down. All you need to do is get home to your man. What's his name?"

"Ryan," Mango murmured. Saying his name hurt. Hurt because Mango wasn't sure what the situation was or how he could fix it.

George nodded, resembling a sprightly bird. "Ryan. I'm sure he needs you more than I do, young man. Now go get your bag. I'll attract the eye of the rather lovely lady over there and get you a taxi. You call me when you're ready. I hope everything is okay, Mango."

Mango was treated to a manly hug and then pushed in the direction of the concierge desk. He managed to mutter a garbled "Thank you very much. I'll call you," and before he knew it, he was being bundled into a taxi and speeding towards the airport.

***

Hours later, Mango ran down the hospital corridor towards Ryan's room. He'd had nothing to do but think—and worry, which turned his stomach into knots—on the way to the airport, on the plane and in the taxi from the airport to the hospital. Lenny had texted the floor and hospital room number, and fucking no one was going to stop Mango from seeing Ryan. Mango knew there might be a battle ahead as he wasn't listed as next of kin or Ryan's significant other but he'd fight the bureaucracy any way he could. Mango had faced down aborigines with poisoned blowpipes, and been attacked by a bull seal on the Arctic ice. He was pretty sure he could face down an officious yet well-meaning doctor or two. And if not, well, Mango was used to sneaking into places he wasn't supposed to be.

His heart lifted when he saw Lenny and Brook in the corridor, standing together outside the room where Mango presumed Ryan lay. He rushed up to them and Lenny reached out an arm to stop him rushing into the hospital room.

"Whoa, pardner. Glad you made it but let me fill you in before you go in there, okay?" Lenny's face was pale but he was smiling, which must mean Ryan was okay, right?

Brook moved closer and gave Mango a reassuring pat on the back. "What he said. Lenny's been, like, the bossy nurse from hell." Brook gave Lenny a fond glance, which was returned.

Mango stared wildly around. "Is he awake? Is he okay? What the hell is going on, why didn't he tell me anything…?"

Lenny pressed a firm finger against his mouth. "Ryan's awake. He's told the doctors who you are and he's waiting to see you, but he's fucking scared. You need to cut him some slack. He's a basket case. He's feeling guilty because he didn't tell you what was going on and, because he's such a dick, now he's pulled you back from your interview and he feels shit about that."

"Has he told you everything? What the problem is? And fuck the interview. He's more important."

Lenny sighed and shook his head, casting a rueful glance at Brook. "Nope. He wanted to tell you first, so we nosy friends will have to wait. I've been second-guessing but Brook tells me, for the sake of my sanity, it doesn't help so best to wait until Ryan's ready to tell us." Lenny cocked a hopeful eyebrow. "Or you do of course. We're not going anywhere. We're going to sit here and be patient." He pursed his lips and blew a strand of hair from his face.

Brook reached over and kissed the top of Lenny's head. "That'll be the day. I'm going to have to ply you with savoury pastries to stop you pacing. A sausage roll or two will calm you down." He grinned but Brook's eyes were worried.

"Jesus, what if something is terribly wrong?" It was all Mango had thought about since hearing the news of Ryan's collapse. "I've been such a fucking idiot, wasting all this time when we could have been spending it together, because I was too damn scared to commit." His hands shook and he fisted them. "What if I lose him, Len? What then? How the hell will I manage without him, he's my life—"

Lenny reached out and enfolded Mango in a strong, comfortable hug. "Shut up, you big lug. You're terrifying me. Don't expect the worse before you hear it." He drew back and regarded Mango. "And those things you just said to me? Tell them to that man in there." He gestured towards Ryan's room. "He needs to hear them right now."

Mango swallowed and nodded his head. "Okay. Let me do this."

Slowly, he pushed open the door, making sure he wore his brave face. When he saw Ryan in the hospital bed, Mango nearly lost it. If it weren't for his dark hair, Ryan's face would have blended into the stark white hospital pillow. He had a drip line going into one arm, and Mango barely stopped a tired smile when he saw the hospital gown Ryan was in. His lover's pride was no doubt deeply injured at having to wear such a prosaic piece of clothing.

Ryan's eyes opened and in them Mango saw guilt, shame and tiredness. Mostly, he saw fear and Mango's chest tightened at the sight of his beautiful, witty, confident lover being reduced to the man currently lying vulnerable in a hospital bed.

Ryan tried to smile but it didn't light up his face. "Mango, hi. I'm so sorry—"

He didn't get a chance to say any more because Mango's mouth met Ryan's, infusing him with everything Mango was feeling. He took Ryan's mouth, which smelt of stale breath and old toothpaste, in a kiss that threatened to consume them both. When Mango had finished, and both of them were breathing raggedly, Mango laid a finger hand across Ryan's mouth.

"Before you say anything, listen to me." He sat down on the bed, watching Ryan's beautiful, expressive eyes widen. "I knew there was something bothering you and I'm sorry I didn't push more. I should have. And whatever you have to tell me about this"—Mango swept his other hand across the room—"I'm there with you, no matter what. It's you and me, baby, so none of this hero shit where you tell me to leave you alone or save myself. Because it isn't going to happen. I'm here no matter what. The thought of losing you scares the shit out of me. You mean the world to me."

He took his hand off Ryan's mouth and waited.

Finally, Ryan spoke. "Are there film cameras outside?" His voice was soft but there was the lilt of laughter in it. It was as if somehow his load had been lightened.

Mango frowned. "Cameras? No, why?"

Ryan reached up his drip-free hand and ran his fingers through Mango's hair, surely messed beyond usual since he'd been running his fingers through it in frustration since he got into the taxi in Madrid.

"Because what you said sounded like the lines to some rom-com where the hero meets the heroine. Or the other way around." His voice quivered. "And honestly, as for the whole sending you away idea? I doubt I could do it." His face crumpled. "I need you. I won't be able to get through this without you." He stopped, closed his eyes for a moment and drew a deep breath. "I have a brain tumour. They want to operate in a couple of weeks." His voice choked up and he collapsed into soft sobs.

Mango pulled Ryan close and wished the world could stop, or go back in time to when Ryan wasn't in such pain. Tears pricked Mango's eyes and he held Ryan's shuddering body tight as his chest ached with his own fear and pain. But he needed to be the strong one now.

"I'm not going anywhere," Mango said, his voice thick with emotion. "I'm right here, love, all the way. We'll get you through this." Inside, though, Mango quailed at the words "brain tumour" and "to operate" and he wanted to be sick. All he knew about those two phrases said together was not good news.

Finally, Ryan stopped crying and gave a hiccupping sniff. "Sorry," he said wanly. "I know I'm being a big baby." He heaved a juddering sigh. "You'd better invite those other two in so they can hear this too. No doubt Lenny has his big ears flapping trying to gather what's going on."

"Hey, I heard that, elf ears." Lenny peered around the doorframe, his eyes shadowed. "Brook wouldn't let me steal the ear horn from the dude in the bed next door. He said it wouldn't be right. Such a party pooper." He moved into the room, Brook behind him.

Ryan gave a watery sniff and chuckled. "Ear horn? Likely story. And don't call me elf ears." He patted the bed. "Sit down and let me tell you my tale of woe. That way I only have to do it once."

Lenny sat gingerly on the bed and Brook folded his large frame into the chair at the side.

Mango still held tight to Ryan but shifted so he was lying on the bed with him, one arm across his shoulders so they were both propped up against the pillows. If the nursing staff didn't like it—tough.

Ryan picked at the covers. "So, you guys know I've been having headaches, yeah? And not feeling too well and being dizzy."

They all nodded.

"Well, turns out after seeing the doctor, the specialist and going for an MRI, I have this growth."

Mango wanted to ask Ryan why he hadn't confided in him but he didn't think now was the right time. Ryan carried on.

"It's called a meningioma, a tumour in the layers of tissue surrounding my brain, the meninges. I've been doing some studying up on it. The one good thing is it's a low grade tumour and I can have surgery to remove it." Ryan's voice shook and Mango rubbed his shoulder comfortingly. His own body was chilled to the bone.

Lenny made a sound of distress and reached for Brook's hand.

"What happened to you today, Ryan?" Brook's deep voice was a welcome distraction. Mango felt as if he was in an alternate reality and he badly wanted to wake and come back to the real and happier world.

Ryan looked shame-faced. "I got the MRI results and the date for the surgery today on the phone—my doctor promised to call me—and I kind of went to pieces. I had a damned panic attack, couldn't breathe and passed out." He shrugged. "I haven't been eating and I've been popping pain pills for the headache. Kyle heard the bang when I fell and came in to find I'd face-planted. Again," he remarked gloomily. He lifted the hand containing the drip. "They have me on some sort of vitamin infusion to get my electrolytes up and rehydrate me."

Mango stiffened. Ryan had *expected* to get his results today? He'd known about this beforehand?

"So you let me go to Spain knowing your doctor was going to call? You went through this hell all on your own rather than have me here with you?" He couldn't keep the hurt from his voice. And from the flinch on Ryan's face, he'd heard it too.

"Babe, this interview was important to you. And to me, because you wanted it. And I'd been convincing myself I was fine and the results weren't going to show anything other than the fact I actually had a brain." Ryan faltered as Mango didn't say anything. "Which I'm beginning to doubt because I know I've hurt you by not telling you sooner. I'm sorry. I thought I was doing the right thing."

Lenny and Brook sat there quietly but Lenny looked stricken. Mango saw Brook's hand cover Lenny's and squeeze it. Lenny shot his lover an affectionate look, and Mango knew it must be tough on Lenny. He and Ryan were good friends.

Mango was hurt and fuming but he decided not to dwell on Ryan's subterfuge. It wouldn't help anything now and the last thing he wanted was to upset his lover even more. Right now wasn't about Mango and his hurt feelings. It was about comforting a man who looked as if the bottom had fallen out of his world and Mango wanted to be the one to pick it up.

"So what's the prognosis on the surgery? Will it fix things?" Mango asked, focused on Ryan's face. The time for hiding things was over. The deep, dark lump in Mango's gut was his fear at having yet another person he loved taken away from him and it was forever present and solidifying with each passing minute.

Ryan reached over and brushed hair from Mango's forehead, his face sad.

"They think so but nothing's sure until they open me up. They're doing what's called a craniotomy."

Mango winced. That word reminded him of something out of the Dark Ages. Dour faced surgeons in shrouded rooms armed with medieval implements drilling holes in people's heads. He knew he was being fanciful since the procedures today were all slick and professional. Despite knowing this, the mediaeval image lingered.

"So this operation gives you the best chance of getting rid of the tumour?" Lenny's aqua eyes narrowed and his hand tightened in Brook's.

Ryan took a deep breath. "It depends on how easy it is to remove and whether they can remove it without damaging anything else in my brain and affecting other things like my memories or bodily functions. Or my sight." Ryan's hands shook and Mango enveloped them in his.

Ryan continued speaking, his voice softer. "They think there's a good chance it will be okay because of where it is but nothing is set in stone. So all we can is wait and see what the surgeon says. Luckily my surgery has been scheduled quicker than expected, because if they act soon, it makes the difference between having a better chance now or making it worse if they delay. I guess I'm one of the lucky ones to get seen quickly." He heaved a resigned sigh and lay back, his face etched with weary resignation.

Mango's protective instincts kicked in. "Right, that's it. You're going to get some sleep and I'm going to stay here with you. But before you do"—he pointed at Ryan—"*you* will tell these doctors who the hell I am and make sure I'm noted as your next of kin. There's no fucking way I'm not being involved in all of this from start to finish. If they so much as swab your balls, I want to know about it."

Ryan gave a strangled chuckle as he settled into the pillows and Mango drew the covers over him. "I don't think they need to touch my balls to operate on my head but point taken. I'll sign whatever needs signing to have you down as my significant other." His voice faltered. "In case, you know…"

Mango leaned in and took hold of Ryan's face, turning it so they were eye to eye. "Don't you dare say it," he warned, panic rising once more in his belly. "Nothing is going to happen to you. I won't fucking let it."

This was the reason he hadn't had a relationship before. In the past some of that had been his fear of becoming too attached. But that ship had sailed a long time ago despite his best efforts to prevent it. Now, greater than past fears of committing to someone he loved, he stood to lose yet another someone who was precious and dear.

Someone who had become his whole world.

And the thought of any world without Ryan in it was unthinkable.

"Right, we'll leave you two alone to have some quality time." Lenny stood and Brook rose with him, standing close, being reassuring. "I'll call you later, see how you're doing. And Mango, any news, you make sure you call me before I hear anything via anyone else. I'm counting on you to keep me up to date."

Mango mock saluted. "Yes, sir." He loved the way Lenny looked out for Ryan. At least when Mango hadn't been around much, Lenny had. A good friend was something to be treasured.

Lenny kissed Ryan on the cheek and ran a hand over his hair. "You keep positive, chicken," he murmured. "I'm counting on you to be up and over this in no time. I have an idea for a little show for Club Delish to celebrate Easter. So you'd better be prepared to don a cute, arse-less bunny costume I've gotten you and hop around stage flashing your backside."

Brook's ears seemed to prick up and he stared at his boyfriend. "You mean I get to see *your* gorgeous cheeks in a bunny suit too?" He winked at Lenny who treated him to an eye roll. Brook continued to leer at Lenny. "I can't wait. Perhaps you should give me a private show first so I can check out what it looks like?"

"Yeah, like that's going to happen anytime soon." But from the wicked smile Lenny threw Brook, Mango had the feeling the scenario might become a reality.

Ryan gave a weak chuckle from the bed. "You guys are crazy." He hesitated. "Thanks for coming down here and making me think it might all work out."

Lenny glanced at him fiercely. "It'll work out," he snorted. "Or my name's not Laverne Debussy-Smith. And *dahling,* you *know* that's who I am." He bobbed his head as he threw his hand up in a campy over-the-top gesture making Ryan giggle. Mango's heart warmed for the first time since Lenny had called hours ago. The cold, dank feeling started to fall away as he looked into Lenny and Brook's reassuring faces and thought perhaps everything might turn out all right.

"Thanks for taking care of him and for calling me." Mango smiled as both men hugged Ryan. "I appreciate it more than you know."

"Always." Lenny nudged him. "Keep us in the loop." He reached a hand out and took Brook's arm. "Come on, let's leave these guys to make out."

Once they'd gone Mango heaved a sigh. He was bone tired and hungry. He looked over at Ryan who appeared to be dozing.

"Love, I'm going to the canteen to grab something to eat. I'm sure they'll have a sandwich or something. Can I get you anything? Are you allowed to eat?"

Ryan opened one bleary eye and smiled. "I'm sure I could manage something. I am a little hungry and they didn't say I couldn't eat. So surprise me."

Mango was torn between wanting to still the grumbling in his belly and his fear of leaving Ryan alone for even a minute. The decision was made for him as an officious male nurse came into the room bearing a chart. He wasn't gorgeous, or hunky, simply a middle-aged man with a goatee and a welcoming style. His name badge read "Jacob."

"Mr Bishop? I'm glad you're awake. I have some observations to do, so perhaps your friend could leave us for a bit while I sort it all out?" Jacob moved over to Ryan's side and began fumbling with the drip.

Ryan waved at him. "I need to speak with someone about getting this sexy guy here down as my significant other. Who would that be?"

Jacob smiled. "I can get the paperwork updated for you. You tell me what to put down and I'll get you to sign it with the doctor present."

Mango saw this as his cue to disappear. He went over to Ryan and pressed a kiss to the top of his head. Ryan's hair was greasy and flattened and Mango knew his boyfriend would pitch a fit if he could see himself in a mirror.

"I'll get us some food and I'll see you in a little while. Behave yourself when I'm gone. No hitting on the nurses."

Jacob grinned and shook his head in amusement.

Once he was out of in the hall, Mango's knees gave way and he was forced to lean against the wall. His head spun and he took a few deep breaths, trying to quell the rising panic.

Shit, fuck, shit.

His world had fallen apart and he had no clue how to put it back together.

**

A few days later, after his unexpected hospital visit, Ryan sat curled on his sofa. Outside, on the busy street, life went on as usual for millions of people. He'd bet every third or fourth person walking by held their own secret or faced something bigger than themselves.

He heaved a deep sigh at the philosophical nature of his mood and reached out to sip at a cup of his special coffee. In the bedroom he heard a muffled "Fuck you," and despite Ryan's contemplative mood, he grinned. It sounded as if the new flat pack item he'd bought was getting the better of Mango.

Ryan was due in the surgery tomorrow and to take his mind off things, he'd decided to revamp his bedroom into French chateau style, complete with chandeliers. It was an affirmative move to convince himself he'd be around to enjoy it.

Ryan was the first to admit he wasn't technical when it came to self-assembly. The new distressed white French armoire he'd purchased, which needed complicated items like screws, dowels, wood glue and drilling and myriad of other things, had arrived yesterday morning. Mango had taken it upon himself to put it together.

Ryan knew Mango was trying to keep busy to take his mind off the upcoming operation. He appeared to be handling things but inside Ryan could still see the small scared boy who'd found his mother dead.

Two minutes after a crash and another "Fuck, fucker, fuck," said DIY man appeared drenched in sweat, a dark blue sweatband across his forehead, behind which his mid-length golden brown hair was tucked. Mango bore a ferocious scowl and held an electric screwdriver in one hand. Ryan noted with approval his lover's open shirt, showing the treasure trail leading down into faded old blue jeans. Mango looked delectably dishevelled and sexy.

Ryan's groin stirred.

"Fucking thing will not get the better of me," Mango growled as his eyes searched the room, looking for... something—Ryan knew not what. "That fucker is going to be owned."

Ryan bit back a chuckle. "The company did offer the option of having their team assemble it here for an extra sixty pounds."

Mango cast him a withering look. "You're not paying so much money for someone to put together a few pieces of damn flat pack shit. I'm quite capable."

Personally Ryan thought the sixty quid would have been well worth it, given the fact he'd been running around fetching this and that, providing Mango with cups of coffee and listening to his filthy invectives for nearly two days now.

"Hmm," Ryan drawled as he stared at Mango. "You look *really* hot. I'm liking this whole handyman look you've got going on."

In truth, the past week had been a little weird sex-wise. Mango had treated Ryan with kid gloves, as if the thing growing in his head had somehow made him fragile and untouchable. Their usual hard and rough sex had been sorely missing. These last few times when Mango was inside Ryan, there wasn't the passion and fervour of their earlier escapades; sex was decidedly restrained. Ryan wanted, no needed, to be pounded so hard he forgot everything else.

Mango grinned, which lit his face and made Ryan lose his breath, as it did each time. "Yeah, you like my new look?" He looked down at himself and when he looked up, his eyes had darkened and there was a distinct smug look Ryan wanted to eat off his face. "Does the owner of the house appreciate my *assets*?"

Ryan moved closer. "I wouldn't know. Those jeans tend to cover your *assets* as well as your arse. Perhaps I should remove them so I can check whether what's under there is to my liking?"

He reached for Mango's jeans and began unbuttoning them, sliding the zipper down slowly.

"Is this something you do a lot? Propositioning the tradesmen?" Mango murmured as he watched Ryan's fingers with smouldering dark eyes. "It's a little dangerous, isn't it? How do you know I'm into this?"

Ryan gave a soft laugh. "Oh, honey, you are *so* into it. *This* tells me."

This was Mango's steadily growing hard-on beneath tight blue boxer briefs, revealed when Ryan shoved Mango's jeans to the floor. "And it's a thing of beauty indeed. And the owner of the house wants you to take it and put it somewhere with extreme prejudice." Ryan grinned at Mango's discomforted expression.

"I thought maybe—" Mango began.

Ryan reached up and laid a finger on Mango's lips. "Shh. I know you're worried about me but I'm not going to break. Nothing's changed. I'm still the same man I was before and will be after."

Please, please, let what I said be true. Don't let this operation make me any less.

The one thing Ryan feared, next to not waking up at all, was waking up and being brain damaged, or losing one of his senses, like his sight, or some other shit. He wasn't sure which one he'd prefer, death or the alternative. He tried not to dwell on it but it was a tough, ever-present thought that circled his brain.

Focusing instead on *much* better things, Ryan reached in and took tight hold of Mango's cock, rubbing his fingers down, tightening his grip.

This was real. *This* was his life and he was damn well going to come back to it, and to the man in front of him, who was regarding him with such adoration it made him feel faint.

Mango sucked in a deep breath, his eyes never leaving Ryan's face.

Ryan leaned in and whispered, "I need you to take me to bed, lover. I need you right now to make me forgot what's going to happen tomorrow."

And if anything does go wrong at least you'll have tonight to remember me by.

From the way Mango fiercely picked him up, it seemed Mango had missed their steamy sessions as much as Ryan had. He gasped at being lifted and wrapped his legs around his lover's waist. Before Ryan knew it, he'd been manhandled into the bedroom, where littered pieces of wood and MDF scattered the floor, like flotsam from a wrecked ship, and the waft of wood glue assaulted their nostrils.

"You want me to help you forget about tomorrow?" Mango growled as he stepped out of the rest of his clothing and stood naked on the bed above Ryan, his cock jutting up from tight balls. "I can do that."

He motioned. "Get out of those damn clothes. You want this in you so badly?" He ran his hand down his hard length and Ryan salivated. "Then show me how much you want it. I want to watch you get yourself ready to take my dick."

Ryan needed no further urging. He got up to kneel on the bed, Mango's beautiful groin only centimetres from Ryan's mouth. The urge to take Mango in his mouth was strong but more overwhelming was the desire for Ryan to be filled, taken. That greediness won out and within minutes he'd stripped and retrieved the lube from on top of the bedside table.

Then, teasingly, he pushed fingers inside himself, groaning artfully as any porn star they'd watched. He sighed with satisfaction when Mango finally could take no more and Ryan was unceremoniously pushed back onto the bed, Mango's hard and wiry body covering his as a hungry mouth sought Ryan's own.

He fell into the rhythmic cadence of being owned, ravished, possessed and loved by the man currently worshiping him. When the world finally ended with a release so strong his ecstatic cry must have rattled windows, Ryan finally felt a kind of fleeting peace.

Chapter 7

Mango sat in the canteen staring unseeingly down at his dried out cheese and tomato sandwich. The one he'd bought an hour ago but had yet to take a bite of.

Hearing Ryan's wishes blatantly reinforced again this morning with the doctors had brought back memories and conversations he'd have preferred never to have had in the first place.

Ryan's soft words of earlier in the week still echoed in Mango's head.

"You know it's what I want. You don't get a say in this one." Ryan's tone had been steely and his blue eyes had brooked no argument. His face had been stubbornly set, the grey hospital gown making the pallor of his face appear even more sickly. "They're fucking around in my brain, for God's sake," he'd said fiercely. "No one knows what could happen when they get in there. I want to be prepared for the worst."

The topic under discussion had been Ryan's living will and Mango being given a lasting power of attorney over Ryan's healthcare. The doctors had reassured them both this wasn't a particularly dangerous operation but it held risks, as did all surgery.

Ryan had stared at him defiantly. "I need you to do this for me. I trust you to make these decisions if I can't. I won't be left a drooling idiot if things go belly-up. No machines keeping me alive, no death without dignity. I know it's tough for you, baby, but you're tough. You'll manage it if the worst comes to worst."

Ryan also made Mango his beneficiary to everything—his savings, his home, his club—apart from some sentimental items that would go to his parents. It was all one mammoth responsibility and Mango was scared but trying to be supportive. Trying to be strong for the man who now sat in a hospital bed waiting for his life to change.

After over two years together, Mango knew how Ryan's mind worked. Last night's lovemaking had been Ryan making sure there was a good memory left behind in case anything bad happened. And Mango had treasured every second of it. Holding Ryan in his arms once they'd both come down from their orgasmic highs had been bittersweet.

He was jolted out of his reverie by the harsh blare of the Tannoy calling out for a Doctor Moodly to pick up a call on line four. Mango blinked down at the sad state of his lunch and grimaced. He laid it on the plastic tray together with his empty coffee cups and stood.

Ryan's surgery was booked for three p.m., another hour to go. Another hour before he was prepped for surgery, when part of his head would be shaved, his vitals checked, pre-med administered and the necessary tubes and lines inserted into his body.

Ryan had seemed more upset at the prospect of having some of his hair shaved off than anything else. The doctor had promised with a small smile they'd keep it to the minimum.

Then the waiting would begin. Three to five hours of patiently sitting and hoping everything went well. His attempts to be strong for Ryan since coming back from Spain had taken their toll.

Teddy and Della had been Mango's steady rocks, as had Lenny and Brook. In their shared affection for Ryan all the friends had come together to help keep Mango sane.

Mango's breathing grew erratic—he needed air. He moved towards the doors leading out into the small garden. His phone vibrated in his pocket and he glanced around guiltily. He made it to the garden and pulled out his mobile. There was a text from Brook.

How are you holding up? Is he okay? Lenny's a basket case. I'm taking him out to the coast to take his mind off things.

Mango texted back.

Make that two basket cases. I've never been so damned scared in my life.

There was a pause. His phone vibrated again.

Lenny says give Ryan a hug from him and we'll call you later, see how things are doing. Stay strong my friend.

Mango texted back a thank you as his throat constricted at their concern. He sat down on the wooden bench, gazing across the rose garden laid out in neat rows.

I fucking hate this waiting. I feel like I'm ten years old again, waiting for my dad to come pick me up. Only he never did, did he. Is this what this is going to be like?

Panic set in and Mango's heart began thrumming, his pulse raced and he swallowed back bile that had suddenly risen as he clenched his hands in his lap.

"I hate being this fucking helpless," he growled. "Hate it. Ryan doesn't deserve this shit." He picked up a stone and threw it moodily across the paving to land in a garden bed. A bird in the bushes gave an indignant squawk and flew off in a flap of wings.

A woman, looking to be in her sixties, sat down next to him and gave him a welcoming smile. She wore a long yellow cotton dress and a blue cardigan. Her face was tired but friendly.

"Did he say something you didn't like?"

Mango flushed at being caught out. "I wasn't trying to hurt the bird. Just letting off steam and he got caught in the cross fire."

She grimaced. "I know the feeling. I've been there myself." She stared across the quadrangle towards the hospital doors, her eyes distant. Mango respected her silence and did the same. He made sure not to throw any more stones.

After a few minutes of contemplation, his visitor spoke. "It's nice to sit and have a quiet moment, isn't it? Especially in this place. It can get to you." She waved a hand, her blue eyes sympathetic. Across the garden, a child's laugh rang out.

Mango nodded. "Yeah. It gets a bit much waiting around."

The woman nodded. "Tell me about it. My husband's here for another chemo session and my life recently seems to have become one endless stream of drinking bad hospital coffee while I wait. But I wouldn't have it any other way."

Mango wasn't sure what to say. "I'm sorry your husband's ill," he said. "I hope things are looking up."

She smiled. "The doctors seem to think it's all going well and that all we can ask for. Graham—that's my husband—is a pretty positive soul and he's managing to keep his hopes up." She cocked her head. "How about you? Who are you waiting for?"

Mango cleared his throat as the ache intensified. "My boyfriend's having surgery for a brain tumour. He's going in an hour or so. I'm just out getting some air."

The woman laid a hand on his arm. "Oh, that's awful, honey. You're so young to go through that. What's the prognosis?"

Mango shrugged. "Good, I guess. The doctors seem quite positive about it all."

She patted his hand. "Then things will be fine. You keep telling yourself that. Is your boyfriend a man who believes he'll get through this?"

Mango snorted. "You have no idea. He's Mr Glass Half Full himself, even though I know he's worried about the surgery."

She laughed. "That's all we can do. My Graham is the same. Hope is a good thing to have."

Mango rolled one shoulder and shifted position on the bench. It was hard on his arse. "Sometimes hope isn't enough," he said quietly. "No matter how much you want something, sometimes it doesn't work out."

The woman's expression softened. "I can tell you speak from experience. There's a sadness in your eyes that tells of loss."

Mango's eyes pricked. He blinked impatiently. "I'm not alone in that. Look where we are. It's a place where hope can sometimes be ripped out of people and leave them wanting."

The woman regarded him appraisingly. "I understand that. But what's the alternative? A good friend of mine always says to ask this of yourself when you have a decision or choice to make. *'What's the alternative?'* It always helps to give me perspective. Sometimes the alternative is worse.

"In your case, if you want to give up hope, the alternative is you lose it altogether. You end up bitter and twisted, thinking nothing will be better and in doing that, you lose a part of yourself." She grinned, a fleeting expression that made her look younger. "And I'd hazard a guess that you like the sum of your parts too much to make that happen. You look like a strong man to me, once that can weather this adversity."

Mango stared at her. "Are you some sort of philosophy teacher or something?" he asked curiously. "Some self-help guru out to deliver homilies to people in need?"

She giggled. "Lord, no. Just a woman who's had double the experience you've had in life and can lend a wise word to a stranger now and then."

"Huh," Mango said. "Well, thanks. I hadn't really thought of things in that way." A faint stirring of hope rose in his chest and wove its warmth through his body and into his mind.

He could do this. He could be Ryan's rock. He had to be, because who else would?

The woman wrapped her blue cardigan tighter around her shoulders. "My Graham once said to me, 'When things go wrong, don't go with them.' I think Elvis said that and Graham lives by it. It's been a long road for both of us and I think we still have a journey to get through but I'm hoping we make it together. Hope is all we have at times like this."

She glanced at her watch. "Speaking of Graham, it's time to go and see if he's settled in." She stood up. "Good luck and I hope everything goes well for you both."

Mango smiled up at her. "Thank you. All the best to you too. And thanks so much for the little pep talk. I appreciate it."

She waved a pale hand in farewell and Mango watched her walk across the garden toward the hospital door, stopping to pat the head of a small boy in hospital pyjamas. The child was wired to a drip, holding his mother's hand. His face lit up when Mango's garden-side visitor took something out of her handbag—it looked like a red lollipop.

Mango smiled at the grin that spread across the child's face at such a simple gesture. It looked as if the hospital had a secret benefactor who gave pep talks to strange men sitting on benches and children in need.

For a split second, discomfort assailed him and he had the ridiculous notion he'd been in the presence of an angel wafting around the hospital stilling the fears in people.

"Don't be bloody stupid," he scoffed. "Now you're just being fanciful. This place does things to you."

Angel or not, Mango wished he'd got her name to thank her again for her kind words that had given him hope. Knowing there were other people out there going through the same trials and tribulations as him—even worse, as the kid only looked to be about eight years old—gave Mango the quiet strength to keep hoping that he and Ryan would make it through together. Because as she'd said, what was the alternative?

Fear was a strong motivator to run and hide away from the world but Mango was determined anew he was going to be strong himself. For Ryan. Just as his mysterious lady had been for her ailing husband.

When Mango went back into Ryan's room, he found him on his mobile, talking animatedly.

"Kyle, tell them not to fuck me about. They gave me a damn quote and they need to stick to it." Ryan passed a hand across his forehead, pushing his hair back in exasperation. "Those workmen needn't think because I'm not there they're going to take advantage of me. Tell them to shut the hell up and get on with their damn job." He scowled fiercely as Mango sat down beside him. "Okay, let me know if those dickheads give you any more trouble. I might be out of commission for a while but leave a message on my phone or call Mango. He'll sort them out if needs be."

Ryan's face softened. "Thanks for holding the fort. I'm sure Mango will keep you updated on things. Speak soon. Bye."

Ryan put his mobile down on the steel cabinet next to his bed and smiled. "Did you eat something? I'm so damn hungry. This whole abstaining from food thing sucks."

Mango reached out and took Ryan's hand, warming the cold fingers in his. "I tried. Not got much of an appetite." He smiled faintly. "Those workmen at the club giving you grief on the renovations? Shitty time to have all that going on too. I'll pop round later and see what's going. Keep them on the straight and narrow."

Ryan's eyes brightened. "Yeah, thank you, I'd appreciate you popping over. Kyle can cope but sometimes it takes a little more than sass and sarcasm to get these guys moving their arses. They tried to stitch us up on the pricing by telling us they'd misquoted. Damn thieves." His face clouded. "Have Mum and

Dad arrived yet? Mum sent me a frantic text ages ago saying something about delays with the airline but they were on their way."

A few days ago, Mango had finally managed to convince his stubborn boyfriend to tell his parents about his surgery. Clarence and Christine Bishop were flying over from their holiday villa on Corfu, and according to a text Mango had received, were currently touching down at the airport.

Mango nodded. "I got the same text. They haven't arrived here yet but I'll make sure to keep an eye out for them." They fell quiet and Mango squeezed Ryan's hand. "Are you okay? Silly thing to ask under the circumstances but..."

Ryan took a deep breath. "Actually, I am. I've made peace with the fact this is how it's got to be and there's nothing I can do about it. And I know when I open my eyes I'll see you. So you keep me strong."

Mango's chest tightened. "Yeah, I'll be here. I'm not going anywhere." He swallowed. "You know I love you, right? I know I don't say it enough but you're it for me. No matter what happens from here on, I'm not going anywhere."

Ryan smiled. "I'm counting on it. I love you too. Always have, always will."

There was a noise at the door and both men turned around. A nurse and an orderly stood there, eyes sympathetic.

"Time to go, Mr Bishop. You get to ride the corridor in your fancy bed-mobile now, and the theatre staff will take it from there. Are you ready?"

Ryan took a deep breath and glanced at Mango. "As ready as I can be." His face was pale but he didn't look scared.

Mango was fucking terrified. He stood as the orderly bustled in, checking the bed and started to slide it away. Mango's throat was choked and he could hardly find the words to tell Ryan what he felt.

Ryan reached out and took his hand. "Breathe, love," he said, eyes soft. "I'm coming back to you, I promise. I won't leave you."

How could Ryan promise such a thing? What if something went wrong?

Despite his fear, Mango nodded, still unable to get anything out past his aching chest and prickling eyes. He drew in a deep breath, thinking of the words he'd heard in the garden. Hope. He needed to believe in it.

"You'll ace this, baby," he finally managed. "Go get 'em, tiger. I love you, Ryan."

Ryan smiled and released his hand as the staff wheeled the bed out the door and into the corridor. "Love you too, baby. Tell my folks not to worry. I'll see you all on the flip side," he whispered with a fleeting grin.

The last image Mango had of the man he loved was Ryan's stoic face, his blue eyes focused on Mango as he was wheeled away. Then they turned a corridor and Ryan was gone.

His legs unsteady, Mango had only sat on a chair outside Ryan's room for a brief moment when he heard his name being called. Startled, he looked up to see a pink-faced Lenny racing down the corridor.

"Shit, did I miss him?" Lenny panted. "The damn trains were on the go-slow today because of some signal failure. I had to get off at a previous station and hail a taxi." Lenny's aqua eyes searched Mango's face anxiously. "Is he okay—has he gone for the surgery already?"

Mango nodded. "Yeah, they took him down."

Lenny plonked down and laid a reassuring hand on Mango's leg. "Well, Ryan's a tough bastard. He's going to be fine, you'll see. Before we know it, we'll have our little diva back as good as new."

Despite the brave words, Mango heard the uncertainty in Lenny's voice. He wasn't aware the tears he'd tried so hard to stave off were rolling down his cheeks until Lenny's soft voice echoed in his ear and a tissue was thrust into his hand.

"He's going to be fine, chicken. Ryan's strong. He'll get through this."

Mango wiped his eyes numbly. "I can't think of him being any other way. Ryan is my world. I held off showing my man I loved him for so damn long and now when I think we have a great chance to be together, something comes along and threatens it. I fucking hate this."

Lenny reached over and laid a warm hand over his. "I know. Have faith in him and in the medical staff here, okay? They're good at what they do." His voice was choked.

They were quiet for a while as people walked past; nurses, patients, visitors were a blur as the two men stared blankly at the passing trade.

Finally Lenny spoke, his voice unsteady. "We're all going to get fucking drunk as sin when this is all over, Ryan included. He's funny when he's pissed. I'll bet I can get him to sing 'I Will Survive' on karaoke night at the club."

Mango snorted. "Good luck with that. The day Ryan has a karaoke night at Club Delish will be the day he throws away his gay man card and goes straight. It's not gonna happen."

"Yeah, he hates shit like that doesn't he?" Lenny's face brightened. "All the more reason to do it as a surprise one night though. It'll be a hoot."

Mango chuckled and gave a watery smile. "On your head, Lenny. Ryan would kill you if he knew what you were plotting."

They were quiet, watching the ebb and flow of hospital duties go on around them.

"Are Ryan's folks on their way?" Lenny asked.

Mango nodded. "Yes. I've not met them so it should be something. Not the most ideal of circumstances under which to meet the boyfriend's parents."

"I've not met them either. I'm glad they made it over though." Lenny scowled. "I can't believe he wasn't going to bloody tell them about this."

Mango heaved a sigh. "That's my Ryan. He gets an idea in his head, it's difficult to change it."

Lenny picked up a fashion magazine and flicked through the pages idly. Mango leaned his head back against the wall and closed his eyes. He was halfway to dozing off when a hand bumped his shoulder.

"I think those must be his folks. I mean, look at the guy. He looks like an older Ryan."

Lenny was staring in wonder at the couple that strode towards them. The woman was tall and blonde, the man was slightly shorter with a trim beard and did indeed resemble an older Ryan. Mango thought if this was how Ryan was going to look when as he aged, he'd have to beat off men with a stick. Any gay man would love the sophistication of a man looking like Clarence Bishop. His wife Christine also had a mature beauty, which would stand out in a crowd. Mango could see where Ryan got his looks from.

The couple looked uncertain and Mango stood. A look of relief came over Clarence Bishop's face. He strode toward him. "Mr Munroe?"

Mango nodded. "Yes, sir. Please call me Mango. I'm glad you made it." He gestured at Lenny. "This is Lenny James, Ryan's best friend."

Clarence huffed as he shook hands. He had long, slim hands like Ryan's and Mango remembered the man was a world famous classical pianist. "It's good to meet you both. I'm glad you convinced my son to call us. The young tyke was remiss to think we wouldn't need to be told about something as serious as this." He waved a hand at his wife. "This is my wife Christine."

Christine Bishop shook Mango's hand. "You look as I expected. Ryan has told me all about you." She grinned but her eyes were shadowed. "He said you were tall, dangerous and sexy."

Mango flushed. "I'm sure he exaggerated."

She smiled. "And Lenny, you're the fashion designer he talks about? My son thinks the world of you both." She stared into the empty hospital room. "So he's gone into surgery already? We missed him?" Her voice was unsteady and a glimmer of tears cast an eerie light on her grey eyes. "We tried so hard to get here on time but the damn plane was delayed. I was spitting blood but there was nothing we could do. I wanted to see my son before he went into surgery."

Mango could only imagine how frustrated they were at not seeing Ryan and immediately wondered whether they'd ever see Ryan, again despite the assurances of doctors and nursing staff.

"He went in about"—Mango looked at his watch—"an hour and a half ago. They said it would take a few hours for the operation."

Clarence blew out his cheeks and looked at his wife. "Then I guess we should get some coffee and something to eat. We haven't had anything yet. We were in such a hurry to get here."

He glanced at Mango. "I suppose we have to simply wait until it's over to get any update?"

"I'm afraid so." Mango sat back down on the chair. "It's a waiting game from here on."

"Then wait we shall," Clarence said quietly. "Come on, darling, let's grab a mouldy sandwich from the cafeteria and stave off the hunger pangs. Would you gentlemen like anything brought back?"

Both Mango and Lenny shook their heads. Clarence gave one last lingering glance into his son's hospital room, then he and his wife made their way down the corridor towards the canteen.

***

The next few hours were spent reading magazines, on which Mango couldn't focus. Eventually he gave up trying. There was sporadic conversation between the four of them, but overall everyone looked shell-shocked and on tenterhooks. Occasionally one of Ryan's parents would disappear to make a telephone call or get more coffee.

Mango paced up and down corridors, went for a short walk in the garden hoping to see his benefactor and tell her how her words had helped him. She was nowhere to be seen. He went back inside and played games on his mobile. Lenny was quieter, more contemplative. He stole away with his mobile to speak in hushed tones to Brook from the seclusion of Ryan's room, while Mango kept an eye out for the nurses.

The few times he'd managed to corner one of the hospital staff to find out how things were going, they'd been firm but sympathetic. Ryan was still in surgery and as soon as there was news, he'd be told. Mango wanted to spit blood and climb the walls with his uncertainty and frustration.

Finally, as he'd sat down for what seemed the thousandth time, someone approached them. Four pairs of eyes stared up hopefully at the doctor clad in green scrubs.

"Mr Munroe?"

Mango stood up, his heart thumping. His throat was dry. "Yes," he croaked. "How is he? Is he okay?" Beside him, Lenny clasped Mango's arm tightly as they waited.

The surgeon nodded. "He's in recovery. It went well."

The sense of relief in the group was palpable.

The surgeon continued. "We managed to remove the tumour, which was fairly small as things go. A sample has been sent for analysis but from the look of the growth, I don't think we have anything to worry about. I'd like to make sure though there's nothing amiss. So while the surgery is over, we need to wait for the results to see if there is anything further needed, like chemo or radiation therapy." He hesitated. "It was a fairly accessible growth so there should be no loss of mental facilities but we will only know for certain when Ryan wakes up."

Clarence put an arm around his wife's shaking shoulders as she sobbed in apparent relief. "Thank you, Doctor. We appreciate all you've done for our son. When can we see him?"

"Give it an hour or so—he's in recovery at the moment. Then we'll get him settled back in the neurology ward where we'll keep an eye on him for a few days. He won't wake up for a while though, he's been through a lot and the medication will make him drowsy, but you can see him. Not all of you at the same time though." He smiled apologetically. "I'd suggest you take it in turns." He gave another smile, turned and walked back down the corridor.

Mango's legs gave way and he sat back down and stared at the floor. His eyes prickled with tears and he wanted to run and scream with joy. Ryan had made it through. Yes, there were other challenges to face but the biggest hurdle was over. The surgeon had seemed confident it was okay so Mango chose to believe him. Hope seemed to be working for him this time around.

He looked up at the faces of the other people in Ryan's life. Lenny gave him a soft grin, looking more relaxed than he had been. Clarence and Christine hugged one another, then Clarence turned to Mango.

"When he's ready to have visitors, you go in and see him first, young man. I'm sure you're anxious to make sure he's okay."

Mango nodded his thanks, unable to speak through the lump in his throat. All he could think of was touching Ryan, having one of their quirky conversations and kissing lips that might not be able to speak yet, but would reassure Mango that Ryan was still there.

Lenny plopped down next to him. "So, I guess this means karaoke is on the cards," he murmured.

Mango gave a strangled chuckle. "I guess so, if that's your idea of a death wish."

***

A little more than an hour later, Mango consulted with the doctors, then finally was permitted to see Ryan. The nurse guided Mango to the bed on the far side of the special ward and he stood there, his heart in his mouth. Ryan's wound was covered in bandages and his face was waxy pale, his lips bloodless. The steady beep of machinery echoed against the stark environment of the cavernous ward. Around them, Mango heard moans, groans, soft whispers and the sounds of people talking. He wanted to shut out the world for a while and pulled the curtains around Ryan's bed to give them some privacy. He was relieved to see only a small portion of Ryan's head had been shaved. His lover would be pleased about that.

Mango leaned over and softly kissed those pale, cracked lips. "You're back with me, my love," he whispered. "I'm so proud of you. I'm not going anywhere until you wake up and I see those beautiful eyes." He sat beside Ryan and took his hand, kissing it. "Your folks and Lenny are outside and they'll be in to see you in a little while. Right now I need you all to myself."

He brushed strands of hair from Ryan's forehead and slowly stroked his cheek. "I hope you can hear me. When you're better, we're going away. I know this little place in Norway by a glacier." Ryan was a little kid when it came to snow. "It has a log cabin, a fireplace perfect for a roaring fire and all the tequila you want. We're going to go there, make snow angels, snuggle under blankets and I'm going to make love to you until you can't think. I'm not letting you out of my sight. There'll be no mobile phones, no contact with the outside world. It'll be you and me." His voice choked up. "I love you, Ry."

Ryan's fingers moved and Mango looked up hopefully. Ryan's eyes were closed but Mango felt sure he'd heard him. He pulled Ryan's iPod out of his pocket and fiddled with it until he found Ryan's favourite Callum Webster album. Mango slid the EarPods into Ryan's ears, then laid his head against Ryan's chest, listening to his steady breaths.

When he woke it was dark outside. The small area was dimly lit by low-glow lamps above the bed. Mango blinked blearily and sat up. His back ached from falling asleep in such an awkward position. He yawned, stretched, scratching his stomach idly as his shirt rode up. A faint snicker sounded from the bed.

"That's some sight." Ryan's voice was scratchy but held a trace of laughter.

Mango leaned forward, every nerve in his body tuned to the beautiful but tired man staring at him. "Oh, it's good to see those baby blues." Mango stood, leaned over and kissed Ryan's now warm lips.

Ryan squeezed his hand and shifted uncomfortably in the bed. "Do you think you can scratch the bottom of my left foot? It's been itching like crazy but you looked so damn peaceful sleeping I didn't have the heart to wake you. And if I move, my head will explode."

Mango would have done anything for this man before. Now, his wish is my command seemed apt. He reached under the covers and couldn't help a grin when he saw what was under there.

"Uhm, don't look now but I don't think much of your new fashion."

Ryan's eyes widened and predictably he moved the cover to stare down at his legs. "What the fuck?"

His slim legs were covered with what looked unflattering stocking bandages.

Mango chuckled at the consternation on Ryan's face. "Relax. They're antithrombotic stockings to help stop any potential blood clots. The doctor told me all about them when we talked earlier." He grimaced. "And you have a catheter in your dick, so don't think we'll be getting up to any funny business."

"Ha-ha," Ryan remarked sourly but his eyes glinted with amusement. "Look at you thinking you're a comedian."

Mango smirked and took Ryan's warm foot in his hands, running his nails firmly down the sole, in steady up and down movements. The stockings were fairly thick but the rubbing should help.

Ryan squirmed but groaned in pleasure. "God, that feels better than an orgasm."

Mango lifted one eyebrow and Ryan laughed. "Well, maybe not as good."

"Have you seen Lenny and your parents?" Mango asked.

Ryan nodded, his face creasing in an expression of pleasure as Mango massaged his foot firmly. "Yeah, they came in while you were sleeping. The nursing staff didn't have the heart to kick you out so they let them in. They thought you looked cute sleeping, even if you were drooling."

Mango reached up and wiped his chin. Ryan smiled at him, tired but beautiful.

"It was good to see the folks. They've gone back to their hotel now. They'll pop back tomorrow. Lenny left about half an hour ago." Ryan's face creased in a grin. "You might want to check your face in the mirror. He had a black eyeliner with him and decided to draw on your face."

"What the fuck?" Mango leapt up. There was no mirror in the cubicle and he scowled. "So what did he do to me?"

"He might have drawn a moustache and a pair of cartoon eyebrows. You were so deep in sleep I think he could have done the *Mona Lisa* on your face and you wouldn't have woken up." Ryan snorted with laughter. That sound did more to raise Mango's spirits than anything else. If Groucho Marx eyebrows were what it took to make Ryan laugh, goddamn it, Mango would have them permanently tattooed on his face.

He sat back down again and took Ryan's hand. "So how do you feel? Or is it a stupid question to ask someone who's had brain surgery?"

Ryan shifted, looking weary. "Fucking exhausted and my head is pounding. But actually, I don't feel as bad as I expected. The doctor was in briefly while you were in the Land of Nod, and he said it all went better than even he expected, so I guess it's a plus. Now we wait for the biopsy results, but he seems to think it will be okay." He licked his dry lips. "What else did the doctor say to you?" He yawned.

Mango shrugged. "He gave me an update, told me all about what happens next."

Ryan snuggled back into his pillows wearily. "So now we have another bout of waiting."

Mango leaned over and placed a soft kiss on Ryan's matted hair. "Stay positive. We've come this far. And you still have most of your hair, which is a fucking miracle."

Ryan's pale face creased in a scowl. "Small mercies. I'm going to be pumped full of anticlotting drugs, cortisone, anticonvulsants in case I pitch a fit and a whole load of other crap. It's going to be a barrel of laughs. I doubt I'll ever get it up again with all the medication they're planning on giving me."

Mango nodded solemnly. "Wow, they actually found a drug to stop your hissy fits? Who knew that kind of magic existed? If I'd known sooner…"

Ryan's eyes narrowed. "Bastard. I so do not have hissy fits." Mango grinned; they both knew that was a lie.

Ryan pretended to toss his hair back diva fashion, then winced as he obviously felt pain in his head. "Christ, I need drugs. Painkillers. Do you think you can call the nurse and tell them her damn patient is dying here?" He fluttered his eyelashes and Mango could no sooner resist the sight than he could his favourite Cherry Chocolate sundae.

"I'll find someone. Didn't they give you a pain drip or anything?"

Ryan's face grew hopeful. When they'd finally determined such a thing wasn't on the cards, Mango was dispatched to find someone to help. He'd completely forgotten about the drawings on his face, remembered only when he saw the strange looks he got as he walked to the nurse's station. The nurses themselves tittered like school kids at the sight and wiped off Lenny's handiwork with sterile wipes.

When he got back to the ward and walked through the curtains to Ryan's bedside, it was to find Ryan fast asleep, EarPods in his ears, lashes dark against pale cheeks and a soft smile on his face. Mango grinned wryly at the nurse with him, who smiled back and left the small plastic container on the metal side cabinet.

"When he wakes up, he can have them if still needs them," she mouthed, and disappeared with a wink.

Mango sighed. He needed a shower and a change of clothes but there was no way he was leaving Ryan without saying a proper good-bye. So resigned to his fate of sweaty armpits and wearing two-day-old underwear by the time the morning rolled around, he settled down in the chair once again to watch Ryan sleep and perhaps catch a few z's himself.

He vaguely heard Ryan mumble, something about snow angels in Norway and fucking him in front of a fire. When he looked up, Ryan was asleep again. Mango gripped the hand in his tighter and thanked all the deities he could think of that the man he loved had made it through.

Chapter 8

Ryan closed the file he'd been working with on his laptop and sighed. He was knackered. It had been three weeks since his operation and he'd only been back at the club for the last one of them. It had driven him crazy the first two weeks, sitting around doing nothing. The past week he'd been tasked with doing nothing too strenuous. He couldn't even drive, for fuck's sake, until the doctor gave him the all clear, which he hoped would be next week.

His door opened and the noise from outside leaked into his office until Kyle shut it behind him.

Ryan smiled. "Hey, everything okay out there? Need me for anything?"

Please say yes. I'm so damned bored sitting here.

"Nope. All under control, boss." Kyle's violet eyes regarded him in amusement. "How are you feeling?"

Ryan shrugged. "I'm fine. Dandy. Chomping at the bit to get back to work without a bunch of fucking nursemaids watching my every move."

Kyle grinned and sat down on the corner of Ryan's desk. "Ooh, full blown bitch alert. Isn't it nearly time for your bedtime?" His eyes twinkled cheekily.

Mango had insisted Ryan be home by ten every night as part of his recovery. It hadn't helped that the doctor had given Ryan the same instruction. It appeared his doctor and lover were in cahoots.

Ryan narrowed his eyes. "Fuck. You." It was only nine p.m.

Kyle sniggered. "Not my rules, boss. Them be Mango's commands." He affected an atrocious Jamaican accent and batted his eyelashes at Ryan who couldn't help smiling. Kyle's sunshiny nature was catching.

"At least those awful stockings have gone," Kyle drawled as he pretended to fan his face like a Southern belle. "I do declare, sir, such a shade of puce I never did see on a gentleman of your standing."

Ryan chuckled. "Shut up, you." He bowed his head in acknowledgement. "Thank fuck they've gone. I hated wearing them. Such passion killers."

"How are things…down there?" Kyle waved in the direction of Ryan's groin.

Not for the first time Ryan regretted in confiding to Kyle that the medication had caused some technical issues in sustaining an erection. It had happened in a weak moment when Ryan had been feeling sorry for himself. The doctor had said it was normal and would resolve itself over time.

"Getting better," he said. "It helps the medication is now maintenance only and not as high a dose as it was. I'll be able to give it up for good in a week or so, I hope."

Kyle nodded, his eyes sympathetic. "You've been through a lot, Ryan," he said softly. "And you came out with flying colours. Not many aftereffects, a clean bill of health, apart from the check-ups. You're a lucky man."

Ryan knew things could be worse. His biopsy could have come back indicating cancer, he could have had worse side effects from the medication, suffered fits—but none of the other bad stuff had happened.

"I am," he acknowledged. "I give thanks every day for coming through it like I did."

Kyle nodded and looked at his watch. "It's time to leave the office, boss," he said firmly. "Mango asked me to get you home a bit earlier."

Ryan frowned. "Why?"

Kyle shrugged. "Dunno." His eyes shone with merriment. "He told me to kick my boss out at nine o'clock or he'd come down and get you himself."

Ryan swore but he stood, looking for his suit jacket. "Damn man is a pain in my arse."

"Isn't that the whole point?" Kyle smirked. His face grew dreamy. "Have you seen Eric lately? He hasn't been around since he saw you a week ago."

Eric had been a constant visitor at both the hospital and the club. Ryan was glad to have him as a friend.

"No, he's away for a few weeks. He went backpacking with some friends in the Grand Canyon, I think." He glanced at Kyle. His manager had a definite thing for Eric but Ryan wasn't sure whether it was going anywhere. Both men seemed skittish.

Kyle's face fell. "Oh. That sounds cool. Well, you'd better get going before that boyfriend of yours comes down and drags you away."

Ryan was ushered out of his office and virtually pushed up the stairs. He got to the flat, opened the door and dropped his man-bag to the floor with a sullen scowl.

"They're still treating me like cotton candy, those arseholes. When will they learn I'm perfectly fine—?"

He stopped his soliloquy and stared around his flat.

Well, that's different. Looks like the bloody gay fairy godmother has been here.

He certainly wasn't prepared for what greeted him. Scented candles cast soft light on the side table and sideboards leading into the lounge. A delicious savoury fragrance wafted through the air and Ryan heard soft strains of music. It was Callum Webster's new album, the one Ryan hadn't gotten around to buying yet. The young singer's moody tones were a perfect backdrop to what appeared to be a planned seduction.

Ryan grinned as he tiptoed slowly toward the kitchen, his ire at work colleagues who insisted on coddling him disappearing. He'd only gotten to the door when Mango appeared, spatula in hand. Ryan's jaw dropped as Mango wagged a hand at him.

"Ah ha. No peeking. Go clean up, put on the little something I put out for you, then go sit down. There's nothing for you to do. I've taken care of it all."

Ryan was stricken speechless not at Mango's words but at the fact Mango wasn't wearing anything—unless an apron counted as clothes. Mango's strong, hairy legs poked out from underneath the short Muscle Man–themed garment, emblazoned with a set of pecs any bodybuilder would have been proud of, and there was a strategic bulge of giant proportions.

When Mango turned to go back into the kitchen, all Ryan saw were two handfuls of arse ripe for the plucking and a lean, contoured back that made his mouth water. To Ryan's joy, his dick livened up like a brass band at an Oompa Loompa wedding.

"What the fuck are you doing?" he groaned as his laughter welled to the surface.

There was a clang from the kitchen and a muttered curse. "Good to see you too. I bought you a new sexy bedtime outfit and put some other stuff in the bathroom. You can change in there. I thought you might like to shower first. Get everything nice and clean for me. Oh, and stay out of the bedroom."

Ryan closed his eyes and opened them again. He surely must be in the twilight zone.

"You bought me a new outfit?" He walked towards the bathroom, manfully resisting the impulse to sneak into his bedroom and see what Mango had hatched in there.

He didn't reply and Ryan pouted and made his way into the dimly lit bathroom. More candles flickered, casting shadows on the pale grey tiles and the white porcelain sink.

"Am I supposed to see what the hell is going on here?" he muttered. "It looks like a rent boy's boudoir."

Ryan had nothing against rent boy boudoirs—in fact he was quite partial to the concept given the appearance of his own French chateau–themed bedroom—but he was a little miffed at being told what to do without actually knowing what was going on.

And when he saw the outfit Mango had laid out for him, he almost had a hernia.

"What the fuck?" he exploded as he held up the tiny set of Lycra shorts and a cropped top in emerald green. He knew it would look delightfully decadent with his skin tone and auburn curls but still. "Has the man got his own brain tumour now? He's having a laugh if he thinks I'm going to put this on."

Ryan was still grumbling when he got out of the shower and his eyes caught sight of the new clothing. To be honest, he'd eyed it all the way through his shower. It was sort of growing on him. It would certainly frame his tight body and arse well.

Once he'd towelled himself dry, he cast another critical eye at the deep green garment and decided he'd be churlish not to try on it after all the trouble Mango had gone to.

The minute he saw himself in the mirror, Ryan knew he'd probably never take it off.

Mango is not going to know what fucking hit him.

The man looking sultrily back at him was flushed from the heat of the water, lips rose pink, blue eyes darkened with anticipation. The hair around his operation site had started growing back and, while not fully grown out, it covered the ugly scar. The shorts barely covered his cock and balls and when Ryan twisted around, the fabric hugged two perfect halves of a taut and perky—if he said it himself—backside. The tight tank top clung to his figure, stopping below his pecs. Ryan's stomach was already toned from his home exercise and dancing so Mango could have no complaints there.

"Darling, you look like fucking sex on legs." Ryan smirked as the man in the mirror smirked back.

He tidied up the bathroom and with the well of anticipation of fun to come filling his belly, he walked out into the hallway, ready to give Mango his dues.

His feeling of well-being, the genuine relief at having made it this far with no more serious implications, made Ryan giddy. He snuck silently into the kitchen where Mango was engrossed in stirring something on the stove and leaned over and murmured, "Boo," into Mango's ear.

Mango jumped as if scalded, which Ryan fervently hoped wasn't the case given he was cooking. He turned to stare angrily.

"Ry, what the hell, you scared the shit…holy fuck."

The hot rise of lust in Mango's eyes coupled with the slow tenting of the apron was validation of Ryan's opinion he looked hot. Swelteringly, blisteringly hot if the way Mango was licking his lips was anything to go by.

"So, you like?" Ryan twirled around, making sure his arse wiggled a bit before turning back to face Mango, whose facial expression was making Ryan's cock inflate. The tight shorts were pinching in all the right—wrong—places. He winced as his dick swelled and moved forward to press himself against Mango's hardness.

Thank God. Looks like I'm working again. Limp dicktitis be damned.

"What say we skip dinner and go straight to the fun part of the evening?"

The feel of his man's warm, hard body against his heated skin was both a blessing and a curse. Ryan wanted so badly to strip off his shorts and feel Mango's own silky steel against his own but he knew if done too quickly, he'd probably come before they were even down his thighs. His throat closed up as Mango laughed huskily.

"You look like my wet dream come true. God, you're every gay man's red-blooded fantasy." His voice grew soft. "Even straight guys would want you. Hell, but you are something, Ryan Bishop. And you're all mine."

The worship and reverence in Mango's tone caught Ryan unprepared and he lost his breath for a moment as he stared into dark tawny eyes reflecting emotions that made his gut clench, his dick harden and his heart race.

"God, I'm glad I'm still here," Ryan whispered, his voice shaking with emotion. "To see that expression in your eyes when you look at me, it's sinful. You make me feel—like I'm all you need."

Mango reached out and pulled Ryan even closer, his mouth nuzzling Ryan's ear. "You *are* all I need. And having you here with me right now—it's all I ever prayed for. The thought of losing you made me cold inside. I couldn't even contemplate it."

Mango's hands drifted down the skin and muscle of Ryan's stomach, ghosting trails of fire down his belly. He fell into the sensations, closing his eyes, able to feel every fibre of the skin on Mango's fingers touching him so intimately.

"I need you." Mango's voice trembled. "God's truth, Ry, I need you so badly."

Ryan pulled away and held out his hand. Mango took it and stared into his face as if he'd discovered the secret of the universe.

"Come on," Ryan murmured, his heart aching. "Let's go."

Mango shook his head. "Yeah, let me switch all this off. It'll keep a little while." He fiddled with dials and pots and turned to Ryan again.

Ryan laughed. "Oh we'll need more than a little while, lover. I'm thinking maybe *this* is going to have to be breakfast tomorrow." He waved around the kitchen at all the food and cooking implements.

"You can't have beef bourguignon for breakfast," Mango grumbled as Ryan led him to the bedroom. "Heathen."

Ryan pushed open the door and stepped inside. He stopped and stared around him in wonder.

Mango fidgeted beside him. "I hope it's not too much," he said, sounding more vulnerable than Ryan had ever heard him. "I wanted to do something special to celebrate…us…you."

Ryan's bedroom, the one he'd worked at replicating French sophistication and chic, was awash with blue and white fairy lights glittering on the ceiling like twinkling stars. A bottle of champagne chilled in an ornately decorated black ice bucket. His blue and gold custom-made bedspread had been folded back to reveal a bed ready to slip into. On the sideboard, a huge bouquet of roses sat in stunning shades of lilac and pink.

Ryan stared at the tableau before him and wanted to burst into happy tears.

"Oh my God," he managed to choke out. "This is too beautiful."

Then his eyes spotted what sat on Mango's bedside table and Ryan held back a hysterical laugh. "You certainly have plans. That's one giant-size lube bottle."

Mango muttered something but Ryan didn't catch it. His attention was focused on the strange looking objects sitting on the table of his side of the bed.

"Babe, why do you have eggs in the bedroom?" Ryan squinted trying to make sense of the pack of multi-coloured eggs sitting there.

Mango cleared his throat. "It's something new I thought we might try. They're Tenga Eggs."

"They're what now?" Ryan moved over to inspect them and Mango moved and held him back.

"Wait. They're mine to play with on you later. Stop being such a quizzy little bastard. Play along with me. I promise I'll make it worth your while."

Ryan ignored him and moved over to prod one of the eggs in the carton.

Mango rolled his eyes. "They won't hatch, you idjit."

Ryan sniffed. "Huh. You are one kinky bastard. I want to see how those translate to fun in the bedroom."

Mango slid off the apron, standing naked in front of Ryan. Ryan's mouth watered at the sight of the treasure trail leading down to the erect cock bobbing against Mango's taut belly.

"Lie down on the bed so I can peel you out of those clothes," Mango said, his voice husky. "Then I'll show you how we use the eggs. Only in a little while though because right now, I want to fuck your beautiful mouth. Hands by your side."

Ryan wasted no time flinging himself dramatically onto the bed, head against the pillows, splaying his legs as he palmed his dick. Such an invitation needed no repeating. There was one thing worrying him, which he needed answered first. He didn't want to ruin the mood but this needed to be said.

"You're not going to shove those things up my arse, are you?" he asked suspiciously. He eyed the eggs with some trepidation. "Because as much as I love something up my arse, an egg is not one of them. They look quite…wide. And like they might get stuck up there." He chortled. "I can see it now. You rushing me to the ER and telling the doctor what the problem is." He warmed to his theme as his dick grew harder with his own touch.

"Doctor, doctor, my boyfriend isn't a freak of nature and actually *laying* an egg, it slipped and fell in while I was pleasuring him." Ryan laughed softly as Mango shook his head. He climbed onto the bed and knelt over Ryan's chest, his beautiful cock only inches from Ryan's needy mouth.

Ryan was dizzy. He'd survived a fucking brain tumour and had lived to enjoy the scent of flowers in the room, Mango's unique woodsy fragrance and the knowledge this whole scene had been orchestrated specially for him. Life was fabulous. Especially the man looking down at him with a mixture of desire, love and amusement.

"Ryan?" Mango's voice was soft, yet commanding. "Shut up."

Ryan licked his lips, hoping he looked as decadent as he felt. "Make me."

The slow smile forming on Mango's face turned Ryan's inside to jelly and he whimpered in pleasure with the knowledge both his mouth and his arse was about to get well and truly ravished.

He opened his mouth at the same time Mango pushed forward into it. Ryan rolled his tongue around thick, salty cock. He raised his gaze to Mango who met his with eyes darkened in sultry need and pleasure. Mango slapped his hands against the iron frame of the bed and thrust forward in slow, deep, measured movements, fucking Ryan's mouth, knowing he belonged there.

Ryan tried to keep his eyes open as long as he could but his lids dropped as the heated flesh assaulting his mouth continued its relentless movement. He groaned around Mango's dick as he sucked and licked, gratified in hearing his lover's answering moan. It was a form of exquisite torture they both enjoyed and Ryan could have done it all night.

Mango groaned loudly. "Look at you, so damned sexy, so fucking hot. You taking my cock like this—God, Ry, you look…" Words failed him as Ryan reached up and grabbed Mango's arse, propelling him even deeper into his eager mouth.

Mango stiffened, his legs tightening against Ryan's torso. "Nearly there, a few more…fuck, oh fuck."

Warm salty fluid flooded Ryan's mouth, and he drank it down then licked Mango clean. Mango leaned forward with ragged breaths, his half-spent dick dangling above Ryan who licked the last remaining spunk off his swollen lips.

"You are one master cocksucker," Mango finally said with a grin.

Ryan quirked an eyebrow as he pulled Mango down on top of him. "A master cocksucker who needs to be fucked," he said, gesturing towards his swollen prick. "You need to take care of this for me. I don't want to lose the opportunity. I think I might be better though." He stroked himself languidly. "It's a fucking miracle."

Mango kissed him, chuckling into his open greedy, wet mouth.

Ryan moaned. "I'm dying here." He reached down to take off his tight shorts and Mango stopped him.

"Oh no. I said I was going to peel it all off you, so wait. Then I'm going to use of those eggs on your dick to show you exactly what they do."

Ryan pouted, then yowled as Mango bit his bottom lip.

"Stop it. It makes you look even sexier and I can't even deal with the sexy man I have, let alone you with your debauched look."

He kissed Ryan again, hard and demanding and while Ryan was still reeling from the sensation, Mango slowly, deliberately, slid the Lycra shorts off Ryan's body.

His dick sprang free, rising against his belly. He grunted his appreciation and relief. "Those shorts make my arse look hot but honestly, my dick needed out of there. Are you going to fuck me now?" He leered. "Can you get it up again after the orgasm I gave you?"

Mango ignored him and leaned over to pluck one of the strange eggs out of the box. Ryan watched, eyes squinted in concentration, as Mango unpeeled a wrapper—huh, who knew there was packaging over the thing— and popped off the top half of the egg. Ryan half expected something to shoot forth, perhaps an alien, but nothing happened. Instead, Mango pursed his lips and drew something out of the bottom half. It was white and soft.

Ryan stared suspiciously. "That's going near my dick? What the fuck is it?" His dick wilted a little.

Mango tut-tutted. "Patience, baby. Watch and enjoy."

He took out a small packet from the spongy thing and tore it open. The tantalising smell of something fruity pervaded the air as Mango poured it inside the strange object.

"Lube?" Ryan was becoming interested now and he tried to sit up to see it clearer. Mango shoved him back.

"Stay down. Put your hands above your head and keep them there this time."

"Fucking pushy sod," Ryan grumbled as he complied and continued to watch Mango carefully to see what came next. Him, he hoped. His cock was aching for release although the waiting was making him even hotter.

Mango grinned and before Ryan knew it, something was being stretched over his cock and pulled down to the base. The lube was cold and the feeling of something foreign over his heated and excited cock—other than a condom—made Ryan squeak a little.

Mango's strong hands began wanking him forcefully, using the covering as friction. He stared down at Ryan with an intensity that made him squirm. He began to relax and push upwards into the fingers gripping him tightly. The *thing* around his dick felt ribbed inside and the sensation was something else.

"Oh," Ryan panted as he tried valiantly to keep his arms where he'd been ordered to keep them. He wanted to reach down and join Mango's hands to bring himself off. "So that's how they work. I—oh fuck. Feels so good…"

The fluid movements up and down Ryan's dick were heaven and, in all truth, he had been ready to blow for some time. His dick had simply needed a little encouraging.

Mango's warm lips sucked on the side of Ryan's neck as he worked him. "I know you've been worried but I wanted to show you it could be good again. I thought these things might help." His fingers gripped Ryan even harder and he gasped. Mango chuckled in his ear as he licked the middle and Ryan moaned loudly. He loved having his ears tongued.

"You feel perfect," Mango whispered as he found Ryan's lips.

He could hardly breathe. The greedy mouth on his and the hands around his cock were causing a meltdown. He felt the start of his orgasm build, the familiar prickling of his skin, the tingling in his balls as they hardened and he got ready to unleash their wrath.

As Mango's tongue slicked with his, Ryan came. He gave a guttural cry as he freed his mouth from Mango's, who was still holding tight to his dick and pushing his sweating body down against it in a gesture of possession.

"Jesus," Ryan panted as his balls emptied themselves in whatever the fuck he had around his dick. "I think I like those eggs."

Mango gave a sly grin as he brushed Ryan's curls away from his sweating face. "Each one has a different texture inside. I thought we could practice on each other, find our own personal favourites. You can do me next time. I planned on finishing the box tonight." He drew the now sticky item gently off Ryan's cock and pushed it back into the bottom half of the egg container.

Ryan gasped. "You are such a pervert. I don't think I can come again."

Mango leaned down and gave a lazy smile. "Oh you will, I promise."

When the box was empty in the early hours of the morning, Ryan was thrilled to admit Mango had been right.

Chapter 9

Club Delish was noisy, packed to the rafters and buzzing. Ryan fucking loved it. Loved seeing all these people who'd come to his club for a special fund-raising benefit for one of the brain tumour charities he'd been in touch with over the previous months.

He was also enjoying the fact he got to be Delilah again for a while. Ryan sashayed across the stage to where Laverne Debussy-Smith waited, a white parasol open and held above her head. As both of them were Mistresses of Ceremonies, they were taking turns announcing the celebrity line-up of people appearing. Mimes, drag queens, comedians, musicians—they were all there.

"Darlings, may I have your attention please?" Ryan called out to the excited audience who were still buzzing, no doubt, because folk singer Lacey Drew had been performing. Lacey was a phenomenal worldwide talent and Ryan was lucky to know her. Luckier still she'd had a hiatus in her schedule and could be here tonight.

The crowd continued being noisy and Ryan stalked to the front of the stage. He smoothed his hand down his one-of-a-kind Kai Morgan design. It was a sweeping ivory and gold organza, lace and sequins concoction, which was *so* his colour.

"Bitches, shut the fuck up," he screeched and the room quietened. Ryan fluttered his false eyelashes. "Thank you, darlings. My, but you people can make a ruckus. Like a herd of randy bulls chasing after a little virgin bull ready to be mounted." He pouted his richly made-up lips. "Make sure it isn't a bullock though, because that would be a fucking waste of energy. I like my men with dicks."

The room tittered and Ryan waved the closed parasol at them. "I said bullock, not bollocks, you dirty perverts. Now, my friend Laverne is going to introduce the next act. I'm not going to steal her thunder—oh fuck, who am I kidding, I'm *totally* going to steal the bitch's thunder."

Laverne gave a loud gasp and turned to look at the audience, then turned and raised her long, satin skirt, with some difficulty. She revealed a pert, lace-clad bottom to the audience with the words "Delilah loves dick" emblazoned across the arse. The crowd erupted in cheers and laugher as Laverne lowered the train on her dress and twirled her parasol cheekily.

Ryan carried on, trying not to laugh. They hadn't rehearsed that bit and it was unexpected. Trust Laverne to have something up her sleeve. Or under her dress. Laverne's boyfriend Brook Hunter stood in the front and he shook his head as his body shook with laughter at his boyfriend's antics. Mango and Kyle stood with him, wide smiles on their faces

"Tonight we have an incredibly talented band from Wales here to perform. Grunge at its best and guaranteed to get you up and dancing. Oh fuck, you're all standing already. Okay, then, bogey on down. Laverne, honey, over to you."

Ryan stepped back behind the curtains as Laverne announced the band called Metallic Grunge. He had to say Laverne rocked in her outfit. Another formfitting Kai creation of navy blue and cream tulle and silk, it puddled softly on the floor and showed off her fake boobs to perfection.

Ryan took one foot out of his high heel, rubbed it, stepped back into it and then did the same with the other. He'd been in the shoes most of the night, and he was glad the final act was now on. That meant he could soon change into something more comfortable, sit back and enjoy the rest of the night with his friends and Mango. Even Eric had made it in time to be there and Ryan was looking forward to sitting down at the table he'd reserved for them and to having a drink.

He grinned. Kyle had been given the night off, with one of the underlings in Ryan's entourage, Becky, taking over. Metallic Grunge finished their set and Laverne called Ryan back onto the stage to close the show. They preened and camped, then after a round of thunderous applause and catcalls, Ryan turned again to make his way back to the small dressing room in the rear. He stopped dead at Laverne's next words.

"And now—it's karaoke time!"

What the fuck?

Ryan watched in horror as Laverne waved an expansive hand, darting a mischievous glance in his direction. He stood frozen on stage trying, not to hyperventilate. His ex–fuck buddy and cross-dressing, traitorous arsehole of a friend Lenny was arranging karaoke—in *his* club.

"Tonight we have something special to end the evening with style. We have a karaoke event taking place—" Laverne shrieked as the room erupted with excited cries and there was a scrabble towards the stage. "Bitches, get back. This is not open to the public right now. Guys in front with big muscles, please stop the fucking hordes from descending. I'd hate to ruin my panty hose kicking them off this stage, because I swear I will."

The bouncers stood impassively in front of the stage and deterred the would-be singers. Laverne cooed down at them. "Thank you, darlings. If any of you have muscles bigger than nine inches, come see me backstage after the party."

Ryan saw Brook's broad shoulders shaking again and the look of affection he threw his lover. Huh, I wouldn't trust that bitch with a nine-inch dick, Ryan thought savagely. I'd beat her to death with it myself.

Kara-fucking-oke?

He strode over to Laverne, hoping his death glare would stop her plans.

"What the fuck are you doing?" he ground out from the side of his mouth as he smiled at the crowd. "Are you batshit crazy? Do you *want* to die by my hand?"

Laverne batted her eyelashes at him as she replied, "Nope. Go with me, baby. It's all in good fun, promise. And try not to burst a blood vessel. You've just had brain surgery after all."

Ryan was left gaping at Laverne as she traversed the stage calling out to the crowd.

"So, grab yourselves a drink or three while our guys set it all up, and I promise you, we'll have some fun when you get back. Spend, spend, spend, ladies, gents and whores, for later—we karaoke."

Laverne swished over to Ryan, took his arm in a firm grip and propelled him into the eaves of the stage. "Come on, before you kill me in full view of any witnesses."

Ryan was sputtering as Laverne manhandled him off stage.

"You can't—I don't know what the hell possessed you—" He stopped his diatribe as Mango stepped out in front of him.

Mango raised an eyebrow at Laverne. "He having a meltdown?"

Laverne chortled. "Oh chicken, and fucking how. Take him away, give him a blowjob. Calm him down before you know who gets up there. I'll change after you get His Majesty into his glad rags."

Laverne pushed Ryan into Mango's arms.

Mango chuckled loudly. "Come on, you. Let's get you all cleaned up and ready for the karaoke event." He drawled the word out. "You'll want to be all dressed up as you before it kicks off."

Ryan followed Mango into the dressing room. "I take it you knew about this," he said frostily. "You and Lenny hatch this up by yourselves? You know I detest fucking karaoke. Bunch of wannabe singers bawling out lyrics they don't have a clue about and making all my fond memories of the original artists disintegrate like fucking snow in the sun. I hate you both."

He stripped down as Mango watched and Ryan was still grumbling when he'd dressed in his black jeans and an emerald green button-down shirt. He began to clean his face.

"So what's the plan? Everybody jumps on my stage, makes a fool of themselves singing and we get to watch? Some fun that is—"

He was effectively shut up when Mango's mouth slanted over his in a kiss, which made Ryan's groin ache. For a moment Ryan forgot about the unauthorised use of his club for singing wannabes and concentrated on the feel of the tongue in his mouth and the hands clasping his arse.

When Mango released him, Ryan stared at him fiercely. "That was nice but I haven't forgiven you yet. Or my ex-arsehole-friend Lenny." He patted his face dry, applied moisturiser and looked across at Mango's amused face in resignation. "So when does the fun start?"

Mango cocked his head as a throbbing dance beat filled the air. He grinned widely. "Right about now. Listen."

Ryan scowled but shut up long enough to hear the voice singing one of his most loved tunes, "Some Kind of Awkward" by Callum Webster. Ryan stared at Mango in both confusion and wonder. "Okay. That guy is truly good. He sounds a lot like Callum." Ryan sniffed. "Of course he could never be as *good* as him."

He wondered why Mango turned away, his shoulders shaking, only to turn back and look as if he'd composed himself. Ryan was getting a little annoyed. He felt he was missing something and he didn't like it.

Mango grasped his hand. "Let's get out there." His voice was choked with laughter. "That'll explain things." He cast an appraising eye over Ryan. "You look sexy as hell, good enough to eat. You'll do."

And with those cryptic words, Ryan was pulled out of the dressing room and through the short corridor to the stage.

The lighting was low, the audience strangely enrapt as the young man standing with the microphone attached to the karaoke machine crooned into its silver depths. His wiry frame was dressed all in black, the Goth look he sported similar to Callum Webster's own. Long black hair spiralled down his back.

Then the young man turned to stare at Ryan with a grin on his pale and entrancing face and Ryan lost his breath.

He swung round to question Mango, whose face was filled with affection and pride. "Fuck me," Ryan whispered in awe. His legs were wobbly. "That *is* Callum Webster. What the hell is he doing in my club?"

Mango wrapped an arm around Ryan's shoulder, a good thing since he might fall to his knees in shock.

"Believe it or not, he knows Kyle. They met in Vegas apparently." Mango winked. "There's some story there, I think. And we all know about your damn man crush on the guy, so we decided to ask him to come here. Callum was only too pleased, apparently he owes Kyle."

"But, he's *here*. In my club." Ryan grew agitated. "Singing on Lenny's stupid karaoke machine. He must think we're a bunch of backwards hicks. We need to get him some proper equipment, he can't do justice to his voice on that stupid fucking thing." Ryan was ready to throw a major hissy fit.

"Ryan, take a deep breath." Mango stifled a chuckle and patted Ryan's back as if he were burping a baby. "Callum knew this was all a bit of a hoax to make you think we were opening the floor to everyone. He thought it was hilarious and he said he could sing without any backing or anything. I think he called it an 'unplugged session.'"

Mango framed Ryan's face in his hands. "Listen to Callum. He sounds awesome. Enjoy your surprise."

Ryan nodded, still shell-shocked. Mango laughed softly and wrapped his arms around Ryan, pulling him back into his chest and enfolding him in a warm, and comforting embrace. Ryan relaxed and watched as the singer he worshiped sang a haunting melody of lost love on *his* stage, in *his* club.

He thought this had to be the most perfect moment he'd ever experienced.

That perfect moment was eclipsed when he got to meet Callum and fangirled like a bitch.

The words, "Oh my God, I love your music," and "You have to tell me how to get my eyes like yours," had spewed forth in a hysterical moment of sheer fandom. Mango hadn't been able to suppress his guffaws.

After Callum's impromptu performance, they all sat at the private table in the exclusive area reserved for VIPs.

Ryan made sure he was next to Callum, with Mango on his other side. He was glad to see Eric talking to Kyle, although the atmosphere didn't seem as warm as he'd hoped. Actually, it seemed a little strained. He made a mental note to speak to one of them and find out what was wrong.

Lenny and Brook sat opposite. Lenny leaned over and nudged Kyle who was shuffling a set of cards lazily in nimble fingers. "Look at him," Lenny said mockingly, gesturing to Ryan. "He looks like a fifteen-year-old girl who saw Bieber naked."

"Fuck off," Ryan said mildly. He grinned at Kyle who did some fancy trick with the cards so they ended up spread in a perfect arc across the table.

Kyle snorted with amusement. "Truth," he murmured. "The man has a serious fanboy crush. I mean, have you seen his Spotify account? It's chock-full of Callum's stuff."

Ryan flushed and tried to deflect the conversation. "You have to tell me how you managed to get Callum here. I mean, however the hell it happened, thanks to you both. This has been an awesome surprise."

Kyle smiled. "No worries." He glanced at Callum. "We met in Vegas at a show and we've kept in touch." His tone was guarded though and Callum looked a little uneasy too. Ryan wondered what their story was. "Callum was happy to help me out."

"I owed him a favour," Callum said. "He saved my bacon once at the card tables. But honestly, it's been a hoot being here. Your club is awesome."

Ryan was happy to have the chance to talk to Callum. The twenty-year-old teen sensation was a charmer and intelligent too. He and Ryan had even spent twenty minutes earnestly debating the value of dating apps and condoms and it had turned into quite an informative discussion. Ryan had slyly mentioned the benefit of Tenga Eggs and Callum's eyes had lit up with interest. Ryan wasn't sure whether he could let him leave—ever. He wondered idly how Mango would feel about adding a third to their relationship.

Mango was smirking into his beer, his eyes on Ryan and Callum. He quirked an eyebrow at Ryan and Ryan blew him a kiss.

In truth, there wasn't anyone else for him but Mango. Callum was cute but Mango was tough, sexy, possessive and everything Ryan wanted in a man. Yeah, he loved the bastard.

The music was pumping in the main club and his feet were itching to dance. It had been a while since he and Mango had gotten down and dirty on the dance floor. Ryan wanted to grind himself against his lover, get him all hot and bothered—then later he thought he might fuck Mango's brains out for a change.

And when "Filthy Sinners" from DJ Kyree started playing, Ryan knew this was one song he wanted to dance to.

He stood. "Dance time," he said to Callum. "Need to get my sex machine over there on the floor."

Ryan danced over to Mango and held out a hand. "Time to par-tay." He swivelled his hips and thrust his pelvis into Mango's face. "Come on. You're with me."

Mango stood, took Ryan's hand and followed him onto the dance floor. Ryan ripped off his shirt and threw it at one of the bouncers. He knew they'd look after it for him.

Bare chested, he began dancing, gyrating and raising his arms. He loved getting lost in the music, feeling the push and shove of sweaty, half-naked bodies around him, interspersed with the occasional boob and crotch of the women who seemed to frequent gay clubs nowadays. He didn't care—a patron was a patron.

Mango smiled sultrily and lost his shirt too. He threw it into the crowd and before Ryan knew it, he was being swung around with Mango behind him and a rock hard cock was prodding his arse in time to the music.

Ryan reached back, wrapping his arms around Mango's neck as his mouth sought a filthy, open-mouthed kiss. There was nothing but the beat of the music, the feel of Mango's body against his, the heady feeling of being alive and the knowledge the man currently ravaging his mouth was his.

Ryan opened his eyes to see Callum nearby, sandwiched between two men. He certainly seemed to be enjoying himself, if the tongue and hands roaming his lithe body were anything to go by. It was one hell of a turn-on.

"You are so enjoying seeing him get off," Mango whispered as he bit Ryan's ear. "Save some of it for me, will you?"

Ryan turned around and pulled Mango's face down. He laid his forehead against Mango's. "I'll always be yours," he promised. "Love you. Going to take you to bed later and make sure you know it."

Mango's eyes flared with heat. "You'd better."

On the other side of the dance floor, Ryan saw Lenny and Brook dancing together, both bare chested and, if he wasn't mistaken, Brook's trousers were open and Lenny's hand was somewhere down there.

The two people he didn't see were Kyle or Eric but with Mango's hand currently sliding its way down Ryan's now unzipped jeans and caressing the crease of his backside, Ryan wasn't going to worry about those two grown men. There was time enough to bring them together if that's what they wanted.

This was what it was all about: Mango, the love of his life. His best friends. His club. And, most important of all, his life.

Ryan closed his eyes and gave into the rush of endorphins flooding his body, the happiness he felt right at this minute as his senses overflowed and he lost himself in the now. He was awed at having his cute and sexy man-crush dancing next to him and the knowledge that the love of his life and his friends had conspired to make a dream come true especially for him.

Ryan was home in every sense of the word. And he had every intention of staying there.

***

Norway in winter at Christmastime was magical. Magical in a fucking cold, white-out, ball-freezing way. Mango shivered as he stood up from making snow angels and gazed down at Ryan, who was still splaying his arms and legs out in an abandon of sheer enjoyment. Puffs of white snow rose in the cold, crisp air and Mango blinked through frosted eyelids. He clutched his thick, damp windcheater tighter round his body.

"I think it's time to go inside, get warm by the fire and drink a bottle of bourbon," Mango managed to get out between chattering teeth. "And maybe do very dirty things to each other on the rug in front of a roaring fire. I'm just saying."

Ryan laughed loudly and the sound warmed Mango, even as it reverberated in the empty expanse of flat, sleek snow around them. He eyed the mountain warily, ever vigilant for avalanches. Ryan had a tendency to be fairly vocal in, well, everything and during one of their lovemaking marathons, Mango had thought they'd be covered by a thick sheet of ice sliding from the mountain as Ryan screamed out in his orgasm. Mango had an irrational fear of someone one day finding their frozen, obscenely intertwined bodies under a layer of snow, displayed in the height of sexual congress. Perhaps even being put on show like the volcano hardened bodies of Vesuvius.

"But I'm having fun." Ryan pouted, his lips blue from the cold. His green woollen beanie held his hair in but an auburn curl escaped and lay red against the snow. "You're horny again."

He resembled a sexy native Norwegian, dressed in a specially purchased sweater and duffle coat, teamed with warm mountain pants, which showcased his slim legs.

Mango appeared to have a permanent hard-on around Ryan this holiday. In the last six months since his surgery, Ryan's bubbly and infectious personality had reasserted itself and Mango had never seen him so happy. He had been fortunate to get time away from his new position as Lecturer in Ecology and Global Change at United University London. Luckily his boss, Professor George Spencer was a bit of a romantic at heart and his husband, Mark, a slim Chinese man with silver hair, concurred. Mango had found them both charming and very much in love after thirty years together.

This round ribbon trip, ending in Flam, in the heart of Norwegian fjord country, had been Mango's gift to Ryan, a promise made good from the darker days when Ryan had been ill. The two-week trip had begun in Oslo, made its way to Kirkenes and the Snowhotel, then Bergen and now Flam was the last leg of their trip before venturing home in four days' time.

Both men had marvelled at their one-night stay in the Snowhotel—one night was all Mango could afford—but both of them agreed their log cabin in the idyllic village of Flam was their favourite. It was private, luxurious, and riding the snowmobiles was as fun as hell.

Mango inclined his head with a grin. "I'm always damn horny around you. You're like this damned drug I have to keep taking. Come on, babe, let's go indoors." He waggled his eyebrows. "I'll make it worth your while, promise."

"Oh well." Ryan stopped his rolling around and flashed Mango a wicked grin. "When you put it that way…"

He leapt nimbly to his feet and as he did, something shot forward from his right arm and smacked Mango in the face. Mango spluttered as snow filled his mouth and began drifting down his cheeks.

"You little bastard," he roared as he chased a chuckling Ryan across the snow towards the cabin. Ryan *kept* catching him out with the fucking snowballs. "I'm going to pound you so hard when I get you. You won't be able to sit down."

Ryan's cackle of laughter was lost as he ran into the cabin. Mango got there before Ryan could shut the door and lock it. He planted his heavy booted foot in the entrance and smirked as Ryan backed away, a look of mock terror on his face.

"Oh please, Mr Rugged Mountain Man, please pound my arse so I don't do it again. Then I promise I'll be a good boy." The twinkle in Ryan's eyes and the smirk on his face belied his words. He edged closer to the fire and began to remove his coat.

"Yeah?" Mango came into the cabin, relishing the heat from the roaring fire they'd started shortly before they went out to play. "I don't think I believe you. I might have to do it a few times to make sure." He began to take his layers off, the heat from the fire beginning to make him sweat. Or it could be the thought of what he was about to do Ryan -he couldn't be sure.

Ryan's tongue came out and he licked his lips. "So come and get it."

He threw his coat down on the comfy couch and took off his sweater. Beneath it he wore only a white FCUK tee shirt, which rode up over his back and belly, revealing pale skin. He slipped out of his trousers and turned to hold his hands out to the fire, revealing a taut backside in a pair of tight yellow CK briefs.

Mango's mouth was dry but he had no problem shrugging out of everything he wore until he was naked. His dick was upright, bobbing against his stomach as he prowled towards Ryan, who was still facing away.

He adjusted the solid heavy-duty fireguard in front of the open fire. The intensity was immediately stifled but remained warm enough to heat the room for a little while.

"Otherwise it's too hot for you to lean over," Mango murmured. "Stand on the hearth and put your hands on the mantelpiece. I'm going to take you from behind like this."

Ryan's body shuddered and Mango knew he was as turned on by the idea as Mango was. Ryan stood on the raised hearth and placed his hands on the wooden mantelpiece.

Mango smiled in satisfaction. He'd scoped out the fireplace earlier, logistics-wise, and Ryan was now exactly the right height for what he had in mind.

Mango slid Ryan's underwear down to his feet. Ryan's cock sprung free. "Stand back a bit and spread your legs," he whispered into Ryan's ear. "Then wait for me."

He saw Ryan swallow, a convulsive motion that made Mango's cock harden more.

"Look at you, all splayed out. You're so fucking sexy, Ry." Mango fetched the lube from one of their various hiding places. He pressed himself against Ryan's back, his leaking and swollen cock jutting against the cheek of Ryan's tight backside. "So goddamn beautiful and eager. And all mine."

A soft moan escaped Ryan's lips as he closed his eyes. Mango opened the lube and slid some onto his fingers. Then he slid two inside Ryan, who gasped at the fingers buried deep in his arse. Mango flexed them in the tight heat of Ryan's channel, finding the spot he wanted and then pushing against it.

Ryan made another low and needy sound as he pushed back onto Mango's fingers. "Fuck the finger play. I am so ready for you. Give me your cock."

Mango grinned against the soft skin of Ryan's back. Flames flickered behind the grate, warming the room and adding a soft light to their foreplay. Ryan's skin shone in the firelight, like golden toast, his scent capturing Mango's imagination as he breathed this lover's fragrance deeper.

Mango slid inside Ryan with the ease and practice borne of two men who knew each other's bodies and emotions. Ryan gave a guttural cry and clenched around Mango's cock.

"You and I, we fit so well together, Ry," Mango whispered as he kept up his steady thrusts and felt Ryan moving in time. His groin was aflame, not with the heat from the fire, but with love, passion and want. "Like fine ink in a pen. One needs the other to function, like us."

Mango wasn't given to poetic sayings but the words flowed from him as they shimmied and swayed together, their mutual sounds of desire muffled and breathless. This was like making love to the soft strains of a waltz, instead of their usual hot and sweaty tango.

Ryan reached back with one hand and pulled Mango's mouth to his in a wet, sloppy kiss, which melted Mango like a marshmallow.

Between Mango's rhythm inside Ryan's body and his hand around Ryan's slick cock, both men's releases were orchestrated to a fine tuning. Mango felt Ryan judder as he spent himself all over Mango's hand, and it only took a few more deep thrusts to bring him to his own climax. He buried his face in Ryan's neck as he came.

Mango couldn't move, so he collapsed against Ryan's back, breathing heavily.

Ryan murmured something, which Mango didn't hear.

"What?" he asked, his voice thick with sexual satiation. Mango didn't think he could go anywhere right now.

"I said my balls are boiling, we need to move." Ryan's voice held laughter and Mango winced as he pulled out of the tight, hot place he'd been so happy in.

Later they lay naked and curled together under a furry blanket, gazing drowsily into the now open flames of the restored fire. Ryan shifted and the movement took his warm body away. Mango murmured a protest.

Ryan chuckled. "Stop being so damn needy. I need to get something."

"What—have we got more bourbon somewhere?" Mango yawned as he watched Ryan clamber quickly from beneath the blanket and walk over to the antique writing desk under the picture window.

Ryan took something out and bounced back under the covers. He climbed onto Mango's lap, straddled his legs and stared down. The blanket bunched behind him in a heap, and all Mango could see was one gloriously naked man whose face was strangely unsure. Ryan was biting his bottom lip, a classic sign he was nervous about something. He cleared his throat and clutched something tightly behind his back.

"So, I know I've told you I love this trip and it's the best Christmas present ever. It was pretty much a surprise, so the thing I had planned, I had to rethink. But honestly, I can't think of anywhere else I'd rather be right now than here, to do this anyway, so I guess I'll just do it. And hope it doesn't blow up in my face. It's pretty fucking nerve-wracking. I'm naked and maybe I should have put some clothes on first. Isn't that how it's done in the movies?"

Mango stared at Ryan in both fascination and confusion as he rambled on. He sat up and frowned as he watched the emotion play across Ryan's face. "Are you okay? I know we had mind-blowing sex but you're acting a little weird."

Ryan swallowed. "I guess it's because I've never asked anyone to marry me before." He brought his hands into view and Mango saw nestled in them a small red velvet bag tied with gold cord.

Mango blinked as his heart raced faster. "What did you say?" His voice came out in a most uncommon squeak.

Ryan opened the bag with trembling hands. His blue eyes were wide and he was still biting his lip as he drew a deep breath. "I said, Manning Munroe, will you marry me? Be my husband one day?"

The ring Ryan held in his hand was stunning, old gold with a rose gold tint. It was simple and elegant, a typical Ryan classic. Mango became aware his jaw had dropped and he closed it. He couldn't find the words to tell the man in front of him what was in his heart. It was too full, aching with too much emotion and to top it off, something was blocking his throat.

Ryan stared down at him, the pulse in his throat throbbing madly. "I'm waiting," he finally said softly, a little uncertainly. "Is it too soon? Oh God, I've fucked this up, haven't I? You're probably not ready for this yet, I should have—"

Mango might not have found his voice but he'd found out how he wanted to tell Ryan yes, he'd marry him and how glad he was to be asked. His hands framed Ryan's anxious face and drew his mouth to his in a kiss and tried to convey his answer until he could find the right words.

He lost himself in the movement of Ryan's mouth against his, the hard heat of his lover's body as he pressed himself against Mango and the breathy sighs escaping both of their names as they devoured each other. It was a moment set in time, in the fjords of Norway, in a log cabin in the snow, which was home as long as Ryan was there with him. It would be a memory he treasured as long he lived.

Mango released Ryan's mouth and found the words. "Yes," he said breathlessly. "I'll marry you, Ry. I wouldn't ever want to marry anyone else. You're all I need."

Ryan's soft smile and the joy on his face made Mango's eyes all prickly and he blinked the tears away. "You're making me cry," Mango growled huskily. "I don't cry. Stop it."

Ryan snorted, Mango thought part in part relief, part happiness. "You big softy," he teased as his lips kissed each one of Mango's erratically blinking eyelids. "Hold out your hand."

Mango complied and Ryan slipped the ring on the fourth finger of Mango's left hand. It was slightly loose and Ryan tut-tutted. "It's the cold. Everything shrinks in the cold."

Mango grinned and wiggled his eyebrows. "Not everything."

The giggle from Ryan's lips was adorable. "Yeah, okay, I'll give you that one. I can feel the proof for myself." He shifted suggestively. Mango hissed and drew in a breath.

Ryan's eyes sparkled in the firelight as he drew out another ring from the bag and handed it over. "Better make it official, fiancé," he murmured. "So everyone knows I'm taken. That I'm yours."

Mango held the ring up and took Ryan's hand. "Oh, you're mine all right." He slid it onto Ryan's ring finger where it fitted perfectly. "You always have been. The same way I've always been yours."

As he drew Ryan's nubile and willing body down onto the rug before the fire, then covered them both with the blanket, Ryan sighed and reached his arms up to pull Mango on top of him.

"Lover, you'd better believe it." Ryan grinned wickedly and Mango couldn't remember anything else other than the feel of Ryan's skin against his as he was taken.

It was time to celebrate all their new beginnings.

SURVIVAL GAME

There can be no question about to whom this book needs to be dedicated. Having experienced their services firsthand, both for myself and for family members, the paramedics and ambulance drivers out there provide an invaluable service. One that is regrettably paid less than what these amazingly dedicated people are worth. All over the world, we've seen their work firsthand during many recent tragic events, and make no mistake, it's a tough career choice dealing day in and day out with injured, dying, and damaged people.

Let's give them their due, not only the ones on the ground, but the ones in the air, and if you can spare a few pennies, or your time and involvement, there are great causes to donate to, such as:

theairambulanceservice.org.uk
www.londonambulance.nhs.uk/getting_involved.aspx
www.theas.org.uk/what-we-do

AUTHOR'S NOTE

Any assumptions or errors in this book about the life of a paramedic, the procedures they use, the ambulance service or the way Las Vegas casinos are run, are my own and may have been adapted for fictional purposes.

ACKNOWLEDGMENTS

Bearing the dedication in mind, there is one single person who deserves this acknowledgement for helping this book get written. His name is Binder Smiff (not his real name), and he was an invaluable help to me on giving generously of his time and experiences as a genuine London Ambulance paramedic.

I found Binder when I was looking around the web for a paramedic blog to get some insight on what really goes on out there. I found this one and was hooked:

www.not-on-my-shift.org
Twitter @Binder999

It opened my eyes to everyday life and events in the London streets, and made me chuckle more than once. Irreverent, true, blunt, and compassionate.

He took time out to write me reams of emails (and boy, they were detailed) on how things get done, to give me the insight I needed and to teach me about the real life out there as a paramedic. While I haven't written overly much about the clinical processes in this story, Binder's help focused me on what NOT to say or assume, and that was equally as important.

Read his blog; you won't be disappointed. He recently coined a phrase with respect to his job and remembering the people he's helped, lost, and continues to help while he carries on learning his trade and from his mistakes: *Remember well and never dwell.*

SPECIAL THANKS to my brilliant editor Michelle Klayman at Boroughs. As always, she tells it straight and makes me write a better book. She is my rock.

And to the readers of my books, thank you from the bottom of my heart. Without you, I'd be truly lost. Every one of you is treasured by me, and never doubt it.

SURVIVAL GAME

Chapter One

Some sounds a man never forgets. It could be his newborn child drawing their first breath, or the whispered exhale of a lover as they climax. It could be the first bars of a song at his wedding or a round of applause at his first big casino win.

Some sounds needed to be forgotten. The slap of a fist hitting flesh; the wheeze of breath as ribs shatter; the ringing in the ears from being hit over and over again.

Kyle Tripper wished he could forget the sounds of his past. Hearing them when sleeping was bad enough. He didn't need to be reminded when he was awake.

He sat in the cinema next to Steve, his blind date, hearing him munch through copious amounts of popcorn. On screen, a senseless and violent film played. The bile in Kyle's mouth soured the taste of the sweet Pepsi he'd just sipped.

He held his phone in his lap, trying to make sure its light didn't disturb people behind him as he texted.

This sucks, boss. My date is an arsehole. Making me watch Fistfight instead of Hackaway. FML.

He'd been looking forward to seeing the acclaimed drama about a group of misspent youths taking part in a corporate project to test corporate security.

Ryan Bishop, his friend and employer, was quick to text back.

Hey, Violet, make an excuse and get out of there. Didn't you have to wash your hair?:)

Kyle smirked at the nickname—courtesy of his purple hair and violet contacts—then winced as a man on screen screamed loudly in pain. The plot of *Fistfight* was nothing more than a badly directed effort at giving brawny men the excuse to beat each other senseless. He wasn't a fan. His hands shook a little when he texted his reply.

Yeah, I'm going to bail once we get out of here. He can forget dinner.

In return, Ryan provided a gif of a man running screaming down the street, together with a thumbs-up emoji and the words: **He gives you any trouble, call me. I'll send Mango along to sort him out.** An angry emoji ended the text.

Kyle was sure Ryan's partner would love to sort someone out. Everyone was wary of Mango Munroe and his fierce stare, and even more protective instincts.

Pushing the phone back into his jacket pocket, Kyle heaved a sigh. The one saving grace was that the film was almost over.

Ten minutes later, they were standing in the chilly early March evening air, huffing clouds of steam from cool lips.

"Wasn't that a great film?" Steve enthused as he huddled into his parka. "I love man-on-man fight action and car chases."

Kyle grimaced. "Not my thing," he muttered, shaken and morose from all the gratuitous on-screen violence. "I mean, come on. There's not much to a film like that, is there? Just some guys with their shirts off beating up on other guys." His dark mood deepened. He needed a drink, something to forget the sordid memories the film had stirred.

Steve shoved his arm playfully. "Come on, gorgeous. You mean all that testosterone and chest hair doesn't turn you on just a little bit? Leave you with a need to maybe get up close and personal with someone?"

Steve edged closer, his intent clear.

Kyle didn't want to be there on the street with a man who thought violence was a turn-on. He'd been down that road before. He wanted to go home to his flat a few blocks down from Club Delish—the nightclub where he worked—make hot chocolate, and crawl under a duvet, alone. The contacts in his eyes hurt, making them gritty and sore.

He shook his head, moving out of Steve's orbit. "I'm not feeling too well, actually. I think I'm going to skip your dinner offer and go home."

Steve stared at him, narrowing his eyes. "Honestly? You're going to leave me here with a boner and expect me to take care of it myself? Especially after paying for the film?"

The first trickling of unease danced across Kyle's spine like sly spider legs. He moved further away from Steve, regarding him warily.

"If I'd known the payment for being treated to a movie was taking care of your boner, I'd rather not have gone," he said quietly. "I didn't realise there was a quid pro quo for being company tonight."

My blind date just got fucking worse. Never again.

"Well, that's how the dating world normally works, Kyle." Steve moved closer, anger threading through his tone. Kyle's vision swam as his personal space was encroached. Panic fluttered in his chest, making his heart skip beats.

"Don't crowd me, Steve," Kyle warned. "Can't we just say we didn't agree on the film choice and leave it at that? I don't want to go home on a bad note."

Steve gripped his arm, his mouth twisting in a smirk. "Maybe just a kiss then?" he wheedled, as Kyle's heart thudded madly. "Or a quick blowjob? I bet those beautiful lips of yours know just how to make a man happy. Your lips and my cock— that's a match." Steve leaned in, and instinctively Kyle raised his arm and pushed back on Steve's hard chest.

"N-no," he stuttered. "I'm not kidding. Don't touch me."

Don't touch me, don't touch me, he chanted in his head. *Not with that fire in your eyes and that aggression in your belly. No dark touches, please.*

Kyle wasn't averse to being touched under the right circumstances. What he feared were those touches he thought of as *the dark*. Hardened, insidious fists pummelling into an already aching belly, rough kicks to ribs and face when he was curled up on the floor; pinches to skin already marked with scratches and bruises. Then there were the more intimate ones, the ones Kyle tried not to think about—rough, punitive sex meant to break him.

Steve's hold tightened. "Fuck that," he snarled. "I at least deserve a goodnight kiss."

Kyle was pushed back against the wall and a greedy, wet mouth invaded his own. He tried to keep his lips pressed together, not wanting to give Steve the satisfaction of gaining access. Steve was determined, though, and within seconds a hot, slick tongue was forced into Kyle's mouth.

Please, please, don't do this. Please.

Stomach roiling in fear, he tried again to push Steve away, memories of being forced taking over and blanking out his brain. Bile rose in his throat, and with a touch of hysteria creeping in, he wondered what Steve would do if Kyle vomited into his hungry mouth.

In a weird twist of fate, it was a homophobic bastard walking down the street that saved him from any further mauling.

"Get a fucking room, you faggots," the man yelled.

Steve let go, his lips releasing Kyle's bruised mouth, then he turned and raised a middle finger at the man on the other side of the street. "Fuck you," he yelled. "Fuck off, you wanker."

Kyle seized his opportunity. Within seconds, he was running back down the street as Steve and the Neanderthal traded insults. Kyle's legs pumped like a sprinter's as fear of being caught threatened to overtake him; his deep, rasping breaths were a staccato accompaniment to the sound of his heavy footsteps on the pavement.

His focus was on getting home. Then, maybe, once safe, he could forget about tonight. Forget he'd made another bad decision, that he was a loser when it came to dating.

He thanked God his instinct for self-preservation had included not giving Steve his home address or number.

As Kyle ran past Club Delish, he glimpsed a light on in the flat above the club. Although tempted, he wasn't going to disturb his friends at this hour. Not the best way to pay back Ryan's offering Mango as backup.

When Kyle reached the relative safety of his building, he ran up the stairs to the fourth floor, not even waiting to get the rickety, ancient lift that wheezed from floor to floor as if on its last legs.

It was only when he was at home, locks bolted and security chain slung across the door that he began to relax. He poured himself a favourite drink, a shot glass of white rum, and gulped it back while he waited for his hands to stop shaking.

"Fuck," he swore as he filled the glass again. "I need to stop this blind date shit. It sucks."

He tossed the second shot down then another before he dragged himself into his bedroom. Bed was a good place to be, even though it wasn't even midnight. Being a night owl, used to working 'til the early morning hours, his body clock wouldn't like this early-to-bed scenario.

Well, tonight his body clock could get stuffed. Sometimes knocking yourself out was the only way to forget the past.

Chapter Two

At seven in the morning, Kyle emerged from his bed tired and headachy. Even after three shots of rum, he hadn't slept well. Memories of the past had chased him in his sleep.

Staring at the bathroom mirror, he grimaced at the dark circles under his eyes, which were bloodshot and swollen. He swore softly. No contacts today then. His trademark deep violet would have to be forgotten. Instead, everyone would have to bear the muddy-brown eyes he was born with.

He'd feel naked without his favourite fashion accessory. He didn't need them—he had virtually perfect vision—but liked the cloaking they seemed to afford him. Eyes behind tiny pieces of coloured hydrogel hid emotions he didn't want seen.

He peered closer into the mirror and winced.

Crap. Even guy-liner might be off the cards today. With the amount of rubbing he would no doubt be doing to alleviate his sore eyes, he'd end up looking like a manic panda.

Thank God it was Monday and he had the day off. Not for the first time he was grateful Club Delish was closed Sundays and Mondays.

"Fuck my life," he said gloomily as he stared into the bathroom mirror. "I really thought Steve might be different. But, no. Once again, I go out with an arsehole and once again I end up alone."

My dick really needs to see some action. It's forgotten how to work.

He pulled his boxers away from his hips and stared down at his groin. Yep, his dick was still there, looking sad with only a smidgen of morning wood nestled in a patch of dark bristles.

Kyle sighed. He needed to man-scape again but right now, he couldn't be bothered. No one was going to see it anyway.

He brushed his fingers over his nipple rings, hissing at the sensation flooding through him. It was a sorry confession to make, but this action was the closest thing to hands on his body for over a month—well, apart from the occasional jackoff.

"I am so pathetic," he groaned. "Jesus, what I'd give—" He clamped his lips together instinctively at his blasphemy. For a split second, he expected the rolling punch of a fist against his cheek, followed by other things he preferred not to think about.

His gut tightened in both panic and relief. Those days were over; he could say what he liked now, use God, or whomever as many times as he liked without penance. The strange thing was, he hardly ever did. His will had been moulded—no, hammered into submission.

After showering, dressing and savouring a cup of coffee— not pods, his boss Ryan had introduced him to the pleasures of a mouth-watering Italian drip blend—he was ready to face the day. Sitting down on the couch, he looked at his telly viewing options, his mood darkening when he saw the offerings.

He could watch more *Banshee*, but pulled a face as he toyed with the remote. Given his dry spell, he wasn't really in the mood to watch Lucas Hood nail yet another willing lady. The guy had the stamina and sex drive of a rabid rabbit.

He did appreciate the nude scenes, though. Watching Lucas's tight arse pistoning in and out of someone—he tried to ignore the fact he was basically watching soft het porn—led to fantasies that it was his arse Lucas was pounding.

Okay. No telly. Kyle could play cards. Forty Thieves was his patience game of choice. He could practise his shuffling skills, which, he had to say, were awesome, but it was never a bad idea to keep them fresh. The casino he'd worked at mostly had automatic card shufflers to get the job done, but an old and wizened casino dealer had taught Kyle the art of the manual shuffle.

When things had gotten past bad with his ex, Kyle used shuffling to occupy his mind—as long as his fingers hadn't been bruised or cut, or at worst, broken.

No. No cards. Perhaps he could watch *Banshee* and jerk off watching Lucas pound flesh. The very fact he'd considered that idea made him groan loudly.

Fuck, how sad am I?

He contented himself with eating half a tub of Ben and Jerry's Rocky Road ice cream for breakfast because he thought the title suited his life. Then he relented and watched Lucas Hood bang yet another bird, ignoring the twinge of jealousy he felt for the woman.

Bloody hell. That man can sure move his hips.

Two hours later, satiated with a morning wank and feeling sick from the ice cream, he was ready to face the day. He cleaned himself up and threw the now empty ice cream carton in the bin, breathing out a guilty sigh as he did. He checked his phone and was thrilled to find a missed call from his best friend Lucinda Drake, whom he'd last seen over a year ago. He grinned with joy when he heard the message delivered in Luce's nasal New York accent.

"Hey jackass, stop wanking off to hot guys and call me back pronto. I'm back in town unexpectedly and thought we could get together for a late brunch and catch up. Talk ta ya later, London."

Shit, she knows me too damn well.

His spirits rose. It was just like Luce to simply turn up as if no time had passed between them, and surprise him. A late brunch sounded like a plan, perhaps at Jackson and Rye. They made the best avocado Florentine eggs he'd ever tasted. He sighed as he dialled her back.

He couldn't recall a time when Luce hadn't called him London. When they'd worked together at The Bohemian Club in Las Vegas, she'd got this crazy idea that London was the be-all of England. He'd been hard-pressed to tell her that there were other great cities.

Luce answered his return call on the fourth ring. "Hey, London Calling. How you doin'?"

Kyle rolled his eyes, wondering if his profile picture was still the same on Luce's phone. It had been one of him, inebriated after a night out, smiling stupidly next to a red Royal Mail telephone box, with the display name of *London Calling*. They'd both found it doubled-over funny at the time.

"I'm good. Better for knowing you're in town. You didn't give me any warning you were coming over though. Is everything okay?"

He and Luce had worked together for years at The Bohemian Club and become firm friends. Luce still worked there and had a crazy, hectic work schedule that had her travelling around the U.S. to the different casinos that club owned. Her job as a slot operations manager involved a huge amount of what Kyle had thought was boring, mundane work—looking at reports and doing a lot of corporate management stuff involving complex mathematics. He'd rather have poked his eyes out with a stick than do that every day.

She gave a loud laugh. "It was a bit all of a sudden. They offered me a position as VP of gaming, but I like what I do, and I didn't see myself licking ass all day like that job would have required me to. They weren't too happy about it. We had a bit of a spat, and when I said I'd go work for the competition, they quickly backtracked and let me be. Since they were nervous I would bolt, I managed to wangle two months off. I'm pretty beat. They owe me like a year of holiday anyway. I got in two days ago and, obviously, I had to call you once the jet lag settled and I caught up on some sleep. So here I am, London, and I'm all yours."

Kyle chuckled. "Only you could be offered a promotion, turn it down and still end up on the winning team on a two-month timeout abroad."

"Yeah, well," she replied wryly. "I had to see my favourite guy and find out how he's doing. I miss you. Skype and Facebook is fine but it doesn't replace honest to goodness face-to-face contact."

He bit back the lump in his throat. "Yeah, I miss you too."

Luce had been his rock during the turbulent and destructive relationship with his ex-boyfriend, dancer Mario Alves. Not only had she saved Kyle's life, her love and support had been instrumental in helping him out of the abusive relationship he'd seemed mired in. He owed her his sanity.

"So, are we doing this whole brunch thing then?" he teased, already wondering what he should wear and whether he'd be able to manage all the interpersonal contacts he'd encounter when he went out in public. "Is Jackson's okay, say about midday?"

She gave a sultry chuckle. "London, that sounds good to me. I'll see you there. Oh, by the way, look for the chick with blue hair."

She rang off before he could say anything else. He grinned as he put down his phone. She had a thing for changing her hair colour like she did her garish, slogan-inspired tee shirts. The last time he'd seen her she'd been a redhead—as in her hair was fire-engine red. She was a flaming beacon on the casino floor when they'd worked together.

With his mood lightened, Kyle sped into the bathroom, took another shower—because the spunk-smell he sported wasn't quite his cologne of the day choice—and dressed into his favourite pair of Firetrap Blackseal Biker jeans. Teamed with a tight-fitting white tee-shirt under a casual grey chambray long-sleeve shirt, Kyle figured he looked good enough to venture out.

He thought if he didn't drink too much, he might go into the club afterward and finish off a few little jobs he had to do on his list.

He hummed to himself as he picked up his keys, checked he had his wallet and shut the door behind him. The day was suddenly looking a lot brighter.

Chapter Three

Eric Kirby drew a deep, shuddering breath and turned his attention to the unholy mess in front of him. The stench of burnt tyres, blood and fuel pushed at his senses as if to say, "You'd better hurry up. Time is short."

He wanted to snarl that he fucking knew time was short.

Only three months into the year and already I'm wishing for things to get better.

He crouched down under a streetlight and held onto the limp hand of a woman who had whispered her name was Sarah, and who was trapped in the wreckage of what had once been a family sedan. He muttered soothing words to Sarah, whose glazed eyes stared up at him in panic and fear. There was resignation there too.

Damn it. He wasn't going to let that emotion defeat the young woman who lay crushed under a mountain of steel.

The firefighters were on their way; he heard the sirens in the distance.

"Not long now." He smiled reassuringly into Sarah's blue eyes. She stared up at him, a mixture of hope and fear swirling in her gaze. "Can you hear that? It's the fire engine on its way to get you out. You hold on, Sarah. Can you do that for me?"

Sarah's eyes fluttered closed briefly but she nodded. Her hand gripped his tighter. "It's my son's birthday celebration this afternoon," she whispered. "Will I still be able to go?"

He had no doubt this woman wouldn't be going anywhere anytime soon. She had a broken leg, a piece of steel in her side, a badly bruised sternum from the deployed air bag, and she probably had internal injuries he couldn't ascertain.

"How old is he today?" he asked, stroking Sarah's hand softly.

A faint smile lit the pale face of the injured woman. "He'll be twelve. We planned dinner at his favourite restaurant." Tears trickled down her face and her face grimaced in pain. "I'm never going to see him again, am I?"

Eric schooled his face to the comforting look that seemed to help victims. Sarah had lost a lot of blood, and while he'd patched her up as best he could, she needed to go to hospital.

"I've stopped the bleeding for now—and listen." His voice rose as the fire engine came into view, screeching to a halt in front of the mangled metal wreck that had been a VW Passat. "Here are the firemen. They'll get you out, and then we'll check you again and get you to the hospital. They'll call your family and let them know what happened. I'm sure you'll be seeing your son in no time at all."

He made to stand up, to get out the way for the firemen to do their job, and Sarah's eyes widened.

"Don't leave me please," she begged. Her fingers held onto his tightly.

Eric motioned towards the men coming his way then bent to speak to Sarah. "I need to get out of the way, let the other guys do their job." The firemen were there now, waiting expectantly, armed with the tools of their trade. "I won't be far. You'll be fine in their hands. I'll see you afterward, and I'll get you all prepped up for the ambulance ride, 'kay?"

He stood up and met the eyes of his crewmate, Aaron, who regarded him with compassion as he mouthed, "You got this one, partner."

Eric nodded tiredly and moved out the way as he turned his hand to its side to smooth hair away from his sweaty, grimy forehead. His neoprene gloves were coated with blood from where he'd tried to staunch the bleeding from pieces of steel embedded in his patient's side and leg. He peeled the gloves off and threw them into the disposal bin in the back of the ambulance.

I'm not sure how much longer I can do this.

Aaron patted him on the shoulder. "Looks like they're getting her out okay," he muttered as they watched the firemen at work. Aaron's round face was weary, dirt coating his forehead and cheeks. He ran a hand through his bristled dark hair. "Poor woman's having a fucking rough day. That arsehole who sideswiped her ought to be locked up." He scowled at the man sitting pale and dejected on the side of the road, surrounded by medical personnel and police alike.

"According to eyewitnesses, the guy was on his phone and didn't see the traffic light was red. Damn, I wish people would understand that it's times like these"—Aaron waved a hand at the scene playing out before them—"that just brings home the whole 'don't check your mobile phone when you're driving because you could kill someone' warnings."

Eric nodded in agreement. "Yep. It's just not worth it." He rubbed his eyes, sudden fatigue stealing through him. "Hopefully the fire department won't be too long getting her out." He squinted through tired eyes at the firemen as the car door pulled away with a screech of metal. He shuddered. He'd never get used to hearing that sound. It went right through him.

Aaron sighed heavily. "No problem. I'm going to check the truck again, see that everything's good for her ride to the hospital. I'll be with you in a sec to load our patient onto the stretcher." He left Eric standing there, watching as the firemen secured the vehicle. After what seemed like a lifetime, one of them raised a hand and waved Eric over.

"She's good to go," the blond-haired guy called out.

Any other time, Eric might have quite fancied getting down and dirty with him. The guy was a cutie. But now, covered once again with someone else's blood, tired to his core and wanting nothing more than to finish the hell-shift and get home to slouch on the couch, he didn't have the energy to worry about what his dick might think.

Before long, his patient was prepped, ready to be taken to the hospital. Together he and Aaron loaded the now semi-conscious woman into the ambulance. Within minutes, Aaron at the wheel, and Eric in the back with their patient, they were speeding their way to the nearest Accident and Emergency centre.

After wheeling Sarah into the A and E ward, and assuring her she was in good hands, they cleaned up the truck as best as they could before the next call out.

There was a young woman who vomited her guts up from drinking too much. Next was an old man suffering from stomach gas who thought it was a heart attack.

Shift finally over, Eric and Aaron travelled back to the Shoreditch station. Both paramedics were permanently stationed there, called having a "line," which was highly sought after. Eric was pleased he and Aaron didn't have to move between stations anymore.

"Can I just say I'm glad you were the attending on this one?" Aaron said with a grimace. "I couldn't face paperwork and reports right now. Honest, I'm so damn tired I couldn't even find my dick to pee."

Eric laughed tiredly. "Me too. I hate paperwork, but some poor sap's got to do it."

"I'll stay and help you if you want, after we clean the truck up." Aaron's grudging response made Eric smile. He knew if he accepted the offer, Aaron would stay. But Aaron had other responsibilities.

"Nah, you get off. Your grandma will be looking forward to seeing you. God forbid I

should detain you from your regular dinner visit. She'll circumcise me herself."

Aaron laughed loudly. "Now there's a thought." He visited his grandmother often to check on her health, often with Eric in tow. He liked Aaron's spitfire of a grandmother, and the feeling was mutual.

"She'll probably force-feed you matzo ball soup and freshly made challah." Eric's mouth watered at the thought of food prepared by Aaron's bubbie, Norma. Eric had eaten there many a time, enjoying the warm yet biting sarcasm of the spry seventy-five-year-old.

With his own family living in another county, he loved the old woman as much as Aaron did. And despite Norma's overprotectiveness and constant belabouring to bring a young man round to meet her, she felt the same about him.

"Yeah, in between her telling me to find a good Jewish woman and settle down to give her great-grandkids," Aaron grumbled as he navigated into the parking garage.

Eric chuckled and they fell silent as they parked the truck. *At least we don't have to restock*, he thought tiredly.

There was a company that came in to replenish the vehicle with what the next team would need for the following shift.

He backslapped an exhausted Aaron. "Come on. Let's get Betty cleaned up and then we can blow this joint."

Betty was the affectionate name for any truck they manned, named after Betty Rizzo from Grease, whom Aaron adored. Eric had been more into Danny himself.

Aaron grinned. "Yeah, let's do it." He looked at his watch. "Shit, it's eight am. A twelve—make that thirteen—hour shift never seemed so long. Thank God we're both off now for a couple of days." He patted Eric on the back.

"Grab your mop, partner. I'll get the bucket."

An hour later, the two tired men laid down their gear and smiled at each other in exhaustion.

"See you in forty-eight hours, buddy." Aaron rolled what were obviously aching shoulders. "I think I might just sleep it away."

"See you, mate. Enjoy your time off." Eric gave Aaron a bro hug then watched him walk away. He heaved a deep sigh and walked into the small, crowded office to finish his paperwork. He thought sleeping in most of today had a good ring to it. Then perhaps later tonight he'd go by and see if his friend Ryan Bishop wanted to go for a drink.

Truth be told, Ryan hadn't been looking so good lately. Normally a bundle of energy, the man seemed to have something on his mind. Perhaps tonight might be the night Eric got to drag it out of him.

He grinned to himself as he powered up the computer. Of course, if Ryan's partner Mango was back in town from eco-warrioring, Eric might not be welcomed. Mango had a streak of jealousy a mile long when it came to him. It was no doubt a remnant of the days Eric and Ryan had tried dating but it hadn't worked out. Ryan had still been too crazy in love with his burly eco-warrior.

Still, there was a silver lining. Perhaps that cute, sexy manager at the club, Kyle, would be there tonight.

The last time Eric had seen Kyle, he'd seemed quite taken with him as well. The young man's beautifully coloured eyes had drifted over in his direction more than once during the conversation.

"Unfortunately, assuming he is gay and interested, a paramedic and a nightclub manager isn't the best match," Eric muttered to himself as he titled his head from side to side, trying to ease the kinks out of his neck. "Chances are we'd never get any time together with the hours we work. Fucking government cutbacks."

He finished his report and powered down the computer. Time to go home, sleep, and then see what the night brought. Assuming when he woke up he still had the energy.

Chapter Four

"Sooo…" Lucinda Drake reached over and stole the last two remaining scallops from Kyle's plate. His indignant "Oi" didn't seem to hold much sway as she popped them both into her mouth. "No new beau on the scene then? No sexy piece of ass in the picture?"

He snorted as he picked around the remaining lettuce on his plate. "Not bloody likely. The blind date I had last night turned out to be a real creep. I have this knack of choosing the wrong people." He didn't want to tell the full extent of what had happened or he'd be subjected to Luce's sympathies and probably be hauled in between scented lady bosoms.

She ran a perfectly manicured hand through her hair. The polished red tips clashed with the strands of bright electric-blue hair that swung down to her shoulders. "Baby, don't say that. You'll find the right guy one day. Just have to pick the truffles out of the pig swill first."

He made a face. "Ugh. Way to go with that analogy. I feel sick right now."

He knew he wasn't the most discerning of people when it came to relationships—thoughts of his ex sent cold chills through him—but surely, he had to get a break sometime.

He wanted to find a man who was warm and funny, and didn't use his fists as a solution to everything. Someone who wouldn't break Kyle and leave him bleeding and ashamed on the floor.

His insides churned and he closed his eyes, thankful that piece of his life was over.

"London? You okay?" Lucinda reached over and covered his hand with her own. "Your hands are freezing. Where did you go right then, or don't I want to know?"

He blinked. "I just closed my eyes for a second."

Lucinda's compassionate gaze washed over him. "You were gone almost a minute; you didn't hear a word I said." Her stare darkened. "London, you have to talk to someone about this. God knows it's been a long time but it's obvious you're still stressing about it. You told me you were going to see someone."

Shit. Here come the bosoms.

His defences went up like solid steel gates. He picked his napkin off his lap and wiped his mouth. "Luce, I told you, I'm fine. I don't need a therapist."

I don't need to relive my life as a puppet, telling some stranger I was a willing, idiotic marionette who didn't have the guts to leave a psychopath. I don't need anyone else knowing how spineless I was.

She leaned back, green eyes sparking emerald fire. "I know you think you deserved it, that you were gutless, but that's not true. People with abusive partners get into this rut—"

He threw down his fancy napkin. "Can we leave this alone please? You didn't come five thousand miles to rehash my past. I want to have fun while you're here, not be browbeaten into submission." He chanced a weak grin. "Been there, done that."

Lucinda gazed at him then exhaled and nodded. "Fine. You want to move onto more sappy subjects, how's that boss of yours? And the nightclub? You still enjoying it there?"

He nodded, grateful to be back to less hurtful memories. "I love it. It's hard work, long hours, and you need the patience of a saint, but it's great. Ryan is a cool boss, his partner Mango is scary on the outside but a kitten at heart, and I get to run the club the way I see fit when Ryan isn't there. Which isn't often. The man's a sucker for work."

"Have you met anyone you'd be interested in working there?" Lucinda asked curiously. "I mean it is a gay club."

Kyle remembered a man dressed in a paramedic's uniform with bright green eyes, chestnut hair and brawny arms. "There was this hunky guy I met a while ago called Eric. He's a paramedic who attended a heart attack incident we had in the club. He's a friend of Ryan's. I think they dated once but it didn't work out."

"And? You interested in him?" Lucinda leaned forward, eyes bright with interest.

He shrugged. "I don't really know that much about him. We didn't get much time to talk when he was there last. He was on his way out with Ryan. He's really yummy though."

And how he'd envied Ryan that night he spent with Eric. He'd seemed like a truly nice bloke.

"So call him. Ask him out. What have you got to lose?" She motioned the waiter over to bring the bill. "Grab that bull by the horns, babe. Maybe we can double date and I can find a nice girl to bring with me. We can hang out, shoot the breeze and have some fun together."

He took the bill the waiter had brought over, only to have it plucked from his hands by scarlet-tipped fingers.

"Mine," she said with a steely eyed glare. "You don't get to pay this one. Don't even argue or I'll shove a Tampax down your throat."

He gaped. "What? That's disgusting. Why would you even say something like that to me in public?"

She gave a wicked grin. "Because talking about lady things was always one way to shut you up. Remember that time we got stoned and we had a whole discussion about vaginas and what we lesbians like to call them? I think the best one was bearded—"

He hurried to press his finger to Lucinda's wicked mouth. "Please, don't say it. You can pay the damn bill."

She smirked and opened her purse to take out her credit card. "You can leave the tip if you like. Don't think I didn't notice you ogling that waiter's groin earlier. He certainly wears tight well. I could see every cock ridge he had to offer."

Kyle groaned. "Dear God, can you keep quiet for a minute before they kick us out of here for all the sex speak?"

She waggled her eyebrows at him. "Then we get to not pay the bill. Win-win all the way."

The bill was duly paid—he winced at the price of a fancy lunch for two in a Covent Garden restaurant—and before long they were standing on the pavement in the cool evening air.

Lucinda wrapped her bright green faux-fur parka around her. "So, what are your plans for tonight then? I'm going over to see my sister and her kids in Edgeware. You're welcome to come along."

He tried to hold back his horror at that suggestion. Lucinda's sister Maggie was a brash, noisy woman with a heart of gold and three rambunctious and rowdy spoilt children. He'd only visited them once before and that had been enough.

"No, sorry, can't make it. I'm going into work to finish off some chores. It'll give me a head start tomorrow—we have a fancy function on at lunchtime. I'll take a rain check."

Lucinda pounced on him and, as expected, he was smothered with warm, female flesh under silk.

"Great to see you, London. We're gonna be doing this bonding thing a lot while I'm here." She released him and he found he could now breathe.

"Sounds good to me. Thanks for lunch. I'll give you a call tomorrow and we can set up another date? Maybe we can go to a West End show. I know you always wanted to see *Wicked*. Perhaps Ryan can get us some cheap tickets. He's got connections in the theatre business."

Her eyes lit up. "Oh yeah, that would be awesome. I'd love to see that show. Call me tomorrow then and let me know what's happening. Lovely to see you, babe. Love you loads, you know that."

She planted a perfumed kiss on his cheek then left with a waft of expensive scent. She clambered into her taxi and Kyle waved as it sped off.

He looked at his watch. Time to do a little work then figure out what he was going to do for the rest of the night.

Around six pm Kyle let himself into the club. He shook his head when he saw the light burning under Ryan's door. His boss always seemed to be working, even when the club was closed.

He huffed. *He* couldn't talk, being here on his day off too.

Bloody hell, we're both losers.

"Boss?" He knocked on Ryan's door, waited a while then tapped again. Sounds emanated from inside the room, so he knew someone was there. He opened the door and walked in. "I thought I'd come in, do the line cleaning, stock some barrels and get everything ready for—"

He stopped short at seeing Ryan on his knees, enthusiastically blowing Mango, who leaned back against the desk with a beatific look upon his face.

Oh shit, I take back my thought about Ryan being a loser.

Suppressing his laughter, Kyle backed out of the door. Maybe they hadn't noticed him.

"What the fuck?" Mango snarled, his voice strangled. "Ry, you in the habit of just letting anyone walk into your office like that? What the hell happened to knocking first?"

He hauled his lover to his feet and then tucked himself away, his face red. Ryan licked his lips and smirked at Kyle.

"Well, hello there," he murmured. "This is a surprise."

"I did knock," Kyle said, trying to keep his amusement at bay. "Twice. Obviously the two of you were preoccupied."

"Yeah, and the club is closed, so no one should be here." Mango hauled his arse up onto the desk. "Ry, talk to your staff," Mango whined. "Tell them they can't just barge in when you and I are having our happy times."

Kyle broke into chuckles at Mango's petulant tone. "Sorry. I didn't mean to *barge* in."

Ryan sauntered over to him looking like a cat who'd got the cream. Kyle was sure he'd interrupted them before *that* happened though. "Ignore Grumpy Puss over there. He's just mad he didn't get to finish. I'll help him out with it in a moment. So, you managed to ditch that douche of a date last night then?"

Kyle couldn't help shuddering. "Yeah, I did. Won't be seeing him again."

Ryan's eyes softened. "You seem out of sorts about it. Anything I need to know?" His tone had an edge to it and Kyle had no doubt that if he so wanted, Ryan and Mango would deal further with the unpleasant Steve.

"No, I left him there, went home and crawled into bed. Nothing to report, boss."

"Hmm." Ryan didn't seem convinced. "Okay. What are you doing here now?"

"I just finished having a late lunch with Luce and rather than go home and eat ice cream again and watch other people getting off on telly, I thought I'd come by here and finish up a few things." He snorted. "I didn't expect to find a free porn show."

Mango raised his middle finger at him but grinned as he did so. Kyle had always found Mango's bark to be far worse than his bite, despite his carefully crafted reputation meant to scare people shitless.

Ever since Ryan had face-planted in the club a while ago, Mango had been a mother hen where Ryan was concerned.

Ryan frowned. "It's your day off, sweetz. You should be out there having fun, not stuck here working." He gave a wicked smile at Mango. "At least I was having fun even though I'm here. My boyfriend here decided he fancied a bit of boss-employee roleplay so we—"

Mango's face flushed. "Okay, Ry, way to tell the world about our sex life. Could we not do that please?" He squirmed uncomfortably.

Ryan chuckled and pressed a kiss to his cheek. "Such a shy boy, aren't you?" He batted his eyelashes. "Well, I know I'm new here, sir, so I don't like to presume, but could I please suck your cock again now? Mr Tripper was just leaving."

"Fuck, Ry…you are so bad." Mango's tone was husky and needy. He looked across at Kyle who was slowly backing out of the office.

"I'm going," he murmured. "You two have fun. See you tomorrow. Remember to breathe, boss." He winked at Mango saucily. He was waved out impatiently as Ryan got busy unbuttoning his lover's Levi's.

Kyle closed the door behind him and stood shaking with laughter—laughter tinged with a little envy and a lot of yearning. The pair had been through some turbulent times recently, what with Ryan breaking up with Mango then taking him back. But they appeared to be stronger than ever and it was clear to see the two men were besotted with each other.

I want that. I want someone to come home to who isn't going to make me lose my breath in fear. Someone who won't treat me like a personal punching bag.

Thoughts of his ex-boyfriend caused his heart to sputter even though the man was thousands of miles away. All Kyle had to see nowadays was the physique of a six-foot, black-haired and muscled man to send chills down his spine.

He was making a last-minute check that he'd put everything away when he felt the presence of someone behind him. An unknown man's cologne teased his nostrils. Heart hammering, Kyle turned swiftly, stepping back defensively. His movement triggered a pile of toilet rolls to go tumbling from the bar countertop to the floor. He'd been about to put them in the gents' loo before he left.

Kyle met the startled gaze of pale jade-green eyes in a tanned complexion, surrounded by short, deep auburn curls. Eric Kirby towered over Kyle by at least six inches and he felt intimidated by the broad shoulders and powerful body.

"Kyle? You okay? You've gone horribly pale." Eric moved toward Kyle, who stepped back again as he tried to get his panic under control.

"Hi, Eric—you surprised me, that's all. I was expecting anyone else. I mean, I'm just putting these away." He waved at the toilet rolls spread across the floor. "I'll pick them up now. No, don't you do it, it was my mistake…"

God, he has beautiful lips. I'd really like to kiss them one day.

"Don't be daft," Eric said, still seeming a little wary of Kyle's overreaction. "I'm sorry I scared you. The door was open and I saw you there, so thought I'd come on over and say hi before I went to see Ryan."

Kyle's gut churned. "You said the door was open? I thought I'd locked it." His hands shook as he piled another roll on the top of a growing mound. He bent down and picked up two errant toilet rolls and put them back on the bar counter.

Eric shook his head as he placed the last straggler on the top of the pile of pink rolls. "No, the keys were still in the lock too. I took them out." He handed over a set of keys. "Here you go."

Kyle stared down at them in bemusement. "I've never done that before. I always make sure I lock the door when we're alone in here and the club's shut. Shit."

Anyone could have walked in. Apparently last night's episode with Steve left me more rattled than I thought.

"Not a big deal. It's all good now." Eric cast a worried glance in Kyle's direction. "Are you sure you're feeling all right?"

"Yeah, I'm good. Thanks." He managed a smile. "Um, about seeing Ryan. I wouldn't go in there right now. He and Mango are kind of in the middle of something. I already interrupted them. I don't think they'd take kindly to another intrusion."

"Ah." Eric's grin lightened the room. "I get it. Well, I only came by to ask him if he wanted to go for a drink. If Mango's here, I guess they'll be busy for a while. Guess I should go then." Sighing, he turned to leave.

Kyle's spirits dropped. He could have done with a bit of a natter but he didn't want to risk Eric giving him the brush off.

With a deep breath, Kyle plastered a false smile on his face just as Eric turned around with a question in his green eyes.

"If you're on your own right now, perhaps you fancy coming for a drink with me?" Eric tilted his head. "There's a great little pub down the road called The Griffith. They make a mean plate of chips with an ale."

Kyle's smile went from false to real in a split second. "Really? Yeah, I guess I could—just wait a sec, will you? I need to put these away in the loo then I'll get my stuff and we can go."

Better freshen up first.

Kyle picked up the toilet roll pile and with arms full, he manoeuvred his way to the bathroom. He'd need to check on the special Deep Purple cloakroom to tidy up, but that could wait.

Once inside the loo, he dumped the supplies in the closet, ensured there was paper in each cubicle, and then retrieved his freshen-up kit from the locked medicine cabinet. He took out his toothbrush and toothpaste, cologne and antiperspirant, scrubbed his teeth 'til they gleamed and made lavish use of the toiletries before stuffing them back in the cabinet.

When he got to the front of the club Eric stood at the front desk, seemingly engrossed in a magazine. Kyle watched as Eric's large, blunt fingers flicked the papers.

Hmm, big hands…

Kyle smirked. In truth, he thought that to be an urban legend. He'd met guys with tiny hands and huge dicks, and guys with big hands, but you'd need an eyeglass to see what nestled between their legs. In Vegas, he'd even met a guy with three balls. One dick, unfortunately.

He cleared his throat and Eric turned around. His face lit up. "You ready to go, then?" He put the magazine down and grinned. "It's only five minutes down the street."

Kyle nodded as he collected his satchel and slid his arms into his faux Hugo Boss padded hoodie.

"That's fine. I could do with the exercise."

"You don't look like you need exercise," Eric murmured. "You look pretty fit to me."

Oh, he was flirting now, was he? This evening promised to be enjoyable.

The walk didn't take long and while they didn't say much weaving through streets teeming with people, it was a companionable silence. Before long they were settled in a quiet corner of the pub, enjoying the local ale.

Kyle may have been a top-notch mixologist and sought-after casino host in Vegas, but at heart he was a simple soul with a love for good beer and rum.

Eric sat back, legs akimbo, beer in hand and regarded Kyle lazily. "So, Ryan and Mango were getting it on when you walked in on them then?"

Kyle laughed. "Yep. Ry was delivering what looked like one helluva blowjob and Mango looked as if he wanted to deck me for interrupting."

Both men chuckled and took a sip of their drinks. Kyle looked at Eric questioningly. "So, tell me if I'm overstepping the mark. You and Ryan tried dating but it didn't work out? What happened?"

Eric shrugged, his long fingers wrapping around his beer bottle as he gestured toward Kyle. "Oh, you know. We thought there were sparks, but there weren't, and it turned out we were better off as friends. Ryan hadn't got over Mango, and, frankly, I thought it was a matter of time until they found their way back together." He grinned. "I'm glad I was right. Those guys deserve each other."

Kyle raised his bottle in a salute. "Amen to that."

He couldn't help noticing the line of Eric's throat as he drank. There was a certain spot—just there—that begged to be licked. Kyle saw himself leaning over the table and dragging his tongue up the stubbled throat then finding Eric's plump lips in a kiss that—

"Earth to Kyle." Eric regarded him with amusement. "Do I have something on my face?"

The warm flush that suffused Kyle wrapped around his body. "Erm, no, sorry. I was thinking of something else."

Eric raised an eyebrow, which Kyle found mouth-wateringly sexy. "Anything I should know about? I almost felt like you were getting ready to serve me up with a slice of lemon and eat me."

Kyle couldn't resist it. "I'd love to eat you," he murmured. "It's one of my favourite things to do."

Eric's eyes widened, and the look of lust that overtook his face left Kyle breathless.

"Oh yeah?" Eric shifted in his seat. "We'll have to try that one night. Now that you've offered, you can't take it back." He grinned and settled back in his chair. "I'm sure I could return the favour." His gaze smouldered as he stared into Kyle's eyes.

Kyle's arse clenched at the thought of Eric's tongue licking his hole, getting deep inside him. His cock was enjoying the idea too.

They were interrupted by their waitress, which probably was just as well. Kyle was sporting a hard-on that threatened to blow. She plunked down their plates of chips, asked if they wanted anything else, barely waited for their head-shakes, and then left.

Kyle lathered his in brown sauce, ignoring Eric's grimace, then popped a hot chip in his mouth and gave a deep groan. "Oh, that tastes good." He licked the sauce off his fingers, while watching Eric's face.

Eric shook his head, and gave a soft laugh. "I see what you're trying to do," he muttered. "God, you are such a tease."

Kyle smirked. "Well, thank you, kind sir. I do try."

Their conversation turned to football, politics and some animated discussion about who was the best James Bond when Eric asked a question that Kyle wasn't ready to answer.

"So, Ryan tells me you used to work in Vegas as a croupier? Must have been fantastic. Sounds glamorous. What made you come back to the UK?" His head was cocked to one side and his expression was one of true curiosity.

Shit, Eric, did you have to go there now? We were having such a good time.

Kyle gulped down the rest of his almost finished drink then shrugged. "I got tired of it all. It's a cutthroat business, and believe me, it looks like a beautiful lifestyle on the outside, but inside it's dirty as hell. Not everything shiny is good; sometimes it's just the dark tarnish that makes it look so inviting."

Especially when that dark tarnish is your ex-boyfriend.

Eric huffed. "Wow, profound. I get where you're coming from. Sometimes people say things like, 'It must feel wonderful saving people in your job.'" His tone was laced with bitterness, face shadowed, and for the first time, Kyle got a glimpse that there were demons lurking within Eric Kirby. "It's the *not* saving people that churns your gut and gives you nightmares." He looked at his plate for a moment then lifted his head with a strained smile. "Sorry. Didn't mean to put a downer on the evening."

Kyle waved a hand. "No problemo. We all have our crosses to bear." He reached around into his jacket pocket. "I did learn a few parlour tricks over there, though. Wanna see a card trick?"

Want misdirection at its best, and a great subject-changer? Always have a deck of cards in your pocket.

Eric nodded eagerly, the shadows disappearing from his eyes. "Fuck, yes. I love card games and tricks. There was this old geezer who used to sit outside the station house in Shoreditch where I work, and he could do this crazy thing with an egg and a pack of cards."

Kyle laughed. "Sounds fun. Mine doesn't have an egg but I hope you'll enjoy it anyway." He winked at Eric.

This would be fun.

As a casino dealer working in Vegas, he'd learnt a few tricks. At any given moment, he'd been expected to deal, pitch cards, move chips, sweep cards, check the players weren't cheating and pay out to the punters. Impressing Eric would be easy.

He started with a couple of easy tricks, like producing a royal flush one after the other.

Eric's eyes boggled. "How the hell do you do that? I thought the odds of dealing one of those was astronomical."

Kyle chuckled as Eric stared at him with disbelief. As did the few fascinated onlookers who watched avidly.

"The probability of receiving a royal flush is slim. I could deal twenty hands of poker every night of the year, and in eight to nine years you would hit one royal flush in the deal." He grinned wickedly. "It's all in the sleight of hands and making the audience focus elsewhere. We call it card manipulation. Here, look at this."

Deftly, he shuffled the deck of cards and dealt four onto the table. With a flip of his wrist, he turned each one over. Eric watched, mouth open, as Kyle revealed four aces. Then he gathered the cards together, shuffled and did it again.

During the parlour tricks, they'd both had a couple more drinks—bought by the clapping onlookers who were enjoying the show—and were fairly buzzed.

Kyle began a running commentary on the card facts he'd learnt over the years.

"Ever notice how the ace of spades always stands out in a deck of cards? There's a reason for that. Once European leaders saw that playing cards had become so popular, they decided there was an opportunity to levy taxes on a deck of cards. Typical, right? Levy tax on a game people enjoy." Kyle waved a hand airily. "The leeches put a stamp on the wrappings of playing cards. Of course, the wrappings got discarded, so to make certain the tax stuck, they decided to stamp one card in a deck to indicate the duty had been paid. In the eighteenth century, the ace of spades commonly received the stamp, probably because it lay on the top of every deck."

"Wow, that's fascinating." Eric watched as Kyle laid out a perfect arc of cards on the table. "You never think about cards having history."

Kyle nodded. "Most playing cards have a story behind them. The king of hearts was fashioned after King Charlemagne, the first Holy Roman Emperor. He was born around seven-forty-two and is the only king in the deck without a moustache, and he has a sword through his head. They used to call him the 'Suicide King.'"

"But how, I mean, you guessed every card I chose, and that thing you do with the royal flush, how do you even...?" Eric's voice trailed off in awe and Kyle basked in the pleasure of it.

"Oh, it's easy when you know how," he sniffed as he shuffled the deck adeptly, loving how it made Eric catch his breath. Practice made perfect after all. "It's all about speed, reading people, misdirection and having fingers the speed of light." He shuffled the cards dexterously then fanned the pile on the table.

Eric nudged his shoulder. "Show off," he muttered. "Do your cocktails taste as good as your mad card skills play?"

Imbued with a sense of confidence that he'd impressed Eric, Kyle threw caution to the wind and decided the flirting could escalate a little.

"Oh, my cock tastes just fine," he murmured, rejoicing at the sight of Eric's face pinking up and his eyes darkening. "Oh, *cocktails*, sorry, I must have misheard you."

If *that* didn't indicate he was interested in the gorgeous man sitting across from him with hunger in his eyes, with lips that were meant to be invaded by Kyle's tongue, then Eric was not the man Kyle thought he was.

Eric leaned over and brushed his fingers over Kyle's eyebrow piercing. It was new, to match the one in his left ear. He'd got rid of the nose piercing a while ago, deciding it was too much.

The feel of calloused fingers on his mouth made Kyle shiver with delight as his cock hardened in his jeans.

"Have you ever had a lip piercing or a tongue stud?" Eric asked as he slid his finger along Kyle's bare lip, gathering up the moisture there.

Kyle swallowed, his cock deflating, cold chills making a slow path down his spine. The memory of Mario trying to rip out Kyle's tongue piercing with his teeth played behind his eyes and he could hear. Mario's disgusted voice as if he were here in the room with them.

Wanton slut. You're a perversion in the sight of God. You tempt me and that's a sin.

"No," Kyle managed to say, as the images and sounds flickered in his head. "Not anymore."

Lip and tongue piercings are too easy to rip out, leaving shredded flesh behind.

Kyle moved back, away from Eric's fingers.

Disappointment and concern registered on Eric's face. "Hey, I hope I didn't step over any line," Eric sat back and drained his drink. "I don't want to spoil what's been a great night."

Kyle shuffled the deck, tidied them up and put them back in the box. He slipped his deck into his jacket pocket.

"It's not you. I just...have...some issues. I'm trying to leave them behind where they belong, but sometimes, it's not so easy, you know?"

Eric sighed heavily. "Looks like we both have our demons." He glanced at his watch, which was a big, masculine timepiece that suited his thick wrist. "It's late anyway. I should be going." He stood up and collected his sheepswool jacket from the back of the chair.

"Sorry," Kyle said wearily. "Way to end an evening." He stayed seated, looking down at the table, wondering whether he should have another drink before going home to his empty flat.

He was surprised when warm hands cupped his chin and forced his eyes upward. Eric regarded him with warmth and compassion. "Don't be sorry. I had fun." White teeth flashed then vanished. "I'm off again tomorrow then back to the grindstone. Shift work is a bit of a bitch to make social arrangements around, but I hope we can make some time to do this again. I know the nightclub life isn't conducive to the normal social thing either."

Kyle stood, having decided against a drink. "I get Sunday and Mondays off, and start work at three in the afternoon generally until close, which is around two am. Ryan's pretty chilled about working hours though. He's a great believer in the flexi-time approach." He pulled a small, tattered card out of his jeans pocket. "Here's a Club Delish card—it has my direct work number on it."

Kyle didn't give out his mobile number to anyone he hadn't known *forever*. He liked Eric but it was too early still to trust the man with something that personal.

"Excellent." Eric shrugged into his coat. "Here's my mobile number. Feel free to text me if you get some spare time." Obviously, Eric didn't suffer from the same reservations.

Kyle nodded. "Sure, will do. Thanks again for the company."

"Anytime." There was an awkward silence then Eric gestured toward the door. "I guess I should say cheerio and get off then."

"What, here? You have a kink for doing it in public?" Kyle was feeling better at the idea he hadn't been written off as being a loser.

"Well, that's for me to know and you to find out." Eric winked.

Kyle watched with a smile as Eric walked out of the pub.

Chapter Five

Walking down to the tube station, Eric felt what he'd said had somehow upset the balance of the relationship between him and Kyle. Well, not quite a relationship—he supposed he couldn't call it that after a couple of chance meetings and one night of drinks together. He certainly wanted to get to know Kyle better. The man was entertaining, sexy as hell with his lithe body, piercings and that eye-catching purple-black hair.

After Eric had brought up the tongue-piercing thing, Kyle had switched off and disappeared into himself. Some old memory had really rattled him.

Eric's mobile rung, and when he saw who it was, his mood lifted.

Deacon.

"Dekes, my man. What's happening? Chrissy kick you out and you need a place to stay for the night?"

His best friend's laugh echoed down the line. "Naw. You know my wife loves me too much to do that. She couldn't live without my hot, sexy bod in her bed for one night, could you, sweetheart?" There was the sound of a scuffle then Chrissy's laughter sounded in Eric's ear.

"Hey, Eric, don't listen to a word my husband says. And when he tells you why he's calling, please tell him no, like you usually do. The survival of our future child depends on it."

Deacon came back on the line sounding put out. "She has no faith in me, that woman. None at all."

Eric chuckled as he leaned against the wall of the tube station. "That's because she knows you. What hare-brained scheme have you found for us to invest in now?"

Deacon was an inveterate believer in weird and wonderful business ventures they could get involved in. The man was a dreamer and an idealist, the thing most people who knew him loved about him. One thing he was not, however, was able to realise when something novel or faddy was a bad idea. He was a successful garden designer in Torquay with green fingers and a top-notch clientele, so his business acumen was impressive.

Deacon ploughed on, enthusiasm growing as he spoke. "I was talking to a lady who has this magnificent greenhouse growing cucumbers. We got around to talking about how much waste there was when you slice the end of a cucumber and then it goes all soggy and you have to throw the whole thing away."

Standing there watching the stream of commuters on the London streets, Eric began to laugh, quietly so as not to offend his friend. He had a feeling he knew where this was going.

"So, I thought about making a cucumber topper, like a clip you could put on the end over the sliced part, to keep it fresh. You could even make them into all sorts of shapes, like cartoon characters, flowers, Christmas themed, that sort of thing. Chrissy thinks I'm crazy but I think it could be a really good idea."

Eric tried to muffle his amusement when he replied. "Well, sounds interesting. Except I'm sure someone tried pitching that on *Dragon's Den* and got laughed out of town. Something about, 'Why would someone buy that when all they need is a bit of tin foil or cling film to wrap around it? Or a plastic salad crisper.' Sorry, mate. I'm not sure there's a huge market for cucumber toppers."

That phrase had his imagination going and for a split second all he saw was Kyle, face down, arse in the air, with Eric behind him with a cucumber.

Now that sounds like something I could invest in.

Deacon huffed angrily. "Those wankers don't know a good idea if they saw it. Look how many ideas they've turned down and the person goes on to make a mint." His voice grew sulky. "I thought you were my best mate."

Eric chuckled. "It's *because* I'm your best mate and Chrissy is your long-suffering wife that we are the voice of reason when you go off on one of your fad phases. Someone has to keep you from spending all my godchild's money. How long does Chrissy have to go now before I get to meet him or her?" He knew any talk of their first child would take Deke's mind off investing in silly ideas.

"She's due in four months, so still a while to go." Yep. Deacon had turned all proud papa in an instant, cucumber toppers forgotten.

Eric felt a tinge of envy and sadness. He and Linc had talked about one day having a child of their own. He swallowed the unbidden picture of his boyfriend's smiling face and spoke quickly.

"Chrissy still feeling all right though, not sick anymore? You know you need to call me if you have any concerns, right?"

"Yes, Doctor. I'm aware you'll come running down here like a mother hen should we need you."

Eric grinned. "You do know I'm not a doctor, don't you? Just a paramedic."

"There's no such thing as 'just a paramedic'," Deacon growled down the phone. "If I'm ever in some sort of accident, you can bet your balls you'd be the one I want looking out for me."

"Yeah, yeah," Eric leaned away from the wall. He needed to get on the tube. "Anyway, I'm freezing my nuts off here outside the tube station. Can I call you back later when I get home?"

"Well, you can, but if you're not interested in my cucumber idea, then I'll have to find someone else to take your place." Deacon teased. "When I make a fortune, you can bet I'll be shoving my naked arse out of the limousine mooning you as I drive by—OW! Hell, Chrissy, those are my balls you're crushing. You need those to make more babies. Don't go man- handling them like that."

Eric winced in sympathy. "I'll leave you two to your marital discord. I'll give you a buzz later, Dekes. Losing signal now. Heading into the tube station."

The air roared with all the power the world could gather, and around him, earth crumbled and split into crevasses that loomed dark and never ending. Eric cried out in fear as Lincoln went sliding toward one of the dark abysses. He scrabbled desperately for something to hold onto, finding a rock, which barely met his fingertips.

"Linc, grab my hand and hold on." Eric lay sprawled across mounds of dust and rocks, cold snow seeping into his skin, which broke and bled as shards of the injured earth sliced into him. His arm was flung out toward his boyfriend; he was trying to grab Linc's hand to stop his slow but interminable slide into dirt and deathly white. All he could see was Linc's panicked, bruised and dirty face as he tried to reach out for Eric's hand to anchor himself.

"Come on, baby, you can do it. Grab my hand." Eric slid further into the crevasse, and behind him someone tugged at his hiking boots, strong hands wrapping around his ankles, grounding him.

"I got you, Eric," shouted his colleague, Anton.

"Not going to reach," Linc panted, looking as if his arms were wrenching out of their sockets with the agonising stretch to clasp Eric's fingers. "I'm too far down to reach up and I can't stop sliding. I'm losing my grip."

"Eric," Anton's anguished voice permeated through Eric's dread. "I'm losing you. I can't hold onto you much longer." The fingers around Eric's ankles were slipping. He was gradually making his own inexorable descent into the seething mass of dust and white powder below.

"I'm not letting him go," Eric screamed against the earth's roar. "You fucking hold on to me, you tosser. Don't let me go until I've got him."

Lincoln shook his head and smiled sadly. "We're not both going." Deep blue eyes gazed into Eric's with love and regret. "Time to save yourself. I love you, baby."

Eric awoke sprawled across his bed, body slick with sweat. His heart ached from loss as fresh as if it happened yesterday. And, for a while, he was right back in Nepal trying to save the love of his life.

He punched his pillow, sobs racking his body. "Fuck. Fuck."

It had been a while since he'd had that nightmare. It had been two and a half years since he'd lost Lincoln but grief had no respect for time. It lurked deep within, ready to strike at whim.

"Fucking triggers," he muttered as he stood and walked naked over to the window of his small mid-terrace house not far from Shoreditch ambulance services. "Sometimes I hate this job."

The daily stress of attending to people in trouble, injured, or even dead, had been steadily wearing him down since he got back from Nepal.

He'd been through therapy after his return—his boss had insisted on it—but he really didn't want to go back to it now. It'd been gut wrenching enough before.

His passion for his job had deflated—losing people on the job did that to you—but he still prided himself on being the best medic he could be. The trouble was he wasn't sure that was enough when his heart wasn't in it.

Eric made himself a cup of tea in his tiny, compact kitchen and sat in the dark, sipping while scrolling through his phone. It would take some time to get back to sleep so he might as well see what was going on in the world.

He couldn't help checking out Kyle's Facebook profile. Most of his public posts were articles about making cocktails, Club Delish, snippets about music he enjoyed —IAMX being one, a group Eric enjoyed too—but there was no personal profile picture of him, only a random image of a deck of cards. In fact, there appeared to be no photos of Kyle out at dinner, with friends and none of those abominable selfies Eric hated with a passion.

Curiouser and curiouser.

Kyle seemed to be a man who preferred to keep his identity a secret. Intrigued, Eric debated whether to send a friend request. His fingers hovered over the Send button. Kyle probably wouldn't see it until tomorrow anyway, and no pain, no gain.

Request sent.

Minutes later, much to his surprise, he got a notification that Kyle had accepted. Messenger showed him as online. Eric thought it would be rude to simply leave it there, so he messaged a simple *Hi. You're up late*.

The reply came back quickly. ***Couldn't sleep. You too?***

He smiled as he replied. ***Same. We're a right pair, aren't we?***

A smiley face came back. Not sure what to reply at four in the morning, he sent back a sleeping kitten emoji. ***Going to try get back to sleep now. Hope you do too.***

Kyle's response was a quick ***Will try. Thanks for the chat:)***

He laid his phone down and went back into his bedroom. He crawled under his duvet and lay back on his pillow, hands behind his head as he stared up at the ceiling.

"Miss you, Linc," he whispered softly into the darkness. "Gonna try to get back to sleep now. Please visit me and leave me good memories this time, will you?"

He shuffled about, punched his pillow into a comfortable nest for his head then lay down and closed his eyes.

It took him a long time to fall asleep.

Unfortunately, with a couple of his teammates calling in ill—one of them Aaron—and a horrific workload, it was impossible for Eric and Kyle to get together. Over the next couple of weeks, they texted short messages about the woe of their respective jobs and consoled themselves with silly gif wars and the occasional meme.

End of shift, he and the cleaning crew were under manpower pressure, with more needs than bodies to do the work. He figured it was a sign of things to come with the current government cutbacks and inspections. Just as he was restocking the truck, his personal mobile rang and he answered his phone with a smile. "Kyle, hey. This is a surprise—"

Out of breath, Kyle sounded panicked. "Eric, Ryan's passed out in his office. I heard this noise and came in to find him slumped over his desk. He's awake, but really out of it."

Eric's paramedic mode kicked in immediately. "Did you call nine-nine-nine? Is an ambulance on its way? I haven't heard anything via my station."

"Yes, I called them first. They're coming. They're only a few blocks away. I just wanted to tell you about it. Mango isn't here. He's abroad. I've told Ryan's bestie, Lenny, and he's going to try to track Mango down."

"Okay. Good. Chances are they'll take him to UCH. University College Hospital."

"I know what UCH stands for, Eric," Kyle said waspishly then let out a shuddering sigh. "Sorry, I'm in a state. I didn't mean to snap."

"Don't worry 'bout that. Just sort out stuff with Lenny, and let me know when they take Ryan in. Do you need to go to the hospital with him?"

Kyle heaved a deep breath. "I can't leave the club. We've got deliveries scheduled this afternoon and I'll catch shit from Ryan if I don't get it sorted. He wouldn't want the club to suffer. Lenny will go to the hospital with his boyfriend Brook. Lenny is Ryan's emergency contact anyway."

Eric didn't have time to wonder why Ryan's boyfriend wasn't down as his contact. "All right. Text me when the ambulance arrives, and I'll make a few calls to the hospital, see if I can find anything out once Ryan has been admitted. Don't worry, mate. I'm sure he's probably not been eating, or has low blood pressure or something. He's been a little off for a while now, but damned if anyone can get him to open up about it."

Kyle heaved a shuddering sigh. "Thanks. Okay. I've got to go. Lenny's on the other line. Hopefully he's got hold of Mango. Speak later."

The phone went dead and Eric swore. "Stupid, secretive arsehole, Ryan. I'm going to kick your backside when you're better."

Later that afternoon, when he had confirmation that Ryan was resting comfortably, Lenny and Brook by his side, and Mango was on his way home from Spain, Kyle texted: *Finished with deliveries. Club ready to open per usual.*

Eric messaged back: *Cool. Luckily Tuesday nights aren't that busy. Hope it goes ok.*

Kyle's reply was short. *Yeah, me too.*

Around ten that night, Eric walked into Club Delish to find it in full swing. He grinned wryly. Life carried on regardless of the owner being in hospital.

Determined to find Kyle, Eric manoeuvred through the writhing throng of half-naked, sweaty bodies, pouting drag queens, and men in various stages of grinding and sex play on the dance floor. He had a feeling he knew where to look.

Sure enough, Kyle was in Ryan's office, standing with arms folded across his chest as he stared out of the large observation window down at the mass below. Eric couldn't help but notice the strain of Kyle's shirt across his shoulders, sleeves rolled up the elbows. His pert arse filled out his well-fitting trousers, one foot tapping to the faint strains of the music floating up from below. His hair colour had changed once again since Eric had seen him last. It was still a deep dark purple but now featured lilac streaks at the tips, and artful splashes that looked casually painted in.

Eric knocked and cleared his throat, announcing himself, knowing Kyle was skittish. Startling the man was the last thing he wanted.

"Kyle?" He waited as Kyle turned swiftly and a look of relief passed over his face when he saw it was Eric.

"Hi. What are you doing here?" Kyle moved away from the window and smiled softly. "Can't keep away, huh?"

Eric walked into the room and laid his jacket on the chair. "I wanted to see how you were doing. And find out if there was any news about Ryan. I imagine things have been a little chaotic here today."

Kyle waved a black-fingernail-tipped hand. He had long fingers, and Eric had seen their dexterity first-hand when Kyle had done his card tricks. A fleeting flash of lust passed through Eric as he wondered what those fingers would feel like milking his cock.

He realised Kyle was talking and brought himself out of his fantasy.

"Not too bad. Rufus and Greg helped offload all the deliveries and get the paperwork done while I made sure the club was ready for opening. The bar needed restocking, like badly, so I gave Jim a hand with that too."

Rufus and Greg were the club's bouncers, both fond of Ryan and Kyle. The head bartender, Jim, was a six-foot muscleman, bald and scary looking, but soft as a pussycat—until you messed with him.

Ryan had a good crew working for him.

"You heard from Lenny?" Eric wandered closer to Kyle, and now saw the dark circles under his eyes and the pallor of his face. The man looked exhausted.

Kyle nodded. "Yeah, Lenny called, said Mango had arrived. I haven't heard anything since, but he said Ryan was fine for now. He sounded worried but I didn't push him. Apparently, Ryan's gonna need some surgery but he didn't elaborate. Ryan wanted to tell me about it himself." Kyle huffed. "I don't know how that's supposed to comfort me. Now I have these horrible thoughts about cancer, or brain tumours and shit. I mean this is Ryan we're talking about." He stopped suddenly and looked uncomfortable, as if he'd said too much.

Eric hadn't missed the tremor in Kyle's voice. Quietly, he asked, "Have you eaten today? Taken a break?"

Kyle closed his eyes momentarily. "I actually can't remember. Greg offered me a doughnut at some stage but I wasn't hungry. I think he said he'd put it down here somewhere for me for later." His eyes roamed the office, looking for the pastry. Eric chuckled and walked over to the desk. He moved a wad of paperwork to reveal a Krispy Kreme doughnut box.

"It's not exactly what I'd call sustenance, but it's sweet and better than nothing." He picked up the box and handed it to Kyle. "Eat. I'll make you a black coffee. Ryan's still got that fancy coffee maker here, hasn't he?"

Kyle swiped the box, opened it and stuffed the doughnut in his mouth. "Yeah, it's in the corner over there." The words were barely distinguishable as he chewed, and he gave a deep groan that immediately had Eric thinking he'd like to be the one that made Kyle groan that way.

"Oh my God, these things are decadent but they taste so good. I could never have another thing in my mouth other than this." He burped, and gave Eric an apologetic smile as he fiddled with the coffee machine. "Sorry, and ignore that last comment. There are some other things I'd like to have in my mouth." He laughed softly.

Eric was glad to see Kyle relaxing but his comment caused desire to flood Eric's body. Those lips wrapped around his cock? Now there was a scenario he could get on board with.

Down boy, he chastised himself. You're supposed to be giving moral support, not perving over everything he says. He brought a cup of black coffee over to Kyle, who took it gratefully.

"Ta." He took a gulp and made another one of those throaty moans. Eric shifted uncomfortably and sat down on the corner of the desk, hoping the bulge in his trousers didn't show too much.

"Was that the only one?" Kyle peered over his shoulder at the desktop. "Greg didn't surprise me with another?"

There were remnants of white, powdery sugar on Kyle's lips, and Eric couldn't resist. "You have something on your lips," he murmured. He ran his thumb across the dusting and watched as Kyle's eyes darkened. He looked wary but not afraid.

"I'd like to kiss you," Eric said softly. "I don't want to scare you though. So if you say no, I'll listen. You have my word."

Kyle's breathing hitched, then with a slow smile he nodded and pulled Eric's face down to his.

Eric gave a soft gasp as their lips touched. He licked the seam of Kyle's luscious lips and his tongue came out, taunting Eric's with warm, fragrant sweetness.

Eric reached out, pulling Kyle between his legs, cupping that firm arse in his hands. Kyle moaned and his kisses became frenzied.

God, he's devouring me, sucking me in.

When they drew apart, Kyle gave a low laugh. "Wow, I didn't expect that."

Eric stared into violet eyes that were languid and glazed. "You should have. That powder on your lips begged to be kissed off."

Kyle's hands, which had been on his shoulders, moved to encircle his neck. "I think I might still have a smidgen of it left."

This time it was Kyle that took the initiative, and before long, Eric's head was swimming in a frothy swirl of desire and need. Kyle rubbed Eric's groin, and fenced him in against the wall. Eric's cock was loving where things were heading and he worried that before long he'd be left with nothing but a sticky mess in his trousers.

Pulling his mouth away from a hungry Kyle, who really seemed to *love* kissing, he managed to gasp out. "Hang on. I need a breath before I blow my load right here."

Kyle's bruised, swollen mouth pouted and his dark eyes shadowed in satisfaction. "I could really make you come just from touching and kissing you?"

"My cock certainly thinks so. Maybe we should slow down."

God, what the fuck am I saying? I've finally gone gaga. But anyone could walk in on us.

Kyle grinned wickedly. "Where's the fun in that?" He reached down and unzipped Eric's jeans as his needy dick said a happy "Hello there" when it poked up from inside his tight briefs.

Kyle licked his lips and bent down, the tip of his tongue sliding along the soft foreskin, teasing Eric to the point of insanity.

"Oh my God." He leaned back on the desk, hands splayed behind him as he watched Kyle's bobbing head. The man sucked cock like he lived for it.

The heat of his mouth, the friction and the sensation of having his cock in that warm, wet mouth drew Eric to the edge. "Kyle, better get off. I'm going to come," he gasped desperately. His legs, buttocks and back tightened at the intense feeling of his impending orgasm.

Kyle looked up, mouth glistening and wet and smiled. "Come on me," he whispered. "Want to see you spurt your spunk all over me."

Eric couldn't hold back after that filthy request. His body shuddered and he watched through glazed eyes as Kyle shrugged off his shirt, revealing a slim, tight body with toned set of abs and a treasure trail of dark hair leading down to an obviously excited thick, long cock.

That sight was all Eric needed to push him to the point of no return. He gave a loud shout and his dick let out what he thought might be a record amount of come, shooting forth in thick white streams, all over Kyle's bare stomach and chest.

Spent yet turned on beyond measure, he slumped back on the desk.

Kyle chuckled. "That's one pretty debauched sight. You flat on your back with your dick sticking out of your trousers looking like you've just been well screwed." His fingers trailed through the wetness on his chest. He dipped his forefinger in Eric's come then slowly sucked off the spunk.

Eric was mesmerised. "Hell, that mouth of yours should be classified as a WMD. In many ways."

"Clean yourself off and zip yourself up, lover boy." Kyle motioned to the bathroom. "I need to check on the club."

Eric sat up, surprised. "You don't want me to get you off? I'm more than happy to return the favour."

Kyle shrugged. "I'm good. I'll sort myself later. I don't mind a little delayed gratification." He turned, bare-chested, and wandered over to the window, where he stood again, gazing down at the strobe lit dance floor.

Eric felt a little disappointed—he'd been looking forward to seeing up-close and in-person what Kyle packed in those trousers. But he did what he was told and went into the bathroom where he tucked himself away and cleaned himself up, then stared in the mirror. His hair was mussed, his lips red and swollen, but the glow of sexual satisfaction was unmistakeable.

Kyle came in behind him and chuckled. "You do look well fucked," he said slyly. He reached over and picked up a hand towel, wetting it under the tap then cleaning the spunk off his chest and stomach. Then he sauntered out into the office. Eric followed, watching as Kyle picked up his shirt and slid it over his head. Within seconds he was the seasoned yet sexy Nightclub Manager again.

Eric picked up a stapler and toyed with it. "So, I'm back on night shift again tomorrow, but maybe we can do something during the day, if you have any time off?"

Kyle nodded absently. "Sure. Let me see how things go with Ryan. I'll message you." He turned and flashed him a smile. "I'd like to see you again."

That is a relief. I really want to see him *again. I don't want this to be a one-hit wonder.*

"Me too. This…" He flapped a hand. "This was fun. And next time, it's my turn to see you get a happy ending, *capisce?*"

"*Capisce*," Kyle acquiesced, amusement in his eyes. "I'll hold you to that."

Eric picked up his jacket and swung it over his shoulder. "Just so you know. Me coming over here tonight—it wasn't for sex or a blowjob. It was because I was worried about you."

Kyle's face softened. "I know. I appreciate it." He moved forward and enveloped Eric in a brief hug that smelt of sex and cologne. "Get home safely and text me when you do. You never know who or what's lurking out there."

"Will do. And let me know about Ryan the minute you hear anything new. I'm worried about him."

"You got it." Kyle's face split in a yawn. "God, I can't wait to get out of here tonight. Only three hours to go." He made a moue of dissatisfaction. "I think I need some more coffee to keep me awake."

Eric took Kyle's movement toward the coffee machine as his cue to leave. "See you soon. Enjoy the rest of the night." He walked out the door to the sound of coffee beans grinding.

Chapter Six

"So, you got any plans to see that hunky paramedic of yours anytime soon?"

Kyle shook his head as he leaned back in his office chair, feet planted firmly on his desk. From the other side of the desk, Lucinda grinned at him as she sucked her iced coffee through a straw. The slurping sounds had been driving him mad for a while now as he tried to finish some Club Delish social media posts and design a promotion planned for a new drag queen event later in the month.

"No, he's been busy." Kyle scowled at the paperwork in front of him. "He's a workaholic, it looks like. Anyway, with Ryan being gone, things haven't exactly been quiet here either. I don't know how he does all the stuff he does, I really don't. He must be fucking Superman."

It had been a rough time for Ryan. As Kyle had feared, things were grave; Ryan had been diagnosed with a brain tumour. After all his posturing that he'd been fine, he hadn't been fine at all. He was home now, but next week he was scheduled to have surgery to remove the bloody thing.

Kyle was scared for his friend, but at the same time angry at Ryan for waiting so long to tell anyone about it. As for Mango— well, the man had been a saint since the diagnosis and Kyle had seen a side of him he'd never expected.

Lucinda gave a loud slurp.

He glared at her. "Really? Can you finish that damn thing already?"

"Ooh, someone's in a pissy mood." She gave one last loud saucy pop as she pulled her mouth off the straw and gestured toward the desk. "Anything I can help you with before you burst a blood vessel?" She stopped as the import of her words struck her. "God, sorry. That was insensitive. Bad form, you'd say. Sorry."

He leaned back in his chair, stretching. "Don't worry. He's in good hands. The operation's scheduled for next week. Mango made him take time off so they can spend it together. I hope it all goes well. It's no picnic having a brain tumour removed."

In truth, he was petrified for Ryan. The idea of his fun-loving, dapper boss and friend having his skull opened and doctors probing around in it? Um, yuck. He shuddered.

"Have you seen him recently? How's he doing?" Lucinda stood and walked around to where he sat. She threw the offending drink container and straw in the bin and perched her bum on the desk. "And more important, sweetz, how are *you* doing? Other than stressing out at work of course. I know Ryan means a lot to you."

"I'm fine. Worried about him, of course. I saw him on Monday. He came in to check how I was coping and that his club was still functioning. He wasn't here for long though." He smiled at the memory. "Mango kept glaring at him and telling him he wasn't supposed to be here at all. Apparently, there was some DIY Ryan wanted done." He snorted with laughter. "Not Mango's forte, I don't think. He's more the 'let's pick up the deadwood and make a bridge so we can save the tigers' type of guy." Kyle batted his eyelashes modestly. "He told me I was doing a great job looking after his club. I'm glad he trusts me."

Lucinda gave an unladylike snort. "Well, duh, sweetie. You're the best at what you do." She glanced down at the trash bin. "Shit. I'm out of coffee and I can't drink that foul stuff you make. I'm gonna run down and grab another. You want one?"

Kyle nodded. "Large mocha for me. None of that pretentious shit you order. Skinny cappuccino with an extra shot, dash of vanilla, extra steaming and a great dollop of *I don't give a fuck*." He smiled wickedly. "That last bit is the free ingredient you get from the hard- done-by barista."

Lucinda tossed her hair over her shoulder with a hand. "Don't get all bitchy with me just because you haven't been boned yet by your man in uniform." Her eyes widened. "Unless you and he have…you know." She made an obscene gesture with her hand and fingers.

He flushed. "Piss off. My sex life is out of bounds to you. I still remember the last time in Vegas when you did that Photoshopped video montage of me as an Easter bunny. Rabbits running from hole to hole? That was your crazy *right* there. I'd dread to think what you'd do if I gave you any details."

She cackled. "Oh yeah. I remember that. You're lucky I only sent it to your phone. I had almost convinced the guys to put it on the big screen in the private casino for your viewing."

He laughed with her, but he was also remembering the sense of relief he'd felt when he'd deleted the vid off his phone before Mario had seen it during one of his routine mobile phone inspections. That video could have cost Kyle a broken arm or leg, or worse.

Lucinda must have sensed his mood change because she put a soft, warm hand on his cheek. "That was before I knew about your situation at home. I felt so damn bad knowing I could have got you into trouble with that douchebag."

Lucinda refused to refer to Mario as anything else. She said he'd deserved to be objectified and the term suited him better than his name. Kyle had been curious and had gone online to research the name "Mario." In various languages, it represented being male, virile, bitter, the God of War and a hammer. He'd given a humourless laugh when he'd discovered that.

"Yeah, well. He's not around anymore. Now are you going to get us that coffee or not?"

Need to change this subject. I don't want to dredge up any more bad memories.

She stuck out her tongue. "Yes, my lord. Her ladyship shall tootle off without delay." Her eyes widened. "Tootle? I never say that. It's your English vernacular rubbing off on me, mate." Her attempt at an English accent made him cringe.

Picking up her bohemian-style shawl, she wrapped it around her shoulders and made her way to the door. "I'll pick us a couple of doughnuts too. Sprinkles for you?"

He nodded, his groin warming at the thought of what had happened the last time he'd eaten a doughnut. "Sounds good.

Now bugger off and leave me in peace for a minute. I have something to finish."

He watched fondly as she flounced out the door. He didn't know where he'd be without her. It was a pity her home was across the pond.

His mobile buzzed. He grinned when he saw the caller ID. Eric. "Hi there. How are things going?"

"They're good. Been working my arse off but got a few days off now." Eric sounded tired. "I have some family commitments. My sister's getting married tomorrow. She's in Somerset with my folks, so I'll be driving there in the morning. I have tonight free though, and I was chancing that we might be able to get together for a drink or something?"

Kyle's stomach gave a strange flutter. "I love the offer, but it's Friday night and the club will be packed. And with Ryan not being here…" His voice trailed off. "Sorry, but I doubt I'll escape long enough to take a pee, let alone have a drink."

Eric's sigh echoed down the phone. "I thought as much. This isn't going to be easy, is it?"

Kyle was confused. "What isn't going to be easy?"

"Getting to see you again." The smile in Eric's voice made those butterflies in Kyle's stomach speed up. "Our working lives are definitely not conducive to courting someone."

He swallowed. "Courting someone?"

He almost felt Eric's shrug. "Well, yeah," he replied. "Trying to at least." He laughed softly and Kyle's insides turned to mush.

God, that man sounds sexy. His laugh is like honey poured over a Belgian waffle. Sweet and decadent.

"I have the usual time off, Sunday and Monday. When do you get back from your family wedding?"

"I plan on leaving Sunday morning. My mum won't let me leave without feeding me a full English before I go. Dad will probably want to shoot the breeze about the latest developments in apple farming."

"Your folks have a farm?" Kyle was enchanted. He'd always lived in cities, even as a kid, and often yearned for a bit of outdoor space and greenery, complete with the requisite baby pig, lamb and, possibly, even a dog.

Eric chuckled. "Yeah, my dad grows apples and makes cider for some of the local markets. It's not a huge place, but it was a great place to grow up in." His tone grew fond. "Shelley—my sister who's getting married tomorrow—and I used to be run around the orchards, helping my dad pick the fruit. We'd eat a lot of it, and give ourselves tummy aches. Good times."

"Sounds great," Kyle said wistfully. "I've never been on a farm before."

"Never?" Eric said in surprise. "We can't have that. I'll have to take you down to see it one day. Meet the folks."

There was a long pause then Eric spoke again, sounding a little uncomfortable. "I mean, you know, as a friend. Not like to introduce you to the parents and declare undying love. Crap, I'm really digging myself a hole here, aren't I?"

Kyle laughed. "I get it. Don't worry. I'm not expecting a ring or anything. Visiting your farm would be cool."

"Good." Eric's relief was palpable. "Anyway, back to the whole date thing. I'm pretty sure I can wangle Monday off somehow. I have a colleague who owes me a favour. Perhaps we can meet for dinner somewhere, maybe that restaurant called Galileo's in Soho? Ryan says it's well worth a visit. Apparently, a lot of people he knows eat there and rave about it."

Kyle was interrupted from replying as Lucinda walked in. She held up his coffee and he nodded his thanks. She sat down in her spot and the slurping noises commenced. He shook his head at her in irritation. Her answer was to slurp louder.

Glaring at his friend, he realised he hadn't replied yet. "Yes, that sounds great. Are you sure it's open? A lot of restaurants close on Mondays."

"It's open," Eric assured him. "They're open all week round, I think. Shall we say seven-thirty?"

"Suits me fine," Kyle confirmed.

"Okay, see you Monday. I look forward to it." Eric rang off.

"You have a date then?" Lucinda asked around a mouthful of what looked like chocolate chip cookie. She nudged the white box over to him, indicating his doughnut inside. He sighed as he picked it up. "Yes. Sort of. Dinner at Galileo's."

Lucinda's eyes lit up. "Ooh, I've heard about that place. Didn't it just win a Glass Clove Award for the most promising venue of the year?"

"I have no idea. I don't read the gossip and social magazines like you do." He bit into his doughnut and gave a blissful moan. "God, this tastes good. Although it's going straight to my damn hips."

His friend stuck her middle finger up. "What damned hips? You're all lean and muscled. It's *my* hips you should be worrying about. I might have to buy two seats to fly back to the U.S. at the rate I'm eating these things." She gestured to her cookie. "I think I might be addicted to these peanut butter choc chip ones."

Kyle knew the feeling. If he didn't watch out, he may be in danger of getting addicted to the sexy stud muffin called Eric Kirby.

Saturday night at the club, Kyle was run off his feet. He'd been persuasive enough to coerce Lucinda into helping him. She'd assisted Jim getting the bar organised, and checked out the restrooms. She had refused to step foot in the hedonistic bathroom known as Deep Purple— Kyle had to face that one himself. Now, from the looks of it, she was entertaining the patrons. She was up on stage with Molly Luscious, one of the regular drag queen acts. Lucinda was dressed up as Charlie Chaplin, hat and cane at the ready, and she and Molly were no doubt trading insults and bitchiness.

He turned to fish out Ryan's secret whisky stash in his bottom desk drawer, opened it up and poured a shot, which Kyle tossed back like a boss.

Wow, that tastes surprisingly good. So smooth.

He took another swig then set the glass down on the desk.

Another two hours to go and he'd be on his way home. Lucinda was staying with him tonight as she planned on having brunch nearby with some friends in the morning. He'd be glad of her company. And he still had his dinner date with Eric to look forward to.

Kyle smiled dreamily. Eric was something else. He was warm and funny, and when he was around, Kyle felt safe. Cherished. It had been a long time since anyone had made him feel that way.

Still daydreaming about the man in his life, he turned and walked over to his office door, intending to walk down and check on how things were going with Rufus and Greg. As he opened the door, he was met with a wall of grey button-down shirt and black jeans. The man reeked of expensive bourbon. He stood there, hand held up as if to knock on his door. His face was flushed, looking truly pissed off. Kyle could feel the waves of anger coming off him.

A frisson of fear crept down his spine, and for a moment he was frozen on the spot. He cleared his throat, hand on the doorknob, ready to smash it closed should this guy be a threat of any kind.

"Can I help you?" Kyle enquired, trying to keep his voice even.

The stairs to the office were marked as "Private/No entry" but there was nothing stopping anyone coming up to see him. It happened all the time.

"I dunno, mate. Can you? Where is she?" the man slurred, taking a step forward. Kyle instinctively stepped back.

"Where is who?"

Man Mountain stepped forward. "My girlfriend, you tosser. She went out to use the bathroom and I haven't seen 'er since. Someone said she came up here."

"She's not here, mate. I haven't seen any ladies up here." He held up a hand, and pointed behind him. "Why don't we go downstairs, see if we can find her? Perhaps she's got lost or stepped out for a smoke."

"Nancy doesn't smoke, you twat." The man's eyes were red, his mouth a snarl, and Kyle tried to stave off the panic rising in his chest.

"Then perhaps she's in the bathroom." He swallowed as the man took another step toward him. There wasn't much saliva in his dry mouth.

Please God, don't let me find her lost in Deep Purple. I don't think Ryan could afford the trauma payments when she sues the club.

"I knew this was a mistake coming here. Gay clubs aren't for ladies like my Nance," the man spat. "Guys can tell a bird they're gay but be straight and get them to do all sorts, like show their tits off. I've seen it." He glared balefully at Kyle. "Have you seen 'em then? Nance's tits?"

"Sir, I can assure you no one has been up here and I most certainly haven't seen anyone's tits." He was finding it hard to breathe as the man pressed closer. The familiar tingle of fear spread from his insides to his extremities. "And I can assure you I have no desire to do so. I'm a real gay, not a pseudo one. Now can we go downstairs to try and find her?"

The man raised his fist menacingly and pushed Kyle back with his other meaty hand. "Not before I check this room, make sure she's not 'ere. Move over."

Kyle stood to one side as Man Mountain brushed roughly past him. He took a few deep breaths and willed his heart to slow down.

This isn't Mario. This is nothing like Mario. One, two, three....

He hoped someone had seen the man come upstairs and had followed to investigate. He wasn't the right size to fight a guy like this, and it wasn't as if he had any ninja skills or anything.

"Nancy, darlin', are you here? Come out, sweetie. I won't be angry, I promise," Man Mountain cooed as he searched the office. It didn't take long. The office wasn't big and apart from the small en-suite bathroom, there were no doors other than the one leading to the stairs.

Man Mountain's face grew darker as his search turned up nothing. He pivoted swiftly and punched the wall next to Kyle. His head swam as he ducked down, instinctively raising his arms in front of his face. His gut churned and he wanted to vomit. Plaster exploded in fragments, covering him with fine dust and shards.

Not the dark touch, please. Not again.

Kyle's vision swam and for one sickening moment Mario's voice echoed in his head.

You asked for it, you slut. It's your fault I'm like this. You've infected me with your body and those cow eyes. Bend over and get ready for a beating. God lets me punish sinners like you.

"I wasn't going to hit you, mate. No need to look so scared." Man Mountain's voice toned softened. When Kyle looked up he could see the guy was puzzled, as if he couldn't believe his behaviour could cause such a reaction.

Kyle wasn't taking chances. He scrabbled up, moving toward the door, and in his haste, his backside hit the desk, the corner sinking deep into the back of his buttock. The pain radiated down his leg and he gasped. "Shit, that hurts."

The guy's expression turned to concern and he shuffled towards him. "You okay, mate?"

Kyle managed to speak. Just. His buttock throbbed and he was coated with fear. "Yes. Go. Away. Your girlfriend isn't here. You can see that." He motioned desperately around him, hating that he felt so helpless. Useless. "Go downstairs and look for her. I'm sure if you look hard enough you'll find her."

Maybe she ran away from your sorry, bullying arse. I wouldn't blame her. That's what I did.

The guy looked confused for a second then his face cleared. "Yeah, she isn't here, is she? Whoever said she'd come up here must have been mistaken."

Give the gorilla a banana, Kyle thought viciously. Hell, give him a fucking bunch.

"No, she isn't. Now piss off."

The guy ambled to the door, looking shamefaced. "Sorry, mate," he said apologetically. "I wasn't goin' to hurt ya. Sometimes my temper gets the better of me."

You don't say.

Now that Kyle was feeling a little safer, his catty side couldn't resist a parting shot. "I'm sure you two deserve each other."

The guy nodded, a dreamy grin on his face. "We're getting married in September. She's gonna be Mrs. Lloyd Glasscock then." He smiled proudly.

Despite his recent panic, Kyle smothered a giggle of hysteria. He thought perhaps he might have to send a sympathy card to the unfortunate Nancy having a surname like that. Poor kids if ever there were any.

"I'm sure you'll be very happy together," he managed between gritted teeth.

Lloyd nodded and left the office.

No sooner had he gone than Kyle closed and locked the door. He strode over to the desk and poured a stiff whisky then knocked it back. He knew that lately he was drinking more than he should, but by God, he needed this right now.

He was starting to feel a little buzzed. Between nearly getting beaten up, not eating anything substantial, and imbibing two hefty glasses of Ryan's treasured ten-year-old Ardbeg, Kyle wasn't surprised he felt his knees wobble.

His hands shook as he poured himself another, and then he closed his eyes, feeling the burn of the whisky as it traced a path down his throat. Perhaps it would wash away the taste of shame and self-loathing at the fact he'd fallen to pieces.

Again.

Light burnt his eyelids and seared into his brain. Kyle opened one bleary eye and looked around. He didn't recognise the place he was lying in, so he closed his eyes again. There was a chuckle from somewhere above him, and once again he opened his eyes and stared about blearily. He vaguely made out the figure of Lucinda sitting curled up in the bench window overlooking the street below.

He was still at the club.

He groaned loudly and sat up. His head throbbed liked two ninjas were battling it out with nunchaku and flying stars. "Oh shit," he croaked. "What did I do?"

"You drank nearly half a bottle of Ryan's treasured whisky, passed out on the desk and spent the night here. As did I." Lucinda uncurled her long limbs and strode over to where he lay. He now recognised the couch in the office as being his resting place.

"Jim and I managed to get your sorry arse onto the couch, and then after we locked up, he made up one of the private cubicles downstairs into a sleeping pad with blankets, and that's where I slept."

"I'm sorry. I didn't mean to pass out. I was just..." his voice tailed off.

Lucinda smirked. "Having a party for one, it looked like. Did you even eat yesterday?"

Kyle shook his head and wished he hadn't. "I don't think so. Fuck, my head hurts."

Lucinda handed him a couple of tablets and a glass of water. "I thought you might need these. It's Advil. Get it down you." She frowned. "What got into you anyway? It's not usual for you to overindulge like that."

He didn't want to tell her the truth—that a man had frightened him, made him think of his past, his inadequacies, his shame. He'd told her he was dealing with it, but there were those loitering pockets of angst and uncertainty when he found himself in situations he thought he couldn't control; then it all came rushing back.

Kyle swallowed the pills with water then lay back on the couch and closed his eyes. "Everything caught up with me, I guess. Worried about Ryan. I just needed to blow off some steam."

She regarded him and for a split second it was as if she knew he was lying. Then she shrugged. "We all have those times. But if anything is wrong, I expect you'd tell me about it, yeah? That's why we're besties."

"Thanks, Luce. I know you're always there for me." He grinned wryly. "Like now. It can't have been comfortable sleeping downstairs and I'm so sorry I made you do that. You could have taken a taxi back to your hotel and left me sleeping it off."

She pulled a moue. "Nah, where's the fun in that? Someone has to look after you." She gestured at the half-full bottle on the desk. "Although you'll need to replace that before Ryan gets back. That'll cost you about fifty dollars."

Kyle sniffed. "I know a man who'll get it for me for much less."

Lucinda frowned. "Unless it was his special bottle of whisky that was bottled in about the nineteen-sixties. Jim said he had one of those somewhere. In which case, it'll cost close to three and a half thousand dollars. Can your friend get you one of *those* cheap?"

Kyle's stomach rebelled and he felt the beginning of a retch. He desperately sought out the dustbin. Lucinda sighed and pushed it over with her foot. Bile left his stomach and splattered at the bottom of the wads of paper that lay there. He wiped his mouth and prayed to every god he knew.

"Please tell me it wasn't that one?" he gasped. "I just picked the bottle from the top tier. Surely he wouldn't keep something worth that much here in his office?"

Lucinda pursed her lips, eyes alight with devilment. "Let me see…" She picked up the bottle and tut-tutted.

He waited, mind racing.

I'll have to empty my savings to buy that. Shit, why didn't I take more notice of what the fuck I was drinking?

He hadn't realised he wasn't breathing until she spoke.

"You're in luck. It's the bog standard one." Her grin flashed and she put the bottle down. Kyle let out a sigh of relief. "But I knew that. God, you are so gullible."

"You bitch," Kyle sputtered. "Why would you do that to me?"

"I had to sleep in a smelly club on a sofa where guys banged each other all night. I'm probably covered in all sorts of disgusting stuff. You deserved it."

His eyes narrowed. "You stepped over a line, there, Missy. I will get you back for that one. You made me hurl."

She stood up and came over to flick his nose. "Nuh-huh. That was all on you, pretty boy. You and that bottle of whisky." Her voice softened, but there was an edge to it he recognised. "God knows what made you drink so much. Are you sure there's nothing you want to tell me?"

He crossed his fingers. In the past, he'd never been able to keep secrets from her. She'd read him like a book. It was just as well, or he'd most likely be dead right now at the hands of his ex-lover. "Give it up, Sherlock. Can't a man get drunk, pass out and have his lady friend take care of him?"

Lucinda's face shadowed. "Yeah, it's just that…"

Kyle knew what she was thinking. *It's just that every time you did that in the past was after Mario had hurt you, and you chose solace in booze and hid away like a cornered animal.*

Kyle had never worried that his self-despair would turn into alcoholism. The one and only thing he'd had control over back then was his drinking, and he'd been damned if Mario would take that away from him as well.

He struggled to his feet, giving a startled yelp as his head buzzed with dizziness. "Honest, I'm good." He sniffed himself and grimaced. "I need to shower though. We'd best get to my place. Unless you want to go back to your hotel?"

Lucinda slid off the edge of the desk. "I'll come home with you, make sure you get there all right. Then I'll probably get a taxi back to the hotel and have a shower myself. I stink of spunk."

She stuck out her tongue and he couldn't help a tired laugh. She was amazing and he missed her so much when she wasn't around.

"Fine. Let me hide the evidence of my self-indulgence and we'll get a taxi. I know it's not far but I don't think I want to walk home looking like this."

Chapter Seven

Eric tapped his fingers on the bar top, picked at the beer bottle's label, then drew a long pull as he glanced towards the restaurant's entrance. Seven-thirty. Kyle should be here any minute.

The butterflies in his stomach intensified as the minutes ticked passed. There was something about Kyle that brought out all Eric's protective instincts. He couldn't shake the feeling that someone, an ex perhaps, hadn't treated Kyle well. He was edgy, skittish and...oh my God, the man was gorgeous.

Eric took a deep breath as Kyle walked in the door. His fluid motion was a thing of beauty as his amazing long legs carried him into the restaurant. When he spotted Eric at the bar, Kyle's face burst into a wide smile, and Eric imagined he was the only person in the room enjoying its warmth and radiance.

God, I'm really into this guy.

Kyle's shock of purple black hair was covered with a grey beanie, giving his face an elfin appearance. His dark burgundy jeans were offset with a tight V-neck white tee-shirt, and covered with a casual black jacket teamed with a funky brown and red patterned scarf. He looked stunningly casual and elegant at the same time.

Eric looked down at his brown chinos with his black button up shirt and felt a little dowdy. But when Kyle's eyes lit up at the sight of him and roved down Eric's body, hovering in a frank, groin-warming inspection, he felt marginally better.

"You look edible," Kyle murmured. "You are red-haired all over, it would seem." He reached out and caressed the chest curls poking out of Eric's shirt. "Of course, I speak from experience." One eyebrow lifted teasingly, the one with the barbell piercing.

Eric felt his face flame at the reminder of that hot, dirty blowjob at the club. He'd be lying if he said he hadn't thought that getting another was on his To Do list tonight, first date or not. "Um, yeah, same colour all over." Eric laughed as the waitress behind the bar gave him a knowing look. "You look really good too. That beanie suits you."

Kyle chuckled. He reached up and tugged it off, running fingers through his hair to tame it. "It itches," he complained. "But it keeps my ears warm. I feel the cold sink into me from head to toe."

Eric touched Kyle's arm. "Do you want a drink at the bar, or do you want to go straight to the table?"

Kyle's eyes gleamed. "Table sounds good," he murmured. "A little more private than here."

Eric cleared his dry throat. "Sure." He gestured to the waitress who was smiling like a Cheshire cat. "Could we be taken to our table please?"

Settled at a small table for two in the back corner, drinks in hand, Kyle looked around in interest. "It's the first time I've been here." He scanned the room as he drank his white wine. "It looks incredible with this décor, and the ambience is great. Really puts you at ease."

Eric nodded. "Yeah, I've been in restaurants where you feel a bit out of place, and can't relax. This one is different. Makes you feel welcome."

"Someone Ryan knows owns it. A guy called Gideon Kent. Apparently, he gave up cooking for a while because of an accident, but now he's back, and his boyfriend is the head chef. Nothing like keeping it in the family." Kyle watched Eric over the rim of his glass then asked, "How did your sister's wedding go?"

The change of subject caught Eric off guard. "It was"—he hesitated—"a wedding. The usual palaver accompanied by a wedding dress, pomp and ceremony plus too much food and drink. My folks did Shelley well. Her husband Greg is a really great guy." Eric grinned. "Luckily, she's the only daughter, so they don't have to splash out on anything for me or my younger brother, Shepherd. I'm not big on the whole being married thing and Shepherd..." He snorted. "That kid is never going to settle down. He's in Thailand now writing his travel journal to add to the video for his YouTube channel. Next week he's in Bangkok and God knows where he'll go from there. He has a girl in every port and loves it." Part of him envied Shep's lifestyle. At twenty-four years old, the world was his oyster.

Kyle's eyebrows rose. "Shepherd is a YouTuber? Wow. It amazes me how people make money out of that. So, you're not into marriage?"

Eric shrugged. "Marriage is just a piece of paper. It's the relationship and how you live your life together that matters. Don't get me wrong, I cheered like a football fan when gay marriage was legalised in the U.K., but it's not important to me personally."

Despite his parents being together for over thirty years, Eric wasn't a believer in the whole formal commitment thing. He and Lincoln had differing views on the matter, which led to a few loud arguments over the years. But now, every so often, Eric wondered if he had been stupid not to accede to Linc's wishes. Hindsight and regret in the rear-view mirror.

Kyle took a sip of his wine, probably contemplating what Eric had said. The waiter came over and they ordered their food.

Eric couldn't help but notice Kyle's nails were clear tonight, no colourful varnish. They were well-maintained, oval-shaped and slightly longer than Eric had seen on a man before. He liked it. Those nails raking down his back...he shuddered. *Down boy*. Stop being so damned shallow. Not everything is about sex.

Although...a lot of the time it was.

"So," Kyle drawled. "We have something else in common. Neither of us are big believers in the whole matrimonial thing." His face darkened. "And having to get married in church or utter those awful wedding vows—that really doesn't work for me."

Eric nodded. "I remember you told Ryan and I once you aren't religious. I'm not either so looks like we have that in common too." He frowned. "You said we have something else in common. What was the other thing?"

Kyle's eyes lit up and his mouth quirked up a little. "We both love dick," he announced, not as quietly as Eric would have liked. Then Kyle sat back and laughed as Eric glanced around quickly to see if anyone had heard.

"Why not proclaim it to the whole restaurant?" Eric murmured, but smiled at his dinner partner. *God, the man was adorable.*

Kyle's fingers grazed Eric's, sending a shock down his arm. "Why shouldn't we? We're two grown gay men on a date. I won't hide who I am." He looked uncertain suddenly, and sat back, biting his lip. It was a most endearing gesture. "You're not, like, in the closet or anything, are you? I mean, I don't expect naked shagging in public, but I won't hide the fact I'm with a man." His voice grew fierce. "That's pretty much a deal breaker for me."

Eric was taken aback. "No. Hell, I'm out and fine with it. I mean, I try to watch what I do in public but it's not like I wouldn't hug or kiss, or hold hands with a guy, as long it's safe."

Kyle leaned forward and traced the blue vein in Eric's hand. "Good. Because I've done that before for someone and I can't do it again."

Eric hadn't missed the pain in Kyle's tone, and once again he wondered who had hurt him. Now wasn't the right time to ask about it.

"So, I've told you about my family. Tell me about yours." Eric waved the waiter over to order more drinks. "I know you're Jewish, non-religious and worked in Vegas as a croupier or something like that, but not much else."

Eric watched the shutters come down over Kyle's face. It reminded him of a veil being drawn over a bride.

"Not much to tell, really. I was born in Chicago. My parents emigrated to the U.K. when I was seven." His fingers toyed nervously with the saltshaker. "I went back to Las Vegas in oh-eight, when I was twenty, waited to turn twenty-one then found work as a croupier-slash-cocktail waiter at The Bohemian Club Casino. That's where I met Lucinda." His face lit up and Eric hoped that one day he might see the same affection on Kyle's face for him. "She's my bestie, although we live on different continents. I'd love you to meet her while she's here."

He put the saltshaker down. "Then in oh-eleven I moved back to the UK and bummed around a bit. A year later I joined Club Delish. I've been there ever since."

Eric nodded. "No family then?"

Kyle looked down at the table. His movements stilled. "I'm an only child. Mum and Dad moved back to Chicago seven years ago. I see them when I go back to the States." His brow furrowed. "That would have been June last year."

"You liked Las Vegas then? It must have been exciting, being out there with all that glam and high rollers."

Kyle's hands clenched on the table, scrunching his napkin into a tight wad. "It was an experience. Let's simply say that." He looked relieved as the food arrived. "This looks scrumptious. Smells amazing."

Eric had a feeling the sharing portion of the evening had concluded. He guessed both of them had their secrets. You couldn't get through your twenties without amassing some baggage. Eric had his Lincoln stuff, and Kyle...well he had something, that was for sure.

Eric was happy to wait until things were at a place that they both felt comfortable to say more. He had high hopes things would progress in that direction.

They ate in companionable silence, joking and putting the world to rights. Eric was all for paramedics being given bulletproof vests and being taught how to deal with potential bombs and explosive devices. Kyle was keen to ensure the future of nightclubs in London, given new legislation, increasing bureaucracy and the focus on shutting down clubs to make way for offices. Money talked in a loud voice in the new London.

Their conversation took them late into the night, and it was close to eleven when they both sat back, replete with coffee, and stared at each other.

Kyle cleared his throat. "I guess we should be getting on our way. The staff keeps giving us the evil eye. I think they want to close." He laughed softly. "I know the feeling, so what do you say we take the chit-chat back to my place, have a nightcap and see what develops."

Eric blinked. He'd never met anyone quite as direct as Kyle before.

"Unless you have an early morning shift tomorrow," Kyle hastened to add. "It's Monday, so I'm off. I guess you don't have the same privilege." He looked hopeful.

"My shift starts at ten," Eric said quietly.

"Oh." Kyle seemed uncomfortable. "Look, I'm sorry if I'm moving too fast for you, it's just...I like you and I'm not one to beat around the bush. I understand if you'd rather let this one go. Just tell me."

Eric laughed softly. He loved the way Kyle tackled everything head on, and wore his heart (or was it his cock?) on his sleeve. After a few tough years of being unable to care about anyone after Linc, this colourful man was a refreshing change, and Eric couldn't wait to get to know him better.

Kyle cocked his head. "Was that a 'I can't wait to kick him to the kerb' laugh or a 'I'm going to take him up on his offer and soon we'll be naked' one?"

Eric stood. "It's an 'I'm going to take a piss and while I'm gone you get the bill so we can go home together' laugh." He watched a grin slide onto Kyle's handsome face then turned to walk to the bathroom. *This guy is going to be a whole load of trouble. But I think I'm ready for it. God, please don't let me have any nightmares tonight.*

Eric hadn't had any bad dreams in the last week so he was hopeful. The thought of going home with Kyle both exhilarated and scared him. Eric did his business, zipped up and by the time he got back, Kyle was already standing with his jacket slung over his shoulder.

"I thought you were getting the bill?"

"I did. Done and dusted." Kyle grinned.

"The idea wasn't that you were paying. How much do I owe you?" Eric reached into his pocket for his wallet. His hand brushed the cock that had been half-hard all night.

Kyle tut-tutted. "Simmer down, gorgeous. You can pay me back later, or get the next one. I thought we could do with getting a move on, that's all." His violet eyes flashed, heat visible in their depths.

Even empty, the restaurant seemed small and crowded suddenly and Eric hoped Kyle didn't live too far. "Let's go then." Eric noticed the huskiness in his voice, and from Kyle's full body shiver, he'd noticed too. "I'm in the mood for a nightcap."

The taxi ride was so brief that as soon as they were settled inside, they were pulling up to the block of flats where Kyle lived. The building's façade was old and Victorian.

Eric insisted on paying the taxi driver then followed Kyle inside.

"It's only four levels," Kyle explained as they walked up the winding stairs. "Three flats on each floor. Mine is at the end of the fourth floor." He flashed a wicked grin. "The lift kinda groans when you get in it, so I prefer the stairs most times."

Eric loved walking behind Kyle. He was almost at full mast already just from watching the globes of the man's arse as they worked together in tandem temptation.

What this man does to me is criminal.

They stopped in front of a scratched, white oak door and Kyle slid the key in and opened it. He stepped inside, flipped on the light switch then shrugged off his scarf and jacket, and threw his beanie casually on a chair.

"Make yourself at home." He gestured to the couch. "I'll grab us a drink. You like whisky?"

Eric nodded as he sat down. "That's fine, thanks."

God, he wanted to make a move on Kyle. To grab him, pull him over Eric's body and kiss the ever-loving fuck out of him. To strip him, see what delights he held hidden beneath those trendy clothes, and to be lust-driven, sweaty beasts together, intent on finding their gratification. The need was so strong Eric could taste it in the air, scent it in the tantalising aroma of spicy cologne and musky male.

Kyle coughed. "Your drink, sir?" He passed the glass to Eric and sat down beside him, close enough that he felt the heat emanating from Kyle's body. The smirk on his face said he knew exactly what he wanted. Eric imagined he mirrored Kyle's open desire.

As Eric's first sip of whisky slid into that mouth, Kyle's gaze was riveted to Eric's throat. Those intriguing violet eyes flared as Eric swallowed and Kyle took a sip of his own drink. His tongue came out and licked the remnants of whisky from his lips. Surely intentional, the tease hit its mark, raising Eric's blood pressure and making his groin ache.

"Maybe the drink can wait." Kyle's raspy voice drifted to Eric's ears like warm air. Kyle—whose hands shook ever so slightly—took Eric's drink from him.

Eric waited, happy to let Kyle take the lead. Kyle leaned over and ran his pink, wet tongue down the length of Eric's throat. Kyle's lips lingered on the throbbing pulse, matching the sensation in Eric's trousers of his hard-on pressing against his chinos.

"You taste so good," Kyle whispered as he licked blissful strokes down Eric's skin. "You should have your own flavour ice cream."

Eric laughed softly as his hands encircled the other man's waist and pulled him closer. Kyle went one better, twisting and straddling Eric's lap, tantalisingly brushing his groin with a tight, round arse.

"I'm not sure about that," Eric murmured, holding Kyle's gaze as Eric unzipped Kyle's jeans, releasing him. Eric swiped his fingers over the tip, loving the velvet-wet smoothness. "I bet you taste just as good."

Kyle's pupils expanded, and his breathing quickened.

The kiss that followed was everything Eric could have hoped for. Kyle's mouth was nubile, eager, and the way he pressed his body against Eric's with each frantic thrust of tongue drove Eric crazy. He didn't even hear or feel his own trousers being unzipped, though he saw Kyle rising above him with a desperation borne of need.

"I need skin, friction," Kyle panted as he pushed his own smooth hardness against Eric's. A warm hand reached down and slicked him up with his own wetness. "I've been waiting all night to do this."

Eric mumbled, "I'm not resisting," between greedy kisses and groping hands that seemed to be everywhere at once. "This is me agreeing with you."

Kyle chuckled, a strangled sound as he ground his shaven groin harder against Eric's. Eric laid his head back on the couch, a moan of pleasure escaping from his ravaged mouth. "We're gonna have friction burns on our dicks." Even as he said it, he slid his hands into the back of Kyle's jeans and roughly held him tighter. The globes of that tight arse felt magical in Eric's hands and he could think of a lot of other things he'd like to do with them.

Kyle's reply was to rub harder and Eric zoned out, closing his eyes as delectable sensations raced through his body.

Time and space disappeared to become only having this sexy man on top of him, taking his mouth with a savage intensity that made Eric see stars. Kyle's soft moans, the tickling of skin as his hair brushed Eric's skin—they all came together in one soul-shattering realisation that Eric had missed this.

Missed having someone so focused on him, giving him pleasure.

It had been too long, and Eric wanted more of it.

"Oh, God," Kyle whispered as he strained above. "I hope you don't mind a mess..." The last words were lost in a deep groan as Kyle came, warm fluid soaking Eric's groin and stomach. Spurts of spunk hit the underside of Eric's chin, catapulting him over the edge. He clasped the bum beneath his hands tighter, fingers clenching as he released.

Again, swollen lips smashed against his. Eric needed to draw breath, so after what seemed like minutes, he pulled away.

There was a moment of blissful silence. Both men lay stuck together by come and sweat.

Kyle chuckled. "Nice. I think we might have invented a new form of liquid Velcro. I don't think I can move away."

Eric grinned, his body coming down from his orgasmic high. "We'd have a lot of gay men volunteering to create the product if it came to that."

The absurdity of that image made them both giggle like kids. It had been a long time since Eric had heard that sound emanating from his own throat.

"We need to clean up," he murmured into Kyle's cute shell of an ear. "Before we stay this way forever."

"Is that such a bad thing?" Kyle murmured back. "I'm pretty comfy here." He nuzzled Eric's neck and planted a soft kiss there. "You make me feel good about myself. Like I'm worth something."

A surge of affection swept through Eric. Kyle was a playful kitten—one with claws, judging from how his sharp fingernails had dug into Eric's arms. Kyle was warm, fragrant and seemed to love cuddling, something Eric was partial to.

He kissed the top of Kyle's fragranced hair. "Whoever it was that made you feel you weren't worth anything was a damned idiot. They had no idea what they had. I guess I'm the lucky one now." He didn't miss Kyle's hitch of breath and the way his hands grasped tighter around Eric's waist.

His playful kitten obviously had some issues. Eric wondered what had happened to make him that way.

Eric cleared his throat. "You're heavy, and I need to piss. I think you're sitting on my bladder."

Kyle grumbled as he lifted himself off. "Fine, spoilsport. Way to ruin the mood with talk of your bodily needs, other than the ones we just satisfied."

Eric couldn't help laughing. "It's either that or I do it here, and as much as I'd like to stay here with you, the idea of wetting myself isn't one I want to entertain." He stood but didn't bother zipping himself up.

"Yeah? You like being with me then?" The vulnerability in Kyle's tone made Eric turn around. Kyle stared up, a picture of debauched beauty lying on the couch. His pale face held a slight frown and he was biting the skin at the side of his nail.

"I think I just proved that, didn't I?"

Kyle pushed himself up on his elbows, an adorable scowl starting on his face.

Eric hastened to qualify his words. "I mean, I'm not here just for the sex, okay? I like you. I like your company." His bladder protested at being delayed but he didn't want to leave while Kyle still thought he was nothing more than a warm body to get off with.

Kyle snorted. "Okay then. Glad we got that sorted. You're sleeping over, right?"

Eric nodded.

Kyle's face softened. "You're jiggling. Go to the bog, for God's sake." He stood and motioned to the door leading off the lounge. "I'll get cleaned up after you. The bedroom is through there."

Eric nodded and sped off to the bathroom to both empty his bursting bladder and clean up. He managed as best he could, taking his briefs and chinos off to wipe off some of the mess. He grimaced. Even so, he'd have to wear them crusty in the morning on his walk of shame. He took a deep breath and wandered out and across to the bedroom.

Kyle was sitting on the side of the bed. He raised an eyebrow when he saw Eric's attire.

"I like the no-pants look." He got up and gestured to the left side of the bed. "Mine's the right side. Get comfortable. I'll be back in a moment." He gestured to the dresser in the corner. "If you fancy sleeping in anything, there's stuff in the top drawer."

Eric took off his shirt and slid naked into the bed. He'd never been able to sleep with clothes on; he hoped Kyle wouldn't mind.

He caught his breath when Kyle walked back into the room. Lithe, with muscles in all the right places and long legs with a smattering of fine hair, he reminded Eric of a thoroughbred colt.

Kyle slipped in beside him. "Mmm, nice," he purred. "I like a man with nothing on lying next to me." He leaned back against the pillows and regarded Eric with a smouldering stare.

"Oh no, mate, no more tonight." Eric got comfortable and snuggled down into the duvet. "As tempting as you are, I need some sleep. If we start again now, it'll be hours before I finish with you and you'll be screaming for more."

"Ooh," Kyle muttered. "You're a confident one. What makes you think I won't be the one making *you* scream?" He smirked. "Next time, we fuck. Properly."

Eric's cock stirred and he ignored it and closed his eyes. "Uh-huh," he managed sleepily. "Maybe next time we can have an all-night fuck fest but tonight, I need some zzzzs. Work tomorrow. Remember? Not like some of us who have Monday off."

He sensed Kyle's face near and his warm breath on Eric's cheeks. He opened his eyes and noticed for the first time Kyle's real eyes were a deep, dark brown. As much as Eric loved the violet contacts, the hue of that brown made him think of warm chestnuts and cold winter days.

"I like the sound of next time," Kyle murmured as his lips found Eric's in a lingering kiss. "I'll hold you to it. 'Night."

Kyle pressed his front against Eric's back. "You don't mind me being the big spoon, do you?" he whispered drowsily. "I promise to keep my bits in control."

"'S fine," Eric mumbled. "Go to sleep, Kyle."

There was another soft drift of lips against the back of Eric's neck and then he remembered no more.

Chapter Eight

"Hey, big guy. What are you smiling about? Looks like you got some last night."

Eric turned to see Aaron watching him. He finished packing in some of the stock he needed for their shift and grinned back.

"Maybe I did, maybe I didn't." He closed the back of the truck and went over to give his partner a shoulder slap. "How are you doing on that front? Did you go on that date your bubbie set up for you?"

Aaron's face brightened. "Actually, I did. It went pretty well. She's a nice girl."

Eric raised an eyebrow. "Go on then, tell me about her. Is she the next Mrs Greenberg?"

Aaron had been married once before, a short-lived, tempestuous relationship which had ended when his bride of six months decided she wanted to volunteer abroad helping wildlife for the rest of her life. He didn't speak about it much. Eric hadn't known Aaron then, but from what he gathered, Aaron had been deeply hurt at the time.

Aaron looked scandalised. "Oi, give me a chance. We've only had the one date. It was nice."

He got a dreamy look on his face and Eric bit back a chuckle. He'd had his reservations about Aaron's crazy, well-meaning grandma arranging a date but it seemed to have worked out.

Eric patted Aaron on the back, putting a sad look on his face. "Mate, if your bubbie has anything to say about it, she's already got the wedding china picked out."

He laughed at the alarmed expression crossing Aaron's face and motioned toward the truck. "Come on. We're ready to rock and roll. Let's go see what lies in store for us today."

"My mam's just got a tummy ache. Can't you just give her some painkillers and be done with it? What the fuck are you waiting around for?"

The baleful glare of the twenty-something-year-old hovering over Eric as he tended to his patient was beginning to rattle him. The young girl had been blabbering on for over five minutes while he was trying to listen to the older woman's heartbeat and pulse.

They'd answered a 999 call for someone who'd collapsed, which had led them to the house in the middle of Tower Hamlets. Entering the grimy premises of the concrete, mass produced apartment on the tenth floor, an older woman had been supine on the floor as a younger one paced around the room, muttering to herself.

He'd known right away the young woman was tripping on something.

Eric took a deep breath. "Your mam hasn't got a stomach ache. She's got a burst appendix and we need to get her to the hospital as soon as possible. Could you please stand back and give me room?"

He waved the unkempt and unwashed girl back. What he didn't expect was the mouthful of spit he got in return. The glob landed on his cheek and he looked up, trying to control his temper, which burned quicker these days.

"Lady, that really wasn't necessary." What he wanted to say was, *Get the fuck out of my face before I give you a syringe of something you won't want, you little bitch.* "I'm only trying to help your mother." He glanced around for Aaron, who'd gone to fetch the board from the truck. "We're taking her to the hospital. She's in a bad way."

"She needs painkillers, you fucker. Not hospital. Who's gonna look after my kids when they come home from school if she's not here?" The wild-eyed girl was definitely on something from the spit surrounding her mouth and the frantic, twitching movements of her body. "And I'm nobody's lady. My name is Jessie."

You're right about that, he thought. *"Lady" is not a word I'd use to describe you.*

A prickle of alarm threaded its way down his spine. Tweakers, at the best of times, were dangerous, but this one looked right on the edge; probably why she was insisting on the painkillers. He had no doubt that, if they had been given, the woman lying on the floor wouldn't have seen any of them.

Eric breathed a sigh of relief when the chunky figure of his partner wheeled in the board.

"Aaron. Help me get her onto the board. We need to get her to the nearest hospital A-sap. I'll call in a blue once we're on the road." A blue call meant radioing ahead to the hospital to ensure someone would be waiting ready to take in their patient.

Aaron wasted no time. Within a few minutes, the unconscious woman was strapped to the board, ready to be transported.

As they wheeled her to the door, Jessie stood in front of it.

"You're not taking my mam anywhere, you tossers. Not until you give me the painkillers." She made a grab for the bag Aaron had on his shoulder.

He shouted and held it tight. "What do you think you're doing? Keep your hands off. This woman is going to the hospital, so I suggest you move away and let us do our job."

The knife appeared out of nowhere.

Dull light glinted off the blade Jessie held in her left hand. Both Eric and Aaron stopped. Eric glanced down at the patient, whose breathing was shallow, sweat beading across her forehead.

It wasn't the first time he and Aaron had been threatened, but a knife pointed at them scared him every time.

Aaron's eyes watched the knife warily. "Do you know how many patients we see who have their own knife turned against themselves? Put the damn thing down, lady."

Eric raised his hands, trying to placate the unstable woman before them. He thought he knew how to jolt her into letting them go.

"Jessie, put that the fuck down," he said quietly. "It's not going to do your mam any good if you hurt either of us or yourself. She's going to die if we don't get her to the hospital soon. Is that what you want? No one to look after your kids, pay your way and let you get on with what you want to do? You'll have to find a job. Maybe let your kids go into care. Is that your plan?"

No doubt the old woman on the board was the sole source of income and babysitting.

Jessie's eyes glittered as she contemplated Eric's argument. A sly smile crossed her face and she cocked her head. "Ya know, I guess you're right. Mam needs to get better and come back 'ere. I'll get me tablets elsewhere seeing as how you two are so bloody stingy with 'em." She waved the knife in their direction. "Go on, then Mr Hero. Get her to the hospital. She'd better make it or I'll come looking for you."

Aaron grunted. "Yeah, and we're both shuddering in our boots. Come on, pal. Let's get this sick woman to hospital where she belongs."

His follow-up, *And get her help to stay the hell away from you*, was unspoken but Eric knew his partner. Any chance he got to report this tweaker and keep the old woman safe, he'd take it, as would Eric.

Aaron cursed as they wheeled the board toward the truck. "Shit. I hate people like that. Freeloaders thinking the world owes them a living. Using their parents to support a drug habit. Thinking violence solves everything."

They loaded the patient into the truck. Eric sighed. "Yeah. It takes all sorts. I guess we'd better report the situation, let Social Services take a look at the kids. I'm not a fan of them, but this case warrants it."

Eric drove carefully, not wanting his patient to jolt around in the back and hurt more. The blue lights were flashing and traffic allowed them easy access.

An hour later they delivered their patient and made their reports to the hospital and Social Services. The prognosis was bleak. They might be able to do something with the kids but the grandmother was another matter. It would be her decision whether to go back to her daughter, or not.

Aaron and Eric got back in the truck in the car park and looked at each other. The radio was silent. Eric breathed a sigh of relief, knowing it would be short-lived. He needed some distracting.

"Tell me more about this lady of yours," he asked idly as he watched his partner complete paperwork. "I don't even know her name."

Aaron looked up. "Her name is Leah. She's twenty-five and works as a paralegal for a company just outside London. She's smart, and she makes me laugh." He gave a self-deprecating sniff. "And she likes short, cuddly men with meat on them, so I'm the ideal man for her."

"You going on another date then?" Eric gazed out the window, watching people walk by.

Aaron shrugged. "I asked her if she wanted to go to a film and she said yes. We need to sort out which one. I think she likes the same ones I do—horror and thrillers, not those horrible rom-com things."

"Oh, she's a keeper all right," Eric said drily. "Hold onto her, mate. Anyone who likes your type of gore is definitely the woman for you."

"Talking about my love life— you still haven't told me much about this new man of yours." Aaron winked. "You came in this morning with a spring in your step. Are you gonna see him again then?"

Eric shrugged. "I guess. Kyle is good fun, and we get on well." In his mind that translated into, *He's smoking hot and I'm really into him*, but he wasn't telling his nosy partner that. In the past, if he'd been even marginally interested in a guy, Aaron had seemed to make it his life's mission to push him into a committed relationship. Aaron knew most of the story about Lincoln and believed Eric needed another warm body in his bed to get over his grief.

His best friend Deke felt much the same way. He was always trying to convince Chrissy to set Eric up on dates with random guys. He hadn't been a priest; he'd had a few sexual exploits since Linc died, but Eric hadn't found someone he really liked. Until now.

Aaron stared at him, eyes narrowed. "You're not telling me everything," he growled. "There's something about this guy. Kyle's special to you. I can feel it."

Eric stared back innocently. "You're not your bubbie, partner," he chuckled. "Don't have me married off like she wants you to be. I'm quite happy with the status quo." For now, he admitted silently. He certainly wasn't averse to things getting a little more serious.

Before Aaron could respond, the radio crackled again with another callout. His partner grunted as Eric started the engine and pulled away from the parking lot. "Maybe we need a double date. You and your man and me and Leah." Aaron's face brightened at that prospect.

Eric shuddered. The last thing he wanted to do was introduce Kyle to an inquisitive Aaron. The two men potentially chatting together gave Eric hives. Who knew what might be revealed in the heat of a relaxed or drunken moment. Aaron knew a lot of embarrassing stories Eric would rather not have revealed.

"Sounds good," he lied as he raced down the road toward their next emergency. "It'll need to wait until I get back from France in a couple of weeks' time. I'm subbing for David at that camping trip at Verdon Gorge, remember?"

One of their paramedic friends, David, had broken a leg skiing in Austria a few weeks ago. He'd been desperate and Eric had agreed to fill in as one of the official medics on call at the camping lodge in France at the so-called Grand Canyon of Europe.

Fortuitously, David happened to be the son of the chief medic at Shoreditch, and strings had been pulled to enable Eric to go as part of his on-going training. He was looking forward to it as a working holiday with pay.

He groaned softly when he realised he hadn't mentioned it to Kyle. Then again, things weren't serious between them, and still too new. Kyle wouldn't be bothered if he went away. Would he?

"Oh, yeah, you're gadding off to Europe to spend time with the rich people," Aaron sniffed. "Leaving me to be paired up with that twat Rosie." He rolled his eyes and Eric grinned.

Ross "Rosie" Corkton was a beefy, hairy brute of a man, who constantly sweated in the truck and gave off a cheesy aroma that made them both gag. Rosie was also one heck of a medic.

"Aww," Eric teased as he glanced at his scowling friend. "You're gonna miss me. How cute."

"Don't get ahead of yourself. I won't miss your sorry arse," Aaron growled. He held on tight as Eric took a corner sharply, avoiding a bicycle courier that had darted out in front of them.

"Stupid tosser," Aaron yelled out of the open window. "You want to be travelling with us then? First-class accommodation in the back, you knucklehead."

Eric sniggered. Aaron certainly had a way with words.

At least the incident had made him forget the double date.

Eric's mobile rang as he was walking down the path to his front door. He grinned when he saw who it was, his spirits instantly lifting.

"Kyle. Hey there. This is a pleasant surprise."

"Yeah." There was the sound of retching and he frowned.

"You okay? You sound sick."

"I am." Kyle's voice was muffled. "I went out today and grabbed a quick doner kebab from a food cart and now I'm fucking puking my guts up." There was another awful sound as Eric fumbled to get his door open.

"You want me to come over and play medic?" he asked as he threw his keys onto the dining table. "I know it's late, but I'm happy to do it." His shift had finished half an hour ago. It was almost eleven pm.

"Oh shit, I'm so sorry." Kyle's voice was panicked. "I've been in bed all afternoon, and didn't realise how late it was. Fuck, I'm a complete plonker…"

"Hey, don't sweat it. You were obviously out of it. Are you sure you don't want me to check you out?" Kyle's tired chuckle made Eric's chest fluttery.

"You know, any other time the chance to get you to play medic and come to check me over would be a resounding yes. But right now, I'm a mess, all barfed out and I just want to get into bed with my bucket. I'll take a rain check though."

"Um, okay." He still wasn't sure why Kyle had called. "Did you need me for anything else?"

The muffled expletive on the other side of the phone made him laugh softly. "Yeah, I was supposed to pass on a message from Ryan for you much earlier but I forgot. Hence the late night call. When he sent me home, saying, and I quote, 'You looked sicker than a goat on fucking crack', he asked if it was possible to remind you about coming around to the club tomorrow before your shift? Apparently, you're going to be a witness for him on some business thingy. He's out somewhere this evening where he has no mobile signal or he'd have called to remind you himself."

Eric had forgotten about that. "Sure. My shift starts at ten, but I'll pop over a bit before then."

"Cool. Okay, I'm going back to bed to puke over my sheets and feel sorry for myself. And before you start on me, I have some boiled ginger ale, a packet of crackers and some anti-nausea pills. I'm all set."

"Hmm. That's a start. Call me in the morning, let me know how you are."

"Ahh, you care 'bout me. That's so sweet." Unfortunately, Kyle's cute sentiment was spoiled by another bout of vomiting. "Yuck, gotta go. The porcelain beckons."

The line went dead. Eric put down his phone and stared at it worriedly. Kyle sounded terrible. What they had was still new, but the last thing Eric wanted to do was be overprotective and scare Kyle away. The man had a stubborn streak that'd piss a mule off. If he said he didn't want company, fine.

Tomorrow when he rang, Eric would see if he could get another date for them to meet up again before...fuck. He still hadn't said anything to Kyle about the upcoming France trip.

Tomorrow, he promised. *I'll let him know then when we speak.*

Unfortunately, Eric didn't get the chance to speak to Kyle before Eric left two days later. Knee-deep in amniotic fluid delivering a pair of twin girls at the time, he'd missed Kyle's call the next afternoon explaining in detail that he felt much better.

After the babies, Eric and Aaron's other call-outs hadn't been as rewarding and were doubly demanding. Over the next two days, London seemed to go crazy. They treated a man with a suspected heart attack, which turned out to be chest pains because he'd taken too much Viagra. They attended two student suicides at a local University, both heart-breaking and sobering. Drug overdoses were rife, as were stabbings. And when they called on an old man with dementia, he was dehydrated and delirious with pain from a beating by a gang of youths. When he saw Aaron, the poor man thought Aaron was his son, and Eric's heart had broken.

In between this were the usual 999 calls that should have been referred to doctors and night clinics.

Already exhausted, disheartened, depressed and grumpy from lack of sleep—more nightmares had kept him up at night—when the time came for Eric to get on the plane to France, he'd sighed with relief.

His inner voice whispered, *I'm sure he's not going to miss me. He doesn't need me being all moody in his life. I'm bad company right now.*

Chapter Nine

Kyle wasn't at work pining over the fact he hadn't heard from Eric in a couple of days. He definitely fucking *wasn't*.

His last message telling Eric he was feeling better had been unanswered. He didn't even know if he'd read it. Not for the first time, Kyle wished he'd used Messenger or WhatsApp so he could tell.

He'd been tempted to call, but a streak of bloody-mindedness had crept in, a little voice whispering that perhaps Eric didn't want to be contacted. That he wasn't interested anymore.

Damn his insecurities. Kyle scowled and kicked the floor moulding moodily. Then he formed his mouth into a fake smile and knocked once on Ryan's door before he opened it, then entered.

He had a job to do on pain of death from a positively scary man.

Ryan smiled up at him from his desk. "Hey, everything okay out there? Need me for anything?"

Kyle kept the smile on his face. "Nope. All under control, boss. How are you feeling?"

Ryan shrugged. "I'm fine and dandy. Chomping at the bit to get back to work without a bunch of fucking nursemaids watching my every move."

Kyle grinned for real now. He sat down on the corner of Ryan's desk. "Ooh, full-blown bitch alert. Isn't it nearly your bedtime?"

Mango had insisted Ryan be home by ten every night as part of his recovery. Kyle was Mango's unwilling accomplice.

Ryan narrowed his eyes. "Fuck. You."

It was only nine pm.

Kyle sniggered. "Not my rules, boss. Them be Mango's commands." He peered over the desk down at Ryan's legs. They were covered with black chinos but Kyle knew what had been under them until a few days ago. "At least those awful stockings have gone," he drawled, fanning his face like a Southern belle. "I do declare, sir, such a shade of puce I never did see on a gentleman of your standing."

Ryan chuckled. "Shut up, you." He bowed his head in acknowledgement. "Thank fuck they've gone. I hated wearing them. Such passion killers."

"How are things…down there?" Kyle waved in the direction of Ryan's groin.

In a weak moment, Ryan had confided that the medication he was on had caused some technical issues in sustaining an erection. The doctor had said it was normal and would resolve itself over time but Kyle knew Ryan was mortified it had happened.

"Getting better," Ryan said. "It helps the medication is now maintenance only and not as high a dose as it was. I'll be able to give it up for good in a week or so, I hope."

Mango will be helping you get it up tonight, Kyle thought wickedly. He's not going to let you off easy. Get you off, more likely.

He nodded, trying to keep the smirk off his face. "You've been through a lot, Ryan. And you came out with flying colours. Not many aftereffects, a clean bill of health, apart from the check-ups. You're a lucky man."

"I am," Ryan acknowledged. "I give thanks every day for coming through it like I did."

Kyle nodded and looked at his watch. "It's time to leave the office, boss. Mango asked me to get you home a bit earlier."

Ryan frowned. "Why?"

Kyle tried to keep the glee out of his voice. He knew exactly what was going on. He'd helped Mango pick out the outfit for Ryan, who was going to look so damned hot in it.

"Dunno. He told me to kick my boss out at nine o'clock sharp or he'd come down and get you himself."

Ryan swore but he stood, looking for his suit jacket. "Damn man is a pain in my arse."

"Isn't that the whole point?" Kyle smirked. "Have you seen Eric lately? He hasn't been around since he came in a while ago."

Or since we had a breathless, heavenly frot at my place.

Ryan shook his head. "No, he's away for a couple of weeks. He went backpacking with some friends in the Grand Canyon, I think."

Kyle's stomach clenched, his chest constricting.

Eric went away to the US and didn't even bother to let me know? Bastard. A text would have sufficed.

He forced himself to stay calm. "Oh. That sounds cool. Well, you'd better get going before that boyfriend of yours comes down and drags you away."

He shooed Ryan out of the office and watched him climb the stairs to his flat. Once he was out of sight, Kyle went into the office and closed the door. He stood, shoulders bowed, staring out of the window.

Kyle sat nursing his drink, staring at the frenzied hordes of hopeful gamblers surrounding him. He'd come down to the Hippodrome Casino in the West End in the hopes it would lift him out of his doldrums. So far all it had done was get him tipsy and make his hands itch to take over from the croupier and earn himself some money at the craps table.

He watched idly as the dealer shuffled the cards and dealt another losing punter his hand.

"So, are you going to drink that or just glare around the room looking sexy?" The lilting Jamaican voice made Kyle look up as a rather attractive black man, perhaps a few years older, sat down next to him. Tall, clean-shaven and dressed in a deep blue suit with a light yellow shirt and matching tie, he looked made for the cover of a fashion magazine. Then the man grinned, making him look even more delicious.

Kyle looked down at the whisky he'd been nursing. "I'm drinking it, just making it last. This place isn't cheap." *Shit, now he's going to think I'm asking him to buy me a drink.*

Sure enough, Jamaica laughed. "Then, my friend, I shall buy you another while you finish that one." He gestured to a passing waitress who swished over and took the order.

Kyle panicked. He didn't tend to take drinks from strange men in casinos. He'd learnt his lesson a long time ago on that one.

"No, shit, that wasn't a hint to buy me a drink. Honestly, I'm fine with this one."

"Nonsense. I insist. A beautiful man like you deserves it."

Kyle frowned. "It's a little risqué to go around paying that type of compliment to strange men in places like this. How do you know I wouldn't pop you one in the nose for trying to come onto me?" He squinted through slightly hazy eyes. Crap, the whisky was starting to go to his head with mega force now.

The man reached out a hand. Kyle shook it, and was engulfed in warm skin and firm fingers. "My name is Louis Devon Thomas. Now we are no longer strangers, Mr Violet Eyes. Now please, could you return the favour by giving me your name?"

"My name is Kyle. And my question still stands."

Louis inclined his head graciously. "You work at Club Delish. I live in this area and frequent it often. I have seen you there. I didn't expect to see you here on a busy Friday night. From what I have seen of you, you are always working. Imagine my delight when I saw you sitting here. Alone."

Kyle's insides constricted and a chill fingered up a spine.

Louis must have seen the flash of panic because he leaned back and shook his head. "I promise you, I'm no stalker. This is a coincidence, nothing more. You have nothing to fear from me."

Kyle's face flushed. "Sorry, I'm being paranoid. Ignore me."

Louis frowned. "I will do no such thing. I saw fear in your eyes just now. You are quite right to question my intentions."

Wow, that's unexpected. Someone who doesn't think I'm a freak.

Kyle toyed with his glass.

"You are not with anyone here tonight?" Louis glanced idly around the busy venue.

Kyle shook his head. "No, the man I'm seeing—or was seeing—disappeared without saying goodbye. I'm on my own."

Shit, way to bear your soul to a stranger, arsehole.

And it wasn't quite true. A week ago Kyle had received a text from Eric saying, "Sorry, forgot to mention I was going away. Will catch up with you when I get back." Then there'd been another text with a photo of a shirtless Eric—looking goddamned tanned and sexy—smiling next to some big-breasted blonde woman in a bikini with the caption "Wish you were here."

Kyle hadn't liked that text one little bit. Not the woman bit anyway.

Louis's eyes brightened. "*Were* seeing? So, you aren't together anymore? I stand a chance?" He had an amused and kind face, and Kyle thought he could really like this man and his gentle demeanour.

He shrugged. "I'm not sure. I thought maybe I scared him away somehow." His tone was wistful.

Louis leaned in. "You like this man very much. He is special to you, yes?"

Kyle started to say no then shut his mouth. He sighed. "I think he could be."

Louis stared at him. "Then I shall not hit on another man's significant other until I am sure there are no emotional attachments. Your man does not know how lucky he is to have you."

Kyle looked down at his empty glass. He wasn't used to compliments. Quite the contrary.

Faggot. Dirty sinner. Cocktease. Mario's hissed words echoed in Kyle's head.

The waitress arrived with their drinks and Louis took them, and offered one to Kyle. "We shall drink as friends and I will sit here hoping that the next time I see you, you are truly alone." He raised his drink. "But somehow I think I am not going to be that fortunate. Cheers." He raised his drink and Kyle clinked his own against the glass.

"Thanks," Kyle said softly. "You seem like a decent bloke. Maybe under different circumstances…"

Louis chuckled. "I won't hold my breath. But it is nice to know."

They drank in comfortable silence.

"I used to work in a casino in Las Vegas," Kyle finally broke the silence. "Much bigger than this one. I did that"—he gestured over to the croupier dealing cards—"along with working the bar sometimes, handling the cash and the back office. It was a lot of fun but your time is never your own. I think I used to get three to four hours a day to myself, max, because of the shifts I worked."

Louis leaned forward curiously. "Las Vegas? That must have been incredible. Why are you here now then instead of there? If I were still a gambler, I would never leave such a place." He made a moue then gave a self-deprecating chuckle. "I would probably die there, either from forgetting to eat, or drinking too much while I play the tables. Or some mobster would decide I owe him money and to teach me a lesson." His face darkened and Kyle saw the shadow in his eyes. "Vegas is not the right place for me."

"I saw those men," Kyle admitted. "The ones with a fever in their eyes and hunger in the bellies to spin yet another wheel or pull another slot machine, or turn over another hand of cards. It's an addiction that's tough to resist."

Louis nodded. "I understand it well. I was one of them. But when I realised how badly I let it control my life, I joined Gamblers Anonymous and it has been four years since I played a table, or held a deck of cards."

Kyle's eyes widened. "Then why come to a place like this? Isn't the temptation too great?"

Louis laughed. "That's like asking a man who has given up drinking whether he can walk into a pub without succumbing. No, I choose to remind myself of how I ruined my life the first time around by coming in here. It tells me what I have achieved so far has been worth it." He flashed a grin at Kyle. "And it allows me to make new friends."

They clicked glasses again.

"You never did answer my original question about why you left there," Louis said musingly. "If you do not wish to say, then please, tell me to mind my own business."

Kyle had no intention of telling anyone why he'd left. Instead he shrugged and put on a blank face. "I got tired of the glitz and glamour and never having any time to myself. I moved back to the U.K. to have an easier life, and I love it here. I'm settled now."

"I see." Louis nodded thoughtfully. "Then we shall leave that as the explanation."

Louis knew there was more to Kyle's leaving than that. Damn, the man was perceptive.

Kyle's mobile vibrated in his pocket and he smiled apologetically. "Let me just get this. It's probably my friend Lucinda. She was going to meet me here after her night out."

He checked the voice message on his phone. Sure enough, it was from Luce. "Hey, London, I'm not gonna make it." Her voice was slurred yet happy. "I met up with this sexy lady who wants to fly me to Paris—don't worry, I know her, she's no stranger—so we're on our way to the airfield now." She giggled. "Oops, sorry, Lanie. Didn't mean to spill my drink on you." There was a soft murmur and Luce burst into a peal of laughter. "Wow, that's just, I don't know what to say. Maybe wait until we're on the plane instead of the taxi?"

There was a crackle and a sound Kyle really didn't want to interpret. It was wet, sloppy and reeked of sexual activity of some sort. Kissing, he hoped. Then Luce's voice spoke again, dreamy and far away. "Anyway, have fun and I'll talk to you when I get back, whenever that it is. Love you, baby."

The message ended. Sighing, Kyle put his phone back into his pocket and met Louis's enquiring gaze. "She's flying to Paris," he murmured. "From the sounds of it, she's having fun."

Louis's eyes gleamed in satisfaction. "Then I have you all to myself for the night. Shall we get another drink?"

Kyle thought he might as well. It was only eleven and he wasn't ready to go home yet. Eric wasn't waiting in his bed so what the fuck did he have to lose?

"Yep, let's do this. Except this is my round. I don't expect to be a kept man."

Oh God, and now he was flirting.

Louis laughed loudly. "Kyle, I am quite sure of it. Yes, you can buy me a cocktail. A hanky-panky if you please."

Kyle hooted with mirth. "One hanky-panky coming up. Although there'll be none of that tonight." He cast a mock glare at Louis who collapsed in amusement.

"Ah, we shall see about that. I am sure we can put our minds to mischief if we think about it."

As Kyle motioned the waiter over, he felt a warm glow inside. Tonight was turning out to be rather pleasant after all. Making new friends wasn't so tough.

A week later, Kyle was in Club Delish helping Ryan take in a new alcohol order. They held their respective stock sheets and ticked off the deliveries one by one. It was a cool day outside but inside the bar it was warm. Sweat trickled down Kyle's back as he stood there.

As usual, Ryan looked completely in control and effortlessly together. The man didn't even have a sheen of perspiration on his face, unlike Kyle who'd rolled up his shirtsleeves and untucked his shirt to let air circulate around his body

"Are you looking forward to Eric coming back tomorrow?" Ryan raised an eyebrow at Kyle, who scowled.

"Oh, did he go away? I hadn't noticed." Kyle turned and placed his stock sheet on the bar as he studied it without seeing. He hadn't had any other texts since the last one of Eric with the busty blonde.

Ryan sniggered. "You've been like a bear whose favourite twink has been taken away, darling. Don't try to fool me. Delilah knows better."

Kyle's face burned. *Am I that transparent? Oh, yeah. This is Ryan.*

"I don't really care whether he's back or not," Kyle declared loftily. "I met some really nice guy at the casino the other night and we've been hanging out. Eric coming back is neither here nor there."

He and Louis had been seeing each other as friends. They'd been to a film and dinner at Galileo's, where Kyle had met the famous and oh-so-cute head chef Eddie. Kyle loved men with red hair and Eddie had been adorable. And from the way Gideon, the restaurant owner, kept a predatory eye on him, he obviously thought so too.

Ryan sidled up to him. "Liar," he said softly. He reached out a hand as if to pat Kyle's arm then pulled it back.

"You don't have to do that," Kyle muttered. "You can touch me if you want to."

Ryan narrowed his eyes. "You seem a little skittish around people who touch you. I don't want to make you feel uncomfortable."

"I'm only uncomfortable with guys who seem…threatening." Kyle couldn't meet Ryan's eyes in case he saw the shame there. "My friends don't count among them."

Ryan growled. Actually, growled. "I knew someone had done a number on you. If you ever want to talk about it, you know I'm here." He gave Kyle an awkward pat on the back then turned to finish his stock count. Kyle was relieved beyond measure Ryan hadn't pushed the issue, and had simply given an offer of support.

"Thanks," Kyle said gruffly and picked up another lengthy stock sheet. They had a lot to go through before the club opened tonight. Wednesday night was Leather Night and they were expecting quite a crowd.

Later that evening, sandwiched between two muscle-bound leather daddies making out on the floor as Kyle tried to navigate back to the bar and check on the stock and general goings-on, he spotted a familiar figure talking to Ryan in a quieter spot of the club.

Eric was back. Kyle's stomach fluttered and he couldn't stop the tingle that spread through his body at seeing his wayward paramedic. He ignored the flush of warmth and pretended he hadn't seen Eric. Kyle knew he was being childish, but he couldn't help it.

His plans were thwarted when someone shouted his name across the floor.

"Kyle." Dammit. "Eric's here. Do you want to say hello?" Kyle scowled at Ryan, whose face shone with glee. Or perhaps Mr Always Perfectly Groomed had sweat on his face, Kyle thought uncharitably. He'd no option but to turn and make his way toward the pair.

Eric looked amazing. Tanned, chestnut hair curly, and he was wearing a white cut-off vest with tight black jeans. The man looked edible enough to eat right there. Kyle wanted to bite the face off the young man behind Eric eyeing him with a distinct look of appreciation and lust.

Mine, he wanted to growl. *All mine*. Fuck off. And yet he had no idea whether Eric was his or not.

Getting closer, he swore inwardly. Crap. Ryan was as impeccable as ever, no trace of perspiration.

Eric smiled uncertainly. "Hey, Kyle. How are you doing?"

Kyle waved a purple-tipped hand airily. "Oh, I'm good. Out and about."

Eric nodded. "That's good. Good." He cleared his throat and glanced around.

Kyle couldn't resist it. "I thought you weren't coming back until tomorrow? At least, that's what someone told me. I didn't know first-hand of course."

His snarky comment had a visible effect on both Eric and Ryan. Ryan snorted with laughter and turned around with a flap of his hand. "I'm going to leave you bitches to sort things out. See ya." He disappeared into the throng.

Eric, however, looked shamefaced. "Yeah, 'bout that. I'm sorry I didn't call but where we were had a bad signal. We had satellite phones up on the mountain, but personal calls weren't really allowed."

Kyle reached up and ran a hand through his hair, trying to look nonchalant. "Oh, don't bother to explain. I understand...wait. What do you mean they didn't allow you personal calls? I thought you were on holiday in the US?"

Eric gaped at him. "The US? No, I was in France for work. I was in a remote holiday spot on a private estate filling in for a friend of mine who broke his leg. Why did you think I was in America?"

"Ryan said you were backpacking in the Grand Canyon. I assumed that was the US?

Eric laughed. "Ah, that would be because I was at Verdon Gorge. It's called the Grand Canyon of Europe. Ryan must have got confused."

Kyle felt a little stupid, but still riled. "I had no idea there was another one in bloody France."

"And I wasn't backpacking." Eric explained. "Not in the true sense. I was a medic up there in one of the fancy retreats run by some billionaire bloke. The guests all go off hiking and skiing, and they like a medic or two on call. It's good work, well paid, so I took it when my mate David couldn't go. He broke his leg."

"Oh." Kyle wasn't sure what to say. It seemed a reasonable something for Eric to do given his day job, and perhaps Kyle had judged Eric too harshly. He'd been out saving lives after all. How could Kyle stay annoyed with him?

Eric reached out with a soft smile and caressed Kyle's cheek. "Did you get my texts? I managed to get away to the town for a little bit when we picked up supplies. Signal wasn't great but I managed to get to the top of the mountain nearby. Thought I'd let you know I was okay."

"Oh, I could see that," Kyle said. "The picture of you with the full-breasted lady was a nice touch. I thought you might have changed sides."

"Someone jealous?" Eric's eyes darkened and Kyle's knees weakened.

Kyle huffed. "No. We don't have a claim on each other. I don't care what you do when you're away." He turned to the barman and asked for a snakebite shot. He needed it.

"I think you do," Eric said with a grin. "That full-breasted lady was the wife of the owner of the resort. Happily married as well."

"Whatever." Kyle knocked back the shot the barman had pushed over to him.

Eric snorted. "No, not jealous at all," he remarked. Then his face shadowed. "Listen, I'm sorry I didn't tell you before I went that I was going away. Things at work got hairy. It was pretty stressful and before I knew it, I was on the plane." He gave a wry grimace. "I wasn't really good company at the time so I didn't think you'd want to hear from me being all depressed."

Kyle motioned for another drink and looked at Eric. "You want anything?"

Eric nodded and Kyle ordered two snakebites.

"Is that the real reason you didn't tell me you were going away?" he snapped. "Because you feared my sensibilities may take offence at the fact you'd had a bad day and felt shitty and you'd taint me with it?"

Eric blinked. "Yeah, I suppose…I wouldn't have put it that way, but yeah, I guess so."

"Well, perhaps next time you can stop thinking I'm some sort of blushing virgin and let me know you're out of town for two weeks, Mister." Kyle's tone rose a faction as he went into drama mode.

Shit. He'd just done exactly what he'd said he wasn't going to. He'd staked a claim on the man. He downed his shot in frustration and slammed it on the bar.

Eric watched him through shuttered eyes, reaching for him and pressing their bodies together. The hard ridge in Eric's pants nudged Kyle's.

"That was the hottest thing I've ever seen—you getting all toppy on my arse." Eric murmured in Kyle's ear.

Kyle opened his mouth to say he absolutely wasn't, and found it filled with tongue. His lips were taken in a kiss that made his cock harder and sent thrills through his body he imagined were akin to being shocked by a pulse of warm electricity.

He heard a moan and was mortified to find out it was him. Eric lavished attention on his mouth as if were the tastiest thing he'd ever eaten. Kyle was thoroughly enjoying being the dish of the day. Dimly he was aware that he was making out during his work shift in the middle of Ryan's club, but he didn't care.

Warm hands slid under his shirt and sent ripples of fire down his skin and straight into his groin. Waves of desire and need spread like warm smoke through his body and he knew if he didn't stop this, he was going to come in his pants.

That would not be a good public look for the house manager of Club Delish. Ryan would castrate him.

Reluctantly, he pulled away, regretting the loss of Eric's hungry mouth the second he did. "I'm still mad with you. And I'm supposed to be working, not fucking about on the dance floor."

"Then maybe later I can fuck you *on* the floor." Eric trailed a finger across Kyle's swollen and wet lips.

Kyle wanted to melt into a puddle of goo simply at the prospect of his promised debauchery. "Oh God, you can't say things like to me here."

He rejoiced as he looked down to see yes, his silk tuxedo jacquard jacket was covering most of his excited groin from view.

Eric slid a hand across Kyle's cock, his eyes dark and liquid. "I can if it gets you to not be mad with me." He squeezed and bent down for another kiss.

Kyle stepped back, noticing the bartender's amused grin along with other patrons who watched them like sharks scenting blood. He had no doubt if he turned around and snapped his fingers right then, he'd have a horde of them begging to be the meat in a Kyle and Eric sandwich.

"No," he said as firmly as he could muster, given his aroused state. "This isn't happening right now. If you really want to apologise to me, you can pick me up after work so I don't have to navigate the tube to yours and take me back to your place. I get off at two." *Only four more hours to go.* "Then we can look at the whole 'fuck on the floor' scenario. If you're not too tired, that is."

"Oh, I'll be fine," Eric drawled, his eyes darting to something behind Kyle. "Not sure you'll make it though." He began to laugh softly.

Kyle turned and looked right into icy blue eyes that bore into his brain like a drill.

"Having fun, are we?" Ryan purred and Kyle's stomach roiled. Delilah was making an appearance. "I confess, I thought I was clear when I said in my job interviews my employees should set an example on the club floor and not commence fucking in plain sight."

"We weren't actually fucking," Kyle said piteously, "We were just—"

Ryan waved a finger. "Tut-tut. It was certainly fucking—of the mouth."

Kyle looked into the crowd, his hard-on now shrivelled to nothing in the face of Ryan's—or was it Delilah's? Sometimes the two were indistinguishable—wilting glare.

"Now, Kyle darling." Ryan's silky voice was both dangerous and teasing. "Do you think you could get back to work and leave your sexual liaisons until you get off at twelve?"

He opened his mouth to say his shift didn't end until two am and shut it promptly at the amused glint in Ryan's eyes. *God, I have the best boss and job ever.* "Yes, I can keep it in my pants until then. Eric, pick me up at twelve, okay? I'll meet you in the staff car park."

Ryan acknowledged Kyle with a regal tilt of his head then winked at Eric. Without a backward glance, in that way he had, he glided off toward the staircase to his office.

Kyle took a deep breath. "Well, that didn't go as badly as it could have. See you later then? I'd better get back to work before Ryan-Delilah really lets me have it."

"It's a date." Eric turned to go, his hair mussed and unruly where Kyle had run his hands through it. "And I look forward to the floor show." He grinned and Kyle's thoughts turned dark and raunchy. He suppressed them manfully.

"Let's hope I'm good enough a performer for you then. See you at twelve."

Kyle blew a kiss to Eric, turned and made his way to the front desk, rolling his eyes in despair at his easy submission into needy pushover.

Chapter Ten

God, that man is going to be the death of me. He kisses like sin.

Kyle's mouth was a sinful smorgasbord of sheer aggression and no-holds-barred tongue action, and for one moment Eric thought he might suffocate. The man knew how to work his body too. Every press of his against Eric's, every sneaky touch of his fingers on skin and the heat-inducing cock rubs against Eric's groin—God. Kyle had no idea how lethal he was to Eric's sanity.

Or maybe he did.

When Eric reached home and got into the shower, anxious to prepare for Kyle's visit, he reran his mental video to recall every moment of that kiss in exquisite detail. More than once his hands drifted down to his cock, which begged for release. He wasn't sure what was better—beating off in the shower to take the edge off, or waiting for Kyle to do it for him.

He settled on rubbing one out, knowing that if he got inside Kyle in his current state Eric would be likely to blow too soon. He wanted to seduce Kyle until he cried Eric's name, and then he would take his time sliding into Kyle as they enjoyed a leisurely session that made them both gasp and come their brains out.

Kyle deserved to be cherished, like a fine port.

Eric dressed in loose sweats and a long-sleeve tee-shirt to pick up Kyle. Eric drove his rarely used white 1972 MGB Roadster, nicknamed Little Lady, which was parked outside his house, ready to go. It had been a birthday present from his parents on his twenty-first birthday.

He'd already fixed the tonneau cover, thinking it was a bit too chilly to have the car's roof down.

He set out into the chilly night air. It might only be a few miles away, but London traffic could be a bitch any time of the night or day.

Eric got to the club just before twelve and parked behind the venue in a small car park reserved only for employees. Ryan had been gracious about letting him park Little Lady there, muttering something about fools with cars and their obsessions with scraps of smoke puking metal.

Eric wasn't even sure Ryan could drive, let alone whether he owned a car.

While he waited, Eric scrolled through his phone, glancing up now and then to check if Kyle was there. It wasn't a particularly savoury place to walk. The parking lot was dark and closed in, and against one wall there was a row of dumpsters.

Eric hated dumpsters. He'd once been called out to a scene to find the man in need of medical assistance had just beaten another human being to death and dumped her in a dumpster like garbage.

Eric had hated every minute of tending to his patient, a crude roughneck of a brute who'd had a major heart attack after his violent assault on a much younger woman, apparently his sister.

Aaron had taken one look inside the bin and shaken his head. There'd been no saving the beaten girl. The brute, however—that was another matter. He'd recovered to face murder charges and was now in prison.

"Why the hell are you thinking about this now, when you're about to go on a date with a sexy bloke?" Eric muttered to himself. "Think sexy thoughts."

He closed his eyes, took a deep breath then squeaked in panic when firm lips pressed against his with a low chuckle. His eyes shot open as the warm mouth left his.

"Are you meditating?" Kyle stood beside the open window, rucksack over his shoulder, jacket slung over his arm. He looked tired but happy. "Aligning your chakras, are we?" He grinned then walked around the front of the car to climb in the passenger seat. He muttered as he tried to stretch out his long legs. "I love the wheels, but she isn't Kyle friendly." He glanced across at Eric. "You look as if you fit, so how come I feel like a sardine?"

"Practice," Eric assured him as he started the car. "I'd suggest you keep your bag on your lap as there isn't room for it in the back."

Finally, Kyle settled in with his seat belt fastened and bag on lap as instructed. Eric pulled out of the dim parking lot and soon they were on the street.

"Thanks for coming to fetch me," Kyle murmured as he rested, half asleep, against the chair back. "I wasn't sure how far away you lived, and after a shift like tonight, I'd have fallen asleep and missed my stop."

Eric placed a hand on Kyle's thigh. "No problem. I love an excuse to get Little Lady out and drive her."

"Little Lady?" Kyle chuckled. "I like it."

Watching Kyle fall asleep was like watching a kid snuggle in under a comforter. He tucked in against the side of the door, hugging his bag possessively. He wore a small smile with those full lips slightly parted. His chest rose and fell evenly under his light pink shirt and a strand of dark purple hair fell across his cheek.

Eric wanted to brush it off but was scared he'd wake up Kyle. This man seemed to bring out all Eric's protective instincts—something he'd last felt with Lincoln.

"He reminds me of you, Linc," Eric whispered in the quiet confines of the car. "Strong on the outside, vulnerable on the inside. Mouthy and too damn sexy for his own good."

He could almost hear Lincoln's chuckle and reply. *You have a type, Eric-bear. Just remember he's not me. I'm gone. You need to find someone new.*

The thought brought a lump to Eric's throat and he was glad when he saw his house and pulled into his parking space. He switched off the engine and looked at Kyle, who slumbered on. It seemed a pity to wake him but he couldn't leave him here squashed in the car.

"Come on, Sleeping Beauty." Eric brushed his fingers down Kyle's bristled cheek. "We're here."

Kyle's eyes opened blearily and then he shot up, staring around him. "Oh, shit. I fell asleep, didn't I? I'm so sorry. Some late-night booty call this is."

Eric stared at him. "Booty call? That's not what this is about, is it? Because that wasn't my intention…"

Kyle swiftly shut him up by pressing cool lips to his. "Hush. It was a figure of speech." He opened his car door and clambered out, stretching and giving a low groan of satisfaction. "Shit, I feel like one of those jack-in-the-boxes that's just popped out."

His tee-shirt drew up and Eric's breath hitched at the glimpse of Kyle's lean, naked torso and the treasure trail leading down, disappearing in his low-slung formal trousers.

"Come on, let's get inside," Eric said gruffly.

Kyle yawned and followed him inside like a lanky puppy. Eric reached up and switched on the light.

Kyle blinked. "Wow, nice. Very white and minimalist. Does the kitchen actually get used?"

Eric frowned. "Well, yeah, of course it does. I don't like stuff being out looking untidy, so it's all packed away until I want to use it. Same for the rest of the place." His home was a simple, clean, white and cream layout, an open-plan kitchen and lounge with two bedrooms to the rear.

Kyle nodded, seemingly fascinated by Eric's lack of ornaments or décor. Apart from his Michael Thompsett prints on the walls, Eric wasn't keen on *stuff* littering his place.

Kyle dropped his bag and bounded over to the long, chenille couch, bouncing on it as he lay down. His face assumed an expression of bliss. Eric despaired whether he was ever going to get to take Kyle to bed tonight. The man looked hell bound to fall asleep.

"This is really comfy." Kyle gave a moan of enjoyment.

Eric sighed and went to the small bar cabinet. "Do you fancy a drink before you go to sleep?" He pulled down the bar top and considered what he had in there. Whisky would do, he knew Kyle enjoyed it.

"Who said anything about sleeping?" came an unexpected murmur in his ear, followed by a warm lick.

Heart thudding, Eric turned to face a smirking and obviously unrepentant Kyle. "You have to stop doing that." Eric exclaimed. "You're going to kill me. And how the hell do you manage to creep up on people so silently?"

Kyle shrugged. "It's a knack." He ran a finger down Eric's jawline, eyes sparkling. "Can I take a quick shower? I'm all sweaty and someone spilled booze on me." He grimaced. "I reek of tequila."

Eric could only nod. "Guest bathroom is through there, down the hallway, first on the right. Spare guest towels in the cupboard under the sink."

Kyle winked, retrieved his bag and disappeared. Eric heard the bathroom door close and the shower start.

The door opened again and Kyle yelled, "You can get ready for me in your bedroom, if you like. I know we said we'd floor-fuck but I'm sure the bed will be much more comfortable on my arse. I'm not partial to rug burn." The door slammed shut again.

Eric needed no further prompting. He turned off the lights and took the two drinks into his bedroom. He placed one on each of the bed's side tables, switching on the bedside light and flooding the room with dim glow. Disrobing quickly, he folded his clothes into a neat pile on the dresser.

When he slid under the duvet, he turned to check he had lube and condoms stashed on the side table. Satisfied he did, he laid back, arms above his head and waited for Kyle.

The wait was worth every minute. Fifteen minutes later, Kyle appeared, fresh and naked, his cock half-mast along his smooth groin. He stopped in the doorway, framed by the light in the bedroom and grinned wickedly as he struck a seductive pose.

"Well," he drawled, watching Eric with hungry eyes. "If it isn't a hunk of paramedic in the bed, waiting to screw me senseless."

He prowled over to the bed, nipple rings glinting in the light. Eric wanted to tug on them with his teeth until he heard Kyle make a small sound of both desire and pain.

Kyle threw back the covers, and like a feral cat, he slinked up the bed to straddle Eric. The air left the room as he wriggled his arse against Eric's rising cock then smiled predatorily.

"Hello there," he purred.

Eric's thoughts jumbled in an already scrambled brain from Kyle's clean scent, the slide of his warm skin against him and the sheer wantonness he gave off as he leaned in to lick a slow trail around Eric's bottom lip.

This man is sex on a stick. I'm not sure I can handle him.

"Stop looking so damn worried," Kyle murmured. "I'm not going to eat you." The eyebrow with the ring in it rose suggestively. "Although that might be a lovely thing to do sometime."

He'd removed his purple contacts and his deep brown eyes shone with both humour and lust.

Eric could stand the teasing no longer. He reached out and pulled Kyle down to him. "I need to taste you."

The wet, open-mouthed kiss that followed sent his senses into further turmoil. From the sounds Kyle was making into his mouth, he was turned on too. His hardened cock pressed against Eric's abs, slicking their stomachs with arousal.

He was dimly aware of Kyle breaking the kiss and lying down beside him, legs akimbo, his desire evident as his hardened cock jutted into Eric's side.

"Enough of that," Kyle said breathlessly. "Time to fuck me."

Eric couldn't take his eyes off Kyle opening the lube bottle and pouring a liberal amount on his fingers. Then, like a sculptor caressing clay, Kyle reached between his legs and slid his finger around his hole, finally pressing inside.

His eyes closed, and his eyelashes fluttered as he fucked himself with his fingers. "Uhhm, yeah," he groaned. The next moan was louder.

Despite his arousal, Eric grinned when Kyle opened one eye, no doubt to gauge his reaction. *God, he's such a fucking tease.* "I think you've had enough fun, mister," he murmured as he slid over Kyle's sweat-sheened body. "It's my turn now. Move your damn hand. That's mine."

Eric caressed the outside of Kyle's rim then slid two fingers inside the warm, tight, wet hole. "This," he promised, and then he removed his fingers from Kyle arse. "And this," he groaned as he gripped Kyle's cock, sliding a clenched hand up and down.

Kyle uttered a strangled moan and Eric felt a surge of satisfaction as he watched those brown eyes grow glassy and unfocused while Kyle's breathing became uneven and deep.

"That feels so good," Kyle murmured breathily. "Imagine how it will feel when I have your beautiful cock inside me."

Eric leaned forward and tugged at the nipple ring with his teeth, causing Kyle's breaths to become erratic. "God, you are incredible," Eric whispered. "So damned responsive."

"Stop with the compliments and fuck me," was Kyle's strained response.

Eric chuckled as he rolled on the condom while Kyle watched avidly, lips wet, pupils flaring. Then, pushing Kyle's hands above his head, Eric held him down as he braced himself for entry into the sexiest creature he'd ever met.

When he breached Kyle's arse, both men gasped and froze, staring at each other.

Fuck, that feels good. He was made for me.

Sweat beaded on Kyle's face. "Stop being such a gentleman and keep going," he snarled, pushing his hips upward, impaling himself deeper. "I didn't say you could stop."

"You're such a bossy bastard," Eric grunted as he did what he was he told.

Then all conversation stopped. There was only the sensation of skin on skin, the taste of salt in his mouth from trickling sweat, and the slow and steady rush of blood in his veins making him feel more alive than he'd been in a long time.

Beneath him Kyle was pumping his hips, scratching sharp nails into Eric's back and uttering nonsensical panting moans as he gave himself over to his bliss.

The primal act of sex, of being as close to another human being as one could get, had always filled Eric with awe. With Kyle, though, he felt—god-like. Thrusting into the willing man writhing under him, feeling his pleasure like electric pulses beating through his cock—this was what it meant to be young and alive; to be part of something bigger than both of them.

And there was no doubt he wanted more of it.

"God," he gasped as his body prickled with heat and his balls contracted. "I'm not sure I can go any longer."

Kyle arched his neck, baring a slender, flushed throat. "Then blow, baby. Give me all you've got."

Eric exploded into the condom as his orgasm hit with avalanche-worthy force. He shuddered as the aftershocks hit, small tremors that shook his body and gave him goose bumps.

"Fuck, that was hot, seeing you come like that." In one fluid motion Kyle pushed Eric onto his back, and straddled him, his cock still inside Kyle. Eric was too spent to react other than look into the heated gaze of the man who currently held him captive in every way.

Kyle reached down and took hold of his own dick. "I want to shoot all over you, paint you like a masterpiece with my come." A few hard jerks resulted in exactly that. Hot, slick semen coated Eric's stomach and chest, and a few stray strands landed on his lips. He licked it away, relishing in the taste of Kyle in his mouth.

Kyle flopped down, boneless and sticky. For a moment neither one said anything then Eric ran a hand down the smooth flanks lying over him. "Epic as that was, we should clean up and get into bed." Eric closed his eyes, loathe to move but needing to breathe.

Kyle nodded, hair brushing Eric's nose and making him sneeze. "Sorry. Yeah, I guess we should do that." He moved off and flung his legs off the bed. "I'll go first." Kyle stood then disappeared into the bathroom.

Eric must have dozed off because when he opened his eyes, a warm body was snuggled up next to him. He rolled his shoulder against heated flesh; his arm had gone to sleep because Kyle was lying on it.

"Ugh," Kyle murmured. "That tickles." He shuffled a little further away and Eric stretched out his arm, trying to relieve the pins and needles.

"Don't worry," Kyle said sleepily as he snuggled a pert, warm arse in against Eric's front. "You were asleep when I came out so I cleaned you up and tucked you in. Go back to sleep."

Eric wrapped an arm around Kyle and drew him closer against him. "Thanks. Sorry I fell asleep."

"S'right," Kyle snuffled from the depths of the pillow. "Not the first time a bloke's gone to sleep afterwards."

Eric kissed the back of the fragranced hair that was still making his nose twitch. "I'm not surprised, if that's what sex with you is like. You really know how to take it out of a guy."

He felt a pang of jealousy for any other man who'd had Kyle this way.

Kyle's head shook fractionally and his muffled words filled Eric with hope. "Not like that with anyone else. Just you. Now go to fucking sleep, will you?"

Eric smiled widely and settled in. He could get used to this.

"No, you can't use a sex swing on the stage tonight. I've told you. The beams above are not strong enough to support you and your partner having bloody simulated sex."

Eric grinned as Kyle, looking more than frazzled, glowered at a two-hundred-pound drag queen who was battering her eyelashes shamelessly at his—boyfriend? He still wasn't quite sure what to call Kyle after the last two weeks. Two incredible weeks of hot sex, cuddles and finding out they both loved Vietnamese food. And Alexander Skarsgård.

They hadn't done much talking about personal stuff, but Eric was at the point where he felt he could talk about Lincoln. He only hoped Kyle would open up soon about whatever gave *him* nightmares.

Eric sighed. *We're a right pair; both of us with our bad dreams and three am wake-up calls. At least the cuddling each other back to sleep makes up for it.*

Cuddling that occasionally led to sleepy, comfort sex.

Tonight, it was the Annual Hoity Toity Tart Fashion Show at Club Delish. It was a major event and had driven Kyle to distraction, even with Ryan's limited help during the recovery stage of his convalescence.

Kyle paced up and down the stage, gesticulating angrily. "Calypso, I don't care what Delilah told you. Those beams won't hold you both and I have to think about health and safety." He glared at Calypso Cockbottom, who simply rolled her eyes at the dramatics.

"And it's not only you two I need to worry about," Kyle said cattily. "I have to worry about you both flattening anyone who might happen to be standing underneath you when the swing gives way."

Calypso opened her mouth and screeched in horror. "Oh, you little bitch. How dare you? It's not my fault you look like one of those candidates for Carnival of the Skinny Man Whore. Some of us love our extra pound of flesh. Don't we, Qunta?"

She flicked the Japanese fan she was holding in the direction of another queen, who stood on the side-lines, smirking at the show playing out centre stage. Eric had been highly entertained for the last ten minutes as the argument escalated, and had seen the amused glint in Calypso's eyes as she baited Kyle.

"Oh, yes, honey," Qunta Kryptonite agreed, as she simpered at her partner. "Some of us like a little something to hold onto while we fuck. We don't want to cut ourselves on the bones of said skinny man whore."

"I am not a man whore," Kyle said between gritted teeth. "And I'm not skinny. Am I, Eric?"

Shocked out of complacency, Eric thought quickly. "No, babe, you're not. Nice and lean is what you are." He sidled up to Kyle, lowering his voice. "You do know these two are just riling you up on purpose, don't you?"

Kyle looked at him and winked. "Oh yeah. It's a game we play. Hang on for the ride."

He strode over to Calypso and prodded her ample chest with each word he spoke. "You.Are.Not.Having.A.Sex.Swing.On.My.Stage. Got it?"

Calypso flapped her fan in his face and glared. "Fine. I'll talk to D. She'll let me have one." She flipped her long black hair over her shoulder and motioned to her partner. "Come on, darling. Let's go find Delilah. She won't be as bitchy as this one."

"Don't go busting her chops," Kyle warned. "She's still recovering from her surgery and you'll have Mango to deal with if you cause her grief."

They both looked worried for a moment. "We'll manage him," Calypso didn't look so sure, but waved a hand in Qunta's direction. "I'm sure two of us weighty bitches can handle little old Mango."

As the two queens exited stage-right, Calypso looked back and flipped her middle finger at Kyle. He flipped her back.

Eric shook his head. "Wow, this is something else. You need some sort of psych education and qualifications to deal with that kind of crazy."

Kyle sniggered. "I have it in spades. In Vegas, they were big, bold and brash, and you had to learn to give as good as you got. Calypso is pretty cool. She might go to Ryan and ask him and he'll tell her the same thing. He was the one who told me to stop the idea in its infancy. Not enough balls to do it himself." Kyle laughed loudly. "And Mango won't let them bug his man. He's become über-protective. That's why Ry hasn't been around much. Too busy being loved up and pampered by a reformed Mango. Mind you, Ry deserves it after all he's been through."

Kyle frowned and stuck out his hip with a turned wrist on it that angled his elbow at forty-five degrees. "So, you really think I'm not too skinny? I don't really care about the man whore comment because, well, there might be a grain of truth in that, but skinny? Pfffft."

Eric pulled Kyle's face toward him and planted a kiss on his lips. "No, you're just the right shape and size. We fit together perfectly."

Kyle smirked. "We do indeed. Like a mortar and pestle. Except my arsehole is tighter."

Eric couldn't help a guffaw at that. "Jeez, you have no filter."

Kyle sidled up and wrapped his arms around Eric's neck "And don't you love it. Thanks for changing your shifts around to help me here today. It's been a bonus." His lips found Eric's and he worked them into a deep and passionate kiss.

All thoughts of oversized drag queens dangling from sex swings disappeared from Eric's mind.

Chapter Eleven

Kyle peered around anxiously at the throng of people waiting to see the fashion show in support of Ryan's chosen charity—supporting brain tumour sufferers. Club Delish was full to brimming; the turnout had exceeded expectations.

"This is great," he muttered to Eric, who stood beside him. "Ryan is as high as a kite on the numbers."

Eric nodded. "I suspect it's *because* of Ryan. His customers hold him in high regard. I guess this is an opportunity for them to see he is well."

Kyle agreed. "It's his first proper public appearances on stage as Delilah Delish since the operation. And of course, Laverne is with him tonight." He laughed. "Those two together are always a hoot."

Ryan's best friend Lenny James a.k.a. Laverne was a well-loved character at Club Delish. It was her designs and those of her students that were being showcased tonight, with sales proceeds going to the charity.

Kyle sniggered. "I know Mango wasn't particularly thrilled that Ryan was performing 'only a month after he'd had fucking brain surgery.' The sight of Ryan giving the deadly laser gaze froze *my* blood, I can tell you. His response to Mango, 'Stop fucking molly coddling me and let me get back to being a normal man.' He's one scary dude."

Eric rolled his eyes.

"No, really. After the argument, they went upstairs and I'm betting there was a slap or two, and then no doubt sizzling make-up sex. That's the way that pair roll." Kyle sighed. "God, I hope everything goes well. I'm a nervous fucking wreck."

"Stop worrying." Eric massaged Kyle's shoulders. "It's all going to go off perfectly."

"You think?" Kyle nibbled on his nail. "There's been so much organisation, I can't help thinking I've forgotten something." *Maybe I didn't order enough booze, or toilet paper. Oh God, did I make sure the kegs were changed earlier?*

Eric chuckled. "Unless Calypso's installed that sex swing you told her not to, I can't see anything going wrong."

Kyle darted a swift glance to the rafters above to check nothing unwanted was swinging down.

Eric stifled a laugh. "Baby, you did good. Ryan even said so himself, didn't he?"

Kyle nodded distractedly. "I s'pose. He seemed pleased with all the arrangements, said he couldn't have done it better himself."

"There you go then. Relax."

"Easy for you to say," Kyle muttered, biting another fingernail.

Eric heaved a sigh and grasped Kyle's hand, moving it away from his mouth. "I can think of better things you can do with that mouth of yours other than bite your nails."

Kyle was about to reply when a female voice behind them startled him. "Hi, London. You look fabulous as usual. And this must be Eric." Kyle looked over to see Lucinda and her date.

Luce's eyes were speculative as she stared at Eric, and he hoped she wasn't going to go too crazy on his arse. This was the first time they were meeting, and Luce had already intimated she was going to grill him about his intentions. After everything she had been through extricating him from Mario's demented grasp, she was an overprotective mama bear.

He pushed that memory from his mind and smiled brightly. "Hey, gorgeous. I'm glad you made it. And who is this beautiful woman beside you?"

Luce laughed, eyes sparkling. "This is Lanie, my date. Lanie, my best pal, Kyle."

Lanie was tall, thin and blonde, and had an air of class Kyle suspected belonged only to the very rich. He presumed this was the Lanie with whom Luce had flown to Paris. Lanie had a charming smile and shook his hand warmly. "I've heard a lot about you from Lucinda. You two have shared some real fun experiences, huh, from your Vegas days?"

Panic shot through Kyle's chest and he flicked a worried glance at Luce. She shook her head slightly and instantly Kyle was relieved. "I'm sure she's told you a lot of lies about me too." He bent over her hand and brushed his lips across her knuckles. "Don't judge. She's a continental bitch." He turned to pull his man forward. "This is Eric."

Lucinda inclined her head toward him. "Good to meet you at last, Eric. I've heard a lot about you."

Eric looked a little awkward. "Likewise. I'm really pleased to meet the woman who keeps him on the straight and narrow."

Kyle watched proudly as everyone shook hands. Eric looked sexy tonight in his black chinos, open dark blue shirt with just a hint of chest hair, and sleeves rolled up to his elbows, which put his strong forearms on display. Kyle had convinced Eric to use a little hair product tonight to tame his unruly curls, and he looked like a model about to walk down the catwalk.

Knowing Luce as he did, Kyle headed her off at the pass before the awkward Eric grilling began. "Well, you know where the bar is, Luce. I suggest you get you and your girl a drink and then sit down to watch the show. It's filling up quickly and I'd hate for you not to get a seat. I need to check on a few things." Kyle kissed Luce on her cheek then crocked a finger at Eric. "C'mon you. I need some help backstage to make sure all the queens are ready to start in fifteen minutes."

"Oh, is that what they're calling a quick shag in the back nowadays?" Luce said archly. "And not so fast, hotshot. I want to get to know Eric a little better first." She smiled like a Cheshire cat.

Kyle's heart sunk. That smile meant business.

"Eric, baby, what are your intentions towards my bestie? He's super special to me, and I want to make sure you treat him right." Beside her Lanie cast a sympathetic glance Kyle's way.

Eric crossed his arms across his chest and grinned at Lucinda. "My intentions? Wow, how much time do you have? Because my intentions are really detailed."

Kyle held back a chuckle. Luce looked taken aback, which was rare.

"I need to know you're not going to break his heart, and you're not in it just for the sex. Which I imagine is wild, given the looks of the two of you."

Kyle blushed scarlet. "Luce, for God's sake. I can look after myself. I don't need you being all mother hen on my arse. We've had this discussion before."

Eric drew him closer, putting a possessive arm around his waist. Kyle sank into the cuddle as his boyfriend's hand drifted down to stroke his arse.

"I can assure you, I have exceptionally good intentions toward Kyle, and he's special to me."

Kyle fluttered his eyelashes. "Aw gee. You gonna be my papa bear?"

Eric mock-growled, "If you like that sort of thing, boy, I'm not objecting. I have a leather harness with your name all over it."

They stared at each and then burst into laughter. Lucinda tossed her hair back but Kyle saw the pleased look on her face.

"Well, all righty then. Come on, Lanie. Let's get those mojitos we promised ourselves. Let these boys have their dirty fun 'helping each other backstage.'"

She pointed a finger at Eric. "But if anything happens to my friend, you'll have me to deal with as well."

She took Lanie's hand and dragged her through the milling crowd.

"She's a little scary," Eric confessed as they watched them go. "And I wouldn't want to face her in a dark alley."

"Yeah," Kyle said fondly. "She's great. We've been through a lot together."

"Maybe one day you'll tell me all about it," Eric murmured.

Kyle ignored that remark, took Eric's hand and drew him through the crowds toward the stage.

"So, is 'helping him backstage' a euphemism?" Eric asked.

"A euphemism for what?" Kyle was distracted by the sight of one of the patrons stripping off to reveal a nice six-pack.

"For us having raunchy sex." Eric flashed him a wicked grin.

Kyle wished it was. "Sorry to disappoint you, baby. It's an actual thing. Speaking to the raving drama queens in the back and making sure when the fashion show starts in"—he looked at his watch—"ten minutes, everyone is ready to go."

Good thing they'd checked. The queens were rebellious, disorganised and ornery. Kyle had to go on stage with a harried apology to the patrons that the show was running late. Finally, everything and everyone was sorted, and he and Eric were able to sit toward the back of the house, both with stiff drinks in their hands, while they watched as Delilah Delish swanned onto the stage.

Kyle's part was over. Now it was up to the performers and models on stage. He took a deep swig of his drink, leant back and closed his eyes in relief.

Eric nudged him. "She looks pretty good, doesn't she? I wish I could wear a white fringe dress and a black feather boa like she can."

Kyle stared at him. "Is that a secret fantasy of yours then? Dressing in drag?" He rather appreciated the idea. He could see that russet hair against a background of pale green headwear and Eric's long, muscled body squeezed into a—hmm, perhaps a dress like the one Alexander McQueen designed. Shades of deep red, bronze and white with a black feather trail.

Oh, yeah. Kyle's dick really liked that idea.

Eric raised an eyebrow. "Would it get you hot? Because I'll do anything that makes you want me."

Kyle leaned forward and ran a finger over Eric's lips. "You don't have to *do* anything to turn me on. You just do." He noted with satisfaction the darkening of Eric's green eyes and the unconscious lick of his lips. *Who's the man? You can still do it to him with just a few words.*

"Could my front of house manager please stop making out with his delicious man in plain sight and pay attention to what *I'm* saying?" The words from on stage echoed in the room. Startled, both looked up to see Delilah glaring at them from heavily made-up eyes. "There's time to suck his dick later."

Kyle snorted with laughter and Eric waved at Delilah who blew him a kiss.

"So, my darlings, you all know I've been a bit in the wars lately."

The room erupted in cheers and cries of "Welcome Back, D. We love you!"

Delilah acknowledged them with an incline of her perfectly coiffed wig. Only someone who knew her well would notice she was quite overcome with the support in the room. She cleared her throat, a sound that resounded into the microphone wired on her front.

"Of course, *someone* in this room"—she cast a withering stare at Mango who sat at the front of the stage—"was an overprotective papa bear and went all dom on my arse, not letting me do as much at the club as I'd have liked."

Mango stood up, a wide grin on his face, and gave a stately bow. He sat down, his gesture having everyone in fits of laughter, interspersed with ribald comments about what he was doing with Delilah's arse.

Sitting beside him was a tall, statuesque black man who said something to Mango. He burst into laughter. Kyle grinned. He'd met Brook Hunter, Laverne's boyfriend, only a few times and had really enjoyed his company.

"In my considerable absence"—an icy stare was once again thrown Mango's way—"my right-hand man, Kyle Tripper, has been running our club."

Kyle noticed the slight emphasis on "our" and his body flushed with warmth at the acknowledgment of his part. Eric squeezed Kyle's hand and looked at him with affection.

"He is my greatest asset, other than these." Delilah cupped her breasts to the support of laughter and jeers. "And I'm fortunate to have him. I'd like to say a huge thank you, my love, for organising tonight and making it such a success, despite the whinges from the bitches backstage. I think we owe this young man a round of applause. He already has my eternal thanks for keeping Club Delish going while I was otherwise indisposed."

Kyle's face heated up as everyone clapped and hooted, and Mango nodded thanks and gave him a thumbs-up.

When the merriment was over, Delilah turned to face the stage wings. She curtsied and as she did so, another queen made her entrance.

Laverne was clad in a slinky black ensemble with grey sleeves resembling bat wings. She glided in on ten-inch heels and the audience erupted into catcalls.

Delilah sported a wide grin as the two women air-kissed, the sound of smacking lips exaggerated before Delilah said, "The delightful Laverne and her assistant Leslie Scott will now announce her designs and the next models. I wish you a wonderful night right through until the end of the show. I'll be back soon, sweethearts. I promise. Just got a little rough and tumble to go take care of." She made a lewd and lascivious gesture to Mango who shook his head in amusement.

Laverne took centre stage. Kyle perked up when a figure he knew quite well swished in next to Laverne. Willowy and black haired, Leslie Scott was the epitome of style in a hand-cut lilac suit crossed with a dove-grey shirt and a darker grey waistcoat. He was a delicious sight to behold, although Kyle knew Leslie's boyfriend, Oliver, would have his guts for garters if he'd ever made a move on him. Besides, he had his own man now.

"Bitches," Laverne shrieked as she surveyed the crowd. "Let's get the party started. The gorgeous Leslie here is going to accompany the models on their way down the catwalk and add a little bit of glam to the proceedings. Because they sure as fuck need it with the bunch of queens we've got down here." She smirked and batted her long eyelashes at the audience.

"Looks like the models are ready for us. First up in an ensemble of violet taffeta and silk bronze trim, designed by me of course, world-famous fashion icon, Laverne Debussy-Smith. And here is the oh-so-edible and charming Calypso Cockbottom."

Laverne flourished a hand toward the woman currently mincing onto the stage as she resumed speaking. Leslie walked over to Calypso, holding out his elbow.

"All these dresses are available to purchase at extremely affordable prices, with all the proceeds going to Club Delish's chosen charity, Going Grey, which supports the work being done on research into brain tumours. Buy a dress for you, your wife, your mistress, your boy, your boyfriend, your favourite drag queen…we thank you for any support you can give us."

Eric laughed beside Kyle. "My God, this place is a hoot tonight. I'm loving all the cattiness."

A voice shouted Kyle's name, and he turned to see his new friend Louis, who looked resplendent in a charcoal grey suit, wine silk shirt and a white and burgundy spotted tie.

Despite being happy to see Louis, Kyle was also a little apprehensive. He hadn't told Eric about his new friend yet. *I hope they get on with each other. Louis can be a bit—intense.*

Kyle stood up to greet Louis, and as he did, he was pulled into a hug and a smacking kiss was planted onto his cheek.

"Hello there, my gorgeous man. This place looks amazing. Those queens look fantastic in those outfits. I may have to invest in one. Perhaps I will wear it out next time we go to dinner." Kyle was enveloped in another hug fragranced with Paco Rabanne and the faint smell of cigars.

"Hi, Louis. It's good to see you too. You're looking as handsome as usual."

Louis finally let him go and Kyle looked over at Eric, whose face was filled with what looked like astonishment and, he hoped, perhaps a tinge of jealousy.

He hastened to introduce the two men. "Louis, I need you to meet Eric. Eric, this is my friend Louis. We met while you were away."

Louis held out a hand to Eric, who took it. "So, you are the man he talks nonstop about. It's a pleasure to meet you." He stepped back and waved a hand toward Kyle. "At the time we met, I was trying to talk him into having a drink with me with an intention to perhaps enjoy a little more of his company. He politely declined. I can see why now. You look enticing in that ensemble. I had no idea black chinos and a grey wool blazer could look so alluring on a man. And I love the black oxfords. Very chic." He grinned, showing white teeth. Kyle stifled a chuckle at the dumbfounded expression on Eric's face, not having been able to get a word in edgeways.

"Babe, Louis will grow on you. He tends to have no filter so he spews stuff out at an alarming rate without even knowing he's doing it. And you know what, I don't think I told you how hot you look tonight. Because you do look sexy as fuck."

Eric blinked and then slowly nodded. "Yeah, thanks, to both of you. So, you two have been seeing each other then?" His gaze landed on Kyle. "You hadn't mentioned it before."

Kyle shrugged. "What with everything going on, it slipped my mind." He turned to Louis. "I reserved you a seat down the front. It has your name on it. Grab yourself a drink and enjoy the rest of the show. I'll catch up with you later."

Louis reached over to hug Kyle again. "Indeed, we will. Do not leave without saying goodbye."

Kyle and Eric watched Louis plunge his way through the crowd. Kyle sat down and reached over to take Eric's hand. "So, what do you think? He's great, isn't he?"

Eric shifted uncomfortably. "I don't know him well enough yet. If you like him, then I guess he must be. He's a bit—handsy, isn't he?"

Kyle made a sound suspiciously like a man giggle and then clapped a hand over his mouth. That sound surely hadn't come out of his mouth, had it?

His man was jealous. Kyle wanted to milk this just a little more.

"Oh, he's a bit affectionate. It's just how he is. Does it bother you?"

Eric looked a little affronted. "I wouldn't ever tell you who can and can't touch you, babe. That's your decision." He leaned in and brushed Kyle's cheek tenderly. "I just don't want him thinking he can ever take you away from me. Because I'm not letting you go without a fight." He smiled softly.

Kyle's eyes filled unexpectedly as the words sunk in. His heart beat erratically and he thought he might explode from the feels.

Eric really wanted him. He would fight for him. And he might be jealous, but he accepted Kyle's responsibility for his own body and his own wellbeing.

He wasn't Mario.

"Wow, that's pretty deep." He tried to make light of it, but his throat was a little choked. "Lucky then I'm not thinking of going anywhere, huh?"

Eric pulled Kyle's chair flush with his, and for a while they were both oblivious to the sounds around them as their kiss became the only thing that mattered.

It was close to two am when an exhausted Kyle was shooed away from the club by an equally exhausted Ryan.

"Go home," he instructed, blue eyes tired yet the look on his face was one of satisfaction. The amount of money raised for the evening had far exceeded expectations. "Rufus is doing the final checks to see we don't have unexpected overnight visitors, and Greg, bless him, is going to close up for me."

Ryan looked as if he couldn't keep his eyes open, and as Mango strode toward him, Kyle had no doubt Ry would be rushed to bed and tucked in before the door was even locked.

Mango's face showed his concerned. "Babe, you've overdone it, as usual. Come on. Let me get you upstairs. I'll carry you if you like." He grinned. "I've done it before, remember?"

Ryan flapped a hand and scowled. "You big ape, I'm not a damsel in distress. I can make it on my own, don't *you* remember?" His tone was fond and the loving glance he gave his boyfriend made Kyle wonder if he might find the same thing with Eric. "Now, shoo, you two. And Kyle, baby?" Ryan reached over and pulled Kyle into a fierce hug. "Thank you. For tonight and every other night. I couldn't have managed to get through all this without you there looking after this place."

Kyle's throat clogged up with emotion and he hugged Ryan back. "No problems, boss. Glad to help anytime. You get to bed, and sweet dreams."

Mango gave him a quick, awkward pat on the back. "Yeah, what he said. Ry's been lucky to have you in his corner. Appreciate you looking out for him."

Kyle spotted Eric on the other side of the room, helping Greg pick up overturned chairs in the private area and setting them right. Eric waved, his smile lighting up his features.

Kyle waved back, and Ryan laughed. "Go on, fuck off you two. Go do the horizontal mamba if you can manage it. Me, I don't think I can even manage to stay awake long enough to enjoy a blowjob." The sly look he gave Mango made Kyle doubt that was true.

He chuckled. "Great. See you Monday." He walked over to Eric who beamed at him. "Ready to go? I'm about to drop where I stand."

Eric's face brightened. "What, right here? Isn't that a bit public?"

Kyle punched Eric on the arm. "Is that all you think about—sex?" He collected his jacket from the back of the reception desk and handed Eric his. "Come on. Let's go home."

Home tonight was Kyle's place. They decided to walk, shift off some cobwebs and the scent of being stuck in the sweaty and testosterone-reeking club all night.

The evening air was chill, the streets still vibrant with people. Eric offered his elbow to Kyle who took it, a warm feeling in his chest that he wasn't averse to displaying affection in public. Kyle wouldn't go further—he'd learnt his lesson about unwanted PDAs the hard way, so kissing or making out in public was a no-no—but the snug feel of his arm tucked into Eric's was soothing. He felt safe and cherished.

The dream was shattered when a sudden push at his back caused him to stumble, twisting to fall awkwardly on the pavement. Instinctively, he put his arms up to shield his body and face. Before he blocked out the view, he caught a glimpse of a familiar figure. A tall, dark-haired man loomed toward him, something swinging from his right arm.

Fuck, he's found me.

Beside him Eric shouted something, but Kyle couldn't hear. His ears were buzzing, bile had collected in the back of his throat and overwhelming fear claimed his body and mind like an invasive entity that drove all rational thought from his brain and made him remember all the abuse he'd suffered.

The words that came out of his mouth were strangled and fearful, ones he thought he'd never utter again. "Mario, I'm sorry. Please don't…."

Something wet hit his face, unwanted and foul smelling. Kyle curled into a ball, waiting for the kicking to start. Instead, strong arms encircled him in their warmth, and dimly he recognised the scent of Eric's aftershave.

"Babe, he's gone. It was just a guy on the lam. I think he snatched a handbag. He ran into you. Are you okay? Are you hurt?"

Kyle shuddered and moved his arms away from his face. Anxious green eyes stared into his, as fingers gently wiped something from his face.

"He spat at you. I want to clean you up. I don't want anything of that bastard's on you. Can you stand? Come on. Hold onto me. We're not far from your flat. Let's get you home."

Eric helped Kyle stand. His body shook but it wasn't from fear alone. He felt ashamed and embarrassed, and was sure Eric would leave him now—because who'd want a man like him?

So indelible, his self-loathing mixed with the current panic, creating a miasma of dark emotions he thought would destroy him.

He let Eric guide him along the busy street, and when they reached his block of flats, it was Eric who led Kyle into the grumbling lift and to the front door of his home. It was Eric who reached into Kyle's pocket and drew out the keys to unlock the door.

But it was Kyle who turned to Eric when they were safely inside, the door shut and locked, and quietly said, "Thank you for seeing me home. I appreciate it. You don't have to stay with me. You can leave. I'd understand if you don't want to come back." Of course he would mind. He'd scream and cry at his own failure until he was drained and comatose.

Eric stared at him, face grim, eyes haunted. "I'm not leaving until I know you're okay. And why the fuck wouldn't I want to come back?"

The bedroom seemed like the right place to be right now, buried under the covers, so Kyle moved toward it, not answering. *I just want to sleep and forget all this for a while. Maybe it'll take this ache in my chest away.*

"Kyle? Talk to me. Please." Eric sounded wounded. He sighed sadly and turned to face Kyle, who had trouble meeting Eric's gaze.

"You must think I'm pathetic. How can you not? I see a person that looks like someone from my past and I fall to pieces. What kind of man does that make me?" Eyes stinging, he walked toward his room. "I won't think any less of you if you don't want to see me anymore."

"Kyle." Eric's tone was fierce. "I'm having trouble with all this."

He laughed harshly. "That's why I said you could leave."

"No." Eric appeared at his side but he made no attempt to touch him. "I meant I'm having trouble with you thinking I'm the sort of man who'd kick you to the kerb because you have some sort of PTSD. I thought you knew me better. I'm disappointed you would even consider I'd do something shitty like that." He didn't wait for an answer. He strode over to Kyle and gathered him into his arms. "I'm not going anywhere. Get used to it. Because you and I—we need to seriously talk about things."

Kyle stopped and let the fatigue wash over him like a veil. Hope flickered in his chest like a small candle. "Are you sure? I mean—"

Soft lips pressed against his and then lingered over his cheek. "I'm sure. You and I—we're the same. I know exactly what you're going through because I've been through it myself. But this isn't about me right now. All I want you to know is that I understand. And I'm not leaving."

Kyle let himself collapse against Eric's broad chest as tears fell while he surrendered to Eric's embrace. Before he knew it, he was undressed, bundled into bed and a duvet was drawn across his body.

"Sleep now. We'll talk in the morning." Eric kissed Kyle's forehead then brushed a strand of hair from his face. "I'm going to take the couch so I don't disturb you. I'll be around if you need me. I'll leave some clean clothes on the dresser for you."

"'Kay," Kyle muttered, his body warm and languid under the covers. "Thanks, baby. For everything."

The light went out and he fell into sleepy darkness.

Tick. Tick. Tick.

Kyle watched the second hand move around the clock at the side of his bed and groaned softly. He'd been lying awake now for over an hour, summoning up the courage to get up. He thought he might be smiling like an idiot.

He's still here.

He heard Eric moving around the kitchen and smelt coffee brewing, which was scented heaven. That alone should have him scrambling out of bed ready to face the day. But he needed another few minutes to gather his thoughts and plan what he was going to say when he faced Eric.

The sharp rap on the door made him jump.

"Hi, sleepy-bones. Get your lazy arse out of bed and come get your coffee. I know you're awake. I heard you sighing like a woman out of some Victorian melodrama."

Kyle bolted upright indignantly. "I so did not. I was thinking."

There was a muffled, amused snort outside the door. "Yeah, well, stop thinking and come have some breakfast. I'm making your favourite."

"You made me French toast?" Kyle swung his legs over the bed, a smile forming.

There was silence. "Oh, French toast is your favourite? I thought it was eggs over easy on rye bread." Eric sounded a bit put out and Kyle chuckled, feeling better. "Anyway, you've got a few minutes to shower—the eggs are going now."

Kyle showered in record time, slung on some sweatpants and a tee-shirt and left his room feeling decidedly better than when he'd gone in the night before. He found Eric in nothing but jeans, his chest bare, dishing out eggs onto already buttered toast.

God, he *looks good enough to eat.*

"This, ermm, all looks good." Kyle waved at the small two-person dining table. The coffee pot was on the table, the mugs already filled. It was the picture of domesticity.

Eric grinned. "I hope you don't mind me taking over your kitchen. I promise I'll clean up, Mr Neat Freak."

Kyle noticed with dismay how untidy his usually pristine kitchen was. Eggshells lurked in plain sight. Crumbs were scattered across every surface and there was even a piece of burnt toast casually flung on top of the tea towel. Fat spattered up the white backsplash tiles. He swallowed, trying not to let the state of his kitchen affect him too much. "No problem. I see you're one of those chefs who really get into what they're doing."

Eric cocked his head to one side as he slid Kyle's plate over to him. "Is that your way of telling me I'm a messy bastard in the kitchen? Because I know I am. I mess first, clean later."

He sat down with his plate and took a slurp of coffee. "God, that's what I needed. Now eat, before it gets cold."

The food was tasty and Kyle hadn't realised how hungry he was. When they'd finished eating, he managed to convince Eric to leave the cleaning up. Kyle found it therapeutic; plus, it meant he could get things cleared the way *he* wanted them. It also delayed their conversation, which he wished there was a way to avoid altogether.

When he'd finished, he went to the lounge to join Eric, who was lying on the couch, legs stretched out. Kyle sat down in the armchair and looked across at him. "That was great, thanks. It's been ages since anyone did that for me."

Eric raised an eyebrow. "Good, I'm glad you enjoyed it. And don't think I didn't notice your attempt at getting me out of your kitchen so you could clean up your way. I would have cleared my own mess."

Kyle nodded. "I know. It's just I like things done a certain way, so…" He fiddled with the drawstring of his sweatpants.

The room went silent.

"Are you going to tell me what happened last night?" Eric shifted on the couch, turning on his side. When Kyle didn't answer, he went straight for the jugular. "Who is Mario?"

Kyle cleared his throat then exhaled. "He was my ex in Vegas. We were together around five months."

Eric's eyes narrowed. "He was abusive?"

Kyle nodded. "You could say that." His fingers clenched together.

What the fuck am I saying? The guy nearly killed me.

He closed his eyes, carefully choosing his next words. He sensed Eric's presence on the arm of the chair before he opened his eyes.

Eric ran a comforting hand down his back. "You going to tell me more? I don't want to push too hard."

Kyle took a deep breath, and then, like a floodgate had opened, it all came out. Torrents of fear, shame and pain mixed in with the need to tell this man next to him, this decent man, exactly why he'd acted like a scared child last night.

"Mario was older than me. He was a backup dancer at the casino. We met during one of the stage shows when I went backstage to deliver some drinks. I worked bar for extra money when I wasn't on the tables."

The memory of the night he'd first seen Mario flooded back. The dressing room had been empty apart from a few men busy disrobing and wiping makeup off their faces. He'd noticed Mario straight away, having seen him perform, and had been smitten.

Mario was dark, tall and muscled, with a dancer's grace. He'd smiled at Kyle when he'd taken his drink, and before Kyle had known it, he'd given Mario his number and arranged to meet him the following day after the show. That had been the start of Kyle's nightmare.

Eric moved over to the couch and patted the seat beside him. "We'll be more comfortable over here," he muttered softly.

Kyle moved to sit next to Eric and leaned in to Eric's side. The contact gave him strength to tell his story.

"Mario was Italian, and Catholic—staunchly so. He was bisexual, but nobody knew. If his family had found out, they'd have disowned him. They were deeply religious. Him having a nice boy slut on the side was all he wanted."

Eric said nothing, but made soothing circles on Kyle's back.

"I thought I was in love with him. He was charismatic, great in bed and spoilt me like crazy. I thought we were a great couple. Then suddenly, everything changed."

He slid closer to Eric. "His uncle Roberto from Italy came to live with the family. He was a priest who was cold and uncompromising. Mario adored him. He began spending time with him, and less with me. At first, I thought it was a family duty thing. Family meant everything to him." Kyle's throat grew tight. "One night he came over to my place in a foul mood after spending the day with his uncle. Roberto must have said something to him, because Mario stormed into my bedroom and..." The memory of that first assault came flooding back. "He hit me. With his fists, again and again, sending me halfway across the room."

Oh God, I can't tell him the rest of it. I can't.

Eric's hands stopped and he moved back, his face a masque of fury. "No reason? He just came in and beat the shit out of you?"

Kyle nodded jerkily. "The scariest thing—he didn't say a word. There was just this disgusted look on his face, as if I were a piece of shit. Then he left the room. I managed to get to the bathroom and clean up, but I was pretty out of it. I went back to bed and must have fallen asleep. When I woke up, he was there beside me, cleaning my face and putting ointment on it. He said he was sorry, that he'd never do it again."

Kyle closed his eyes and heaved a juddering sigh. "And I believed him. For a while, we were okay, went back to normal. That was when I met Luce at the club. She came to my rescue one night when he was getting mouthy. Told him to piss off and find someone his own size to pick on." He smiled at a better memory this time, one of meeting a crazy woman with pink hair telling his boyfriend exactly what she thought of him.

Of course, he'd never told her that had led to a beating when he got home. Luce would never have forgiven herself. It had been worth that beating to hear someone stand up to Mario like Kyle never had.

"Did you tell her about Mario beating you?" Eric's face was stony.

"No, not then. Things seemed all right, so I thought...no need for anyone else to get involved. Until it happened again. And kept happening. It was as if Mario was a different person. An evil, sadistic bastard, whose only intent was to hurt me. He said I brought out the 'dark touches' in him." Kyle laughed cynically. "Apparently what we did sexually was all my fault."

Kyle looked at the floor. "It's why that time we first went out I got spooked when you asked me about a lip ring. I used to have one, and a tongue stud, but the bastard tried to rip them out with his teeth a couple of times." He stroked his upper lip. "You can still see a faint scar if you look really closely."

He cleared his throat and continued, "Finally, I had to tell Luce about the fucked-up relationship I'd had with Mario. I had too many bruises and she was observant. Hell, she was so pissed off I had to stop her going to the cops. She had no idea what Mario was like. He wouldn't have gone quietly, and I didn't want her getting hurt." He grimaced. "As it happened, it wasn't long after that it all came to a head anyway."

Eric blew out a puff of air. "Didn't you have anywhere else to go? What kept you there?"

Kyle stared at him. "What kept me there was his threat to harm Luce if I left him, or went to the police. He threatened to beat her face in if I didn't stay with him. And he would have done it too. I had no doubt. He hated her, was jealous of the time we spent together. I tried to explain we worked together, so we had to see a lot of each other, but he didn't like it. I could have gone back to my parents in Chicago, but then what would have happened to Luce? Her life was there at that club."

"You stayed to keep her safe."

"Not just for that, but mainly. I thought I loved the man. Each time he beat me, I forgave him. I was stupid. His uncle was telling him about the sins of homosexuality, and it was driving him crazy. Mario needed the sex, the kink, but he thought it was a sin. He took it out on me, the so-called 'instrument' of his failing with God. If I even uttered a swear word which he thought was blasphemous, it led to another beating. I was in over my head. I didn't know what to do."

Eric squinted, "What kink?"

"Huh?"

"You said he had a kink. What was it?"

Kyle's bones chilled. "Oh, nothing, it was just an expression."

"Kyle." Eric's tone was compassionate. "Speaking from experience, if you're to have any hope of dealing with your PTSD, you're going to have to face the demon who put it there."

"Why don't you tell me *your* story?" Kyle spat, trying desperately to head Eric off. "You said you've got experience—well, tell me about it."

Eric's face clouded over with pain and Kyle felt like a heel for causing it. "I promise I will. But first, you need to finish yours."

The shame of Kyle's past washed over him. "Rough sex, okay? Mario liked rough sex when he went all Avenging Angel on my arse. He used to beat me, bloody me up then fuck me—no condoms, no lube, just straight. He said it would teach me a lesson and I deserved to be hurt for what I did to tempt him into sinning. The last time he did it, I suffered a ruptured rectum and had to be rushed to hospital. He'd hurt me so badly, I was in there over a week. They said I could have died. If Luce hadn't found me, I would have." Kyle was hyperventilating now, his hands shaking and body trembling.

"I'm sorry, baby, so sorry. I shouldn't have pushed you. Forgive me." Eric's whispered anguished words were heartfelt and Kyle tucked himself into Eric's chest, listening to the heartbeat under his ear.

"It's okay," Kyle murmured as tears slid down his cheeks, their saltiness lingering on his lips. "I feel better for having told you." He brushed Eric's jawline with his fingertips. He did feel better letting that out.

Finally, Eric looked up, eyes shining. "God, what you went through. I can't believe it. I hope that bastard got locked up for everything he did to you. If he didn't, I'll hunt him down and fucking kill him." The violence in Eric's tones was scary, and something Kyle hadn't heard from him before. A frisson of fear breathed cold air down his spine.

Eric would never hurt me. He saves lives; he doesn't damage them.

"Unfortunately, no. After the ambulance took me away, he rushed home to his uncle. I assumed he told him what he'd done because when I told the police about it, they went to his house and were told he'd gone away. I think his uncle spirited him back to Italy. The cops looked for him, but he'd gone to ground. Luce said there was a rumour he'd gone to a seminary in Europe somewhere to become a priest, but that was unverified."

"Did the police contact Interpol? He almost killed you, for God's sake." Eric hugged Kyle tighter.

"They did, but I think they gave up when there were no sightings of Mario anywhere. You know how it is. Something else more important comes up than a gay man being beaten by his lover." Kyle leaned into his boyfriend's comforting embrace. "The last time I heard from him was a crazy telephone call telling me how I'd messed up his life, that God may never forgive him, and that he was going to hunt me down and make sure I never did it to anyone else."

"Did the cops take the threat seriously?" Eric asked between clenched teeth.

Kyle nodded. "I think it's over, but seeing someone who looks or acts like him still triggers the trauma all over again." The telling had been cathartic and he was exhausted. "Now you know it all. I'm sorry I ended up a whimpering mess last night." He picked at his fingernails. "Luce has been telling me to see someone about it. A therapist. Maybe I will." He had the number of someone she'd recommended. He thought perhaps now was a time to call him.

"I think that's good advice." Eric shifted away and stood. "I feel like I've been through an emotional wringer, so I can imagine how you feel. What say I go make some cocoa, then we can sit on the couch, watch a film and snuggle under the duvet for a while? That work for you?"

Kyle smiled weakly. "That sounds fabulous." He hesitated. "Don't forget you owe me some details too. Maybe when we're in a better place, you can tell me. I think we've both had enough angst for one day."

Eric nodded. "Why don't you get the duvet? I'll get the drinks."

Kyle leaned back and closed his eyes, curling in the safe warmth of the spot Eric had just vacated.

Yawning, Kyle stretched and untangled himself from the duvet. Peering outside, he saw London enveloped in drizzle and mist. Dim shapes of people huddled under umbrellas were reminiscent of a painting by Rauf Janibekov, one of his favourite artists.

There was a sudden crash in the street and he jumped. Walking over to the window, he saw two people in the road gesticulating wildly as they each surveyed the damage to their cars. People passed by in the torrential rain, seemingly oblivious to the heated discussion of insurance culpability.

He shook his head and walked over to the kitchen. He found Eric in there, peering out into the road, coffee mug in hand. He turned when he heard Kyle come in. "Hi, sleepyhead." He gestured outside. "Silly buggers playing bumper cars out in this weather. I was checking to see they were okay, but they look unharmed. I hope you don't mind me taking over your kitchen but I needed coffee."

"As long as there's enough left for me." Kyle ran a hand over his bare chest, catching a glimpse of himself in the cupboard glass. He winced. His tousled hair stuck up like porcupine spikes and he had dark circles under his eyes. He hitched up his sweatpants.

Eric nodded and took down a fresh mug to fill it with strong black coffee. "I always make loads of extra coffee," he said as he handed the mug over. "It's the only thing that keeps me on time for my shifts most days."

Kyle took the mug gratefully and padded to the couch. He sat down to look out the window at the rain.

Eric plonked down beside him. "Did you have a good nap? You looked so relaxed. I didn't have the heart to wake you. You must have been exhausted."

Kyle nodded. "I was, a bit," he confessed. "Baring your soul takes it out of you." He hesitated. "Thanks for being there for me earlier. I'm not used to telling people that story. I know I'm a weakling who should have had the balls to stand up to a bully, but that's easier than it sounds."

Eric reached over and took Kyle's hands in his, rubbing them gently. "You have nothing to apologise for. And I get it— truly, I do. I see people every day in bad situations just like the one you were in and you can't judge them. No one knows what's going on in their heads. All you can do is lend support and try and get them to take care of themselves."

He scowled. "And you're no weakling. You re-made your life, and not everyone can say that about themselves."

Kyle gave a happy sigh, feeling safe and warm as he snuggled into Eric's chest and placed a kiss against his throat. "Thank you. That means a lot to me."

They sat together, Kyle listening to the beat of Eric's heart. "What are your plans for the rest of today?"

Eric hugged him closer. "It's raining out, as you can see, so indoors sounds like a good call. Maybe you can show me some more of those tricky card games. Teach me a couple, maybe?"

Kyle grinned, feeling more relaxed. "I'm sure I have a few up my sleeve you could learn."

"Then cards it is." Eric went to the dresser and pulled out an old deck of cards. "Show me how you did it in Vegas, baby."

661

Chapter Twelve

"Hell's bells," Eric muttered to Aaron in disgust. "Look at those fucking people. Like hyenas." He scowled at them fiercely. These last three days had been a bitch, so why should today be any different? The crowd around them had phones out, taking pictures of their latest incident and Eric wanted to swear at them, run over and yank the gadgets out of their hands.

They'd taken a call out for a woman who'd collapsed during the busy Saturday morning rush hour. After fighting their way through traffic and cursing at cars blocking their way, Eric and Aaron had finally arrived at the scene.

It took all of Eric's skills to move the man hovering over the woman's supine body away to let Aaron look at her. His partner's eyes conveyed the result to him even before he'd spoken the words. Aaron stood up and faced the middle-aged man in front of him.

"Sir, what's your name?" he asked gently.

"Jeremy. Jeremy Woden. My wife's name is Emily."

The man clenched his hands together as he gazed down at his stricken wife. "Emily, Emily, wake up," he sobbed, reaching down and pulling at her lifeless body. "The ambulance is here, you have to wake up."

Aaron's face was grave with sadness. "Jeremy, I'm so sorry to tell you this. Emily is gone. I think she might have been dead a little while. How long were you trying to wake her up?"

"Emily isn't gone," Jeremy spat out, tears rolling down gaunt cheeks. "She can't be. I've been talking to her for the last fifteen minutes."

Aaron threw a look of compassion at the man. "My gut feeling is she's had an aneurysm. It would have been quick.

What do you mean, you talked to her for fifteen minutes? Did she respond at all?"

Jeremy's face clouded. "No, she didn't answer, but I swear I saw her eyes move. I thought if I talked to her, she'd wake up."

Eric stifled a weary sigh. The chances were that they wouldn't have been able to do anything if it had been an aneurysm, but waiting that long to call an ambulance had certainly lessened the woman's chances.

"Who called you anyway?" Jeremy asked wildly. "I didn't ask for anyone to come. I was going to wake her up and take her home."

A voice called out from the crowd. A slim Asian woman waved at them. "I did. I thought she needed an ambulance." Eric walked over to her. She was one of the few that didn't have a phone in her hand, merely a concerned expression on her face.

"Thank you," he said softly. "I think it's too late but you did what you could."

"Oh my God." The petite woman's face paled and her eyes filled with tears. "How tragic. That poor man."

The screech of absolute pain and grief from behind him made Eric's skin crawl, and goose bumps crept over his body. He turned around just in time to see Jeremy Woden run like a scared rabbit toward the entrance to the parking garage. His face was white but determined, and instinct made Eric run after him.

"Jeremy, stop, let's talk," he shouted as he followed the man up the winding turns of the driveways. Jeremy seemed intent on getting as high as he could. Eric had a bad feeling about this.

The sudden constriction in his chest had little to do with the fact he was exerting himself—he was fit—and more to do with the onset of something that felt very much like a panic attack.

If Jeremy was going to do what Eric thought he was going to, he wasn't sure he could deal with it.

I have to stop him.

Jeremy must have been a runner because he sprinted away fast, leaving Eric behind. The next thing Eric knew as he reached the fourth floor level was that he was too late. Jeremy was perched on the ledge, crouched low, muttering words Eric couldn't hear. He swallowed as he moved toward the determined man. "Jeremy, please calm down. I just need you not to move, 'kay?"

Jeremy stared back at him with dulled eyes. "It's all right," he reassured Eric, his face relaxing. "I know what I'm doing." He shrugged. "I can't live without her, don't you see? It's not something I can do."

He smiled at Eric and peace had suffused his face. "Thank you for trying to help anyway."

Eric could see the decision in his eyes. He'd seen it before. Adrenaline, shock, whatever it was, it propelled him forward to grab at Jeremy's arm. Before Eric could do anything more, the ledge was empty and all he held was the pale blue cardigan Jeremy had been wearing.

"No," he screamed as he dashed forward and looked over the side. He'd never forget the sight of the broken body lying four floors down, Aaron running toward it. It bore no resemblance to the man who only a few seconds ago had been on the ledge.

Bile rose in his throat as his chest tightened. He retched over and over again. Memories of another time and another man lying broken among rock and dust blinded him and pressed shards of sharp glass into his heart.

"Fuck," he coughed up as yellow fluid splashed onto the concrete floor. "Why did he jump?"

He dropped to his knees, uncaring of the fact he'd just coated his trousers with his own vomit as he knelt. The light around him grew dimmer; it was harder to breathe. He was dimly aware of a strong arm pulling him to his feet and forcing bottled water down his throat.

He barely registered the walk to the ambulance, supported by Aaron who murmured words of comfort in his ear. It was only when he was in the passenger side of the truck, eyes wet, chest heaving with sobs, that he realised he still held the cardigan in his hands.

Later that night, stretched out on the couch, Eric couldn't relax. Memories of the day played in his brain in a permanent loop. Aaron had gotten him back to the station and explained to their boss what had happened—panic attack, yes, like PTSD, past loss, needs a bit of time—while Eric looked on, feeling ashamed.

His protests had held no weight with either Aaron or their boss, Jim, and now Eric found he had an unscheduled couple of days off. Taken home like a fucking damsel in distress, he thought grumpily as he tried to get comfortable. What a clusterfuck.

His mobile chirped and he glanced at it and sighed.

Kyle.

He forced a note of normality into his voice. He simply wasn't ready to talk about the day yet. "Hey," he said, plumping up a cushion with his free hand and leaning back on it. "Everything all right?"

He and Kyle had only managed to see each other once in the past few days, work pressures being as they were. It had seemed strange being apart so long after their last intimate conversation when Kyle had revealed all.

"Yeah, all good. I was wondering if you were in the mood for company?" Kyle's tone was hopeful. "For some reason, Ryan seems intent on helping me with my love life and giving me more time off. I'm not complaining. He has someone else starting next week as a trainee manager. Her name's Kellie. She's a fun lady. I'm hopeful she'll do well and we'll both get some more time off."

"That sounds so like Ryan. He's a good man." Eric picked a thread off the couch. "How can she not be a good fit if you like her?"

I really want to see him, but I'm in no mood for company tonight, not even Kyle. He doesn't deserve my shit. He's been through enough.

"Mmm, flattery gets you everywhere." Kyle sounded as if he was smiling. "So, you up for it? Me popping round? I'll even bring pizza. You owe me a conversation too. Fair's fair."

Eric chose his words carefully. There was no way he was telling Kyle about anything from his past tonight. Maybe not ever, on second thought. "Um, do you mind if I take a rain check? I've had a shitty day, and I'm awful company."

There was silence.

Then Kyle spoke brightly. "Oh, okay. You need some time to yourself. I get it. No worries. Have a good night and let me know when you're feeling better. See you."

The phone went dead.

Eric slapped a hand against his forehead. Crap, had he just pissed Kyle off or not?

"Shit, shit, shit." He threw the TV remote across the room, watching as it hit a potted plant and dirt scattered in all directions.

"Great," he groaned. "More shit to clean up. It can wait till tomorrow."

He sagged back again on the couch and closed his eyes.

The following morning, Eric got out of bed, determined to stop his pity party. He'd faced rough times before and this was nothing like that time.

He needed to get a grip.

His dreams hadn't been welcome, and had involved mixed and random occurrences, some of which had featured Kyle broken on the pavement. But Eric told himself that's all they were. Dreams. *His* Kyle was alive. Real.

After coffee, Eric sorted out some buttered toast then texted Kyle.

Soz bout lst nite. I wz shit comp. FanC a drink tonight?

Twenty minutes later—thinking he'd messed things up—he got a text back.

I have no idea what you said. Please translate. Queens English please. :)

Ha. The smiley face must mean Kyle wasn't mad. Instead of regaling Kyle with text slang, he called him. The phone rang five times before it was picked up.

"I hope this is Eric and not some snot-faced teenage skateboard dude. Honestly, I have no clue what half of that message said. All I recognised was the word drink." Kyle's tone was dry but there was a trace of wary amusement.

Eric snorted. "Sorry, I automatically assume everyone knows text slang. I said I'm sorry about last night. I was shit company and do you fancy a drink tonight?"

I can throw this mood off and make time for him. I need to. I miss him.

"Oh, I can't." Kyle said regretfully. "Luce leaves at midnight to go back to the US and we have a girls' night out. Just the two of us. Because no doubt there will be tears and snot. And plenty of drama when we wave goodbye." He snorted in amusement. "Plus Luce and I have been tasked with getting something special organised for the club."

Eric tried to hide the disappointment in his voice. "Oh. She's off already? It was only last week we all had dinner together. Her departure came around quickly. Maybe another night then. I'll text her, say goodbye before she goes."

After what Luce had done for Kyle in Vegas, they deserved time together, and Eric certainly didn't begrudge them it.

There was silence, then Kyle spoke softly. "I heard that there's a great Impressionism exhibition at the National Gallery. Maybe you'd like to join me and we can go for dinner afterward? It's Monday night, so I guess you'll be off?"

Eric didn't have a clue what Impressionism meant but he wouldn't disappoint Kyle a second time.

"I like Impressionism." He made a mental note to look it up before they went out. "And Monday is good. And the best thing is it's only two days away. It's a date. Just let me know where to meet you."

"I'll do that. I'll text you but it won't be that stupid stuff you do." The smile in Kyle's voice warmed Eric. "Okay then, I'll speak to you soon. Looking forward to it."

Eric smiled at his phone. "Me too." He ended the call and slumped down into the armchair. His stomach was still queasy with the aftermath of yesterday's events.

Perhaps Aaron was right. Perhaps Eric needed to talk to someone again about the recurrence of the nightmares, the fact his job meant less and less to him each day and that he might have found someone else who was special.

Eric knew Kyle was important to him and was becoming more so every day. It was time to begin living again, to place his trust and caring in another person. Carrying the shadow of Lincoln's death in his soul and the still-twisted remnants of the similar event of yesterday was not going to bring him that solace.

With a sigh, Eric picked up his phone again and scrolled through the numbers. Then, with a resolve he drew up from his soul, he dialled a number he knew off by heart.

"Wow, that exhibition was amazing. The brushstrokes on that Cezanne were so intricate they were breath-taking." Kyle's enthusiasm about the art they'd seen should have lifted Eric's spirits more. Instead, he smiled and continued walking down the busy street, avoiding people coming in the opposite direction. The streets were packed, and he was irritated at the constant pushes and shoves as people strode past, uncaring of whether or not they knocked into anybody.

I should have known better than to go the therapist this morning. I should have cancelled. But Kyle was so looking forward to the exhibition.

This morning's session with his old doctor, Louisa Kenton, had been rough. A specialist in PTSD and survival guilt related disorders, she'd been soft-spoken yet thorough and it had left Eric feeling shattered and drained.

Dredging up old feelings had been tougher than he'd imagined. He'd never had thought his guilt at not saving Lincoln and surviving was a living thing, a despotic malingerer intent on destroying him from within. Dr Kenton had shown him a glimpse of the monster and Eric wasn't a fan. The fact he felt he'd failed at saving the suicide jumper hadn't helped either.

"I'm surprised you're so chipper when you got in at one this morning," Eric said dryly. "You sound as if you and Luce had a really good time."

Eric was glad that he'd managed to pull off normal. Sure, he'd been quiet—but then, Kyle said enough for both of them.

"Oh, we did," Kyle chirped. "We pub crawled, did the whole dance scene thing, then she caught her taxi to the airport around ten." His face clouded. "There was a lot of snot and drama. We were both a mess when we said goodbye, but she said she's coming back in six months' time." He bounced happily. "It's something to look forward to."

Eric frowned. "If she left at about ten, how come you got in at one?"

Kyle made puppy dog eyes at him. "I met up with an old friend. We had a few drinks afterward because I was still upset, and he was a shoulder to cry on."

"Anyone I know?" Eric asked. He felt a teeny bit put out Kyle hadn't called him, and yet, he'd been the one to tell him not to come over, hadn't he?

Kyle glanced at him slyly. "Maybe." He grinned widely. "Is that a hint of jealousy I detect there?"

Eric grunted. "No. I'm just being polite. You can be friends with whomever you want, you know that."

"Ooh, Mr Grumpy Pants," Kyle chided. He squeezed Eric's hand. "It was Ryan, you doofus. He'd dropped Mango off at the airport for some gung-ho conference he was going to and decided to pop in at the bar on his way home. That's where he saw me and we spent some time together."

Eric felt much better knowing it had been Ryan, but he wasn't going to give the satisfaction of letting Kyle know that. "I'm glad he's back to his old self now, and is getting out and about. That's cool."

"So, where do you want to go to get something to eat?" Kyle chattered beside him.

Eric glanced over and grinned. "Anywhere you like. What kind of cuisine do you fancy, my liege? The night is yours to command."

Kyle raised an eyebrow. "Oh, yeah? I can have anything I want?" He reached down and clasped Eric's hand tentatively. "This work?"

Eric's throat clogged up at the simple gesture. "That feels good." He squeezed Kyle's chilled hand harder.

The blinding smile Kyle gave him made Eric want to give him the world. *God, he's beautiful. I don't want to lose this— what we have. What we're building. I hope the feeling is mutual.*

"Hmm. Maybe we should try Korean? There's a great place a couple of blocks away," Kyle suggested.

"Sounds good. I don't think I've eaten Korean before. What's it like?"

As Kyle burbled on enthusiastically about tofu and kimchi, Eric's attention was diverted to an elderly man further away coming toward them with a guide dog. Eric deftly manoeuvred him and Kyle out of the way to allow him to pass unhindered.

Someone else, however, was not as courteous. A woman in front of them, carrying a shit ton of designer-labelled bags barrelled toward the man as if expecting him to give way. She was talking on a headset of some sort.

Eric opened his mouth to warn her to watch out. Before he could, the dog changed course, no doubt to attempt to change the owner's direction to avoid a collision. But the crowds were too thick and, as Eric watched in horror, the woman barrelled into the unseeing man, causing him to stagger and lose his balance.

He shouted in surprise and the dog gave a deep woof.

Leaving a startled Kyle behind him, Eric rushed forward to try and break the man's fall. He managed to grab an arm and used all his strength to curtail the man's descent. If he'd fallen to the pavement, the rushing throng of traffic may well have trampled on him.

"Sir, it's okay, I've got you. Here, let me help."

The man righted himself and threw a smile of gratitude toward Eric. "Thank you so much. I must have not been paying attention to Kirby…"

Eric presumed Kirby was the dog, who now sat patiently waiting for instructions.

"No," he said grimly, glaring at the woman who was clutching her parcels to her chest as if he were a thief attempting to take them from her. "It wasn't your fault. It was this woman who knocked you over. She was the one not watching where she was going." He stared at her. "Perhaps next time you could be more careful, madam."

"Fuck you," she spat, her face contorted with anger. "People like him shouldn't be allowed on the streets in rush hour. They're a bloody nuisance, them and their animals." Around them some curious eyes stared, but for the most part people scurried by uncaring.

A slow flare of temper crept through Eric's chest and he clenched his fists to keep it in check. "People like him," he said caustically. "You mean blind people? You're a nasty piece of work, aren't you?"

Kyle was at Eric's side now, a hand on his arm. "Calm down, babe." He moved over to the blind man. "Are you okay, sir? Can I help at all?"

"I'm good, young man." He waved a hand. "Thank you for asking though." He shook his head wearily. "And honestly, please don't get riled on my account. I'm used to it."

"Well, you shouldn't have to get used to it," Eric growled. "It's not right. You have as much right to be here with your dog as she has, selfish cow."

"Eric," Kyle said warningly. "Come on, let it go. She's not worth it."

The woman's eyes opened wider. "Not worth it? And what would you know about it, you freak?" She scrutinised Kyle, who stared back defiantly. "Fucking purple hair, piercings, and showing your body off. You're a sight, you are. I bet your mum's not proud of you, looking like that."

Kyle looked at her pityingly. "My mum's just fine with who I am, thanks. So am I."

Eric's fury welled at the bitch's biting words. In his opinion, Kyle looked perfect, and his tight stomach showing beneath the crop-top shirt he wore was fabulous.

His frustration at his therapy session and the emotions still surging beneath the surface got the better of him. "Better than being a bitch, lady. And leave my boyfriend alone. You want someone to insult, you can insult me."

Kyle pulled his arm, his face pale. "Eric, let's go. The gentleman is fine and there's no point causing a scene in public."

"I agree," the elderly man said. "Kirby and I need to get home to my wife. But thank you, both of you, for standing up for me. I appreciate it." He cast a glare in the direction of the now red-faced woman. "And you, madam, need to learn some manners. Good day."

With a farewell wave and Kirby leading the way, he set off. The woman harrumphed and turned to leave. But Eric couldn't let it go. "Enjoy the rest of your night," he called after her as she sashayed away. "Try not to knock any more elderly people down, why don't you?"

"Eric," Kyle hissed, face darkening. "That's enough. You're being a prick now."

Eric turned to Kyle in angry surprise. "A prick? For defending an old blind man? Jesus Christ, Kyle."

Kyle flinched. Eric moved toward him, arm out, intending on taking his hand to continue their walk home. His gut roiled at the sudden look of panic rising on Kyle's face. Kyle gathered his jacket closer around him in a defensive gesture and motioned to the street. "Let's go home. I've had enough of tonight." He moved swiftly forward, through the crowd. Eric followed, stricken at how the ending to their night had turned out.

Perhaps he had overreacted, but God, Kyle hadn't thought he was going to get violent with him, had he? Fuck it, surely, he knew him better than that?

Confused, awash with dread that he'd fucked up—again— and with the beginnings of a quiet flame of resentment that Kyle could even *think* that of him, Eric followed his lover home in silence.

Chapter Thirteen

Kyle opened the door to his flat and strode inside. He switched on the light and went to the kitchen for a glass of water. His hands were shaking slightly and he willed them still. Behind him, he heard Eric throw his jacket over the back of the couch and sit down in the armchair.

What the fuck had that all been about? He'd never seen Eric so aggressive, so in someone's face. It was as if the man he knew, the one who helped people and who had held him at night in some of the darkest of his times, was another person.

"Would you like a drink?"

Eric grunted, "No thanks."

Kyle turned back and poured another glass of water, downing it. He went over to the couch and sat down. Eric stared at him moodily.

"I'm sorry," he muttered. "For causing such a scene. I overreacted."

"Yes, you fucking did," Kyle retorted. "Care to tell me what had you in such a mood tonight? Don't think I couldn't see you were trying so hard to appear normal. I knew something was off the minute I saw you."

Eric shrugged. "It was a rough week. Not much to tell."

Kyle took a deep breath, trying to ignore the prickling irritation at Eric's reticence. *I spilt my guts and that's all I get?* "That's what *boyfriends* do, isn't it? Listen to your tales of woe?"

He hadn't missed the use of the word when Eric shouted it at the woman back on the street. At the time, it had given him a warm, fuzzy feeling that he'd been described that way.

Eric's nostrils flared at the word boyfriend.

"Unless of course, that was said in the heat of the moment and you didn't mean to use it." Kyle cocked an eyebrow.

Eric scowled. "I meant to use it. Duh. I mean, we are, aren't we?"

Even Kyle wasn't a hundred percent on that one, although he hoped so. "If you tell me what's bugging you. Otherwise, I'll have to recant the honorific." Kyle played his ace. "And you still owe me some payback, remember? A little something for me telling you my story. We agreed."

At that, something happened. Eric jumped to his feet and paced around the room like a caged animal.

"You want to see the inside of me? Try to figure me out and see if you can fix me? She tried that this morning and all it did was make me feel more miserable." He picked up a cushion and glared at it before flinging it back on the couch.

Kyle blinked. "Who tried what this morning? Who the fuck is *she*?"

The way Eric's arms folded across his chest told Kyle he wasn't happy about spilling the beans.

"I don't want to talk about it," he said. "It's my business."

Kyle had heard enough. "For fuck's sake. You just answered your own question about being boyfriends. If you're not ready to talk to me about whatever bug you have up your arse, I don't think that's a term we can call ourselves." His chest ached and his heart was bleeding but he had to say it. "I think the word fuckbuddies is more what you have in mind. And that's not something I want to be for you."

Eric remained silent and shut off. He folded his arms across his chest and looked down at the floor.

"The fact you aren't denying it makes me think it's the truth." The lump in Kyle's throat made the words hard. His eyes prickled but he was damned if he was going to cry. "Look, maybe we need to be alone tonight. You have issues. I have issues. Maybe this isn't a good idea right now." *Say something. Tell me I'm wrong and this is as serious for you as it is for me.*

Eric remained tight lipped. Kyle closed his eyes briefly then opened them to see Eric staring at him. His stormy gaze showed both pain and guilt but his face was unreadable.

Kyle reached for his phone. "I think maybe you should go home. I'll call you a taxi then we can see how things are tomorrow when we're both not so hyped up."

Eric stood up and pushed Kyle's hand away from the mobile. "That's not necessary," he said. "I'll find my own way home. Perhaps you're right. We need to think about things for a while. Alone."

Before Kyle could say anything, Eric had picked up his jacket and was out the door. It swung shut behind him and all Kyle could do was stand there and wonder how everything had suddenly turned to shit.

"And now—it's karaoke time!"

The audience in Club Delish roared in delight, anticipating the entertainment that was to come. Seated at the table in front of the stage, Kyle laughed out loud at how those words must have stricken fear and fury into Ryan. He knew how his boss felt about the dreaded curse of patrons butchering his favourite songs.

The fund-raising benefit had taken some organising; the little surprise they'd all planned for Ryan's unofficial welcome-back party had been hard to keep secret. Between himself, Luce, Mango and Lenny, though, they'd managed.

And now the object of that surprise, young teen singer and Goth sensation Callum Webster was pouring his heart out on stage. Kyle was sure when Ryan realised exactly who they'd convinced to karaoke at his club, all would be forgiven. His boss had an unholy crush on the singer. Luckily Kyle had an in with Callum from his days in Vegas and he'd been happy to oblige with a favour.

Kyle took another sip of his drink and looked around the room. He stared at the name badge on the table next to his, and wondered if Eric was still coming tonight. Since their argument a week ago, he hadn't heard a word from him.

He reflected drolly that it was just as well Eric had been out of the picture, as Kyle had had more time to devote to the event tonight. He was still hurt by the fact Eric hadn't even tried to get in touch.

And since Kyle had been left with plenty of time on his hands, he made sure his flat was sparkling and tidy. He tended to clean when he got upset.

"Penny for your thoughts?" Brook Hunter leaned across the table, his smile dazzling. Lenny's boyfriend, with his dark, debonair good looks, was a delicious specimen of man who wore a suit like a fashion model.

Kyle forced a grin. "Just thinking about Ryan's reaction when he heard the word 'karaoke.' I bet he threw a hissy fit the likes of which even Mango hasn't seen before."

Brook's hearty laugh rang out around the room. On stage, Laverne glanced their way and blew Brook a kiss.

"The lady is looking mighty fine tonight." Kyle waved a hand at Laverne. "She certainly knows how to put on a show."

"You know it," Brook said fondly as he regarded his partner. "And I wouldn't have it any other way for either of them."

"Evening."

Kyle's heart leapt at the familiar voice.

"Am I still welcome at the table?"

Kyle looked up. Eric looked splendid in a pair of dark blue smoothies and a pale blue shirt teamed with a trendy open waistcoat in differing shades of blue and grey. His auburn hair curled around his ears and Kyle noticed it had grown a little.

He shrugged. "Sure, feel free. It says your name right there." He felt a little better when Eric rolled his eyes at his sass as he sat down.

Brook nodded at him. "Hi Eric—you're looking good. How's things at work?"

Kyle tried not to listen to their conversation, affecting an air of disdain he didn't feel. He watched the show but kept his ears pricked for mentions of him or signs that Eric was missing him. They didn't come.

Why doesn't Eric look more upset that he hasn't seen me for a week? Why doesn't he talk to me, or apologise? Well, two can play that game.

For the rest of the evening, Kyle put on a great show of his card skills, amazing everyone with his dexterity. He chatted civilly to Eric, as if nothing had changed, and was gratified to see the confusion in his face that Kyle seemed unaffected by their parting.

Secretive bastard, Kyle thought savagely. See me not give a fuck. See me getting over you. And yet the whole time he was performing his famous croupier shuffling skills and showing his friends the magic tricks he'd learnt in Vegas at the side of the Great Hazzy Houzzini, Kyle was dying a little bit inside.

The 606 Club in Soho was one of Kyle's favourite jazz places. Intimate and bohemian, it was one of his go-to places when he needed cheering up. And cheering up was just what he needed.

It had been two days since he'd seen Eric at Club Delish, and since then he'd received one short message saying that it had been good to see him and Eric would be in touch soon. Kyle had responded back with a thumbs-up icon, and that had been as much as he could manage. So, when he sat in his favourite booth with a whisky sour—a drink of sheer perfection created by the legendary bartender Sergio—tapping his fingers to the strains of jazz floating across the room, the last thing he expected to see when he opened his eyes was Eric.

He looked tired; his eyes were shadowed, and he seemed thinner. He still looked good though, in ripped jeans and a white long-sleeved tee-shirt.

"Hey." Eric said, slipping his thumbs into his belt loops and leaning forward slightly.

"Hey, back." Kyle stared for a moment, and then realising it was getting them nowhere, he motioned to the seat beside him. "Want to sit down?"

Eric slid into the booth, the heat and touch of his body in the closed space instantly causing Kyle's groin to react.

"How did you know I was here?" Kyle asked then chuckled. "Don't tell me. Ryan."

Eric nodded. "He said you were coming down here tonight. That he'd given you the night off while he sees how Kellie does managing the club on her own." He frowned slightly. "She seems to be settling in well. Is everything okay there? Ryan's not thinking of replacing you or anything is he? Because you're one of the best things to happen to that club—"

Kyle reached over and pressed a firm finger over Eric's lips. "Don't be daft. I'm quite happy with having a bit more time off, to be honest. You know what my days off are usually like— popping down to check on things, catch up on paperwork I can't do when I'm there at night and do stock takes and shit. It's nice to not be the only one anymore. And Ryan would never do me wrong."

Eric didn't look convinced and Kyle's chest filled with warmth. *He's worried about my job. That's too sweet.*

"Well, okay. As long as you're happy."

Kyle decided the time had come to let Eric know exactly how he felt. It couldn't do any harm. After all, Eric had taken the time to seek him out, hadn't he? That must mean something.

"I haven't been happy for a while," he admitted, raising his glass and taking a sip while Eric beckoned a waitress over. "I missed you." *There, I said it. Deal with it.*

Instead of backing off as he half expected, Eric leaned over and fixed his eyes on Kyle's. They really are like peridot, he thought dreamily. So damn beautiful.

"I missed you too." Eric reached up and traced a warm finger along Kyle's cheekbone. "Like crazy. That's why I swung around tonight. To apologise and tell you I care about you and I'm not going to let you go over a stupid spat." He shrugged. "I had plenty of time to think about things and I think I'm in a better place to talk to you about it."

Kyle struggled to draw a breath after that admission. His insides were all tingly, and something else was getting happy too. Finally, he managed to respond.

"Glad to hear it," he murmured. "Maybe I should finish up my drink and we can go back to my place, finish what we started the other night?"

He gasped as Eric's hand reached under the table and squeezed his thigh. " Let me finish the drink I just ordered, watch this next set and then we can go. Deal?"

"Deal," Kyle agreed.

They sat in contemplative silence as the next band came on. Kyle's body swayed to the saxophone and drum work, and for a while, he lost himself in the rhythm.

Jazz, whisky and a sexy—and hopefully repentant—man beside him, willing to take whatever punishment Kyle offered.

Things were looking up.

They reached Kyle's house around eleven o'clock and he mixed them a drink. Eric looked around the flat with surprise.

"Your place is looking really tidy," he muttered as he took in the obsessively re-organised in alphabetical order DVD collection. His eyes drifted to Kyle's dice collection. "And you've added a few more of those."

Kyle looked over at his pride and joy fondly. He'd been acquiring dice for years and had quite the collection. "I had some time to hunt them out and buy a few more. Pretty cool, huh?"

"A few more?" Eric snorted in amusement. "You've bought a lot more than a few."

"Did you come here to talk about my dices—dice? Dicii? I never remember the plural for the damn things—or do you want to tell me what happened the other day that put you in such a bad mood?" Kyle plonked down beside Eric, making sure their legs touched.

The sigh Eric heaved seemed to have been dragged from deep inside. "I guess." He took a deep gulp of his drink and Kyle could see he was garnering courage for whatever he was about to tell him.

"That day we went to the gallery, I went to a therapist to talk about my 'problems.'" Eric used air quotes. "I knew I needed to talk to someone about it again given what happened the other day but…" He shook his head fiercely. "I wasn't prepared."

Kyle was mystified. "What the hell is 'it?' Are you being deliberately cryptic?"

Eric swung around to face him, eyes dark. "*It* was losing a man to suicide. The other day, when I was working a case, the guy jumped and I couldn't save him. It rehashed all the inadequacies and guilt I felt when I lost my partner in Nepal. I watched the man I loved fall to his death while saving me."

Kyle gasped in horror. "Eric, I'm so sorry. I can't even imagine—" He broke off as Eric made a cutting motion with his hand.

"It was the most unselfish and noble thing anyone has ever done for me. And I fucking hated him for it." The room fell silent. The bleak look in Eric's eyes spoke volumes and Kyle wasn't sure what to say.

Finally, he dragged up the courage to be the friend Eric had been a couple of weeks before when Kyle bared his soul. "Can you tell me what happened? I'd like to hear about it if you can tell me. You kind of scared me the other night." *So, this is what he's been hiding. God, he must have been devastated.*

A pang of fear, selfish but nonetheless real, took him by surprise. *Can I compete with a man who gave his life for his lover? How does anyone beat that? Especially me, who couldn't even stand up for himself with his psycho ex.*

It was the shuddering breath Eric took as he passed a hand over his eyes that made Kyle want to rush over and hug the life out of him. At least he was good for that.

After another minute of pacing, Eric sat down in his chair and closed his eyes. When he opened them, he stared at Kyle fiercely.

"First things first. You know I would *never* hurt you, right? I'm not a violent guy, and after what you went through, the idea of doing anything harmful to you appals me. The other night, I was on edge. No excuse, just…" He gazed at Kyle imploringly. "I'd never touch you in any way you didn't want."

Kyle rubbed his fingers along the top of Eric's hand. "I know," he said. "I do, honest. It's just sometimes, I get spooked."

"I'm sorry, babe," Eric said softly. "I never wanted to make you think of *him*. That's the last thing I ever want you to do. He's in your past, and let's hope he'll stay there."

He took a shuddering breath. "I guess I should start at the beginning. My boyfriend's name was Lincoln Dunbar. He was a couple of years older than me. I met him through a rock-climbing group. It used to be a thing of mine." He stopped, his face growing contemplative. "Linc was an experienced instructor and he taught me everything I knew about climbing. One thing led to another and we became a couple. I'd just joined the ambulance service so time together wasn't easy. But we managed. God, we managed."

A faint smile crossed his face at a memory and Kyle swallowed, feeling it was not becoming of him to be jealous of a dead man.

"In twenty-twelve, a group of us went to Nepal to do some climbing." Eric's face turned bleak. "We were on our way up to the summit of Everest when there was an earthquake." He looked down at his entwined hands in his lap. "It triggered an avalanche. Linc was bringing up the rear. My buddy Anton was at the top and Katherine was below me. We managed to swing into a cave. God knows how we managed it, but we did. Lincoln wasn't so lucky. The rope slipped, cut, fuck knows, and he went dangling off into the abyss." He halted, taking a deep, tortured breath.

Kyle's eyes stung as he fought to choke back tears at the distraught look on Eric's face. He couldn't speak for love or money, too caught up in the tragedy.

Eric continued, his voice rough. "I managed to pull him up, Anton was holding me, but he couldn't sustain it." He stood up, taking agitated strides around the room. "I told him, Aaron, don't you fucking let go of me. I'm going to pull Linc in." He gave a shuddering sigh. "And he tried, God he tried. But I kept slipping, going down the same way as Lincoln, while he kept telling me to leave him. But I couldn't. I had hold of his arm so tightly, but it was only his jacket and I—" he choked, tears running down his face. "Then he looked at me and said, "Time to save yourself. I love you, baby." And he let go. Just...let go."

Staring into space, seeing what had to be etched into him memory, he sputtered, "The bastard left me there holding his jacket and watching him fall into a fucking abyss." His face was ghastly pale and Kyle couldn't help the tears flowing freely down his face. His heart ached with pain and grieved for the man who'd given his life so Eric could live—and oh the tragedy for Eric to have seen it. Who wouldn't be traumatised by that experience?

This time, Kyle didn't care whether Eric wanted him close or not. Kyle needed to hold him.

"Oh, baby, I'm so sorry," he murmured helplessly as he pulled Eric into his chest and wrapped arms around him. Eric fell into him and his body shook with sobs.

"I hated him for leaving me," he stuttered, words muffled against Kyle's chest. "I put it behind me, tried to carry on. It was hard and I still miss him every day. But I was dealing with it, even with the nightmares, the memories. Then a few days ago, the day I blew you off, someone went and jumped off a building. I tried to stop him but I couldn't." He lifted his head and stared at Kyle with swollen eyes. "All I was left with was his damn cardigan. Just like before."

Kyle's heart broke in two right then. That Eric had been through this with someone he'd loved, and now, to bring it all to the fore again, a stranger had done the same. No wonder Eric was falling apart, and on the edge.

And it sounds like he still loves Lincoln.

Kyle swallowed, trying to relieve the ache in his throat at the thought Eric might not want him after all and he might have misjudged things.

"Let it out," he whispered against Eric's hair. "I'm here for you. No matter what the outcome is, I'll always be around."

Eric stilled then pulled free from Kyle's embrace. "What do you mean?" he choked out. "That sounds like you're planning on going somewhere." He sounded desperate.

"I'm not going anywhere," Kyle murmured. "Promise." *Not until you ask me to leave.*

Eric's face flooded with relief. "Oh, that's good. I thought…" His voice trailed off.

His face lighting up gave Kyle hope. "He sounds like a remarkable man, your Lincoln."

Eric nodded. "He was. We had good times together." He took Kyle's hand and rubbed his fingers gently across the top. Kyle watched the movement, mesmerised.

"When he died, I resented that I'd lived and he hadn't. Aaron calls it survivor's guilt. He says it's common enough." Eric traced circles on Kyle's palm. "Being in my current job doesn't help when I lose a patient. It's been worrying me a lot lately."

Kyle nodded. "I've read about that." He wrinkled his nose as he thought about the two of them. "I suppose you and I have that in common. We both survived something traumatic, although you lost someone dear to you and I didn't."

Eric chuckled weakly. "This isn't a competition, babe. When I think of the guy that hurt you that way, used you like a punching bag, did other foul things to you, I want to beat his lights out." He stopped and raised Kyle's hand to his lips, placing a soft kiss on his skin. "We both suffered, just in different ways."

Then bright green eyes looked into Kyle's. "So, I'm seeing my therapist again," Eric muttered. "She's helping me with some stuff."

Kyle wanted to laugh at the irony of it all. "That's good. I don't want to detract from your story, but"—he hesitated—"I am too. I finally caved in and am seeing someone about what happened to me in Vegas. Luce will be thrilled." He shrugged. "I understand what you're going through is what I'm trying to say."

Eric's eyes widened. "Wow, look at us. We're a truly modern couple, both in therapy and talking about our issues."

Kyle cleared his throat, not quite knowing how to phrase his next words. "Is this therapy bringing out old feelings? Are you, like…" he stuttered, "…discovering you still have unresolved feelings, anything I need to know about?"

"Are you asking me if I still love Lincoln?" Eric leaned forward and ran his finger along Kyle's bottom lip. "I'll always love him in my own way, in here." He touched his chest, and Kyle's throat went dry. "But he's not around now. I have plenty of room in my heart for someone else to love, and you fit perfectly. Like you were made for me."

683

Kyle's stomach fluttered and his body tingled as Eric face split into the most genuine smile Kyle had seen all day.

"Now kiss me, please. You have this habit of making me feel like nothing else matters. I need some of your Kyle magic right now."

The kiss that followed was like no other kiss Kyle had experienced. Eric's lips were a mix of salt and sweet, his hands clutching tightly to the back of Kyle's head, holding him there. Poignant and sweet, he didn't want to let go.

Being needed this way was a heady euphoria, and when the kiss changed from soft and subtle to deep, wet necessity, where tongues duelled and lips bit, there was no going back.

Standing as if they were one, the kiss went from one of support and compassion to a place where there were only two naked, desperate men, eager to touch and feel each other as if there would be no other chance to do so.

Eric manoeuvred them to the couch, his lips swollen with the force of their kisses, his beautiful body stretched out like a smorgasbord of something Kyle wanted to sample.

"I want you to make love to me," Eric whispered as he lay down, pulling Kyle on top of him. He opened his legs and beckoned Kyle in. "Need to be as close to you as I can get. You inside me…"

He reached his arms above his head, deliberately teasing Kyle. He resembled an infinitely sexier and debauched image of "Boy on the Bed" by Lucian Freud, another one of Kyle's favourite works of art.

"Oh, I'm happy to oblige," he said as he rubbed their cocks together, eliciting an appreciative moan from the man sprawled beneath him. He rummaged around under one of the cushions then produced the lube with a "Ta-dah." A condom was located too, and in record time, he was suited up and ready to go.

He watched, entranced, as Eric's fingers circled his own entrance, and couldn't hold back a moan when Eric plunged a finger inside himself, throat muscles straining.

"God, I could watch you do that all day." Kyle reached down and covered Eric's fingers with his own, slicking them with lube. "Now it's my turn."

He pushed Eric's legs up, gaining access to the enticing hole. He slid inside, watching Eric's mouth opening with a satisfied grunt. Emboldened, he thrust deeper, and this time, Eric groaned loudly and took firm hold of Kyle's arse, pulling him farther inside.

Heated flesh around Kyle's cock pulsed and gripped him, and he thought he'd lose his mind being so at one with a man he was falling in love with.

"God, baby, so good," Eric panted, eyes half shut, as he rutted upwards. "Fuck me harder."

"I thought we were calling this making love, not fucking," Kyle teased as he gained momentum and pounded into Eric's arse.

Eric's eyes flashed open dangerously. "I don't care what you want to call it," he said between gritted teeth. "All I know is that I want to come, and you doing exactly what you're doing right now is going to make that happen. Now shut the fuck up and get me off."

Kyle laughed and reached down to claim Eric's lips. He wasn't far off his own orgasm and knowing he could make a man come just by being inside him like this gave him a thrill of pride.

The slap of flesh against flesh and the silken slide of their sweat-sheened bodies was all Kyle needed. He came with a startled cry at the unexpected force of it, body tensing and hands gripping Eric's legs enough to make him growl with pain.

Eric's own release was impressive. Spurts of his spunk covered them both in sticky residue, the shockwaves of his climax taking hold of his body as he rode out the sensations.

At last, they lay still, supine and stuck together with come.

"That was something," Eric said drowsily. "You fucked my brains out."

Kyle smiled, his cheek stuck against his boyfriend's sticky chest hair. "You're welcome anytime."

He rolled off Eric reluctantly and stood, wincing at the rawness of his dick and the ache in his back where he'd probably pulled a muscle with his efforts.

"I think it's time to wash up and get into bed." He had a thought. "You know, we didn't even have any dinner." As if it heard him, his stomach rumbled. "I think I might make us something to eat then we can settle in."

Eric flapped a hand as he clambered off the couch. "Sure. I'll go take a pee and clean up. I'll come give you a hand in a minute."

Kyle was already planning what he was going to cook as he walked into the kitchen. "No problem."

Half an hour later there was no sign of Eric but there were two plates of carbonara pasta on a plate, with two glasses of wine. Kyle wandered into the bedroom and stood still.

Eric was face down on the bed covers, naked and snoring heavily. Kyle took a moment to enjoy the sight before he laid the tray on the chest of drawers.

"Nice," he muttered. "I slave away in the kitchen and you come in here and take over my bed. Huh."

He pulled the extra duvet from the cupboard, not wanting to roll Eric over and disturb him. Then he covered him with it and crawled into bed. He made sure to bring his pasta and wine with him.

"You might not want this, but I'm bloody starving." Kyle leaned down and kissed Eric's cheek. "Sleep tight, babe." He hesitated then whispered, "I'm falling hard for you, you know that?"

He didn't think he was at any risk of Eric hearing. His man was out for the count.

Chapter Fourteen

Eric clapped his hands over his ears at the caterwauling coming from inside of the truck. Great partner Aaron may be, but singer, he was not. And hearing "It's Raining Men" sung in his off-key tones caused Eric's arse to clench and his ears to bleed.

"You're killing me," he complained as Aaron hit a particularly high note. "Can you not do that please? I think you just pierced my eardrum."

"I don't think so," Aaron sang along with the lines. "Hallelujah, I don't think so, amen."

Eric reached out and switched the radio off. Aaron looked at him, an injured expression on his face.

"Hey," he protested. "I was just getting to the good bit."

"There are no good bits," Eric grumbled as he fiddled with the paperwork on his lap. "Only *really* bad bits."

Aaron huffed and waved a hand dramatically. "I was bringing out my inner queen," he stated. "Leah said I was in touch with my feminine side the other night, so I decided to enjoy it a little bit more. Heathen."

"Yeah, yeah." Eric grinned as Dispatch crackled into sound. "I think I prefer your man side when it comes to your singing."

The radio operator announced a new call and Eric frowned.

"Isn't that the same address we attended a while ago? The nutty lady who pulled a knife on us, with the mom and kids?"

"Yeah." Aaron's face was grim. "Sounds like something's gone down there again. Maybe this time she's gone too far." He looked at Eric. "Should we call in for police backup?"

They stared at each other for a minute then both shook their heads at the same time.

"Nah," Aaron said. "The police are busy enough as it is. I'm sure we can manage one crazy lady between us now we know what to watch out for."

Eric nodded in agreement. They drove in silence then Eric looked at his partner. "So, you and Leah still going strong? I bet your bubbie is happy."

Aaron smiled, a wide beam that split his face. "Yeah, Leah's great. She and my gran get on well, and now bubbie is even bossier than before, which I didn't think was humanly possible." He smiled wryly. "'Cut your hair; you'd look more handsome for her. Don't forget to take that lovely flower arrangement home with you for Leah—she'll love it. When is the wedding day? You don't want to lose that one, she's a keeper—'" He rolled his eyes. "Two strong women in my life is more than I bargained for."

From the beatific look on his face, Aaron didn't seem too worried about that, Eric thought.

"So how are you and Kyle getting on? It's been, what, over three months now you've been dating? You practically live at his place. When are you two moving in together?"

Eric grinned. "Too soon for that. But, yeah, I do spend a lot of time at his place since it's closer to the club. Our work rotas are a bitch to try and get time together."

Aaron peered at him. "With that grin on your face, mate, I'd say the two of you are coping well enough. I'm glad you got over your little spat. You were an insufferable bastard when the two of you were arguing."

Eric opened his mouth to deny it then closed it. Aaron was right; he had been a moody git at the time. But that had been nearly two months ago. They had now reached a level of what Kyle laughingly called "boyfriendship" they both were comfortable with.

Toothbrushes at each other's homes, spare clothes in the closet, microwave popcorn for Kyle in Eric's cupboards and bags of crisps for Eric in Kyle's—these were all signs of their rapidly evolving relationship.

Friends, lovers, partners—whatever you wanted to call it, Eric was glad it had happened. He couldn't imagine a life without his purple-haired, vivacious and sexy boyfriend. He had a feeling Kyle felt the same but neither of them had really committed to the L-word yet. Like Kyle—who was quick, quirky and full of depth—Eric's emotions had grown the same way.

"Get that soppy look off your face, you lovesick sap. We're here." Aaron stopped outside the house they'd been to before.

Eric blinked himself back to reality and looked around. He sighed. They were once again in a tough part of the city and they needed to be wary. And last time they'd been threatened. This call was not going to be a walk in the park.

They picked up their bags and approached the house. All the radio operator had said was another potential heart attack victim needing assistance.

Eric knocked on the door. There was no response. He knocked again.

This time the door opened and the same woman who'd held a knife on them last time stood there. Eric was pleased to note this time she had nothing in her hand except a ragged dishcloth. Sunglasses covered her eyes.

"Thank God you're here," the woman said. "It's my mum again. She's not well."

Jessie, Eric thought suddenly. Her name was Jessie. He smiled at her as he and his partner brushed past the narrow doorway into the dingy living room.

"Can you tell us what happened, Jessie? Did she have another heart—?"

He stopped short, Aaron swearing as he bumped into him. "Damn, Eric, warn me next time, will you?"

Eric's sarcastic reply was choked off, his throat going dry as he observed the scene before him. The older woman—Jessie's mother, he guessed—lay in a pool of blood on the carpet, eyes unstaring, her head a mess of blood, tissue and bone. Next to her was a large brick covered in gore.

"Aaron, this isn't a fucking heart attack. Call in backup. We need the police for this one." He moved swiftly to the woman's side, but from the mess her skull was in, he knew she was dead.

Obviously not hearing him, Aaron barrelled into the room, crouching beside him and feeling for a pulse. He looked up, his dark eyes meeting Eric's. The two of them swivelled their heads around to see a smirking Jessie standing above them. Her sunglasses had gone, but in her left hand was a large kitchen knife.

Fear tingled its way down Eric's spine.

Shit, not again. This woman is insane. She's also as high as a kite.

As if pulled by an invisible puppeteer's string, both men stood together and faced the unstable woman before them.

"I told you," Jessie hissed as she blocked the doorway. "I told *her*"—she motioned with the knife to the dead woman on the floor—"what would happen if I didn't get my kids back. Now those fuckers at DSS have decided to keep them. I warned you all I wouldn't be happy."

"Jessie, we've been in this place before," Eric said softly. "Put the knife down and let's talk."

Jessie cackled loudly, eyes dilated and spittle in the corners of her mouth. "Talk? It was you talking that got me into this mess, you wanker. You told them Social Services bitches about me and they took my kids away. I never got no money no more. Then she—" She gave one savage gesture at the woman on the floor. "She had the fuckin' cheek to tell them she didn't think it was a good idea to give 'em back to me." Her eyes narrowed and a smirk crossed her face. "But I showed her. I bricked her one and she fucking stopped talking, didn't she?" She nodded. "Yeah, I showed the mummy bitch who was boss."

Eric's gorge rose at the sheer malevolence in her voice. Beside him Aaron moved, and the knife moved his way threateningly.

"You need help, Jessie," Aaron said, his voice soothing. "We can do that. Give you something to calm you down, get you to a hospital so they can look after you. Wouldn't you like that—someone looking after you, not worrying about bills or cleaning up this mess?"

Jessie tilted her head to one side, considering his suggestions. "What, three shitty meals a day, wipe my bum, put me in fucking prison care? I'm better off here, turning tricks. At least those blokes give me a good dinner now and then. That's what you made me do, you know? Fuck people for money. Because you took away my income."

Eric was pretty sure that had been what Jessie had been doing as a living even before their first call out.

Not going to argue with the crazy bitch with a knife. We need her to surrender it.

He moved forward, Aaron's hissed "Eric, no." ringing in his ears. Outside, he heard sirens.

"Jessie, come on. Let go of the knife, and we'll sit and have a talk, 'kay? I've got something in my bag I can give you to help you come down from wherever you are. Then we can get someone in to take your mum away, so she has some dignity. Come on. Let us help you. Please."

Jessie's lips thinned and she looked from him to Aaron. Finally, she looked down at the body on the floor and a faint expression of fear crossed her face.

Eric held his breath as he waited for her answer. Finally, she nodded and the knifepoint slowly descended down.

"Just drop the knife on the floor," Eric said as he moved toward her warily. Aaron made a sound behind him but Eric ignored it. The knife fell harmlessly to the floor and Eric let out a breath of relief as he reached her.

"Great, now let's sit down and—"

At first, the sharp pain in his left side didn't register. It was only a split second of agony followed by a sudden breathlessness as the shock of being stabbed hit him. He reeled backward, hearing Aaron's agonised cry and Jessie's peal of cruel laughter.

She must have had another knife somewhere. Shit, I need to see what the damage is. I hope she didn't hit an artery. His paramedic mind in full throttle despite the pain, Eric staggered backward, wondering why the room was growing dim and fuzzy, his eyes losing focus. Between his fingers, copious amounts of blood seeped in puddles onto an already blood-spattered floor.

He was aware of someone bending over him—not Aaron, another uniformed man. He tried to keep his eyes open, see if Aaron was safe, but it was just too much.

His last thought before he succumbed to unconsciousness was of violet eyes and a warm smile.

"Hey, baby. I'm not sure if you can hear me. The nurse says you can, so I hope so. You're doing okay. The doctor says the knife hit a blood vessel, but Aaron got you all fixed up quickly. I guess that's the one benefit of having a paramedic and a truck on call, right? Anyway, Aaron said to tell you he's fine and he needs his partner back because the one he's got now is driving him fucking crazy."

There was a soft giggle followed by a sniffle. "That's his words, not mine." There was the sound of rustling. "I bought you some grapes, because everyone knows that's what you bring to a hospital, right? And I also got you a beautiful bunch of flowers, only the hospital wouldn't let me bring it in because apparently, it's not healthy. And the sister on the ward didn't stop sneezing. It's a pity 'cause I chose them myself and did the arrangement. I had to take them home again." Kyle sounded terribly peeved.

Eric tried to laugh but it was too painful. He felt as if he'd gone three rounds with a heavyweight boxer. But the insane boyfriend babbling was adorable and he wanted to kiss him.

"Oh my God, you can hear me? Eric, open your eyes, love. Please open your eyes." The desperation in Kyle's voice energised Eric into finally doing what he was told. The first sight that greeted him was Kyle's face, anxious and pale, with red-rimmed eyes. Eric had never seen anything more welcoming.

"Hi," he croaked, throat burning. His eyes watered with the bright light of the room. "I'm glad you're here."

Kyle loomed over him, fussing with his pillows to raise his head up. "Where else would I be?" he asked waspishly. "You decided to go and get yourself stabbed. This is generally where those people end up, with the people who love them worrying over them."

Despite the snark in the comment, Eric heard the vulnerability beneath. And the roundabout declaration of love that made his heart race.

"Come here," he instructed, raising one arm carefully so as not to dislodge whatever drips were in it. "I need to hold you.

Just be careful. I have been in the wars with a knife-wielding maniac."

Kyle leaned down and buried his face in Eric's neck so close it was as if they were joined by damp skin. "I thought I'd lost you, you bastard," he whispered tremulously against Eric's skin. "I was so worried about you."

Eric gave him a one-armed hug, as strong as he could manage. "I'm here," he murmured, stroking Kyle's hair. "You think I'd go anywhere without you?"

"Well, okay," Kyle retorted, his words muffled. "I wouldn't want to have followed you down there." He waved a hand at the floor. "But I'm good with anywhere else."

Eric grinned. "What makes you think I would have gone to Hell?" he said teasingly.

Kyle looked up, a smile in his eyes. "Duh, don't all sexy bad boys go there? I think it's the law." He cupped Eric's face in cool hands. "God, when they told me you were here, I didn't know what to do. Ryan kicked me out of the club, told me to stay here until I was sure you were okay."

"So how long have I been out? And what happened from the time I hit the deck?" Eric shifted uncomfortably. His whole body ached and his left side burnt like hell.

"Two days. They brought you in on Wednesday. Today's Friday afternoon." Kyle scowled. "The crazy bitch that stabbed you was taken down by the police who'd already been on route. She had another knife on standby it looked like, hidden on the mantelpiece." He scowled. "What is it with people and knives in this country? Anyway, the poor old lady screaming on the phone to Social Services as her head was bashed in generated some warning bells." He grimaced. "They called the coppers and they arrived in time to save your arses. Aaron did his magic and you were rushed into surgery. And poof, here you are."

Eric leaned back on his pillows, exhausted. "I'm going to be okay then? Nothing vital damaged?"

Kyle nodded. "The doctor says you'll be fine. Just need rest, and a lot of sex."

Eric gaped. "What?"

Kyle's face was mischievous. "Oh, yeah, he said I was the cutest guy he'd ever seen and as long as I gave you loads of love and sex, your recovery was guaranteed. I couldn't let the best advice of the medical profession go to waste so I wrote down a plan, see?" He held up a calendar with red crosses all over it. Hardly any of the page could be seen.

He pointed at one line. "This is where we have butt sex, me on the bottom. This one," he dragged his finger along, "is sixty-nine sex. This one here is a blowjob for you, and here again we have—butt sex. You on the bottom this time. I have your medical recovery programme all planned out." He looked pleased with himself and Eric choked as he laughed.

"*This* is what you've been doing while I've been lying here unconscious? Did you perhaps do anything more personal while I was out?" He lifted his covers with difficulty. "I look as if I'm intact. No cock cage or anal beads up my arse. I think."

Kyle reached over and pressed warm lips to his. "I might have peeked now and then, just to see you were still functioning." He chuckled against Eric's mouth.

"God, you are so crazy, but I love you." Eric yawned, wondering why Kyle's eyes widened and his mouth dropped. He was also becoming dizzy and floaty.

"Do you think you could ask the nurse if I could have some water or something? I'm parched." His voice sounded slurred and he frowned.

Perhaps he should go to sleep for a bit. After he had his water.

"Yeah, sure," Kyle stammered. "I'll, erm, go fetch her." He scuttled out of the room as if all the demons from hell were at his heels.

Closing his eyes, Eric imagined he and Kyle were on a soft, white beach somewhere, with cocktails. Kyle was in a tiny, dark blue Speedo and had never looked so delicious. His body was tanned and toned, his arse framed by the tight trunks and all Eric wanted to do was throw him down on the sand and...

"He looks weird, like he's dreaming." Kyle's whisper made him come back to the present. "Is it the drugs you're giving him?"

There was a soft laugh. "Dearie, he's on so much medication I'm surprised he's awake and lucid. It must be you he came back for from the deep, dark doldrums. He's a tough bugger, this one."

Eric's eyes remained closed because they were heavy and he couldn't bother opening them right now. *Yep, you're the one that I want, Kyle baby. Only you...*

"Oh, so he might not be saying things he'll remember later, when he's not on the meds?" Kyle sounded disappointed.

"I think the medicine has just caught up with him now, that's all. He's been through a lot, what with the surgery. I'm sure whatever he said to you meant something to him at the time."

What did I say to him? Oh, yeah, I think I told him I love him.

Eric tried to nod to assure Kyle that, yes, indeed, he'd meant every word and he'd tell him again when he was up and about just in case he needed to hear it again.

The nod seemed to grow heavier and Eric surrendered to the warmth of the darkness of sleep calling his name.

"I'm not an invalid. I can make it on my own," Eric grumbled as Kyle helped him out of the car. Little Lady *was* tough to get out of when you were still stitched up and sore, but he was determined he could get out of his Roadster without help.

Kyle dangled the car keys in front of him. "Says the man who insisted he could drive us here then ended up having a mini stroke when he pushed down on the pedals." He slammed the door shut and beamed at his boyfriend. "Lucky I was there to help out. She's awesome to drive."

"Yeah, well, don't get used to it," Eric said.

Kyle sniggered. "God, you are such a grump. Come here. Perhaps this will make you feel better."

In full view of the neighbours outside Aaron's bubbie's house, Kyle drew him close and kissed him thoroughly. When he finally let go, Eric was breathless, hard and feeling better. Kyle's kisses should have been declared a natural amphetamine the way they made his heart beat so fast.

"Tell me again what this visit is in aid of?" Kyle reached into the back of the car and took out a bottle of wine and a bouquet of flowers. "I remember you said something about meeting Aaron's girlfriend. Is this his house?"

Eric bit back a laugh. "Nope." He walked slowly up the path towards the small, terraced house in the middle of Islington. His side still hurt but he was a lot better than he'd been three weeks ago.

Kyle's tender ministrations, some great medical care and a lot of rest had got him back on his feet quicker than anyone had expected. Kyle still swore it was due to the gentle, yet exhilarating sex sessions prescribed on his calendar.

His boyfriend caught up with him. "Oh, so it's her house?"

"Nope." Eric smiled to himself at Kyle's exasperated grumble behind him.

"Why do you have to be so damned secretive? What is it with you?" He swatted away a bumblebee and scowled.

Eric knocked on the door. *You'll soon find out. Welcome to your baptism of fire.*

The door opened to reveal a tiny sprite of a woman with jet-black hair streaked with silver-grey and a myriad of coloured baubles around her neck, dangling across her flat chest. She was dressed in multi-coloured paisley trousers and wore a bright orange blouse, stained with something Eric wasn't sure about.

"Shalom, Eric, my boy. It's been ages since I've seen you. You look a bit pale. Are you eating properly since your accident?" Shrewd pale blue eyes turned to assess Kyle. "Is this the mensch Aaron told me about? Oy vay, he's skinny. And what's with all that metal in that pretty face?" She shook her head. "I'll never understand it."

Eric stifled a laugh at Kyle's gobsmacked expression.

"Bubbie Norma, it's good to see you again. And yes, this mensch is my boyfriend, Kyle."

Norma waved them in. "Come in, don't stand there on the doorway. The neighbours will think I'm having a sex party."

Kyle's jaw dropped even further. He was speechless for the first time since Eric had known him. *Mission accomplished. Thank you, Norma.*

As Norma propelled Kyle into a small lounge, his wide eyes stared back at Eric in panic.

"Come, sit," she fussed as she pushed Kyle physically down into an armchair covered with varying degrees of what looked like knotted multi-coloured cords. She swept them onto the floor with an impatient flip of her hand and turned back to Eric.

"Tea? Aaron and Leah will be here in a while. They walked to the shop to get me some more milk, although I'm sure they've taken the opportunity to make out somewhere along the way. They've been gone a while."

She motioned to the chair full of ropes. "Chuck that on the floor if you need room—it's only my macramé project for the local Women's Institute."

"Tea would be good, thank you. We'll sit and wait for Aaron." Eric smiled at Norma who gave him a beaming smile and scurried off into the kitchen.

Kyle was up in a shot, standing in front of Eric. "What the hell? You didn't warn me some crazy Yiddish grandmother was going to accost me. I'm assuming that's Aaron's bubbie." He glanced uneasily toward the kitchen. "I mean, she seems nice enough but she gets a bit personal, doesn't she?" He fingered his eyebrow stud nervously then his fingers drifted to the one in his lip. He'd finally taken the plunge and had it done. "Should I have taken these out to visit? I would have if I'd known—"

Eric silenced him with a swift kiss. "No, never. I love you just the way you are, so I'd never ask you to remove anything that makes you, you."

Kyle looked down at the floor. "That's the second time you've said that to me," he muttered. "I'll be starting to think you mean it soon." His violet eyes flashed with emotion and Eric choked back the words that sprung to his lips.

No, not yet. You have a plan, remember? Stick to the plan or Aaron will kill you. He spent hours shopping with you for the right thing. His hand drifted to his pocket, and satisfied the item was still there he gave a sigh of relief.

"Yes, that's her. She's quite the character. And, as you can tell, forthright. She's amazing though."

He didn't miss the disappointment on Kyle's face. They hadn't really talked about their expressions of loving each other since the accident. It had been a time devoted to healing and recovery, but Eric was damned sure that was going to change tonight, with his close friend and a woman he counted as a surrogate mother.

Ten minutes later, Aaron arrived with a pretty, dark-haired woman he introduced as his girlfriend, Leah. She was tall, curvy and had short, spiky hair that suited her round face. Eric could see the couple were besotted with each other.

They all sat down while Norma forced slices of cake, homemade rugelach and copious amounts of tea upon them.

Eric sat next to Kyle, his hand loosely resting on his thigh.

"So, my Eric, what happened to that bad woman who stabbed you? And her poor mother. Oy." Norma fanned herself. "What a terrible thing to happen."

"She was admitted to hospital and is undergoing psychiatric evaluation," Eric said. "We'll have to see what happens when they finish with that."

"Well, I hope they lock her up forever," Kyle spat out fiercely. "She deserves to go to prison for what she did. Bashing the poor woman's brains in and nearly killing you."

Norma laughed. "You have a little spitfire there, Eric. I like him already. So, when is the—"

Aaron cut her off with a glare and a wave of his hand. "Cut it out, bubbie. Don't even ask that question."

Leah giggled beside him and he took her hand. "And don't start on us either. I told you, when we're ready, we're ready."

Norma sat back and folded her arms across her chest. She pouted. "You don't let me have any fun, do you? I have a yen to plan a wedding. Someone get married, please."

Her eyes glinted as she leaned in toward Kyle. He made an instinctive movement back. She raised one finger and waggled it at him.

"A little bird told me—"

"Bubbie, could you please fetch the stuff from the kitchen? You know—the stuff we need to do the thing?" Aaron's voice was desperate. He shot an apologetic glance at Eric, who was having trouble breathing with the need to laugh and the knowledge of what he was about to do.

"The thing? What thing?" Norma looked confused. Then, as Aaron's glare grew fiercer, she nodded slowly. "Oh, *that* thing. My wish is your command, grandson. I am but a slave here to do your bidding." Muttering under her breath, she disappeared once again into the kitchen.

Eric swallowed down his nervousness and turned to Kyle, who looked like a hare caught in headlights. "What's going on?" he asked dazedly. "I swear I feel like I've stepped into the Twilight Zone. Have I missed something?"

"No, baby." Eric shuffled closer to Kyle and reached up to draw a hand through the spiky hair. "I have something to tell you and I wanted to do it with my friend and his crazy grandmother present."

Kyle looked visibly nervous. "Oh, wow. Way to pressure a guy. That sounds ominous." He fiddled with his lip ring again.

Norma came in bearing flute glasses and a bottle of champagne. She set them down and then settled in her armchair again, cherubic smile on her face.

"Go on," she commanded to Eric. "Do it."

"Oh, God," Kyle said faintly. His lip ring twiddling got worse.

Eric reached out and took his hand away from his mouth. "I said something to you when I was in the hospital. Something I meant then and I mean now. Do you remember what I said? You were worried I'd forget about it."

Kyle nodded. "Yeah, I remember."

"What did I say to you?" Eric prompted.

Kyle stared around at the faces watching him and closed his eyes momentarily. When he opened them, they were shiny. "That you loved me."

Eric reached out and caressed Kyle's face tenderly. "I love you. It wasn't the drugs talking, it was all me. Being there, knowing I might not have made it—I needed you to know that."

He reached into his pocket and grinned at the panic on Kyle's face. "Don't worry. Despite bubbie's need to have a wedding, I'm not going to ask you to marry me. Yet."

Kyle's shoulders sagged in relief but he stared at Eric, entranced, as he continued speaking. "We both know it's too soon for that."

Norma made a noise like a fart. Eric ignored her and removed a small velvet bag from his pocket. He reached in and drew out one of the two platinum bracelets he'd had made.

"They're commitment bracelets. Yours says 'I'm His' and mine says 'I'm Yours.' Or we can swap them around if you fancy a change." He chuckled. "Either way, it means I want you by my side as long as you'll have me."

Kyle's eyes were wet with tears as he nodded. "I love you too. And I'm not fussy about what mine says. Either way, it's true."

Heart full, Eric took Kyle's slim wrist and slid the "I'm His" bracelet over, rubbing at the soft skin with his thumb. Then, among soft claps from Aaron and Leah, and a series of noisy hoots interspersed with Yiddish gibberish Eric couldn't even hope to understand, Eric kissed his man.

As they sat drinking their celebratory champagne, Eric's mobile rang. He mouthed at Kyle—"Deacon"—then whispered, "Did I tell you we were all meeting them for dinner tonight so they can say congratulations?"

Kyle shook his head, smiling. "No, babe, you didn't. You're just full of surprises today, aren't you? Sounds good though." He and Eric'd had dinner with Deacon and his wife Chrissy a couple of times, and he'd found Deacon to be a real character. In a way, he felt sorry for Chrissy and Eric, what with Deke's hare-brained enthusiasm for get-rich-quick schemes.

"Hey, Deke, what's up?" Eric's grin grew wider as he listened. "Buddy, I'm not sure that's a good idea." His shoulders shook with laughter. "I get the whole concept, but hanging your baby up on a wall or a door so you have your hands free sounds like a pretty radical idea. Isn't that what those baby knapsack thingies are for?"

Kyle's jaw dropped. He mouthed, "What the hell?" at Eric who was struggling to contain himself. Everyone else was laughing too.

"Deke, hang on, Kyle wants to ask you about your idea— he's dying to find out what it's all about." With a wicked grin, Eric thrust his phone into Kyle's hand, and he stared mystified at his boyfriend, who had tears rolling down his cheeks.

Kyle sighed and raised the phone to his ear. "Hey, Deke."

"My man, Kyle. Please tell my wife and my stupid, ignorant friend that a baby carrier that you can hang on a wall, or a door or in a tree, is a great idea. You could, like, push him as well, like a swing if you hung it in a tree, have a bit of fun too." Deacon's voice became higher with enthusiasm. "It gives the parents their hands back and the baby can just hang around until they're done. You know, like in a bathroom when you need to wash your hands or do your business. You hang baby up with this device, like a strap that you can carry him around in on your body but adapts to hang up elsewhere. A bit like a sturdy coat-hanger that goes over the door."

Kyle blinked. "What does, err, Chrissy think about this?"

Deacon snorted. "Please, she thinks people will end up forgetting the baby and walking out of the bathroom leaving him hanging, or that the tree branch might break, or that the baby will break free and fall down or something. I mean, as a parent, you'd make sure the kid was safe, right? And you'd never forget your baby in a bloody bathroom. As if. What do you think?"

Kyle walked over toward Eric. "I think it's a great idea."

Aaron hooted with laughter and Norma gave a smile of satisfaction. "That'll teach you to put Kyle on the spot like that," she smirked.

Eric's head shot up and he stared at Kyle in horror. He smirked. "In fact, Eric agrees with me. He's even got a name for it. The Kiddy Keeper. Here. I'll hand him back over so you two can discuss it more. Oh, and I believe we're seeing you for dinner later. I look forward to it."

With a snigger, Kyle handed the phone back to Eric, who glared daggers. Aaron, Leah and Norma chuckled as they looked on.

Kyle slapped palms with the others in triumph as Eric tried to convince his best friend that, no, he didn't think the Kiddy Keeper was a good idea after all.

Later, lying at home after a slow, steamy session of lovemaking, Eric decided it was time to tell Kyle his other bit of good news.

"I have something else to tell you." He *oomphed* as Kyle moved on top of him, straddling his hips. His arse was still slick from Eric's come. They'd dispensed with condoms weeks ago. Eric was tested in the hospital as a matter of course, and Kyle decided to get it done then too.

"More to tell me?" He wiggled his bum suggestively against Eric's rapidly rising dick. "Is it my birthday or something that I'm being spoilt?" He squinted down at Eric. "It's good news, right? I don't want bad news when I'm on a high."

"It's good news to me." Eric lifted his arms and laid them above his head, stretching out. "I'm leaving the ambulance service."

Kyle's sexy movements stopped. "What? Since when? Why?"

"You know I've been burning out in this job. My heart isn't in it anymore. I applied for a job as an advanced paramedic practitioner for a large GP practice. I got it."

Kyle leaned down and placed a soft kiss on Eric's cheek. "What does that mean for you?"

Eric reached up and drew Kyle down to lie flat on his chest and nuzzled his neck. "It means I get to see you more often. I won't be working crazy shifts. It will still be damned hard work and I'll have some further studying to do, but I'm happy with it. I think I'll fit in there. The people seem really nice."

Kyle sighed. "Have you told Aaron yet? He's going to be mad."

Eric nodded. "Yes, he knows. I needed his advice about the new job. He's not happy. But he understands. He knows you're more important now."

Kyle sat up, hands splayed on Eric's chest. "Then I approve. Whatever makes you happy, babe. That's all I want." He gave a wicked grin and wrapped his hand around Eric's cock. "And this. This makes me happy too."

Wet, warm lips found Eric's, and as Kyle proceeded to ride him into oblivion, Eric thought dreamily he couldn't have wished for a better way to finish his day.

NOT SO SECRET SANTA

*You wanted more Leslie,
and since you love him the way I do –
this story is for you*

AUTHOR'S NOTE

There's something about Leslie. He wormed his sassy way into our hearts and lingered there. Lately, he's been murmuring in my ear, in that way he has, to write a soupçon more about his love for Oliver. After all, he adores the man. This story is a fitting tribute to Leslie's warm heart and his ability to make anything into yet more drama, it's a seasonal tale that had to be told...and, there's no one else that deserves another happy ending more than this couple.

Not So Secret Santa features the best proposal of the year done in true Leslie fashion. Oliver and Leslie get so gooey mushy that you'll end up needing a visit to your dentist. I make no apologies for that, so please don't send me your dental bills for reimbursement.

Chapter 1

D-Day—three weeks and counting

I'm fucking stuck in here and I have no idea how to get myself out.

It wasn't the first time Leslie had been in a pickle. Much like his predilection to put his foot in his mouth, his pickles were numerous. However, it was the first time in his life he'd been trapped in a roll of fabric, in a container, with his rear end (perky as it may be) jutting out of the roll for all the world to see.

It appeared his Gucci belt had snagged on something as he'd wriggled through the bolt of material trying to rescue the treasured Mont Blanc pen Oliver, his adored boyfriend, had given him.

Leslie had known today was going to be a bad day the minute he'd gotten out of bed. First, he'd found a nasty spot on his chin. Second, he'd managed to spill the sugar all over the kitchen floor in his haste to leave this morning. Because of that, he'd been late—again. And third, Laverne, damn her evil heart, had sent him on this stupid mission to deal with customs agents at the docks and to oversee the delivery of a large consignment from Hong Kong.

Of course, she'd insisted Leslie look in the container to make sure it was all there. "Darling," she'd drawled, "you know these customs places. I order suit fabric and end up with a million years' worth of fuzzy children's bunnies. Or is that children's fuzzy bunnies?" She'd waved a manicured hand. "Never mind. You simply *must* check it before you sign the acceptance form."

Grudgingly, Leslie had done just that, trying to charm the grizzled veteran of the docks with little success (Leslie had nicknamed him Bear Growls) but had achieved his goal nonetheless. Then, as he'd bent down to check a tag on the bolt of cloth, his pen had fallen out of his shirt pocket, rolled into the wide damn cardboard tube that the fabric was wrapped around, and landed with a *plink* on the other side of the roll. With no way to get to the other side since the container was packed to the brim, Leslie had thought he was being clever slinking his way into the roll to rescue his pen.

Unfortunately, he'd not given a thought as to how he would get out. And now, here he was, snagged on something, he knew not what, unable to retreat or advance.

Leslie thanked all the Gods above he'd worn proper underwear today and not a thong.

When the time came for him to be found, desiccated and limp, looking for all the world like a mummy the world had forgotten, at least he'd be halfway decent.

"If there's anyone behind me, could they please either pull me out, or give me a push?" he yelled, as a bead of sweat rolled into his eye. The eyeliner he wore rolled with it, and he swore at the sting. "Fucking poxy stupid belt, let me the fuck go," he demanded.

The cardboard roll remained uncooperative, his belt didn't budge, and Leslie remained stuck. His profanity didn't appear to be working as a tactic. Perhaps, if he stretched out as far as he could, he'd be able to grab the end of the pen between his fingertips. He blew a lock of hair out of his face in irritation as he glowered at the pen lying innocently out of reach, unaware of its owner's dilemma.

He reached out, bit by bit, and finally his index finger and thumb caught the nib of the pen and grasped it. "Got you," he muttered. He pulled the item toward him and heaved a thankful sigh at having it back in his possession. Now all he had to do was extricate himself from the predicament he was in.

"Hello?" he shouted, hoping Bear Growls might have come back from making his tea. "I'm stuck. I need help."

Behind him, someone cleared his throat. "Well, this is a fine sight," the voice rasped. "You bit off a tad more than you could chew there, lad."

Leslie breathed a sigh of relief on recognising Bear Growls's distinctive, well, growl.

"Oh, thank God," he muttered, "Saved by the bear. Could you pull me out please? My belt got stuck and I'm hoping a bit of force might shift it."

"Well, I *can*," Bear Growls drawled, "but I'm enjoying the scenery too much. Can I finish my tea first?"

Leslie's jaw dropped. "No, you cannot finish your tea," he snarled. "I'm sweating, my shirt is creased to hell, and my eyeliner is running. I really would like to get out of here, now."

Part of him, the smug bit, was rather tickled that the burly docksman seemed to be enjoying the sight before him.

He's looking at my arse? Well, I never. But the man does have great taste.

Bear gave a chuckle and Leslie felt two hands grab hold of his ankles.

"Mind the boots please," he muttered. "They're Jo Ghost, and I'd hate them to get scuffed."

There was a loud snort behind him and hands like melons with fingers wrapped around his sock-clad ankles and pulled hard. "I'll do my best, lad. Now you just lie there and let me do all the work."

"Huh, like I haven't heard that one before," Leslie murmured sarcastically as he found himself being tugged backward. "You should be on the stage." He yelped as his belt came free and he slid along the cardboard floor into the bright sunshine of the dockyard. He lay there for a minute, his belly to the asphalt, as Bear knelt beside him and peered into his face.

"You all right there, lad? I guess I could say I've pulled and all." Bear sniggered.

"Oh, for God's sake." Leslie stood himself up and glared at the short, burly man who stood there, shaking with laughter. "Thank you very much for getting me out, but please, enough with the silly jokes."

He frowned as he stared down at his shirt, all crumpled and creased around his stomach. He rearranged his suit jacket with as much dignity as he could, having been extricated from a cardboard roll by a bear with a sense of humour.

Bear Growls grinned at him. Leslie had to admit the man was quite a fine specimen, in his late thirties, with a short, dark beard and bright blue eyes. Underneath his open-necked shirt Leslie saw the start of a chest covered with thick, dark hair. He was only a few inches taller than Leslie and built like a bricklayer. There would have been a time, had Leslie met such a man in a club, he might have gone home with him.

Not now, of course. He had his sexy, adorable Oliver, who'd come a long way since being the reclusive former porn star with a nasty scar. In the past three years, Leslie had made it his mission to drag Oliver into the social circles Leslie lived and breathed in. The new Oliver, imbued with more confidence than before, was the by-product of Leslie's tough love and owned Leslie's heart like no other.

Bear Growls gestured at him. "I hope you found what you were looking for," he said. "I have to say this was the most entertaining event I've participated in this week."

Leslie grasped the recalcitrant pen tightly in his hand and nodded. "I did," he acknowledged gracefully. After all, the man had rescued him from what could have been a living hell. What if the container had been closed, with him inside? What if it had been shipped to Outer Mongolia where there was no Internet, and people with no fashion sense?

He shuddered.

"So, was everything all right then, apart from the getting stuck bit?" Bear held out a clipboard and a pen with a chewed top. "I'll need your signature, please, and I don't mind if you give me your number either." He winked.

Leslie shook his head regretfully. "Alas, I am spoken for," he said. "However, if you give me *your* number, I do know of someone who might like to meet you." His assistant Chester, who worked with him at Debussy, had been looking for someone like Bear Growls for a long time. Perhaps they could arrange a blind date together.

Bear shrugged. "Story of my life. All the best ones are taken or straight." He squinted at Leslie, who took the board and signed it with a flourish. "This mate of yours, is he a nice bloke? I'm not looking for a fly-by-night. I'm not into one-night stands."

Leslie rolled his eyes. "Chester is the picture boy for the whole 'relationship' scene. He's a home and hearth man."

Bear Growls's eyes lit up. "He sounds like my type. Do you think he'd agree to go on a date with me?" His tone grew uncertain. "I mean, I'm nothing special, I work here at the London docks, and I'm not much to look at—"

Leslie reached over and placed a finger on Bear's lips, effectively shutting him up. Leslie tut-tutted. "Oh no, no, we don't do self-deprecation here. You seem like a nice man and while I can't speak for Chester, there was a time when *I* might have considered a date with you." He waved his hand. "Of course, I have my own man now and he's perfect, thank you very much."

He glanced at his watch. "As much as I love being matchmaker, I really do need to get back to work. My boss will have my balls if I don't."

He held up a warning finger as Bear's lips parted. "No ball jokes, please. I don't think I could take it."

Bear smiled, and Leslie was taken aback by the way it transformed his face. Bear was stunning when he smiled. Chester was going to be so delighted. He felt it necessary to warn Bear who he was dealing with. "I will pass on your number to my friend, and if it works for you both, fine, but I'm warning you now, that if you harm a hair on his head or break his heart, I will hunt you down and beat you to death with my Jimmy Choos." He tried to make his face as menacing as possible, but Oliver had always told him he looked adorably cute when he was trying to be mean, so he wasn't sure if it worked.

Bear blinked and then gave one of his huge, beautiful smiles again. "Duly noted. I am shaking in my boots."

Leslie took out his phone and quirked an eyebrow at Bear. "I can't put Bear Growls in my phone, so you'll need to tell me your real name."

Bear hooted in laughter. "Oh, I like that one. You're a cute bit of trouble, I can tell." He looked a little sheepish. "I prefer that to my real names."

Leslie's curiosity was piqued. He leaned in and laid a hand on Bear's impressive bicep. "Ooh do tell. What did your parents saddle you with?"

Bear cleared his throat. "My full names are Enoch Andrew Michael Jenkins."

Leslie blinked. "That's a lot of names. Enoch doesn't sound so bad though?"

Bear snorted. "I've heard so many knock-knock jokes about my name, you can't imagine. Oh, hi, Enoch, knock-knock, who's there? I prefer to use Andrew. Or Andy."

Leslie nodded sympathetically. "People can be tossers about names and teasing. Andy it is then."

He took down the number then grinned at Andy. "Right, I'd better be off to work before I get stabbed with a letter opener by my boss. She doesn't take kindly to me larking about." He checked he had everything—including his pen, after all the trouble it had gotten him into—and with a final wave at Andy, Leslie departed the docks on route back to Debussy Fashion.

Chapter 2

"Well, well, well. Lovely of you to join us, chicken. I thought for one moment the universe had sucked you into a black hole, never to be seen again."

Leslie stopped what he was doing, which was trying to sneak surreptitiously into his office. He had one now as he'd been promoted to senior buyer, but was still Laverne's general factotum, a chore he bore with grumbling acceptance, even though he loved every minute. He turned to face Laverne Debussy-Smith, his boss, with a wide and brilliant smile.

"Laverne. You're looking lovely. That suit looks amazing on you." He waved a hand. "And you've done something to your hair?"

Laverne, known as Lenny James when she *wasn't* dressed to kill, was as much of a friend to Leslie as Laverne, gazed down at her apparel and then back up at Leslie with a lazy smile.

"Fancy that. It looks equally as amazing as it did this morning when you saw me in it. And as for my hair, I suppose me running my hands through it, wondering where you were, concerned for one of my most valued employees, has given it that *je ne sais quoi* appearance." She smiled evilly and prowled toward Leslie. "You have a good time at the docks?"

Leslie nodded fervently as he made his way behind his desk. He sat down in the chair and pulled his computer keyboard to him. "Yes, I managed to get the consignment sorted, and it will be here tomorrow morning."

Laverne tapped her chin with a long fingernail in contemplation. "I'm glad to hear it. You'll notice a few emails in your inbox, some marked 'Urgent,' so I'd appreciate it if you could handle them, especially the one from Robert Kingsman.

He's fretting about his exhibition tonight and has a few last-minute things he needs done. That will get him off *my* back. He's been calling for you all afternoon." She rolled her eyes and fanned herself. "The man is a complete tosser with everyone else but for some strange reason, he loves you. One has no clue why." The sparkle of amusement in her eyes took the sting out of the comment.

Leslie smirked. Laverne loved Leslie too. Oliver told him everyone did. That he was a loveable sort of person. He nodded. "Of course, boss. I'm right on it."

Laverne perched one linen-clad buttock on the corner of Leslie's desk and regarded him thoughtfully. "What took so long? Was there a problem with the shipment?"

"Er, no, we had a bit of a logistical issue that needing resolving, so that took a while." He crossed his fingers under the desk. "The dock person was a decent kind of guy, so he helped me sort everything."

"Hmmm." Laverne didn't sound convinced. "Well, I'm glad about that because I need to finish up the new Christmas range. It's only a few weeks away and we've still got a lot to do." Her eyes grew dreamy. "That suit fabric is going to look fabulous on the finished product in the stores, and our Nutcracker range is going to be the talk of the town this season."

Leslie breathed a sigh of relief. While Laverne was thinking about her fashion and clothing, he wouldn't have to explain any further why he'd been late. The word Christmas made him starry-eyed as well. He had big plans this season. *Big plans* with his Oliver Brown. Leslie wondered dreamily how he could ever have thought that name was boring. Oliver was the moon, the stars, and the rainbow over the soft, wispy clouds. Oliver was the unicorn who regularly used his big, ever-so-tasty horn to—

His thoughts were caught short by a slap to the hand with a ruler. He glared at his boss, who flipped the ruler at him, narrowly missing his nose. Laverne's face was creased in merriment, her blonde bangs swinging down over her face as she laughed.

"Do you mind?" Leslie snapped, moving out of range. "You could have broken my nose with that."

Laverne winked. "The look on your face right then... That was a 'thinking of Oliver' look if ever there was one. I know when you have those sexy thoughts about him, chicken. Your face is an open book." She gazed at him speculatively. "In fact, come to think of it, you've been rather secretive of late. Spending time with Chester—where is he, by the way—and scrounging more fabric in the recycling room. Have you both got a secret project I should know about?"

Leslie's throat closed in panic. He did indeed have a secret project, but he wasn't about to tell Laverne about it. The woman would make a sumptuous feast of his plan and before you knew it, his secret would be escalated to the likes of a Liberace show. Leslie wanted quiet and simple on this one.

The actual wedding- well, that was another thing entirely. A show by Liberace would look pale in comparison to what Leslie had planned.

"Uhmm, Chester was in The Arbour when I came in, checking stock. And you know me, I'm always on the lookout for bits and pieces to make my outfits pop. Nothing says 'I'm trendy' more than a well-placed piece of lace or leather."

Or a whole bolt of red satin that just happened to fall into my arms when I was there last. Oh, and let's not forget the white faux fur that somehow found its way into my man bag.

Laverne huffed. "Uh-huh. I'm on to you, chicken." She pointed her fingers at her eyes then back at Leslie, who blinked as innocently as he could. "I know something's up. And I intend to find out what in due course. You can't fool me." She stood up, and straightened her blouse, then her jacket, finally running her hands down her hips to smooth her trousers. "Now I have another one of those boring bank manager meetings, followed by a lengthy debate with Herbert Chessingham on exactly why I can't make him a suit with PVC see-through butt cheeks."

Leslie snorted a giggle. "Oh God, is he still going on about that? I thought you'd talked him out of it."

Laverne sighed wearily. "So did I, chicken. But his lady friend thinks it's sexy and I haven't got the heart to tell him his scrawny backside will not do my suits any favours." She flipped her hair back indignantly. "A Debussy will not be lowered to what appears to be a passing fantasy for some little gold digger.

No way, José." She made a moue with her raspberry-coloured lips. "He can go to fucking Tracy Trey for that pleasure."

Leslie chuckled. There was no love lost between Laverne and her rival. During their last encounter, Tracy had come off second best when Laverne had kneed him in the balls.

"In fact," Laverne said eagerly, her face lighting up, "I have had the most wonderful idea. I'll refer him to Tracy, professional courtesy and all that. I don't know why I didn't think of that before." She leaned over and kissed Leslie on the top of his head. "Always good shooting the breeze with you, sexiness. Now sort out Robert for me, will you? If he calls me one more time today, I will come in and shove that red satin you misappropriated down your lovely throat." Laverne grinned wickedly as Leslie gaped at her. "I know everything. You should know that by now." She waved a hand and disappeared into the main corridor with a swish.

I was so careful. How does she know? The woman is a witch, I swear. I need to find a charm that will stop her from reading my thoughts.

He thought smugly she didn't seem to know about the faux fur. *Leslie—1, Laverne—0.* He wasn't about to tempt fate though, and was a moment away from researching a local Wiccan shop on his computer for a spell or charm when someone slid in through his door and shut it swiftly behind him.

"Good, she's gone. I waited ages." Chester Romero winked at Leslie. "I have something for you." Dark eyebrows over even darker eyes waggled as Chester reached down the front of his trousers and drew out a furry white and gold glitter pom-pom.

Leslie stared at him in horror. "That was down your pants? Yuck."

Chester shrugged. "I am wearing underwear, and I couldn't fit it in my shirt because of my suspenders, and my shirt is a bit tight." He gestured down his lithe little body at the white long-sleeve shirt he wore rolled up to the elbows, and his dark green suspenders. "So down here was the best place." He was only about five feet four in his boots and even Leslie towered over him.

Chester's dark face wreathed in a grin, showing white teeth. His Cuban heritage was something Leslie envied—all that beautifully tanned skin and hair as black and thick as molasses. Leslie seemed to burn every time he tried tanning in the sun. Ah, the joys of being British.

"I thought this could go on top of the hat." Chester gestured animatedly toward the pom-pom that sat on Leslie's desk. "We can sew it on, and it will look *fabuloso*, yes?"

Leslie picked up the item with a slight grimace and held it up. "It is rather nifty," he acknowledged, and flashed a smile at his friend. "Thank you so much, it's perfect." They smiled at each in their shared secret.

"We can finish cutting the fabric this weekend, and then I will start sewing it all together." Chester made a scissoring motion with his fingers. "Oliver is going to be so surprised, *mi amigo*. He will love it." As one of the trainee fashion designers and Leslie's one and only direct report, Chester was well versed to take on the task of Leslie's "secret project."

Leslie sighed. "I hope so."

Chester looked affronted. "Sure, he will love it. It's not every boyfriend who gets to see his beautiful partner in a special Santa Claus outfit, designed by an up-and-coming young mover and shaker in the industry. This will be a Romero special. With the assistance of a Leslie, of course."

"I'm not doing much," Leslie confessed, "other than telling you what I want. You're the one doing most of the work." He had indeed been helping Chester with the pattern, and cutting the fabric, but Chester refused to let him sew. He'd said that was his job. Leslie thought Chester didn't trust him enough not to make a mistake. Chester could be quite the perfectionist.

The Santa Claus outfit was going to be epic though. Leslie wanted this Christmas to be special for a lot of reasons, and creating the sexiest Santa outfit he could think of was part of his plan. This plan included tight red satin trousers and a form-hugging shirt, with white fur around the cuffs and collar, and a pointy soft velvet hat with the pom-pom adorned on the top.

Of course, it was all easy unfastening too. He already had the shoes, a pair of red patent leather Kurt Geiger stilettos he'd purchased specially for the occasion.

Leslie was going to rock Oliver's world dressed in this outfit. And of course, there was the other thing as well…the thing that caused him sleepless nights and made his stomach gurgle in panic. He smiled back at Chester, who was eagerly explaining his plans for the intricate stitching across the back seams. Enough thinking about that, he remonstrated himself sharply.

It's all under control and it's going to be fine.

Chapter 3

Oliver understood having a boyfriend like Leslie Tiberius Scott meant life was often somewhat exhausting. As much as he adored Leslie, there were times he wished he could find his OFF switch and press it. He'd been busy creating websites all day, he had a bitch of a headache, a weird churning feeling in his belly, and he wanted nothing more than to curl up in his easy chair with a glass of wine and finish his book.

Then Leslie, gorgeous, sexy as fuck, but oh so excitable Leslie, had swooshed into the living room, and while Oliver's world had gotten brighter, it had also shrunk with the power of his boyfriend's presence. Thinking about it, ever since Leslie had moved into Oliver's home in Wembley, the place seemed smaller.

And it wasn't only because of Leslie's clothes, shoes, and handbags. The man had a huge, sparkling personality and it seeped out of every window and doorframe. Oliver was sure the neighbours must have a touch of it in their own homes. He grinned at the old memory of making love on top of a pile of coats lying on the floor when they'd been trying to unpack when Leslie moved in. While Leslie had fussed over them afterward, the sight of his boyfriend riding his cock while clad only in a pair of dark blue heels had been spectacular.

"And I told her, well, you'll have to put up with it, or risk having a face-lift in later life and looking like wrinkled old prune. Honestly, nowadays, who wouldn't want to wear sunscreen?" Leslie huffed vexedly and leaned forward from the couch where he sat, his toned, tanned legs clad in denim shorts curled under him. "Oliver, baby, are you okay? You've hardly said anything since I got home."

Oliver sighed wearily. "That's because you haven't let me, love. You seem a little more…" He paused. Like a squirrel on crack was what he wanted to say, but he didn't dare.

"Enthusiastic than usual," he finished lamely. "You must have really had a great day at work."

Leslie's eyes narrowed. "Well, I did, apart from getting stuck in a rather uncompromising position, and having to have Bear Growls pull me out, oh, and I managed to get a date for Chester with him, they've made contact and it's all systems go. I told them about Galileo's so they'll give it whirl." Galileo's was the renowned Soho restaurant owned by the boyfriend of one of Leslie's best mates, Eddie Tripp.

"Bear Growls," Oliver said faintly. "Who is he? And stuck how?"

Leslie waved a hand. "Oh, it was a silly misunderstanding with me and my pen. Andy managed to extricate me."

"Who the fuck is Andy?" Oliver's headache grew worse and he reached up a hand and rubbed his forehead.

Leslie huffed in frustration. "He's Bear Growls. Honestly, Oliver, have you not heard a word I've said?"

Oliver couldn't reply. Instead, he leapt up from his chair and barely made it to the loo to kneel before upchucking his meagre lunch of marmite toast down into the porcelain bowl. He gripped the loo seat as everything spewed forth.

"Oh babe, hang on, I'll get you a wet cloth to wipe your mouth." Leslie's warm fingers brushed the top of his head. "What the heck did you eat today? Oh God, there you go again. I'll, uhm, wait here until you've finished."

When Oliver finally thought he could be sick no more, he leaned back against the wall of the bathroom, legs splayed in front of him. Leslie crouched beside him, sapphire blue eyes filled with concern.

"Sweetie, let's get you cleaned up and then it's off to bed with you. I'll get you some of that electrolyte stuff. You must have caught a bug or something."

He helped Oliver to his feet. He was feeling decidedly dizzy, but a lot better now that he'd gotten what was bothering him out into the open, so to speak.

"I've been feeling a little shitty all week," he husked out, throat still raw. "I thought I was over it, but obviously not."

Leslie's brow furrowed as he wiped a soft wet cloth over Oliver's face and chin. His lips pursed in a classic Leslie indication of faint disapproval. His boyfriend squeezed toothpaste onto Oliver's toothbrush and held it out. "There you go. Brush your teeth and I'll go get that fluid replacement thingy." Leslie walked out of the bathroom. Oliver finished brushing his teeth, then made his way wearily to the bedroom. He undressed, down to his wine-red briefs, and got between the covers with a sigh of relief.

No sooner had he pulled up the duvet, Leslie was there with a glass of something pink. He perched down on the side of the bed. "Drink," he ordered.

Oliver did as he was told. Leslie's eyes bore into him and Oliver had the feeling that even though he was sick, he wasn't about to be let off the hook that easily. "So, all those times you told me you felt fine, you really weren't?" Leslie asked pointedly. "Looks to me like you've got this stomach bug that's doing the rounds."

Oliver flapped a hand. "It was no big deal," he protested. "I thought I was over it. I've been watching what I eat, nothing too rich."

"Uh-huh." Leslie's lips tightened. "Oliver, when I ask how you're feeling, I actually *want* to know. I don't need you keeping the situation from me."

Oliver closed his eyes and tried to look pathetic, which in all honesty wasn't such a big stretch given the way he felt. "Baby, I'm sorry, I didn't want to worry you. You've had a lot on your plate lately and I didn't want to add to it. Really."

Leslie nodded, eyes softening. "And now look at you, babe." He reached down and stroked a lock of hair from Oliver's forehead and those soft lips he loved so much kissed Oliver's cheek. "Get some sleep. I've got a few things to sort out then I'll come to bed."

The room lapsed into silence when Leslie left and seemed to get that little bit darker as well. Oliver rolled over onto his side and closed his eyes. He'd make it up to Leslie in the morning. He'd take him for breakfast at that French place down the road.

Then they'd come back and have a lazy Saturday afternoon together, doing nothing. Well, perhaps not nothing. Oliver's face creased in a smile as he drifted off to oblivion.

***

Oliver chuckled sleepily when Leslie slid into bed beside him later and wrapped an arm around his waist. His boyfriend's body was chilled, and Oliver heaved a sigh even as he flinched at the cool skin against his.

"Where the hell have you been that you're so cold?" he asked groggily as Leslie planted a feather-light kiss to the nape of Oliver's neck.

"I was sitting outside watching the stars." Leslie wriggled and Oliver's body responded pleasantly. "I had a few things on my mind."

Oliver shifted. "What kind of things?" he murmured drowsily, enjoying the feel of Leslie's firm body behind him, skin to skin.

"Secret things," Leslie whispered. "Good things, though. Nothing to worry about." His hand slid over Oliver's stomach. "Are you feeling better?"

"Uh-huh. My stomach feels a little less as if it was a washing machine, and that nauseous feeling has gone. I think being sick got it all out."

Leslie snuggled closer. "Would you like me to take care of this?"

His fingers slid around Oliver's hardening length and he groaned, "I'll never say no to your hands on my body." He hitched a breath. "Yes, baby. That feels good."

Leslie's hardness prodded against Oliver's backside and he closed his eyes as the strong, sure touch of the man he adored rocked his world. In the intimacy of their bedroom, with the clock ticking softly on the wall, marking down exquisite seconds, and the steady pull of Leslie's hand on his cock, Oliver wanted for nothing more.

***

Sex with his boyfriend was always a pleasure. Waking up the morning after to a snarling Leslie, however, was not.

"Motherfucker. I am so going to kill him when I see him."

Something hit the dresser top, causing bottles of aftershave, makeup, and Oliver's treasured figure of Star Trek's Spock—bought at the last comic con they'd gone to—to go crashing to the floor. He peered out from beneath the covers with one eye. "Babe, what's got you all riled up?"

He noticed the offending item thrown at the dresser was one of Leslie's favourite waistcoats, a vintage Gothic brocade one with chains on the pockets. Leslie turned to stare at him, one hand on a trouser-clad hip. Oliver had to admit he looked delicious standing there in his work clothes: tight tailored trousers, a pale blue shirt, and a tie that only Leslie could love, dark blue featuring yellow Minions.

He'd seen another tie at a local suit shop he thought Leslie would love—a grey one with penguins, another Leslie favourite—and had made a mental note to pop out and buy it today for him.

Leslie deserved presents and a little something special.

"That new apprentice at work agreed to take in my waistcoat, I wanted an extra pleat in the back. I don't think he measured correctly. He's made the damn thing too tight now. I can't wear it today and I'm going to have get the whole thing unpicked and redone."

Oliver didn't think that issue merited a sonic Leslie meltdown but he daren't say it. He certainly wasn't going to suggest his lover might have picked up a teensy-weensy bit of weight since the waistcoat had been altered. That would be suicide. Instead, he made a noncommittal sound of comfort and snuggled back under the duvet. He was due up in half an hour, so he might as well make the most of it. He did, however, feel morally bound to help the poor unfortunate soul who may face Leslie's wrath when he got into work.

Call it my good deed for the day.

"He is an apprentice, though. Perhaps you can teach him what he's done wrong, make it a learning curve kind of thing. I mean, you are a manager now and that's one of your responsibilities, isn't it?"

Leslie hummed thoughtfully. "I suppose that's true. Maybe I won't castrate him after all." He scowled adorably. "But he's going to need to get his backside into gear and fix it. I want to wear it this weekend." He nodded to himself. "It'll go well with those new trousers I bought to wear to the event this Saturday night. You do remember we're going to Taylor and Draven's for dinner, right?"

Crisis averted, Oliver smiled. "I remember. It's all you bloody Musketeers have been talking about for the last month and a half." Taylor Abelard was another good friend of Leslie's, and together with Eddie, the three friends were dubbed the Gay Musketeers.

Leslie rummaged through his cupboard, no doubt looking for another waistcoat. "We have so not. Well, maybe a bit. It is three years they've been engaged for after all, and it's about time they started thinking about getting married."

Something landed on Oliver's feet. He stayed where he was, being used to having various items of clothing draped over him when Leslie was trying to find something.

Oliver sighed. "Leslie, not everyone wants to get married. Some people are quite happy being in a relationship without all the bells and whistles."

The rummaging stopped and there was silence. Oliver hoped Leslie had found what he was looking for, so he could go back to sleep. Instead, Leslie sat down on the bed and Oliver moved the duvet to look at him. His boyfriend's usually bright face looked shadowed, his lovely lips pursed together.

"What are you saying? That them being engaged isn't a big thing and getting married isn't something you want to do?"

Oliver sat up, covers falling to his waist, and he regarded Leslie with more scrutiny than usual.

I think I should give up on getting back to sleep.

"I'm saying plenty of people don't need the pomp and ceremony to know they love someone and that they want to spend the rest of their lives together. That's all."

Leslie's brow furrowed then he smiled, but it looked a little forced. "Oh, yeah. I get it. Is that the category we fall into then?" He stood up and started pushing the clothes apart, still looking for whatever he wanted, with a bit more force than before.

"Yes, no. God, I don't know. I think sometimes people put too much faith in rings and ceremonies when all they need to do is love the other person and things will work out. I know I adore you. I hope you do the same back. What else do we need?"

Leslie finally found what he was looking for, another waistcoat of dark grey with yellow and white flowers on the lapels. "I s'pose. Hey, do you think this will go well with what I'm wearing?"

He held the waistcoat against himself and looked over at Oliver, who nodded and grinned, thankful the moment of awkwardness seemed to have passed. "Baby, you rock anything you wear. And absolutely, that looks good with your outfit."

Ten minutes later, after one filthy kiss and a quick flounce of Leslie's manicured hands, his boyfriend was out the bedroom door on his way to work. Oliver stood up, stretched, and regarded the chaos that was their bedroom with dismay. He certainly wasn't picking up after Leslie. Oliver attempted to make the bed, artfully shifting aside the clothes that lay on top to make it look presentable, then made his way to the bathroom for a shower.

Might as well get to work. Those websites won't build themselves.

Chapter 4

"What's up, Leslie? You don't seem yourself today." Chester's voice filtered into Leslie's office. "You haven't even eaten the doughnut I bought you."

Leslie looked up from his paperwork and stared sadly at the yummy sprinkled and strawberry-cream-filled doughnut gracing his desk.

"I know. I don't have the appetite right now." He'd gotten to work and remonstrated with Kaden, the apprentice, about the too-small waistcoat, and while doing so, he'd had a horrific thought that had curled his toes and plummeted his spirits to the bottom of Mount Leslie.

What if I've put on weight and that's why the waistcoat didn't fit?

That thought had been too horrible to contemplate, and the calorie-laden doughnut sitting forlornly on his desk seemed to smirk at him like an evil temptress. The fact Oliver didn't seem to believe in getting married had burst his happy bubble first thing this morning. Leslie's heart ached at the thought that his plans for Christmas seemed to be falling apart.

Chester came inside the office and perched on the corner of the desk. "*Mi amigo*, everyone is talking. You have been shuttered inside this office all day and hardly said a word. Even Laverne threatened to come and drag you out into the cutting room to see for herself how sick you are."

Leslie sighed and shook his head. "I'm not sick." *Heart sick, maybe.* "It's just—" He glanced at the door.

I have to tell someone, and Chester will keep the secret. I haven't been able to tell Taylor or Eddie, because, honestly, those two and keeping secrets are like drag queens without makeup. Not going to happen.

"Close the door, will you? I need some advice."

Chester jumped up, shut the door, then sat back down with a look of curiosity on his face. "Of course. Anything I can do to help."

Leslie took a deep breath. "You know I'm making this outfit, but I haven't told you the reason I'm making it." He swallowed nervously.

What if he thinks it's a stupid idea, like Oliver seems to?

Chester leaned in eagerly. "Oooh. I am all ears."

"I'mgoingtoaskOlivertomarrymeatChristmasbutIdon'tthinkhewantstoandIdon'tknowwhattodo." The words came out in panic-speak and no sooner had he said them, Leslie wished he could take them back. The secret he'd hugged to himself for so long, revelled in, taking joy in, was now out, and somehow, with Oliver's reaction this morning, the words seemed—tainted.

Chester gazed at him, and for a minute Leslie thought the man hadn't understood a word he'd said. Then Chester beamed, and it was like the window blinds had been opened and the sun was shining in.

Huh. I haven't even opened the blinds yet. I suppose I should. No wonder everyone is worried about me.

"Oh my God," Chester squealed, coming around the desk and wrapping sinewy arms around Leslie. "That is epic. Oh, Leslie, why would you think Oliver would say no?"

Leslie shrugged, feeling a little better at Chester's reaction, and relayed the gist of this morning's conversation to his friend. Chester stood up, cocked his head like a cute puppy and frowned. "I think perhaps you read too much into it," he remarked wisely. Leslie nodded sagely, knowing he was prone to fly off the handle first, ask questions later. "You are talking about the man who rented a whole cinema for you so you could see a secret showing of *The Birdcage* again on the big screen for your anniversary." He perched back on the desk, suggesting the image of a dark little bird. "And he arranged for thirty red roses to be delivered to your place of work the same day. Remember that lady in Accounting complained about the strong smell then you went all Amazonian on her arse. After that, and countless other displays, you think Oliver wouldn't want to marry you when you ask him?"

Leslie picked up the doughnut and bit into it, sprinkles falling down his chin and onto his desk blotter. He smiled whimsically. That had indeed been a wonderful day. Oliver had made sure of it.

"I know he's awesome, and I adore him. I suppose I'm worrying too much. We've been together nearly three years now and I really want to be able to call him my fiancé, then my husband." Leslie took another bite of the half-eaten doughnut. "I've even chosen the ring. It's beautiful. Simple but elegant, just like him.

"I thought I'd do it at Club Delish, in that little room Ryan has off the stage, under a Christmas tree—good food, wine, and Cher playing in the background." He sighed dreamily. "It will be perfect." He popped the last bit of doughnut into his mouth and scowled. "Then he spoiled my fantasy by saying he didn't believe in it all. What kind of monster doesn't believe in getting married?"

Chester tut-tutted. "From what you told me, he didn't say he didn't believe in it, but that you didn't need it to prove two people love each other. That's a big difference."

Leslie regarded his sticky fingers glumly. "I s'pose. You think I'm overreacting then?" He put his fingers in his mouth and sucked off the doughnut glaze.

Chester cackled loudly. "Leslie, this is you we're talking about. Of course, you are." He stood and pulled at Leslie's sleeve. "I know how to cheer you up. Come take a look at the progress I've made on your outfit. It's starting to take shape."

Leslie stood, wiping his hands on the donut napkin, his spirits lifting. Maybe Chester was right, and everything would go according to plan. "Lead away, MacDuff. Let me see how damn sexy I'm going to look so I can blow my future husband's socks off."

He followed Chester out of the room, keeping a sharp eye out for Laverne. He didn't fancy being interrogated to within an inch of his life about his current mood. "By the way, Ches, did you organise your date with Bear?"

Chester nodded as they walked across the office. "I did. Saturday night. And his name is Andy, not Bear."

Leslie huffed. "I found him, I get to call him what I want." He looked slyly at his friend. "And believe me, when you see him, Bear is going to be the first thing you think of. He's all muscly and growly and *so you.*"

Chester's face pinked. "He does sound nice. He sent me a picture of himself."

"A dick picture?" Leslie asked, and sniggered.

Chester turned to him crossly. "No, a real one of him all dressed up in jeans and tank top. Not all of us use Grindr as our personal spank bank photo gallery."

"I have no need for that anymore," Leslie declared loftily. "I have my own spank bank experience waiting for me at home, thank you very much." That thought lifted his mood as he and Chester entered the back room where the secret project was being created (it was an old stockroom no one really used anymore), and he decided there and then not to worry about his Christmas proposal.

"Remember this is a secret," he told Chester as they walked into the room. "No one else knows yet, so you have to promise me you'll say nothing to anyone."

They pinkie-swore and Chester solemnly assured Leslie that not a word about the exciting event would leave his lips. Leslie believed him. Chester was a pretty good egg.

It was all going to work out fine, exactly the way Leslie had planned.

***

"Sean Connery. Has to be. Anyone else is an absolute no." Draven Samuels sat on the living room floor of the home he shared with his partner, Taylor Abelard. He leaned back against Taylor's long, jeans-clad legs. "Don't even get me started on Pierce Brosnan."

Taylor, seated on the couch behind him, gasped in mock horror. "How the fuck can you say that? It's Daniel Craig. Got to be him." He ran a hand through his long, dark hair and nodded his head firmly.

"You would say that," Draven smirked. "'Cause he looks like me." Taylor ruffled Draven's hair, causing his fiancé to grasp his hand and growl, "Leave my fucking hair alone. You know I hate it when you do that."

"Ooh, temper, temper, babe." Taylor ruffled harder and yelped when Draven turned and dragged him down onto the floor beside him. The two men tussled like teenagers. The six friends were gathered together to celebrate Taylor and Draven's third "being engaged" anniversary.

It wasn't strictly their idea, to be fair. The couple couldn't have cared less, but for some reason, Eddie and Leslie insisted that it was something worth celebrating each year, and they all ended up gathered together like tonight. Oliver wondered if it was some plan on Eddie and Leslie's part to hurry the couple along to get married. The two of them were earmarked to be best men and Leslie already had the wedding's fashion statement planned.

"God's truth, do you two ever not argue?" Leslie leaned against Oliver's shoulder as his body shook with mirth. "I swear, I don't know how you two have been together this long without killing each other."

Oliver looked around at the gathering of his friends and chuckled.

These guys are *batshit crazy.*

He glanced over at Gideon Kent, partner of Leslie's other bestie, Eddie Tripp.

Gideon winked at him. "I'm with Draven on this one," he declared loftily. "The best James Bond was Sean Connery. Period."

Eddie turned his head slowly to stare at his boyfriend. Under his tousled red curls, green eyes regarded Gideon with disdain. "Sean might have been the best until Daniel came along. Come on, you can't look at those steely blue eyes and strong jawline and not feel a little turned on when he goes all macho on the bad guys' arses."

Oliver felt honour bound to weigh in on this most important discussion. "So am I the only one who thinks Timothy Dalton made the best Bond?"

The room quieted as five pairs of eyes swivelled to regard him in disbelief.

"Timothy Dalton?" Leslie gasped. "Oliver, are you feeling okay? I could have sworn you just made the worst statement ever." He flung a lock of black hair back from his face in true diva fashion, and not for the first time Oliver wondered how much more he could fall in love with this man.

Draven grunted. "He must have hit his head when we weren't looking." His fingers played idly with Taylor's curls as they sat huddled together on the carpet.

Gideon nodded. "Or been transported to a parallel universe and returned as the village idiot." Everyone turned to stare at Gideon, who flushed, and rubbed his dark chin stubble nervously. "What?"

Eddie sniggered. "That was a totally un-Gideon like thing to say. You've been playing too many medieval Xbox games, I think."

"But still," Taylor said doubtfully. "Timothy Dalton?"

Oliver laughed loudly. "Guys, I was joking. I happen to agree with Taylor. Daniel Craig was the best." There were hoots and cheers around the table, and then Eddie turned to Taylor.

"So come on, Mr Psychic, who do you think the next Bond will be? Use your third eye and see the future." He made the sound of the Twilight Zone theme music. "Idris, one of the Toms, or Luke Evans?"

Taylor's eyes shadowed. "My Spidey senses aren't quite working the way they used to, guys." He tried to smile. "Anyway, you know it doesn't work like that."

Eddie gasped.

Leslie turned to look at Taylor with narrowed eyes. "What do you mean?" he asked suspiciously. "Have you lost your power for good or what? Spill the beans, Tay."

Oliver felt sorry for Taylor. Having the "Power of Leslie" targeted against him was difficult to resist. Although having been friends for so long, he was sure Taylor was used to it.

Taylor shrugged uncomfortably. "Things have changed a bit, is all. I don't feel stuff the same way I used to." He stared down at his hands, lost in thought.

Draven leaned forward and rubbed a thumb against Taylor's hand comfortingly. "Babe, it's not all doom and gloom." He looked around at the curious faces in the room. "Taylor doesn't seem to be able to process stuff like he used to. Like when you were being hurt, Eddie? Remember how he felt it? Well now, that doesn't happen anymore. Instead he only seems to be able to read things by touch."

Oliver frowned. That didn't sound so bad. Before, Taylor had been haunted by visions and sounds he'd been unable to suppress. It had caused him many sleepless nights and a lot of angst. "Taylor, I don't mean to be ignorant or anything, but isn't that better? Before you had no control over it. Now it seems like you do if touch is the main catalyst. It's more your choice."

Draven looked at him, gratitude written all over his face. "Exactly what I've been trying to tell him. The nights of waking up screaming after seeing stuff have disappeared. Tay's sleeping better and he's able to choose whether he wants to get involved with his Spidey senses. That doesn't sound like a bad compromise to me. But Tay feels different about it…" His words trailed off.

Taylor heaved a huge sigh and finally looked up. "I know you guys mean well, but it's something I was born with and now it's gone. I spoke to an auntie in Mauritius about it and she says it's not unusual. I'm not the first in the family line to have this happen to them."

Leslie rushed over to hug his friend and Oliver's heart warmed at the sight. His boyfriend was one of the most caring people he knew. "Sweetie, I know you think you've lost something. And we could never even understand how that feels. But look on the bright side." Oliver bit back a chuckle. That sentiment was so Leslie. "You've got your sleep back. You don't have this grumpy fiancé of yours complaining he was woken up in the middle of the night with your nightmares, and…you still get to help people because it's still there, your gift, only different."

Taylor nodded wearily. "I know. You make a good case. I suppose I need to get used to the idea. I'm still doing police work, and it seems to be going along fine, but there's a little bit of me that feels empty inside."

Eddie laughed evilly. "Well, Draven can make up for that—" He broke off, going bright red. "Christ, I'm sorry. Wrong time for a joke?"

Everyone was chuckling now, and Gideon rolled over and rumpled Eddie's unruly red hair in affection. "You always know how to choose your moments, love. That mouth of yours knows no boundaries."

The room erupted into sniggers and dirty one-liners and Taylor seemed more at ease now that he'd told his friends about his dilemma.

Oliver decided it was time for pudding. He stood up. "Now that we've sorted the world out, do you think we can have dessert? I'm dying to tuck into that delicious celebration cake over there." He waved toward the mouth-watering profiterole layered extravagance sitting on the kitchen top that had been taken out to defrost a while ago and had probably melted by now.

Taylor stood up and ambled over to the open-plan kitchen. "Shit, I forgot about this." He clattered around between the counters and Draven got up to help.

Oliver took the lull in conversation to pull Leslie tighter against him and kiss him softly. "Our friends are insane, you know that?"

Leslie grinned. "Aren't they just? They are so cray-cray, but I love them madly."

Oliver frowned. "Talking of cray-cray, what's this I hear about some big event going down at Club Delish over Christmas? Some sort of dancing show Lenny and Ryan are putting on?"

Leslie sat up, eyes sparkling with excitement. "You heard right, lover. We're doing this whole Kissmas Drag Stravaganza on Christmas Eve, with go-go dancers and drag queens, and a whole load of other entertainment. It's the first time the club has done something like this, so it will be epic. And I get to be part of the fashion team for the event." He smirked. "You will be there, too, I've already bought the tickets."

"Huh." Oliver sat back against the couch. "Sounds like fun. Going to keep you busy then, I imagine."

Leslie smiled enigmatically. "You have no idea. I have plans. Lots of plans…." His voice trailed off and he got that faraway Leslie look Oliver knew so well. He felt a tinge of misgiving.

"What kind of plans?" he asked.

Leslie leaned forward. "Don't you worry that handsome head about it. Let's just say it will be a Christmas to remember and leave it at that, shall we?" His eyes widened. "Ooh, look, Taylor's brought out the chocolate wine, I need to get me some of that. I'll get you a glass too, babe." He bounded off the couch over to the kitchen counter and Oliver watched his pert arse disappear.

Oliver wasn't sure about the whole Christmas event, and less about whatever surprise Leslie might have up his sleeve. God help him if Leslie had organised any form of karaoke and expected Oliver to make a fool of himself. That simply wasn't going to happen. He hated karaoke. With Leslie though, anything was possible. And, Oliver admitted, that was part of his charm.

Later that evening they all sat replete and comfortable as soft music played, and the warmth of the room soaked into Oliver's bones. He watched Leslie talk, entranced by the way his hands waved away animatedly, and his long eyelashes batted at his friends when he was trying to make a point about something.

"What do you think, Oliver?"

"Huh?" He was interrupted in his sappy contemplation of his boyfriend and brought back to the present.

Draven laughed loudly. "Leslie, your man was looking all gaga there, watching you." He grinned. "You looked away with the fairies there, Olly."

His words were teasing, and Oliver grinned shamefacedly. "Sorry, guys, I zoned out a bit."

"We were discussing the fact Draven and Taylor can't get married in church," Leslie said firmly. "Not that they want to, but that shouldn't be the point. How sucky is that? I thought we were moving forward with the whole gay rights thing here in England."

Oliver puffed out his cheeks. "I agree they should be able to, of course. But attitudes take time to change, and we're slowly chipping away at them."

"Not fast enough," Leslie huffed. "I know some religions allow same-sex marriages, but that's so not the point. They all should."

"Meh." Taylor waved a lazy hand. "I'm not fussed. I'm an atheist anyway. A civil partnership will do me when we decide it's time. It's not the piece of paper that makes the marriage. It's the two people involved."

Oliver nodded. "I think that too. It's wonderful to be able to have the whole shebang, and we need to keep fighting for it so people who do want it can have it, but I've got Leslie and that's all I need. Anything else is irrelevant."

A shadow crossed Leslie's beautiful face.

"You okay, sweetheart?" Oliver asked. "Something else on your mind?"

Leslie crossed his arms across his chest. "What about if something happens to you?

You hear all these stories about someone's boyfriend going to hospital and then the same-sex partner isn't recognised so he can't visit. Surely even a civil partnership will make sure both people have the same rights to be there for each other the same way heterosexual couples do?"

Oliver blinked as the room went quiet. "I hear you, sweetheart. And I agree with you. It would break my heart if I couldn't be with you when you were sick or hurt. It's something we should think about, definitely."

Eddie stared at Leslie with concern. "Hopefully people are more open to it nowadays, at least, I'd like to think so. If not, we'll take a pair of your heels and make our point known." He cackled. "Get it, make our point—"

Gideon reached over and laid a large finger on his lips. "We get it, babe. You're such a funny man." He flicked Eddie's ear and his lover yowled in pain.

"God, would you stop doing that? My ears are big enough as they are, I don't need them any more noticeable."

Once again, the room exploded into chaos as Gideon teased Eddie about his ears and

Taylor fed Draven chocolate profiteroles, in a manner that made Oliver want to tell them to get a room. As it was their house, he thought that would be wasted, or worst, they'd take him up on it. Instead, he watched Leslie try to join in the horsing about by trying to protect Eddie's poor ears from Gideon's unrelenting attention.

Oliver sighed as he picked up his glass of wine and tried to avoid being jostled by the horseplay of grown men. Deep down inside, he acknowledged that Leslie had a point about their relationship.

It would certainly be something to discuss at a later stage, to ensure that they both had some say over each other's lives should it ever come to the worst.

I'll do anything to make you happy, he thought as he watched Leslie joking with his friends.

And in truth, it would probably make Oliver feel better too.

Chapter 5

D-Day—two weeks and counting

Leslie sat in The Arbour at work, eating his lunchtime BLT as he contemplated life and the strange being that was Oliver Brown.

"I'd like to know," he said to no one in particular, waving his sandwich in the air, "whether I'm being stupid with my plan. Am I old-fashioned wanting a proper commitment to the man I love? Am I being unreasonable hoping that one day we'll get married and I'll be able to call Oliver my husband?"

He bit down fiercely on his sandwich. As he chewed, he scowled at the people passing in the busy lunchtime street crowd below. He wondered ungraciously how many of them had a recalcitrant boyfriend at home who didn't seem to think a ring and a wedding ceremony were all that important.

"Leslie, are you all right?" Laverne's worried voice cut through his dark musings.

"Someone said you'd chosen to sit here alone and I told them surely not. Leslie Scott would never choose to do that unless something was really bothering him."

She entered and sat down next to him at the staff table, regarding him with an amused gaze.

Leslie snorted. "I have a few things on my mind." He stared down moodily at the remains of his sandwich. "I wanted to be alone and think."

Laverne chuckled. "I can leave if you want." Her hand came across the table and covered his. "Then again, they always say a problem shared is a problem halved. Want to talk about it?"

That soft touch on his hand seemed to be the catalyst for Leslie to unleash the word devil that dwelt within him, together with the fact he couldn't keep a burning secret to himself any more than he could give up wearing heels or sexy lingerie. Truth be told, he had no idea how he'd lasted so long not telling Taylor and Eddie. It had to be a world record for him.

"I'mgoingtoaskOlivertomarrymeatChristmasandIdon'tthink he'llsayyes," Leslie wailed.

"Honestly, I'm dying here. Oliver doesn't seem so keen, and I have all these fucking plans, and I'm not even sure I should do it anymore."

He sat back in his chair, staring down miserably at his feet. Laverne tapped one manicured fingernail on the table, her head cocked to one side as she regarded him with interest. A smile played around her full lips. Leslie had expected more of a verbal reaction, so he was a little miffed when she didn't say anything.

"Some reassurance would be nice," he finally muttered, looking up to stare darkly at Laverne's thoughtful face. "Why, Leslie, the man adores you, of course he'll say yes. Oh, Leslie, just because he isn't over the moon about it now doesn't mean he won't be when you ask him."

He was nonplussed when Laverne simply smiled mysteriously and stood up. "I do believe, chicken, that you've just single-handedly reassured yourself." She sighed and squeezed Leslie's shoulder. "That man would do anything to make you happy."

Leslie's heart sank. "But that's just it," he said quietly. "I don't want him to do it because it makes *me* happy. I want him to do it because it will make *him* happy."

"I put that badly," Laverne said hastily. "Leslie, chicken, not all of us go around thinking of getting married one day, or even getting engaged. Look at Brook and me. We're perfectly happy right now, and neither one of us is chomping at the bit to take things further.

"But, darling, if he turned around tonight and pressed a ring in my hand and asked me to marry him, I'd say yes in a heartbeat. And you," she leaned in and kissed the top of Leslie's head, "you'll be asking something right from that beautiful heart of yours, and in that moment ,Oliver will only see your gesture for what it is. Love for him. No man can resist that."

She patted Leslie's shoulder. "And we *are* talking about the Oliver Brown who took you to the fair and spent a fortune on the shooting stall so he could win you the fuzzy bunny you wanted." She chuckled. "If I recall, the man finally gave it to him because he couldn't bear to leech any more money out of poor, dear Oliver. *And, too,* there was a queue of sticky-fingered kids getting restless because they wanted a turn."

Leslie nodded, thinking of the ginormous purple bunny he'd called Rags sitting on his bed at home. "He was such a bad shot," he murmured fondly. He felt marginally better as he pushed his half-eaten sandwich away and stood to give Laverne a hug.

"Thank you," he murmured into Laverne's fragranced wig. He frowned and squeezed Laverne's bicep. "My, what a big arm you have. Have you been working out with Brook?"

Laverne moved away and grinned. "I have. Like my new muscles? Brook always tells me they're all the better to fu—"

"I don't want to hear any more," Leslie stated firmly, making a shooing motion to Laverne, who chuckled wickedly. "It's like hearing my parents have sex in the room next door to me." He grimaced. "That used to happen often. My mum and dad were like bloody rabbits."

Laverne laughed. "The vision that conjures up as to how you were created makes more sense about who you are. The mind boggles." Her face grew serious. "I'm so excited about you proposing to Oliver. Stop worrying about it and go with your heart. It's what you do best." She glanced at her watch. "Fuck, I'm late. I'm having lunch with Brook and you know how that man gets when people are late. He's got such a stick up his arse about things like that." She gave Leslie another quick hug and hurried out the door.

He looked down at the remains of his unappetising, dry sandwich and sighed. He hadn't had a chance to swear Laverne to secrecy but he thought her nature was such that she'd keep it anyway. He had to admit he'd been surprised about the ease with which she'd accepted the news without any grand plans being made. Laverne was clearly mellowing in her approach, probably the influence of the easy-going Brook.

Leslie heaved a huge sigh and stared out of the window dreamily.

God, why can't Christmas hurry up and get here already? All this secret keeping is killing me.

***

"Honey? I'm home." Oliver walked into the hallway around eight pm and raised an eyebrow when there was no resultant squeal of delight. Normally he could count on a Leslie whirlwind to welcome him home. The last two days he'd been working at a customer's home in Surrey, taking a train in the early hours and arriving back in the evenings much later than he'd expected. His business as a website designer had grown, and he was now doing corporate websites for multinational companies who expected to at least see the man who was responsible for creating their outlet to the digital world once or twice.

Being with Leslie had certainly broadened Oliver's horizons—extended them even. No longer was he hidden away, scared to show his scarred face to the world.

He'd even been tempted onto the stage at Club Delish a few times to be part of a drag act that Delilah and Laverne had performed. If Oliver was honest, it had been fun being in the spotlight again, having people cheer and clap when as his alter ego, Nicky Starr, former porn actor, had been part of the act for a few dirty, raunchy minutes. Before Leslie, or *BL* as he thought of it, he would never have been able to face doing that.

Oliver thanked God each day that Leslie had found him and dragged him into the world again. Oliver attributed his flourishing website business due to his ability to get out and meet people. And that success was all because of Leslie.

That said, his last customer had been a nightmare. Livia Alcott was a self-made businesswoman in her late sixties who needed the personal touch when being shown around her new website. The business she'd built, a global Plc, selling custom-made wigs made with real hair, had been a fascinating study for Oliver. He'd enjoyed researching and creating the website and using Leslie as a guinea pig to wear the wigs and create images for use on the site.

Oliver dropped his briefcase onto the floor and made his way into the bedroom. Perhaps Leslie was catnapping. Oliver would often come home and find his lover curled up on the bed, book in hand. Frequently he fell asleep reading.

The bedroom was empty.

Oliver pulled his phone out and squinted down at the messages. There was nothing new there so Leslie hadn't contacted him to say he'd be late. Oliver rolled his shoulders and decided to take a shower. Perhaps his missing boyfriend would turn up soon. He might have stayed for a drink at work or been asked to help at a fashion show. Still, Oliver felt a twinge of misgiving. It wasn't like Leslie not to message him to tell him he'd be late.

Oliver was in the shower washing his hair in a stream of steaming hot water when he heard the bathroom door open. He half turned to check it was Leslie and not some crazy serial killer about to slice and dice him, but was stopped from clubbing an intruder with his favourite crème rinse when a warm, sinewy body pressed itself against Oliver's back and long fingers ran down his soapy sides. He grinned, his body responding to the familiar scent of his lover in its usual, predictable way.

With his dick.

With Leslie, the only way was up.

"I think we'll have to be quick," he murmured as he rinsed soap out of his eyes. "My boyfriend will be home soon and he's not going to like me having a sexy creature like you in my shower."

"Oh really?" Leslie purred behind him, nimble fingers skimming Oliver's flat stomach. "Is he the jealous type then?"

Oliver drew a breath as soft lips nibbled at the nape of his neck, then slid round to softly bite his earlobe. "He's been known to pitch a fit when he thinks someone is trying to make out with me," he murmured, enjoying the feel of Leslie's hard-on against his backside. "Last time someone did that, they ended up with hot chocolate in their lap, scalding their privates."

Leslie's sultry chuckle made Oliver's groin heat level increase even more. "That guy was an arsehole, and he was less than subtle with the eye winks and head tilts toward the bathroom and the 'My name is Jed Steele but you can call me Stainless' comment. I mean, how tacky was that?"

Oliver hitched a breath as his cock was grasped tightly and Leslie began his long, slow pulls. Behind him, Leslie slid his dick against Oliver's arse. It was something his lover had down to an art, being able push and pull at the same time. Oliver tended to go off stroke when he tried it.

"God, you feel good," Oliver gasped as he veered between pushing his dick farther into Leslie's hands, which were skillfully causing mayhem, and pushing backward to feel Leslie's cock slip in between his cheeks. "So damn good. Yes, like that, please. Harder, baby."

Leslie gripped him tighter as he drove Oliver into that space where time seemed to disappear, and the only sensation was the primal need to climax. To feel his balls tighten and the rush of heat and pleasure fill his groin.

Leslie's soft pants and moans behind him as he rubbed against Oliver's wet skin indicated he was close to climaxing too. Three years of amazing sex together had taught them to read each other's signals and know them intimately. Tonight was no exception.

Water ran into Oliver's eyes, and he fluttered his eyelashes in pleasure, lost in the sensation of the hard tugging of his aching and straining cock, and the insistent feel of Leslie's cock across his hole. If they'd been in the bedroom, Oliver would have begged Leslie to take him right then, to fill him and make love to him the way only Leslie could. He would have spread his legs like a slut and watched Leslie enter him as that long, beautiful cock of his disappeared inside.

But now he was too close to erupting and from the sounds of it, Leslie was too. The low keening sound that emanated from his beautiful lips as he came was something Oliver treasured. That he could drive this sexy, sassy, beautiful human being to this was something he was proud of.

He clenched his backside tighter, and Leslie swore softly, filthy words getting lost beneath the sounds of water and Oliver's own cries as he spilt over Leslie's hand, body shaking and jerking until he was spent and boneless pressed against the shower wall.

Leslie's body tightened and with a sudden rush of heat between his arse cheeks, and then a shudder that Oliver felt right down to his core, Leslie orgasmed and then slumped against Oliver with a satisfied grunt. For a moment, neither of them moved. Then Oliver turned around and cradled Leslie's face in his hands.

"I love you, you know that," he murmured softly. "This is all I ever need. Only you."

Leslie's blue eyes were barely visible between his half-shut lids, his lips parted in a soft smile. His black hair was plastered to his head, stray strands against his cheeks and forehead. "I love you too. I'm so glad I was the one to deliver that suit that day."

Oliver reached over and turned off the water as it was now tepid, and then pulled his lover to him. His lips found Leslie's as he gave a happy sigh and surrendered his mouth to be plundered by Oliver's questing tongue.

It was only when Oliver became aware that Leslie was shivering that he broke the kiss. "Babe, you're cold. Come on. Let's get out of here. There's a warm towel with your name on it." Twenty minutes later, warm and cozy, Oliver dressed in boxers and a tee shirt, Leslie in a set of royal blue silk pyjamas, they sat snuggled together on the couch, with tea and biscuits, idly watching the latest news.

"Laverne keep you late tonight?" Oliver asked as he munched on another chocolate biscuit. "I was a little worried when you weren't home."

The locks of dark hair resting on his chest moved as Leslie shook his head sleepily. "No, I have a special project I'm working on and I stayed behind to finish up. Sorry I didn't text. I didn't really think I'd be as late as I was."

"Special project? Sounds interesting. What are you doing?" Oliver filched another biscuit and dipped it into his tea.

Leslie stilled. "I, uh, can't tell you about it. It's a secret."

Oliver ran fingers through Leslie's soft hair, and his lover purred with satisfaction.

He's like a damn cat, Oliver thought in amusement. An exotic, beautiful Siamese cat. The Christmas present he'd had custom made for Leslie would be perfect. It was a white gold choker with a pearl set in the middle. Leslie had seen a picture of one in a magazine and talked about it for days.

Oliver couldn't wait to see the look in his man's eyes when Leslie saw his present.

"Do I get to find out what this special secret project is at any stage?" Olive enquired.

Leslie nodded and shifted on the couch, his strong legs stretching to top the couch arm. "Uh-huh. You will, soon enough."

"Is it a new suit for me?" Oliver enquired.

Leslie sat up and perched cross-legged on the couch. He raised one eyebrow. "What makes you think the surprise is for you? And just because last Christmas you got a bit of fancy tat to wear doesn't mean I'm doing it again this year." He huffed. "Perhaps it's a secret project for someone else."

Oliver reached over and tickled Leslie's side, where Oliver knew Leslie was most susceptible. "I bet it's for me and I bet I can tickle it out of you."

Leslie squealed and tried to evade Oliver's searching fingers. "Bastard, don't do that. And I will not be tortured into spilling the beans by tickling."

Leslie's squeals turned to helpless giggles as Oliver proceeded to tickle him unmercifully, and when Oliver ended up with a lap of warm, fragrant man trying to distract the not-so-torture torture by kissing him, all thoughts of the Christmas secret were forgotten.

Chapter 6

D-Day—one week and counting

Eddie and Taylor stared at the item on the table in horror. "You did *what*?" they chorused.

Leslie smiled smugly. "Don't look so surprised," he chided. "You knew it was going to happen someday. I've always said I wanted another one."

Eddie looked a little green around the gills. "But, Leslie, you don't have the best luck with them. I mean, remember what happened to Glenda, and then little Rollo. Do you really want to go through that heartbreak again?"

Leslie's face fell. "I really don't. I loved those fish. But I'm older now and I feel I can deal with anything that happens. But it won't. Nothing bad, I mean."

Taylor cleared his throat. "Not being bitchy or anything but, Leslie, you know your track record with pets. It's not exactly been…successful. Look at poor Monty."

All three of them turned to look at the small fish tank on the dining room table of Leslie's home.

"I know," Leslie muttered. "But these looked so cute in the window and I couldn't resist."

It was his day off and he'd gone and picked them up from the pet shop down the road. Now he was proud to show his new pets to his two best friends, who had the same day off due to a little creative juggling. Oliver was having lunch with his old friend and former fuck-buddy Maxwell Lewis, while Max's boyfriend Gibson was off at some gaming seminar in Bristol.

Inside the tank, three fish swam in circles, one a clown fish, the other ones Leslie wasn't sure of. The pet shop man, whose name was Reggie, had seemed knowledgeable enough, and he'd promised that even Leslie couldn't kill these fish. He'd also promised they wouldn't eat each other.

Eddie peered into the tank, which was lovely enough, with a castle in the corner, lots of green fronds, and even a sunken ship. "Huh. Oliver will be surprised," he said with a laugh in his voice.

"Pffftt." Leslie waved an elegant hand. "Oliver will come to love Sushi, Finn, and Gill as much as I do." He regarded the fish fondly as Taylor and Eddie gawked at each other.

"Besides, Monty only escaped because the stupid dog next door bounded in while the cage was on the floor, getting some sunshine." He scowled. "That woman needs to learn to control her stupid poodle. If she hadn't knocked the cage door open, poor Monty would still be with us."

Leslie's heart ached still for the loss of his dwarf guinea pig. He hoped Monty was somewhere enjoying a fruitful life with another guinea pig and having loads of sex and babies.

"Still," Taylor muttered. "I don't want to be here when he finds out he has new family members."

Leslie laughed. "Oh, I'm sure he'll be okay with it," he murmured. "I'll initiate mind-blowing sex and make him feel good about it."

Eddie guffawed. "Is that your answer to everything? Because I try it with Gideon and it doesn't always work out. He sees right through me."

Taylor nodded. "Draven too. He's happy to take advantage of it but after he's gotten what he wanted, he still doesn't change his mind. Wily fucker."

Leslie sauntered over to the kitchen to fetch the half-empty wine bottle. "Apparently, you boys don't know how to do it."

His jaw dropped when he spotted the red satin ribbon on the kitchen top, together with a sketch of his Christmas suit, and his to-do list. He'd forgotten to tuck it away before company arrived. He slid a hand across the counter, hoping to snag it, and screamed in panic when a deep voice said, "Whatcha doing?" in his ear.

"Jesus, Ed, do you have to creep up on someone like that?" Leslie tried to hide the items under his hand, but part of the ribbon and sketch peeked out. "I swear, you almost gave me a heart attack."

Taylor had joined them and he stared in interest at the bit of the sketch showing.

"What's that, some new drag costume or something? Looks very Christmassy. Is it for the Drag Stravaganza?"

Eddie pushed some hair from his face and behind his ears as he bent down to look. "Looks pretty sexy to me. Come on, Leslie, let's have a peek."

Leslie swallowed, trying to stop the panic from bubbling up as he struggled to keep his secret. If word got out to these two, there would be no surprise for Oliver. The whole of London would know by the time they'd hopped on the tube to go to their respective homes.

"It's a secret," he hissed, "so stop being so fucking nosy. You'll learn about it in good time." He scooped up the items and turned to walk away to hide them in the sideboard drawer where he kept all his fashion articles and cuttings. The old secret of stashing private stuff in an underwear drawer didn't work with Oliver. His boyfriend took too much pleasure in finding items for Leslie to wear when he was in "the mood."

Leslie stashed the ribbon and sketch away, and as he closed the drawer he frowned. Wasn't there supposed to be something else with it? The lack of noise should have been his first clue that all was not right. He turned slowly to see Taylor sheepishly holding out a piece of paper. "You dropped this," he said awkwardly, with a quick glance at Eddie.

It was Leslie's to-do list, with the number one action being "Ask Oliver to marry me on Christmas Eve." They had to have seen it. It was written in bright pink, with hearts and the initials LTSB written all down the side. Leslie had been practicing his signature as a Scott-Brown, which sounded so much better than Brown-Scott, which sounded like some fungal disease a Highlander might have had.

Both men stared at Leslie, and Leslie had no idea how they were restraining themselves from asking him what the fuck was going on. He rolled his eyes. Perhaps he could tell them what he planned and invoke some mid-earth demon to promise to rot their penises off if they spilled the beans too soon.

"Fine. Here's the thing." He took a deep breath and continued, "I'm going to ask Oliver to marry me and you're not allowed to tell anyone or else your penises will fall off."

Eddie and Taylor gawped at him, then, as understanding of the garbled Leslie-speak became clear, their faces burst into sunny smiles. Both men bounded over to him and enveloped him in bear hugs that threatened to break his ribs.

"Oh my God, that's so cool," Eddie gushed. "How exciting. When are you going to do it?" His eyes grew dreamy. "Are you going away to Venice, and you'll propose on a gondola as you pass under the Bridge of Sighs?"

Both Taylor and Leslie undid their embrace and turned to stare at Eddie.

"Wow," Leslie murmured. "That's pretty specific. Think about it much then?"

Taylor sniggered. "I think we know how dear Ed wants to be asked to tie the knot."

Eddie was beet red, flushing to the tips of his fiery red hair. "I might have given it some thought." He scowled. "Anyway, we're not to here to talk about me. This is Leslie's moment. And what do you mean, our penises will fall off?"

Leslie sank down exhausted onto the couch and his friends followed suit. "I'm going to ask him on Christmas Eve at the club. I mean, it's supposed to be a secret, but I seem to make a habit of blurting it out to people." He reached over and took both of their hands. "Chaps, you two are my besties, but if you breathe a word of this to anyone, I will summon a demon from hell and I will ask him to rot your extremities until there's nothing left."

"We can't even tell our other halves?" Eddie asked, aghast. "It will kill me knowing this and not telling Gideon I know."

Leslie sighed. "Fine, tell them but please, please, don't let Oliver find out about it. I've been planning this for months."

Taylor nodded solemnly. "We promise." He chuckled. "Draven is the world's best at keeping secrets, so he's no problem. Gideon's the same, I think."

"It's not as much them as you two flibbertigibbets," Leslie remarked drily.

Eddie and Taylor shared a look, then turned to regard Leslie in earnest. "We promise we won't say a word," Eddie muttered. "Pinkie-swear." He held out his pinkie and Leslie clasped it with his in silent agreement.

Taylor agreed. "I rather fancy my dick right where it is, thank you very much." He smirked. "And Draven will no doubt agree."

By the time they'd left later that afternoon, once again promising to keep their lips sealed, Leslie was ready to tackle the worrying sentiment that perhaps Oliver might not be as happy with their new house additions as he was. He decided to tackle the problem head on, Leslie-style. The new lacy underwear he'd bought, together with a pair of high heels and a bottle of bubbly might do the trick to distract his lover so he could make his argument for his fish.

After all, a relationship was all about negotiation and compromise.

***

Oliver sprinkled more fish food into the tank and closed the top. He sat down in his chair at the dining room table and watched as the fish darted to the top to eat. The tank resided on the sideboard, having forced out a glass lamp and a small photo of him and Leslie. Those pieces had now been relegated to other places in their home.

Oliver admitted he'd been worried about having more fish given Leslie's tender heart and the fact that when something bad happened to them, he'd be inconsolable for days. Oliver hated seeing him upset.

So far, Gill, Finn, and Sushi seemed to be doing well. And, of course, the plan Leslie had come up with to convince him the fish were acceptable new family members had been fun too. Being greeted by his sexy boyfriend dressed in little more than lace, bearing champagne and then proceeding to screw his brains out had certainly made him feel better about it. Of course, that had been Leslie's plan all along, and Oliver adored how his lover didn't seem to realise that he was on to him.

He stared at his computer screen, reviewing the images he'd uploaded. Rubbing a hand over his tired eyes, Oliver contemplated going down to Debussy's to take Leslie to lunch. It had been while since he'd been there.

Decision made, he showered, dressed into one of his favourite casual suits, and journeyed down to Hackney to surprise his boyfriend. The new receptionist—he thought her name was Frederika—greeted him warmly when he arrived.

"Oliver." Her accented German voice purred out over the hub and bub of the reception area. "How nice to see you here. We haven't seen you for a long time."

He nodded and grinned. "I know. Bad me. I think the last time I was here was for a suit fitting when Leslie and I went to that film premiere of *Totally Thomas*."

Her eyes widened. "That was a great film. I adored it." She gave him a huge grin.

"I'm so glad you decided to go. I remember you being unsure about it when it was first mentioned."

Oliver shrugged. "Leslie can be convincing." With Leslie's guidance, and to be honest, forcefulness, in the past two years Oliver had revisited his past and gradually got back in touch with men he'd worked with in his adult film career. He'd been flabbergasted that a lot of them had remembered him, and was even more gobstruck by the fact none of them cared about the scar on his face. Indeed, some of them thought it had given him a certain bad boy panache.

He sniggered to himself at the memory of one unfortunate incident involving an actor who'd dared to grab Oliver's crotch uninvited. Leslie had staked his claim, declaring in a loud voice (showing his teeth in a menacing smile that crocodiles would have envied) that he was so glad Luke Thighwalker's terrible case of gonorrhea had cleared up and wasn't modern medicine miraculous.

After that, people had been less handsy with Oliver. When he'd been invited to the one film Leslie had been dying to see, he'd felt honour bound to attend. *Totally Thomas* was a gay erotic film, being screened by a small, exclusive theatre in the heart of Soho. His old working buddy, Chris Lancaster, had landed the lead in his first role outside of the porn industry.

Frederika chuckled. "Your young man could charm a snake into giving him their last skin," she murmured. "Anyway, please go on down to his office. He should be there."

Oliver smiled at her, even as he wondered at her comment, because, *ugh, snakes.* He shuddered then sauntered down to the small office at the end of the corridor. Despite the fact it was his boyfriend's office, Oliver still felt it was only good manners to knock on the door before he walked in. Leslie might be on the phone with a customer. He knocked and twisted the door handle. It didn't open. He frowned. "Leslie? Babe, are you in there? Why's the door locked?"

There was a deathly silence from within. He knocked again. This time, he heard frantic whispers and scuffling as if someone was moving around in a hurry.

"Leslie, you in there? I thought I'd take you for lunch." He stared at the door, waiting for a response. There was more muttered whispers and the sound of what appeared to be a door slamming and then Leslie's panicked voice confirmed he was indeed in his office.

"Oh, hi there. Give me a minute. I'll open the door in a second."

Oliver waited patiently, his curiosity growing.

He's up to something in there. Wonder if it has anything to do with my Christmas suit?

Finally, the door opened to reveal a pink-faced and flustered Leslie, hair suspiciously out of shape and with silver glitter on his face. He beamed at Oliver. "I'll get my jacket, and my man bag and be with you in a mo."

The door shut in Oliver's face and he stared at it in disbelief.

What the hell is going on in there?

He opened the door and entered. Leslie looked up with a start and Oliver couldn't help but notice another man bent over in the corner, covering something with a piece of fabric. A man who had a nice arse, and when he finally stood up to face him, looked like a Latin wet dream. The man was petite and utterly gorgeous. And looked as guilty as hell.

"What's up, sweetheart?" Oliver strode over to his boyfriend and pulled him close for a kiss. Leslie melted against him and returned the kiss with fervour. When they finally drew apart, Leslie seemed to realise someone else was in the room with them.

"Uh, honey, this is Chester. He works here with me. Chester, my boyfriend Oliver, if you hadn't already guessed by that kiss. That yummy *possessive* kiss." Leslie's eyes glinted dangerously and he brushed a strand of glittered hair back from his face. Oliver didn't care if he'd overstepped the mark. He wasn't a jealous man and trusted Leslie, but this situation was a little weird. If Leslie could embarrass porn stars on his behalf, Oliver could stake a claim.

He held out his hand to Chester. "Nice to meet you." Huh. So *this* gorgeous man was the talented Chester, who Leslie chatted about nonstop and thought was the next best thing to hit fashion design since men's lace underwear had been invented.

"Good to meet you too," Chester stuttered. "Leslie has told me a lot about you." He cleared his throat. "I really enjoyed your films back in the day. You were incredible. The industry is not the same since you left."

Oliver's chest warmed at the words. "Thanks. I appreciate that."

Leslie sniffed, stalked over to his desk, retrieved his bag, and picked up his jacket with a flounce. "I didn't know you were coming. You should have texted me."

Oliver blinked. "It was a split-second decision. I wanted to see you, thought we could go for a bite to eat."

Leslie patted Oliver's cheek as he walked past him into the corridor. "I know I'm irresistible, darling, but that door was locked for a reason." He smirked. "And not the reason you might have thought. Chester and I are working on something together and we'd rather no one saw it until it's ready."

Ohhhhh, Oliver thought in satisfaction. *They must be working together on my new suit. That's why they look so put out.* Chester was still staring at Oliver with a "deer in the headlights" look. Perhaps he was in awe of meeting one of his favourite former porn stars who would get to wear a suit to which Chester had contributed.

"No worries," he said magnanimously. "I'm sorry if I interrupted anything. Come on, tiger, let's get you fed then perhaps we can come back here, and you can show me some of your, er, designs?" Oliver grinned. "Chester, enjoy the rest of your afternoon. Great to meet you."

It was only much later, after he'd given his boyfriend an after-lunch blowjob in the confines of Leslie's once-again-locked office, that he wondered what the potential significance of glitter might have to do with his Christmas present.

Chapter 7

D-Day—and a Leslie meltdown

"I can't fucking do this. It was a fucking stupid idea and I've changed my mind." Leslie paced around the dressing room at the nightclub, hands furling and unfurling at his sides. His feet hurt from all the pacing he'd done, and for once, his designer boots didn't feel quite as comfortable as they usually were.

What the fuck was I thinking? And I'm getting a fucking blister on my toe. Life sucks.

Christmas Eve had snuck up on him sooner than he'd expected, and the thought of what he was going to do tonight made his stomach churn and his throat dry. Lenny, standing in the dressing room with him as he checked his own costume for the show tonight, rolled his eyes and sighed. His bright blue eyes lit with amusement as he ran a hand through his mid-length blond hair. "Leslie, you're driving yourself crazy. Sit down and I'll get you some chamomile tea."

He went over to the small kitchen station on which sat a kettle, some faded white canisters, and assorted mugs. As he busied himself making Leslie his favourite go-to pacifying drink, Leslie continued to pace.

"I don't know what came over me, thinking I could do this. Of course, the costume will look delectable, I'll be in it, but the thought of actually proposing..." His throat dried up. "I don't think I can do it, Len."

Lenny turned and motioned Leslie toward the dilapidated couch in the corner. "Sit down, for God's sake. If Ryan has to replace this damn carpet again, he's going to pitch a hissy fit. That man does diva like no one else."

"This is what you do when I'm not around? Complain and gossip about me? Well, bitches, I can tell you a few things about yourselves." The low, modulated, and husky tone made them turn around.

Ryan Bishop, owner of the club in whose break room they sat in, Club Delish, and famed drag queen Delilah Delish, glared at them with fire in his blue eyes. "And as for this carpet, Mr High and Mighty Know It All," he hissed at a smiling Lenny, "I think you contributed to the last refurb when you spilt not one, but two bottles of nail polish on the former carpet then proceeded to vomit like a geyser all over it." He shuddered. "I couldn't get the smell of rancid sea bass puke out for love or money."

Ryan was slim and toned with dark auburn hair and the cutest ears Leslie had ever seen. He often wanted to ask the man whether he ever wanted to be an extra on the set of *Lord of the Rings*, but Lenny had laughed hard and told him never to broach the subject. Apparently, Ryan was sensitive about his slightly pointy ears and Leslie didn't quite fancy being on the other end of that spitfire tongue. He'd seen Mango Munroe, Ryan's significant other, quake when Ryan got going. And Mango was six feet and then some of rangy, hard-arse eco-warrior.

"I wasn't gossiping, Lenny was," Leslie proclaimed. He'd throw his friend to the wolves anytime when it came to Ryan. Lenny came over, bearing hot tea, and set it down on the table next to the couch.

"Thanks," he said drily. "Way to drop your buddies in the shit."

Leslie sank down exhausted on the couch and sipped his drink. "You're bigger than I am. And thanks for the tea." He sighed.

Ryan slumped into the other easy chair, long jeans-clad legs draping over the armchair's sides. "So, Leslie, how are things going? Is the venue to your satisfaction?" He bit at a fingernail as Leslie narrowed his eyes and stared at Lenny. Lenny stared back, a slight tic in his jaw. Leslie had reserved the plush dining room for dinner tonight but hadn't told Ryan the whole story.

"It's all beautifully done, thank you," he acknowledged. "The Christmas bouquet looks amazing. Oliver loves orchids."

"This is a special Christmas Eve dinner then, is it?" Ryan proclaimed silkily. "You'd know, given you've made sure his favourite flowers are there."

"Ryan," Lenny hissed, rubbing his chin nervously. "What did I tell you?"

Ryan's eyes widened guilelessly. "What? I'm a concerned host, trying to ascertain whether my customer is happy with the service."

Leslie closed his eyes in resignation. Ryan knew. Lenny had spilled the beans. When he opened them again, both men were staring at him, Ryan with a distinct smug air, Lenny in trepidation.

"This really isn't going how I planned," Leslie murmured sadly. "It was supposed to be fun, something I'd dreamed about, and now it's all going to pot. Is there anyone left who doesn't know what I was going to do tonight?"

Ryan sat up. "Sweetie, there is no 'was going to do' about this. You *are* going to do it." He sniffed. "I didn't have my people bring out the best cutlery, order you the best bottles of champagne and deck the fucking halls with boughs of holly so you can wuss out."

Lenny cleared his throat. "Sorry, Leslie, but Ryan is like a damn bloodhound. He could smell the secret on me. He made me tell him."

Ryan waved a hand. "Bitch, it didn't take much doing. And I know—I have mad skills." He smirked. "So, Leslie darling, you are going to do your thing this afternoon before the show starts, put your big boy panties on, and later tonight you'll have the happiest man alive at your beck and call." His face softened as he reached over and clasped Leslie's hand. "The room looks incredible. You'll look as sexy as anything, and it's all going to go like clockwork. We queens," he gestured to Lenny then himself, "will make sure of it. Tonight's show is going to be the best Kissmas Drag Stravaganza ever, and you are going to be part of it."

Lenny nodded in agreement. "Chicken, when I get dressed for the show and stand with this be-atch here, believe me, Laverne and Delilah will support you on that stage in any way we can. All you have to do is pop the question."

Leslie sighed. "I s'pose." He brightened up a little. "You are going to *love* my costume. I can't wait for you to see it. Chester did such a fabulous job."

Lenny regarded him in amusement. "I can't wait to see what your stockroom pilfering has turned into." He batted his eyes. "And your use of employee time to make this masterpiece." His tone was dry but fond.

Leslie had the grace to blush, but only for a moment. "Well, at least you know it contributed to a good cause. To make one of your favourite employees happy." He frowned. "Oh, wait, I mean your *all-time favourite* employee happy."

He scuttled out of the room before the other men could even comment on that.

***

An hour later, Leslie was feeling much better. He stood with Chester on the stage at Club Delish and gazed in wonder at himself in the full-length mirror.

"*Wow*," he breathed. "I look fantabulous." He turned and regarded his skin-tight costume with delight. "Chester, this is utterly perfect."

Chester nodded in excitement. "*Sí*, it is stunning. And you are so going to entrance that man of yours tonight when you wear it."

Leslie swanned around the stage, getting used to the feel of the fabric and feeling the give and take. He had to admit there was very little give. His red heels added inches to his height and the Santa hat perched on his head with its glittery pom-pom added a distinctly cheerful air.

"The other day when Oliver came to see you so unexpectedly, I thought we would be caught. Thank God you locked the door when we did that fitting." Chester walked over and examined his work with critical eyes. "It would have spoilt the surprise."

"I'm shocked we'd managed to get me out of this so quickly." Leslie blew up a puff of air to move a strand of hair from his eyes, all the better to see himself with. "I think he thought we were, you know...." He flapped his hand meaningfully.

Chester let out a peal of laughter. "I think so too. He had this crazy look in his eye that said he would break me in two if I was doing something naughty."

"Do you think?" Leslie asked, a warm glow suffusing his body. "That's so hot." He fanned himself. "Talking of hot, I'd better get this off. The show is in a few hours and there's still loads of drag queens to boss around."

Laverne had commandeered Leslie for the event to help dress and primp the queens for the show tonight. He and Chester began peeling the slinky suit off Leslie's slightly sweaty body. He'd have to shower before tonight's big event.

"What is the plan?" Chester enquired as he helped peel the top over Leslie's head. "The show starts at eight pm, yes? There are drinks and your friends will be here?"

Leslie nodded underneath the top, which was proving decidedly stubborn in its removal. "Yes," he said, his words muffled beneath the red satin. "I'm helping out in the dressing room. Those queens need some attention. Then we'll all be having cocktails and watching the show. Before it finishes, around ten thirty, I'm going back to the dressing room. I'll get changed into my sexy suit, and go check to make sure everything is good in the proposal room."

The top came off with a slither and Leslie was finally free. He breathed a sigh of relief as Chester folded and packed the clothes away with reverence. "Delilah will make an announcement for Oliver to make his way to the room after the show, and then..." Leslie blinked. "Well, then he'll see me in my costume, I'll pretend I'm his present, we'll have dinner, and then I'll propose."

He swallowed. "And then we'll come on out and everything will be as it should be." His face brightened. "I wanted to show you the ring. It's in my man bag." He tottered his way across the stage to his bag, retrieved the small velvet box, and tottered back to Chester, who held his hand to his chest over his heart.

"I get to see the ring? *Me siento honrado*, Leslie." Leslie opened the box and Chester gasped. "*Oh Dios mío. Eso es hermoso.*"

The ring sparkled against the blue velvet, and once again Leslie's eyes prickled at the sight of something he intended to give to the man he loved, along with his heart, which Oliver had already, but this time it would be formal.

The ring was a *Ogham Le Chéile* Faith Ring, in white and yellow gold, two halves in different colours, representing Oliver and Leslie. He'd been entranced with the colouring and the beautiful Le Chéile design, together with an inscription from the ancient Ogham alphabet. The jeweller had told him *Le Chéile* was Gaelic for "together" and had been used in many ancient Irish texts, the *Book of Kells* being the most famous.

Neither he nor Oliver had any Irish roots, but it had been love at first sight for Leslie, and the intention of the ring was all about them.

"It is pretty, isn't it?" Leslie sighed dreamily as he struggled out of the tight trousers and heels, and back into his work clothes. The pair of them sighed in unison and gazed at the sparkling item in Leslie's hand. Their admiration was rudely interrupted by a panicked shout from side stage.

"Leslie," Ryan was whisper shouting. "Oliver is here. He's right here, coming to see you." Ryan turned back to face the stage wings. "Hi Oliver, long time no see. Can I interest you in a drink first?" Ryan was obviously aware Leslie and Chester were in dress rehearsal and was trying to head Oliver off at the pass.

Chester looked around in desperation as he stuffed the costume into a dress bag. "What is it with that man and his untimely appearances? He should have a bell around his neck."

Leslie snorted in laughter at the image of Oliver with a cat or cow bell around his neck.

Chester stared at him. "You are laughing. This is an *emergency*," he hissed.

"Leslie?" Oliver's voice grew nearer. "You forgot your phone at home, sweetheart. I thought I'd drop it over, in case anyone needed to get hold of you for tonight."

Leslie had indeed forgotten his phone this morning, only realising once he'd gotten to the club. He'd meant to borrow someone's phone earlier to text Oliver to ask him to bring it with him tonight.

"Blast him being my white knight," he muttered as he slipped his feet back into his socks and shoes.

"The ring," Chester spluttered. "We must hide it. Here, let me do it." Before Leslie could protest, Chester snatched the ring box from the floor beside Leslie and scampered over to the fake fireplace at the back of the stage. The scene from the *Nutcracker*—drag queen style—was all set up. Chester reached into the recess of the fireplace and the box disappeared.

"There is a little shelf in here, the box fits nicely. We can get it later."

Leslie was left wondering why it couldn't have been put back in his man bag, or tucked into his suit pocket, but he'd no time to argue. He'd only barely got his jacket on—no tie—and was busy running a hand over his hair when Oliver appeared, Ryan close on his heels.

"Uhmm, thanks for the sightseeing tour, Ryan. You do know I've been backstage in the club before?" Oliver looked perplexed, but his face lit up when he saw Leslie. It darkened when he saw Chester. "Hi, babe. Oh, and you again, Chester. Wow, you two really have taken working together to a new art form, haven't you?" He laughed, but Leslie thought it sounded a little false.

He refrained from giving his patented eye roll, but a small part of him revelled in the fact his boyfriend seemed a tad jealous.

Ryan grimaced and mouthed, "I tried to distract him, but he was a man on a mission."

Leslie hugged Oliver tightly. "I'm sorry. I wasn't all that bothered about it, because I've been really busy here, but thank you for bringing it down."

"No problem. I know tonight is a big deal for you, so I wanted to make sure you didn't miss out on anything. I was in the area for a meeting with a new customer." Oliver looked around the stage with interest, his gaze focusing on the faux fireplace and the cut-outs surrounding it. "Huh. That's different. I've never seen the *Nutcracker* performed with naked full-frontal soldiers before. And what the hell are they holding?"

"Leslie? Are you here?" Laverne's strident tones echoed across the stage. "The ladies require your services, *tout suite*."

"Fuck me, it's like London Liverpool Station here." Leslie swore as he moved out of Oliver's arms. "Why don't we invite the cast of Dr Who. I heard they're shooting an episode a block away." He cast a desperate glance at the faux fireplace.

I need to get that damn ring back.

Laverne strode over, splendid in a dark blue dress, ruched in the front and showing off her toned legs in four-inch heels. She leaned in and flicked Leslie's ear, casting a beady eye around her. "Chicken, those damn queens are chomping at the bit to get dressed, and you're *the* person to make it happen. Now shoo, off with you. Chester, don't you be sidling out that side door. I see you. Go give Leslie a hand. It will keep the two of you out of mischief." She drew a deep breath. "Everyone else, follow me. It's time for a Pimm's."

She swept off the stage in a flourish of exuberance. Ryan shrugged and followed her. "Pimm's works for me."

Leslie watched them go and sighed. "I suppose we'd better get down to the dressing rooms and help the ladies. Babe, I'll see you later when the show starts. Love you." He cast another sneaky peek at the ring's hiding place.

Damn it. I'll have to sneak back later after the show and get it. I hope nobody finds it.

He beckoned to Chester and they left a bewildered-looking Oliver alone on the stage still marvelling at the grinning, naked Nutcracker soldiers with their blue and red dildos held before them like swords.

Chapter 8

D Day—and an unexpected performance

"Ladies, gentlemen, people of indiscriminate gender, and those who remain in a state of flux, may I present *The Nutcracker*— Club Delish style."

Oliver had never seen a glam of drag queens doing Psy's "Gangnam Style" dance before, set to lyrics and with lewd gestures that certainly weren't suitable for minors. As the queens sashayed and shimmered across the stage, he turned to Gideon, who sat beside him, looking equally fascinated.

"It's pretty disturbing," Gideon muttered. "That I'm enjoying this. I mean, it's so camp we should pitch a tent. But I love it."

On Gideon's other side, Eddie chuckled as he too enjoyed the onstage antics. "It's something all right. Tay, what do you think?"

Taylor was watching the show with morbid fascination. "It's like a bunch of crazed loonies have escaped from a Victorian asylum and swallowed crack. Strangely mesmerising."

The table they sat at was crowded, and the club was packed to the rafters.

"Christ, I'm thinking a riot of brightly dressed puppets have escaped from a circus and are trying to St Vitus dance their way out of the place," Draven growled. "But what Taylor said. I can't stop watching."

Oliver chuckled and sipped his drink as he waited for Leslie to come back from the bathroom. His boyfriend had been strangely in need of many pees tonight, and he seemed nervous. "Wait 'til you see what they have planned for later, when it gets to the scene under the Christmas tree. Whoever designed this set had to be on something, I swear." He smiled as Leslie appeared and sat down next to him. "Everything okay, love?"

Leslie nodded distractedly. "Fine, fine. I think the wine is going right through me."

Oliver noticed the quick glances the others all gave each other. He had no time to ponder it as Brook, the dark god who was Lenny's boyfriend, sat down across the table and set his bottle of beer down.

"Evening, all." Brook sounded like velvet chocolate, if such a thing existed. "I see my other half has outdone herself this evening with this show of extreme sass. Only Laverne and Delilah could come up with such a spectacle."

"Oh, it gets better," Leslie murmured. "Depending on your definition of better." He sniggered, then his eyes widened. "Oh my God, Mango is coming across. I didn't think he'd join us. He's normally all, 'I'm a strong silent type and I'll just stand here in this corner and glower.'"

Oliver rather liked Mango Munro. He was indeed the quiet man, the complete opposite to the excitable Ryan, but Mango had a sardonic humour and a jaded outlook on life that spoke to Oliver. And there was no doubt Mango adored Ryan Bishop.

Mango reached their table and nodded. "Evening," he said and sat down in the one remaining chair, still gripping his bottle of beer. Leslie visibly gulped, and Oliver had to bite back a smile. Leslie wasn't in awe of many people, but Mango was one of them. There was a chorus of "hellos" and "'evening" around the table.

Brook inclined his head toward Mango. "Looks like our respective SOs have set up a fine performance tonight." He gave a deep belly laugh. "I hate to think what else is planned."

Mango squinted at the stage. "If I know mine, it won't be pretty." A faint smile crossed his face. "But it will be fun." He leaned back, stretching his long legs out in front of him like a rangy cowboy and drank from his bottle.

Oliver leaned into Leslie. "Where's your friend Chester tonight, then?" he asked. "I thought he'd be here too, seeing as how you two have been working so closely together." He couldn't help the faint tinge of green that slipped into his tone.

Leslie smiled. "Honestly, you have nothing to worry about from Chester. He's my friend. And he's not sitting with us because he has a second date with Bear Growls. There they are, over there." He indicated to another table where Chester sat with a man older than him, and rather hirsute. Oliver thought they made a cute couple.

"I didn't think anything," he lied mildly. "I know you're mine."

"You *were* a little jealous." Leslie pursed his lips. Oliver wanted to kiss them so he did, to the catcalls around the table of, "Get a room, you two."

"Oh, no doubt that'll happen later, afterwards," Eddie murmured wickedly. Gideon reached out and tweaked his ear.

"Ow, what was that for?" Eddie rubbed his ear. Gideon scowled.

"Reminding you of your obligation," he muttered. "You and that mouth of yours are trouble."

Eddie grinned. "I thought you liked my mouth."

Taylor added, "He does. But not when it might, you know." He winked at Eddie and waved his hand. Eddie nodded in understanding.

Draven shook his head. "Give me strength," he growled. "Can you two musketeers behave yourselves and enjoy the show, please? Or do I have to take out my gun and shoot you?"

Brook chortled loudly. "This is better than the show."

Oliver blinked. He wasn't sure what the hell was going down, and beside him, Leslie was fidgeting.

"Excuse me," his boyfriend whispered faintly. "I need to pee again." He stood up and left the table, leaving Oliver staring at his retreating arse. After whispered consultation, Taylor and Eddie stood up and followed him.

"What the fuck is going on?" Oliver asked faintly. "I feel like the only man at the table who isn't in the loop. Whatever the hell the loop is." Panic flashed across Brook's, Gideon's, and Draven's faces. Mango remained impervious, but a grin traced the corners of his full lips. He pulled out his phone and started scrolling through it.

"You know what those three are like," Gideon offered. "They have this secret code none of us get, and sometimes it makes them do crazy things."

"Amen," Draven agreed. "Like the time I came home from abroad and found them all paralytic on the floor after holding their own fashion show." He shuddered. "I don't even want to tell you what my eyeballs saw that night. There's a reason I call them the Unholy Trinity."

Oliver laughed. "Amen indeed. I think we can all drink to that." He raised his wineglass in a toast.

They continued to watch the show and Oliver was about to get up to find Leslie when he saw him navigating across the dance floor with his two friends beside him. As Leslie sat down, Oliver reached over to take his hands.

"You okay? I feel as if I should know something, but don't."

Leslie's blue eyes stared into his. "I'm fine. I think I must have eaten something bad at lunchtime. It's making my stomach feel a little upset." He leaned in and kissed Oliver's cheek. "Honest, everything's good."

Oliver picked up his wine and took a sip. He wasn't convinced.

Something else is going on. And I need to find out what.

"Well, hello there, darlings. My name is Sass Parilla." Her Southern accent, unmistakably from the US, sounded sweet, like overly sugared lemonade. "You all looked lonely, so I thought I'd bring my gorgeous self over here to keep you all company." Sass Parilla placed a hand on Oliver's shoulder. "And you, my hunk of male goodness, look as if you could use a little Sass in your life."

Oliver looked up at the six-foot-plus woman towering over him, with long blonde hair and eyelashes that could put Dumbo to shame. He waved at Leslie. "Madam, I have all the sass I need right there. But thank you."

Sass draped a hand along his unscarred cheek. "Darling, you can never have too much sass. And oh my. *Madam.* Such a gentleman." Her fingers ruffled his hair as her eyes glinted wickedly. "I'd love to put a little Sass in you and hear you scream my name." She gestured to her groin and made a lewd gesture.

Oliver grinned, leaned back in his chair, spread his legs so his package was on full display, and grabbed his crotch. "Sweetheart, you couldn't handle this," the Nicky Starr in him drawled. "Many a good man and drag queen has tried and failed. Come back when you've been around the block a few more times."

The table exploded into laughter. The easy transition from Oliver Brown, reclusive website designer, to his alter ego Nicky Starr, man of porn moments in many films, rose to the surface like an easy second skin. Oliver was surprised to have Nicky emerge after so long. He blamed the alcohol, and mostly, nestled in his heart like a secret weapon, a certain wonderful human being named Leslie Tiberius Scott.

Sass shrieked loudly and slapped his shoulder. "Now who's the sassy one?" She simpered at Leslie. "Darling, you are one lucky man. I guess you can handle him quite fine."

Leslie was staring at Oliver with such heat and lust in his eyes that Oliver thought the table might catch fire. They'd role-played to Nicky Starr's films more than once before and Oliver had the feeling this would become another firm favourite.

Oh God. He's giving me such a chubby right here. What he does to me is criminal.

Sass Parilla turned her attention to Taylor, who was grinning widely. "And who's this handsome fellow? Love what you've done to the hair, sweetheart. Very Renaissance." She levelled her gaze at Mango, who saluted her with his beer bottle. "As for you, sexy, I know better than to poach on Delilah's belongings. She says hello, and there's a blowjob waiting for you after the show." She winked.

Mango chuckled. "Tell her I'll be there."

Sass Parilla motioned to Eddie. "Pull me up a chair, honey. I'm going to entertain you boys tonight."

Eddie blushed but pulled up a chair with alacrity. Over the next hour, between the show and Sass's flirting with them all, treating them to dirty jokes and innuendo, Oliver had no time to think about Leslie's strange behaviour. His boyfriend seemed more relaxed though, and Oliver thought he must have imagined that there was something else going on.

***

Oh. My. Fucking God. Oliver is so going to get it tonight. I want to do such filthy things to him. Leslie pushed down on his aching dick, willing it to settle down. The sight of Oliver, eyes dark, mouth twisted in that easy grin, had sent his senses reeling and his body tingling. His man was without doubt the sexiest person on the planet. Once Leslie got his breath back and calmed his racing heart, he acknowledged he'd never been so pleased to see a drag queen invade his small party of friends. Sass was doing a wonderful job of keeping them all entertained, and Leslie couldn't help feeling that had been the plan all along.

Whoever had orchestrated the welcome distraction was a hero. He glanced around the table. Mango caught his eye and mock saluted with his beer bottle. Then he winked. *He really is a superhero*, Leslie thought in awe. *I don't care how he did it, but I know it was him.* He raised his wineglass back and mouthed his thanks.

His frequent trips to the bathroom to perform a few deep breaths of meditation and focus his core on what was going to happen tonight had helped.

Now all I have to do is go get changed, wait for the show to finish, and grab the ring from that stupid place Chester hid it. Then I can propose to my boyfriend and hope he doesn't say no.

Leslie finished his wine, checked his watch, and then nudged Oliver, who was enraptured by something on stage. "The show's nearly finished," Leslie spoke loud enough to make sure Oliver heard over the caterwauling and jeers of the audience. "I need to go check on the supplies for the dressing room, make sure they have bottled water, and that Miss Kiki Heavens has her fruit smoothie, and Misty Faithful has her packets of Skittles." He was aware that he was blathering. He stood up and planted a kiss on Oliver's head. "I'll be back soon."

Please don't let anyone say anything. Please make Tyler and Eddie hold their wicked tongues.

He was amazed they'd gotten this far without one or both of them having taken out an ad in *The Times*. It seemed when it came to the important things, Leslie could count on his two besties. He didn't have to worry anyway. Gideon's tongue was stuck so far down Eddie's throat, they could have been conjoined twins. Taylor appeared merry as Draven patted his back and told him to breathe. That extra tequila Taylor had enjoyed appeared to be causing him some issues. Brook and Mango watched him go, and Leslie saw a glimmer of support in their eyes for what he was about to do. He hurried to the dressing room and sought out his costume. It would be tough but he'd assured Chester he'd get into it on his own with no problem.

The Santa suit was cleverly designed with easy zippers and Velcro (Leslie had insisted the trousers could be ripped off at a moment's notice to reveal his red thong underneath). It took ten minutes of huffing and puffing, and a calisthenics workout better suited to a gym, but finally Leslie was almost ready. As he perched the jaunty Christmas hat on his black curls and arranged them artfully to frame his face, he heard the closing number of the show, a raucous medley of show tunes mixed with Tchaikovsky's Nutcracker Suite. As the last bars played, he dashed out of the dressing room as fast as he could, given he was in heels.

I'll wait here until it's over and then it's my showtime. Despite his nervousness, Leslie's heart beat with excitement.

He lingered behind the side curtain as the queens came off the stage, chattering and joking as they made their way to the open enclosure behind him which held bottled water and the stronger stuff. Leslie thought they'd probably grab a drink then be off to their changing rooms.

As the stage curtains closed, Leslie breathed a sigh of relief. He slinked across to the fireplace and reached up, looking for the alcove that held the box. His fingers couldn't find what he was looking for and he swore.

"Damn thing. Where are you?" He stretched up farther, even as he thought logically that Chester wasn't taller than him, so it was unlikely to be higher up, Leslie still felt around to find nothing there. Leslie's throat went dry and he was sure the whole world could hear the hammering of his heart as it sped up in panic. He lowered his arm and tried rummaging around again. Finally, his fingers hit something square and solid, and he grasped hold of it with a victorious exclamation.

"And now, sit yourselves down and grab another drink, darlings, because the ladies are coming back with that encore you know you want."

Behind him, Leslie heard the familiar swish of the curtains as they began to open.

His body went cold.

Encore? What the hell were they doing an encore for? Club Delish didn't do encores. It was a nightclub for fuck's sake, not a theatre. All he could do was stand there, close his eyes and wish the earth would swallow him whole. The nightclub erupted in catcalls, and shouts of encouragement and Leslie was sure he heard Eddie calling out, a little drunkenly, "Way to go, you sexy thing. Shake that booty."

Oh, he would so *kill Eddie later for that comment.*

"Leslie, what *are* you doing out there?" Laverne's panicked whisper echoed across the stage. There was a heated discussion between what appeared to be her and Delilah and then

Delilah's voice rang out. "Before the ladies come back on stage, we are thrilled to announce that our very own Leslie Scott has graced us with his delightful presence, and in an even more delightful piece of sexy apparel. He'll be performing a short number for us. Leslie, darling, sashay away. The floor is yours."

There were more calls to shake his arse and show them what he'd got. Leslie closed his eyes, trying not to hyperventilate. There was an element of hysteria in Delilah's voice and it made him waaay nervous.

"Dance, chicken," hissed Laverne from the shadows. "Christ, Leslie, do something before your plan is completely fucked."

It was when he heard someone singing drunkenly, "When Santa got stuck in the chimney"—he thought it might have been Taylor—that Leslie knew he had to act quickly before it all became a little too farcical and not the truly romantic moment he'd wanted.

He drew in a deep breath. He was Leslie fucking Tiberius damn Scott, and if anything, he knew how to entertain an audience. Grasping the box tightly in his hand, he wiggled his bum seductively. Twice. The audience cheered, and he was encouraged with ribald calls to do a lot more. Then he heard

Oliver's voice carrying above the crowd, and he knew that he had this.

"Go, Leslie. Show these people what's mine. Love you, baby."

Leslie bit his lower lip in determination and wriggled his bum a bit more as he extricated himself from the chimney. The crowd seemed to love it and, his confidence growing, he turned around. As he did, the glorious tones of his favourite diva, Cher, rang out stridently, encouraging him to turn back time.

Leslie glanced to the wings where Laverne stood, holding a thumb up. She knew what tunes he liked, and by God, he was going to make this dance count before he figured out what the hell he was going to do next. For the next few minutes, Leslie sashayed and danced his way across the stage as if he'd been born to do it. His dancing skills weren't bad, and in his time he'd had plenty of chance to perfect them on the club dance floors and at various karaoke bars.

The audience clapped and sang along, and all the time he was aware of the little blue box in his hand. There'd been no time to put it down, and in all honesty, with the chorus girl kicking he was doing, the last thing he wanted was to send it hurtling into the crowd.

As he kicked and minced across the stage, Leslie gave silent thanks to the fashion god that was Chester for making his costume seams tight and sturdy enough to cope with Leslie's shenanigans.

Oliver was up front, closer to the stage, his face beaming as he stomped and cheered to Leslie's performance. Their friends stood beside him, rocking away too, and Leslie's heart stuttered at seeing his brilliantly supportive close-knit group of friends together. Even Chester and Bear were there, and if Leslie wasn't mistaken, Bear had Chester's hand in his.

When the final strains of music faded away, Leslie, gasping and no doubt pink-faced, took his bow and stood trembling. Crap, his legs were wobbly, and his feet hurt like hell.

But he'd Cher'd on stage, and fuck, it had felt good.

"That's my boyfriend," Oliver called out, shining with pride. "Eat your heart out, everyone, because he's going home with me."

Laverne and Delilah flounced onstage as Delilah addressed the crowd on her penis mic. "Wasn't that fabulous? This young man has a future in construction, because I know for a fact something's been erected in my basement."

The crowd erupted once again with cheers and entreaties for "More, more." Leslie huffed and puffed trying to gain his breath back—he really needed to do more cardiovascular at the gym—as Laverne stage-whispered, "That was a good save but what the hell are you going to do *now*?"

She looked meaningfully down at the box Leslie still clutched in sweaty fingers. He made one of those split-second decisions and hoped like hell Oliver would understand. He grabbed the microphone from Delilah, who looked at him, startled. He held it up to his lips and started to speak.

"Oliver—" His voice sounded soft, and nothing else came out.

Laverne leaned over with a roll of her perfectly mascaraed eyes and pressed her finger to his lips. "Hold the button when you speak, chicken." She stroked his hand softly and whispered, "You can do this."

Leslie gulped and pressed down on the switch. Before he could say anything, Oliver shouted out again. "I knew you were hiding something, sweetheart, and now I know what it was. That was amazing, fantastically amazing."

Leslie switched on the microphone. "Uhmm, babe, that wasn't really the surprise, but thanks. Could you come onto the stage please?" He had to smile when he noticed Oliver didn't have a choice. Leslie's friends began pushing his boyfriend toward the stage, then shoved him up the narrow side staircase to the top.

"Oliver. Oliver," the crowd chanted.

Oliver was grinning but looked a little apprehensive. Leslie sashayed over to where Oliver stood and held out a hand. "Come on," he murmured. "I promise this will be good, sweetie."

Oliver took Leslie's hand and let himself be led to the centre. He waved at the audience and gave a short bow. Leslie's heart warmed at the sight and he leaned in and pressed his lips to Oliver's in a soothing kiss.

God, you have come so far, my beautiful man. There was a time when I wouldn't have dared to do this to you.

"Thank you for doing this," he whispered. Then he knelt on one knee, wincing a little because the trousers were tight and were almost bisecting his balls.

"Blowjob, blowjob, blowjob," was the rousing cry he heard, and he'd had enough. He raised the microphone to his lips as Oliver gazed down mystified.

"Shut the fuck up, you randy bunch of perverts. I'm trying to propose to my boyfriend."

The entire club went silent. Leslie nodded in satisfaction and opened his hand to reveal the box. He looked back up at Oliver, whose mouth was open, a look of pure astonishment on his face.

"Oliver, we've been together three years now, and I know you're the man for me. I hope I'm the man for you, because if I'm not, that will really suck big hairy donkey balls. I know you don't feel that rings and marriage are important if two people love each other and, baby, I get that." Leslie's throat clogged up and he sniffed. His eyes were starting to prickle. "But *I* believe in those things, and there's no one else I'd want to make a commitment to, so I'm asking you, Oliver Brown, will you be my husband one day?" he finished then whispered softly, "Please say yes."

Leslie stood up, wincing at hearing his one knee crackle. He couldn't look into Oliver's eyes. He didn't want to see the answer until it was spoken. Speaking words gave them the power. They gave promise, and oh God, Leslie wanted promise so much.

Beside him, Laverne was blowing her nose and Delilah was making noises that sounded suspiciously like goose honks. There was a small moment of agony as Leslie waited for Oliver's reply. The crowd was so still they might not have been there. Then Oliver's fingers reached out and lifted Leslie's chin. The microphone was removed from his trembling hands and there was a dull click as it went live.

"Leslie, sweetheart, look at me. Let me see those gorgeous blues," Oliver whispered reverently. Leslie took a chance and glanced up. Oliver's face was wreathed in a smile, his dark eyes loving and joyful, and the look of adoration Leslie saw there made him want to sink to his knees and pray.

"My incredible, sassy, lovable, and adorable man, how could you even think I'd ever say no? I know you think I'm not interested in this stuff but, sweetheart, this is *you*." The room erupted in cheering and somewhere party hooters went off. There was full-on sobbing now from somewhere on the dance floor below.

Oliver's eyes shone with love. "I might talk the talk about not having to have anything formal between two people who adore each other but, babe, the fact you've asked me?" Oliver swallowed, his throat working. "I can't tell you how honoured I feel." His eyes shone with something else now, a tiny teardrop at one corner giving credence to his words.

Leslie felt a bit like crying himself, the relief was so great. A niggle of doubt wormed its way into his head. Wait. Oliver hadn't *actually* said yes.

"Is that a yes?" He sniffled. "Because I really need to hear you say the word."

Oliver reached over and drew him into a kiss that held every promise Leslie had ever wanted. When he was released, Leslie felt trembly for a whole different reason. "That's a big yes."

Leslie collapsed into his boyfriend's arms. "Oh thank God," he said fervently.

"Oh, thank the fuck," Delilah and Laverne said simultaneously, fanning themselves with manicured talons. Oliver smiled at Leslie, love radiating in rainbow waves as the coloured strobe lights flickered above.

"You know me, I'm not good at public stuff." He reached out and caressed Leslie's cheek. "Three years ago, you came into my life to bring me a suit, and I'm a lucky man—you never left."

Leslie swallowed, his eyes filling with tears at the love in Oliver's voice as he continued. "You took a reclusive, scared man and gave him nothing but your unconditional love. You gave me back something I'd lost. My life. And now," Oliver's voice broke and he moved closer, "I am as privileged as hell that you've asked me to be your husband. I can't think of anything I'd rather do than marry you."

Finally. Leslie kissed his fiancé to the clapping and cheering from the watching crowd.

"Give him the bloody ring then," came the roar from the watching crowd. Leslie remembered the thing that had caused all the trouble in the first place as he opened the box and lifted out the ring. He took Oliver's hand, a hand that was also trembling, and slid the ring home.

"Oh my God, Leslie. It's stunning," Oliver whispered. "I've only ever seen something as beautiful as this once before." He smiled so sweetly, Leslie thought his heart would break free and float into the air above. "Only that was a certain someone I'd really love to kiss right now."

He pulled Leslie over to him and any noise the crowd made, or music that played, or drag queens that danced, were forgotten in the warmth of Oliver's embrace and the taste of his mouth against Leslie's.

Oliver's mouth left his and Leslie huffed his displeasure.

"You know," Oliver murmured with a smile, "I thought I was getting a new suit for Christmas. I thought that was your secret. But this," he gestured around him, "this was so much better."

Leslie reached out a hand and smirked. "Sweetie, the next suit I have made for you is going to be a special one," he purred, loving the shine of the light as it played on Oliver's ring. "I'm thinking white tuxedos, perhaps a splash of teal—and peacocks." He sighed. "I'm seeing peacocks at our wedding."

Oliver's answer to that was to pull Leslie in for another mind-bending kiss, and as his fiancé's arms kept him tight in a warm embrace, all Leslie could do was hold on for the ride.

This Kissmas Drag Stravaganza has been the best event ever, he thought dreamily.

They'd have to do it next year.

This time, it could be Taylor and Draven's turn.

Leslie would make sure of it.

The Men of London thank you for living their love.
Don't worry, chickens, you'll see them again.

ABOUT THE AUTHOR

The 'Official' stuff

Susan writes steamy, sexy, and fun contemporary romance stories, some suspenseful, some gritty and dark, and she hopes, always entertaining. She's also Editor-in-Chief at Divine Magazine, an online LGBTQ e-zine, and a member of The Society of Authors, the Writers Guild of Great Britain, and the Authors Guild in the U.S.

Susan is also an award-winning screenplay writer, with scripts based on two of her own published works. *Sight Unseen* has garnered no less than five awards to date, and her TV pilot, *Reel Life*, based on her debut novel, *Cassandra by Starlight*, was also a winner at the Oaxaca Film Fest.

The 'Unofficial' stuff

Susan loves going to the theatre, live music concerts (especially if it's her man-crush Adam Lambert), walks in the countryside, a good G and T, lazing away afternoons reading a good book, and watching re-runs of *Silent Witness*.

Her chequered past includes stories like being mistaken for a prostitute in the city of Johannesburg, being chased by a rhino on a dusty Kenyan road, getting kicked out of a youth club for being a bad influence (she encouraged free thinking), and having an aunt who was engaged to Cliff Richard.

<u>Connect with Susan:</u>

website: authorsusanmacnicol.com
facebook: Author-Susan-Mac-Nicol
twitter: SusanMacNicol7
instagram: susiemax77
linkedin: susanmacnicol

www.BOROUGHSPUBLISHINGGROUP.com

If you enjoyed this book, please write a review. Our authors appreciate the feedback, and it helps future readers find books they love. We welcome your comments and invite you to send them to info@boroughspublishinggroup.com. Follow us on Facebook, Twitter and Instagram, and be sure to sign up for our newsletter for surprises and new releases from your favorite authors.

Are you an aspiring writer? Check out www.boroughspublishinggroup.com/submit and see if we can help you make your dreams come true.